Lew Wallace

The Fair God or the Last of the 'Tzins

A Tale of the Conquest of Mexico

Lew Wallace

The Fair God or the Last of the 'Tzins
A Tale of the Conquest of Mexico

ISBN/EAN: 9783337076696

Printed in Europe, USA, Canada, Australia, Japan

Cover: Foto ©Andreas Hilbeck / pixelio.de

More available books at **www.hansebooks.com**

WARNE'S "CROWN" LIBRARY

THE FAIR GOD

OR,

THE LAST OF THE 'TZINS

A Tale of the Conquest of Mexico

BY

LEW. WALLACE

AUTHOR OF "BEN HUR"

"From Mexico . . . a civilisation that might have instructed Europe was crushed out. . . . It has been her [Spain's] evil destiny to ruin two civilisations, Oriental and Occidental, and to be ruined thereby herself. . . . In America she destroyed races more civilised than herself."—DRAPER, *Int. Development of Europe.*

LONDON AND NEW YORK
FREDERICK WARNE AND CO.
1887

NOTE BY THE AUTHOR.

A PERSONAL experience, though ever so plainly told, is, generally speaking, more attractive to listeners and readers than fiction. A circumstance from the tongue or pen of one to whom it actually happened, or who was its hero or victim, or even its spectator, is always more interesting than if given second-hand. If the makers of history, contradistinguished from its writers, could teach it to us directly, one telling would suffice to secure our lasting remembrance. The reason is, that the narrative so proceeding derives a personality and reality not otherwise attainable, which assist in making way to our imagination and the sources of our sympathy.

With this theory or bit of philosophy in mind, when the annexed book was resolved upon, I judged best to assume the character of a translator, which would enable me to write in the style and spirit of one who not merely lived at the time of the occurrences woven in the text, but was acquainted with many of the historical personages who figure therein, and was a native of the beautiful valley in which the story is located. Thinking to make the descriptions yet more real, and therefore more impressive, I took the liberty of attributing the composition to a literator who, whatever may be thought of his works, was not himself a fiction. Without meaning to insinuate that THE FAIR GOD would have been the worse for creation by Don Fernando de Alva, the Tezcucan, I wish merely to say that it is not a translation. Having been so written, however, now that publication is at hand, change is impossible ; hence, nothing is omitted,—title-page, introductory, and conclusion are given to the reader exactly as they were brought to the publisher by the author.

L. W.

CONTENTS.

BOOK ONE.

BOOK TWO.

BOOK THREE.

BOOK FOUR.

BOOK FIVE.

BOOK SIX.

BOOK SEVEN.

INTRODUCTORY.

FERNANDO DE ALVA,[1] a noble Tezcucan, flourished, we are told, in the beginning of the sixteenth century. He was a man of great learning, familiar with the Mexican and Spanish languages, and the hieroglyphics of Anahuac. Ambitious to rescue his race from oblivion, and inspired by love of learning, he collected a library, availed himself of his knowledge of picture-writing, became master of the songs and traditions, and, in the Castilian language, composed books of merit.

It was scarcely possible that his labours should escape the researches of Mr. Prescott, who, with such incomparable genius, has given the world a history of the Conquest of Mexico. From him we have a criticism upon the labours of the learned Fernando, from which the following paragraph is extracted.

[1] Fernando De Alva Iztlilzochitl.

"Iztlilzochitl's writings have many of the defects belonging to his age. He often crowds the page with incidents of a trivial, and sometimes improbable, character. The improbability increases with the distance of the period; for distance, which diminishes objects to the natural eye, exaggerates them to the mental. His chronology, as I have more than once noticed, is inextricably entangled. He has often lent a too willing ear to traditions and reports which would startle the more sceptical criticism of the present time. Yet there is an appearance of good faith and simplicity in his writings, which may convince the reader that, when he errs, it is from no worse cause than the national partiality. And surely such partiality is excusable in the descendant of a proud line, shorn of its ancient splendours, which it was soothing to his own feelings to revive again—though with something more than their legitimate lustre—on the canvas of history. It should also be considered that, if his narrative is sometimes startling, his researches penetrate into the mysterious depths of antiquity, where light and darkness meet and melt into each other; and where everything is still further liable to distortion, as seen through the misty medium of hieroglyphics."

Besides his *Relaciones* and *Historia Chichemeca*, De Alva composed works of a lighter nature, though equally based upon history. Some were lost; others fell into the hands of persons ignorant of their value; a few only were rescued and given to the press. For a considerable period he served as interpreter to the Spanish Viceroy. His duties as such were trifling: he had **ample** time for literary pursuits; his enthusiasm as a scholar permitted **him no relaxation or idle-ness.** Thus favoured, **it is** believed he composed the books now for the first time given to the world.

The MSS. were found among a heap **of old despatches** from the Viceroy Mendoza to **the** Emperor. **It is quite** probable that **they** became mixed with **the** State papers through accident; if, however, they were purposely ad-dressed to His Majesty, it must have been to give **him a** completer idea of the Aztecan people and their civilisation, **or to** lighten the burdens **of** royalty by **an** amusement to which, it is known, Charles **V.** was not averse. Besides, Mendoza, in his difficulty **with** the Marquess of the Valley (Cortes), failed not **to** avail himself **of** every means likely to propitiate his cause with the court, and especially with the Royal Council **of the** Indies. **It** is **not** altogether improbable, therefore, that the MSS. were forwarded for the entertainment of the members of the Council and the lordly personages of the court, who not only devoured with avidity, but, as the wily Mendoza well knew, were vastly obliged **for,** everything relative to **the** New World, and particularly the dazzling Conquest of Mexico.

In the translation, certain liberties have been taken, for which, if wrong has been done, pardon **is** besought both from the public and **the** shade **of the** author. Thus, The Books in the original are unbroken narratives; but, with infinite care and trouble, they have all been brought out of the confusion, and arranged **into chapters.** So, there were names, some of which have been altogether changed; while others, **for the** sake of **euphony,** have been **abbreviated,** though without sacrificing **the identity of the** heroes who **wore them so proudly.**

And thus beginneth the FIRST BOOK.

THE FAIR GOD.

BOOK ONE.

CHAPTER I.

OUR MOTHER HAS A FORTUNE WAITING US YONDER.

THE Spanish Calendar is simpler than the Aztecan. In fact, Christian methods, of whatever nature, are better than heathen.

So, then, by the Spanish Calendar, March 1519 had about half spent itself in the valley of Anahuac, which was as yet untrodden by gold-seeker, with cross-hilted sword at his side, and on his lips a Catholic oath. Near noon of one of its fairest days a traveller came descending the western slope of the Sierra de Ahualco. Since the dawn his path had been amongst hills and crags; at times traversing bald rocks that towered to where the winds blew chill, then dipping into warm valleys, where were grass, flowers, and streamlets, and sometimes forests of cedar and fir,—labyrinths in which there reigned a perpetual twilight.

Toilsome as was the way, the traveller, young and strong, marched lightly. His dress, of the kind prevalent in his country, was provincial, and with few signs of rank. He had sandals of buffalo-hide, fitted for climbing rocks and threading pathless woods; a sort of white tunic, covering his body from the neck to the knees, leaving bare the arms from the shoulder; *maxtlatl* and *tilmatli*—sash and mantle—of cotton, blue-tinted, and void of ornament; on the wrist of his left arm he wore a substantial golden bracelet, and in both ears jewelled pendants; while an ebony band, encircling his head, kept his straight black locks in place, and permitted a snow-white bird's-wing for decoration. There was a shield on his left arm, framed of wood, and covered with padded cloth, and in the left hand a javelin barbed with

B

'itzli ; at his back swung a *maquahuitl*, and a quiver filled with
arrows ; an unstrung bow in his right hand completed his
equipments, and served him in lieu of staff. An ocelot, trudging
stealthily behind him, was his sole companion.

In the course of his journey he came to a crag that sank
bluffly down several hundred feet, commanding a fine prospect
Though the air was cold, he halted. Away to the north-west
stretched the beautiful valley of Anahuac, dotted with hamlets
and farmhouses, and marked with the silver tracery of streams.
Far across the plain, he caught a view of the fresh waters of
Lake Chalco, and beyond that, blue in the distance and faintly
relieved against the sky, the royal hill of Chapultepec, with its
palaces and cypress forests. In all the New World there was
no scene comparable with that he looked upon,—none its rival
for beauty, none where the heavens seemed so perfectly melted
into earth. There were the most renowned cities of the
Empire ; from that plain went the armies whose marches
were all triumphs ; in that air hovered the gods awaiting
sacrifices ; into that sky rose the smoke of the inextinguishable fires ; there shone the brightest suns, and lingered the
longest summers ; and yonder dwelt that king—in youth a
priest, then a warrior, now the terror of all nations—whose
signet on the hand of a slave could fill the land with rustling
of banners.

No traveller, I ween, could look unmoved on the picture ; ours
sat down, and gazed with brimful eyes and a beating heart.
For the first time he was beholding the matchless vale so overhung with loveliness, and full of the monuments of a strange
civilisation. So rapt was he that he did not observe the ocelot
come and lay its head in his lap, like a dog seeking caresses.
"Come, boy !" he said, at last rousing himself ; "let us on. Our
Mother [1] has a fortune waiting us yonder."

And they resumed the journey. Half an hour's brisk walk
brought them to the foot of the mountain. Suddenly they came
upon company.

It was on the bank of a considerable stream, which, pouring in
noisy torrent over a rocky bed, appeared to rush with a song
forward into the valley. A clump of giant oaks shaded a level
sward. Under them a crowd of *tamanes*,[2] tawny, half-clad,
broad-shouldered men, devoured loaves of cold maize bread.
Near the roots of the trees their masters reclined comfortably
on *petates*, or mats, without which an Aztec trader's outfit was
incomplete. Our traveller understood at a glance the character
of the strangers ; so that, as his road led directly to them, he

---

[1] The goddess Cioacoatl, called "Our Lady and Mother." Sahagun,
Hist de Nueva Esp.
[2] Carrier slaves, or porters.

went on without hesitation. As he came near, some of them sat up to observe him.

"A warrior going to the city," said one.

"Or rather a king's courier," suggested another.

"Is not that an ocelot at his heels?" asked a third.

"That it is. Bring me my javelin!"

"And mine! And mine!" cried several of them at once, all springing to their feet.

By the time the young man came up, the whole party stood ready to give him an armed welcome.

"I am very sorry to have disturbed you," he said quietly, finding himself obliged to stop.

"You seem friendly enough," answered one of the older men; "but your comrade there,—what of him?"

The traveller smiled. "See, he is muzzled."

The party laughed at their own fears. The old merchant, however, stepped forward to the young stranger.

"I confess you have greatly relieved me. I feared the brute might set on and wound somebody. Come up, and sit down with us."

The traveller was nowise disinclined, being tempted by the prospect of cheer from the provision baskets lying around.

"Bring a mat for the warrior," said the friendly trader. "Now give him bread and meat."

From an abundance of bread, fowl, and fruit the wayfarer helped himself. A running conversation was meantime maintained.

"My ocelot? The story is simple; for your sakes, good friends, I wish it were better. I killed his mother, and took him when a whelp. Now he does me good service hunting. You should see him in pursuit of an antelope!"

"Then you are not a warrior?"

"To be a warrior," replied the hunter modestly, "is to have been in many battles, and taken many captives. I have practised arms, and, at times, boasted of skill,—foolishly, perhaps; yet, I confess, I never marched a day under the banner of the great king."

"Ah," said the old man quizzically, "I understand you! You have served some free-trading company like our own."

"You are shrewd. My father is a merchant. At times he has travelled with strong trains, and even attacked cities that have refused him admission to their market."

"Indeed! He must be of renown. In what province does he live, my son?"

"In Tihuanco."

"Tepaja! old Tepaja, of Tihuanco! Are you son of his?" The good man grasped the young one's hand enthusiastically.

" I knew him well ; many years ago we were as brothers together ; we travelled and traded through many provinces. That was the day of the elder Montezuma, when the Empire was not as large as now ; when, in fact, most gates were closed against us, because our king was an Aztec, and we had to storm a town, then turn its square into a market for the sale of our wares. Sometimes we marched an army, each of us carrying a thousand slaves ; and yet our tasks were not always easy. I remember once, down on the bank of the Great River, we were beaten back from a walled town, and succeeded only after a four days' fight. Ah, but we made it win ! We led three thousand slaves back to Tenochtitlan, besides five hundred captives,—a present for the gods."

So the merchant talked until the hunger of his new acquaintance was appeased ; then he offered a pipe, which was declined.

" I am fond of a pipe after a good meal ; and this one has been worthy a king. But now I have no leisure for the luxury ; the city to which I am bound is too far ahead of me."

" If it is your first visit, you are right. Fail not to be there before the market closes. Such a sight never gladdened your dreams ! "

" So I have heard my father say."

" Oh, it never was as it will be to-night ! The roads for days have been thronged with visitors going up in processions."

" What is the occasion ? "

" Why, to-morrow is the celebration of Quetzal' ! Certainly, my son, you have heard the prophecies concerning that god."

" In rumours only. I believe he was to return to Anahuac."

" Well, the story is long, and you are in a hurry. We also are going to the city, but will halt our slaves at Iztapalapan for the night, and cross the causeway before the sun to-morrow. If you care to keep us company, we will start at once ; on the way I will tell you a few things that may not be unacceptable."

" I see," said the hunter pleasantly, " I have reason to be proud of my father's good report. Certainly, I will go a distance with you at least, and thank you for information. To speak frankly, I am seeking my fortune."

The merchant spoke to his companions, and, raising a huge conch-shell to his mouth, blew a blast that started every slave to his feet. For a few minutes all was commotion. The mats were rolled up, and, with the provision-baskets, slung upon broad shoulders ; each *tamane* resumed his load of wares, and took his place ; those armed put themselves, with their masters, at the head ; and at another peal from the shell all set forward. The column, if such it may be called, was long, and not without a certain picturesqueness as it crossed the stream, and entered a tract covered with tall trees, amongst which the palm was strangely intermingled with the oak and the cypress. The whole valley, from the lake to the mountains, was irrigated, and under cultivation. Full of wonder, the hunter marched beside the merchant.

CHAPTER II.

QUETZAL', THE FAIR GOD.

" I was speaking about Quetzal', I believe," said the old man, when all were fairly on the way. "His real name was Quetzalcoatl.[1] He was a wonderfully kind god, who, many ages ago, came into the valley here, and dwelt awhile. The people were then rude and savage; but he taught them agriculture, and other arts, of which you will see signs as we get on. He changed the manners and customs: while he stayed, famine was unknown; the harvests were abundant, and happiness universal. Above all, he taught the princes wisdom in their government. If to-day the Aztec Empire is the strongest in the world, it is owing to Quetzal'. Where he came from, or how long he stayed, is not known. The people and their governors after a time proved ungrateful, and banished him; they also overthrew his religion, and set up idols again, and sacrificed men, both of which he had prohibited. Driven away, he went to Cholula; thence to the sea-coast, where, it is said, he built him a canoe of serpent-skins, and departed for Tlapallan, a heaven lying somewhere toward the rising sun. But before he went he promised to return some day and wrest away the Empire and restore his own religion. In appearance, he was not like our race; his skin was white, his hair long and wavy and black. He is said to have been wise as a god, and more beautiful than men. Such is his history; and, as the prophecy has it, the time of his return is at hand. The king and Tlalac, the *teotuctli*,[2] are looking for him; they expect him every hour, and, they say, live in continual dread of him. Wishing to propitiate him, they have called the people together, and celebrate to-morrow with sacrifices and combats and more pomp than was ever seen before, not excepting the time of the king's coronation."

The hunter listened closely, and at the conclusion said, "Thank you, uncle. Tell me now of the combats."

" Yes. In the days of the first kings it was the custom to go into the temples, choose the bravest warriors there set apart for

---

[1] In Aztec mythology, God of the Air.
[2] Equivalent to Pontiff, or Pope.

sacrifice, bring them into the *tianguez*, and make them do battle in the presence of the people. If they conquered, they were set free and sent home with presents." [1]

"With whom did they combat?"

"True enough, my son. The fight **was deemed a** point of **honour** amongst the Aztecs, and the best of them volunteered. **Indeed,** those were royal times! Of late, I am sorry to say, the custom of which I was speaking has been neglected, but to-morrow it **is to be** revived. The scene will be very grand. The king and **all** the nobles **will be there."**

The description excited the listener's fancy, and he said, **with** flushed cheeks, "I would not lose the chance for the world. **Can** you tell me who of the Aztecs will combat?"

"In the city we could easily find out; but you must recollect I am going home after a long absence. The shields of the combatants are always exhibited in the *tianguez* the evening before the day of the fight. In that way the public are notified beforehand of those who take the field. As the city is full of caciques, you may be assured our champions will be noble."

"Thank you again, uncle. And now, as one looking for service, like myself, is anxious **to** know with whom to engage, tell me of the caciques and chiefs."

"Then you intend entering **the army?"**

"Well, yes. I am tired of hunting; **and though** trading is honourable, I have no taste for it."

The merchant, as if deliberating, took out a box of snuff and helped himself; and then he replied,—

"The caciques **are** very numerous; in no former reign, probably, were there so many of ability and renown. With some of them I have personal acquaintance; others I know only by sight or reputation. You had better mention those of whom **you** have been thinking."

Well," said the hunter, "there is Iztlil', the Tezcucan." [2]

"**Do** not think of him, I pray you!" And the good man spoke earnestly. "He is brave as any, and perhaps as skilful, but proud, haughty, soured, and treacherous. Everybody fears him. I suppose you have heard of his father?"

"You mean the wise 'Hualpilli?"

"Yes. Upon his death, not long since, Iztlil' denied his brother's right to the Tezcucan throne. There was a quarrel which would have ended in blood, had not Montezuma interfered, and given the city **to** Cacama, and all the northern part of the province **to** Iztlil'. **Since** that, the latter has been discontented with the great king. So, **I** say **again, do** not think of him, unless you are careless about honour."

[1] Sahagun, *Hist. de Nueva Esp.*
[2] Ixtlilxochitl, son of Nezahualpilli, king of Tezcuco.

"Then what of Cacama?[1] Tezcuco is a goodly city."

"He has courage, but is too effeminate to be a great warrior. A garden and a soft couch delight him more than camps, and dancing women better than fighting men. You might grow rich with him, but not renowned. Look elsewhere."

"Then there is the lord Cuitlahua."[2]

"The king's brother, and governor of Iztapalapan!" said the merchant promptly. "Some have thought him better qualified for Chapultepec than Montezuma, but it is not wise to say so. His people are prosperous, and he has the most beautiful gardens in the world; unlike Cacama, he cares nothing for them when there is a field to be fought. Considering his influence at court and his love of war, you would do well to bear shield for him; but, on the other hand, he is old. Were I in **your** place, **my son**, I would attach myself to some young man."

"That brings me to Maxtla, the Tesoyucan."

"I know him only by repute. With scarcely a beard, he is chief of the king's guard. There was never anything like his fortune. Listen now, I will tell you a secret which may be of value to you some time. The king is not as young as he used to be by quite forty summers."

The hunter smiled at the caution with which the old man spoke of the monarch.

"You see," the speaker continued, "time and palace life have changed him: he no longer leads the armies; his days are passed in the temples with the priests, or in the gardens with his women, of whom there are several hundreds; his most active amusement now is to cross the lake to his forests, and kill birds **and** rabbits by blowing little arrows at them through a reed. Thus changed, you can very well understand how he can be amused by songs and wit, and make favourites of those who best lighten his hours of satiety and indolence. In that way Maxtla rose,—a marvellous courtier, but a very common soldier."

The description amused the young man, but he said gravely, "You have spoken wisely, uncle, and I am satisfied you know the men well. Really, I had no intention of entering the suite of either of them: they are not of my ideal; but there is a cacique, if reports **are** to be credited, beyond all exception,—learned and brave, honoured alike by high and low."

"Ah, you need not name him to me! I know him, as who does not?" And now the merchant spoke warmly. "A nobler than Guatamozin[3]—or, as he is more commonly called, the 'tzin

---

[1] King of Tezcuco.

[2] See Prescott's *Conq. of Mexico.*

[3] Guatamozin, nephew to Montezuma. Of him Bernal Diaz says: "This monarch was between twenty-three and twenty-four years of age, and could in all truth be called a handsome man, both as regards his

Guatamo—never dwelt in Anahuac. He is the people's friend,
and the Empire's hope. His valour and wisdom,—ah, you should
see him, my son! Such a face! His manner is so full of sweet
dignity! But I will give you other evidence."

He clapped his hands three times, and a soldier sprang forward
at the signal.

"Do you know the 'tzin Guatamo?" asked the merchant.

"I am a humble soldier, my master, and the 'tzin is the great
king's nephew; but I know him. When he was only a boy, I
served under him in Tlascala. He is the best chief in Anahuac."

"That will do."

The man retired.

"So I might call up my *tamanes*," the merchant resumed, "and
not one but would speak of him in the same way."

"Strange!" said the Tihuancan, in a low tone.

"No, if you allude to his popularity, it is not strange; if you
mean the man himself, you are right. The gods seldom give the
qualities that belong to him. He is more learned than Tlalac or
the king; he is generous, as becomes a prince; in action, he is a
hero. You have probably heard of the Tlascalan wall in the
eastern valley;[1] few warriors ever passed it and lived; yet he
did so when almost a boy. I myself have seen him send an
arrow to the heart of an eagle in its flight. He has a palace and
garden in Iztapalapan; in one of the halls stand the figures of
three kings—two of Michuaca, and one of the Ottomies. He
took them prisoners in battle, and now they hold torches at his
feasts."

"Enough, enough!" cried the hunter. "I have been dreaming
of him while among the hills. I want no better leader."

The merchant cast an admiring glance at his beaming countenance, and said, "You are right; enter his service."

In such manner the conversation was continued, until the sun
fast declined towards the western mountains. Meantime, they
had passed through several hamlets and considerable towns. In
nearly the whole progress, the way on either hand had been lined
with plantations. Besides the presence of a busy, thriving
population, they everywhere saw evidences of a cultivation and
science, constituting the real superiority of the Aztecs over their
neighbours. The country was thus preparing the stranger for the
city, unrivalled in splendour and beauty. Casting a look toward

countenance and figure. His face was rather of an elongated form, with
a cheerful look; his eye had great expression, both when he assumed a
majestic expression, or when he looked pleasantly around; the colour of
his face inclined to white more than to the copper-brown tint of the
Indians in general."—Diaz, *Conquest of Mexico*, Lockhart's Trans., Vol.
IV., p. 110.

[1] Prescott's *Conq. of Mexico*, Vol. I., p. 417.

the sun, he at length said, "Uncle, I have much to thank you for,—you and your friends. But it is growing late, and I must hurry on, if I would see the *tianguez* before the market closes."

"Very well," returned the old trader. "We will be in the city to-morrow. The gods go with you!"

Whistling to his ocelot, the adventurer quickened his pace, and was soon far in the advance.

CHAPTER III.

A CHALLENGE.

In the valley of Anahuac, at the time I write, are four lakes,— Xaltocan, Chalco, Xochichalco, and Tezcuco. The latter, besides being the largest, washed the walls of Tenochtitlan, and was the especial pride of the Aztecs, who, familiar with its ways as with the city, traversed them all the days of the year, and even the nights.

"Ho, there!" shouted a *voyageur*, in a voice that might have been heard a long distance over the calm expanse of the lake. "Ho, the canoe!"

The hail was answered.

"Is it Guatamozin?" asked **the** first speaker.

"Yes."

"And going to Tenochtitlan?"

"The gods willing,—yes."

The canoes of the *voyageurs*—I use that term because it more nearly expresses the meaning of the word the Aztecs themselves were wont to apply to persons thus abroad—were, at the time, about the middle of the little sea. After the 'tzin's reply, they were soon alongside, when lashings were applied, and together they swept on rapidly, for the slaves at the paddles vied in skill and discipline.

"Iztlil' of Tezcuco!" said the 'tzin lightly. "He is welcome; but had a messenger asked me where at this hour he would most likely be found, I should have bade him search the *chinampas*, especially those most notable for their perfume and music."

The speech was courteous, yet the moment of reply was allowed to pass. The 'tzin waited until the delay excited his wonder.

"There is a rumour of a great battle with the Tlascalans," he said again, this time with a direct question. "Has my friend heard of it?"

"The winds that carry rumours seldom come to me," answered Iztlil'.

"Couriers from Tlascala pass directly through your capital"—

The Tezcucan laid his hand on the speaker's shoulder.

"My capital!" he said. "Do you speak of the city of Tezcuco?"

The 'tzin dashed the hand away, and arose, saying, "Your meaning is dark in this dimness of stars."

"Be seated," said the other.

"If I sit, is it as friend or foe?"

"Hear me; then be yourself the judge."

The Aztec folded his cloak about him and resumed his seat, very watchful.

"Montezuma, the king"—

"Beware! The great king is my kinsman, and I am his faithful subject."

The Tezcucan continued. "In the valley the king is next to the gods; yet to his nephew I say I hate him, and will teach him that my hate is no idleness, like a passing love. 'Tzin, a hundred years ago our races were distinct and independent. The birds of the woods, the winds of the prairie, were not more free than the people of Tezcuco. We had our capital, our temples, our worship, and our gods; we celebrated our own festivals, our kings commanded their own armies, our priesthood prescribed their own sacrifices. But where now are king, country, and gods? Alas! you have seen the children of 'Hualpilli, of the blood of the Acolhuan, suppliants of Montezuma, the Aztec." And, as if overcome by the recollection, he burst into apostrophe. "I mourn thee, O Tezcuco, garden of my childhood, palace of my fathers, inheritance of my right! Against me are thy gates closed. The stars may come, and as of old garland thy towers with their rays; but in thy echoing halls and princely courts never, never shall I be known again!"

The silence that ensued the 'tzin was the first to break.

"You would have me understand," he said, "that the king has done you wrong. Be it so. But, for such cause, why quarrel with me?"

"Ah yes!" answered the Tezcucan in an altered voice. "Come closer, that the slaves may not hear."

The Aztec kept his attitude of dignity. Yet lower Iztlil' dropped his voice.

"The king has a daughter whom he calls Tula, and loves as the light of his palace."

The 'tzin started, but held his peace.

"You know her?" continued the Tezcucan.

"Name her not!" said Guatamozin passionately.

"Why not? I love her; and but for you, O 'tzin, she would have loved me. You, too, have done me wrong."

With thoughts dark as the waters he rode, the Aztec looked long at the light of fire painted on the sky above the distant **city.**

"Is Guatamozin turned woman?" asked Iztlil' tauntingly.

"Tula is my cousin. We have lived the lives of brother and sister. In hall, in garden, on the lake, always together, I could not help loving her."

"You mistake me," **said the other.** "**I seek** her for wife, but you seek her for ambition ; **in her eyes you see** only her father's throne."

Then **the** Aztec's manner changed, and he assumed the mastery.

"Enough, Tezcucan! I listened calmly while you reviled the **king,** and now I have somewhat to say. In your youth the wise men prophesied evil from you ; they said you were ingrate and blasphemer then : your whole life has but verified their judgment. Well for your royal father and his beautiful city had he cut you off as they counselled him to do. Treason to the king,— defiance to me! By the holy Sun, for each offence you should answer me shield to shield! But I recollect that I am neither priest to slay a victim nor officer to execute the law. I mourn **a** feud, still more the blood of countrymen shed by my hand ; yet the wrongs shall not go unavenged or without challenge. To-morrow is the sacrifice to Quetzal'. There will be combat with the best captives in the temples ; the arena will be **in** the *tianguez;* Tenochtitlan, and all the valley, and all the nobility of the empire, will look on. Dare you prove your kingly blood? I challenge the son of 'Hualpilli to share the danger with me."

The cacique was silent, and the 'tzin did not disturb him. **At** his order, however, the slaves bent their dusky forms, and **the** vessels sped on, like wingless birds.

CHAPTER IV.

TENOCHTITLAN AT NIGHT.

THE site **of the** city of Tenochtitlan was chosen by the gods. In the south-western border of Lake Tezcuco, one morning in 1300, a wandering tribe of Aztecs saw an eagle perched, with outspread wings, upon a cactus, and holding a serpent in its talons. At a word from their priests, they took possession of the marsh, and there stayed their migration and founded the city : such is the tradition. As men love to trace their descent back to some storied greatness, nations delight to associate the gods with their origin.

Originally the Aztecs were barbarous. In their southern march, they brought with them only their arms and a spirit of sovereignty. The valley of Anahuac, when they reached it, was already peopled ; in fact, had been so for ages. The cultivation and progress they found and conquered there reacted upon them. They grew apace ; and as they carried their shields into neighbouring territory, as by intercourse and commerce they crept from out their shell of barbarism, as they strengthened in opulence and dominion, they repudiated the reeds and rushes of which their primal houses were built, and erected enduring temples and residences of Oriental splendour.

Under the smiles of the gods, whom countless victims kept propitiated, the city threw abroad its arms, and, before the passage of a century, became the emporium of the valley. Its people climbed the mountains around, and, in pursuit of captives to grace their festivals, made the conquest of "Mexico." Then the kings began to centralize. They made Tenochtitlan their capital ; under their encouragement the arts grew and flourished ; its market became famous ; the nobles and privileged orders made it their dwelling-place ; wealth abounded ; as a consequence, a vast population speedily filled its walls and extended them as required. At the coming of the "conquistadores," it contained sixty thousand houses and three hundred thousand souls. Its plat testifies to a high degree of order and regularity, with all the streets running north and south, and intersected by canals, so as to leave quadrilateral blocks. An ancient map, exhibiting the city proper, presents the face of a checker-board, each square, except those of some of the temples and palaces, being meted with mathematical certainty.

Such was the city the 'tzin and the cacique were approaching. Left of them, half a league distant, lay the towers and embattled gate of Xoloc. On the horizon behind paled the fires of Iztapalapan, while those of Tenochtitlan at each moment threw brighter hues into the sky, and more richly empurpled the face of the lake. In mid air, high over all others, like a great torch, blazed the pyre of Huitzil'.[1] Out on the sea, the course of the *voyageurs* was occasionally obstructed by *chinampas* at anchor, or afloat before the light wind ; nearer the walls, the floating gardens multiplied until the passage was as if through an archipelago in miniature. From many of them poured the light of torches ; others gave to the grateful sense the melody of flutes and blended voices ; while over them the radiance from the temples fell softly, revealing white pavilions, orange-trees, flowering shrubs, and nameless varieties of the unrivalled tropical vegetation. A breeze, strong enough to gently ripple the lake, hovered around the

---

[1] The God of War,—aptly called the "Mexican Mars."

undulating retreats, scattering a largesse of perfume, and so ministering to the voluptuous floramour of the locality.

As the *voyageurs* proceeded, the city, rising to view, underwent a number of transformations. At first, amidst the light of its own fires,[1] it looked like a black sea-shore; directly its towers and turrets became visible, some looming vaguely and dark, others glowing and purpled, the whole magnified by the dim duplication below; then it seemed like a cloud, one half kindled by the sun, the other obscured by the night. As they swept yet nearer, it changed to the likeness of a long, ill-defined wall, over which crept a hum wing-like and strange,—the hum of myriad life.

In silence still they hurried forward. Vessels like their own, but with lanterns of stained *aguave* at the prows, seeking some favourite *chinampa*, sped by with benisons from the crews. At length they reached the wall, and, passing through an interval that formed the outlet of a canal, entered the city. Instantly the water became waveless; houses encompassed them; lights gleamed across their way; the hum that hovered over them while out on the lake realized itself in the voices of men and the notes of labour.

Yet farther into the city, the light from the temples increased. From towers, turreted like a Moresco castle, they heard the night-watchers proclaiming the hour. Canoes, in flocks, darted by them, decked with garlands, and laden with the wealth of a merchant, or the trade of a market-man, or full of revellers singing choruses to the stars or to the fair denizens of the palaces. Here and there the canal was bordered with sidewalks of masonry, and sometimes with steps leading from the water up to a portal, about which were companies whose flaunting, parti-coloured costumes, brilliant in the mellowed light, had all the appearance of Venetian masqueraders.

At last the canoes gained the great street that continued from the causeway at the south through the whole city; then the Tezcucan touched the 'tzin, and said,—

"The son of 'Hualpilli accepts the challenge, Aztec. In the *tianguez* to-morrow."

Without further speech, the foemen leaped on the landing, and separated.

---

[1] There was a fire for each altar in the temples which was inextinguishable; and so numerous were the altars, and so brilliant their fires, that they kept the city illuminated throughout the darkest nights. Prescott, *Conq. of Mexico*, Vol. I., p. 72.

CHAPTER V.

THE CHILD OF THE TEMPLE.

THERE were two royal palaces in the city ; one built by Axaya',
the other by Montezuma, the reigning king, who naturally pre-
ferred his own structure, and so resided there.　It was a low,
irregular pile, embracing not only the king's abode proper, but
also quarters for his guard, and edifices for an armoury, an aviary,
and a menagerie.　Attached to it was a garden, adorned with the
choicest shrubbery and plants, with fruit and forest trees, with
walks strewn with shells, and fountains of pure water conducted
from the reservoir of Chapultepec.

At night, except when the moon shone, the garden was lighted
with lamps ; and, whether in day or night, it was a favourite
lounging-place.　During fair evenings, particularly, its walks, of
the whiteness of snow, were thronged by nobles and courtiers.

Shortly after the arrival of Iztlil' and Guatamozin, a party,
mostly of the sons of provincial governors kept at the palace as
hostages, were gathered in the garden, under a canopy used to
shield a fountain from the noonday sun.　The place was fairly
lighted, the air fresh with the breath of flowers, and delightful
with the sound of falling water.

Maxtla, chief of the guard, was there, his juvenility well hidden
under an ostentatious display.　That he was "a very common
soldier" in the opinion of the people was of small moment : he
had the king's ear ; and that, without wit and courtly tact,
would have made him what he was,—the oracle of the party
around him.

In the midst of his gossip, Iztlil', the Tezcucan, came suddenly
to the fountain.　He coldly surveyed the assembly.　Maxtla
alone saluted him.

"Will the prince of Tezcuco be seated ?" said the chief.

"The place is pleasant, and the company looks inviting,"
returned Iztlil' grimly.

Since his affair with Guatamozin, he had donned the uniform
of an Aztec chieftain.　Over his shoulders was carelessly flung a
crimson *tilmatli*,—a short, square cloak, fantastically embroidered
with gold, and so sprinkled with jewels as to flash at every movement ; his body was wrapped closely in a *escaupil*, or tunic, of
cotton lightly quilted, over which, and around his waist, was a
maxtlatl, or sash, inseparable from the warrior.　A casque of
silver, thin, burnished, and topped with plumes, surmounted his
head.　His features were gracefully moulded, and he would have
been handsome but that his complexion was deepened by black,
frowning eyebrows.　He was excessively arrogant ; though some-

times, when deeply stirred by passion, his manner rose into the
royal. His character I leave to history.

"I have just come from Iztapalapan," he said, as he sat upon
the proffered stool. "The lake is calm, the way was very pleasant,
I had the 'tzin Guatamo for comrade."

"You were fortunate. The 'tzin is good company," said
Maxtla.

Itzlil' frowned, and became silent.

"To-morrow," continued the courtier, upon whom the discontent,
slight as it was, had not been lost, "is the sacrifice to Quetzal'.
I am reminded, gracious prince, that at a recent celebration you
put up a thousand cocoa,[1] to be forfeited if you failed to see the
daughter of Mualox, the paba. If not improper, how runs the
wager, and what of the result?"

The cacique shrugged his broad shoulders.

"The man trembles!" whispered one of the party.

"Well he may! Old Mualox is more than a man."

Maxtla bowed and laughed. "Mualox is a magician; the stars
deal with him. And my brother will not speak, lest he may cover
the sky of his fortune with clouds."

"No," said the Tezcucan proudly; "the wager was not a
sacrilege to the paba or his god; if it was, the god, not the man,
should be a warrior's fear."

"Does Maxtla believe Mualox a prophet?" asked Tlahua, a
noble Otompan.

"The gods have power in the sun; why not on earth?"

"You do not like the paba," observed Itzlil' gloomily.

"Who has seen him, O prince, and thought of love? And the
walls and towers of his dusty temple,—are they not hung with
dread, as the sky on a dark day with clouds?"

The party, however they might dislike the cacique, could not
listen coldly to this conversation. They were mostly of that
mystic race of Azatlan, who, ages before, had descended into the
valley, like an inundation, from the north: the race whose religion
was founded upon credulity; the race full of chivalry, but horribly
governed by a crafty priesthood. None of them disbelieved in
star-dealing. So every eye fixed on the Tezcucan, every ear drank
the musical syllables of Maxtla. They were startled when the
former said abruptly,—

"Comrades, the wrath of the old paba is not to be lightly pro-
voked; he has gifts not of men. But, as there is nothing I do
not dare, I will tell the story."

The company now gathered close around the speaker.

"Probably you have all heard," he began, "that Mualox keeps

---

[1] The Aztec currency consisted of bits of tin, in shape like a capital T,
of quills of gold-dust, and of bags of cocoa, containing a stated number
of grains. Sahagun, *Hist. de Nueva Esp.*

in his temple somewhere a child or woman too beautiful to be
mortal. The story may be true; yet it is only a belief; no
eye has seen footprint or shadow of her. A certain lord in the
palace, who goes thrice a week to the shrine of Quetzal', has faith
in the gossip and the paba. He says the mystery is Quetzal' himself, already returned, and waiting, concealed in the temple, the
ripening of the time when he is to burst in vengeance on Tenochtitlan. I heard him talking about it one day, and wagered him a
thousand cocoa that, if there was such a being I would see her
before the next sacrifice to Quetzal'."

The Tezcucan hesitated.

" Is the believer to boast himself wealthier by the wager?" said
Maxtla, profoundly interested. " A thousand cocoa would buy a
jewel or a slave: surely, O prince, surely they were worth the
winning!"

Iztlil' frowned again, and said bitterly, "A thousand cocoa I
cannot well spare; they do not grow on my hard northern hills
like flowers in Xochimilco. I did my best to save the wager.
Old habit lures me to the great *teocallis;* [1] for I am of those who
believe that a warrior's worship is meet for no god but Huitzil'.
But, as the girl was supposed to be down in the cells of the old
temple, and none but Mualox could satisfy me, I began going
there, thinking to bargain humilities for favour. I played my
part studiously, if not well; but no offering of tongue or gold
ever won me word of friendship or smile of confidence. Hopeless
and weary, I at last gave up, and went back to the *teocallis.* But
now hear my parting with the paba. A short time ago a mystery
was enacted in the temple. At the end, I turned to go away,
determined that it should be my last visit. At the eastern steps,
as I was about descending, I felt a hand laid on my arm. It was
Mualox; and not more terrible looks Tlalac when he has sacrificed
a thousand victims. There was no blood on his hands; his beard
and surplice were white and stainless; the terror was in his eyes,
that seemed to burn and shoot lightning. You know, good chief,
that I could have crushed him with a blow; yet I trembled.
Looking back now, I cannot explain the awe that seized me. I
remember how my will deserted me,—how another's came in its
stead. With a glance he bound me hand and foot. While I
looked at him, he dilated, until I was covered by his shadow.
He magnified himself into the stature of a god. 'Prince of
Tezcuco,' he said, 'son of the wise 'Hualpilli, from the sun Quetzal'
looks down on the earth. Alike over land and sea he looks.
Before him space melts into a span, and darkness puts on the glow
of day. Did you think to deceive my god, O prince?' I could
not answer; my tongue was like stone. 'Go hence, go hence!'

---

[1] Temple. The term appears to have applied particularly to the temples
of the god Huitzil'. – Tr.

he cried, waving his hand. 'Your presence darkens his mood. His wrath is on your soul ; he has cursed you. Hence, abandoned of the gods !' So saying, he went back to the tower again, and my will returned, and I fled. And now," said the cacique, turning suddenly and sternly upon his hearers, " who will deny the magic of Mualox ? How may I be assured that his curse that day spoken was not indeed a curse from Quetzal' ?"

There was neither word nor laugh,—not even a smile. The gay Maxtla appeared infected with a sombreness of spirit ; and it was not long until the party broke up, and went each his way.

CHAPTER VI.

THE CÛ OF QUETZAL', AND MUALOX, THE PABA.

OVER the city from temple to temple passed the wail of the watchers, and a quarter of the night was gone. Few heard the cry without pleasure ; for to-morrow was Quetzal's day, which would bring feasting, music, combat, crowd, and flowers.

Among others the proclamation of the passing time was made from a temple in the neighbourhood of the Tlateloco *tianguez*, or market-place, which had been built by one of the first kings of Tenochtitlan, and, like all edifices of that date properly called Cûs, was of but one story, and had but one tower. At the south its base was washed by a canal ; on all the other sides it was enclosed by stone walls, high, probably, as a man's head. The three sides so walled were bounded by streets, and faced by houses, some of which were higher than the Cû itself, and adorned with beautiful porticoes. The canal on the south ran parallel with the Tlacopan causeway, and intersected the Iztapalapan street at a point nearly half a mile above the great pyramid.

The antique pile thus formed a square of vast extent. According to the belief that there were blessings in the orient rays of the sun, the front was to the east, where a flight of steps, wide as the whole building, led from the ground to the *azoteas*, a paved area constituting the roof, crowned in the centre by a round tower of wood most quaintly carved with religious symbols. Entering the door of the tower, the devotee might at once kneel before the sacred image of Quetzal'.

A circuitous stairway outside the tower conducted to its summit, where blazed the fire. Another flight of steps about midway the tower and the western verge of the *azoteas* descended into a court-yard, around which, in the shade of a colonnade, were doors and windows of habitable apartments and passages leading far into the interior. And there, shrouded in a perpetual twilight and darkness, once slept, ate, prayed, and studied or dreamed the members of a fraternity powerful as the Templars and gloomy as the Fratres Minores.

The interior was cut into rooms, and long, winding halls, and countless cellular dens.

Such was the Cû of Quetzal',—stern, sombre, and massive as in its first days; unchanged in all save the prosperity of its priesthood and the popularity of its shrine. Time was when every cell contained its votaries, and kings, returning from battle, bowed before the altar. But Montezuma had built a new edifice, and set up there a new idol; and, as if a king could better make a god than custom, the people abandoned the old ones to desuetude. Up in the ancient cupola, however, sat the image said to have been carved by Quetzal's own hand. Still the fair face looked out benignly on its realm of air; carelessly the winds waved "the plumes of fire" that decked its awful head; and one stony hand yet grasped a golden sceptre, while the other held aloft the painted shield,—symbols of its dominion.[1] But the servitors and surpliced mystics were gone; the cells were very solitudes; the last paba lingered to protect the image and its mansion, all unwitting how, in his faithfulness of love, he himself had assumed the highest prerogative of a god.

The fire from the urn on the tower flashed a red glow down over the *azoteas*, near a corner of which Mualox stood, his beard white and flowing as his surplice. Thought of days palmier for himself and more glorious for his temple and god struggled to his lips.

"Children of Azatlan, ye have strayed from his shrine, and dust is on his shield. The temple is of his handiwork, but its chambers are voiceless; the morning comes and falls asleep on its steps, and no foot disturbs it, no one seeks its blessings. Where is the hymn of the choir? Where the prayer? Where the holiness that rested, like a spell, around the altar? Is the valley fruitless, and are the gardens without flowers, that he should be without offering or sacrifice? . . . Ah! well ye know that the day is not distant when he will glisten again in the valley; when he will come, not as of old he departed, the full harvest quick ripening in his footsteps, but with the power of Mictlan,[2] the owl on his skirt, and death in his hand. Return, O children, and Tenochtitlan may yet live!"

In the midst of his pleadings there was a clang of sandalled feet on the pavement, and two men came near him, and stopped. One of them wore the hood and long black gown of a priest; the

---

[1] Sahagun, *Hist. de Nueva Esp.*
[2] The Mexican Hell. The owl was the symbol of the Devil, whose name signifies "the rational owl."

other the full military garb,—burnished casque crested with plumes, a fur-trimmed *tilmatli*, *escaupil*, and *maxtlatl*, and sandals the thongs of which were embossed with silver. He also carried a javelin, and a shield with an owl painted on its face. Indeed, one will travel far before finding, among Christians or unbelievers, his peer. He was then not more than twenty-five years old, tall and nobly proportioned, and with a bearing truly **royal.** In Spain I have seen eyes as large and lustrous, but **none of such** power and variety of expression. His complexion was merely the brown of the **sun.** Though very masculine, his features, especially when the spirit was in repose, were softened by an expression unusually gentle and attractive. Such was the 'tzin Guatamo, or, as he is more commonly known **in history, Guata-** mozin,—the highest, noblest type of his race, **blending in one its** genius and heroism, **with** but few of **its** debasements.

"Mualox," said the priestly **stranger.**

The paba turned, and knelt, **and kissed** the pavement.

"O king, pardon your slave! **He was** dreaming of his country."

"No slave of mine, but Quetzal's. Up, Mualox!" said Monte- zuma, throwing back the hood that covered his head. "Holy should be the dust that mingles in your beard!"

And the light from the tower shone full **on** the face of him,— the priest of lore profound, and monarch wise of thought, for whom Heaven **was** preparing a destiny most memorable among the melancholy episodes of history.

A slight mustache shaded his **upper lip, and a** thin, **dark** beard covered his chin and throat **; his nose was** straight; his brows curved archly; his forehead **was** broad and full, while he seemed possessed of height and strength. His neck was round, muscular, and encircled by **a** collar **of** golden wires. His **manner was** winsome, and he spoke to the kneeling man in **a** voice clear, distinct, and sufficiently emphatic for the king he was.[1]

Mualox arose, and stood with downcast eyes, and hands crossed over his breast.

"Many a coming of stars it has been," he said, "since the old shrine has known the favour of gift from Montezuma. Gloom of clouds in a **vale** of firs is not darker than the mood of Quetzal'; but to the poor paba, your voice, O king, is welcome as the song of the river in the ear of the thirsty."

The king looked up at the fire on the tower.

"Why should the mood of Quetzal' be dark? A new *teocallis* holds his image. His priests are proud; and they say he is happy, and that when he **comes** from the golden land his canoe will be full of blessings."

[1] Bernal Diaz, *Hist. de la Conquista.*

Mualox sighed, and when he ventured to raise his eyes to the king's, they were wet with tears.

"O king, have you forgotten that chapter of the *teoamoxtli*,[1] in which is written how this Cû was built, and its first fires lighted, by Quetzal' himself? The new pyramid may be grand; its towers may be numberless, and its fires far reaching as the sun itself: but hope not that will satisfy the god, while his own house is desolate. In the name of Quetzal', I, his true servant, tell you, never again look for smile from Tlapallan."

The paba's speech was bold, and the king frowned; but in the eyes of the venerable man there was the unaccountable fascination mentioned by Iztlil'.

"I remember the Mualox of my father's day; surely he was not as you are!" Then, laying his hand on the 'tzin's arm, the monarch added, "Did you not say the holy man had something to tell me?"

Mualox answered, "Even so, O king! Few are the friends left the paba, now that his religion and god are mocked; but the 'tzin is faithful. At my bidding he went to the palace. Will Montezuma go with his servant?"

"Where?"

"Only into the Cû."

The monarch faltered.

"Dread be from you!" said Mualox. "Think you it is as hard to be faithful to a king as to a god whom even he has abandoned?"

Montezuma was touched. "Let us go," he said to the 'tzin.

CHAPTER VII.

THE PROPHECY ON THE WALL.

MUALOX led them into the tower. The light of purpled lamps filled the sacred place, and played softly around the idol, before which they bowed. Then he took a light from the altar, and conducted them to the *azoteas*, and down into the courtyard, from whence they entered a hall leading on into the Cû.

The way was labyrinthine, and both the king and the 'tzin became bewildered; they only knew that they descended several stairways, and walked a considerable distance; nevertheless, they submitted themselves entirely to their guide, who went forward without hesitancy. At last he stopped; and, by the light which

[1] The Divine Book, or Bible. Ixtlil's *Relaciones MS.*

he held up for the purpose, they saw in the wall an aperture roughly excavated, and large enough to admit them singly.

"You have read the Holy Book, wise king," said Mualox. "Can you not recall its saying that, before the founding of Tenochtitlan, a Cû was begun, with chambers to lie under the bed of the lake? Especially, do you not remember the declaration, that in some of those chambers, besides a store of wealth so vast as to be beyond the calculation of men, there were prophecies to be read, written on the walls by a god?"

"I remember it," said the king.

"Give me faith, then, and I will show you all you there read."

Thereupon the paba stepped into the aperture, saying,—

"Mark! I am now standing under the eastern wall of **the old Cû.**"

He passed through, and **they** followed him, **and were amazed.**

"**Look** around, O king! **You are in** one of the chambers mentioned in the Holy Book."

The light penetrated but a short distance, so that Montezuma could form no idea of the extent of the apartment. He would **have** thought it a great natural cavern but for the floor smoothly paved with alternate red and grey flags, and some massive stone blocks rudely piled up in places to support the roof.

As they proceeded, Mualox said, "On every side of us there are rooms through which we might go till, in stormy weather, the waves of the lake can be heard breaking overhead."

In a short time they again stopped.

"We are nearly there. Son of a king, is your heart strong?" said Mualox solemnly.

Montezuma made no answer.

"Many a time," continued the paba, "your glance has rested on the tower of the old Cû, then flashed to where, in prouder state, your pyramids rise. You never thought the grey pile you smiled at was the humblest of all Quetzal's works. Can a man, though a king, outdo a god?"

"I never thought so, I never thought so!"

But the mystic did not notice the deprecation.

"See," he said, speaking louder, "the pride of man says, I will build upward that the sun may show my power; but the gods **are too** great for pride; so the sun shines not on their especial glories, which as frequently lie in the earth and sea as in the air and heavens. O mighty king! You crush the worm under your sandal, never thinking that its humble life is more wonderful than all your temples and state. It was the same folly that laughed at the simple tower of Quetzal', which has mysteries"—

"Mysteries!" said the king.

"I will show you wealth enough to restock the mines and visited valleys with all their plundered gold and jewels."

"You are dreaming, paba."

"Come, then ; let us see ! "

They moved past some columns, and came before a great arched doorway, through which streamed a brilliance like day.

"Now, let your souls be strong ! "

They entered the door, and for a while were blinded by the glare, and could see only the floor covered with grains of gold large as wheat. Moving on, they came to a great stone table, and stopped.

"You wonder ; and so did I, until I was reminded that a god had been here. Look up, O king ! look up, and see the handiwork of Quetzal' ! "

The chamber was broad and square. The obstruction of many pillars, forming the stay of the roof, was compensated by their lightness and wonderful carving. Lamps, lit by Mualox in anticipation of the royal coming, blazed in all quarters. The ceiling was covered with lattice-work of shining white and yellow metals, the preciousness of which was palpable to eyes accustomed like the monarch's. Where the bars crossed each other, there were fanciful representations of flowers, wrought in gold, some of them large as shields, and garnished with jewels that burned with star-like fires. Between the columns, up and down, ran rows of brazen tables, bearing urns and vases of the royal metals, higher than tall men, and carved all over with gods in *bas-relief*, not as hideous caricatures, but beautiful as love and Grecian skill could make them. Between the vases and urns there were heaps of rubies and pearls and brilliants, amongst which looked out softly the familiar, pale-green lustre of the *chalchuites*, or priceless Aztecan diamond.[1] And here and there, like guardians of the buried beauty and treasure, statues looked down from tall pedestals, crowned and armed, as became the kings and demi-gods of a great and martial people. The monarch was speechless. Again and again he surveyed the golden chamber. As if seeking an explanation, but too overwhelmed for words, he turned to Mualox.

"And now does Montezuma believe his servant dreaming?" said the paba. "Quetzal' directed the discovery of the chamber. I knew of it, O king, before you were born. And here is the wealth of which I spoke. If it so confounds you, how much more will the other mystery ! I have dug up a prophecy ; from darkness plucked a treasure richer than all these. O king, I will give you to read a message from the gods ! "

[1] A kind of emerald, used altogether by the nobility. Sahagun, *Hist. de Nueva Esp.*

The monarch's face became bloodless, and it had now not a trace of scepticism.

"I will show you from Quetzal' himself that the end of **your** Empire is at hand, and that every wind of the earth is full sown with woe to you and yours. The **writing is on** the walls Come!"

And he led **the** king, followed by Guatamozin, to the northern corner of the eastern wall, on which, in square marble panels, *bas-relief* style, were hierograms and sculptured pictures of men, executed apparently by the same hand that chiselled the statues in the room. The ground of the carvings was coated with coarse grey **coral,** which had the effect **to** bring out **the white** figures with marvellous perfection.

"This, O king, is the writing," said Mualox, **"which begins** here, and continues around the walls. I will **read, if you please** to hear."

Montezuma waved his hand, and the paba proceeded.

"This figure is that of the first king of Tenochtitlan; the others are his followers. The letters record the time of the march from the north. Observe that the first of the writing—its commencement—is here in the north."

After a little while, they moved on to the second panel.

"Here," said Mualox, "is represented the march of the king. It was accompanied with battles. See, he stands with lifted javelin, his foot on the breast of a prostrate foe. His followers dance and sound shells; the priests sacrifice a victim. The king has won a great victory."

They stopped before the third panel.

"And here the monarch is still on the march. He is in the midst of his warriors; no doubt the crown he is receiving is that of the ruler of a conquered city."

This cartoon Montezuma examined closely. The chief, or king, was distinguished by a crown in all respects like that then in the palace; the priests, by their long gowns; and the warriors, by their arms, which, as they were counterparts of those still in use, sufficiently identified the wanderers. Greatly was the royal inspector troubled. And as the paba slowly conducted him from panel to panel, he forgot the treasure with which the chamber was stored. What he read was the story of his race, the record of their glory. The whole eastern wall he found, when he had passed before it, given to illustrations of the crusade from Azatlan, the fatherland, northward so far that corn was gathered in the snow, and flowers were the wonder of the six weeks' summer.

In front of the first panel on the southern wall Mualox said,—

"All we have passed is the first era in the history; this is the beginning of the second; and the first writing on the western

wall will commence a third. Here the king stands on a rock ; a
priest points him to an eagle on a cactus, holding a serpent. At
last they have reached the place where Tenochtitlan is to be
founded."

The paba passed on.

"Here," he said, "are temples and palaces. The king reclines
on a couch ; the city has been founded."

And before another panel,—"Look well to this, O king ! A
new character is introduced ; here it is before an altar, offering a
sacrifice of fruits and flowers. It is Quetzal' ! In his worship,
you recollect, there is no slaughter of victims. My hands are
pure of blood."

The Quetzal', with its pleasant face, flowing curls, and simple
costume, seemed to have a charm for Montezuma, for he mused
over it a long time. Some distance on, the figure again appeared,
stepping into a canoe, while the people, temples, and palaces of
the city were behind it. Mualox explained, "See, O king ! The
fair god is departing from Tenochtitlan ; he has been banished.
Saddest of all the days was that !"

And so, the holy man interpreting, they moved along the
southern wall. Not a scene but was illustrative of some incident
memorable in the Aztecan history. And the reviewers were
struck with the faithfulness of the record not less than with the
beauty of the work.

On the western wall, the first cartoon represented a young man
sweeping the steps of a temple. Montezuma paused before it
amazed, and Guatamozin for the first time cried out, "It is the
king ! It is the king !" The likeness was perfect.

After that came a coronation scene. The *teotuctli* was placing a
panache[1] on Montezuma's head. In the third cartoon, he was
with the army, going to battle. In the fourth, he was seated,
while a man clad in *nequen*,[2] but crowned, stood before him.

"You have grown familiar with triumphs, and it is many
summers since, O king," said Mualox ; "but you have not yet
forgotten the gladness of your first conquest. Here is its record.
As we go on, recall the kings who were thus made to stand before
you."

And counting as they proceeded, Montezuma found that in
every cartoon there was an additional figure crowned and in
nequen. When they came to the one next the last on the western
wall, he said,—

"Show me the meaning of all this : here are thirty kings."

[1] Or *capilli*,—the king's crown. A *panache* was the head-dress of a
warrior.

[2] A garment of coarse white material, made from the fibre of the aloe,
and by court etiquette required to be worn by courtiers and suitors in the
king's presence. The rule appears to have been of universal application.

"Will the king tell **his slave the** number of cities he has conquered?"

He thought awhile, and replied, "Thirty."

"Then the record is faithful. It started with the first king of Tenochtitlan; it came down **to** your coronation; now, it has numbered your conquests. See you not, O king? Behind us, all the writing is of the past; this is Montezuma and Tenochtitlan as they are: the present is before us! Could the hand that set this chamber and carved these walls have been a man's? Who but a god six cycles ago could have foreseen that a son of **the son** of Axaya' would carry the rulers of thirty conquered cities **in his** train?"

The royal visitor listened breathlessly. He began to comprehend the writing, and thrill with fast-coming presentiments. Yet he struggled with his fears.

"Prophecy has to do with the future," he said; **"and you** have shown me nothing that the sculptors and jewellers in my palace cannot do. Would you have me believe all this from Quetzal', show me something that is to come."

Mualox led him to the next scene, which represented the king sitting in state; above him a canopy; his nobles and the women of his household around him; at his feet the people; and all were looking at a combat going on between warriors.

"You have asked for prophecy,—behold!" said Mualox.

"I see nothing," replied the king.

"Nothing! Is not this the celebration to-morrow? **Since** it was ordered, could your sculptors have executed what **you see?**"

Back to the monarch's face **stole the pallor.**

"Look again, O king! You only saw yourself, **your people** and warriors. But what is this?"

Walking up, he laid his finger on **the representation of** a man landing from a canoe.

"The last we beheld of Quetzal'," he continued, "was on the southern wall; his back was to Tenochtitlan, which he was leaving with a curse. All you have heard about his promise to return is true. He himself has written the very day, and here it is. Look! While the king, his warriors and people, are gathered to the combat, Quetzal' steps from the canoe to the seashore."

The figure in the carving was scarcely two hands high, but exquisitely wrought. With terror poorly concealed, Montezuma recognised it.

"And now my promise is redeemed. I said I would give you to read a message from the sun."

"Read, Mualox: I cannot."

The holy man turned to the writing, and said, with a swelling voice, "Thus writes Quetzal' to Montezuma, the king! In the last day he will seek to stay my vengeance; he will call together his people; there will be combat in Tenochtitlan; but in the midst of the rejoicing I will land on the sea-shore, and end the days of Azatlan for ever."

"For ever!" said the unhappy monarch. "No, **no!** Read the next writing."

"There is no other; this is the last."

The eastern, southern, and western walls had been successively **passed,** and interpreted. Now the king turned to the northern **wall:** *it was blank!* His eyes flashed, and he almost shouted,—

"**Liar!** Quetzal' **may come** to-morrow, but it will be as friend. **There is no curse!**"

The paba humbled himself before the speaker, and said, slowly and tearfully, "The wise king is blinded by his hope. When Quetzal' finished this chapter, his task was done; he had recorded the last day of perfect glory, and ceased to write because, Azatlan being now to perish, there was nothing more to record. O unhappy king! that is the curse, and it needed no writing!"

Montezuma shook with passion.

"Lead me hence, lead me hence!" **he cried.** "I will watch; and if Quetzal' comes not on the morrow,—comes not during the celebration,—I swear to level this temple, and let the lake into its chambers! And you, paba though you be, I will drown you like a slave! Lead on!"

Mualox obeyed without a word. Lamp in hand, he led his visitors from the splendid chamber up to the *azoteas* of the ancient house. **As** they descended the eastern steps, he knelt and kissed the pavement.

CHAPTER VIII.

A BUSINESS MAN IN TENOCHTITLAN.

XOLI, the Chalcan, was supposed to be the richest citizen, exclusive of the nobles, in Tenochtitlan. Amongst other properties he owned a house on the eastern side of the Tlateloco *tianguez,* or market-place, which, whether considered architecturally, **or** with reference to the business to which it was devoted, or as the device of an unassoilzied heathen, **was** certainly very remarkable. Its portico had six great columns **of** white marble alternating six **others** of green porphyry, with a roof guarded by a parapet intricately and tastefully carved; while cushioned lounges, heavy curtains festooned and flashing with cochineal, and a fountain of water pure enough for the draught of a king, all within the columns, perfected it as a retreat from the sultry summer sun.

The house thus elegantly garnished was not a *meson*, or a café, or a theatre, or a broker's office; but rather a combination of them all, and therefore divided into many apartments; of which one was for the sale of beverages favourite among the wealthy and noble Aztecs,—Bacchic inventions, with *pulque* for chief staple, since it had the sanction of antiquity, and was mildly intoxicating; another was a restaurant, where the *cuisine* was only excelled at the royal table; indeed, there was a story abroad that the king had several times borrowed the services of the Chalcan's *artistes;* but, whether derived from the master or his slaves, the shrewd reader will conclude from it, that the science of advertising was known and practised as well in Tenochtitlan as in Madrid. Nor were these all. Under the same roof were rooms for the amusement of patrons,—for reading, smoking, and games; one in especial for a play of hazard called *totoloque*, then very popular, because a passion of Montezuma's. Finally, as entertainments not prohibited by the *teotuctli*, a signal would at any time summon a minstrel, a juggler, or a dancing-girl. Hardly need I say that the establishment was successful. Always ringing with music, and of nights always resplendent with lamps, it was always overflowing with custom.

"So old Tepaja wanted you to be a merchant," said the Chalcan in his full, round voice, as, comfortably seated under the curtains of his portico, he smoked his pipe, and talked with our young friend, the Tihuancan.

"Yes. Now that he is old, he thinks war dangerous."

"You mistake him, boy. He merely thinks with me, that there is something more real in wealth and many slaves. As he has grown older, he has grown wiser."

"As you will. I could not be a merchant."

"Whom did you think of serving?"

"The 'tzin Guatamo." [1]

"I know him. He comes to my portico sometimes, but not to borrow money. You see, I frequently act as broker, and take deposits from the merchants and securities from the spendthrift nobles; he, however, has no vices. When not with the army, he passes the time in study; though they do say he goes a great deal to the palace to make love to the princess. And now that I reflect, I doubt if you can get place with him."

"Why so?"

"Well, he keeps no idle train, and the time is very quiet. If he were going to the frontier it would be different."

[1] *'Tzin* was a title equivalent to *lord* in English. *Guatamotzin*, as compounded, signifies *Lord Guatamo.*

" Indeed ! "

" You see, boy, he is the bravest man and best fighter in the army ; and the sensible fellows of moderate skill and ambition have no fancy for the hot place in a fight, which is generally where he is."

" The discredit is not to him, by Our Mother ! " said Hualpa, laughing.

The broker stopped to cherish the fire in his pipe,—an act which the inexperienced consider wholly incompatible with the profound reflection he certainly indulged. When next he spoke, it was with smoke wreathing his round face, as white clouds sometimes wreathe the full moon.

" About an hour ago a fellow came here, and said he had heard that Iztlil', the Tezcucan, had challenged the 'tzin to go into the arena with him to-morrow. Not a bad thing for the god Quetzal', if all I hear be true ! "

Again the pipe, and then the continuation.

" You see, when the combat was determined on, there happened to be in the temples two Othmies and two Tlascalans, warriors of very great report. As soon as it became known that by the king's choice they were the challengers, the young fellows about the palace shunned the sport, and there was danger that the god would find himself without a champion. To avoid such a disgrace, the 'tzin was coming here to-night to hang his shield in the portico. If he and the Tezcucan both take up the fight, it will be a great day indeed."

The silence that ensued was broken by the hunter, whom the gossip had plunged into reverie.

" I pray your pardon, Xoli ; but you said, I think, that the lords hang back from the danger. Can any one volunteer ? "

" Certainly ; any one who is a warrior, and is in time. Are you of that mind ? "

The Chalcan took down the pipe, and looked at him earnestly.

" If I had the arms "—

" But you know nothing about it,—not even how such combats are conducted ! "

The broker was now astonished.

" Listen to me," he said. " These combats are always in honour of some one or more of the Aztecan gods,—generally of Huitzil', god of war. They used to be very simple affairs. A small platform of stone, of the height of a man, was put up in the midst of the *tianguez,* so as to be seen by the people standing around ; and upon it, in pairs, the champions fought their duels. This, however, was too plain to suit the tastes of the last Montezuma ; and he changed the ceremony into a spectacle really honourable and great. Now, the arena is first prepared,—a central space in a great many rows of seats erected so as to rise one above the other. At the proper time, the people, the priests, and the soldiers go in and take possession of their allotted places. Some time previous, the quarters of the prisoners taken in battle are examined, and two or more of the best of the warriors found there are chosen by the king, and put in training for the occasion. They are treated fairly, and are told that, if they fight and win, they shall be crowned as heroes, and returned to their tribes. No need, I think, to tell you how brave men fight when stimulated by hope of glory and hope of life. When chosen, their names are published, and their shields hung up in a portico on the other side of the square yonder; after which they are understood to be the challengers of any equal number of warriors who dare become champions of the god or gods in whose honour the celebration is had. Think of the approved skill and valour of the foe; think of the thousands who will be present; think of your own inexperience in war, and of your youth, your stature hardly gained, your muscles hardly matured; think of everything tending to weaken your chances of success,—and then speak to me."

Hualpa met the sharp gaze of the Chalcan steadily, and answered, "I am thought to have some skill with the bow and *maquahuitl.* Get me the opportunity, and I will fight."

And Xoli, who was a sincere friend, reflected awhile. "There is peril in the undertaking, to be sure; but then he is resolved to be a warrior, and if he survives, it is glory at once gained, fortune at once made." Then he arose, and, smiling, said aloud, "Let us go to the portico. If the list be not full, you shall have the arms,—yes, by the Sun! as the lordly Aztecs swear,—the very best in Tenochtitlan."

And they lifted the curtains, and stepped into the *tianguez.*[1] The light of the fires on the temples was hardly more in strength than the shine of the moon; so that torches had to be set up at intervals over the celebrated square. On an ordinary occasion, with a visitation of forty thousand busy buyers and sellers, it was a show of merchants and merchantable staples worthy the chief mart of an empire so notable; but now, drawn by the double attraction of market and celebration, the multitude that thronged it was trebly greater; yet the order was perfect.

An officer, at the head of a patrol, passed them with a prisoner.

"Ho, Chalcan! If you would see justice done, follow me."

"Thanks, thanks, good friend; I have been before the judges too often already."

So the preservation of the peace was no mystery.

[1] The great market-place or square of Tlateloco. The Spaniards called it *tianguez.* For description, see Prescott, *Conq. of Mexico,* Vol. II., Book IV. Bernal Diaz's Work, *Hist. de la Conq.*

The friends made way slowly, giving the Tihuancan time to gratify his curiosity. He found the place like a great national fair, in which few branches of industry were unrepresented. There were smiths who worked in the coarser metals, and jewellers skilful as those of Europe; there were makers and dealers in furniture, and sandals, and *plumaje*; at one place men were disposing of fruits, flowers, and vegetables; not far away fishermen boasted their stock caught that day in the fresh waters of Chalco; tables of pastry and maize bread were set next the quarters of the hunters of Xilotepec; the armourers, clothiers, and dealers in cotton were each of them a separate host. In no land where a science has been taught or a book written have the fine arts been dishonoured; and so in the great market of Tenochtitlan there were no galleries so rich as those of the painters, nor was any craft allowed such space for their exhibitions as the sculptors.

They halted an instant before a porch full of slaves. A rapid glance at the miserable wretches, and Xoli said pitilessly, "Bah! Mictlan has many such. Let us go."

Farther on they came to a platform on which a band of mountebanks was performing. Hualpa would have stayed to witness their tableaux, but Xoli was impatient.

"You see yon barber's shop," he said; "next to it is the portico we seek. Come on!"

At last they arrived there, and mixed with the crowd, curious like themselves.

"Ah, boy, you are too late! The list is full."

The Chalcan spoke regretfully.

Hualpa looked for himself. On a clear white wall, that fairly glistened with the flood of light pouring upon it, he counted eight shields, or gages of battle. Over the four to the left were picture-written, "Othmies," "Tlascalans." They belonged to the challengers, and were battered and stained, proving that their gathering had been in no field of peace. The four to the right were of the Aztecs, and all bore devices except one. A sentinel stood silently beneath them.

"Welcome, Chalcan!" said a citizen, saluting the broker. "You are in good time to tell us the owners of the shields here."

"Of the Aztecs?"

"Yes."

"Well," said Xoli slowly and gravely, "the shields I do not know are few and of little note. At one time or another I have seen them all pass my portico going to battle."

A bystander, listening, whispered to his friends,—

"The braggart! He says nothing of the times the owners passed his door to get a pinch of his snuff."

"Or to get drunk on his abominable *pulque*," said another.

"Or to get a loan, leaving their palaces in pawn," said a third party.

But Xoli went on impressively,—

"Those two to the left belong to a surly Otompan and a girl-faced Cholulan. They had a quarrel in the king's garden, and this is the upshot. That other,—surely, O citizens, you know the shield of Iztlil', the Tezcucan !"

"Yes ; but its neighbour ?"

"The plain shield ! Its owner has a name to win. I can find you enough such here in the market to equip an army. Say, soldier, whose gage is that ?"

The sentinel shook his head. "A page came not long ago, and asked me to hang it up by the side of the Tezcucan's. He said not whom he served."

"Well, maybe you know the challengers."

"Two of the shields belong to a father and son of the tribe of Othmies. In the last battle the son alone slew eight Cempoallan warriors for us. Tlascalans, whose names I do not know, own the others."

"Do you think they will escape ?" asked a citizen.

The sentinel smiled grimly, and said, "Not if it be true that yon plain shield belongs to Guatamo, the 'tzin."

Directly a patrol, rudely thrusting the citizens aside, came to relieve the guard. In the confusion, the Chalcan whispered to his friend, "Let us go back. There is no chance for you in the arena to-morrow ; and this new fellow is sullen ; his tongue would not wag though I promised him drink from the king's vase."

Soon after they reached the Chalcan's portico and disappeared in the building, the cry of the night-watchers arose from the temples, and the market was closed. The great crowd vanished ; in stall and portico the lights were extinguished ; but at once another scene equally tumultuous usurped the *tianguez.* Thousands of half-naked *tamanes* rushed into the deserted place, and all night long it resounded, like a Babel, with clamour of tongues and notes of mighty preparation.

CHAPTER IX.

THE QUESTIONER OF THE MORNING.

WHEN Montezuma departed from the old Cû for his palace, it was not to sleep or rest. The revelation that so disturbed him, that held him wordless on the street, and made him shrink from his people, wild with the promise of pomp and combat, would not be shut out by gates and guards; it clung to his memory, and with him stood by the fountain, walked in the garden, and laid down on his couch. Royalty had no medicine for the trouble; he was restless as a fevered slave, and at times muttered prayers, pronouncing no name but Quetzal's. When the morning approached, he called Maxtla, and bade him get ready his canoe: from Chapultepec, the palace and tomb of his fathers, he would see the sun rise.

From one of the westerly canals they put out. The lake was still rocking the night on its bosom, and no light other than of the stars shone in the east. The gurgling sound of waters parted by the rushing vessel, and the regular dip of the paddles, were all that disturbed the brooding of majesty abroad thus early on Tezcuco.

The canoe struck the white pebbles that strewed the landing at the princely property just as dawn was dappling the sky. On the highest point of the hill there was a tower from which the kings were accustomed to observe the stars. Thither Montezuma went. Maxtla, who alone dared follow, spread a mat for him on the tiles; kneeling upon it, and folding his hands worshipfully upon his breast, he looked to the east.

And the king was learned; indeed, one more so was not in all his realm. In his student days, and in his priesthood, before he was taken from sweeping the temple to be arch-ruler, he had gained astrological craft, and yet practised it from habit. The heavens, with their blazonry, were to him as pictured parchments. He loved the stars for their sublime mystery, and had faith in them as oracles. He consulted them always: his armies marched at their bidding; and they and the gods controlled every movement of his civil polity. But as he had never before been moved by so great a trouble, and as the knowledge he now sought directly concerned his throne and nations, he came to consult and question the Morning, that intelligence higher and purer than the stars. If Quetzal' was angered, and would that day land for vengeance, he naturally supposed the Sun, his dwelling-place, would give some warning. So he came seeking the mood of the god from the Sun.

And while he knelt, gradually the grey dawn melted into purple and gold. The stars went softly out. Long rays, like radiant spears, shot up and athwart the sky. As the indications multiplied, his hopes arose. Farther back he threw the hood from his brow; the sun seemed coming clear and cloudless above the mountains, kindling his heart no less than the air and earth.

A wide territory, wrapped in the dim light, extended beneath his feet. There slept Tenochtitlan, with her shining temples and blazing towers, her streets and resistless nationality; there were the four lakes, with their blue waters, their shores set with cities, villages, and gardens; beyond them lay eastern Anahuac, **the** princeliest jewel of the empire. What with its harvests, its orchards, and its homesteads; its forests of oak, sycamore, and cedar; its population busy, happy, and faithful, contented as tillers of the soil, and brave as lions in time of need, it was all of Aden he had ever known or dreamed.

In the south-east, above a long range of mountains, rose the volcanic peaks poetized by the Aztecs into "The White Woman"[1] and "The Smoking Hill."[2] Mythology had covered them with sanctifying faith, as, in a different age and more classic clime, it clothed the serene mountain of Thessaly.

But the king saw little of all this beauty; he observed nothing but the sun, which was rising a few degrees north of "The Smoking Hill." In all the heavens round there was not a fleck; and already his heart throbbed with delight, when suddenly a cloud of smoke rushed upward from the mountain, and commenced gathering darkly about its white summit. Quick to behold it, he scarcely hushed a cry of fear, and instinctively waved his hand, as if, by a kingly gesture, to stay the eruption. Slowly the vapour crept over the roseate sky, and, breathless and motionless, the seeker of the god's mood and questioner of the Morning watched its progress. Across the pathway of the sun it stretched, so that when the disc wheeled fairly above the mountain-range, it looked like a ball of blood.

The king was a reader of picture-writing, and skilful in deducing the meaning of men from cipher and hieroglyph. Straightway he interpreted the phenomenon as a direful portent; and because he came looking for omens, the idea that this was a message sent him expressly from the gods was but a right royal vanity. He drew the hood over his face again, and dropped his head disconsolately upon his breast. His mind filled with a host of gloomy thoughts. The revelation of Mualox was prophecy here confirmed,—Quetzal' was coming! Throne, power, people, —all the glories of his country and Empire,—he saw snatched from his nerveless grasp, and floating away, like the dust of the valley.

After a while he rose to depart. One more look he gave the sun before descending from the roof, and shuddered at the sight of city, lake, valley, the cloud itself, and the sky above it, all coloured with an ominous crimson.

"Behold!" he said tremulously to Maxtla; "to-day we will sacrifice to Quetzal': how long until Quetzal' sacrifices to himself?"

[1] Iztaccihuatl.   [2] Popocatepetl.

D

The chief cast down his eyes; for he knew how dangerous it was to look on royalty humbled by fear. Then Montezuma shaded his face again, and left the proud old hill, with a sigh for its palaces and the beauty of its great cypress-groves.

CHAPTER X.

GOING TO THE COMBAT.

As the morning advanced, the city grew **fully** animate. A festal spirit was abroad, seeking display in masks, mimes, and processions. Jugglers performed on the street corners; dancing-girls, with tambours, and long elf-locks dressed in flowers, possessed themselves of the smooth side-walks. Very plainly, the evil omen of the morning affected the king more than his people.

The day advanced clear and beautiful. In the eastern sky the smoke of the volcano still lingered; but the sun rose above it, and smiled on the valley, like a loving god.

At length the tambour in the great temple sounded the signal of assemblage. Its deep tones, penetrating every recess of the town and rushing across the lake, were heard in the villages on the distant shores. Then, in steady currents, the multitudes set forward for the *tianguez*. The *chinampas* were deserted; hovels and palaces gave up their tenantry; canoes, gay with garlands, were abandoned in the waveless canals. The women and children came down from the roofs; from all the temples—all but the old one with the solitary grey tower and echoless court—poured the priesthood in processions, headed by chanting choirs, and interspersed with countless sacred symbols. Many were the pomps, but that of the warriors surpassed all others. Marching in columns of thousands, they filled the streets with flashing arms and gorgeous regalia, roar of *attabals* and peals of minstrelsy.

About the same time the royal palanquin stood at the palace portal, engoldened, jewelled, and surmounted with a *panache* of green plumes. Cuitlahua, Cacama, Maxtla, and the lords of Tlacopan, Tepejaca, and Cholula, with other nobles from the provinces far and near, were collected about it in waiting, sporting on their persons the wealth of principalities. When the monarch came out, they knelt, and every one of them placed his palm on the ground before him. On the last stone at the portal he stopped, and raised **his eyes to** the sky. A piece of *aguave*, fluttering like a leaf, **fell so near** him that he reached out his hand and caught it.

" Read it, my lords," he said, after a moment's study.

The paper contained only the picture of an eagle attacked by an owl, and passed from hand to hand. Intent on deciphering the writing, none thought of inquiring whether its coming was of design or accident.

" What does it mean, my lord Cacama?" asked the monarch gravely.

Cacama's eyes dropped as he replied,—

" When we write of you, O king, we paint an eagle ; when we write of the 'tzin Guatamo, we paint an owl."

" What !" said the lord Cuitlahua ; " would the 'tzin attack his king?"

And the monarch looked from one to the other strangely, saying only, " The owl is the device on his shield."

Then he entered the palanquin ; whereupon some of the nobles lifted it on their shoulders, and the company, in procession, set out for the *tianguez*. On the way they were joined by Iztlil', the Tezcucan ; and it was remarkable that, of them all, he was the only one silent about the paper.

The Iztapalapan street, of great width, and on both sides lined with gardens, palaces, and temples, was not only the boast of Tenochtitlan ; its beauty was told in song and story throughout the Empire. The signal of assemblage for the day's great pastime found Xoli and his provincial friend lounging along the broad pave of the beautiful thoroughfare. They at once started for the *tianguez*. The broker was fat, and it was troublesome for him to keep pace with the hunter ; nevertheless, they overtook a party of *tamanes* going in the same direction, and bearing a palanquin richly caparisoned. The slaves, very sumptuously clad, proceeded slowly and with downcast eyes, and so steadily that the carriage had the onward, gliding motion of a boat.

" Lower,—down, boy ! See you not the green *panache?*" whispered Xoli, half frightened.

Too late. The Chalcan, even as he whispered, touched the pavement, but Hualpa remained erect : not only that ; he looked boldly into the eyes of the occupants of the palanquin,—two women, whose beauty shone upon him like a sudden light. Then he bent his head, and his heart closed upon the recollection of what he saw so that it never escaped. The picture was of a girl, almost a woman, laughing: opposite her, and rather in the shade of the fringed curtain, one older, though young, and grave and stately ; her hair black, her face oval, her eyes large and lustrous. To her he made his involuntary obeisance. Afterwards she reminded many a Spaniard of the dark-eyed *hermosura* with whom he had left love-tokens in his native land.

"They are the king's daughters, the princesses Tula and Nenetzin," said Xoli, when fairly past the carriage. "And as you have just come up from the country, listen. Green is the royal colour, and belongs to the king's family; and wherever met, in the city or on the lake, the people salute it. Though what they meet be but a green feather in a slave's hand, they salute. Remember the lesson. By the way, the gossips say that Guatamozin will marry Tula, the eldest one."

"She is very beautiful," said the hunter, as to himself, and slackening his steps.

"Are you mad?" cried the broker, seizing his arm. "Would you bring the patrol upon us? They are not for such as you. Come on. It may be we can get seats to see the king and his whole household."

At the entrance to the arena there was a press which the police could hardly control. In the midst of it, Xoli pulled his companion to one side, saying, "The king comes! Let us under the staging here until he passes."

They found themselves, then, close by the spears, which, planted in the ground, upheld the shields of the combatants; and when the Tihuancan heard the people, as they streamed in, cheer the champions of the god, he grieved sorely that he was not one of them.

The heralds then came up, clearing the way; and all thereabout knelt, and so received the monarch. He stopped to inspect the shields; for in all his realm there was not one better versed in its heraldry. A diadem, not unlike the papal tiara, crowned his head; his tunic and cloak were of the skins of green humming-birds brilliantly iridescent; a rope of pearls large as grapes hung, many times doubled, from his neck down over his breast; his sandals and sandal-thongs were embossed with gold, and, besides anklets of massive gold, *cuishes* of the same metal guarded his legs from knee to anklet. Save the transparent, lustrous grey of the pearls, his dress was of the two colours, green and yellow, and the effect was indescribably royal; yet all the bravery of his trappings could not hide from Hualpa, beholding him for the first time, that, like any common soul, he was suffering from some trouble of mind.

"So, Cacama," he said pleasantly, after a look at the gages, "your brother has a mind to make peace with the gods. It is well!"

And thereupon Iztlil' himself stepped out and knelt before him in battle array, the javelin in his hand, and bow, quiver, and *maquahuitl* at his back; and in his homage the floating feathers of his helm brushed the dust from the royal feet.

"It is well!" repeated the king, smiling. "But, son of my friend, where are your comrades?"

Tlahua, the Otompan, and the young Cholulan, equipped like Iztlil', rendered their homage also. Over their heads he extended his hands, and said softly, "They who love the gods, the gods love. Put your trust in them, O my children! And upon you be their blessing!"

And already he had passed the spears: one gage was forgotten, one combatant unblessed. Suddenly he looked back.

"Whose shield is that, my lords?"

All eyes rested upon the plain gage, but no one replied.

"Who is he that thus mocks the holy cause of Quetzal'? Go, Maxtla, and bring him to me!"

Then outspake Iztlil'.

"The shield is Guatamozin's. Last night he challenged me to this combat, and he is not here. O king, the owl may be looking for the eagle."

A moment the sadly serene countenance of the monarch knit and flushed as from a passing pain; a moment he regarded the Tezcucan. Then he turned to the shields of the Othmies and Tlascalans.

"They are a sturdy foe, and I warrant will fight hard," he said quietly. "But such victims are the delight of the gods. Fail me not, O children!"

When the Tihuancan and his chaperon climbed half-way to the upper row of seats, in the quarter assigned to the people, the former was amazed. He looked down on a circular arena, strewn with white sand from the lake, and large enough for manœuvring half a thousand men. It was bounded by a rope, outside of which was a broad margin crowded with rank on rank of common soldiery, whose shields were arranged before them like a wall impervious to a glancing arrow. Back from the arena extended the staging, rising gradually seat above seat, platform above platform, until the whole area of the *tianguez* was occupied.

"Is the king a magician, that he can do this thing in a single night?" asked Hualpa.

Xoli laughed. "He has done many things much greater. The timbers you see were wrought long ago, and have been lying in the temples; the *tamanes* had only to bring them out and put them together."

In the east there was a platform, carpeted, furnished with lounges, and protected from the sun by a red canopy; broad passages of entrance separated it from the ruder structure erected for the commonality; it was also the highest of the platforms, so that its occupants could overlook the whole amphitheatre. This lordlier preparation belonged to the king, his household and nobles. So, besides his wives and daughters, under the red canopy sat the three hundred women of his harem,—soft testimony that Orientalism dwelt not alone in the sky and palm-trees of the valley.

As remarked, the margin around the arena belonged to the soldiery ; the citizens had seats in the north and south ; while the priesthood, superior to either of them in sanctity of character, sat aloof in the west, also screened by a canopy. And, as the celebration was regarded in the light of a religious exercise, not only did women crowd the place, but mothers brought their children, that, from the examples of the arena, they might learn to be warriors.

Upon the appearance of the monarch there was a perfect calm. Standing awhile by his couch, he looked over the scene ; and not often has royal vision been better filled with all that constitutes royalty. Opposite him he saw the servitors of his religion ; at his feet were his warriors and people almost innumerable. When, at last, the minstrels of the soldiery poured their wild music over the theatre, he thrilled with the ecstasy of power.

The champions for the god then came in ; and as they strode across to the western side of the arena the air was filled with plaudits and flying garlands ; but hardly was the welcome ended before there was a great hum and stir, as the spectators asked each other why the fourth combatant came not with the others.

"The one with the bright *panache*, asked you ? That is Iztlil', the Tezcucan," said Xoli.

"Is he not too fine ?"

"No. Only think of the friends the glitter has made him among the women and children."

The Chalcan laughed heartily at the cynicism.

"And the broad-shouldered fellow now fixing the thongs of his shield ?"

"The Otompan,—a good warrior. They say he goes to battle with the will a girl goes to a feast. The other is the Cholulan ; he has his renown to win, and is too young."

"But he may have other qualities," suggested Hualpa. "I have heard it said that, in a battle of arrows, a quick eye is better than a strong arm."

The broker yawned. "Well, I like not those Cholulans. They are proud ; they scorn the other nations, even the Aztecs. Probably it is well they are better priests than soldiers. Under the red canopy yonder I see his father."

"Listen, good Xoli. I hear the people talking about the 'tzin ? Where can he be ?"

Just then within the wall of shields there came a warrior, who strode swiftly toward the solitary cage. His array was less splendid than his comrades': his helm was of plain leather without ornament ; his *escaupil* was secured by a simple loop : yet the people knew him, and shouted ; and when he took down the plain shield and fixed it to his arm, the approbation of the common soldiery arose like a storm. As they bore such shields to battle, he became, as it were, their peculiar representative. It was Guatamozin.

And under the royal canopy there was rapid exchange of whispers and looks; every mind reverted to the paper dropped so mysteriously into the king's hand at the palace door; and some there were, acuter than the rest, who saw corroboration of the meaning given the writing in the fact that the shield the 'tzin now chose was without the owl, his usual device. Whether the monarch himself was one of them might not be said; his face was as impassive as bronze.

Next, the Othmies and Tlascalans, dignified into common challengers of the proudest chiefs of Tenochtitlan, were conducted into the arena.

The Tlascalans were strong men used to battle; and though, like their companions in danger, at first bewildered by the sudden introduction to so vast a multitude, they became quickly inured to the situation. Of the Othmies, a more promising pair of gladiators never exhibited before a Roman audience. The father was past the prime of life, but erect, broad-shouldered, and of unusual dignity; the son was slighter, and not so tall, but his limbs were round and beautiful, and he looked as if he might outleap an antelope. The people were delighted, and cheered the challengers with scarcely less heartiness than their own champions. Still the younger Othmi appeared hesitant, and, when the clamour somewhat abated, the sire touched him, and said,—

"Does my boy dream? What voice is in his ear that his heart is so melted? Awake! the shield is on the arm of the foe."

The young man aroused. "I saw the sun on the green hills of Othmi. But see!" he said proudly, and with flashing eyes; "there is no weakness in the dreamer's arm." And with the words he seized a bow at his feet, fitted an arrow upon the cord, and, drawing full to the head, sent it cleaving the sunshine far above them. Every eye followed its flight but his own. "The arm, O chief, is not stronger than the heart," he added, carelessly dropping the bow.

The old warrior gazed at him tenderly; but as that was no time for the indulgence of affection, he turned to the Tlascalans, and said, "We must be ready: let us arm."

Each donned a leathern helm, and wrapped himself in a quilted *escaupil*; each buckled the shield on his arm, and tightened the thongs of his sandals. Their arms lay at hand.

Such were the preparations for the combat, such the combatants. And as the foemen faced each other, awaiting the signal for the mortal strife, I fancy no Christian has seen anything more beautiful than the theatre. Among the faces the gaze swam as in a sea; the gleaming of arms and ornaments was bewildering; while the diversity of colours in the costumes of the vast audience was without comparison. With the exception of the arena, the royal platform was the cynosure. Behind the king, with a shield faced with silver, stood Maxtla, vigilant against treachery or despair. The array of nobles about the couch was imperial; and, what with them, and the dark-eyed beauties of his household, and the canopy tinging the air and softly undulating above him, and the mighty congregation of subjects at his feet, it was with Montezuma like a revival of the glory of the Hystaspes. Yet the presence of his power but increased his gloom: in a short time he heard no music and saw no splendour; everything reminded him of the last picture on the western wall of the golden chamber.

CHAPTER XI.

THE COMBAT.

THE champions for the god drew themselves up in the west, while their challengers occupied the east of the arena. This position of parties was the subject of much speculation with the spectators, who saw it might prove a point of great importance if the engagement assumed the form of single combats.

Considering age and appearance, the Tlascalans were adjudged most dangerous of the challengers,—a palm readily awarded to the Tezcucan and the 'tzin on their side. The common opinion held also, that the Cholulan, the youngest and least experienced of the Aztecs, should have been the antagonist of the elder Othmi, whose vigour was presumed to be affected by his age; as it was, that combat belonged to Tlahua, the Otompan, while the younger Othmi confronted the Cholulan.

And now the theatre grew profoundly still with expectancy.

"The day grows old. Let the signal be given." And so saying, the king waved his hand, and sank indolently back upon his couch.

A moment after there was a burst of martial symphony, and the combat began.

It was opened with arrows; and to determine, if possible, the comparative skill of the combatants, the spectators watched the commencement with closest attention. The younger Othmi sent his missile straight into the shield of the Cholulan, who, from precipitation probably, was not so successful. The elder Othmi and his antagonist each planted his arrow fairly, as did Iztlil' and the Tlascalans. But a great outcry of applause attended Guatamozin, when his bolt, flying across the space, buried its barb in the crest of his adversary. A score of feathers, shorn away, floated slowly to the sand.

"It was well done! by Our Mother, ɪt **was** well done!" murmured Hualpa.

"Wait!" said the Chalcan patronizingly. "Wait till they come to the *maquahuitl!*"

Quite a number of arrows were thus interchanged by the parties without effect, as they were always dexterously intercepted. The passage was but the preluding skirmish, participated in by all but the 'tzin, who, after his first shot, stood a little apart from his comrades, and, resting his long bow on the ground, watched the trial with apparent indifference. Like the Chalcan, he seemed to regard it as play; and the populace after a while fell into the same opinion: there was not enough danger to fully interest them. So there began to arise murmurs and cries, which the Cholulan was the first to observe and interpret. Under **an** impulse which had relation, probably, to his first failure, he resolved to avail himself of the growing feeling. Throwing down his bow, he seized the *maquahuitl* at his back, and, without a word to his friends, started impetuously across the arena. The peril was great, for every foeman at once turned his arrow against him.

Then the 'tzin stirred himself. "The boy is mad, and will **die** if we do not go with him," he said; and already his foot was advanced to follow, when the young Othmi sprang forward **from** the other side to meet the Cholulan.

The eagerness lest an incident should be lost became intense; even the king sat up to see the duel. The theatre rang with cries of encouragement,—none, however, so cheery as that of the elder Othmi, whose feelings of paternity were, for the moment, lost in his passion of warrior.

"On, boy! Remember the green hills, and the hammock by the stream. Strike hard, strike hard!"

The combatants were apparently well matched, being about equal in height and age; both brandished the *maquahuitl*, the deadliest weapon known to their wars. Wielded by both hands, and swung high above the head, its blades of glass generally clove their way to the life. About midway the arena the foemen met. At the instant of contact the Cholulan brought **a** downward blow, well aimed, at the head of his antagonist; but the lithe Othmi, though at full speed, swerved like **a** bird on the wing. A great shout attested the appreciation of the audience. The Cholulan wheeled, with his weapon uplifted for another blow ; the action called his left arm into play, and drew his shield from its guard. The Othmi saw the advantage. One step he took nearer, and then, with a sweep of his arm and an upward stroke, he drove every blade deep into the side of his enemy. The lifted weapon dropped in its half-finished circle, the shield flew wildly up, and with a groan the victim fell heavily to the sand, struggled once to rise, fell back again, and his battles were ended for ever. A cry of anguish went out from under the royal canopy.

"Hark!" cried Xoli. "Did you hear the old Cholulan? See! they are leading him from the platform!'

Except that cry, however, not a voice was heard ; from rising apprehension as to the result of the combat, or touched by a passing sympathy for the early death, the multitude was perfectly hushed.

"That was a brave blow, Xoli ; but let him beware now!" said Hualpa excitedly.

And in expectation of instant vengeance, all eyes watched the Othmi. Around the arena he glanced, then back to his friends. Retreat would forfeit the honour gained : death was preferable. So he knelt upon the breast of his enemy, and, setting his shield before him, waited sternly and in silence the result. And Iztlil' and Tlahua launched their arrows at him in quick succession, but Guatamozin was as indifferent as ever.

"What ails the 'tzin?" said Maxtla to the king. "The Othmi is at his mercy."

The monarch deigned no reply.

The spirit of the old Othmi rose. On the sand behind him, prepared for service, was a dart with three points of copper, and a long cord by which to recover it when once thrown. Catching the weapon up, and shouting, "I am coming, I am coming!" he ran to avert or share the danger. The space to be crossed was inconsiderable, yet such his animation that, as he ran, he poised the dart, and exposed his hand above the shield. The 'tzin raised his bow, and let the arrow fly. It struck right amongst the supple joints of the veteran's wrist. The unhappy man stopped bewildered ; over the theatre he looked, then at the wound ; in despair he tore the shaft out with his teeth, and rushed on till he reached the boy.

The outburst of acclamation shook the theatre.

"To have seen such archery, Xoli, were worth all the years of a hunter's life!" said Hualpa.

The Chalcan smiled like a connoisseur, and replied, "It is nothing. Wait!"

And now the combat again presented a show of equality. The advantage, if there was any, was thought to be with the Aztecs, since the loss of the Cholulan was not to be weighed against the disability of the Othmi. Thus the populace were released from apprehension, without any abatement of interest; indeed, the excitement increased, for there was a promise of change in the character of the contest; from quiet archery **was** growing bloody action.

The Tlascalans, alive **to** the necessity **of** supporting their friends, advanced to where the Cholulan lay, but more cautiously. When they were come up, the Othmies both **arose,** and calmly perfected the front. The astonishment at this was very great.

"Brave fellow! He is worth ten live Cholulans!" said Xoli. "But now look, boy! The challengers have advanced half-**way;** the Aztecs must meet them."

The conjecture was speedily verified. **Iztlil'** had, in fact, ill brooked the superior skill, or better fortune, of the 'tzin; the applause of the populace had been worse than wounds to his jealous heart. Till this time, however, **he** had restrained his passion; now the foe were ranged **as** if challenging attack: he threw away his useless bow, and laid his hand on his *maqua-huitl.*

"**It** is not for **an Aztec god that we are** fighting, O comrade!" he cried to Tlahua. "**It is for ourselves.** Come, let us show yon king a better war!"

And without waiting, he set on. **The** Otompan followed, leaving the 'tzin alone. The call had not been to him, and, as he was fighting for the god, and the Tezcucan for himself, he merely placed another arrow on his bow, and observed **the attack.**

Leaving the Otompan to engage the Othmies, **the fierce** Tezcucan assaulted the Tlascalans, an encounter **in which there was** no equality; but the eyes of Tenochtitlan **were upon him,** and at his back was a hated rival. His antagonists **each** sent an arrow to meet him; but, as he skilfully caught them on his shield, they too betook themselves to the *maquahuitl.* Right on he kept, until his shield struck theirs; it was gallantly done, and won a furious outburst from the people. Again Montezuma sat up, momentarily animated.

"Ah, my lord Cacama," he said, "if your brother's love were but equal to his courage, I would give him an army!"

"All the gods forfend!" replied the jealous prince. "**The** viper would recover his fangs."

The speed with which he went was all that saved Iztlil' from the blades of the Tlascalans. Striking no blow himself, he strove to make way between them, and get behind, so that, facing about to repel his returning onset, their backs would be to the 'tzin. But they were wary, and did not yield. As they pushed against him, one, dropping his more cumbrous weapon, struck him in **the** breast with a copper knife. The blow was distinctly seen **by the** spectators.

Hualpa started from his seat. "He has it; they will finish him now! No, he recovers. Our Mother, what a blow!"

The Tezcucan disengaged himself, and, maddened by the blood that began to flow down his quilted armour, assaulted furiously. He was strong, quick of eye, and skilful; the blades of his weapon gleamed in circles around his head, and resounded against the shields. At length a desperate blow beat down the guard of one of the Tlascalans; ere it could be recovered, or Iztlil' avail himself of the advantage, there came a sharp whirring through the air, and an arrow from the 'tzin pierced to the warrior's heart. Up he leaped, dead before he touched the sand. Again Iztlil' heard the acclamation of his rival. Without a pause, he rushed upon the surviving Tlascalan, as if to bear him down by stormy dint.

Meantime the combat of Tlahua, the Otompan, was not without its difficulties, since it was not singly with the young Othmi.

"Mictlan take the old man!" cried the lord Cuitlahua, bending from his seat. "I thought him done for; but, see! he defends, the other fights."

And so it was. The Otompan struck hard, but was distracted by the tactics of his foemen: if he aimed at the younger, both their shields warded the blow; if he assaulted the elder, he was in turn attacked by the younger; and so, without advantage to either, their strife continued until the fall of the Tlascalan. Then, inspired by despairing valour, the boy threw down his *maquahuitl*, and endeavoured to push aside the Otompan's shield. Once within its guard, the knife would finish the contest. Tlahua retreated; but the foe clung to him,—one wrenching at his shield, the other intercepting his blows, and both carefully avoiding the deadly archery of the 'tzin, who, seeing the extremity of the danger, started to the rescue. All the people shouted, "The 'tzin, the 'tzin!" Xoli burst into ecstasy, and clapped his hands. "There he goes! Now look for something!"

The rescuer went as a swift wind; but the clamour had been as a warning to the young Othmi. By a great effort he tore away the Otompan's shield. In vain the latter struggled. There was a flash, sharp, vivid, like the sparkle of the sun upon restless waters. Then his head drooped forward, and he staggered blindly. Once only the death-stroke was repeated; and so still was the multitude that the dull sound of the knife driving home was heard. The 'tzin was too late.

The prospect for the Aztecs was now gloomy. The Cholulan and Otompan were dead; the Tezcucan, wounded and bleeding, was engaged in a doubtful struggle with the Tlascalan; the 'tzin was the last hope of his party. Upon him devolved the fight with the Othmies. In the interest thus excited Iztlil's battle was forgotten.

Twice had the younger Othmi been victor, and still he was scatheless. Instead of the *maquahuitl*, he was now armed with the javelin, which, while effective as a dart, was excellent to repel assault.

From the crowded seats of the theatre not a sound was heard. At no time had the excitement risen to such a pitch. Breathless and motionless, the spectators awaited the advance of the 'tzin. He was, as I have said, a general favourite, beloved by priest and citizen, and with the wild soldiery an object of rude idolatry. And if, under the royal canopy, there were eyes that looked not lovingly upon him, there were lips there murmuring soft words of prayer for his success.

When within a few steps of the waiting Othmies, he halted. They glared at him an instant in silence ; then the old chief said tauntingly, and loud enough to be heard above the noise of the conflict at his side,—

"A woman may wield a bow, and from a distance slay a warrior ; but the *maquahuitl* is heavy in the hand of the coward, looking in the face of his foeman."

The Aztec made no answer ; he was familiar with the wile. Looking at the speaker as if against him he intended his first attack, with right hand back he swung the heavy weapon above his shoulder till it sung in quickening circles ; when its force was fully collected, he suddenly hurled it from him. The old Othmi crouched low behind his shield : but his was not the form in the 'tzin's eyes ; for right in the centre of the young victor's guard the flying danger struck. Nor arm nor shield might bar its way. The boy was lifted sheer above the body of the Otompan, and driven backward as if shot from a catapult.

Guatamozin advanced no farther. A thrust of his javelin would have disposed of the old Othmi, now unarmed and helpless. The acclamation of the audience, in which was blent the shrill voices of women, failed to arouse his passion.

The sturdy chief arose from his crouching ; he looked for the boy to whom he had so lately spoken of home ; he saw him lying outstretched, his face in the sand, and his shield, so often bound with wreaths and garlands, twain-broken beneath him ; and his will, that in the fight had been tougher than the gold of his bracelets, gave way,—forgetful of all else, he ran, and, with a great cry, threw himself upon the body.

The Chalcan was as exultant as if the achievement had been his own. Even the prouder souls under the red canopy yielded their tardy praise ; only the king was silent.

As none now remained of the challengers but the Tlascalan occupied with Iztlil',—none whom he might in honour engage,— Guatamozin moved away from the Othmies ; and as he went, once he allowed his glance to wander to the royal platform, but with thought of love, not wrong.

The attention of the people was again directed to the combat of the Tezcucan. The death of his comrades nowise daunted the Tlascalan; he rather struck the harder for revenge; his shield was racked, the feathers in his crest torn away, while the blades were red with his blood. Still it fared but ill with Iztlil' fighting for himself. His wound in the breast bled freely, and his equipments were in no better plight than his antagonist's. The struggle was that of the hewing and hacking which, whether giving or taking, soon exhausts the strongest frame. At last, faint with loss of blood, he went down. The Tlascalan attempted to strike a final blow, but darkness rushed upon him; he staggered, the blades sank into the sand, and he rolled beside his enemy.

With that the combat was done. The challengers might not behold their "land of bread" again; nevermore for them was hammock by the stream or echo of tambour amongst the hills.

And all the multitude arose and gave way to their rejoicing; they embraced each other, and shouted and sang; the pabas waved their ensigns, and the soldiers saluted with voice and pealing shells; and up to the sun ascended the name of Quetzal' with form and circumstance to soften the mood of the most demanding god; but all the time the audience saw only the fortunate hero, standing so calmly before them, the dead at his feet, and the golden light about him.

And the king was happy as the rest, and talked gaily, caring little for the living or the dead. The combat was over, and Quetzal' not come. Mualox was a madman, not a prophet; the Aztecs had won, and the god was propitiated: so the questioner of the Morning flattered himself!

"If the Othmi cannot fight, he can serve for sacrifice. Let him be removed. And the dead— But hold!" he cried, and his cheeks blanched with mortal pallor. "Who comes yonder? Look to the arena,—nay, to the people! By my father's ashes, the paba shall perish! White hairs and prophet's gifts shall not save him."

While the king was speaking, Mualox, the keeper of the temple, rushed within the wall of shields. His dress was disordered, and he was bareheaded and unsandalled. Over his shoulders and down his breast flowed his hair and beard, tangled and unkempt, wavy as a billow and white as the foam. Excitement flashed from every feature; and far as his vision ranged,—in every quarter, on every platform,—in the blood of others he kindled his own unwonted passion.

CHAPTER XII.

MUALOX AND HIS WORLD.

MUALOX, after the departure of the king and 'tzin, ascended the tower of the old Cû, and remained there all night, stooped beside the sacred fire, sorrowing and dreaming, hearkening to the voices of the city, or watching the mild-eyed stars. So the morning found him. He too beheld the coming of the sun, and trembled when the Smoking Hill sent up its cloud. Then he heaped fresh faggots on the dying fire, and went down to the courtyard. It was the hour when in all the other temples worshippers came to pray.

He took a lighted lamp from a table in his cell, and followed a passage on deeper into the building. The way, like that to the golden chamber, was intricate and bewildering. Before a door at the foot of a flight of steps he stopped. A number of earthen jars and ovens stood near; while from the room to which the door gave entrance there came a strong, savoury perfume, very grateful to the sense of a hungry man. Here was the kitchen of the ancient house. ·The paba went in.

This was on a level with the water of the canal at the south base; and when the good man came out, and descended another stairway, he was in a hall which, though below the canal, was dusty and perfectly dry. Down the hall farther he came to a doorway in the floor, or rather an aperture, which had at one time been covered and hidden by a ponderous flagstone yet lying close by. A rope-ladder was coiled up on the stone. Flinging the ladder through the door, he heard it rattle on the floor beneath; then he stooped, and called,—

"Tecetl, Tecetl!"

No one replied. He repeated the call.

"Poor child! She is asleep," he said in a low voice. "I will go down without her."

Leaving the lamp above, he committed himself to the unsteady rope, like one accustomed to it. Below all was darkness; but, pushing boldly on, he suddenly flung aside a curtain which had small silver bells in the fringing; and, ushered by the tiny ringing, he stepped into a chamber lighted and full of beauty,— a grotto carven with infinite labour from the bed-rock of the lake.

And here in the day mourned by the paba, when the temple was honoured, and its god had worshippers, and the name of Quetzal' was second to no other, not even Huitzil's, must have been held the secret conclaves of the priesthood,—so great were the dimensions of the chamber, and so far was it below the roll of

waters.   But now it might be a place for dwelling, or for thought
and dreaming, or for pleasure, or in which the eaters of the
African lotus might spend their hours and days of semi-conscious-
ness sounding of a life earthly yet purely spiritual.   There were
long aisles for walking, and couches for rest ; there were pictures,
flowers, and a fountain ; the walls and ceiling glowed with frescoing ; and wherever the eye turned it rested upon some cunning
device intended to instruct, gladden, comfort, and content.   Lamplight streamed into every corner, ill supplying the perfect sunshine, yet serving its grand purpose.   The effect was more than
beautiful.   The world above was counterfeited, so that one
ignorant of the original and dwelling in the counterfeit could
have been happy all his life long.   Scarcely is it too much to say
of the master who designed and finished the grotto, that, could
he have borrowed the materials of nature, he had the taste and
genius to set a star with the variety and harmony that mark the
setting of the earth's surface, and of themselves prove its Creator
divine.

In the enchantment of the place there was a peculiarity indicative of a purpose higher than mere enjoyment, and that was the
total absence of humanity in the host of things visible.   Painted
on the ceiling and walls were animals of almost every kind
common to the clime ; birds of wondrous plumage darted hither
and thither, twittering and singing ; there, also, were flowers the
fairest and most fragrant, and orange and laurel shrubs, and
pines and cedars and oaks, and other trees of the forest, dwarfed,
and arranged for convenient carriage to the *azoteas;* in the
pictures, moreover, were the objects most remarkable in the face
of nature,—rivers, woods, plains, mountains, oceans, the heavens
in storm and calm ; but nowhere was the picture of man, woman,
or child.   In the frescoing were houses and temples, grouped as
in hamlets and cities, or standing alone on a river's bank, or in
the shadow of great trees ; but of their habitants and builders
there was not a trace.   In fine, the knowledge there taught was
that of a singular book.   A mind receiving impressions, like a
child's, would be carried by it far enough in the progressive
education of life to form vivid ideas of the world, and yet be left
in a dream of unintelligence to people it with fairies, angels,
or gods.   Almost everything had there a representation but
humanity, the brightest fallen nature.

Mualox entered as one habituated to the chamber.   The air
was soft, balmy, and pleasant, and the illumination mellowed, as
if the morning were shut out by curtains of gossamer tinted with
roses and gold.   Near the centre of the room he came to a fountain of water crystal-clear and in full play, the jet shooting from
a sculptured stone up almost to the ceiling.   Around it were
tables, ottomans, couches, and things of *vertu,* such as would have

adorned the palace ; there, also, were vases of flowers, culled and growing, and of such colour and perfume as would have been estimable in Cholula, and musical instrument, and pencils and paints.

It was hardly possible that this conception, so like the **Restful** World of Brahma, should be without its angel ; for the atmosphere and all were for a spirit of earth or heaven softer than man's. And by the fountain it was,—a soul fresh and pure as the laughing water.

The girl of whom I speak was asleep. Her head lay upon **a** cushion ; over the face, clear and almost white, shone a lambent transparency, which might have been the reflection of the sparkling water. The garments gathered close about her did not conceal the delicacy and childlike grace of her form. One foot was exposed, and it was bare, small, and nearly lost in the tufted mattress of her couch. Under a profusion of dark hair, covering the cushion like the floss of silk, lay an arm ; a hand, dimpled and soft, rested lightly on her breast. The slumber was very deep, giving the face the expression **of** dreamless repose, with the promise of health and happiness upon waking.

The paba approached her tenderly, and knelt down. **His** face was full of holy affection. He bent his cheek close to her parted lips, listening to her breathing. He brought the straying locks back, and laid them across her neck. Now and **then** a bird came and lighted on the table, and he waved his **mantle** to scare **it** away. And when the voice of the fountain **seemed,** under an increased pulsation of the water, to grow louder, he looked around, frowning lest it might disturb her. She slept on, his love about her like a silent prayer that has found its consummation in perfect peace.

And as he knelt, he became sad and thoughtful. The events that were to come, and his faith in their coming, **were** as actual sorrows. His reflections were like **a** plea addressed **to** his conscience.

"God pardon me, if, after all, **I** should be mistaken ! The wrong would be so very great as to bar me from the Sun. Is any vanity like that which makes sorrows for our fellows ? And such is not only the vanity of the warrior, and that of the ruler of tribes ; sometimes it is of **the** priests who go into the temples thinking **of** things that do not pertain to the gods. What if mine were such ?

"The holy Quetzal' knows that I intended to be kind **to** the child. I thought my knowledge greater than that of ordinary mortals ; I thought it moved in fields where only the **gods** walk, sowing wisdom. The same vanity, taking words, **told** me, ' Look up ! There is no abyss between you and the gods ; they cannot make themselves of the dust, but you can reach their summit

E

almost a god.' And I laboured, seeking the principles that
would accomplish my dream, if such it were. Heaven forgive
me, but I once thought I had found them! Other men looking
out on creation could see nothing but Wisdom—Wisdom everywhere; but I looked with a stronger vision, and wherever there
was a trace of infinite WISDOM, there was also for me an infinite
WILL.

"Here were the principles, but they were not enough. Something said me, 'What were the Wisdom and Will of the gods
without subjects?' It was a great idea: I thought I stood almost
upon the summit!

"And I set about building me a world. I took the treasure of
Quetzal', and collected these marvels, and bought me the labour
of art. Weavers, florists, painters, masons,—all toiled for me.
Gold, labour, and time are here,—there is little beauty without
them. Here is my world," he said aloud, glancing around the
great hall.

"I had my world; next I wanted a subject for my will. But
where to go? Not among men,—alas, they are their own slaves!
One day I stood in the *tianguez* where a woman was being sold.
A baby in her arms smiled, it might have been at the sunshine,
it might have been at me. The mother said, 'Buy.' A light
flashed upon me—I bought you, my poor child. Men say of the
bud, It will be a rose, and of the plant, It will be a tree; you
were so young then that I said, 'It will be a mind.' And into
my world I brought you, thinking, as I had made it, so I would
make a subject. This, I told you, was your birthplace; and here
passed your infancy and childhood; here you have dwelt. Your
cheeks are pale, my little one, but full and fresh; your breath is
sweet as the air above a garden; and you have grown in beauty,
knowing nothing living but the birds and me. My will has a
subject, O Tecetl, and my heart a child. And judge me, holy
Quetzal', if I have not tried to make her happy! I have given
her knowledge of everything but humanity, and ignorance of that
is happiness. My world has thus far been a heaven to her; her
dreams have been of it; I am its god!"

And yet unwilling to disturb her slumber, Mualox arose, and
walked away.

CHAPTER XIII.

THE SEARCH FOR QUETZAL'.

By and by he returned, and, standing by the couch, passed his hand several times above her face. Silent as the movements were, she awoke, and threw her arms around his neck.

"You have been gone a long while," she said in a childish voice. "I waited for you; but the lamps burned down low, and the shadows, from their hiding among the bushes, came creeping in upon the fountain, and I slept."

"I saw you," he answered, playing **with her hair. "I saw** you; I always see you."

"I tried to paint the fountain," she went on; "but when I watched the water to catch its colours, I thought its singing changed to voices, and, listening to them, they stole my thoughts away. Then I tried to blend my voice with them, and sing as they sung; but whenever mine sank low enough, it seemed sad, while they went on gayer and more ringing than ever. I can paint the flowers, but not the water; I can sing with the birds, but not with the fountain. But you promised to call me,—that you would always call me."

"I knew you were asleep."

"But you had only to think to waken me."

He smiled at this acknowledgment of the power of his will. Just then a bell sounded faintly through the chamber; hastening away, he shortly returned with breakfast on a great shell waiter; **there** were maize bread and honey, quails and chocolate, figs and oranges. Placing them on a table, he rolled up an ottoman for the girl; and, though she talked much and lightly, the meal was soon over. Then he composed himself upon the couch, and in the quiet, unbroken save by Tecetl, forgot the night and its incidents.

His rest was calm; when he awoke, she was sitting by the basin of the fountain talking to her birds gleefully as a child. She had given them names, words more of sound pleasant to the ear than of signification; so she understood the birds, whose varied cries were to her a language. And they were fearless and tame, perching on her hand, and courting her caresses; while she was as artless, with a knowledge as innocent, and a nature as happy. If Quetzal' was the paba's idol in religion, **she** was his idol in affection.

He watched her awhile, then suddenly sat up; though he said not a word, she flung her birds off, and came to him smiling.

"You called me, father."

He laid his hand upon her shoulder, all overflowed with the dark hair, and said in a low voice, "The time approaches when Quetzal' is to come from the home of the gods; it may be he is near. I will send you over the sea and the land to find him; you shall have wings to carry you into the air; and you shall fly swifter than the birds you have been talking to."

Her smile deepened.

"Have you not told me that Quetzal' is good, and that his voice is like the fountain's, and that when he speaks it is like singing? I am ready."

He kissed her, and nearer the basin rolled the couch, upon which she sat reclined against a heap of cushions, her hands clasped over her breast.

"Do not let me be long gone!" she said. "The lamps will burn low again, and I do not like to have the shadows come and fold up my flowers."

The paba took a pearl from the folds of his gown, and laid it before her; then he sat down, and fixed his eyes upon her face; she looked at the jewel, and composed herself as for sleep. Her hands settled upon her bosom, her features grew impassive, the lips slowly parted; gradually her eyelids drooped, and the life running in the veins of her cheeks and forehead went back into her heart. Out of the pearl seemed to issue a spell that stole upon her spirits gently as an atomy settles through the still air. Finally, there was a sigh, a sob, and over the soul of the maiden the will of Mualox became absolute. He took her hand in his.

"Wings swifter than the winds are yours, Tecetl. Go," he said, "search for the god; search the land."

She moved not, and scarcely breathed.

"Speak," he continued; "let me know that I am obeyed."

The will was absolute; she spoke, and though at first the words came slowly, yet he listened like a prophet waiting for revelation. She spoke of the land, of its rivers, forests, and mountains; she spoke of the cities, of their streets and buildings, and of their people, for whom she knew no name. She spoke of events transpiring in distant provinces, as well as in Tenochtitlan. She went into the temples, markets, and palaces. Wherever men travelled, thither her spirit flew. When the flight was done, and her broken description ceased, the holy man sighed.

"Not yet, Tecetl; he is not found. The god is not on the land. Search the air."

And still the will was absolute, though the theme of the seer changed. It was not of the land now, but of the higher realm. She spoke of the sunshine and the cloud, of the wind rushing and chill, of the earth far down, and grown so small that the mountains levelled with the plains.

"Not yet, not yet," he cried; "the god is not in the **air.** Go search the sea!"

In the hollow of his hand he lifted water, and sprinkled **her** face; and when he resumed his seat she spoke, not slowly **as** before, but fast and free.

"The land is passed; behind me are the cities and lakes, and the great houses and **blue** waters, such as I have seen in my pictures. I am hovering now, father, where there is nothing before me but waves and distance. White birds go skimming about careless of the foam; the winds pour upon **me** steadily; and in my **ear** is **a** sound as of a great voice. I **listen,** and it is the **sea;** or, father, it may be the voice of **the god** whom you seek."

She was silent, as if waiting for an answer.

"The water, is it? Well, well,—whither shall I go now?"

"Follow the shore; it may lead where only gods have been."

"Still the waves and the distance, and the land, where it goes down into the sea sprinkled with shells. Still the deep voice in my ear, and the wind about me. I hurry on, but it is all alike,— all water and sound. No! Out of the waves rises a new land, the sea, a girdle of billows, encircling it everywhere; yet there are blue clouds ascending from the fields, and I see palm-trees and temples. May not thy god dwell here?"

"No. You see but an island. On!"

"Well, well. Behind me fades the island; before me is nothing **but** sheen and waves and distance again; far around runs the line separating the sea and sky. Waste, all waste; the sea all **green,** the sky all blue; **no** life; no god. But stay!"

"Something moves on the waste: speak, child!"

But for a time she was still.

"Speak!" he said earnestly. "Speak, Tecetl!"

"They are far off,—far off," she replied slowly and in a doubt-ing way. "They move and live, but I cannot tell whether they come or go, or what they are. Their course is unsteady, and, like the flight of birds, now upon the sea, then in air, a moment seeming of the waves, then of the sky. They look like white clouds."

"You are fleeter than birds or clouds,—nearer!" he said sternly, **the** fire in his eyes all alight.

"I go,—I approach them,—I now see them coming. O father, father! I know not what your god is like, nor what shape he takes, nor in what manner he travels; but surely these are his! There are many of them, and as they sweep along they are a sight to be looked at with trembling."

"What are they, Tecetl?"

"How can I answer? They are not of the things I have seen in my pictures, nor heard in my songs. The face of the sea is whitened by them; the largest leads the way, looking like a shell,—of them I have heard you speak as coming from the sea,—a great shell streaked with light and shade, and hollow, so that the sides rise above the reach of the waves,— wings"—

"Nay, what would a god of the air with wings to journey upon the sea?"

"Above it are clouds,—clouds white as the foam, and such as a god might choose to waft him on his way. I can see them sway and toss, but as the shell rushes into the hollow places, they lift it up, and drive it on."

A brighter light flashed from his eyes. "It is the canoe, the canoe!" he exclaimed. "The canoe from Tlapallan!"

"The canoe, father! The waves rush joyously around it; they lift themselves in its path, and roll on to meet it; then, as if they knew it to be a god's, in peace make way for its coming. Upon the temples in my pictures I have seen signs floating in the air"—

"You mean banners—banners, child," he said tremulously.

"I remember now. Above the foremost canoe, above its clouds, there is a banner, and it is black"—

"'Tis Quetzal's! 'Tis Quetzal's!" he muttered.

"It is black, with golden embroidery, and something picture-written on it, but what I cannot tell."

"Look in the canoe."

"I see—oh, I know not what to call them!"

"Of what shape are they, child?"

"Yours, father."

"Go on: they are gods!" he said; and still the naming of men was unheard in the great chamber.

"There are many of them," she continued; "their garments flash and gleam; around one like themselves they are met; to me he seems the superior god,—he is speaking, they are listening. He is taller than you, father, and has a fair face, and hair and beard like the hue of his banner. His garments are the brightest of all."

"You have described a god; it is Quetzal', the holy, beautiful Quetzal'!" he said, with rising voice. "Look if his course be toward the land."

"Every canoe moves towards the shore."

"Enough!" he cried. "The writing on the wall is the god's!" And, rising, he awoke the girl.

As Tecetl awake had no recollection of her journey, or of what she had seen in its course, she wondered at his trouble and excitement, and spoke to him, without answer.

"Father dear, what has Tecetl done that you should be so troubled?"

He put aside her arms, and in silence turned slowly from the pleasant place, and retraced his steps back through the halls of the Cû to the court-yard and *azoteas.*

The weight of the secret did not oppress him; it rested upon him lightly as the surplice upon his shoulders; for the humble servant of his god was lifted above his poverty and trembling, and, vivified by the consciousness of inspiration, felt more than a warrior's strength. But what should he do? Where proclaim the revelation? Upon the temple?

"The streets are deserted; the people are in the theatre; the king is there with all Anahuac," he muttered. "The coming of Quetzal' concerns the Empire, and it shall hear the announcement: so not on the temple, but to the *tianguez.* The god speaks to me! To the *tianguez!*"

In the chapel he exchanged his white surplice for the **regalia of** sacrifice. Never before, to his fancy, wore the idol such seeming of life. Satisfaction played grimly about its mouth; upon its brow, like a coronet, sat the infinite Will. From the chapel he descended to the street that led to the great square. Insensibly, as he hurried on, his steps quickened; and bareheaded and un-sandalled, his white beard and hair loose and flowing, and his face beaming with excitement, he looked the very embodiment of direful prophecy. On the streets he met only slaves. At **the** theatre the entrance was blocked by people; soldiery guarded **the** arena: but guard and people shrunk at his approach; and thus, without word or cry, he rushed within the wall of shields, where were none but the combatants, living and dead.

Midway the arena he halted, his face to the king. Around ran **his** wondrous glance, and, regardless of the royalty present, the people shouted, "The paba, the paba!" and their many voices shook the theatre. Flinging the white locks back on his shoulders, he tossed his arms aloft; and the tumult rose into the welkin, and a calm settled over the multitude. Montezuma, with the malediction warm on his lips, bent from his couch to hear his words.

"Woe is Tenochtitlan, the beautiful!" he cried in the un-measured accents of grief. "Woe **to** homes, and people, and armies, and king! Why this gathering of dwellers on the hills and in the valley? Why the combat of warriors? Quetzal' **is** at hand. He comes for vengeance. Woe is Tenochtitlan, the beauti-ful! . . . This, O king, is the day of the fulfilment of prophecy. From out the sea, wafted by clouds, even now the canoes of the god are coming. His power whitens the waves, and the garments of his warriors gleam with the light of the sky. Woe is Tenoch-titlan! This day **is** the last of her perfect glory; to-morrow

Quetzal' will glisten on the sea-shore, and her Empire vanish for
ever. . . . People, say farewell to peace! Keepers of the temples,
holy men, go feed the fires, and say the prayer, and sacrifice the
victim! And thou, O king! summon thy strong men, leaders in
battle, and be thy banners counted, and thy nations marshalled.
In vain! Woe is Tenochtitlan! Sitting in the lake, she shines
lustrously as a star; and though in a valley of gardens, she is like
a great tree shadowing in a desert. But the ravager comes, and
the tree shall be felled, and the star go out darkling for ever.
The fires shall fade, the bones of the dead kings be scattered,
altars and gods overthrown, and every temple levelled with the
streets. Woe is Tenochtitlan! Ended,—ended for ever is the
march of Azatlan, the mighty!"

His arms fell down, and without further word, his head bowed
upon his breast, the prophet departed. The spell he left behind
him remained unbroken. As they recovered from the effects of
his bodement, the people left the theatre, their minds full of
indefinite dread. If perchance they spoke of the scene as they
went, it was in whispers, and rather to sound the depths of each
other's alarm. And for the rest of the day they remained in their
houses, brooding alone, or collected in groups, talking in low
voices, wondering about the prescience of the paba, and looking
each moment for the development of something more terrible.

The king watched the holy man until he disappeared in the
crowded passage; then a deadly paleness overspread his face, and
he sank almost to the platform. The nobles rushed around, and
bore him to his palanquin, their brave souls astonished that the
warrior and priest and mighty monarch could be so overcome.
They carried him to his palace, and left him to a solitude full of
unkingly superstitions.

Guatamozin, serene amid the confusion, called the *tamanes*, and
ordered the old Othmi and the dead to be removed. The Tezcucan
still breathed.

"The reviler of the gods shall be cared for," he said to himself.
"If he lives, their justice will convict him."

Before the setting of the sun, the structure in the *tianguez* was
taken down and restored to the temples, never again to be used.
Yet the market-place remained deserted and vacant; the whole
city seemed plague-smitten.

And the common terror was not without cause, any more than
Mualox was without inspiration. That night the ships of Cortes,
eleven in number, and freighted with the materials of conquest,
from the east of Yucatan, came sweeping down the bay of Cam-
peachy. Next morning they sailed up the Rio de Tabasco,
beautiful with its pure water and its banks fringed with man-

groves. Tecetl had described the fleet, the sails of which from afar looked like clouds, while they did, indeed, whiten the sea.

Next evening a courier sped hotly over the causeway and up the street, stopping at the gate of the royal palace. He was taken before the king; and, shortly after, it went flying over the city how Quetzal' had arrived, in canoes larger than temples, wafted by clouds, and full of thunder and lightning. Then sank the monarch's heart; and, though the Spaniard knew it not, his marvellous conquest was half completed before his iron shoe smote the shore at San Juan de Ulloa.[1]

[1] Cortes' squadron reached the mouth of the river Tabasco on the 12th of March 1519.

BOOK TWO.

—◆—

CHAPTER I.

WHO ARE THE STRANGERS?

MARCH passed, and April came, and still the strangers, in their great canoes, lingered on the coast. Montezuma observed them with becoming prudence; through his look-outs he was informed of their progress from the time they left the Rio de Tabasco.

The constant anxiety to which he was subjected affected his temper; and, though roused from the torpor into which he had been plunged by the visit to the golden chamber, **and** the subsequent prophecy of Mualox, his melancholy was a thing of common observation. He renounced his ordinary amusements, even *totoloque,* and went no more to the hunting-grounds **on** the shore of the lake; in preference, he took long walks **in** the gardens, and reclined in the audience-chamber **of** his palace; yet more remarkable, conversation with his councillors and nobles delighted him more than the dances of his women or the songs of his minstrels. In truth, the monarch was himself a victim of the delusions he had perfected for his people. Polytheism had come to him with the Empire; but he had enlarged upon it, and covered it with dogmas; and so earnestly, through a long and glorious reign, had he preached them, that at last he had become his own most zealous convert. In all his dominions there was not one whom faith more inclined to absolute fear of Quetzal' than himself.

One evening he passed from his bath to the dining-hall for the last meal of the day. Invigorated, and, as was his custom, attired for the fourth time since morning in fresh garments, he walked briskly, and even droned a song.

No monarch in Europe fared more sumptuously than Montezuma. The room devoted to the purpose was spacious, and, on this occasion, brilliantly lighted. The floor was spread with figured matting, and the walls hung with beautiful tapestry; and in the centre of the apartment a luxurious couch had been rolled for him, it being his habit to eat reclining ; while, to hide him from the curious, a screen had been contrived, and set up between the couch and principal door. The viands set down by his steward as the substantials of the first course were arranged upon the floor before the couch, and kept warm and smoking by chafing-dishes. The table, if such it may be called, was supplied by contributions from the provinces, and furnished, in fact, no contemptible proof of his authority, and the perfection with which it was exercised. The ware was of the finest Cholulan manufacture, and, like his clothes, **never** used by him but the once, a royal custom requiring him to present it to his friends.[1]

When he entered the room the evening I have mentioned, there were present only his steward, four or five aged councillors, whom he was accustomed to address as "uncles," and a couple of women, who occupied themselves in preparing certain wafers and confections which he particularly affected. He stretched himself comfortably upon the couch, much, I presume, after the style of the Romans, and at once began the meal. The ancients moved back several steps, and a score of boys, noble, yet clad in the inevitable *nequen*, responding to a bell, came in and posted themselves **to answer** his requests.

Sometimes, **by** invitation, the councillors were permitted to **share the** feast ; oftener, however, the only object of their presence was to afford him the gratification of remark. The conversation was usually irregular, and hushed and renewed as he prompted, and not unfrequently extended to the gravest political and religious subjects. On the evening in question he spoke to them kindly.

"I feel better this evening, uncles. My good star is rising above the mists that have clouded it. We ought not to complain of what we cannot help ; still, I have thought that when the gods retained the power to afflict us with sorrows, they should have given us some power to correct them."

One of the old men answered reverentially, "A king should **be too great** for sorrows ; he should wear his crown against them as we **wear** our mantles against the cold winds."

"A good idea," said the monarch, smiling ; "but you forget that the crown, instead of protecting, is itself the trouble. Come nearer, uncles ; there is a matter more serious about which I would hear your minds."

They obeyed him, and he went on.

"The last courier brought me word that the strangers were yet on the coast, **hovering about** the islands. **Tell** me, who say you they are, and whence do **they come?**"

"How may we know **more than our wise master?**" said one of them.

---

[1] Prescott, *Conq. of Mexico.*

"And our thoughts,—do we not borrow them from **you**, O king?" added another.

"What! Call you those answers? Nay, uncles, my fools can better serve me; if they cannot instruct, they can at least amuse."

The king spoke bitterly, and looking at one, probably the oldest of them all, said,—

"Uncle, you are the poorest courtier, but you are discreet and honest. I want opinions that have in them more wisdom than flattery. Speak to me truly; who are these strangers?"

"For your sake, O my good king, I wish I were wise; for the trouble they have given my poor understanding is indeed very great. I believe them to be gods, landed from the Sun." And the old man went on to fortify his belief with arguments. In the excited state of his fancy, it was easy for him to convert the cannon of the Spaniards into engines of thunder and lightning, and transform their horses into creatures of Mictlan mightier than men. Right summarily he also concluded that none but gods could traverse the dominions of Haloc,[1] subjecting the variant winds to their will. Finally, to prove the strangers irresistible, he referred to the battle of Tabasco, then lately fought between Cortes and the Indians.

Montezuma heard him in silence, and replied,—

"Not badly given, uncle; your friends may profit by your example; but you have not talked as a warrior. You have forgotten that we too have beaten the lazy Tabascans. That reference proves as much for my caciques as for your gods."

He waved his hand, and the first course was removed. The second consisted for the most part of delicacies in the preparation of which his *artistes* delighted; at this time appeared the *choclatl*, a rich, frothy beverage served in *xicaras*, or small golden goblets. Girls, selected for their rank and beauty, succeeded the boys. Flocking around him with light and echoless feet, very graceful, very happy, theirs was indeed the service that awaits the faithful in Mahomet's Paradise. To each of his ancients he passed a goblet of *choclatl*, then continued his eating and talking.

"Yes. Be they gods or men, I would give a province to know their intention; that, uncles, would enable me to determine my policy,—whether to give them war or peace. As yet, they have asked nothing but the privilege of trading with us; and, judging them by our nations, I want not better warrant of friendship. As you know, strangers have twice before been upon our coast in such canoes, and with such arms;[2] and in both instances they sought gold, and getting it they departed. Will these go like them?"

[1] God of the sea.
[2] The allusion was doubtless to the expeditions of Hernandez de Cordova in 1517, and Juan de Grijalva in 1518.

" Has my master forgotten the words of Mualox ? "

" To Mictlan with the paba ! " said the king violently. " He
has filled my cities and people with trouble."

" Yet he is a prophet," retorted the old councillor boldly.
" How knew he of the coming of the **strangers** before it was
known in the palace ? "

The flush of the king's face faded.

" It is a mystery, uncle,—a mystery too deep for me. **All the**
day and night before he was in his Cû ; he went **not into the**
city even."

" If the wise master will listen to the words of his **slave**, he
will not again curse the paba, but make him **a** friend."

The monarch's lip curled derisively.

" My palace is now a house of prayer and sober life ; he would
turn it into a place of revelry."

All the ancients but the one laughed at the irony ; that one
repeated his words.

" A friend ; but how ?' asked Montezuma.

" Call him from the Cû to the palace ; let him stand here with
us ; in the councils give him a voice. He can read the future ;
make of him an oracle. O king, **who like** him can stand between
you and Quetzal' ? "

For a while Montezuma toyed idly with the *xicara*. He also
believed in the prophetic gifts of Mualox, and it was not the first
time he had pondered the question of how the holy man had
learned the coming of the strangers ; to satisfy himself as to his
means of information, he had even instituted inquiries outside
the palace. And yet it was but one of several mysteries ; behind
it, if not superior, were the golden chamber, its wealth, and the
writing on the walls. They were not to be attributed to the
paba : works so wondrous could not have been done in one life-
time. They were the handiwork of a god, **who** had chosen Mualox
for his servant and prophet ; such was the judgment of the king.

Nor was that all. The monarch had come to believe that the
strangers **on** the coast were Quetzal' and his followers, whom it
were vain **to** resist, if their object was vengeance. But the
human heart is seldom without its suggestion of hope ; and he
thought, though resistance was impossible, might he not propitiate ? This policy had occupied his thoughts, and most likely
without result, for the words of-the councillor seemed welcome.
Indeed, he could scarcely fail to recognise the bold idea they
conveyed,—nothing less, in fact, than meeting the god with his
own prophet.

" Very well," he said in his heart. " I will use the paba. He
shall come and stand between me and the woe."

Then he arose, took a string of pearls from his neck, and with
his own hand placed it around that of the ancient.

"Your place is with me, uncle. I will have a chamber fitted
for you here in the palace. Go no more away. Ho, steward!
The supper is done; let the pipes be brought, and give me music
and dance. Bid the minstrels come. A song of the olden time
may make me strong again."

CHAPTER II.

A TEZCUCAN LOVER.

TRACES of the supper speedily disappeared. The screen was
rolled away, and pipes placed in the monarch's hand for distri-
bution among his familiars. Blue vapour began to ascend to the
carved rafters, when the tapestry on both sides of the room was
flung aside, and the sound of cornets and flutes poured in from
an adjoining apartment; and, as if answering the summons of
the music, a company of dancing-girls entered, and filled the
space in front of the monarch; half nude were they, and flashing
with ornaments, and aerial with gauze and flying ribbons;
silver bells tinkled with each step, and on their heads were
wreaths, and in their hands garlands of flowers. Voluptuous
children were they of the voluptuous valley.

Saluting the monarch, they glided away, and commenced a
dance. With dreamy, half-shut eyes, through the scented cloud
momently deepening around him, he watched them; and in the
sensuous, animated scene was disclosed one of the enchantments
that had weaned him from the martial love of his youth.

Every movement of the figure had been carefully studied, and
a kind of æsthetic philosophy was blent with its perfect time
and elegance of motion. Slow and stately at first, it gradually
quickened; then, as if to excite the blood and fancy, it became
more mazy and voluptuous; and finally, as that is the sweetest
song that ends with a long decadence, it was so concluded as to
soothe the transports itself had awakened. Sweeping along, it
reached a point, a very climax of abandon and beauty, in which
the dancers appeared to forget the music and the method of the
figure: then the eyes of the king shone brightly, and the pipe
lingered on his lips forgotten; and then the musicians began,
one by one, to withdraw from the harmony, and the dancers to
vanish singly from the room, until, at last, there was but one
flute to be heard, while but one girl remained. Finally, she also
disappeared, and all grew still again.

And the king sat silent and listless, surrendered to the enjoy-

ment which was the object of the diversion ;—yet he heard the
music ; yet he saw the lithe and palpitating forms of the dancers
in posture and motion ; yet he felt the sweet influence of their
youth and grace and beauty, not as a passion, but rather a spell
full of the suggestions of passion, when a number of men came
noiselessly in, and, kneeling, saluted him. Their costume was
that of priests, and each of them carried an instrument of music
fashioned somewhat like a Hebrew lyre.

"Ah, my minstrels, my minstrels!" he said, his face flushing
with pleasure. "Welcome in the streets, welcome in the camp,
welcome in the palace also! What have you to-night?"

"When last we **were** admitted to your presence, O king, you
bade us compose hymns to the god Quetzal'"—

"Yes ; I remember."

"We pray you not to think ill of your slaves if we say that
the verses which come unbidden are the best ; no song of the
bird's so beautiful as the one it sings when its heart is full."

The monarch sat up.

"Nay, I did not command. I know something of the spirit of
poetry. **It is not a thing to** be driven by the will, like a canoe
by a strong arm ; **neither is** it a slave, **to come** or go at a signal.
I bid my warriors march ; I order the sacrifice ; but the lays of
my minstrels have ever been of their free will. Leave me now.
To you are my gardens and palaces. I warrant the verses you
have are good ; but go ask your hearts for better."

They retired with their faces toward him until hidden behind
the tapestry.

"I love a song, uncles," continued the king ; "I love a hymn
to the gods, and a story of battle chanted in a deep voice. In
the halls of the Sun every soul is a minstrel, and every tale a
song. But let them go ; it is well enough. I promised Iztlil',
the Tezcucan, to give him audience to-night. He comes to the
palace but seldom, and he **has** not asked a favour since I settled
his quarrel with the lord Cacama. **Send** one to see if he is now
at the door."

Thereupon **he** fell to reflecting and smoking ; and when next
he spoke, it was from the midst of an aromatic cloud.

"I loved the wise 'Hualpilli ; for his sake, I would have his
children happy. He was a lover of peace, and gave more to
policy than to war. It were grievous to let his city be disturbed
by feuds and fighting men ; therefore I gave it to the eldest son.
His claim was best ; and, besides, he has the friendly heart to
serve me. Still—still, I wish there had been two Tezcucos."

"There was but **one voice about** the judgment in Tezcuco,
O king ; the citizens all said it was just."

"And they would have said the same if **I** have given them
Iztlil'. I know the **knaves**, uncle. It was not their applause

I cared for; but, you see, in gaining a servant, I lost one. Iztlil' is a warrior. Had he the will, he could serve me in the field as well as his brother in the council. I must attach him to me. A strong arm is pleasant to lean on; it is better than a staff."

Addressing himself to the pipe again, he sat smoking, and moodily observing the vapour vanish above him. There was silence until Iztlil' was ushered in.

The cacique was still suffering from his wounds. His step was feeble, so that his obeisance was stopped by the monarch himself.

"Let the salutation go, my lord Iztlil'. Your courage has cost you much. I remember you are the son of my old friend, and bid you welcome."

"The Tlascalans are good warriors," said the Tezcucan coldly.

"And for that reason better victims," added the king quickly. "By the Sun, I know not what we would do without them. Their hills supply our temples."

"And I, good king—I am but a warrior. My heart is not softened by things pertaining to religion. Enough for me to worship the gods."

"Then you are not a student?"

"I never studied in the academies."

"I understand," said the king with a low laugh. "You cannot name as many stars as enemies whom you have slain. No matter. I have places for such scholars. Have you commanded an army?"

"It pleased you to give me that confidence. I led my companies within the Tlascalan wall, and came back with captives."

"I recollect now. But as most good warriors are modest, my son, I will not tell you what the chiefs said of your conduct; you would blush"—

Iztlil' started.

"Content you, content you; your blush would not be for shame."

There was a pause, which the king gave to his pipe. Suddenly he said, "There have been tongues busy with your fame, my son. I have heard you were greatly dissatisfied because I gave your father's city to your elder brother. But I consider that men are never without detractors, and I cannot forget that you have perilled your life for the gods. Actions I accept as the proofs of will. If the favour that brought you here be reasonable, it is yours for the asking. I have the wish to serve you."

"I am not surprised that I have enemies," said Iztlil' calmly. "I will abuse no one on that account; for I am an enemy, and can forgive in others what I deem virtue in myself. But it moves me greatly, O king, that my enemies should steal into

your palace, and, in my absence, wrong me in your opinion. But
pardon me; I did not come to defend myself"—

"You have taken my words in an evil sense," interposed the
king, with an impatient gesture.

"Or to conceal the truth," the Tezcucan continued. "There
is kingly blood in me, and I dare speak as my father's son. So
if they said merely that I was dissatisfied with your judgment,
they said truly."

Montezuma frowned.

"I intend my words to be respectful, most mighty king. A
common wisdom teaches us to respect the brave man and dread
the coward. And there is not in your garden a flower as beautiful, nor in your power a privilege as precious, as free speech;
and it would sound ill of one so great and secure as my father's
friend if he permitted in the streets and in the farmer's hut what
he forbade in his palace. I spoke of dissatisfaction; but think
not it was because you gave Tezcuco to my brother, and to me
the bare hills that have scarcely herbage enough for a wolf-
covert. I am less a prince than a warrior; all places are alike
to me; the earth affords me royal slumber, while no jewelled
canopy is equal to the starred heavens; and as there is a weakness in pleasant memories, I have none. To such as I am,
O king, what matters a barren hill or a proud palace? I murmured—nay, I did more—because, in judging my quarrel, you
overthrew the independence of my country. When my father
visited you from across the lake, he was not accustomed to stand
before you, or hide his kingly robes beneath a slave's garb."

Montezuma half started from his seat. "Holy Gods! Is
rebellion so bold?"

"I meant no disrespect, great king. I only sought to justify
myself, and in your royal presence say what I have thought while
fighting under your banner. But, without more abuse of your
patience, I will to my purpose, especially as I came for peace and
friendship."

"The son of my friend forgets that I have ways to make peace
without treating for it," said the king.

The Tezcucan smothered an angry reply.

"By service done, I have shown a disposition to serve you,
O king. Very soon every warrior will be needed. A throne
may be laid amid hymns and priestly prayers, yet have no
strength; to endure, it must rest upon the allegiance of love.
Though I have spoken unpleasant words, I came to ask that, by
a simple boon, you give me cause to love. I have reflected that
I too am of royal blood, and, as the son of a king, may lead
your armies, and look for alliance in your house. By marriage,
O king, I desire, come good or evil, to link my fortune to yours."

Montezuma's countenance was stolid; no eye could have detected upon it so much as surprise. He quietly asked, "Which of my daughters has found favour in your eyes?"

"They are all beautiful, but only one of them is fitted for a warrior's wife."

"Tula?"

Iztlil' bowed.

"She is dear to me," said the king softly,—"dearer than a city; she is holy as a temple, and lovelier than the morning; her voice is sweet as the summer wind, and her presence as the summer itself. Have you spoken to her of this thing?"

"I love her, so that her love is nothing to me. Her feelings are her own, but she is yours; and you are more powerful to give than she to withhold."

"Well, well," said the monarch, after a little thought; "in my realm there are none of better quality than the children of 'Hualpilli,—none from whom such demand is as proper. Yet it is worthy deliberation. It is true, I have the power to bestow; but there are others who have the right to be consulted. I study the happiness of my people, and it were unnatural if I cared less for that of my children. So leave me now, but take with you, brave prince, the assurance that I am friendly to your suit. The gods go with you!"

And Iztlil', after a low obeisance, withdrew; and then the overture was fully discussed. Montezuma spoke freely, welcoming the opportunity of securing the bold, free-spoken cacique, and seeing in the demand only a question of policy. As might be expected, the ancients made no opposition; they could see no danger in the alliance, and had no care for the parties. It was policy.

CHAPTER III.

THE BANISHMENT OF GUATAMOZIN.

THE palace of Montezuma was regarded as of very great sanctity, so that his household, its economy, and the exact relation its members bore to each other, were mysteries to the public. From the best information, however, it would seem that he had two lawful and acknowledged wives, the queens Tecalco and Acatlan,[1] who, with their families, occupied spacious apartments secure from intrusion. They were good-looking, middle-aged women, whom the monarch honoured with the highest respect and con-

[1] These are the proper names of the queens. MSS. of Munoz. Also, note to Prescott, *Conq. of Mexico*, Vol. II., p. 351.

fidence. By the first one, he had a son and daughter; by the second, two daughters.

"Help me, Acatlan! I appeal to your friendship, to the love you bear your children,—help me in my trouble!" So the queen Tecalco prayed the queen Acatlan in the palace the morning after the audience given the Tezcucan by the king.

The two were sitting in a room furnished with some taste. Through the great windows, shaded by purple curtains, streamed the fresh breath of the early day. There were female slaves around them in waiting; while a boy, nearly grown, at the eastern end of the apartment was pitching the golden balls in *tutoloque.* This was prince Io', the brother of Tula and son of Tecalco.

"What is the trouble? What can I do?" asked Acatlan.

"Listen to me," said Tecalco. "The king has just gone. He came in better mood than usual, and talked pleasantly. Something had happened; some point of policy had been gained. Nowadays, you know, he talks and thinks of nothing but policy; formerly it was all of war. We cannot deny, Acatlan, that he is much changed. Well, he played a game with Io', then sat down, saying he had news which he thought would please me. You will hardly believe it, but he said that Iztlil', the proud Tezcucan, asked Tula in marriage last night. Think of it! Tula, my blossom, my soul!—and to that vile cacique!"

"Well, he is brave, and the son of 'Hualpilli," said Acatlan.

"What! You!" said Tecalco despairingly. "Do you too turn against me? I do not like him, and would not if he were the son of a god. Tula hates him!"

"I will not turn against you, Tecalco. Be calmer, and tell me what more the king said."

"I told him I was surprised, but not glad, to hear the news. He frowned, and paced the floor, now here, now there. I was frightened, but could bear his anger better than the idea of my Tula, so good, so beautiful, the wife of the base Tezcucan. He said the marriage must go on; it was required by policy, and would help to quiet the Empire, which was never so threatened. You will hardly believe I ventured to tell him that it should not be, as Tula was already contracted to Guatamozin. I supposed that announcement would quiet the matter, but it only enraged him; he spoke bitterly of the 'tzin. I could scarcely believe my ears. He used to love him. What has happened to change his feeling?"

Acatlan thrummed her pretty mouth with her fingers, and thought awhile.

"Yes, I have heard some stories about the 'tzin "—

"Indeed!" said Tecalco, opening her eyes.

"He too has changed, as you may have observed," continued

Acatlan. "He used to be gay and talkative, fond of company, and dance ; latterly, he stays at home, and when abroad, mopes, and is silent ; while we all know that no great private or public misfortune has happened him. The king appears to have noticed it. And, my dear sister,"—the queen lowered her voice to a confidential whisper,—"they say the 'tzin aspires to the throne."

"What ! Do you believe it ? Does the king ?" cried Tecalco, more in anger than surprise.

"I believe nothing yet, though there are some grounds for his accusers to go upon. They say he entertains at his palace near Iztapalapan none but men of the army, and that, while in Tenochtitlan, he studies the favour of the people, and uses his wealth to win popularity with all classes. Indeed, Tecalco, somehow the king learned that, on the day of the celebration of Quetzal', **the** 'tzin was engaged in a direct conspiracy against him."

"It is false, Acatlan, it is false ! The king has not **a more** faithful subject. I know the 'tzin. **He** is worth a thousand of the Tezcucan, who is himself the traitor." And the vexed queen beat the floor with her sandalled foot.

"As to that, Tecalco, I know nothing. But what more from the king ? **"**

"He told me that Tula should never marry the 'tzin ; he would use all his power against it ; he would banish him from the city first. And his rage increased until, finally, he swore by the gods he would order a banquet, and, in presence of all the lords of the Empire, publicly betroth Tula and the Tezcucan. He said he would do anything the safety of the throne and the gods required of him. He never was so angry. And that, O Acatlan, my sister, that is my trouble ! How can I save my child from such a horrid betrothal ? **"**

Acatlan shook her head gloomily. **"The** king brooks defeat better than opposition. We would not be safe to do anything openly. I acknowledge myself afraid, and **unable** to advise you."

Tecalco burst into tears, and wrung her hands, overcome by fear and rage. Io' then left his game, and came to her. He was not handsome, being too large for his years, and ungraceful ; this tendency to homeliness was increased by the smallness of his face and head ; the features were actually childish.

"Say no more, mother," he said, tears standing in his eyes, as if to prove his sympathy and kindliness. "You know it would be better to play with the tigers than stir the king to anger."

"Ah, Io', what shall I do ? I always heard you speak well of the 'tzin. You loved him once."

"And I love him yet."

Tecalco was less pacified than ever.

"What would I not give to know who set the king so against

him! Upon the traitor be the harm there is in a mother's curse! If my child must be sacrificed, let it be by a priest, and as a victim to the gods."

"Do not speak so. Be wise, Tecalco. Recollect such sorrows belong to our rank."

"Our rank, Acatlan! I can forget it sooner than that I am a mother! Oh, you do not know how long I have nursed the idea of wedding Tula to the 'tzin! Since their childhood I have prayed, plotted, and hoped for it. With what pride I have seen them grow up,—he so brave, generous, and princely, she so staid and beautiful! I have never allowed her to think of other destiny : the gods made them for each other."

"Mother," said Io' thoughtfully, "I have heard you say that Guatamozin was wise. Why not send him word of what has happened, and put our trust in him?"

The poor queen caught at the suggestion eagerly ; for, with a promise of aid, at the same time it relieved her of responsibility, of all burdens the most dreadful to a woman. And Acatlan, really desirous of helping her friend, but at a loss for a plan, and terrified by the idea of the monarch's wrath incurred, wondered they had not thought of the proposal sooner, and urged the 'tzin's right to be informed of the occurrence.

"There must be secrecy, Tecalco. The king must never know us as traitors : that would be our ruin."

"There shall be no danger ; I can go myself," said Io'. "It is long since I was at Iztapalapan, and they say the 'tzin has such beautiful gardens. I want to see the three kings who hold torches in his hall ; I want to try a bow with him."

After some entreaty, Tecalco assented. She required him, however, to put on a costume less likely to attract attention, and take some other than a royal canoe across the lake. Half an hour later, he passed out of a garden gate, and, by a circuitous route, hurried to the canal in which lay the vessels of the Iztapalapan watermen. He found one, and was bargaining with its owner when a young man walked briskly up, and stepped into a canoe close by. Something in the gay dress of the stranger made Io' look at him a second time, and he was hardly less pleased than surprised at being addressed,—

"Ho, friend! I am going to your city. Save your cocoa, and go with me."

Io' was confused.

"Come on!" the stranger persisted, with a pleasant smile. "Come on! I want company. You were never so welcome."

The smile decided the boy. He set one foot in the vessel, but instantly retreated—an ocelot, crouched in the bottom, raised its round head and stared fixedly at him. The stranger laughed, and reassured him, after which he walked boldly forward. Then

the canoe swung from **its** mooring, and in a few minutes, under
the impulsion of three strong slaves, went flying down the canal.
Under bridges, through incoming flotillas, and past the great
houses on either hand, they darted, until the city was left behind,
and the lake, coloured with the borrowed blue **of** the sky, spread
out rich and billowy before them. The **eyes** of the stranger
brightened at the prospect.

"I like this. By Our Mother, I **like it!**" he said **earnestly.**
"We have lakes in Tihuanco on which **I have spent days riding**
waves and spearing fish ; but they were **dull to this.** See the
stretch of **the** water ! Look yonder at the **villages, and here at**
the city and Chapultepec ! Ah, that you were **born in Tenoch-**
titlan be proud ! There is no grander birthplace **this side of the**
Sun !"

"I am an Aztec," said Io', moved by the words.

The other smiled, and added, "Why not go further, and **say,**
'and son of the king'?"

Io' was startled.

"Surprised ! Good prince, **I am a** hunter. From habit, I
observe everything,—a track, a tree, a place, once seen is never
forgotten ; and since I came **to** the city, the night before the
combat of Quetzal', the habit has not left me. That day you were
seated under the red canopy with the princesses Tula and Nenetzin. So I came to know the king's son."

"Then you saw the combat ?"

"And how brave it was ! There never was its match,—never
such archery as the 'tzin's. Then the blow with which he killed
the Othmi ! I only regretted that the Tezcucan escaped. I do
not like him ; he is envious and spiteful ; it would have **been**
better had he fallen instead of the Otompan. **You know**
Iztlil' ?"

"Not to love him," said **Io'.**

"Is he like the 'tzin ?"

"Not at all."

"So I have heard," said the hunter, shrugging **his** shoulders.
"But— Down, fellow ! he cried to the ocelot, whose approaches
discomposed the prince. "I was going to say," he resumed, with
a look which as **an** invitation to confidence was irresistible,
"that there is no reason why you and I should not be friends.
We **are** both going to see the 'tzin."

Io' **was** again much confused.

"I only heard you say so to the waterman on the landing. **If**
your visit, good prince, was intended as a secret, you are a careless
messenger. But have no fear. I intend entering **the** 'tzin's
service ; that is, if he will take me."

"Is the 'tzin enlisting men ?" asked Io'.

"No. I am merely weary of hunting. **My** father is a good

merchant whose trading life is too tame for me. I love excitement. Even hunting deer and chasing wolves are too tame. I
will now try war, and there is but one whom I care to follow.
Together we will see and talk to him."

"You speak as if you were used to arms."

"My skill may be counted nothing. I seek the service more
from what I imagine it to be. The march, the camp, the battle,
the taking captives, the perilling life, when it is but a secondary
object, as it must be with every warrior of true ambition, all have
charms for my fancy. Besides, I am discontented with my condition. I want honour, rank, and command,—wealth I have.
Hence, for me, the army is the surest road. Beset with trials, and
needing a good heart and arm, yet it travels upward, upward, and
that is all I seek to know."

The *naïveté* and enthusiasm of the hunter were new and charming to the prince, who was impelled to study him once more. He
noticed how exactly the arms were rounded ; that the neck was
long, muscular, and widened at the base, like the trunk of an
oak ; that the features, excited by the passing feeling, were noble
and good ; that the very carriage of the head was significant of
aptitude for brave things, if not command. Could the better
gods have thrown Io' in such company for self-comparison ? Was
that the time they had chosen to wake within him the longings of
mind natural to coming manhood ? He felt the inspiration of an
idea new to him. All his life had been passed in the splendid
monotony of his father's palace ; he had been permitted merely
to hear of war, and that from a distance ; of the noble passion for
arms he knew nothing. Accustomed to childish wants, with
authority to gratify them, ambition for power had not yet disturbed him. But, as he listened, it was given him to see the
emptiness of his past life, and understand the advantages he
already possessed ; he said to himself, "Am I not master of grade
and opportunities, so coveted by this unknown hunter, and so far
above his reach ?" In that moment the contentment which had
canopied his existence like a calm sky, full of stars and silence
and peace, was taken up, and whirled away ; his spirit
strengthened with a rising ambition and a courage royally
descended.

"You are going to study with the 'tzin. I would like to be
your comrade," he said.

"I accept you, I give you my heart !" replied the hunter with
beaming face. "We will march, and sleep, and fight, and practise
together. I will be true to you as shield to the warrior. Hereafter, O prince, when you would speak of me, call me Hualpa ;
and if you would make me happy, say of me, 'He is my comrade !'"

The sun stood high in the heavens when they reached the

landing. Mounting a few steps that led from the water's edge, they found themselves in a garden rich with flowers, beautiful trees, running streams, and trellised summer-houses,—the garden of a prince—of Guatamozin, the true hero of his country.

— ⚬ —

CHAPTER IV.

GUATAMOZIN AT HOME.

GUATAMOZIN inherited a great fortune, ducal rank, and **an estate** near Iztapalapan. Outside the city, midst a garden that **extended** for miles around, stood his palace, built in the prevalent style, one storey high, but broad and wide enough to comfortably accommodate several thousand men. His retainers, a legion in themselves, inhabited it for the most part ; and whether soldier, artisan, or farmer, each had his quarters, his exclusive possession as against every one but the 'tzin.

The garden was almost entirely devoted to the cultivation of fruits and flowers. Hundreds of slaves, toiling there constantly under tasteful supervision, made and kept it beautiful **past** description. Rivulets of pure water, spanned by bridges **and** bordered with flowers, ran through every part over beds of **sand** yellow as gold. The paths frequently led to artificial lagoons, delightful for the coolness that lingered about them, when the sun looked with his burning eye down upon the valley ; for they were fringed with willow and sycamore trees, all clad with vines **as** with garments ; and some were further garnished with little islands, plumed with palms, and made attractive by kiosks. Nor **were** these all. Fountains and cascades filled the air with sleepy songs ; orange-groves rose up, testifying to the clime they adorned ; and in every path small *teules*, on pedestals of stone, so mingled religion with the loveliness that there could be no admiration without worship.

Io' and Hualpa, marvelling at the beauty they beheld, pursued a path strewn with white sand, and leading across the garden to the palace. A few armed men loitered about the portal, but allowed them to approach without question. From the ante-chamber they sent their names to the 'tzin, and directly the slave returned with word to Io' to follow him.

The study into which the prince was presently shown was furnished with severe plainness. An arm-chair, if such it may **be** called, some rude tables and uncushioned benches, offered small encouragement to idleness.

Sand, glittering like crushed crystal, covered the floor, and, instead of tapestry, the walls were hung with maps of the Empire, and provinces the most distant. Several piles of MSS.,—the books of the Aztecs,—with parchment and writing-materials, lay on a table; and half concealed amongst them was a harp, such as we have seen in the hands of the royal minstrels.

"Welcome, Io', welcome!" said the 'tzin in his full voice. "You have come at length, after so many promises,—come last of all my friends. When you were here before, you were a child, and I a boy like you now. Let us go and talk it over." And leading him to a bench by a window, they sat down.

"I remember the visit," said Io'. "It was many years ago. You were studying then, and I find you studying yet."

A serious thought rose to the 'tzin's mind, and his smile was clouded.

"You do not understand me, Io'. Shut up in your father's palace, your life is passing too dreamily. The days with you are like waves of the lake: one rolls up, and, scarcely murmuring, breaks on the shore; another succeeds,—that is all. Hear, and believe me. He who would be wise must study. There are many who live for themselves; a few who live for their race. Of the first class, no thought is required; they eat, sleep, are merry, and die, and have no hall in heaven: but the second must think, toil, and be patient; they must know, and, if possible, know everything. God and ourselves are the only sources of knowledge. I would not have you despise humanity, but all that is from ourselves is soon learned. There is but one inexhaustible fountain of intelligence, and that is Nature, the God Supreme. See those volumes! they are of men, full of wisdom, but nothing original; they are borrowed from the book of deity,—the always-opened book, of which the sky is one chapter, and earth the other. Very deep are the lessons of life and heaven there taught. I confess to you, Io', that I aspire to be of those whose lives are void of selfishness, who live for others, for their country. Your father's servant, I would serve him understandingly; to do so, I must be wise; and I cannot be wise without patient study."

Io's unpractised mind but half understood the philosophy to which he listened; but when the 'tzin called himself his father's servant, Acatlan's words recurred to the boy.

"O 'tzin," he said, "they are not all like you, so good, so true. There have been some telling strange stories about you to the king."

"About me?"

"They say you want to be king,"—the listener's face was passive,—"and that on Quetzal's day you were looking for opportunity to attack my father." Still there was no sign of emotion. "Your staying at home, they say, is but a pretence to cover your designs."

"And what more, Io'?"

"They **say** you are taking soldiers into your pay; **that** you give money, and practise all manner of arts, to become popular in Tenochtitlan; and that your delay in entering the arena on the day of the combat had something to do with your conspiracy."

For a moment the noble countenance of the 'tzin was disturbed.

"A lying catalogue! But is that all?"

"No,"—and Io's voice trembled,—"I am a secret messenger from the queen Tecalco, my mother. She bade me say to you, that last night Iztlil', the Tezcucan, had audience with the king, and asked Tula for his wife."

Guatamozin sprang from his seat more pallid than ever in battle.

"And what said Montezuma?"

"This morning he came to the queen, my mother, and told her about it. On your account she objected; but he became angry, spoke harshly of you, and swore Tula should not wed with you; he would banish you first."

Through the silent cell the 'tzin strode gloomily; the blow weakened him. Mualox was wrong,—men cannot make themselves almost gods; by having many ills, and bearing them bravely, they can only become heroes. After a long struggle he resumed his calmness and seat.

"What more from the queen?"

"Only that, as she was helpless, she left everything to you. She dares not oppose the king."

"I understand!" exclaimed the 'tzin, starting from the bench again. "The Tezcucan is my enemy. Crossing the lake, night before the combat, he told me he loved Tula, and charged me with designs against the Empire, and cursed the king and his crown. Next day he fought under my challenge. The malice of a mean soul cannot be allayed by kindness. But for me the *tamanes* would have buried him with the Tlascalans. I sent him to my house; my slaves tended him; yet his hate was only sharpened."

He paced the floor to and fro, speaking vehemently.

"The ingrate charges me with aspiring to the throne. Judge me, holy gods! Judge how willingly I would lay down my life to keep the crown where it is! He says my palace has been open to men of the army. It was always so,—I am a warrior. I have consulted them about the Empire, but always as a subject, never for its ill. Such charges I laugh at; but that I sought to slay the king is too horrible for endurance. On the day of the combat, about the time of the assemblage, I went to the Cû of Quetzal' for blessing. I saw no smoke or other sign of fire upon the tower. Mualox was gone, and I trembled lest the fire should be dead. I climbed up, and found only a few living embers. There were no faggots on the roof, nor in the courtyard; the shrine was abandoned, Mualox old. The desolation appealed to me. The god seemed to claim my service. I broke my spear and shield, and flung the fragments into the urn, then hastened to the palace, loaded some *tamanes* with wood, and went back to the Cû. I was not too late there; but, hurrying to the *tianguez*, I found myself almost dishonoured. So was I kept from the arena; that service to the god is now helping my enemy as proof that I was waiting on a housetop to murder my king and kinsman! Alas! I have only slaves to bear witness to the holy work that kept me on the temple. Much I fear the gods are making the king blind for his ruin and the ruin of us all. He believes the strangers on the coast are from the Sun, when they are but men. Instead of war against them, he is thinking of embassies and presents. Now, more than ever, he needs the support of friends; but he divides his family against itself, and confers favours on enemies. I see the danger. Unfriendly gods are moving against us, not in the strangers, but in our own divisions. Remember the prophecy of Mualox, 'The race of Azatlan is ended for ever.'"

The speaker stopped his walking, and his voice became low and tremulous.

"Yet I love him. He has been kind; he gave me command; through his graciousness I have dwelt unmolested in this palace of my father. I am bound to him by love and law. As he has been my friend, I will be his; when his peril is greatest, I will be truest. Nothing but ill from him to Anahuac can make me his enemy. So, so,—let it pass. I trust the future to the gods."

Then, as if seeking to rid himself of the bitter subject, he turned to Io'. "Did not some one come with you?"

The boy told what he knew of Hualpa.

"I take him to be no common fellow; he has some proud ideas. I think you would like him."

"I will try your hunter, Io'. And if he is what you say of him, I will accept his service."

And they went immediately to the antechamber, where Hualpa saluted the 'tzin. The latter surveyed his fine person approvingly, and said, "I am told you wish to enter my service. Were you ever in battle?"

The hunter told his story with his wonted modesty.

"Well, the chase is a good school for warriors. It trains the thews, teaches patience and endurance, and sharpens the spirit's edge. Let us to the garden. A hand to retain skill must continue its practice; like a good memory, it is the better for exercise. Come, and I will show you how I keep prepared for every emergency of combat." And so saying, the 'tzin led the visitors out.

They **went** to the garden, followed by the retainers lounging at the **door**. A short walk brought them to a space surrounded by a copse of orange-trees, strewn with sand, and broad enough for a mock battle; a few benches about the margin afforded accommodation to spectators; a stone house at the northern end served for armoury, and was full of arms and armour. A glance assured the visitors that the place had been prepared expressly for training. Some score or more of warriors, in the military livery of the 'tzin, already occupied a portion of the field. Upon his appearance they quitted their games, and closed around him with respectful salutations.

"How now, my good Chinantlan!" he said pleasantly. "**Did** I not award you a prize yesterday? There are few in the **valley** who can excel you in launching the spear."

"The plume is mine no longer," replied the warrior. "**I was** beaten last night. The winner, however, is a countryman."

"A countryman! You Chinantlans seem born to the spear. Where is the man?"

The victor stepped forward, and drew up before the master, who regarded his brawny limbs, sinewy neck, and bold eyes with undisguised admiration; so an artist would regard a picture or a statue. Above the fellow's helm floated a plume of scarlet feathers, the trophy of his superior skill.

"Get your spear," said the 'tzin. "**I** bring **you a com**petitor."

The spear was brought, an ugly weapon in any **hand. The** head was of copper, and the shaft sixteen feet long. **The rough** Chinantlan handled it with a loving grip.

"Have you such in Tihuanco?" asked Guatamozin.

Hualpa balanced the weapon and laughed.

"We have only javelins,—mere reeds to this. Unless to hold an enemy at **bay,** I hardly know its use. Certainly, it is not for casting."

"Set the mark, men. **We** will give the stranger a lesson. Set it to the farthest throw."

A pine picket was then set up a hundred feet away, presenting a target of the height and breadth of a man, to which a shield was bolted breast-high from the sand.

"Now give the Chinantlan room!"

The wearer of the plume took his place; advancing one foot, he lifted the spear above his head with the right hand, poised it a moment, then hurled it from him, and struck the picket a palm's breadth below the shield.

"Out, out!" cried the 'tzin. "Bring me the **spear; I** have a mind **to** wear the plume myself."

When it was brought him, he cast it lightly as a child would toss a **weed;** yet the point drove clanging through the brazen base of the shield, and into the picket behind. Amid the applause of the sturdy warriors he said to Hualpa,—

"Get ready; the hunter must do something for the honour of his native hills."

"I cannot use a spear in competition with Guatamozin," said Hualpa with brightening eyes; "but if he will have brought a javelin, a good comely weapon, I will show him my practice."

A slender-shafted missile, about half the length of the spear, was produced from the armoury, and examined carefully.

"See, good 'tzin, it is not true. Let me have another."

The next one was to his satisfaction.

"Now," he said, "set the target thrice a hundred feet away. If the dainty living of Xoli have not weakened my arm, I will at least strike you shield."

The bystanders looked at each other wonderingly, and the 'tzin was pleased. He had not lost a word or a motion of Hualpa's. The feat undertaken was difficult, and but seldom achieved successfully; but the aspirant was confident, and he manifested the will to which all achievable things are possible.

The target was reset, and the Tihuancan took the stand. Resting the shaft on the palm of his left hand, he placed the fingers of his right against the butt, and drew the graceful weapon arm-length backward. It described an arc in the air, and to the astonishment of all fell in the shield a little left of the centre.

"Tell me, Hualpa," said Guatamozin, "are there more hunters in Tihuanco who can do such a deed? I will have you bring them to me."

The Tihuancan lowered his eyes. "I grieve to say, good 'tzin, that I know of none. I excelled them all. But I can promise that in my native province there are hundreds braver than I, ready to serve you to the death."

"Well, it is enough. I intended to try you further, and with other weapons, but not now. He who can so wield a javelin must know to bend a bow and strike with a *maquahuitl*. I accept your service. Let us to the palace."

Hualpa thrilled with delight. Already he felt himself in the warrior's path, with a glory won. All his dreams were about to be realized. In respectful silence he followed Guatamozin, and as they reached the portal steps, Io' touched his arm.

"Remember our compact on the lake," he whispered.

The hunter put his arm lovingly about the prince, and so they entered the house. And that day Fate wove a brotherhood of three hearts which was broken only by death.

CHAPTER V.

NIGHT AT THE CHALCAN'S.

THE same day, in the evening, Xoli lay on a lounge by the fountain under his portico. His position gave him the range of the rooms, which glowed like day, and resounded with life. He could even distinguish the occupations of some of his guests. In fair view a group was listening to a minstrel ; beyond them he occasionally caught sight of girls dancing ; and every moment peals of laughter floated out from the chambers of play. A number of persons, whose arms and attire published them of the nobler class, **sat** around the Chalcan in the screen of the curtains, conversing, or listlessly gazing out on the square.

Gradually Xoli's revery became more dreamy ; sleep stole upon his senses, and shut out the lullaby of the fountain, and drowned the influence of his *cuisine*. His patrons after a while disappeared, and the watchers on the temples told the passing time without awakening him. Very happy was the Chalcan.

The slumber was yet strong upon him when an old man and a girl came to the portico. The former, decrepit and ragged, seated himself on the step. Scanty hair hung in white locks **over** his face ; and grasping a staff, he rested his head wearily upon his hands, and talked to himself.

The girl approached the Chalcan with the muffled tread **of** fear. She was clad in the usual dress of her class,—a white chemise, with several skirts short and embroidered, over which, after being crossed at the throat, a red scarf dropped its tasselled ends nearly to her heels. The neatness of the garments more than offset their cheapness. Above her forehead, in the fillet **that** held the mass of black hair off her face, leaving it fully exposed, there was the gleam of a common jewel ; otherwise she **was** without ornament. In all beauty there is—nay, must be— an idea ; so that a countenance to be handsome even, must in some way at sight quicken a sentiment or stir a memory in the beholder. It was so here. To look at the old man's guardian was to know that she had a sorrow to tell, and to pity her before it was told,—to be sure that under her tremulous anxiety there was a darksome story and an extraordinary purpose, the signs of which, too fine for the materialism of words, but plain to the sympathetic inner consciousness, lurked in the corners of her mouth, looked from her great black eyes, and blent with every action.

Gliding over the marble, she stopped behind the sleeper, and spoke without awakening him ; her voice **was** too like the murmur of the fountain. Frightened at the words, low as they were, she hesitated ; but a look **at the old** man reassured her, and she called again. Xoli started.

"How now, mistress !" he **said** angrily, reaching for her hand.

"I want to see Xoli, the **Chalcan,**" she replied, escaping his touch.

"What have you to do with him ?"

He sat up, and looked at her in wonder.

"What have you to do with him ?" he repeated in a kindlier tone.

Her face kindled with a sudden intelligence. "Xoli ! **The gods be praised !** And their blessing on you, if you will **do a kind deed** for a countryman !"

"Well ! But what beggar is that ? Came he with you ?"

"It is of him I would speak. Hear me !" she asked, drawing near him again. "He is poor, but a Chalcan. If you have memory of the city of your birth, be merciful to his child."

"**His** child ! **Who ?** Nay, it is a beggar's tale ! Ho, fellow ! **How many times have I** driven you away already ! How dare **you return !**"

Slowly the old man raised his head from his staff, and turned **his face to the** speaker : there was no light there ; he was blind !

"**By the** holy fires, **no trick** this ! Say on, girl. He is a **Chalcan,** you said."

"A countryman **of** yours ;" and her tears fell fast. "A hut is standing where the causeway leads from Chalco to Iztapalapan ; it is my father's. He was happy under its roof ; for, though blind and poor, he could hear my mother's voice, which was the kindliest thing on earth to him. But Our Mother called her on the coming of a bright morning, and since then he has asked for bread, when I had not a *tuna*[1] to give him. O Xoli ! did you but know what it is to ask for bread when there is none ! I am his child, and can think of but one way to quiet his cry." And she paused, looking in his face for encouragement.

"Tell me your name, girl ; tell me your name, then go on," he said with a trembling lip, for his soul was clever.

At that instant the old man moaned querulously, "**Yeteve, Yeteve !**"

She went, and clasped his neck, and spoke to him soothingly. Xoli's eyes became humid ; down in the depths of his heart an emotion grew strangely warm.

"Yeteve, Yeteve !" he repeated musingly, thinking the syllables soft and pretty. "Come ; stand here again, Yeteve," said he aloud, when **the dotard was** pacified. "He wants bread, you say ; how would you supply him ?"

"You are rich. You want many slaves ; and the law permits

---

[1] A species of fig.

the poor to sell themselves.[1] I would be your slave,—asking no price, except that you give the beggar bread."

"A slave! Sell yourself!" he cried in dismay. "A slave! Why, you are beautiful, Yeteve, and have not bethought yourself that some day the gods may want you for a victim."

She was silent.

"What can you do? Dance? Sing? Can you weave soft veils and embroider golden flowers, like ladies in the palaces? If you can, no slave in Anahuac will be so peerless; the lords will bid more cocoa than you can carry; you will be rich."

"If so, then can I do all you have said."

And she ran, and embraced the old man, saying, "Patience, patience! In a little while we will have bread, and be rich. Yes," she continued, returning to the Chalcan, "they taught me in the *teocallis*, where they would have had me as priestess."

"It is good to be a priestess, Yeteve; you should have stayed there."

"But I did so love the little hut by **the causeway.** And I loved the beggar, and they let me go."

"And now you wish to sell yourself? I want slaves, but not such as you, Yeteve. I want those who can work,—slaves whom **the** lash will hurt, but not kill. Besides, you are worth more cocoa than I can spare. Keep back your tears. I will do better than buy you myself. I will sell you, and to-night. Here in my house you shall dance for the bidders. I know them all. He shall be brave and rich and clever who buys,—clever and brave, and the owner of a palace, full of bread for the beggar, and love for Yeteve."

Clapping his hands, a slave appeared at the door.

"Take yon beggar, and give him to eat. Lead **him,—he is** blind. Come, child, follow me."

He summoned his servants, and bade them publish the sale in every apartment; then he led the girl to the hall used for the exhibition of his own dancing-girls. It was roomy and finely lighted; the floor was of polished marble; a blue drop-curtain extended across the northern end, in front of which were rows of stools, handsomely cushioned, for spectators. Music, measured for the dance, greeted the poor priestess, and had a magical effect upon her; her eyes brightened, a smile played about her mouth. Never was the chamber of the rich Chalcan graced by a creature fairer or more devoted.

"A priestess of the dance needs no teaching from me," said Xoli, patting her flushed cheek. "Get ready; they are coming. Beware of the marble; and when I clap my hands, begin."

She looked around the hall once; not a point escaped her. Springing to the great curtain, and throwing **her** robe away,

[1] Prescott, *Conq. of* **Mexico.**

she stood before it in her simple attire; and no studied effect of art could have been more beautiful: motionless and lovely, against the relief of the blue background, she seemed actually *spirituelle.*

Upon the announcement of the auction, the patrons of the house hurried to the scene. Voluntary renunciation of freedom was common enough among the poorer classes in Tenochtitlan, but a transaction of the kind under the auspices of the rich broker was a novelty; so that curiosity and expectation ran high. The nobles, as they arrived, occupied the space in front of the curtain, or seated themselves, marvelling at the expression of her countenance.

The music had not ceased; and the bidders being gathered, Xoli, smiling with satisfaction, stepped forward to give the signal, when an uproar of merriment announced the arrival of a party of the younger dignitaries of the court,—amongst them Iztlil', the Tezcucan, and Maxtla, chief of the guard, the former showing signs of quick recovery from his wounds, the latter superbly attired.

"Hold! What have we here?" cried the Tezcucan, surveying the girl. "Has this son of Chalco been robbing the palace?"

"The temples, my lord Iztlil'! He has robbed the temples! By all the gods, it is the priestess Yeteve!" answered Maxtla, amazed. "Say, Chalcan, what does priestess of the Blessed Lady in such unhallowed den?"

The broker explained.

"Good, good!" shouted the new-comers.

"Begin, Xoli! A thousand cocoa for the priestess,—millions of bread for the beggar!" This from Maxtla.

"Only a thousand?" said Iztlil' scornfully. "Only a thousand? Five thousand to begin with, more after she dances."

Xoli gave the signal, and the soul of the Chalcan girl broke forth in motion. Dancing had been her *rôle* in the religious rites of the temple; many a time the pabas around the altar, allured by her matchless grace, had turned from the bleeding heart indifferent to its auguration. And she had always danced moved by no warmer impulse than duty; so that the prompting of the spirit in the presence of a strange auditory free to express itself, like that she now faced, came to her for the first time. The dance chosen was one of the wild, quick, pulsating figures wont to be given in thanksgiving for favourable tokens from the deity. The steps were irregular and difficult; a great variety of posturing was required; the head, arms, and feet had each their parts, all to be rendered in harmony. At the commencement she was frightened by the ecstasy that possessed her; suddenly the crowd vanished, and she saw only the beggar, and him

wanting bread. Then her form became divinely gifted,—she
bounded as if winged, advanced and retreated, a moment
swaying like a reed, the next whirling like a leaf in a circling
wind. The expression of her countenance throughout was so full
of soul, so intense, rapt, and beautiful, that the lords were spell-
bound. When the figure was ended, there was an outburst of
voices, some bidding, others applauding; though most of the
spectators were silent from pity and admiration.

Of the competitors the loudest was Iztlil'. In his excitement,
he would have sacrificed his province to become the owner of the
girl. Maxtla opposed him.

"Five thousand cocoa! Hear, Chalcan!" shouted the
Tezcucan.

"A thousand better!" answered Maxtla, laughing at the
cacique's rage.

"By all the gods, I will have her! Put me down a thousand
quills of gold!"

"A thousand quills above him! Not bread, but riches for the
beggar!" replied Maxtla, half in derision.

"Two thousand,—only two thousand quills! More, noble
lords! She is worth a palace!" sung Xoli, trembling with
excitement; for in such large bids he saw an extraordinary loan.
Just then, under the parted curtain of the principal doorway, he
beheld one dear to every lover of Tenochtitlan; he stopped. All
eyes turned in that direction, and a general exclamation followed,
—"The 'tzin, the 'tzin!"

Guatamozin was in full military garb, and armed. As he
lingered by the door to comprehend the scene, what with his
height, brassy helm, and embossed shield, he looked like a Greek
returned from Troy.

"Yeteve, the priestess!" he said. "Impossible!"

He strode to the front.

"How?" he said, placing his hand on her head. "Has Yeteve
flown the temple to become a slave?"

Up to this time, it would seem that, in the fixedness of her
purpose, she had been blind to all but the beggar, and deaf to
everything but the music. Now she knelt at the feet of the
noble Aztec, sobbing broken-heartedly. The spectators were
moved with sympathy,—all save one.

"Who stays the sale? By all the gods, Chalcan, you shall
proceed!"

Scarcely had the words been spoken, or the duller faculties
understood them, before Guatamozin confronted the speaker, his
javelin drawn, and his shield in readiness. Naturally his countenance was womanly gentle; but the transition of feeling was
mighty, and those looking upon him then shrank with dread; it
was as if their calm blue lake had in an instant darkened with

storm. Face to face he stood with the Tezcucan, the latter unprepared for combat, but in nowise daunted. In their angry attitude a seer might have read the destiny of Anahuac.

One thrust of the javelin would have sent the traitor to Mictlan,—the Empire, as well as the wrongs of the lover, called for it ; but before the veterans, recovering from their panic, could rush between the foemen, all the 'tzin's calmness returned.

"Xoli," he said, "a priestess belongs to the temple, and cannot be sold ; such is the law. The sale would have sent your heart, and that of her purchaser, to the Blessed Lady. Remove the girl. I will see that she is taken to a place of safety. Here is gold ; give the beggar what he wants, and keep him until to-morrow. And, my lords and brethren," he added, turning to the company, "I did not think to behave so unseemly. It is only against the enemies of our country that we should turn our arms. Blood is sacred, and accursed is his hand who sheds that of a countryman in petty quarrel. I pray you, forget all that has passed." And with a low obeisance to them, he walked away, taking with him the possibility of further rencounter.

He had just arrived from his palace at Iztapalapan.

CHAPTER VI.

THE CHINAMPA.

BETWEEN Tula, the child of Tecalco, and Nenetzin, daughter and child of Acatlan, there existed a sisterly affection. The same sports had engaged them, and they had been, and yet were, inseparable. Their mothers, themselves friends, encouraged the intimacy ; and so their past lives had vanished, like two summer clouds borne away by a soft south wind.

The evening after Iztlil's overture of marriage was deepening over Lake Tezcuco ; the breeze became murmurous and like a breath, and all the heavens filled with starlight. Cloudless must be the morrow to such a night !

So thought the princess Tula. Won by the beauty of the evening, she had flown from the city to her *chinampa*, which was lying anchored in a quarter of the lake east of the cause-way to Tepejaca, beyond the noise of the town, and where no sound less agreeable than the plash of light waves could disturb her dreams.

A retreat more delightful would be a task for fancy. The artisan who knitted the timbers of the *chinampa* had doubtless

been a lover of the luxuriant, and built as only a lover can
build. The waves of the lake had not been overlooked in
his plan; he had measured their height, and the depth and
width of their troughs, when the weather was calm and the
water gentle. So he knew both what rocking they would
make, and what rocking would be pleasantest to a delicate
soul; for, as there were such souls, there were also such artisans
in Tenochtitlan.

Viewed from a distance, the *chinampa* looked like an island of
flowers. Except where the canopy of a white pavilion rose from
the midst of the green beauty, it was covered to the water's edge
with blooming shrubbery, which, this evening, was luminous
with the light of lamps. The radiance, glinting through the
foliage, tinted the atmosphere above it with mellow rays, and
seemed the visible presence of enchantment.

The humid night breeze blew softly under the raised walls of
the pavilion, within which, in a hammock that swung to and
fro regularly as the *chinampa* obeyed the waves, lay Tula and
Nenetzin.

They were both beautiful, but different in their beauty. Tula's
face was round and of a transparent olive complexion, without
being fair; her eyes were hazel, large, clear, and full of melancholy earnestness; masses of black hair, evenly parted, fell over
her temples, and were gathered behind in a simple knot; with a
tall, full form, her presence and manner were grave and very
queenly. Whereas, Nenetzin's eyes, though dark, were bright
with the light of laughter; her voice was low and sweet, and
her manner that of a hoyden. One was the noble woman, the
other a jocund child.

"It is late, Tula; our father may want us. Let us return."

"Be patient a little longer. The 'tzin will come for us; he
promised to, and you know he never forgets."

"Patience, sister! Ah! you may say it, you who *know;* but
how am I to practise it,—I, who have only a *hope?*"

"What do you mean, Nenetzin?"

The girl leaned back, and struck a suspended hoop, in which
was perched a large parrot. The touch, though light, interrupted
the pendulous motion of the bird, and it pecked at her hand,
uttering a gruff scream of rage.

"You spoke of something I know, and you hope. What do
you mean, child?"

Nenetzin withdrew her hand from the perch, looked in the
questioner's face, then crept up to win her embrace.

"O Tula, I know you are learned and thoughtful. Often
after the banquet, when the hall was cleared, and the music
begun, have I seen you stand apart, silent, while all others
danced or laughed. See, your eyes are on me now, but more in

thought than love. Oh, indeed, you are wise! Tell me, did you ever think of me as a woman?"

The smile deepened on the lips, and burned in the eyes of the queenly auditor.

"No, never as a woman," continued Nenetzin. "Listen to me, Tula. The other night I was asleep in your arms,—I felt them in love around me,—and I dreamed so strangely."

"Of what?" asked Tula, seeing she hesitated.

"I dreamed there entered at the palace door a being with a countenance white like snow, while its hair and beard were yellow, like the silk of the maize; its eyes were blue, like the deep water of the lake, but bright, so bright that they terrified while they charmed me. Thinking of it now, O Tula, it was a man, though it looked like a god. He entered at the palace door, and came into the great chamber where our father sat with his chiefs; but he came not barefooted and in *nequen*; he spoke as he were master, and our father a slave. Looking and listening, a feeling thrilled me,—thrilled warm and deep, and was a sense of joy, like a blessing of Tlalac. Since then, though I have acted as a girl, I have felt as a woman."

"Very strange, indeed, Nenetzin!" said Tula playfully. "But you forget: I asked you what I know, and you only hope?"

"I will explain directly; but, as you are wise, first tell me what that feeling was."

"Nay, I can tell you whence the water flows, but I cannot tell you what it is."

"Well, since then I have had a hope"—

"Well?"

"A hope of seeing the white face and blue eyes."

"I begin to understand you, Nenetzin. But go on: what is it I know?"

"What I dreamed,—a great warrior, who loves you. You will see him to-night, and then, O Tula,—then you may tell of the feeling that thrilled me so in my dream."

And with a blush and a laugh, she laid her face in Tula's bosom.

Both were silent awhile, Nenetzin with her face hidden, and Tula looking wistfully up at the parrot swinging lazily in the perch. The dream was singular, and made an impression on the mind of the one as it had on the heart of the other.

"Look up, O Nenetzin!" said Tula after a while. "Look up, and I will tell you something that has seemed as strange to me as the dream to you."

The girl raised her head.

"Did you ever see Mualox, the old paba of Quetzal'? No. Well, he is said to be a prophet; a look of his will make a warrior tremble. He is the friend of Guatamozin, who always goes to his shrine to worship the god. I went there once to make an offering. I climbed the steps, went in where the image is, laid my gift on the altar, and turned to depart, when a man came and stood by the door, wearing a surplice, and with long, flowing white beard. He looked at me, then bowed, and kissed the pavement at my feet. I shrank away. 'Fear not, O Tula!' he said. 'I bow to you, not for what you are, but for what you shall be. *You shall be queen in your father's palace!*' With that he arose, and left me to descend."

"Said he so? How did he know you were Tula, the king's daughter?"

"That is part of the mystery. I never saw him before; nor, until I told the story to the 'tzin, did I know the paba. Now, O sister, can the believer of a dream refuse to believe a priest and prophet?"

"A queen! You a queen! I will kiss you now, and pray for you then." And they threw their arms lovingly around each other.

Then the bird above them awoke, and, with a fluttering of its scarlet wings, cried, "Guatamo! Guatamo!"—taught it by the patient love of Tula.

"Oh, what a time that will be!" Nenetzin went on with sparkling eyes. "What a garden we will make of Anahuac! How happy we shall be! None but the brave and beautiful shall come around us; for you will be queen, my Tula."

"Yes; and Nenetzin shall have a lord, he whom she loves best, for she will be as peerless as I am powerful," answered Tula, humouring the mood. "Whom will she take? Let us decide now,—there are so many to choose from. What says she to Cacama, lord of Tezcuco?"

The girl made no answer.

"There is the lord of Chinantla, once a king, who has already asked our father for a wife."

Still Nenetzin was silent.

"Neither of them! Then there are left but the lord of Tlacopan, and Iztlil', the Tezcuean."

At the mention of the last name, a strong expression of disgust burst from Nenetzin.

"A tiger from the museum first! It could be taught to love me. No, none of them for me; none, Tula, if you let me have my way, but the white face and blue eyes I saw in my dream."

"You are mad, Nenetzin! That was a god, not a man."

"All the better, Tula! The god will forgive me for loving him."

Before Tula spoke again, Guatamozin stepped within the pavilion. Nenetzin was noisy in expressing her gladness, while the elder sister betrayed no feeling by words; only her smile and the glow of her eyes intensified.

The 'tzin sat down by the hammock, and with his strong hand staying its oscillation, talked lightly. As yet Tula knew nothing of the proposal of the Tezcucan, or of the favour the king had given it; but the ken of love is as acute as an angel's—sorrow of the cherished heart cannot be hidden from it; so in his very jests she detected a trouble; but, thinking it had relation to the condition of the Empire, she asked nothing, while he, loath to disturb her happiness, counselled darkly of his own soul.

After a while, as Nenetzin prayed to return to the city, they left the pavilion; and, following a little path through the teeming shrubbery, and under the bows of orange-trees, overarched like an arbour, they came to the 'tzin's canoe. The keeper of the *chinampa* was there with great bundles of flowers. Tula and Nenetzin entered the vessel; then was the time for the slave; so he threw in the bundles until they were nearly buried under them,—his gifts of love and allegiance. When the rowers pushed off, he knelt with his face to the earth.

Gliding homeward through the dusk, Guatamozin told the story of Yeteve; and Tula, moved by the girl's devotion, consented to take her into service,—at least until the temple claimed its own.

CHAPTER VII.

COURT GOSSIP.

"A PINCH of your snuff, Xoli! To be out thus early dulls a nice brain, which nothing clarifies like snuff. By the way, it is very strange that when one wants a good article of any kind, he can only get it at the palace or of you. So, a pinch, my fat fellow!"

"I can commend my snuff," said the Chalcan, bowing very low, "only a little less than the good taste of the most noble Maxtla."

While speaking,—the scene being in his *pulque* room,—he uncovered a gilded jar sitting upon the counter.

"Help yourself; it is good to sneeze."

Maxtla snuffed the scented drug freely, then rushed to the door, and, through eyes misty with tears of pleasure, looked at the sun rising over the mountains. A fit of sneezing seized him, at the end of which a slave stood by his elbow with a ewer of water and a napkin. He bathed his face. Altogether, it was apparent that sneezing had been reduced to an Aztec science.

"Elegant! By the Sun, I feel inspired!"

"No doubt," responded the Chalcan. "Such ought to be the effect of tobacco and rose-leaves, moistened with dew. But tell me; that *tilmatli* you are wearing is quite royal,—is it from the king?"

The young chief raised the folds of the mantle of *plumaje*, which he was sporting for the first time. "From the king? No; my tailor has just finished it."

"Certainly, my lord. How dull I was! You are preparing for the banquet at the palace to-morrow night."

"You recollect the two thousand quills of gold I bid for your priestess the other evening," said Maxtla, paying no attention to the remark. "I concluded to change the investment; they are all in that collar and loop."

Xoli examined the loop.

"A *chalchuite*! What jeweller in the city could sell you one so rich?"

"Not one. I bought it of Cacama. It is a crown jewel of Tezcuco."

"You were lucky, my lord. But, if you will allow me, what became of the priestess? Saw you ever such dancing?"

"You are late inquiring, Chalcan. The beggar was fast by starvation that night; but you were nearer death. The story was told the king,—ah! you turn pale; well you may,—and he swore, by the fires of the temple, if the girl had been sold he would have flayed alive both buyer and seller. Hereafter we had both better look more closely to the law."

"But she moved my pity as it was never moved before; moreover, she told me they had discharged her from the temple."

"No matter; the peril is over, and our hearts are our own. Yesterday I saw her in the train of the princess Tula. The 'tzin cared for her. But speaking of the princess,—the banquet to-morrow night will be spicy."

The Chalcan dropped the precious loop. Gossip that concerned the court was one of his special weaknesses.

"You know," continued Maxtla, "that the 'tzin has always been a favourite of the king's"—

"As he always deserved to be."

"Not so fast, Chalcan! Keep your praise. You ought to know that nothing is so fickle as fortune; that what was most popular yesterday may be most unpopular to-day. Hear me out. You also know that Iztlil', the Tezcucan, was down in the royal estimation quite as much as the 'tzin was up; on which account, more than anything else, he lost his father's city."

Xoli rested his elbow on the counter, and listened eagerly.

"It has been agreed on all sides for years," continued Maxtla in his modulated voice, "that the 'tzin and Tula were to be married upon her coming of age. No one else has presumed to pay her court, lest it might be an interference. Now, the whole thing is at an end. Iztlil', not the 'tzin, is the fortunate man."

"Iztlil'! And to-morrow night!"

"The palace was alive last evening as with a swarming of bees. Some were indignant,—all astonished. In fact, Xoli, I believe the 'tzin had as many friends as the king. Several courtiers openly defended him, notwithstanding his fall,—something that, to my knowledge, never happened before. The upshot was, that a herald went in state to Iztapalapan with a decree prohibiting the 'tzin from visiting Tenochtitlan, under any pretence, until the further pleasure of the king is made known to him."

"Banished, banished! But that the noble Maxtla told me, I could not believe what I hear."

"Certainly the affair is mysterious, as were the means by which the result was brought about. Look you, Chalcan: the 'tzin loved the princess, and was contracted to her, and now comes this banishment just the day before the valley is called to witness her betrothal to the Tezcucan. Certainly it would ill become the 'tzin to be a guest at such a banquet."

"I understand," said Xoli with a cunning smile. "It was to save his pride that he was banished."

"If to be a Chalcan is to be so stupid, I thank the gods for making me what I am!" cried Maxtla impatiently. "What cares the great king for the pride of the enemy he would humble? The banishment is a penalty,—it is ruin."

There was a pause, during which the Chalcan hung his head.

"Ah, Xoli! The king has changed; he used to be a warrior, loving warriors as the eagle loves its young. Now—alas! I dare not speak. Time was when no envious-hearted knave could have made him believe that Guatamozin was hatching treason in his garden at Iztapalapan. Now, surrounded by mewling priests, he sits in the depths of his palace, and trembles, and, like a credulous child, believes everything. 'Woe is Tenochtitlan!' said Mualox; and the days strengthen the prophecy. But enough,—more than enough! Hist, Chalcan! What I have said and you listened to — yea, the mere listening — would suffice, if told in the right ears, to send us both straightway to the tigers. I have paid you for your snuff, and the divine sneeze. In retailing recollect, I am not the manufacturer. Farewell."

"Stay a moment, most noble chief,—but a moment," said the Chalcan. "I have invented a drink which I desire you to inaugurate. If I may be counted a judge, it is fit for a god."

"A judge! You? Where is the man who would deny you that excellence? Your days have been spent in the practice; nay, your whole life has been one long, long drink. Make haste. I will wager *pulque* is chief in the compound."

The broker went out, and directly returned, bearing on a waiter a Cholulan goblet full of cool liquor, exquisitely coloured with the rich blood of the cactus apple. Maxtla sipped, drank, then swore the drink was without a rival.

"Look you, Chalcan. They say we are indebted to our heroes, our minstrels, and our priests, and I believe so; but hereafter I shall go farther in the faith. This drink is worth a victory, is pleasant as a song, and has all the virtues of a prayer. Do not laugh. I am in earnest. You shall be canonized with the best of them. To show that I am no vain boaster, you shall come to the banquet to-morrow, and the king shall thank you. Put on your best *tilmatli*, and, above all else, beware that the vase holding this liquor is not empty when I call for it. Farewell!"

CHAPTER VIII.

GUATAMOZIN AND MUALOX.

Up the steps of the old Cû of Quetzal', early in the evening of the banquet, went Guatamozin unattended. As the royal interdiction rested upon his coming to the capital, he was muffled in a priestly garb, which hid his face and person, but could not all disguise the stately bearing that so distinguished him. Climbing the steps slowly, and without halting at the top to note the signs of the city, all astir with life, he crossed the *azoteas*, entered the chamber most sanctified by the presence of the god, and before the image bowed awhile in prayer. Soon Mualox came in.

"Ask anything that is not evil, O best beloved of Quetzal', and it shall be granted," said the paba solemnly, laying a hand upon the visitor's shoulder. "I knew you were coming; I saw you on the lake. Arise, my son."

Guatamozin stood up, and flung back his hood.

"The house is holy, Mualox, and I have come to speak of the things of life that have little to do with religion."

"That is not possible. Everything has to do with life, which

has all to do with heaven. Speak out. This presence will keep
you wise ; if your thoughts be of wrong, it is not likely you will
give them speech in the very ear of Quetzal'."

Slowly the 'tzin then said,—

"'Thanks, father. In what I have to say, I will be brief, and
endeavour not to forget the presence. You love me, and I am
come for counsel. You know how often those most discreet in
the affairs of others are foolish in what concerns themselves.
Long time ago you taught me the importance of knowledge ;
how it was the divine secret of happiness, and stronger than a
spear **to** win victories, and better in danger than a shield seven
times quilted. Now I have come to say that my habits of study
have brought evil upon me ; out of the solitude in which I was
toiling **to** lay up a great knowledge, a misfortune has arisen,
father, to my ruin. My stay at home has been misconstrued.
Enemies have said I loved books less than power ; they charge
that in the quiet of my gardens I have been taking council of
my ambition, which nothing satisfies but the throne ; and so
they have estranged from me the love of the king. Here against
his order, forbidden the city,"—and as he spoke he raised his head
proudly,—"forbidden the city, behold me, paba, a banished man !"

Mualox smiled, and grim satisfaction was in the smile.

"If you seek sympathy," he said, "the errand **is** fruitless.
I have no sorrow for what you call your misfortune."

"Let me understand you, father."

"I repeat, I have no sorrow for **you.** Why should I ? I see
you as you should see yourself. **You** confirm the lessons of
which you complain. Not vainly that you wrought in solitude
for knowledge, which, while I knew it would make you a mark
for even kingly envy, I also intended should make you superior
to misfortunes and kings. Understand you now ? What matters
that you are maligned ? What is banishment ? They only liken
you the more to Quetzal', whose coming triumph,—heed me well,
O 'tzin,—whose coming triumph shall be your triumph."

The look and voice of the holy man were those of one with
authority.

"**For this time,**" he continued, "and others like it, yet to come,
I thought **to arm** your soul with a strong intelligence. Your life
is to be **a battle** against evil ; fail not yourself in the beginning.
Success **will** be equal **to** your wisdom and courage. But your
story was not all told."

The 'tzin's face flushed, and he **replied, with** some faltering,—

"You have known and **encouraged the** love I bear **the** princess
Tula, and counted **on it as the means** of some great fortune in
store for me. Yet, in part at least, **I am** banished on that account.
O Mualox, the banquet which the king holds to-night is to make
public the betrothal of Tula to Iztll', the Tezcucan !"

"Well, what do you intend?"

"Nothing. Had the trouble been a friend's, I might have **advised him**; but being my own, I have no confidence in myself. I repose **on** your discretion and friendship."

Mualox softened his manner, and said, pleasantly at first, **"O** 'tzin, is humanity all frailty? Must chief and philosopher bow to the passion, like a slave or a dealer in wares?" Suddenly he became serious; his eyes shone full of the magnetism he used so often and so well. "Can Guatamozin find nothing higher to occupy his mind than a trouble born of a silly love? Unmanned by such a trifle? Arouse! Ponder the mightier interests **in** peril! What is a woman, with all a lover's gild about her, **to** the nation?"

"The nation?" repeated the 'tzin slowly.

The paba looked reverently up to the idol. "I have withdrawn from the world; I live but for Quetzal' and Anahuac. Oh, generously has the god repaid me! He has given me to look out upon the future; all that is to come affecting my country he has shown me." Turning to the 'tzin again, he said with emphasis, "I could tell marvels,—let this content you: words cannot paint the danger impending over our country, over Anahuac, the beautiful and beloved; her existence, and the glory and power that make her so worthy love like ours, are linked to your action. Your fate, O 'tzin, and hers, and that of the many nations, are one and the same. Accept the words as a prophecy; wear them in memory; and when, as now, you are moved by a trifling fear **or** anger, they should and will keep you from shame and folly."

Both then became silent. The paba might have been observing the events of the future, as, one by one, they rose and passed before his abstracted vision. Certain it was, with the thoughts of the warrior there mixed an ambition no longer selfish, but all his country's.

Mualox finally concluded. "The future belongs to the gods; only the present is ours. Of that let us think. Admit your troubles worthy vengeance: dare you tell me what you thought of doing? My son, why are you here?"

"Does my father seek to mortify me?"

"Would the 'tzin have me encourage folly, if not worse?—and that in the presence of my god and his?"

"Speak plainly, Mualox."

"So I will. Obey the king. Go not to the palace to-night. If the thought of giving the woman to another is so hard, could you endure the sight? Think: if present, what could you do to prevent the betrothal?"

A savage anger flashed from the 'tzin's face, and **he** answered, "What could I? Slay the Tezcucan on the step **of the** throne, though I died!"

"It would come to that. And Anahuac!—what then of her?" said Mualox in a voice of exceeding sorrow.

The love the warrior bore his country at that moment surpassed all others, and his rage passed away.

"True, most true! If it should be as you say, that my destiny"—

"If? O 'tzin, if you live! If Anahuac lives! If there are gods!"—

"Enough, Mualox! I know what you would say. Content you; I give you all faith. The wrong that tortures me is not altogether that the woman is to be given to another; her memory I could pluck from my heart as a feather from my helm. If that were all, I could curse the fate, and submit; but there is more: for the sake of a cowardly policy I have been put to shame; treachery and treason have been crowned, loyalty and blood disgraced. Hear me, father! After the decree of interdiction was served upon me, I ventured to send a messenger to the king, and he was spurned from the palace. Next went the lord Cuitlahua, uncle of mine, and true lover of Anahuac; he was forbidden the mention of my name. I am not withdrawn from the world; my pride will not down at a word; so wronged, I cannot reason,—therefore I am here."

"And the coming is a breach of duty; the risk is great. Return to Iztapalapan before the midnight is out. And I,—but you do not know, my son, what a fortune has befallen me.' The paba smiled faintly. "I have been promoted to the palace; I am a councillor at the royal table."

"A councillor! You, father?"

The good man's face grew serious again. "I accepted the appointment, thinking good might result. But, alas! the hope was vain. Montezuma, once so wise, is past counsel. He will take no guidance. And what a vanity! O 'tzin, the asking me to the palace was itself a crime, since it was to make me a weapon in his hand with which to resist the holy Quetzal'. As though I could not see the design!"

He laughed scornfully, and then said, "But be not detained, my son. What I can, I will do for you; at the council-table, and elsewhere, as opportunity may offer, I will exert my influence for your restoration to the city and palace. Go now. Farewell; peace be with you. To-morrow I will send you tidings."

Thereupon he went out of the tower, and down into the temple.

CHAPTER IX.

A KING'S BANQUET.

At last the evening of the royal banquet arrived,—theme of incessant talk and object of preparation for two days and a night, out of the capital no less than in it; for all the nobler classes within a convenient radius of the lake had been bidden, and, with them, people of distinction, such as successful artists, artisans, and merchants.

It is not to be supposed that a king of Montezuma's subtlety in matters governmental could overlook the importance of the social element, or neglect it. Education imports a society; more yet, academies, such as were in Tenochtitlan for the culture of women, always import a refined and cultivated society. And such there was in the beautiful valley.

My picture of the entertainment will be feeble, I know, and I give it rather as a suggestion of the reality, which was gorgeous enough to be interesting to any nursling even of the court of His Most Catholic Majesty; for, though heathen in religion, Montezuma was not altogether barbarian in taste; and, sooth to say, no monarch in Christendom better understood the influence of kingliness splendidly maintained. About it, moreover, was all that makes chivalry adorable,—the dance, the feast, the wassail; brave men, fair women, and the majesty of royalty in state amidst its most absolute proofs of power.

On such occasions it was the custom of the great king to throw open the palace, with all its accompaniments, for the delight of his guests, admitting them freely to aviary, menagerie, and garden, the latter itself spacious enough for the recreation of thirty thousand persons.

The house, it must be remembered, formed a vast square, with *patios* or courtyards in the interior, around which the rooms were ranged. The part devoted to domestic uses was magnificently furnished. Another very considerable portion was necessary to the state and high duties of the monarch; such were offices for his functionaries, quarters for his guards, and chambers for the safe deposit of the archives of the Empire, consisting of maps, laws, decrees and proclamations, accounts and reports financial and military, and the accumulated trophies of campaigns and conquests innumerable. When we consider the regard in which the king was held by his people, amounting almost to worship, and their curiosity to see all that pertained to his establishment, an idea may be formed of what the palace and its appurtenances were as accessories to one of his entertainments.

Passing from the endless succession of rooms, the visitor might go into the garden, where the walks were freshly strewn with shells, the shrubbery studded with coloured lamps, the fountains all at play, and the air loaded with the perfume of flowers, which were an Aztec passion, and seemed **everywhere a** part of everything.

And all this convenience and splendour was not wasted upon an inappreciative horde,—ferocious Caribs or simple children of Hispaniola. At such times the order requiring the wearing of *nequen* **was suspended ; so** that in the matter of costume there **were no limits** upon the guest, except such as were prescribed by **his taste** or condition. In the animated current that swept from **room to room** and from **house** to garden might be seen citizens in plain **attire, and warriors** arrayed in regalia which permitted **all** dazzling **colours, and** pabas hooded, surpliced, and gowned, brooding darkly even there, and stoled minstrels with their harps, **and** pages gay as butterflies, while over all was the beauty of the presence of lovely women.

Yet, withal, the presence of Montezuma was more attractive **than the** calm night in the garden ; neither stars, nor perfumed summer airs, nor singing fountains, nor walks strewn with shells, nor chant of minstrels could keep the guests from the great hall where he sat in state ; so that it was alike the centre of all coming and **all going.** There the aged and sedate whiled away the hours **in conversation ;** the young danced, laughed, and were happy ; and **in the** common joyousness none exceeded the beauties of the harem, transiently released from the jealous thraldom that made the palace their prison.

From the house-tops, or from the dykes, or out on the water, **the** common people of the capital, in vast multitudes, witnessed **the** coming of the guests across the lake. The rivalry of the great lords and families was at all times extravagant in the matter of **pomp** and show ; a king's banquet, however, seemed its special opportunity, and the lake its particular field of display. The king Cacama, for example, left his city in a canoe of exquisite workmanship, pranked with pennons, ribbons, and garlands ; **behind him, or at** his right and left, constantly ploying and **deploying, attended** a flotilla of hundreds of canoes only a little **less rich in decoration** than his own, and timed in every movement, **even that of** the paddles, by the music of conch-shells and tambours ; **yet,** princely as **the turn-out** was, it did not **exceed** that of the lord Cuitlahua, governor of Iztapalapan. And if others were inferior to them in extravagance, nevertheless they helped clothe the beloved sea with a beauty and interest scarcely to be imagined by people **who never witnessed** or read of the grand Venetian pageants.

Arrived at the capital, the younger warriors proceeded to the **palace** afoot ; while the matrons and maids, and the older and more dignified lords, were borne thither in palanquins. By evening the whole were assembled.

About the second quarter of the night two men came up the great street to the palace, and made their way through the palanquins stationed there in waiting. They were guests; so their garbs bespoke them. One wore the gown and carried the harp of a minstrel; very white locks escaped from his hood, and a staff was required to assist his enfeebled steps. The other was younger, and with consistent vanity sported a military costume. To say the truth, his extremely warlike demeanour lost nothing by the flash of a dauntless eye and a step that made the pave ring again.

An official received them at the door, and, by request, conducted them to the garden.

"This is indeed royal!" the warrior said to the minstrel. "It bewilders me. Be yours the lead."

"I know the walks as a deer his paths, or a bird the brake that shelters its mate. Come," and the voice was strangely firm for one so aged,—"come, let us see the company."

Now and then they passed ladies, escorted by gallants, and frequently there were pauses to send second looks after the handsome soldier, and words of pity for his feeble companion. By and by, coming to an intersection of the walk they were pursuing, they were hailed,—"Stay, minstrel, and give us a song."

By the door of a summer-house they saw, upon stopping, a girl whose beauty was worthy the tribute she sought. The elder sat down upon a bench and replied,—

"A song is gentle medicine for sorrows. Have you such? You are very young."

Her look of sympathy gave place to one of surprise.

"I would I were assured that minstrelsy is your proper calling."

"You doubt it! Here is my harp: a soldier is known by his shield."

"But I have heard your voice before," she persisted.

"The children of Tenochtitlan, and many who are old now, have heard me sing."

"But I am a Chalcan."

"I have sung in Chalco."

"May I ask your name?"

"There are many streets in the city, and on each they call me differently."

The girl was still perplexed.

"Minstrels have patrons," she said directly, "who"—

"Nay, child, this soldier here is all the friend I have."

Some one then threw aside the vine that draped the door.

H

While the minstrel looked to see who the intruder was, his inquisitor gazed at the soldier, who, on his part, saw neither of them; he was making an obeisance so very low that his face and hand both touched the ground.

"Does the minstrel intend to sing, **Yeteve?**" asked Nenetzin, stepping into the light that flooded the walk.

The old man bent forward on his seat.

"Heaven's best blessing on the child of the **king**! It should **be a nobler** hand than mine that strikes a **string to one so** beautiful."

The comely princess replied, her face beaming with pleasure, "**Verily**, minstrel, **much** familiarity with song has given you courtly speech."

"I have courtly friends, **and only borrow** their words. This place is fair, but to my dull fancy it seems that a maiden would prefer the great hall, unless she has a grief to indulge."

"Oh, I have a great grief," she returned; "though I do borrow it as you your words."

"Then you love some one who is unhappy. I understand. Is this child in your service?" he asked, looking at Yeteve.

"Call it mine. She **loves** me well enough to serve me."

The minstrel struck the strings of his harp softly, as if commencing a mournful story.

"I have a friend," he said, "a prince and warrior, whose presence here is banned. He sits in his palace to-night, and is visited by thoughts such as make men old in their youth. He has seen much of life, and won fame, but is fast finding that glory does not sweeten misfortune, and that of all things ingratitude is the most bitter. His heart is set upon a noble woman; and now, when his love is strongest, he is separated from her, and may not say farewell. Oh, it is not in the ear of a true woman that lover so unhappy could breathe his story in vain! What would **the** princess Nenetzin do, if she knew a service of hers might soothe his great grief?"

Nenetzin's eyes were dewy with **tears**.

"**Good** minstrel, I know the story; it is the 'tzin's. Are you **a friend** of his?"

"His **true friend**. I bring his farewell to Tula."

"I **will serve him**." And, stepping to the old man, she laid her hand **on his**. "**Tell** me what to do, and what you would have."

"Only a moment's speech with her."

"With Tula?"

"A moment to say the farewell he cannot. **Go to** the palace, **and** tell her what I seek. I will follow directly. Tell her she **may** know me in the throng by these locks, whose whiteness will **prove my** sincerity and devotion. And further, I will twine my harp with a branch of this vine; its leaves will mark me, and at the same time tell her that his love is green as in the day a king's smile sunned it into ripeness. Be quick. The moment comes when she cannot in honour listen to the message I am to to speak."

He bent over his harp again, and Nenetzin and Yeteve hurried away.

CHAPTER X.

THE 'TZIN'S LOVE.

THE minstrel stayed a while to dress his harp with the vine.

"A woman would have done it better; they have a special cunning for such things; yet it will serve the purpose. Now let us on!" he said, when the task was finished.

To the palace they then turned their steps. As they approached it, the walk became more crowded with guests. Several times the minstrel was petitioned to stay and sing, but he excused himself. He proceeded, looking steadily at the ground, as is the custom of the very aged. Amongst others, they met Maxtla, gay in his trappings as a parrot from the Great River.

"Good minstrel," he said, "in your wanderings through the garden, have you seen Iztlil', the Tezcucan?"

"I have not seen the Tezcucan. I should look for him in the great hall, where his bride is, rather than in the garden, dreaming of his bridal."

"Well said, uncle! I infer your harp is not carried for show; you can sing! I will try you after a while."

When he was gone, the minstrel spoke bitterly,—

"Beware of the thing known in the great house yonder as policy. A week ago the lord Maxtla would have scorned to be seen hunting the Tezcucan, whom he hates."

They came to a portal above which, in a niche of the wall, sat the *teotl*[1] of the house, grimly claiming attention and worship. Under the portal, past the guard on duty there, through many apartments full of objects of wonder to the stranger, they proceeded, and, at last, with a current of guests slowly moving in the same direction, reached the hall dominated by the king, where the minstrel thought to find the princess Tula.

"O my friend, I pray you, let me stay here a moment," said the warrior, abashed by dread of the sudden introduction to the royal presence. The singer heard not, but went on.

[1] A household god.

Standing by the door, the young stranger looked down a hall of great depth eastwardly, broken by two rows of pillars supporting vast oaken girders, upon which rested rafters of red cedar. The walls were divided into panels, with borders broad and intricately arabesqued. A massive bracket in the centre of each panel held the image of a deity, the duplicate of the idol in the proper sanctuary; and from the feet of the image radiated long arms of wood, well carved, crooked upward at the elbows, and ending with shapely hands, clasping lanterns of *aguave* which emitted lights of every tint. In the central space, between the rows of pillars, immense chandeliers dropped from the rafters, so covered with lamps that they looked like pyramids aglow. And arms, and images, and chandeliers, and even the huge pillars, were wreathed in garlands of cedar boughs and flowers, from which the air drew a redolence as of morning in a garden.

Through all these splendours, the gaze of the visitor sped to the farther end of the hall, and there stayed as charmed. He saw a stage, bright with crimson carpeting, rising three steps above the floor, and extending from wall to wall; and on that, covered with green *plumaje*, a dais, on which, in a chair or throne glittering with burnished gold, the king sat,—above him spread a canopy fashioned like a broad sunshade, the staff resting on the floor behind the throne, sustained by two full-armed warriors, who, while motionless as statues, were yet vigilant as sentinels. Around the dais, their costumes and personal decorations sharing the monarch's splendour, were collected his queens, and their children, and all who might claim connection with the royal family. The light shone about them as the noonday, so full that all that portion of the hall seemed bursting with sunshine. Never satin richer than the emerald cloth of the canopy, inwoven, as it was, with feathers of humming-birds! Never sheen of stars, to the eyes of the wondering stranger, sharper than the glinting of the jewels with which it was fringed!

And the king appeared in happier mood than common, though the deep, serious look which always accompanies a great care came often to his face. He had intervals of silence also; yet his shrewdest guests were not permitted to see that he did not enjoy their enjoyment.

His queens were seated at his left, Tecalco deeply troubled, sometimes tearful, and Acatlan cold and distant; for, in thought of her own child, the beautiful Nenetzin, she trembled before the remorseless policy.

And Tula, next to the king the recipient of attention, sat in front of her mother, never more queenly, never so unhappy. Compliments came to her, and congratulations, given in courtly style; minstrels extolled her grace and beauty, and the prowess and martial qualities of the high-born Tezcucan; and priest and warrior laid their homage at her feet. Yet her demeanour was not that of the glad young bride; she never smiled, and her eyes, commonly so lustrous, were dim and hopeless; her thoughts were with her heart, across the lake with the banished 'tzin.

As may be conjectured, it was no easy game to steal her from place so conspicuous; nevertheless, Nenetzin awaited the opportunity.

It happened that Maxtla was quite as anxious to get the monarch's ear for the benefit of his friend, the Chalcan,—in fact, for the introduction of the latter's newly-invented drink. Experience taught the chief when the felicitous moment arrived. He had then but to say the word: a page was sent, the liquor brought. Montezuma sipped, smiled, quaffed deeper, and was delighted.

"There is nothing like it!" he said. "Bring goblets for **my** friends, and fill up again!"

All the lordly personages **about** him had then to follow **his** example,—to drink and approve. At the end, Xoli was summoned.

Nenetzin saw the chance, and said, "O Tula, such a song as we have heard! It was sweeter than that of the bird that wakes us in the morning, sweeter than all the flutes in the hall."

"And the singer,—who was he?"

Neither Nenetzin nor Yeteve could tell his name.

"He charmed us so," said the former, "that we thought **only** of taking you to hear him. Come, go with us. There never **was** such music or musician."

And the three came down from the platform unobserved by the king. When the minstrel's message was delivered, then was shown how well the Tezcucan had spoken when he said of the royal children, "They are all beautiful, but only one is fitted to be a warrior's wife."

"Let us see the man," said Tula. "How may we know him, Nenetzin?"

And they went about eagerly looking for the singer with the grey locks and the vine-wreathed harp. They found him at last about midway the hall, leaning on his staff, a solitary amidst the throng. No one thought of asking him for a song; he was too old, too like one come from a tomb with unfashionable stories.

"Father," said Tula, "we claim your service. You look weary, yet you must know the ancient chants, which, though I would not like to say it everywhere, please me best. Will you sing?"

He raised his head, and looked at her. She started; something she saw in his eyes that had escaped her friends.

"A song from me!" he replied, as if astonished. "No, it cannot be. I have known some gentle hearts, and studied them to remember; but long since they went to dust. You do not

know me. Imagining you discerned of what I was thinking, you
were moved ; you only pitied me, here so desolate."

As he talked, she recovered her composure.

"Will you sing for me, father?" she again asked.

"Oh, willingly! My memory is not so good as it used to be ;
yet one song, at least, I will give you from the numberless ills
that crowd it."

He looked slowly and tremulously around at the guests who
had followed her, or stopped, as they were passing, to hear the
conversation.

"As you say," he then continued, "I am old and feeble, and
it is wearisome to stand here ; besides, my theme will be sad, and
such as should be heard in quiet. Time was when my harp had
honour,—to me it seems but yesterday ; but now—enough! Here
it were not well that my voice should be heard."

She caught his meaning, and her whole face kindled ; but .
Nenetzin spoke first.

"Oh yes ; let us to the garden!"

The minstrel bowed reverently. As they started, a woman,
who had been listening, said, "Surely the noble Tula is
not going! The man is a dotard ; he cannot sing ; he is
palsied."

But they proceeded, and through the crowd and out of the hall
guided the trembling minstrel. Coming to a passage that seemed
to be deserted, they turned into it, and Nenetzin, at Tula's request,
went back to the king. Then a change came over the good man ;
his stooping left him, his step became firm, and, placing himself
in front, he said in a deep, strong voice,—

"It is mine to lead now. I remember these halls. Once again,
O Tula, let me lead you here, as I have a thousand times in childhood."

And to a chamber overlooking the garden, by the hand he led
her, followed by Yeteve, sobbing like a child. A dim light from
the lamps without disclosed the walls hung with trophies captured
in wars with the surrounding tribes and nations. Where the
rays were strongest, he stopped, and removed the hood, and said
earnestly,—

"Against the king's command, and loving you better than life,
O Tula, Guatamozin has come to say farewell."

There was a great silence ; each heard the beating of the other's
heart.

"You have passed from me," he continued, "and I send my
grief after you. I look into your face, and see fade our youth,
our hopes, and our love, and all the past that bore it relation.
The days of pleasantness are ended ; the spring that fed the
running brook is dry. O Tula, dear one, the bird that made us
such sweet music is songless for ever!"

Her anguish was too deep for the comfort of words **or tears**. Closer he clasped her hand.

"Oh that power should be so faithless! Here are banners that I have taken. Yonder is a shield of a king of Michuaca whom I slew. I well remember the day. Montezuma led the army; the fight was hard, the peril great; and after I struck the blow, he said I had saved his life, and vowed me boundless love and a splendid reward. What a passion the field of fighting men was! And yet there was another always greater. I had dwelt in the palace, and learned that in the smile of the noble Tula there was to my life what the sunshine is to the flower."

He faltered, then continued brokenly,—

"He had honours, palaces, provinces, and crowns to bestow; but witness, O gods, whose sacred duty it is to punish ingratitude, **—witness** that I cared more to call Tula wife than for all the multitude of his princeliest gifts!"

And **now** fast ran the tears of **the** princess, through sorrow rising to full womanhood, while the murky chamber echoed with the sobs of Yeteve. If the ghost of the barbarian king yet cared for the shield he died defending, if **it** were there present, seeing and hearing, its revenge was perfect.

"If Guatamozin—so dear to me now, so dear always—will overlook the womanly selfishness that could find a pleasure in his grief, I will prove that he has not loved unworthily. You have asked nothing of me, nor urged any counsel, and I thank you for the moderation. I thank you, also, that you have spoken as if this sorrow were not yours more than mine. Most of all, O 'tzin, I thank you for not accusing me. Need I say how I hate the Tezcucan? or that I am given away against my will? I am **to** go as a price, as so much *cocoa*, in purchase of the fealty **of** a wretch who would league with Mictlan to humble my father. I **am a** weak woman, without tribes or banner, and therefore the wrong is put upon me. But have I no power?" And, trembling with the strong purpose, she laid her hand upon his breast. "Wife will I never be except of Guatamozin. I am the daughter of a king. My father, at least, should know me. He may sell me, but, thank the holy gods, I am the keeper of my own life! And what would life be with the base Tezcucan for my master? Royal power in a palace of pearl and gold would not make it worth the keeping. O 'tzin, you never threw a worthless leaf upon the lake more carelessly than I would then fling this poor body there!"

Closer to his heart he pressed the hand on his breast.

"To you, to you, O Tula, be the one blessing greater than all others which the gods keep back in the Sun! So only can you be rewarded. I take your words as an oath. Keep them, only keep them, and I will win for you all that can be won by man. What **a time is** coming"—

Just then a joyous cry and a burst of laughter from the garden interrupted his passionate speech, and recalled him to himself and the present,—to the present, which was not to be satisfied with lovers' rhapsodies. And so he said, when next he spoke,—

"You have answered my most jealous wish. Go back now ; make no objection to the Tezcucan ; the betrothal is not the bridal. The king and Iztil' cannot abide together in peace. I know them."

And, sinking his voice, he added, "Your hand is on my heart, and by its beating you cannot fail to know how full it is of love. Take my blessing to strengthen you. Farewell ! I will return to my gardens and dreams."

"To dreams ! And with such a storm coming upon Anahuac!" said Tula. "No, no ; to dream is mine."

Up, clear to his vision, rose the destiny prophesied for him by Mualox. As he pondered it, she said tearfully,—

"I love my father, and he is blind or mad. Now is his peril greatest, now most he needs friendship and help. O 'tzin, leave him not,—I conjure you by his past kindness ! Remember I am his child."

Thereupon he dropped her hand, and walked the floor, while the banners and the shields upon the walls, and the mute glory they perpetuated, whispered of the wrong and shame he was enduring. When he answered, she knew how great the struggle had been, and that the end was scarcely a victory.

"You have asked that of me, my beloved, which is a sore trial," he said. "I will not deny that the great love I bore your father is disturbed by bitterness. Think how excessive my injury is,— I who revered as a son, and have already put myself in death's way for him. In the halls, and out in the gardens, my name has been a jest to-night. And how the Tezcucan has exulted ! It is hard for the sufferer to love his wrong-doer,—oh, so hard ! But this I will, and as an oath take the promise : as long as the king acts for Anahuac, not imperilling her safety or glory, so long will I uphold him ; this, O Tula, from love of country, and nothing more !"

And as the future was veiled against the woman and dutiful child, she replied simply, "I accept the oath. Now lead me hence."

He took her hand again, and said, "In peril of life I came to say farewell for ever ; but I will leave a kiss upon your forehead, and plant its memory in your heart, and some day come again to claim you mine."

And he put his arm around her, and left the kiss on her forehead, and, as the ancient he entered, conducted the unhappy princess from the chamber of banners back to the hall of betrothal.

CHAPTER XI

THE CHANT.

"If you have there anything for laughter, Maxtla, I bid you welcome," said the king, his guests around him.

And the young chief knelt on the step before the throne, and answered with mock solemnity, "Your servant, O king, knows your great love of minstrelsy, and how it delights you to make rich the keeper of a harp who sings a good song well. I have taken one who **bears** him like **a** noble singer, and has **age to** warrant his experience."

"Call you that the man?" asked the king, pointing **to Guata-** mozin.

"He is the man."

The monarch laughed, and all the guests listening laughed.

Now minstrels were common on all festive occasions ; indeed, **an** Aztec banquet was no more perfect without them than without guests ; but it was seldom the royal halls were graced by one so very aged ; so that the bent form and grey locks, that at other places and times would have insured safety and respect, **now** excited derision. The men thought his presence there **pre-** sumptuous, the women laughed at him as a dotard. In **brief,** the 'tzin's peril was very great.

He seemed, however, the picture of aged innocence, and **stood** before the throne, his head bowed, his face shaded **by the hood,** leaning humbly on his staff, and clasping the harp close **to his** breast, the vines yet about it. So well did he observe his disguise, that none there, save Tula and Yeteve, might dream that the hood and dark gown concealed the boldest warrior in Tenoch-titlan. The **face** of the priestess was turned away, but the princess sat a calm witness of the scene ; either she had too much pride to betray her solicitude, or a confidence in his address so absolute that she felt none.

"He is none of ours," said the king, when he had several times scanned the minstrel. "If **the** palace ever knew him, it was **in** the days of Axaya', from whose tomb he seems to have come."

"As I came in from the garden, I met him going out," said Maxtla in explanation. "I could not bear that my master should lose such a promise of song. Besides, I have heard the veterans in service often say that the ancient chants were the best, and I thought it a good time to test the boast."

The grey courtiers frowned, and the king laughed again.

"My minstrel here represented that old time **so** well," con-tinued Maxtla, "that at first I was full of reverence ; therefore

I besought him to come, and **before** you, O king, sing the **chants** that used to charm your mighty father. I thought it no dishonour for him to compete with the singers now in favour, they giving us something of the present time. He declined in courtliest style ; saying that, though his voice was good, he was too old, and might shame the ancient minstrelsy ; and that, from what he had heard, my master delighted only in things of modern invention. A javelin in the hand of a sentinel ended the argument, and he finally consented. Wherefore, O king, I claim him captive, to whom, if it be your royal pleasure, I offer liberty, if he will sing in competition before this noble company."

What sport **could be more royal** than such poetic contest, —the old **reign** against **the new?** Montezuma welcomed the idea.

"The condition is reasonable," he said. "Is there a minstrel in the valley to call it otherwise?"

In a tone scarcely audible, though all were silent that they might hear, the 'tzin answered,—

'Obedience was the first lesson of every minstrel of the old **time ;** but as the master we served loved us as his children, we never had occasion to sing for the purchase of our liberty. And more,—the capture of a harmless singer, though he were not aged as your poor slave, O king, was not deemed so brave a deed as to be rewarded by our master's smile."

The speech, though feebly spoken, struck both **the king and** his chief.

"Well done, uncle!" said the former, laughing. "And since you have tongue so sharp, we remove the condition"—

"Thanks, many thanks, most mighty king! May the **gods** mete you nothing but good! I will depart." And the **'tzin** stooped till his harp struck the floor.

The monarch waved his hand. "Stay. I merely spoke of the condition that made your liberty depend upon your song. Go, **some** of **you,** and call my singers." A courtier hurried away, then the king added, "It shall be well for him who best strikes the strings. I promise a prize that shall raise him above trouble, and make his life what a poet's ought to be."

Guatamozin advanced, and knelt on **the** step **from which** Maxtla had risen, and said, his voice sounding tremulous with age and infirmity,—

"If the great king will deign to heed his servant again,—I am old and weak. There was a time when I would have rejoiced to hear a prize so princely offered in such a trial. But that was many, many summers ago. And this afternoon, in my hut by the lake-shore, when I took my harp, all covered with dust, from the shelf where it had so long lain untouched and neglected, and wreathed it with this fresh vine, thinking a gay dress might give it the appearance of use, and myself a deceitful likeness to the minstrel I once was, alas! I did not think of my trembling hand and my shattered memory, or of trial like this. I only knew that a singer, however humble, **was** privileged at your banquet, and that the privilege was a custom of the monarchs now in their halls in the Sun,—true, kingly men, who at time like this would have put gold in my hand, and bade me arise and go in peace. Is Montezuma more careless of his glory? Will he compel my song, and dishonour my grey hair, that I may go abroad in Tenochtitlan and tell the story? In pity, O king, suffer me to depart."

The courtiers murmured, and **even** Maxtla relented, but **the** king said,—

"Good uncle, you **excite** my curiosity the more. **If** your common speech have in it such a vein of poetry, what must the poetry be? And then, does not your obstinacy outmeasure my cruelty? Get ready, I hold the fortune. Win it, and I am no king if it be not yours."

The interest of the bystanders now exceeded their pity. It was novel to find one refusing reward so rich, when the followers of his art were accustomed to gratify **an** audience, even **one** listener, upon request.

And, seeing that escape from the trial was impossible, the 'tzin arose, resolved to act boldly. Minstrelsy, as practised by **the** Aztecs, it must be remembered, was not singing so much **as a** form of chanting, accompanied by rhythmical touches of the lyre or harp,—of all kinds of choral music the most primitive. This he had practised, but in the solitude of his study. The people present knew the 'tzin Guatamo, supposed to be in his palace across the lake, as soldier, scholar, and prince, but not as poet or singer of heroic tales. So that confident minstrelsy was now but another, if not a surer, disguise. And the eyes of the princess Tula shining upon him calmly and steadily, he said, his voice this time trembling with suppressed wrath,—

"Be it so, O king! Let the singers come,—let them come! Your slave will fancy himself before the great Axaya', or your father, not less royal. He will forget his age, and put his trust in the god whose story he will sing."

Then other amusements were abandoned, and, intelligence of the trial flying far and fast, lords and ladies, soldiers and priests, crowded about the throne and filled the hall. That any power of song could belong to one so old and unknown was incredible.

"He is a provincial,—the musician of one of the hamlets," said a courtier derisively.

"Yes," sneered another; "he will tell how the flood came, and drowned the harvest in his neighbourhood."

"Or," ventured a third, "how a ravenous vulture once descended from the hills, and carried off his pet rabbit."

By and by the royal minstrels came,—sleek, comely men, wearing long stoles fringed with gold, and having harps inlaid with pearl, and strung with silver wires. With scarce a glance at their humble competitor, they ranged themselves before the monarch.

The trial began. One after another, the favourites were called upon. The first sang of love, the next of his mistress, the third of Lake Tezcuco, the fourth of Montezuma, his power, wisdom, and glory. Before all were through, the patience of the king and crowd was exhausted. The pabas wanted something touching religion, the soldiers something heroic and resounding with war; and all waited for the stranger, as men listening to a story wait for the laughter it may chance to excite. How were they surprised! Before the womanly tones of the last singer ceased, the old man dropped his staff, and, lifting his harp against his breast, struck its chords, and, in a voice clear and vibratory as the blast of a shell,—a voice that filled the whole hall, and startled maid and king alike,—began his chant.

QUETZAL'.

Beloved of the Sun! Mother of the
Brave! Azatlan, the North-born! Heard be thou
In my far-launched voice! I sing to thy
Listening children of thee and Heaven.
Vale in the Sun, where dwell the Gods! Sum of
The beautiful art thou! Thy forests are
Flowering trees; of crystal and gold thy
Mountains; and liquid light are thy rivers
Flowing, all murmurous with songs, over
Beds of stars. O Vale of Gods, the summery
Sheen that flecks Earth's seas, and kisses its mountains,
And fairly floods its plains, we know is of thee,—
A sign sent us from afar, that we may
Feebly learn how beautiful is Heaven!

The singer rested a moment; then, looking in the eyes of the king, with a rising voice he continued,—

Richest hall in all the Vale is Quetzal's—

At that name Montezuma started. The minstrel noted well the sign.

O, none so fair as Quetzal's! The winds that
Play among its silver columns are Love's
Light laughter, while of Love is all the air

About.   From its orient porch the young
Mornings glean the glory with which they rise
On earth.

First God and fairest was Quetzal'.
As him O none so full of holiness,
And by none were men so lov'd !   Sat he always
In his hall, in deity rob'd, watching
Humanity, its genius, and its struggles
Upward.   But most he watch'd its wars,—no hero
Fell but he call'd the wand'ring soul in love
To rest **with** him for ever.

Sat he once
Thus watching, and where least expected, in
The far North, by stormy Winter rul'd, up
From the snows he saw a Nation rise.   Shook
Their bolts, glistened their shields, flashed the
Light of their fierce eyes.   A king, in wolf-skin
Girt, pointed Southward, and up the hills, through
The air, to the Sun, flew the name—Azatlan.
Then march'd they ; by day and night they march'd,—march'd
Ever South, across the desert, up the
Mountains, down the mountains ; leaping rivers,
Smiting foes, taking cities,—thus they march'd ;
Thus, a cloud of eagles, roll'd they from the
North ; **thus on** the South they fell, **as autumn**
Frosts upon **the** fruits of summer fall.

And now the priests were glad,—the singer sang of Heaven ;
and the warriors were aroused,—his voice was like a battle-cry,
and the theme was the proud tradition of the conquering march
of their fathers from the distant North.   Sitting with clasped
hands and drooped head, the king followed the chant, like one
listening to an oracle.   Yet stronger grew the minstrel's voice,—

Pass'd
Many years of toil, and still the Nation march'd ;
Still Southward strode the king ; still Sunward rose
The cry of *Azatlan ! Azatlan !*   And
Warmer, truer, brighter grew the human
Love **of** Quetzal'.   He saw them reach a lake ;
As dew its waves were clear ; like lover's breath
The wind flew o'er it.   'Twas in the clime of
Starry nights,—the clime of orange-groves and
Plumy palms.

Then Quetzal' from his watching
Rose.   Aside he flung his sunly symbols.
Like **a** falling star, from the Vale of Gods

He dropp'd ; like a falling star shot through the
Shoreless space ; like a golden morning reach'd
The earth,—reach'd the lake. Then stay'd the Nation's
March. Still Sunward rose the cry, but Southward
Strode the king no more.

     In his roomy **heart, in**
The chambers of its love, Quetzal' took the
Nation. He swore its kings should be his sons,—
They should conquer, by the Sun, he swore ! In
The laughing Lake he bade them build ; and up
Sprang Tenochtitlan, of the human love
Of Quetzal' child ; up rose its fire-lit towers,
Outspread **its piles,** outstretched its streets
Of stone and wave. And as the city grew,
Still stronger grew the love of Quetzal'.

        Thine
Is the Empire. To the shields again, O
Azatlan ! 'Twas thus he spoke ; and feather'd
Crest and oaken spear, the same that from the
North came conquering, through the valley,
On a wave of war went swiftly floating.
Down before the flaming shields fell all the
Neighbouring tribes ; open flew the cities' gates ;
Fighting kings gave up their crowns ; from the hills
The Chichimecan fled ; on temple towers
The Toltec fires to scattering ashes
Died. Like a scourge upon the city, like
A fire across the plain, like storms adown
The mountain,—such was Azatlan that day
It went to battle ! Like a monarch 'mid
His people, like a god amid the Heavens,
O such was Azatlan, victor from the
Battle, the Empire in its hand !

At this point the excitement of the audience rose into inter-
ruption : they clapped their hands and stamped ; some shouted.
As the strong voice rolled the grand story on, even the king's
dread of the god disappeared ; and, had the 'tzin concluded then,
the prize had certainly been his. But when the silence was
restored, he resumed the attitude so proper to his disguise, and,
sinking his voice and changing the measure of the chant, solemnly
proceeded,—

As the river runneth ever, like the river ran the love of
Quetzal'. The clime grew softer, and the Vale fairer. To weave, and
  trade,

And sow, and build, he taught, with countless other ways of peace. **He broke**
The seals of knowledge, and unveiled the mystic paths of wisdom ;
Gathered gold from the earth, and jewels from the streams ; **and happy in**
Peace, as terrible in war, became Azatlan. Only one more
Blessing,—a religion sounding of a quiet heaven and a
Godly love,—this only wanted Azatlan. And alas, for the
Sunly Quetzal' ! He built a temple, with a single tower, a
Temple over many chambers.

Slowly the 'tzin repeated the last sentence, and under his **gaze** the monarch's face changed visibly.

Worship he asked, and offerings,
And sacrifices, not of captives, heart-broken and complaining,
But of blooming flowers, and ripened fruits, emblems **of** love, and peace,
And beauty. Alas, for the gentle Quetzal' ! Cold grew the people
Lov'd so well. A little while they worshipped ; then, as bees go no
More to a withered flower, they forsook his shrine, and mock'd his
Image. His love, longest lingering, went down at last, but slowly
Went, as the brook, drop by drop, runs dry in the drought of **a rainless**
Summer. Wrath rose **instead. Down in a** chamber **below the** temple,
A chamber full of gold and unveiled splendour, beneath the Lake that
Long had ceased its laughing, thither went the god, and **on the walls,**
On the marble and the gold, he wrote—

The improvisation, if such **it** was, now wrought its full effect upon Montezuma, who saw the recital coming nearer and nearer to the dread mysteries of the golden chamber in the old Cû. At the beginning of the last sentence, the blood left his face, and he leaned forward as if to check the speech, at the same time some master influence held him wordless. His look was that of one seeing a vision. The vagaries of a mind shaken by days and nights of trouble are wonderful ; sometimes they are fearful. How easy for his distempered fancy to change the minstrel, with his white locks and venerable countenance, into a servant of Quetzal', sent by the god to confirm the interpretation and prophecies of his other servant Mualox. At the last word he arose, and, with an imperial gesture, cried,—

" Peace—enough ! "

Then his utterance failed him,—another vision seemed to fix **his** gaze. The audience, thrilling with fear, turned to see what he saw, and heard a commotion, which, from the farther end of

the hall, drew slowly near the throne, and ceased not until
Mualox, in his sacrificial robes, knelt upon the step in the
minstrel's place. Montezuma dropped into his throne, and,
covering his eyes with his hands, said faintly,—

"Evil betides me, father, evil betides me! But I am a king.
Speak what you can!"

Mualox prostrated himself until his white hair covered his
master's feet.

"Again, O king, your servant comes speaking for his god."

"For the god, Mualox?"

The hall became silent as a tomb.

"I come," the holy man continued, "to tell the king that
Quetzal' has landed, this time on the sea-shore in Cempoalla.
At set of sun his power was collected on the beach. Summon all
your wisdom,—the end is at hand."

All present and hearing listened awestruck. Of the warriors,
not one, however battle-tried, but trembled with undefined terror.
And who may accuse them? The weakness was from fear of a
supposed god; their heathen souls, after the manner of the
Christian, asked, Who may war against Heaven?

"Rise, Mualox! You love me; I have no better servant,"
said the king with dignity, but so sadly that even the prophet's
heart was touched. "It is not for me to say if your news be
good or evil. All things, even my Empire, are in the care of the
gods. To-morrow I will hold a council to determine how this
visit may be best met." With a mighty effort he freed his spirit
of the influence of the untimely visitation, and said, with a show
of unconcern, "Leave the morrow to whom it belongs, my children. Let us now to the ceremony which was to crown the
night. Come forward, son of 'Hualpilli! Room for the lord
Iztlil', my friends!"

Tula looked down, and the queen Tecalco bowed her face upon
the shoulder of the queen Acatlan; and immediately, all differences lost in loving loyalty, the caciques and chiefs gathered
before him,—a nobility as true and chivalric as ever fought
beneath an infidel banner.

And they waited, but the Tezcucan came not.

"Go, Maxtla. Seek the lord Iztlil', and bring him to my
presence."

Through the palace and through the gardens they sought the
recreant lover. And the silence of the waiting in the great hall
was painful. Guest looked in the face of guest, mute, yet asking
much. The prince Cacama whispered to the prince Cuitlahua,
"It is a happy interference of the gods!"

Tecalco wept on, but not from sorrow, and the eyes of the
devoted princess were lustrous for the first time; hope had come
back to the darkened soul.

And the monarch said little, and ere long retired. **A** great portion of the company, despite his injunction, speedily followed his example, leaving the younger guests, with what humour they could command, to continue the revel till morning.

Next day at noon couriers from Cempoalla confirmed the announcement of Mualox. Cortes had indeed landed ; and that Good Friday was the last **of** the perfect glory of Anahuac.

Poor king ! Not long now until I may sing for thee the lamentation of the Gothic Roderick, whose story is but little less melancholy than thine.

He look'd for the brave captains that led the hosts of Spain,
But all were fled, except the dead,—and who could count the slain ?
Where'er his eye could wander all bloody was the plain ;
And while thus he said, the tears he shed ran down his cheeks like rain :—

Last night I was the king of Spain : to-day no king am I.
Last night fair castles held my train : to-night where shall I lie ?
Last night a hundred pages did serve me on the knee :
To-night not one I call my own,—not one pertains to me. [1]

---

[1] The fifth and sixth verses **of the famous Spanish ballad,** "The Lamentation of Don Roderic." **The translation I have borrowed** from Lockhart's *Spanish Ballads.*—TR.

BOOK THREE.

CHAPTER I.

THE FIRST COMBAT.

THE 'tzin's companion the night of the banquet, as the reader has no doubt anticipated, was Hualpa, the Tihuancan. To an adventure of his, more luckless than his friend's, I now turn.

It will be remembered that the 'tzin left him at the **door of** the great hall. In a strange scene, without a guide, **it was** natural for him to be ill at ease; light-hearted and fearless, however, he strolled leisurely about, at **one** place stopping to hear a minstrel, at another to observe a dance, **and** all the time half confused by the maze and splendour of all he beheld. **In** such awe stood he of the monarch, that he gave the throne a wide margin, contented from a distance to view the accustomed interchanges of courtesy between the guests and their master. Finding, at last, that he could not break through the bashfulness acquired in his solitary life among the hills, and imitate the ease and nonchalance of those born, as it were, to the lordliness of the hour, he left the house, and once more sought the retiracy of the gardens. Out of doors, beneath the stars, with the fresh air in his nostrils, he felt at home again, the whilom hunter, ready for any emprise.

As to the walk he should follow he had no choice, for in every direction he heard laughter, music, and conversation; everywhere were flowers and the glow of lamps. Merest chance put him in a path that led to the neighbourhood of the museum.

Since the night shut in,—be it said in a whisper,—a memory of wonderful brightness had taken possession of his mind. Nenetzin's face, as he saw it laughing in the door of the kiosk when Yeteve called the 'tzin for a song, he thought outshone the lamplight, the flowers, and everything most beautiful about his path; her eyes were as stars, rivalling the insensate ones in the mead above him. He remembered them, too, as all the brighter for the tears through which they had looked down,—alas! not on him, but upon his reverend comrade. If Hualpa was not in love, he was, at least, borrowing wings for a flight of that kind.

Indulging the delicious reverie, he came upon some nobles conversing, and quite blocking up the way, though going in his direction. He hesitated; but considering that, as a guest, the freedom of the garden belonged equally to him, he proceeded, and became a listener.

"People call him a warrior. They know nothing of what makes a warrior; they mistake good fortune, or what the traders in the *tianguez* call luck, for skill. Take his conduct at the combat of Quetzal' as an example; say he threw his arrows well: yet it was a cowardly war. How much braver to grasp the *maquahuitl*, and rush to blows! That requires manhood, strength, skill. To stand back, and kill with a chance arrow,—a woman could do as much."

The 'tzin was the subject of discussion, and the voice that of Iztlil', the Tezcucan. Hualpa moved closer to the party.

"I thought his course in that combat good," said a stranger; "it gave him opportunities not otherwise to be had. That he did not join the assault cannot be urged against his courage. Had you, my lord Iztlil', fallen like the Otompan, he would have been left alone to fight the challengers. A fool would have seen the risk; a coward would not have courted it."

"That argument," replied Iztlil', "is crediting him with too much shrewdness. By the gods, he never doubted the result,—not he! He knew the Tlascalans would never pass my shield; he knew the victory was mine, two against me as there were. A prince of Tezcuco was never conquered!"

The spirit of the hunter was fast rising; yet he followed, listening.

"And, my friends," the Tezcucan continued, "who better judged the conduct of the combatants that day than the king? See the result. To-night I take from the faint heart his bride, the woman he has loved from boyhood. Then this banquet. In whose honour is it? What does it celebrate? There is a prize to be awarded,—the prize of courage and skill; and who gets it? And further, of the nobles and chiefs of the valley, but one is absent,—he whose prudence exceeds his valour."

In such strain the Tezcucan proceeded. And Hualpa, fully aroused, pushed through the company to the speaker, but so quietly that those who observed him asked no questions. Assured that the 'tzin must have friends present, he waited for some one to take up his cause. His own impulse was restrained by his great dread of the king, whose gardens he knew were not fighting-grounds at any time or in any quarrel. But, as the boastful prince continued, the resolve to punish him took definite form with the Tihuancan,—to such degree had his admiration for the 'tzin already risen! Gradually the auditors dropped behind or disappeared; finally, but one remained,—a middle-aged, portly noble, whose demeanour was not of the kind to shake the resolution taken.

Hualpa made his first advance close by the eastern gate of the garden, to which point he held himself in check lest the want of arms should prove an apology for refusing the fight.

"Will the lord Iztlil' stop?" he said, laying his hand on the Tezcucan's arm.

"I do not know you," was the answer.

The sleek courtier also stopped, and stared broadly.

"You do not know me! I will mend my fortune in that respect," returned the hunter mildly. "I have heard what you said so ungraciously of my friend and comrade,"—the last word he emphasized strongly,—"Guatamozin." Then he repeated the offensive words as correctly as if he had been a practised herald, and concluded, "Now, you know the 'tzin cannot be here to-night; you also know the reason; but, for him and in his place, I say, prince though you are, you have basely slandered an absent enemy."

"Who are you?" asked the Tezcucan, surprised.

"The comrade of Guatamozin, here to take up his quarrel."

"You challenge me?" said Iztlil' in disdain.

"Does a prince of Tezcuco, son of 'Hualpilli, require a blow? Take it then."

The blow was given.

"See! do I not bring you princely blood?" And, in his turn, Hualpa laughed scornfully.

The Tezcucan was almost choked with rage. "This to me,—to me,—a prince and warrior!" he cried.

A danger not considered by the rash hunter now offered itself. An outcry would bring down the guard; and, in the event of his arrest, the united representations of Iztlil' and his friend would be sufficient to have him sent forthwith to the tigers. The pride of the prince saved him.

"Have a care,—'tis an assassin! I will call the guard at the gate!" said the courtier, alarmed.

"Call them not, call them not! I am equal to my own revenge. Oh for a spear or knife,—anything to kill!"

"Will you hear me,—a word!" the hunter said. "I am without arms also; but they can be had."

"The arms, the arms!" cried Iztlil' passionately.

"We can make the sentinels at the gate clever by a few quills of gold; and here are enough to satisfy them." Hualpa produced a handful of the money. "Let us try them. Outside the gate the street is clear."

The courtier protested, but the prince was determined.

"The arms! Pledge my province and palaces,—everything for a *maquahuitl* now!"

They went to the gate and obtained the use of two of the weapons and as many shields. Then the party passed into the street, which they found deserted. To avoid the great thoroughfare to Iztapalapan, they turned to the north, and kept on as far as the corner of the garden wall.

"Stay we here," said the courtier. "Short time is all you want, lord Iztlil'. The feathers on the hawk's wings are not full-fledged."

The man spoke confidently; and it must be confessed that the Tezcucan's reputation and experience justified the assurance. One advantage the hunter had which his enemies both overlooked,—a surpassing composure. From a temple near by a red light flared broadly over the place, redeeming it from what would otherwise have been vague starlight; by its aid they might have seen his countenance without a trace of excitement or passion. One wish, and but one, he had,—that Guatamozin could witness the trial.

The impatience of the Tezcucan permitted but few preliminaries.

"The gods of Mictlan require no prayers. Stand out!" he said.

"Strike!" answered Hualpa.

Up rose the glassy blades of the Tezcucan, flashing in the light; quick and strong the blow, yet it clove but the empty air. "For the 'tzin!" shouted the hunter, striking back before the other was half recovered. The shield was dashed aside; a groan acknowledged a wound in the breast, and Iztlil' staggered; another blow stretched him on the pavement. A stream of blood, black in the night, stole slowly out over the flags. The fight was over. The victor dropped the bladed end of his weapon, and surveyed his foe with astonishment, then pity.

"Your friend is hurt; help him!" he said, turning to the courtier; but he was alone,—the craven had run. For one fresh from the hills, this was indeed a dilemma! A duel and a death in sight of the royal palace! A chill tingled through his veins. He thought rapidly of the alarm, the arrest, the king's wrath, and himself given to glut the monsters in the menagerie. Up rose, also, the many fastnesses amid the cedared glades of Tihuanco. Could he but reach them! The slaves of Montezuma, to please a whim, might pursue and capture a quail or an eagle; but there he could laugh at pursuit, while in Tenochtitlan he was nowhere safe.

Sight of the flowing blood brought him out of the panic. He raised the Tezcucan's arm, and tore the rich vestments from his breast. The wound was a glancing one ; it might not be fatal after all ; to save him were worth the trial. Taking off his own *maxtlatl*, he wound it tightly round the body and over the cut. Across the street there was a small, open house ; lifting the wounded man gently as possible, he carried him thither, and laid him in a darkened passage. Where else to convey him he knew not ; that was all he could do. Now for flight,—for Tihuanco. Tireless and swift of foot shall they be who catch him on the way !

He started for the lake, intending to cross in a canoe rather than by the causeway ; already a square was put behind, when it occurred to him that the Tezcucan might have slaves and a palanquin waiting before the palace door. He began, also, to reproach himself for the baseness of the desertion. How would the 'tzin have acted ? When the same Tezcucan lay with the dead in the arena, who nursed him back to life ?

If Hualpa had wished his patron's presence at the beginning of the combat, now, flying from imaginary dangers,—flying like a startled coward from his very victory,—much did he thank the gods that he was alone and unseen. In a kind of alcove, or resting-place for weary walkers, with which, by the way, the thoroughfares of Tenochtitlan were well provided, he sat down, recalled his wonted courage, and determined on a course more manly, whatever the risk.

Then he retraced his steps, and went boldly to the portal of the palace, where he found the Tezcucan's palanquin. The slaves in charge followed him without objection.

"Take your master to his own palace. Be quick !" he said to them, when the wounded man was transferred to the carriage.

" It is in Tecuba," said one of them.

" To Tecuba then."

He did more ; he accompanied the slaves. Along the street, across the causeway, which never seemed of such weary length, they proceeded. On the road the Tezcucan revived. He said little, and was passive in his enemy's hands. From Tecuba the latter hastened back to Tenochtitlan, and reached the portico of Xoli, the Chalcan, just as day broke over the valley.

And such was the hunter's first emprise as a warrior.

CHAPTER II.

THE SECOND COMBAT.

It is hardly worth while to detail the debate between Hualpa and Xoli; enough to know that the latter, anticipating pursuit, hid the son of his friend in a closet attached to his restaurant.

That day, and many others, the police went up and down, ferreting for the assassin of the noble Iztlil'. Few premises escaped their search. The Chalcan's, amongst others, was examined, but without discovery. Thus safely concealed, the hunter throve on the *cuisine*, and for the loss of liberty was consoled by the gossip and wordy wisdom of his accessory, and, what was better, the gratitude of Guatamozin. In such manner two weeks passed away, the longest and most wearisome of his existence. How sick at heart he grew in his luxurious imprisonment; how he pined for the old hills and woodlands; how he longed once more to go down the shaded vales free-footed and fearless, stalking deer or following his ocelot. Ah, what is ambition gratified to freedom lost!

Unused to the confinement, it became irksome to him, and at length intolerable. "When," he asked himself, "is this to end? Will the king ever withdraw his huntsmen? Through whom am I to look or hope for pardon?" He sighed, paced the narrow closet, and determined that night to walk out and see if his old friends the stars were still in their places, and take a draught of the fresh air, to his remembrance sweeter than the new beverage of the Chalcan. And when the night came he was true to his resolution.

Pass we his impatience while waiting an opportunity to leave the house unobserved; his attempts unsuccessfully repeated; his vexation at the "noble patrons" who lounged in the apartments and talked so long over their goblets. At a late hour he made good his exit. In the *tianguez*, which was the first to receive him, booths and porticoes were closed for the night; lights were everywhere extinguished, except on the towers of the temples. As morning would end his furlough and drive him back to the hated captivity, he resolved to make the most of the night; he would visit the lake, he would stroll through the streets. By the gods! he would play freeman to the full.

In his situation, all places were alike perilous,—houses, streets, temples, and palaces. As, for that reason, one direction was good as another, he started up the Iztapalapan street from the *tianguez*. Passengers met him now and then; otherwise the great thoroughfare was unusually quiet. Sauntering along in excellent imitation of careless enjoyment, he strove to feel cheerful; but, in spite

of his efforts, he became lonesome, while his dread of the patrols
kept him uneasy. Such freedom, he ascertained, **was not** all his
fancy coloured it ; yet it was not so bad as his prison. On he
went. Sometimes on a step, or in the shade of a portico, he
would sit and gaze at the houses as if they were old friends
basking in the moonlight ; at the bridges he would also stop,
and, leaning over the balustrades, watch the waveless water in
the canal below, and envy the watermen asleep in their open
canoes. The result was a feeling of recklessness, sharpened by
a yearning for something to do, some place to visit, some person
to see ; in short, a thousand wishes, so vague, however, that they
amounted **to** nothing.

In this **mood** he thought of Nenetzin, who, in the **tedium of**
his imprisonment, had become to him a constant dream,—a vision
by which his fancy was amused and his impatience soothed,—a
vision that faded not with the morning, but **at** noon was **sweet**
as at night. With the thought **came** another,—the idea **of** an
adventure excusable only in a lover.

"The garden !" he said, stopping and thinking. "The garden!
It **is** the king's ; so is the street. It is guarded ; so is the city. I
will be in danger ; but that is around me everywhere. By the gods!
I will go to the garden, and look at the house in which she sleeps."

Invade the gardens of the great king at midnight ! The
project would have terrified the Chalean ; the 'tzin would **have**
forbade it ; at any other time, the adventurer himself **would**
rather have gone unarmed into the den of a tiger. The gardens
were chosen places sacred to royalty ; otherwise they would have
been without walls and without sentinels at the gates. **In** the
event of detection and arrest, the intrusion at such a time would
be without excuse ; death was the penalty.

But the venture was agreeable to the mood **he** was in ; he
welcomed it as a relief from loneliness, as a rescue from his
tormenting void of purpose ; if he saw the dangers, they were
viewed in the charm of his gentle passion,—griffins and goblins
masked by Love, the enchanter. He started at once ; and now
that he had an object before him, there was no more loitering
under porticoes or on the bridges. As the squares were put
behind him, he repeated over and over, as a magical exorcism, "I
will look **at the** house **in** which she sleeps,—the house in which
she sleeps."

Once in his progress he turned aside from the great street, and
went up a footway bordering a canal. At the next street, however, he crossed a bridge, and proceeded to the north again.
Almost before he was aware of it, he reached the corner of the
royal garden, always to be remembered by him **as** the place of
his combat with the Tezcucan. But so intent was he upon his
present project he scarcely gave it **a** second look.

The wall was but little higher than his head, and covered with
snowy stucco; and where, over the coping, motionless in the
moonshine, a palm-tree lifted its graceful head, he boldly climbed
and entered the sacred enclosure.   Drawing his mantle close
about him, he stole toward the palace, selecting the narrow walks
most protected by overhanging shrubbery.

A man's instinct is a good counsellor in danger; often it is the
only counsellor.   Gliding through the shadows, cautiously as if
hunting, he seemed to hear a recurrent whisper,—

"Have a care, O hunter! This is not one of thy familiar
places. The gardens of the great king have other guardians than
the stars. Death awaits thee at every gate."

But as often came the reply, "Nenetzin,—I will see the house
in which she sleeps."

He held on toward the palace, never stopping until the top,
here and there crowned with low turrets, rose above the highest
trees.   Then he listened intently, but heard not a sound of life
from the princely pile. He sought next a retreat, where, secure
from observation, he might sit in the pleasant air, and give wings
to his lover's fancy. At last he found one, a little retired from
the central walk, and not far from a tank, which had once been,
if it were not now, the basin of a fountain.   Upon a bench, well
shaded by a clump of flowering bushes, he stretched himself at
ease, and was soon absorbed.

The course of his thought, in keeping with his youth, was
to the future. Most of the time, however, he had no distinct
idea; reverie, like an evening mist, settled upon him. Sometimes he lay with closed eyes, shutting himself in, as it were,
from the world; then he stared vacantly at the stars, or into
those blue places in the mighty vault too deep for stars; but
most he loved to look at the white walls of the palace. And for
the time he was happy; his soul may be said to have been
singing a silent song to the unconscious Nenetzin.

Once or twice he was disturbed by a noise, like the suppressed cry of a child; but he attributed it to some of the restless
animals in the museum at the farther side of the garden. Half
the night was gone; so the watchers on the temples proclaimed;
and still he stayed,—still dreamed.

About that time, however, he was startled by footsteps coming
apparently from the palace. He sat up, ready for action. The
appearance of a man alone and unarmed allayed his apprehension
for the moment. Up the walk, directly by the hiding-place, the
stranger came. As he passed slowly on, the intruder thrilled at
beholding, not a guard or an officer, but Montezuma in person!
As far as the tank the monarch walked; there he stopped, put
his hands behind him, and looked moodily down into the
pool.

Garden, palace, Nenetzin,—everything but the motionless figure by the tank,—faded from Hualpa's mind. Fear came upon him; and no wonder: there, almost within reach, at midnight, unattended, stood what was to him the positive realization of power, ruler of the empire, dispenser of richest gifts, keeper of life and death! Guilty, and tremulously apprehensive that he had been discovered, Hualpa looked each instant to be dragged from his hiding.

The space around the tank was clear, and strewn with shells perfectly white in the moonlight. While the adventurer sat fixed to his seat watching the king, watching also a chance of escape, he **saw** something come from the shrubbery, move stealthily out into **the** walk, then crouch down. Now, as I have shown, he **was** brave; but this tested all his courage. Out farther **crept the** object, moving with the stillness of a spirit. Scarcely **could he** persuade himself at first that it was not **an** illusion begotten of his fears; but **its** form and movements, the **very** stillness of its advance, at last identified it. In all his hunter's experience, he had never seen **au** ocelot so large. The screams he had heard were now explained,—the monster had escaped from the menagerie!

I cannot say the recognition wrought a subsidence of Hualpa's fears. He felt instinctively for his arms,—he had nothing but a knife of brittle *itzli.* Then he thought of the stories he had heard of the ferocity of the royal tigers, and of unhappy wretches flung, by way of punishment, into their dens. He shuddered, and turned to the king, who still gazed thoughtfully **over** the wall of the tank.

Holy Huitzil'! the ocelot was creeping upon the monarch! The flash of understanding that revealed the fact to Hualpa was like the lightning. Breathlessly he noticed the course the brute was taking; there could be no doubt. Another flash, and he understood the monarch's peril,—alone, unarmed, before the guards at the gates or in the palace could come, the struggle would be over; child of the Sun though he was, there remained for him but one hope of rescue.

As, in common with provincials generally, he cherished a reverence for the monarch hardly secondary to that he felt for the gods, the Tihuancan was inexpressibly shocked to see **him** subject to such a danger. An impulse aside from native chivalry urged him to confront the ocelot; but under the circumstances, —and he recounted them rapidly,—he feared the king more than **the** brute. Brief time was there for consideration; each **moment the** peril increased. He thought of the 'tzin, then of Nenetzin.

"Now or never!" he said. "If the gods do but help me, I will prove myself!"

And he unlooped the mantle, and wound **it** about his left arm;

the knife, poor as it was, he took from his *maxtlatl;* then he was ready. Ah, if he only had a javelin!

To place himself between the king and his enemy was what he next set about. Experience had taught him how much such animals are governed by curiosity, and upon that he proceeded to act. On his hands and knees he crept out into the walk. The moment he became exposed, the ocelot stopped, raised its round head, and watched him with a gaze as intent as his own. The advance was slow and stealthy; when the point was almost gained, the king turned about.

"Speak not, stir not, O king!" he cried, without stopping. "I will save you,—no other can."

From creeping man the monarch looked to crouching beast, and comprehended the situation.

Forward went Hualpa, now the chief object of attraction to the monster. At last he was directly in front of it.

"Call the guard and fly! It is coming now!"

And through the garden rang the call. Verily, the hunter had become the king!

A moment after the ocelot lowered its head, and leaped. The Tihuancan had barely time to put himself in posture to receive the attack, his left arm serving as a shield; upon his knee, he struck with the knife. The blood flew, and there was a howl so loud that the shouts of the monarch were drowned. The mantle was rent to ribbons: and through the feathers, cloth, and flesh, the long fangs craunched to the bone,—but not without return. This time the knife, better directed, was driven to the heart, where it snapped short off, and remained. The clenched jaws relaxed. Rushing suddenly in, Hualpa contrived to push the fainting brute into the tank. He saw it sink, saw the pool subside to its calm, then turned to Montezuma, who, though calling lustily for the guard, had stayed to the end. Kneeling upon the stained shells, he laid the broken knife at the monarch's feet, and waited for him to speak.

"Arise!" the king said kindly.

The hunter stood up, splashed with blood, the fragments of his *tilmatli* clinging in shreds to his arm, his tunic torn, the hair fallen over his face,—a most uncourtierlike figure.

"You are hurt," said the king directly. "I was once thought skilful with medicines. Let me see."

He found the wounds, and, untying his own sash, rich with embroidery, wrapped it in many folds around the bleeding arm.

Meantime there was commotion in many quarters.

"Evil take the careless watchers!" he said sternly, noticing the rising clamour. "Had I trusted them,—but are you not of the guard?"

"I am the great king's slave,—his poorest slave, but not of his guard."

Montezuma regarded him attentively.

"It cannot be ; an assassin would not have interfered with the ocelot. Take up the knife, and follow me."

Hualpa obeyed. On the way they met a number of the guard running in great perplexity ; but, without a word to them, the monarch walked on, and into the palace. In a room where there were tables and seats, books and writing-materials, maps on the walls and piles of them on the floor, he stopped, and seated himself.

"You know what truth is, and how the gods punish falsehood," he began ; then, abruptly, " How came you in the garden ?"

Hualpa fell on his knees, laid his palm on the floor, and answered without looking up, for such he knew to be a courtly custom.

"Who may deceive the wise king Montezuma ? I will answer as to the gods : the gardens are famous in song and story, and I was tempted to see them, and climbed the wall. When you came to the fountain, I was close by ; and while waiting a chance to escape, I saw the ocelot creeping upon you ; and—and—the great king is too generous to deny his slave the pardon he risked his life for."

"Who are you ?"

"I am from the province of Tihuanco. My name is Hualpa."

"Hualpa, Hualpa," repeated the king slowly. "You serve Guatamozin ?"

"He is my friend and master, O king."

Montezuma started. "Holy gods, what madness ! My people have sought you far and wide to feed you to the tiger in the tank."

Hualpa faltered not.

"O king, I know I am charged with the murder of Iztlil', the Tezcucan. Will it please you to hear my story ?"

And, taking the assent, he gave the particulars of the combat, not omitting the cause. "I did not murder him," he concluded. "If he is dead, I slew him in fair fight, shield to shield, as a warrior may, with honour, slay a foeman."

"And you carried him to Tecuba ?"

"Before the judges, if you choose, I will make the account good."

"Be it so !" the monarch said emphatically. "Two days hence, in the court, I will accuse you. Have there your witnesses : it is a matter of life and death. Now, what of your master, the 'tzin ?"

The question was dangerous, and Hualpa trembled, but resolved to be bold.

"If it be not too presumptuous, most mighty king,—if a slave may seem to judge his **master's judgment** by the offer of a word "—

"Speak! I give you liberty."

"I wish to say," continued Hualpa, "that **in** the court there are many noble courtiers who would die for you, O king; but, of them all, there is not one who so loves you, or whose love could be made so profitable, being backed by skill, courage, and wisdom, as the generous prince whom you call my master. In **his** banishment he has chosen to serve you; for the night the **strangers** landed in Cempoalla, he left his palace in Iztapalapan, **and** entered their camp in the train of the governor of Cotastlan. Yesterday a courier, whom you rewarded richly for his speed **in** coming, brought you portraits of the strangers, and pictures of their arms and camp; that courier was Guatamozin, and his was the hand that wrought the artist's work. Oh, much as your faculties become a king, you have been deceived: he is not a traitor."

"Who told you such a fine minstrel's tale?"

"The gods judge me, O king, if, without your leave, I had so much as dared kiss the dust at your feet. What you have graciously permitted me to tell I heard from the 'tzin himself."

Montezuma sat a long time silent, then asked, "Did your master speak of the strangers, or of the things he saw?"

"The noble 'tzin regards me kindly, and therefore spoke with freedom. He said, mourning much that he could not be at your last council to declare his opinion, that you were mistaken."

The speaker's face was cast down, so that he could not see the frown with which the plain words were received, and he continued,—

"'They are not *teules*,'[1] so the 'tzin said, 'but men, as you and I are; they eat, sleep, drink, like us; nor is that all,—they die like us; for in the night,' he said, 'I was in their camp, and saw them, by torchlight, bury the body of one that day dead.' And then he asked, 'Is that a practice among the gods?' Your slave, O king, is not learned as a paba, and therefore believed him."

Montezuma stood up.

"Not *teules!* How thinks he they should be dealt with?"

"He says that, as they are men, they are also invaders, with whom an Aztec cannot treat. Nothing for them but war!"

To and fro the monarch walked. After which he returned to Hualpa and said,—

"Go home now. To-morrow I will send you a *tilmatli* for the one you wear. Look to your wounds, and recollect the trial. As you love life, have there your proof. I will be your accuser."

"As the great king is merciful to his children, the gods will

[1] Gods.

be merciful to him. I will give myself to **the guards,**" said the
hunter, to whom anything was preferable **to the closet** in the
restaurant.

" No, you are free."

Hualpa kissed the floor, **and arose,** and hurried from **the** palace
to the house of Xoli on the *tianguez.* The effect of his appearance
upon that worthy, and the effect of the story afterwards, may be
imagined. Attention to the wounds, a bath, and sound slumber
put the adventurer in a better condition by the next noon.

And from that night he thought more than ever of glory and
Nenetzin.

CHAPTER III.

THE **PORTRAIT.**

NEXT **day,** after the removal of the noon comfitures, and when
the princess Tula had gone to the hammock for the usual *siesta,*
Nenetzin rushed into her apartment unusually excited.

" Oh, I have something so strange to tell you,—something so
strange ! " she cried, throwing herself upon the hammock.

Her face was bright and very beautiful. Tula looked at her a
moment, then put her lips lovingly to the smooth forehead.

" By the Sun ! **as** our royal father sometimes swears, **my** sister
seems in earnest."

" Indeed I am ; and you will go with me, will you not ? "

" Ah ! you want to take me to the garden to see the dead tiger,
or, perhaps, the warrior who slew it, or—now I have it—you
have seen another minstrel."

Tula expected the girl to laugh, but was surprised to see her
eyes filled with tears. She changed her manner instantly, and
bade **the** slave who had been sitting by the hammock fanning her
to retire. Then she said,—

" You jest so much, Nenetzin, that I do not know when you
are serious. I love you : now tell me what has happened."

The answer was given in a low voice.

" You will think me foolish, and so I am, but I cannot help
it. Do you recollect the dream I told you the night on the
chinampa ? "

" The night Yeteve came to us ? I recollect."

" You know I saw a man come and sit down in our father's
palace,—a stranger with blue eyes and fair face, and hair and
beard like the silk of the ripening maize. I told you I loved
him, and would have none but him ; and you laughed at me, and

said he was the god Quetzal'. O Tula, the dream has come back to me many times since ; so often that it seems, when I am awake, to have been a reality. I am childish, you think, and very weak ; you may even pity me ; but I have grown to look upon the blue-eyed as something lovable and great, and thought of him is a part of my mind,—so much so that it is useless for me to say he is not, or that I am loving a shadow. And now, O dear Tula, now comes the strange part of my story. Yesterday, you know, a courier from Cempoalla brought our father some pictures of the strangers lately landed from the sea. This morning I heard there were portraits among them, and could not resist a curiosity to see them ; so I went, and almost the first one I came to,—do not laugh,—almost the first one I came to was the picture of him who comes to me so often in my dreams. I looked and trembled. There indeed he was : there were the blue eyes, the yellow hair, the white face, even the dress, shining as silver, and the plumed crest. I did not stay to look at anything else, but hurried here, scarcely knowing whether to be glad or afraid. I thought if you went with me I would not be afraid. Go you must ; we will look at the portrait together." And she hid her face, sobbing like a child.

"It is too wonderful for belief. I will go," said Tula.

She arose, and the slave brought and threw over her shoulders the long white scarf so invariably a part of an Aztec woman's costume. Then the sisters took their way to the chamber where the pictures were kept,—the same into which Hualpa had been led the night before. The king was elsewhere giving audience, and his clerks and attendants were with him. So the two were allowed to indulge their curiosity undisturbed.

Nenetzin went to a pile of manuscripts lying on the floor. The elder sister was startled by the first picture exposed ; for she recognised the handiwork, long since familiar to her, of the 'tzin. Nor was she less surprised by the subject, which was a horse, apparently a nobler instrument for a god's revenge than man himself.

Next she saw pictured a horse, its rider mounted, and in Christian armour, and bearing shield, lance, and sword. Then came a cannon, the gunner by the carriage, his match lighted, while a volume of flame and smoke was bursting from the throat of the piece. A portrait followed ; she lifted it up, and trembled to see the hero of Nenetzin's dream !

"Did I not tell you so, O Tula ?" said the girl in a whisper.

"The face is pleasant and noble," the other answered thoughtfully ; "but I am afraid. There is evil in the smile, evil in the blue eyes."

The rest of the manuscripts they left untouched. The one absorbed them ; but with what different feelings ! Nenetzin was a-flutter with pleasure, restrained by awe. Impressed by the singularity of the vision, as thus realized, a passionate wish to see the man or god, whichever he was, and hear his voice, may be called her nearest semblance to reflection. Like a lover in the presence of the beloved, she was glad and contented, and asked nothing of the future. But with Tula, older and wiser, it was different. She was conscious of the novelty of the incident; at the same time a presentiment, a gloomy foreboding, filled her soul. In slumber we sometimes see spectres, and they sit by us and smile; yet we shrink, and cannot keep down anticipations of ill. So Tula was affected by what she beheld.

She laid the portrait softly down, and turned to Nenetzin, who had now no need to deprecate her laugh.

"The ways of the gods are most strange. Something tells me this is their work. I am afraid; let us go."

And they retired; and the rest of the day, swinging in the hammock, they talked of the dream and the portrait, and wondered what would come of them.

CHAPTER IV.

THE TRIAL.

HUALPA'S adventure in the garden made a great stir in the palace and the city. Profound was the astonishment, therefore, when it became known that the saviour of the king and the murderer of the Tezcuean were one and the same person, and that, in the latter character, he was to be taken into court and tried for his life, Montezuma himself acting as accuser. Though universally discredited, the story had the effect of drawing an immense attendance at the trial.

"Ho, Chalcan! Fly not your friends in that way!"

So the broker was saluted by some men nobly dressed, whom he was about passing on the great street. He stopped, and bowed very low.

"A pleasant day, my lords! Your invitation honours me; the will of his patrons should always be law to the poor keeper of a portico. I am hurrying to the trial."

"Then stay with us. We also have a curiosity to see the assassin."

"My good lord speaks harshly. The boy, whom I love as a son, cannot be what you call him."

K

The noble laughed. "Take it not ill, Chalcan. So much do I honour the hand that slew the base Tezcucan that I care not whether it was in fair fight or by vantage taken. But what do you know about the king being accuser to-day?"

"So he told the boy."

"Incredible!"

"I will not quarrel with my lord on that account," rejoined the broker. "A more generous master than Montezuma never lived. Are not the people always complaining of his liberality? At the last banquet, for inventing a simple drink, did he not give me, his humblest slave, a goblet fit for another king?"

"And what is your drink, though ever so excellent, to the saving his life? Is not that your argument, Chalcan?"

"Yes, my lord, and at such peril! Ah, you should have seen the ocelot when taken from the tank! The keepers told me it was the largest and fiercest in the museum."

Then Xoli proceeded to edify his noble audience with all the gossip pertaining to the adventure; and as his object was to take into court some friends for the luckless hunter more influential than himself, he succeeded admirably. Every few steps there were such expressions as, "It would be pitiful if so brave a fellow should die!" "If I were king, by the Sun, I would enrich him from the possessions of the Tezcucan!" And as they showed no disposition to interrupt him, his pleading lasted to the house of justice, where the company arrived not any too soon to procure comfortable seats.

The court-house stood at the left of the street, a little retired from the regular line of buildings. The visitors had first to pass through a spacious hall, which brought them to a court-yard cemented under foot, and on all sides bounded with beautiful houses. Then, on the right, they saw the entrance to the chamber of justice, grotesquely called the Tribunal of God,[1] in which for ages had been administered a code, vindictive, but not without equity. The great door was richly carved; the windows high and broad, and lined with fluted marble; while a projecting cornice, tastefully finished, gave airiness and beauty to the venerable structure.

The party entered the room with profoundest reverence. On a dais sat the judge; in front of him was the stool bearing the skull with the emerald crown and gay plumes. Turning from the plain tapestry along the walls, the spectators failed not to admire the jewels that blazed with almost starry splendour from the centre of the canopy above him.

The broker, not being of the class of privileged nobles, found a seat with difficulty. To his comfort, however, he was placed by the side of an acquaintance.

---

[1] Prescott, *Conq. of Mexico*, Vol. I., p. 33.

" You should have come earlier, Chalcan ; **the judge has twice**
used the arrow this morning."

" Indeed ! "

" Once against a boy too much given to *pulque*,—a drunkard.
With the other doubtless you were acquainted."

" Was he noble ? "

" He had good blood, at least, being the son of a Tetzmellocan,
who died immensely rich. The witnesses said the fellow squan-
dered his father's estate almost as soon as it came to him."

" Better had he been born a thief," [1] said Xoli coolly.

Suddenly, four heralds, with silver maces, entered the court-
room, announcing the monarch. The people fell upon their
knees, and so remained until he was seated before the dais.
Then they arose, and, with staring eyes, devoured the beauty of
his costume, and the mysterious sanction of manner, office, power,
and custom, which the lovers of royalty throughout the world
have delighted to sum up in the one word,—majesty. The hum
of voices filled the chamber. Then, by another door, in charge
of officers, Hualpa apppeared, and **was** led to the dais opposite
the king. Before an Aztecan court there was no ceremony. The
highest and the lowliest **stood upon a** level : such, at least, was
the beautiful theory.

So intense was the curiosity to see the prisoner that the spectators pressed upon each other, for the moment mindless of the
monarch's presence.

" A handsome fellow ! " said an old cacique approvingly.

" Only a boy, my lord ! " suggested the critic.

" And not fierce-looking either."

" Yes "—

" No "—

" He might kill, but in fair fight : so I judge him."

And that became the opinion amongst the nobles.

" Your friend seems confident, Xoli. I like him," remarked
the Chalcan's acquaintance.

" Hush ! The king accuses."

" The king, said you ! " And the good man, representing the
commonalty, was frozen into silence.

In another quarter, one asked, " Does he not wear the 'tzin's
livery ? "

The person interrogated covered his mouth with both hands,
then drew to the other's ear, and whispered,—

" Yes ; he's a 'tzin's man, and that, they say, is his crime."

The sharp voice of the executive officer of the court rang out,
and there was stillness almost breathless. Up rose the clerk, a
learned man, keeper of **the** records, and read the indictment ;

---

[1] A thief might be punished with slavery : death was the penalty for
prodigalism and drunkenness.

that done, he laid the portrait of the accused on the table before the judge ; then the trial began.

The judge, playing carelessly **with the** fatal arrow, said,— "Hualpa, son of Tepaja, the Tihuancan, stand up and answer."

And the prisoner arose and saluted **court** and king, and answered, "It is true that, on the night of **the** banquet, I fought **the** Tezcucan ; by favour of the gods, I defeated, without slaying him. He is here in person to acquit me."

"**Bring the** witness," said the judge.

Some of the officers retired ; during their absence **a solemn** hush prevailed ; directly they returned, carrying a palanquin. Right before the dais they **set** it down, and drew aside **the curtains.** Then slowly the Tezcucan came forth, weak, but unconquered. At the judge he looked, and at the king, and all the fire of his haughty soul burned in the glance. Borrowing strength from his pride, he raised his head high, and said scornfully,—

"The power of my father's friend **is** exceeding great ; he **speaks,** and all things obey him. I **am** sick and suffering ; but he bade me come, and I **am here.** What new shame awaits me ?"

Montezuma answered, never more **a king** than then : "'Hualpilli was wise ; his son is foolish : for **the memory of the one I** spare the other. The keeper of this **sacred place will answer** why you are brought **here.** Look that **he pardons you lightly as** I have."

Then the judge said, "Prince of Tezcuco, you are here by my order. There stands one charged with your murder. Would you have had him suffer the penalty ? You have dared **be** insolent. See, O prince, that before **to-morrow** you pay the treasurer ten thousand quills of gold. See to it." And, returning the portrait to the clerk, he added, "Let the accused go acquit."

"Ah ! said I not so, said **I not so?**" muttered the Chalcan, **rubbing** his hands joyfully, **and disturbing** the attentive people about him.

"Hist, hist !" they said impatiently. "What more ? hearken !"

Hualpa **was** kneeling before the monarch.

"Most mighty king," he said, "if what I have done be worthy reward, grant **me** the discharge of this fine."

"How !" **said** Montezuma, amazed. "The Tezcucan is **your** enemy !"

"Yet he fought me fairly, **and is** a warrior."

The eyes of the king sought those of Iztlil'.

"What says the son of 'Hualpilli ?"

The latter raised his head with a **flash** of the old pride. "He **is a slave** of Guatamozin's : I scorn **the** intercession. I am yet a prince of Tezcuco."

Then the monarch went forward, and sat by the judge. **Not a** sound was heard, till he spoke.

"Arise, and come near," he **said to Hualpa.** "**I will do what** becomes me."

His voice was low and tremulous with feeling, and over his **face** came the peculiar suffusion of sadness afterwards its habitual expression. The hunter kissed the floor at his feet, and remained kneeling. Then he continued,—

"Son of the Tihuancan, I acknowledge I owe my life to you, and I call all to hear **the** acknowledgment. If the people have thought this prosecution **part of** my gratitude,—if they have marvelled at my appearing as your accuser,—much have **they** wronged **me.** I thought of reward higher than they **could have** asked for you ; but I also thought to try you. A slave **is not fit to be a** chief, nor is every chief fit **to be a** king. I thought to **try you : I am** satisfied. When your fame goes abroad, as it **will ; when the minstrels** sing your valour ; when Tenochtitlan **talks of the** merchant's son who **in** the garden slew the tiger, and **saved** the life of Montezuma,—let them also tell how Monte- zuma rewarded him ; let them say I made him noble."

Thereupon he arose, and transferred **the** *panache* from his head to Hualpa's. Those close by looked at **the** gift, and saw, for the first time, that it was not the **crown,** but the crest of a chief or cacique. Then they knew **that the trial** was **merely** to **make** more public the honours designed.

"Let them say further," he continued, "that with my own hand I made him a warrior of the highest grade." And, bending **over** the adventurer, he clasped around his neck the collar of the supreme military order of the realm.[1] "Nor is that all. Rank, without competence, is a vexation and shame. At the foot of Chapultepec, on the shore of the lake, lie an estate and a palace **of** which I have been proud. Let it be said, finally, that I gave them to enrich him and his for ever." He paused, and turned coldly to the Tezcucan. "But as **to** the son of 'Hualpilli, his fine must stand ; such pride must be punished. He shall pay the gold, **or** forfeit his province." Then, outstretching toward the audience both his arms, he said, so as to be heard throughout the chamber, "Now, O my children, justice has been done !"

The words **were** simple ; but the manner, royal as a king's **and** patriarchal as a pontiff's, brought every listener to his knees.

"Stand up, my lord Hualpa ! Take **your** place in **my train.** I will return to the palace."

With that he passed out.

And soon there was but one person remaining,—Iztlil', the

---

[1] **The** authorities touching the military orders of the Aztecs are full and complete. Prescott, *Conq. of Mexico,* Vol. I., p. 45 ; Acosta, Book VI., ch. 26 ; Mendoza's *Collec. Antiq. of Mexico,* Vol. I., pl. 65.

Tezcucan. Brought from Tlacopan by officers of the court, too weak to walk without slaves to help him, at sight of the deserted hall his countenance became haggard, the light in his hollow eyes came and went, and his broad breast heaved passionately ; in that long, slow look he measured the depth of his fall.

"O Tezcuco, Tezcuco, city of my fathers !" he cried aloud. "This is the last wrong to the last of thy race of kings."

A little after he was upon a bench exhausted, his head covered by his mantle. Then a hand was laid upon his shoulder ; he looked up and saw Hualpa.

"How now ! Has the base-born come to enjoy his triumph ? I cannot strike. Laugh and revile me ; but remember, mine is the blood of kings. The gods loved my father, and will not abandon his son. In their names I curse you !"

"Tezcucan, you are proud to foolishness," said the hunter calmly. "I came to serve you. Within an hour I have become master of slaves"—

"And were yourself a slave !"

"Well, I won my freedom ; I slew a beast and conquered a— But, prince, my slaves are at the door. Command them to Tlacopan."

"Play courtier to those who have influence ; lean your ambition upon one who can advance it. I am undone."

"I am not a courtier. The service I offer you springs from a warrior's motive. I propose it, not to a man of power, but to a prince whose courage is superior to his fortune."

For a moment the Tezcucan studied the glowing face ; then his brows relaxed, and, sighing like a woman, and like a woman overcome by the unexpected gentleness, he bowed his head, and covered his face with his hands, that he might not be accused of tears.

"Let me call the slaves, O prince," said Hualpa.

Thrice he clapped his hands, whereat four tattooed *tamanes* stalked into the chamber with a palanquin. Iztlil' took seat in the carriage, and was being borne away, when he called the hunter.

"A word," he said, in a voice from which all passion was gone. "Though my enemy, you have been generous, and remembered my misfortunes when all others forsook me. Take with you this mark. I do not ask you to wear it, for the time is nearly come when the son of 'Hualpilli will be proscribed throughout the valley ; but keep it in witness that I, the son of a king, acknowledged your right and fitness to be a noble. Farewell !"

Hualpa could not refuse a present so delicately given ; extending his hand, he received a bracelet of gold, set with an Aztec diamond of immense value. He clasped it upon his arm, and followed the carriage into the street.

BOOK FOUR.

CHAPTER I.

THE KING GIVES A TRUST TO HUALPA.

AND now was come the time of all the year most pleasant,—the time when the *maguey* was greenest, when the cacti burst into flowers, and in every field women and children, with the strong men, went to pluck the ripened maize. Of the summer, only the wealth and beauty remained. The Goddess of Abundance divided the worship which, at other seasons, was mostly given to Huitzil' and Tezca' ;[1] in her temples the days were all of prayer, hymning, and priestly ceremony. No other towers sent up such columns of the blue smoke so grateful to the dwellers in the Sun ; in no other places were there such incessant burning of censers, presentation of gifts, and sacrifice of victims. Throughout the valley the people carolled those songs the sweetest and most millennial of men,—the songs of harvest, peace, and plenty.

I have before said that Tezcuco, the lake, was the especial pride of the Aztecs. When the sky was clear, and the air tranquil, it was very beautiful ; but when the king, with his court, all in state, set out for the hunting-grounds on the northern shore, its beauty rose to splendour. By his invitation great numbers of citizens, in style suited to the honour, joined their canoes to the flotilla composing the retinue. And let it not be forgotten that the Aztec loved his canoe as in Christendom the good knight loves his steed, and decorated it with all he knew of art ; that its prow, rising high above the water, and touched by the master sculptors, was dressed in garlands and fantastic symbols ; that its light and shapely canopy, elegantly trimmed within, was shaded by curtains, and surmounted by trailing streamers ; and that the slaves, four, six, and sometimes twelve in number, dipped and drew their flashing paddles in faultless time, and shone afar

---

[1] Tezcatlipoca, a god next in rank to the Supreme Being. Supposed creator of the world.

brilliant in livery. So, when the multitude of vessels cleared the city walls, and with music and songs dashed into the open lake, the very water seemed to dance and quiver with a sensuous pleasure.

In such style did Montezuma one pleasant morning leave his capital. Calm was the lake, and so clear that the reflection of the sky above seemed a bed of blue below. There were music, and shouts, and merry songs, and from the city the cheers and plaudits of the thousands who from the walls and housetops witnessed the pageant. And his canoe was the soul of the pomp, and he had with him his favourite minstrel and jester, and Maxtla ; yet there was something on his mind that made him indifferent to the scene and prospective sport. Some distance out, by his direction, the slaves so manœuvred that all the flotilla passed him ; then he said to Maxtla, "The will has left me. I will not hunt to-day ; yet the pastime must go on ; a recall now were unkingly. Look out for a way to follow the train, while I return."

The chief arose, and swept the lake with a bright glance. "Yonder is a *chinampa;* I can take its master's canoe."

"Do so. Give this ring to the lord Cuitlahua, and tell him to conduct the hunt."

And soon Maxtla was hurrying to the north with the signet, while the monarch was speeding more swiftly to the south.

"For Iztapalapan," said the latter to his slaves. "Take me there before the lords reach the hunting-grounds, and you shall have a feast to-night."

They bent to the paddles, and rested not until he saw the white houses of the city, built far into the lake in imitation of the capital.

"Not to the town, but the palace of Guatamozin," he then said. "Speed ! the sun is rising high."

Arrived at the landing, Montezuma set forward alone to the palace. The path led into a grove of cedar and wild orange-trees, interspersed with *ceibas*, the true kings of the forests of New Mexico. The air was sweet with perfume ; birds sang to each other from the coverts ; the adjacent cascades played their steady, muffled music ; and altogether morning on the lake was less beautiful than morning in the 'tzin's garden. In the multitude of walks he became bewildered ; but, as he was pleased by all he beheld, he walked on without consulting the sun. At length, guided by the sound of voices, he came to the arena for martial games ; and there he found Hualpa and Io' practising with the bow.

He had been wont to regard Io' as a child, unripe for any but childish amusements, and hardly to be trusted alone. Absorbed in his business of governing, he had not observed how increase of years brought the boy strength, stature, and corresponding tastes. Now he was admonished of his neglect: the stripling should have been familiarized with bow, sling, and *maquahuitl;* **men** ought to have been given him for comrades; the warrior's school, even the actual field, had been better for him than the nursery. An idea of ambition also occurred to the monarch. When he himself was gathered to his fathers, who was to succeed him on the throne? Cuitlahua, Cacama, the lord of Tlacopan? Why not Io'?

Meanwhile the **two** diligently pursued their sport. **At the** moment the **king** came upon them, Hualpa was giving some directions as **to the** mode of holding the brave weapon. The boy listened eagerly,—**a** sign that pleased the observer, for nothing is so easy as to flatter the hope of a dreamy heart. Observing them further, he saw Io' take the stand, draw the arrow quite to the head, and strike the target. At the second trial, he pierced **the** centre. Hualpa embraced the scholar joyously; and thereupon the king warmed toward the warrior, and tears blinded his eyes. Advancing into the arena, the clanging of his golden sandals announced his presence.

And they knelt and kissed the earth.

"Stand up!" he said, with the smile which gave his countenance a womanly beauty. And to Hualpa he added, "I thought your palace by Chapultepec would be more attractive than the practice of arms; more credit should have been given the habits of a hunter. I was right to make you noble. But what can you make of Io'?"

"If you will **give** the time, **O king, I can make him** of excellent skill."

"And what says the son of Tecalco?"

Io' knelt again, saying, "I have a pardon to ask "—

"A pardon! For wishing to be a warrior?"

"If the king will hear me,—I have heard you say that in your youth you divided your days between the camp and the temples, learning at the same time the duties of the priest and the warrior. That I may be able some day to serve you, O king, I have stolen away from Tenochtitlan "—

Montezuma laid his hand tenderly on the boy's head and **said,** "No more. I know all you would say, and will ask the great Huitzil' to give you strength and courage. Take my permission to be a warrior. Arise now, and give me the bow. It is long since I pulled the cord, and my hand may have weakened, and **my eyes** become dim; but I challenge you both! I have a shield **wrought** of pearl and gold, unfit for the field, yet beautiful as a prize **of** skill. Who plants an arrow nearest yon **target's** heart, his **the** shield shall be."

The challenge was accepted, and, after preparation, the mon-

arch dropped his mantle and took the stand. He drew the shaft
to his ear with a careless show of skill ; and when it quivered in
the target about a palm's breadth below the mark, he said, laughing, "I am at least within the line of the good bowman. A
Tlascalan would not have escaped scarless."

Io' next took the bow, and was so fortunate as to hit the lower
edge of the heart squarely above the king's bolt.

"Mine is the shield, mine is the shield!" he cried exultantly.
"Oh that a minstrel were here ! I would have a song,—my first
song !"

"Very proud !" said the king good-humouredly. "Know you,
boy, the warrior counts his captives only when the battle is ended.
Here, lord Hualpa, the boaster should be beaten. Prove your
quality. To you there may be more in this trial than a song or a
golden shield."

The hunter took the vacant place ; his arrow whistled away,
and the report came back from the target. By a happy accident,
if such it were, the copper point was planted exactly in the middle
of the space between the other two.

More joyous than before arose the cry of Io', "I have beaten a
king and a warrior! Mine is the shield, mine is the shield!"

And the king, listening, said to himself, "I remember my own
youth, and its earliest victory, and how I passed from successes at
first the most trifling. Ah ! who but Huitzil', father of all the
gods, can tell the end ? Blessed the day when I can set before
him the prospect of a throne instead of a shield!"

The target was brought him, and he measured the distance of
each arrow from the centre ; and when he saw how exactly
Hualpa's was planted between the others, his subtle mind detected
the purpose and the generosity.

"The victory is yours, O my son, and so is the shield," he said
slowly and thoughtfully. "But ah ! were it given you to look
with eyes like mine,—with eyes sharpened by age for the discovery of blessings, your rejoicing would be over a friend found,
whose love is proof against vanity and the hope of reward."

Hualpa understood him, and was proud. What was the prize
lost to Montezuma gained ?

"It grows late ; my time is sacred," said the king. "Lord
Hualpa, stay and guide me to the palace. And Io', be you my
courier to the 'tzin. Go before, and tell him I am coming."

The boy ran ahead, and, as they leisurely followed him, the
monarch relapsed into melancholy. In the shade of a *ceiba* tree
he stopped, and said, "There is a service you might do me, that
lies nearer my heart than any other."

"The will of the great king is mine," Hualpa replied, with a
low reverence.

"When I am old," pursued Montezuma, "when the things of

earth begin to recede from me, it would be pleasant to have a son worthy to lift the Empire from my shoulders. While I am going up the steps of the temple, a seeker of the holy peace that lies in worship and prayer, the government would not then be a care to disturb me. But I am sensible that no one could thus relieve me unless he had the strong hand of a warrior, and was fearless except of the gods. Io' is my only hope. From you he first caught the desire of greatness, and you can make him great. Take him as a comrade; love him as a brother; teach him the elements of war,—to wield spear and *maquahuitl;* to bear shield, to command, and to be brave and generous. Show him the ways of ambition. Above all,"—as he spoke he raised his head and hand, and looked the impersonation of his idea,—"above all, let him know that a king may find his glory as much in the love of his people as in his power. Am I understood?"

Hualpa did not look up, but said, "Am I worthy? I have the skill of hand; but have I the learning?"

"To make him learned belongs to the priests. I only asked you to make him a warrior."

"Does not that belong to the gods?"

"No; he derives nothing from them but the soul. They will not teach him to launch the arrow."

"Then I accept the charge. Shall he go with me?"

"Always,—even to battle."

O mighty king! was the shadow of the coming fate upon thy spirit then?

CHAPTER II.

THE KING AND THE 'TZIN.

THE visit was unexpected to Guatamozin, and its object a mystery; but he thought only of paying the guest meet honour and respect, for he was still the great king. And so, bareheaded and unarmed, he went forth, and, meeting him in the garden, knelt, and saluted him after the manner of the court.

"I am glad to say the word of welcome to my father's brother. Know, O king, that my house, my garden, and all you behold are yours."

Hualpa left them; then Montezuma replied, the sadness of his voice softening the austerity of his manner,—

"I have loved you well, Guatamozin. Very good it was to mark you come up from boyhood, and day by day grow in strength and thought. I never knew one so rich in promise.

Ours is a proud race, and you seemed to have all its genius. From the beginning you were thoughtful and provident ; in the field there was always a victory for you, and in council your words were the soul of policy. Oh, ill was the day evil came between us, and suspicion shattered the love I bore you ! Arise ! I have not crossed the lake for explanations ; there is that to speak of more important to us both.'

The 'tzin arose, and looked into the monarch's face, his own suffused with grief.

"Is not a king punished for the wrong he does?"

Montezuma's brows lowered, chilling the fixed look which was his only answer ; and the 'tzin spoke on.

"I cannot accuse you directly ; but this I will say, O king : a just man, and a brave, never condemns another upon suspicion."

The monarch's eyes blazed with sudden fire, and from his *maxtlatl* he drew a knife. The 'tzin moved not ; the armed hand stopped ; an instant each met the other's gaze, then the weapon was flung away.

"I am a child," said the king, vexed and ashamed. "When I came here I did not think of the past, I thought only of the Empire ; but trouble has devoured my strength of purpose, until my power mocks me, and, most miserable of men, I yearn to fly from myself, without knowing where to find relief. A vague impulse—whence derived, except from intolerable suffering of mind, I know not—brought me to you. O 'tzin, silent be the differences that separate us. Yours I know to be a tongue of undefiled truth ; and if not for me now, for our country, and the renown of our fathers, I believe you will speak."

The shame, the grief, and the self-accusation moved the 'tzin more than the deadly menace.

"Set my feet, O king !—set my feet in the way to serve or save my country, and I will tread it, though every step be sown with the terrors of Mictlan."

"I did not misjudge you, my son," the king said, when he had again perfectly mastered his feelings.

And Guatamozin, yet more softened, would have given him all the old love, but that Tula, contracted to the Tezcucan, rose to memory. Checking the impulse, he regarded the unhappy monarch sorrowfully.

And the latter, glancing up at the sun, said,—

"It is getting late. I left the train going to the hunting-grounds. By noon they will return, and I wish to be at the city before them. My canoe lies at the landing ; walk there with me, and on the way I will speak of the purpose of my visit."

Their steps as they went were slow, and their faces downcast and solemn. The king was first to speak.

"As the time requires, I have held many councils, and taken

the voice of priest, warrior, and merchant; and they agree in nothing but their confusion and fear."

"The king forgets,—I have been barred his councils, and know not what they considered."

"True, true; yet there is but one topic in all Anahuac,—in the Empire. Of that, the *tamanes* talk gravely as their masters; only one class asks, 'Who are the white men making all this trouble?' while the other argues, 'They are here; they are gods. What are we to do?'"

"And what say the councils, O king?"

"It could not be that all would speak as one man. Of different castes, they are differently moved. The pabas believe the Sun has sent us some godly warriors, whom nothing earthly can subdue. They advise patience, friendship, and peace. 'The eye of Huitzil' is on them, numbering their marches. In the shade of the great temple he awaits, and there he will consume them with a breath,' —so say the pabas. The warriors are dumb, or else borrow and reassert the opinions of the holy men. 'Give them gold, if they will depart; if not that, give them peace, and leave the issue to the gods,'—so they say. Cuitlahua says war; so does Cacama. The merchants and the people have no opinion,—nothing but fear. For myself, yesterday I was for war, to-day I am for peace. So far, I have chosen to act upon the advice of the pabas. I have sent the strangers many presents and friendly messages, and kept ambassadors in their camp; but, while preserving such relations, I have continually forbade their coming to Tenochtitlan. They seem bolder than men. Who but they would have undertaken the march from Cempoalla? What tribes or people could have conquered Tlascala as they have? You have heard of their battles. Did they not in a day what we have failed to do in a hundred years? With Tlascala for ally, they have set my word at naught, and, whether they be of the sun or the earth, they are now marching upon Cholula, most sacred city of the gods. And from Cholula there is but one more march. Already, from the mountains, they have looked wistfully down on our valley of gardens, upon Tenochtitlan. O 'tzin, 'tzin! can we forget the prophecy?"

"Shall I say what I think? Will the king hear me?" asked Guatamozin.

"For that I came. Speak!"

"I obey gladly. The opportunity is dearer to me than any honour. And, speaking, I will remember of what race I am."

"Speak as if you were king."

"Then—I condemn your policy."

The monarch's face remained placid. If the bluff words wounded him, he dissembled consummately.

"It was not well to go so often to the temple," Guatamozin

continued. "Huitzil' is not **there**; the pabas have only **his** name, his image and altar; your breast is his true temple; there ought you to find him. Yesterday, you say, you were for war; the god was with you then: to-day you are for peace; the god has abandoned you. I know not in what words the lords Cuitlahua and Cacama urged their counsel, **nor on** what grounds. By the Sun! theirs is the only policy that comports with the fame of a ruler of Aztecs. Why speak of any other? For me, I would **seek the strangers in** battle and die, sooner **than a** minstrel should sing, **or tradition tell,** how Guatamozin, overcome by fear, **dwelt in** their camp praying peace as the beggar prays **for** bread."

Literally, Guatamozin was speaking like a king.

"I have heard your pearl-divers say," he continued, "that they **never** venture into a strange sea without dread. Like the new sea to them, this subject has been to your people; but however the declaration may strike your ears, O king, I have sounded all its depths. While your priests were asking questions of speechless hearts; while your lords were nursing their love of ease in **the** shade **and** perfume of your palace; while your warriors, **forgetful of** their glory, indulged the fancy that the new enemy **were gods;** while Montezuma was watching stars, and studying omens, and listening to oracles which the gods know not, hoping for wisdom to be found nowhere as certainly as in his own royal instincts,—face to face with the strangers, in their very camp, I studied them, their customs, language, and nature. Take heart, O king! Gods, indeed! Why, like men, I have seen them hunger and thirst; like men, heard them complain; on the other hand, like men, I have seen them feed and drink to surfeit, and heard them sing from gladness. What means their love of gold? If they come from the Sun, where the dwellings of the gods and the hills they are built on are all of gold, why should they be seeking it here? Nor is that all. I listened to the **interpreter,** through whom their leader explained his religion, **and they** are worshippers, like us—only they adore a woman, **instead of a great,** heroic god"—

"A woman!" exclaimed the king.

"Nay, the argument is that they worship **at all. Gods do not** adore each other!"

They had now walked some distance, and so absorbed had Montezuma been that he had not observed the direction they were pursuing. Emerging suddenly from a cypress-grove, he was surprised to find the path terminate in a small lake, which at any other time would have excited his admiration. Tall trees, draped to their topmost boughs in luxuriant vines, encircled the little expanse of water, and in its midst **there** was an island, crowned with a kiosk or summer-house, **and** covered with orange shrubs and tapering palms.

"Bear with me, O king," said Guatamozin, observing his wonder. "I brought you here that you may be absolutely convinced of the nature of our enemies. On that island I have an argument stronger than the vagaries of pabas or the fancies of warriors,—a visible argument."

He stepped into a canoe lying at the foot of the path, and, with a sweep of the paddle, drove across to the island. Remaining there, he pushed the vessel back.

"Come over, O king, come over, and see."

Montezuma followed boldly, and was led to the kiosk. The retreat was not one of frequent resort. Several times they were stopped by vines grown across the path. Inside the house, the visitor had no leisure for observation; he was at once arrested by an object that filled him with horror. On a table was a human head. Squarely severed from the body, it stood upright on the base of the neck, looking with its ghastly white face directly toward the entrance. The features were swollen and ferocious; the black brows locked in a frown, with which, as was plainly to be seen, nature had as much to do as death; the hair was short, and on the crown almost worn away; heavy, matted beard covered the cheeks and chin; finally, other means of identification being wanted, the coarse, upturned mustache would have betrayed the Spaniard. Montezuma surveyed the head for some time; at length, mastering his deep loathing, he advanced to the table.

"A *teule!*" he said in a low voice.

"A man,—only a man!" exclaimed Guatamozin, so sternly that the monarch shrank as if the blue lips of the dead had spoken to him. "Ask yourself, O king, Do the gods die?"

Montezuma smiled, either at his own alarm or at the ghastly argument.

"Whence came the trophy?" he asked.

"Have you not heard of the battle of Nauhtlan?"

"Surely; but tell it again."

"When the strangers marched to Tlascala," the 'tzin began, "their chief left a garrison behind him in the town he founded. I was then on the coast. To convince the people, and particularly the army, that they were men, I determined to attack them. An opportunity soon occurred. Your tax-gatherers happening to visit Nauhtlan, the township revolted, and claimed protection of the garrison, who marched to their relief. At my instance the caciques drew their bands together, and we set upon the enemy. The Totonaques fled at our first war-cry; but the strangers welcomed us with a new kind of war. They were few in number, but the thunder seemed theirs, and they hailed great stones upon us, and after a while came against us upon their fierce animals. When my warriors saw them come leaping on, they fled. All was lost. I had but one thought more,—a captive taken might

save the Empire. I ran where the strangers clove their bloody
way. This"—and he pointed to the head—"was the chief, and I
met him in the rout, raging like a tiger in a herd of deer. He
was bold and strong, and, shouting his battle-cry, he rushed upon
me. His spear went through my shield. I wrenched it from
him, and slew the beast; then I dragged him away, intending to
bring him alive to Tenochtitlan; but he slew himself. So look
again! What likeness is there in that to a god? O king, I ask
you, did ever its sightless eyes see the glories of the Sun, or its
rotting lips sing a song in heaven? Is Huitzil' or Tezca' made of
such stuff?"

The monarch, turning away, laid his hand familiarly on the
'tzin's arm, and said,—

"Come, I am content. Let us go."

And they started for the landing.

"The strangers, as I have said, my son, are marching to
Cholula. And Malinche—so their chief is called—now says he
is coming to Tenochtitlan."

"To Tenochtitlan! In its honoured name, in the name of its
kings and gods, I protest against his coming!"

"Too late—too late!" replied Montezuma, his face working as
though a pang were at his heart. "I have invited him to come."

"Alas, alas!" cried Guatamozin solemnly. "The day he
enters the capital will be the commencement of the woe, if it has
not already commenced. The many victories will have been in
vain. The provinces will drop away, like threaded pearls when
the string is broken. O king, better had you buried your
crown,—better for your people, better for your own glory!"

"Your words are bitter," said the monarch gloomily.

"I speak from the fulness of a heart darkened by a vision of
Anahuac blasted, and her glory gone," returned the 'tzin. Then
in a lament, vivid with poetic colouring, he set forth a picture of
the national ruin,—the armies overthrown, the city wasted, the
old religion supplanted by a new. At the shore where the canoe
was waiting, Montezuma stopped, and said,—

"You have spoken boldly, and I have listened patiently. One
thing more: what does Guatamozin say the king should do?"

"It is not enough for the servant to know his own place; he
should know his master's also. I say not what the king should
do, but I will say what I would do if I were king."

Rising from the obeisance with which he accompanied the
words, he said boldly,—

"Cholula should be the grave of the invaders. The whole
population should strike them in the narrow streets where they
can be best assailed. Shut up in some square or temple, hunger
will fight them for us, and win. But I would not trust the
citizens alone. In sight of the temples, so close that a conch could

summon them to the attack, I would encamp a hundred thousand
warriors. Better the desolation of Cholula than Tenochtitlan.
If all things else failed, I would take to the last resort ; I would
call in the waters of Tezcuco and drown the city to the highest
azoteas. So would I, O king, if the crown and signet were mine."

Montezuma looked from the speaker to the lake.

"The project is bold," **he** said musingly ; "but **if** it failed,
my son?"

"The failure should be but the beginning of the war."

"What would the nations say?"

"They would **say,** 'Montezuma is still **the** great king.' **If**
they do not **that**"—

"What then?"

"Call **on the** *teotuctli.* The gods **can be made speak** whatever your policy demands."

"Does my son blaspheme?" said Montezuma angrily.

"Nay, I but spoke of what has happened. Long rule the good
god of our fathers !"

Yet the monarch was not satisfied. Never before had dis-
course been addressed to him in strain so bold.

"They see all things, even our hearts," he said, turning coldly
away. "Farewell. A courier will come for you when your
presence is wanted in the city."

And so they separated, conscious that no healing had been
brought to their broken friendship. As the canoe moved off,
the 'tzin knelt, but the king looked not that way again.

CHAPTER III.

LOVE ON **THE LAKE.**

"WHAT can they mean? Here have they been loitering since
morning, as if the lake, like the *tianguez,* were a place for idlers.
As I love the gods, if I knew them, they should be punished !"

So the farmer of the *chinampa* heretofore described as the
property of the princess Tula gave expression to his wrath ; after
which he returned to his employment ; that is, he went crawling
among the shrubs and flowers, pruning-knife in hand, here
clipping **a** limb, there loosening the loam. Emerging from the
thicket after **a** protracted stay, his ire was again aroused.

L

"Still there! Thieves maybe, watching a chance to steal. But we shall see. My work is done, and I will not take eyes off of them again."

The good man's alarm was occasioned by the occupants of a canoe, which since sunrise had been plying about the garden, never stationary, seldom more than three hundred yards away, yet always keeping on the side next the city. Once in a while the slaves withdrew their paddles, leaving the vessel to the breeze; at such times it drifted so near that he could see the *voyageurs* reclining in the shade of the blue canopy, wrapped in *escaupils* such as none but lords or distinguished merchants were permitted to wear.

The leisurely *voyageurs*, on their part, appeared to have a perfect understanding of the light in which they were viewed from the *chinampa*.

"There he is again! See!" said one of them.

The other lifted the curtain, and looked, and laughed.

"Ah! if we could send an arrow there, just near enough to whistle through the orange-trees. Tula would never hear the end of the story. He would tell her how two thieves came to plunder him; how they shot at him; how narrowly he escaped"—

"And how valiantly he defended the garden. By Our Mother, Io', I have a mind to try him!"

Hualpa half rose to measure the distance, but fell back at once. "No. Better that we get into no difficulty. We are messengers, and have these flowers to deliver. Besides, the judge is not to my liking."

"Tula is merciful, and would forgive you for the 'tzin's sake."

"I meant the judge of the court," Hualpa said soberly. "You never saw him lift the golden arrow, as if to draw it across your portrait. It is pleasanter sitting here, in the shade, rocked by the water."

"And pleasanter yet to be made noble and master of a palace over by Chapultepec," Io' answered. "But see! Yonder is a canoe."

"From the city?"

"It is too far off; wait awhile."

But Hualpa, impatient, leaned over the side and looked for himself. At the time they were up in the northern part of the lake, at least a league from the capital. Long, regular swells, something like those of the sea when settling into calm, tumbled the surface; far to the south, however, he discerned the canoe, looking no larger than a blue-winged gull.

"It is coming; I see the prow this way. Is the vase ready?"

"The vase! You forget; there are two of them."

Hualpa looked down confused.

"Does the 'tzin intend them both for Tula?"

Hualpa was the more embarrassed.

"Flowers have a meaning; sometimes they tell tales. Let me see if I cannot read what the 'tzin would say to Tula."

And Io' went forward and brought the vases, and, placing them before him, began to study each flower.

"Io'," said Hualpa in a low voice, "but one of the vases is the 'tzin's."

"And the other?" asked the prince, looking up.

Hualpa's face flushed deeper.

"The other is mine. Have you not two sisters?"

Io's eyes dilated; a moment he was serious, then he burst out laughing.

"I have you now! Nenetzin,—she too has a lover."

The hunter never found himself so at loss; he played with the loops of his *escaupil*, and refused to take his eyes off the coming canoe. Through his veins the blood ran merrily; in his brain it intoxicated, like wine.

"I have heard how love makes women of warriors; now I will see,—I will see how brave you are."

"Ho, slaves! Put the canoe about; yonder are those whom I would meet," Hualpa shouted.

The vessel was headed to the south. A long distance had to be passed, and in the time the ambassador recovered himself. Lying down again, and twanging the chord of his bow, he endeavoured to compose a speech to accompany the delivery of the vase to Tula. But his thoughts would return to his own love; the laugh with which Io' received his explanation flattered him; and, true to the logic of the passion, he already saw the vase accepted, and himself the favoured of Nenetzin. From that point the world of dreams was but a step distant; he took the step, but was brought back by Io'.

"They recognise us; Nenetzin waves her scarf!"

The approaching vessel was elegant as the art of the Aztecan shipmaster could make it. The prow was sculptured into the head and slender curved neck of a swan. The passengers, fair as ever journeyed on sea wave, sat under a canopy of royal green, above which floated a *panache* of long, trailing feathers, coloured like the canopy. Like a creature of the water, so lightly, so gracefully, the boat drew nigh the messengers. When alongside, Io' sprang aboard, and, with boyish ardour, embraced his sisters.

"What has kept you so?"

"We stayed to see twenty thousand warriors cross the causeway," replied Nenetzin.

"Where can they be going?"

"To Cholula."

The news excited **the boy**; turning to speak to Hualpa, he was reminded of his duty.

"Here is a messenger from Guatamozin,—the lord Hualpa, who slew the tiger in the garden."

The heart of the young warrior beat violently; he touched the **floor of the** canoe with his palm.

And Tula spoke. "We have heard **the minstrels sing the** story. Arise, lord Hualpa."

"The words of the noble Tula are pleasanter **than any song.** Will she hear the message **I** bring?"

She looked at Io' and Nenetzin, and assented.

"Guatamozin salutes the noble Tula. He hopes the blessings of the gods are about her. He bade me say, that four mornings ago the king visited him at his palace, but talked of nothing but the strangers; so that the contract with Iztlil', the Tezcucan, still holds good. Further, the king asked his counsel as to what should be **done** with the strangers. He advised war, whereupon the king became angry, and departed, saying that a courier would **come** for **the** 'tzin when his presence was wanted in the city; **so the** banishment also holds good. And so, finally, there is **no** more hope from interviews with the **king. All** that remains is to leave the cause to time and the gods."

A moment her calm face was troubled; **but she recovered, and** said with simple dignity,—

"I thank you. Is the 'tzin well and **patient?**"

"He is a warrior, noble Tula, and foemen are marching through the provinces, like welcome guests; he thinks of them, and curses the peace as a season fruitful of dishonour."

Nenetzin, who had been quietly listening, was aroused.

"Has he heard **the news? Does** he not know a battle is to be fought in Cholula?"

"Such tidings will be medicine to his spirit."

"**A battle!**" cried Io'. "Tell me about it, Nenetzin."

"**I too** will listen," said Hualpa; "**for** the gods have given me **a** love of words spoken with **a voice** sweeter than the flutes of Tezca'."

The girl laughed aloud, **and was** well pleased, although she answered,—

"My father gave me a bracelet this morning, but he did not carry his love so far **as to** tell me his purposes; and I am not yet a warrior **to talk** to warriors about battles. The lord Maxtla, **even Tula here, can better** tell you of such things."

"Of what?" asked Tula.

" Io' and his friend wish to know all about the war."

The elder princess mused a moment, and then said gravely, " You may tell the 'tzin, as from me, lord Hualpa, that twenty thousand warriors this morning marched for Cholula ; that the citizens there have been armed ; and to-morrow, the gods willing, Malinche will be attacked. The king at one time thought of conducting the expedition himself ; but, by the persuasion of the paba, Mualox, he has given the command to the lord Cuitlahua."

Io' clapped his hands. " The gods are kind ; let us rejoice, O Hualpa ! What marching of armies there will be ! What battles ! Hasten, and let us to Cholula ; we can be there before the night sets in."

" What !" said Nenetzin. " Would you fight, Io' ? No, no ; come home with us, and I will put my parrot in a tree, and you may shoot at him all day."

The boy went to his own canoe, and, returning, held up a shield of pearl and gold. " See ! With a bow I beat our father and the lord Hualpa, and this was the prize."

" That a shield !" Nenetzin said. " A toy,—a mere brooch to a Tlascalan. I have a tortoise-shell that will serve you better."

The boy frowned, and a rejoinder was on his lips when Tula spoke.

" The flowers in your vases are very beautiful, lord Hualpa. What altar is to receive the tribute ?"

Nenetzin's badinage had charmed the ambassador into forgetfulness of his embassy ; so he answered confusedly, " The noble Tula reminds me of my duty. Before now, standing upon the hills of Tihuanco, watching the morning brightening in the east, I have forgotten myself. I pray pardon "—

Tula glanced archly at Nenetzin. " The morning looks pleasant ; doubtless its worshipper will be forgiven."

And then he knew the woman's sharp eyes had seen into his inner heart, and that the audacious dream he there cherished was exposed ; yet his confusion gave place to delight, for the discovery had been published with a smile. Thereupon he set one of the vases at her feet, and touched the floor with his palm, and said,—

" I was charged by Guatamozin to salute you again, and say that these flowers would tell you all his hopes and wishes."

As she raised the gift, her hand trembled ; then he discovered how precious a simple Cholulan vase could become ; and with that his real task was before him. Taking the other vase, he knelt before Nenetzin.

" I have but little skill in courtierly ways," he said. " In flowers I see nothing but their beauty ; and what I would have these say is, that if Nenetzin, the beautiful Nenetzin, will accept them, she will make me very happy."

The girl looked at Tula, then at him; then she raised the vase, and, laughing, hid her face in the flowers.

But little more was said; and soon the lashings were cast off, and the vessels separated.

On the return Hualpa stopped at Tenochtitlan, and in the shade of the portico, over a cup of the new beverage, now all the fashion, received from Xoli the particulars of the contemplated attack upon the strangers in Cholula; for, with his usual diligence in the fields of gossip, the broker had early informed himself of all that was to be heard of the affair. And that night, while Io' dreamed of war, and the hunter of love, the 'tzin paced his study or wandered through his gardens, feverishly solicitous about the result of the expedition.

"If it fail," he repeated over and over,—"if it fail, Malinche will enter Tenochtitlan as a god!"

CHAPTER IV.

THE KING DEMANDS A SIGN OF MUALOX.

NEXT morning Mualox ascended the tower of his old Cû. The hour was so early that the stars were still shining in the east. He fed the fire in the great urn until it burst into cheery flame; then, spreading his mantle on the roof, he laid down to woo back the slumber from which he had been taken. By and by, a man, armed with a javelin, and clad in cotton mail, came up the steps, and spoke to the paba.

"Does the servant of his god sleep this morning?"

Mualox arose, and kissed the pavement.

"Montezuma is welcome. The blessing of the gods upon him!"

"Of all the gods, Mualox?"

"Of all,—even Quetzal's, O king!"

"Arise! Last night I bade you wait me here. I said I would come with the morning star; yonder it is, and I am faithful. The time is fittest for my business."

Mualox arose, and stood before the monarch with bowed head and crossed hands.

"Montezuma knows his servant."

"Yet I seek to know him better. Mualox, Mualox, have you room for a perfect love aside from Quetzal'? What would you do for me?"

"Ask me rather what I would not do."

"Hear me, then. Lately you have been a counsellor in my palace; with my policy and purposes you are acquainted; you knew of the march to Cholula, and the order to attack the strangers; you were present when they were resolved"—

"And opposed them. Witness for me to Quetzal', O king!"

"Yes; you prophesied evil and failure from them, and for that I seek you now. Tell me, O Mualox, spake you then as a prophet?"

The paba ventured to look up and study the face of the questioner as well as he could in the flickering light.

"I know the vulgar have called me a magician," he said slowly; "and sometimes they have spoken of my commerce with the stars. To say that either report is true, were wrong to the gods. Regardful of them, I cannot answer you; but I can say—and its sufficiency depends on your wisdom—your slave, O king, is warned of your intention. You come asking a sign; you would have me prove my power, that it may be seen."

"By the Sun"—

"Nay,—if my master will permit,—another word."

"I came to hear you; say on."

"You spoke of me as a counsellor in the palace. How may we measure the value of honours? By the intent with which they are given? O king, had you not thought the poor paba would use his power for the betrayal of his god; had you not thought he could stand between you and the wrath"—

"No more, Mualox, no more!" said Montezuma. "I confess I asked you to the palace that you might befriend me. Was I wrong to count on your loyalty? Are you not of Anahuac? And further, I confess I come now seeking a sign. I command you to show me the future!"

"If you do indeed believe me the beloved of Quetzal' and his prophet, then are you bold,—even for a king."

"Until I wrong the gods, why should I fear? I too am a priest."

"Be wise, O my master! Let the future alone; it is sown with sorrows to all you love."

"Have done, paba!" the king exclaimed angrily. "I am weary,—by the Sun! I am weary of such words."

The holy man bowed reverently, and touched the floor with his palm, saying,—

"Mualox lays his heart at his master's feet. In the time when his beard was black and his spirit young, he began the singing

of two songs,—one of worship to Quetzal', the other of love for
Montezuma."

These words he said tremulously; and there was that in the
manner, in the bent form, in the low obeisance, which soothed
the impatience of the king, so that he turned away, and looked
out over the city. And day began to gild the east; in a short
time the sun would claim his own. Still the monarch thought,
still Mualox stood humbly waiting his pleasure. At length the
former approached the fire.

"Mualox," he said, speaking slowly, "I crossed the lake the
other day, and talked with Guatamozin about the strangers.
He satisfied me they are not *teules*, and, more, he urged me to
attack them in Cholula."

"The 'tzin!" exclaimed Mualox in strong surprise.

Montezuma knew the love of the paba for the young cacique
rested upon his supposed love of Quetzal'; so he continued,—

"The attack was planned by him,—only he would have sent
a hundred thousand warriors to help the citizens. The order is
out; the companies are there; blood will run in the streets of
the holy city to-day. The battle waits on the sun, and it is
nearly up. Mualox,"—his manner became solemn,—"Mualox,
on this day's work bides my peace. The morning comes;
by all your prophet's power, tell me what the night will
bring!"

Sorely was the paba troubled. The king's faith in his qualities
as prophet he saw was absolute, and that it was too late to deny
the character.

"Does Montezuma believe the Sun would tell me what it
withholds from its child?"

"Quetzal', not the Sun, will speak to you."

"But Quetzal' is your enemy."

Montezuma laid his hand on the paba's. "I have heard you
speak of love for me; prove it now, and your reward shall be
princely. I will give you a palace, and many slaves, and riches
beyond count."

Mualox bent his head, and was silent. Enjoyment of a palace
meant abandonment of the old Cû and sacred service. Just then
the wail of a watcher from a distant temple swept faintly by; he
heard the cry, and from his surplice drew a trumpet, and through
it sung with a swelling voice,—

"Morning is come! Morning is come! To the temples, O
worshippers! Morning is come!"

And the warning hymn, the same that had been heard from
the old tower for so many ages, heard heralding suns while the
city was founding, given now, amid the singer's sore perplexity,
was an assurance to his listening deity that he was faithful

against kingly blandishments as well as kingly neglect. **While** the words were being repeated from the many temples, he stood attentive to them, then he turned, and said,—

"Montezuma is generous to his slave ; but ambition is a goodly **tree** gone to dust in my heart ; and if it were not, O king, what are all your treasures to that in the golden chamber? Nay, keep your offerings, and let me keep the temple. I hunger after no riches except such **as** lie in the love of Quetzal'."

"Then tell me," said the monarch impatiently,—"without price, tell me his will."

"I cannot, I am but a man; but this much I can"— He faltered ; the hands crossed upon his breast closed tightly, and the breast laboured painfully.

"I am **waiting.** Speak ! What can you ?"

"Will the **king** trust his servant, and **go with him down into** the Cû again ?"

"To talk with the Morning, this is the place," said the monarch, **too** well remembering the former introduction to the mysteries of the ancient house.

"My master mistakes me for a juggling soothsayer ; he thinks I will look into the halls of the Sun through burning drugs, and the magic of unmeaning words. I have nothing to do with the Morning ; I have no incantations. I am but the dutiful slave of Quetzal', the god, and Montezuma, the king."

The royal listener looked away again, debating **with** his fears, which, it is but just to say, were not of harm from the paba. Men unfamiliar with the custom do not think lightly of encountering things unnatural ; in this instance, moreover, favour was not to be hoped from the god through whom the forbidden knowledge was to come. But curiosity and an uncontrollable interest in the result of the affair in Cholula overcame his apprehensions.

"I will go with you. I am ready," he said.

The old man stooped, and touched **the roof,** and, rising, said,—

"I have a little world of my own, O king ; and though without sun and stars, and the grand harmony which only the gods can give, it has its wonders and beauty, and is to me a place of perpetual delight. Bide my return a little while. I will go and prepare the way for you."

Resuming his mantle, he departed, leaving the king to study the new-born day. When he came back, the valley and the sky were full of the glory of the sun full risen. And they descended **to** the *azoteas,* thence to the court-yard. Taking a lamp hanging **in** a passage-door, the holy man, with the utmost reverence, conducted his guest into the labyrinth. At first, the latter tried to recollect the course taken, the halls and stairs passed, and the storeys descended; but the thread was too often broken, the light too dim, the way too intricate. Soon he yielded himself entirely to his guide, and followed, wondering much at the massiveness of the building, and the courage necessary to live there alone. Ignorant of the zeal which had become the motive of the paba's life, inspiring him with incredible cunning and industry, and equally without a conception of the power there is in one idea long awake in the soul and nursed into mania, it was not singular that, as they went, the monarch should turn the very walls into witnesses corroborant of the traditions of the temple and the weird claims of its keeper.

Passing the kitchen, and descending the last flight of steps, they came to the trap-door in the passage, beside which lay the ladder of ropes.

"Be of courage a little longer, O king," said Mualox, flinging the ladder through the doorway. "We are almost there."

And the paba, leaving the lamp above, committed himself confidently to the ropes and darkness below. A suspicion of his madness occurred to the king, whose situation called for consideration; in fact, he hesitated to follow farther; twice he was called to; and when, finally, he did go down, the secret of his courage was an idea that they were about to emerge from the dusty caverns into the freer air of day; for, while yet in the passage, he heard the whistle of a bird, and fancied he detected a fragrance as of flowers.

"Your hand now, O king, and Mualox will lead you into his world."

The motives that constrained the holy man to this step are not easily divined. Of all the mysteries of the house, that hall was by him the most cherished; and of all men the king was the last whom he would have voluntarily chosen as a participant in its secrets, since he alone had power to break them up. The necessity must have been very great; possibly he felt his influence and peculiar character dependent upon yielding to the pressure: the moment the step was resolved upon, however, nothing remained but to use the mysteries for the protection of the abode; and with that purpose he went to prepare the way.

Much study would most of us have required to know what was essential to the purpose; not so the paba. He merely trimmed the lamps already lighted, and lighted and disposed others. His plan was to overwhelm the visitor by the first glance; without warning, without time to study details, to flash upon him a crowd of impossibilities. In the mass, the generality, the whole together, a god's hand was to be made apparent to a superstitious fancy.

CHAPTER V.

THE MASSACRE IN CHOLULA.

INSIDE the hall, scarcely a step from the curtain, the monarch stopped bewildered ; half amazed, half alarmed, he surveyed the chamber, now glowing as with day. Flowers blooming, birds singing, shrubbery thick and green as in his own garden. Whence came they ? how were they nurtured down so far ? And the countless subjects painted on the ceiling and walls, and woven in colours on the tapestry,—surely they were the work of the same master who had wrought so marvellously in the golden chamber. The extent of the hall, exaggerated by the light, impressed him. Filled with the presence of what seemed impossibilities, he cried out,—

"The abode of Quetzal' !"

"No," answered Mualox, "not his abode, only his temple,— the temple of his own building."

And from that time it was with the king as if the god were actually present.

The paba read the effect in the monarch's manner,—in his atti- tude, in the softness of his tread, in the cloudy, saddened expression of his countenance, in the whisper with which he spoke ; he read it, and was assured.

"This way, O king ! Though your servant cannot let you see into the Sun, or give you the sign required, follow him and he will bring you to hear of events in Cholula even as they transpire. Remember, however, he says now that the Cholulans and the twenty thousand warriors will fail, and the night bring you but sorrow and repentance."

Along the aisles he conducted him, until they came to the fountain, where the monarch stopped again. The light there was brighter than in the rest of the hall. A number of birds flew up, scared by the stranger ; in the space around the marble basin stood vases crowned with flowers ; the floor was strewn with wreaths and garlands ; the water sparkled with silvery lustre : yet all were lost on the wondering guest, who saw only Tecetl,— a vision, once seen, to be looked at again and again.

Upon a couch, a little apart from the fountain, she sat, leaning against a pile of cushions, which was covered by a mantle of *plumaje.* Her garments were white, and wholly without orna- ment ; her hair strayed lightly from a wreath upon her head ; the childish hands lay clasped in her lap ; upon the soft mattress rested the delicate limbs, covered, but not concealed, the soles of the small feet tinted with warmth and life, like the pink and rose lining of certain shells. So fragile, innocent, and beautiful looked she, and so hushed and motionless withal,—so like a spirituality,—that the monarch's quick sensation of sympathy shot through his heart an absolute pain.

"Disturb her not ; let her **sleep**," **he** whispered, waving his hand.

Mualox smiled.

"Nay, the full battle-cry of your armies would not waken her."

The influence of the Will was upon her, stronger **than** slumber. Not yet was she to see a human being other than **the** paba,—not even the great king. A little longer was she to be **happy in** ignorance of the actual world. Ah, many, many are **the victims** of affection unwise in its very fulness !

Again and again the monarch scanned the girl's face, charmed, yet awed. The paba had said the sleep was wakeless ; and that was a mystery unreported by tradition, unknown to his philosophy, and rarer, if not greater, than death. If life at all, what kind was **it ?** The longer he looked and reflected, the lovelier she grew. So completely was his credulity gained that he thought not once of questioning Mualox **about** her ; he was content with believing.

The paba, meantime, **had** been holding one of her hands, and gazing intently **in her face. When he** looked **up, the** monarch was startled by his appearance ; **his air was imposing, his eyes** lighted with the mesmeric force.

"Sit, O king, and give ear. Through the lips **of his child,** Quetzal' will speak, and tell you of the day in Cholula."

He spoke imperiously, and the monarch obeyed. Then, disturbed only by the chiming of the fountain, and sometimes by the whistling of the birds, Tecetl began, and softly, brokenly, unconsciously told of the massacre in the holy city of Cholula. Not a question was asked her. There was little prompting aloud. Much did the king marvel, never once doubted he.

"The sky is very clear," said Tecetl. "I rise into the air ; **I** leave the city **in** the lake, and the lake itself ; now the mountains **are** below me. Lo, another city ! I descend again ; the *azoteas* **of a** temple receives me ; around are great houses. Who are these **I see ?** There, in front of the temple, they stand, in lines ; even **in the** shade their garments glisten. They have shields ; some bear long lances, some sit on strange animals that have **eyes of** fire and ring the pavement with their stamping."

"Does the king understand ?" asked Mualox.

"She describes the strangers," was the reply.

And Tecetl resumed. "There is one standing **in** the midst of a throng ; he speaks, they listen. I **cannot** repeat his words, or understand them, for they are not like ours. Now I see his face, and **it** is white ; his eyes are black, and his cheeks bearded ; he is angry ; he points to the city around the temple, and his **voice** grows harsh, and his face dark."

The king approached a step, and whispered, "Malinche !"

But Mualox replied, with flashing eyes, "The **servant** knows his god ; it is Quetzal' !"

"He speaks, I listen," Tecetl continued, after a rest, and thenceforth her sentences were given at longer intervals. "Now he is through ; he waves his hand, and the listeners retire and go to different quarters ; in places they kindle fires ; the gates are open, and some station themselves there."

"Named she where this is happening ?" asked Montezuma.

"She describes the strangers ; and are they not in Cholula, O king ? She also spoke of the *azoteas* of a temple "—

"True, true," replied the king moodily. "The preparations must be going on in the square of the temple in which Malinche was lodged last night."

Tecetl continued. "And now **I** look down the street ; a crowd approaches from the city "—

"Speak of them," said Mualox. "I would know who they are."

"Most of them wear long beards and robes, like yours, father, —**robes** white and reaching to their feet ; in front a few come, swinging censers "—

"They are pabas from the temples," said Mualox.

"Behind them I see a greater crowd," **she** continued. "**How** stately their step ! how beautiful their plumes !"

"The twenty thousand ! the army !" said Mualox.

"No, she speaks of them as plumed. They must be lords and caciques going to the temple." While speaking, the monarch's eyes wandered restlessly, and he sighed, saying, "Where can the companies be ? It is time they were in the city."

So his anxiety betrayed itself.

Then Mualox said grimly, "**Hope** not, O king. The priests and caciques go to death ; the **army** would but swell the flow of blood."

Montezuma clapped his hands, and drooped his head.

"Yet more," said Tecetl, almost immediately ; "another crowd comes on, a band reaching far down the street ; they are naked, and come without order, bringing "—

"The *tamanes*," said Mualox, without looking from her face.

"And now," she said, "the city begins to stir. I look, and **on** the housetops and temples hosts collect ; from all the towers the smoke goes up in bluer columns : yet all is still. Those who carry the censers come near the gate below me ; now **they are** within it ; the plumed train follows them, and the square begins **to** fill. Back by the great door, on one of the animals, the god "—

"Quetzal'," muttered Mualox.

" A company, glistening, surrounds him ; his face seems whiter than before, his eyes darker ; a shield is on his arm, white plumes toss above his head. The censer-bearers cross the square, and the air thickens with a sweet perfume. Now he speaks to them ; his voice is harsh and high ; they are frightened ; some kneel, and begin to pray as to a god ; others turn and start quickly for the gate."

" Take heed, take heed, O king ! " said Mualox, his eyes aflame.

And Montezuma answered, trembling with fear and rage, " Has Anahuac no gods to care for her children ? "

" What can they against the Supreme Quetzal'? **It is a trial of** power. The end is at hand ! "

Never man spoke more confidently than the paba.

By this time Tecetl's **face was** flushed, and her voice faint. Mualox filled the hollow of **his hand** with water, and laved her forehead. And she sighed wearily and continued,—

" The fair-faced god "—

" Mark the words, O king,—mark the words ! " said the paba.

" The fair-faced god quits speaking ; he waves his hand, and one of **his** company on the steps of the temple answers with a shout. Lo ! a stream of fire, and a noise like the bursting of a cloud ! a rising, rolling cloud of smoke veils the whole front of the house. How the smoke thickens ! How the strangers rush into the square ! The square itself **trembles** ! I do not understand it, father."

".It is battle ! On, child ! a king waits to see a god in battle."

" In my pictures there is nothing like this, nor have you told me of anything like it. Oh, it is fearful ! " she said. " The crowd in the middle of the square, those who came from the city, are broken, and rush here and there ; at the gates they are beaten back ; some, climbing the walls, are struck by arrows, and fall down screaming. Hark ! how they call on the gods,—Huitzil', **Tezca'**, Quetzal'. And why are they not heard ? Where, **father, where is** the good Quetzal' ? "

Flashed the paba's eyes with the superhuman light,—other answer he deigned not ; and she proceeded.

" What a change has come over the square ? Where are they that awhile ago filled it **with** white robes and dancing plumes ? "

She shuddered visibly.

" I look again. The pavement **is** covered with heaps of the fallen, and among them I see some with plumes and some with robes ; even the censer-bearers lie still. What can it mean ? And all the time the horror grows. When the thunder and fire and smoke burst from near the temple-steps, how the helpless in the square shriek with terror and run blindly about ! How **many** are torn to pieces ! Down they go ; I cannot count them, they fall so fast, and in such heaps! Then—ah, the pavement looks red! Oh, father, it is blood!"

She stopped. Montezuma covered his face with his hands; the good heart that so loved his people sickened at their slaughter.

Again Mualox bathed her face. Joy flamed in **his** eyes; Quetzal' was consummating his vengeance, and confirming the prophecies of his servant.

"Go on; stay not!" **he said** sternly. "The story is not told."

"Still the running **to and** fro, and the screaming; still the fire flashing, and **the** smoke rising, and the hissing of arrows **and** sound of **blows; still** the prayers to Huitzil'!" said Tecetl. "I look down, **and** under the smoke, which has **a** choking **smell**, I see the fallen. **Red** pools gather in the hollow places, plumes **are** broken **and robes** no longer white. Oh, the piteous looks **I see**, the moans I hear, the many faces, brown like oak-leaves **faded**, turned stilly up to the sun!"

"The people of the god,—tell **of** them," said Mualox.

"I search for them,—I see them **on** the steps and out by the walls **and** the gates. They are all in their places yet; not one of them is down; theirs the arrows, and the fire and thunder."

"Does the king hear?" asked Mualox. "Only the pabas and caciques perish. Who may presume to oppose Quetzal'? Look further, child. Tell us of the city."

"Gladly, most gladly! Now, abroad over **the city, the** people quit the housetops; they run from all directions **to the** troubled temple; they crowd the streets; about the gates, **where** the gods are, they struggle to get into the square, and the **air** thickens with their arrows. The god"—

"What god?" asked Mualox.

"The white-plumed one."

"Quetzal'! Go **on**!"

"He **has**"— **She** faltered.

"What?"

"In my pictures, father, there is nothing like them. Fire leaps from their mouths, and smoke, and the air and earth tremble when they speak; and see—ah, how the crowds in the streets go down before them!"

Again she shuddered, and faltered.

"Hear, O king!" said Mualox, who not only recognised the cannon of the Spaniards in the description, but saw their weight at that moment as an argument. "What can the slingers, and the spearmen of Chinantla, and the swordsmen of Tenochtitlan, against warriors of the Sun, with their lightning and thunder?"

And he looked at the monarch, sitting with his face covered, and was satisfied. With faculties sharpened by **a** zeal too fervid

for sympathy, he saw the fears of the proud but kindly soul, and
rejoiced in them. Yet he permitted no delay.

"Go on, child! Look for the fair-faced god; he holds the
battle in his hand."

"I see him,—I see his white plumes nodding in a group of
spears. Now he is at the main gate of the temple, and speaks.
Hark! The earth is shaken by another roar,—from the street
another great cry; and through the smoke, out of the gate, he
leads his band. And the animals,—what shall I call them?"

"Tell us of the god!" replied the enthusiast, himself ignorant
of the name and nature of the horse.

"Well, well,—they run like deer; on them the god and his
comrades plunge into the masses in the street; beating back and
pursuing, striking with their spears, and trampling down all in
their way. Stones and arrows are flung from the houses, but
they avail nothing. The god shouts joyously, he plunges on;
and the blood flows faster than before; it reddens the shields, it
drips from the spear points"—

"Enough, Mualox!" said Montezuma, starting from his seat,
and speaking firmly. "I want no more. Guide me hence!"

The paba was surprised; rising slowly, he asked,—

"Will not the king stay to the end?"

"Stay!" repeated the monarch, with curling lip. "Are my
people of Cholula wolves that I should be glad at their slaughter?
It is murder, massacre, not battle! Show me to the roof again.
Come!"

Mualox turned to Tecetl; touching her hand, he found it cold;
the sunken eyes, and the lips, vermeil no longer, admonished him
of the delicacy of her spirit and body. He filled a vase at the
fountain, and laved her face, the while soothingly repeating,
"Tecetl, Tecetl, child!" Some minutes were thus devoted;
then kissing her, and replacing the hand tenderly in the other
lying in her lap, he said to the monarch,—

"Until to-day, O king, this sacredness has been sealed from
the generations that forsook the religion of Quetzal' Eye of
mocker has not seen, nor foot of unbeliever trod this purlieu, the
last to receive his blessing. You alone—I am of the god—you
alone can go abroad knowing what is here. Never before were
you so nearly face to face with the Ruler of the Winds! And
now, with what force a servant may, I charge you, by the glory
of the Sun, respect this house; and when you think of it, or of
what here you have seen, be it as friend, lover, and worshipper.
If the king will follow me, I am ready."

"I am neither mocker nor unbeliever. Lead on," replied
Montezuma.

And after that the king paid no attention to the chamber; he moved along the aisles too unhappy to be curious. The twenty thousand warriors had not been mentioned by Tecetl; they had not, it would seem, entered the city or the battle, so there was a chance of the victory; yet was he hopeless, for never a doubt had he of her story. Wherefore, his lamentation was twofold,—for his people and for himself.

And Mualox was silent **as the** king, though for a different cause. To him, suddenly, **the object** of his life put on the garb of quick possibility. **Quetzal', he** was sure, would fill the streets of Cholula with the **dead, and crown** his wrath amid the ruins of the city. In the face **of example** so dreadful, none would dare oppose him, **not** even Montezuma, whose pride broken was next to his faith gained. And around the new-born hope, as cherubs around the Madonna, rustled the wings of fancies most exalted. He saw the supremacy of Quetzal' acknowledged above all others, the Cû restored to its first glory, and the silent cells repeopled. O happy day! Already he heard the court-yard resounding with solemn chants as of old; when before the altar, in the presence-chamber, from morn till night he stood, receiving offerings, and dispensing blessings to the worshippers who, with a faith equal to his own, believed the ancient image the ONE SUPREME GOD.

At the head of the eastern steps of the temple, as **the king** began the descent, the holy man knelt, and said,—

"For peace to his people let the wise Montezuma look **to** Quetzal'. Mualox gives him his blessing. Farewell!"

CHAPTER VI.

THE CONQUEROR WILL **COME.**

A FEW weeks more,—weeks of pain, vacillation, embassies, and distracted councils to Montezuma; of doubt and anxiety to the nobles; of sacrifice and ceremonies by the priests; of fear and wonder to the people. In that time, if never before, the Spaniards became the one subject of discourse throughout Anahuac. In the *tianguez*, merchants bargaining paused **to** interchange opinions about them; craftsmen in the shops entertained and frightened each other with stories of their marvellous strength and ferocity; porters, bending under burdens, speculated **on** their character and mission; and never a waterman passed an acquaintance on the lake without lingering awhile to ask or give

M

the latest news from the **Holy City**, which, with the best grace it could, still entertained its **scourgers**.

What Malinche—for by that name Cortes was now universally known—would do was the first conjecture ; what the great king intended **was** the next.

As a matter of policy, the dismal massacre in Cholula accomplished all Cortes purposed. It made him a national terror ; it smoothed the causeway for his march, and held the gates of Xoloc open for peaceful entry into Tenochtitlan. Yet the question on the many tongues was, Would he come ?

And **he himself** answered. One day a **courier ran** up the great **street** of Tenochtitlan to the king's palace ; immediately the portal was thronged by anxious citizens. That morning Malinche began his march to the capital,—he was coming, was actually on the way. The thousands trembled as they heard the news.

After that the city was not an hour without messengers reporting the progress of the Spaniards, whose every step and halt and camping-place was watched with the distrust of fear and the sleeplessness of jealousy. The horsemen and footmen were all numbered ; the personal appearance of each leader was painted over and over again with brush and tongue ; the devices on the shields and pennons were described with heraldic accuracy. And though, from long service and constant exposure and repeated battles, the equipments of the adventurers had lost the freshness that belonged to them the day of the departure from Cuba ; though plumes and scarfs were stained, and casques and breastplates tarnished, and good steeds tamed by strange fare and wearisome marches,—nevertheless the accounts that went abroad concerning them were sufficiently splendid and terrible to confirm the prophecies by which they were preceded.

And the people, made swift by alarm and curiosity, outmarched Cortes many days. Before he reached Iztapalapan, the capital was full of them ; in multitudes, lords and slaves, men, women, and children, like Jews to the Passover, scaled the mountains, and hurried through the valley and across the lakes. Better opportunity to study the characteristics of the tribes was never afforded.

All day and night the public resorts—streets, houses, temples— were burdened with the multitude, whose fear, as the hour of entry drew nigh, yielded to their curiosity. And when, at last, the road the visitors would come by was settled, the whole city seemed to breathe easier. From the village of Iscalpan, so ran the word, they had boldly plunged into the passes of the Sierra, and thence taken the most direct route, by way of Tlalmanalco. And now they were at Ayotzinco, a town on the eastern shore of Lake Tezcuco ; to-morrow they would reach Iztapalapan, and then Tenochtitlan. Not a long time to wait, if they brought the vengeance of Quetzal'; yet thousands took canoes, and crossed to the village, and, catching the first view, hurried back, each with a fancy more than ever inflamed.

A soldier, sauntering down the street, is beset with citizens.

"A pleasant day, O son of Huitzil'!"

"A pleasant day; may all that shine on Tenochtitlan **be like it**!" he answers.

"What news?"

"I have been to the temple."

"And what says the *teotuctli* **now**?"

"Nothing. There are no signs. Like the stars, the **hearts of** the victims will not answer."

"What! Did not Huitzil' speak last night?"

"Oh yes!" and the warrior smiles with satisfaction. "**Last** night he bade the priests tell the king not to oppose the entry **of** Malinche."

"Then what?"

"Why, here in the city he would cut the strangers off to the **last** one."

And all the citizens cry in chorus, "Praised be Huitzil'!"

Farther on the warrior overtakes a comrade in arms.

"Are we to take our shields to the field, O my brother?" **he** asks.

"All is peaceful yet,—nothing but embassies."

"Is it true that the lord Cacama is to go in **state, and invite** Malinche to Tenochtitlan?"

"He sets out to-day."

"Ha, ha! Of all voices for war, his was the loudest. **Where** caught he the merchant's cry for peace?"

"In the temples; it may be from Huitzil'."

The answer **is** given in a low voice, and with an ironic laugh.

"Well, well, comrade, there are but two lords fit, in time like this, for the love of warriors,—Cuitlahua and Guatamozin. They still talk of war."

"Cuitlahua, Cuitlahua!" And the laugh rises to boisterous contempt. "Why, he has consented to receive Malinche in Iztapalapan, **and** entertain him with a banquet in his palace. He has gone **for that** purpose now. The lord of Cojohuaca is with him."

"Then we have only the 'tzin!"

The fellow sighs like one sincerely grieved.

"Only the 'tzin, brother, only the 'tzin! and he is banished!"

They shake their heads, and look what they dare **not** speak, and go their ways. The gloom they take with them **is** a sample of that which rests over the whole valley.

When the Spaniards reached Iztapalapan, the excitement in the capital became irrepressible. The cities were but an easy march apart, most of it along the causeway. The going and coming may be imagined. The miles of dyke were covered by a continuous procession, while the lake, in a broad line from town to town, was darkened by canoes. Cortes' progress through the streets of Iztapalapan was antitypical of the grander reception awaiting him in Tenochtitlan.

In the latter city there was no sleep that night. The *tianguez* in particular was densely filled, not by traders, but by a mass of newsmongers, who hardly knew whether they were most pleased or alarmed. The general neglect of business had exceptions ; at least one portico shone with unusual brilliancy till morning. Every great merchant is a philosopher : in the midst of calamities he is serene, because it is profit's time ; before the famine, he buys up all the corn ; in forethought of pestilence, he secures all the medicine ; and the world, counting his gains, says delightedly, What a wise man ! I will not say the Chalcan was of that honoured class ; he thought himself a benefactor, and was happy to accommodate the lords, and help them divide their time between his palace and that of the king. It is hardly necessary to add that his apartments were well patronized, though, in truth, his *pulque* was in greater demand than his *choclatl.*

The drinking-chamber, about the close of the third quarter of the night, presented a lively picture. For the convenience of the many patrons, tables from other rooms had been brought in. Some of the older lords were far gone in intoxication ; slaves darted to and fro, removing goblets, or bringing them back replenished. A few minstrels found listeners among those who happened to be too stupid to talk, though not too sleepy to drink. Every little while a new-comer would enter, when, if he were from Iztapalapan, a crowd would surround him, allowing neither rest nor refreshment until he had told the things he had seen or heard. Amongst others, Hualpa and Io' chanced to find their way thither. Maxtla, seated at a table with some friends, including the Chalcan, called them to him ; and, as they had attended the banquet of the lord Cuitlahua, they were quickly provided with seats, goblets, and an audience of eager listeners.

"Certainly, my good chief, I have seen Malinche, and passed the afternoon looking at him and his people," said Hualpa to Maxtla. "It may be that I am too much influenced by the 'tzin to judge them ; but, if they are *teules*, so are we. I longed to try my javelin on them."

"Was their behaviour unseemly ?"

"Call it as you please. I was in the train when, after the

banquet, the lord Cuitlahua took them to see his gardens. As they strode the walks, and snuffed the flowers, and plucked the fruit,—as they moved along the canal with its lining of stone, and stopped to drink at the fountains,—I was made feel that they thought everything, not merely my lord's property, but my lord himself, belonged to them : they said as much by their looks and actions, by their insolent swagger."

"Was the 'tzin there?"

"From the *azoteas* of a temple he saw them enter the city ; but he was not at the banquet. I heard a story showing how he would treat the strangers if he had the power. One of their priests, out with a party, came to the temple where he happened to be, and went up to the tower. In the sanctuary one of them raised his spear and struck the image of the god. The pabas threw up their hands and shrieked ; he rushed upon the impious wretch, and carried him to the sacrificial stone, stretched him out, and called to the pabas 'Come, the victim is ready!' When the other *teules* would have attacked him, he offered to fight them all. The strange priest interfered, and they departed."

The applause of the bystanders was loud and protracted ; when it had somewhat abated, Xoli, whose thoughts, from habit, ran chiefly upon the edibles, said,—

"My lord Cuitlahua is a giver of good suppers. Pray, tell us about the courses "—

"Peace! be still, Chalcan!" cried Maxtla angrily. "What care we whether Malinche ate wolf-meat or quail?"

Xoli bowed ; the lords laughed.

Then a grey-haired cacique behind Io' asked, "Tell us rather what Malinche said."

Hualpa shook his head. "The conversation was tedious. Everything was said through an interpreter,—a woman born in the province Painalla ; so I paid little attention. I recollect, however, he asked many questions about the great king, and about the Empire, and Tenochtitlan. He said his master, the governor of the universe, had sent him here. He gave much time, also, to explaining his religion. I might have understood him, uncle, but my ears were too full of the rattle of arms."

"What! Sat they at the table armed?" asked Maxtla.

"All of them ; even Malinche."

"That was not the worst," said Io' earnestly. "At the same table my lord Cuitlahua entertained a band of beggarly Tlascalan chiefs. Sooner should my tongue have been torn out!"

The bystanders made haste to approve the sentiment, and for a time it diverted the conversation. Meanwhile, at Hualpa's order, the goblets were refilled.

"Dares the noble Maxtla," he then asked, "tell what the king will do?"

"The question is very broad;" and the chief smiled. "What special information does my comrade seek?"

"Can you tell us when Malinche will enter Tenochtitlan?"

"Certainly. Xoli published that in the *tianguez* before the sun was up."

"To be sure," answered the Chalcan. "The lord Maxtla knows the news cost me a bowl of *pulque*."

There was much laughter, in which the chief joined. Then he said gravely,—

"The king has arranged everything. As advised by the gods, Malinche enters Tenochtitlan day after to-morrow. He will leave Iztapalapan at sunrise, and march to the causeway by the lake shore. Cuitlahua, with Cacama, the lord of Tecuba, and others of like importance, will meet him at Xoloc. The king will follow them in state. As to the procession, I will only say it were ill to lose the sight. Such splendour was never seen on the causeway."

Ordinarily the mention of such a prospect would have kindled the liveliest enthusiasm; for the Aztecs were lovers of spectacles, and never so glad as when the great green banner of the Empire was brought forth to shed its solemn beauty over the legions, and along the storied street of Tenochtitlan. Much, therefore, was Maxtla surprised at the coldness that fell upon the company.

"Ho, friends! One would think the reception not much to your liking," he said.

"We are the king's,—dust under his feet,—and it is not for us to murmur," said a sturdy cacique, first to break the disagreeable silence. "Yet our fathers gave their enemies bolts instead of banquets."

"Who may disobey the gods?" asked Maxtla.

The argument was not more sententious than unanswerable.

"Well, well!" said Hualpa. "I will get ready. Advise me, good chief: had I better take a canoe?"

"The procession will doubtless be better seen from the lake; but to hear what passes between the king and Malinche, you should be in the train. By the way, will the 'tzin be present?"

"As the king may order," replied Hualpa.

Maxtla threw back his look, and said with enthusiasm, real or affected, "Much would I like to see and hear him when the Tlascalans come flying their banners into the city! How he will flame with wrath!"

Then Hualpa considerately changed the direction of the discourse.

"Malinche will be a troublesome guest, if only from the

number of his following. Will he be lodged in one of the temples?"

"A temple, indeed!" and Maxtla laughed scornfully. "A temple would be fitter lodging for the gods of Mictlan! At Cempoalla, you recollect, the *teules* threw down the sacred gods, and butchered the *pabas* at the altars. Lest they should desecrate a holy house here, they are assigned to the old palace of Axaya'. To-morrow the *tamanes* will put it in order."

Io' then asked, "Is it known how long they will stay?"

Maxtla shrugged his shoulders, and drank his *pulque*.

"Hist!" whistled a cacique. "That is what the king would give half his kingdom to know!"

"And why?' asked the boy, reddening. "Is he not master? Does it not depend upon him?"

"It depends upon no other!" cried Maxtla, dashing his palm upon the table until the goblets danced. "By the holy gods! he has but to speak the word, and these guests will turn to victims!"

And Hualpa, surprised at the display of spirit, seconded the chief: "Brave words, O my lord Maxtla! They give us hope."

"He will treat them graciously," Maxtla continued, "because they come by his request; but when he tells them to depart, if they obey not,—if they obey not,—when was his vengeance other than a king's? Who dares say he cannot, by a word, end this visit?"

"No one!" cried Io'.

"Ay, no one! But the goblets are empty. See! Io', good prince,"—and Maxtla's voice changed at once,—"would another draught be too much for us? We drink slowly; one more, only one. And while we drink, we will forget Malinche."

"Would that were possible!" sighed the boy.

They sent up the goblets, and continued the session until daylight.

CHAPTER VII.

MONTEZUMA GOES TO MEET CORTES.

CAME the eighth of November, which no Spaniard, himself a Conquistador, can ever forget; that day Cortes entered Tenochtitlan.

The morning dawned over Anahuac as sometimes it dawns over

the Bay of Naples, bringing an azure haze in which the world seemed set afloat.

"Look you, uncles," said Montezuma, yet at breakfast, and speaking to his counsellors: "they are to go before me, my heralds; and as Malinche is the servant of a king, and used to courtly styles, I would not have them shame me. Admit them with the *nequen* off. As they will appear before him, let them come to me."

And thereupon four nobles were ushered in, full-armed, even to the shield. Their helms were of glittering silver; their *escaupils*, or tunics of quilted mail, were stained vivid green, and at the neck and borders sparkled with pearls; over their shoulders hung graceful mantles of *plumaje*, softer than cramoisy velvet; upon their breasts blazed decorations and military insignia; from wrist to elbow, and from knee to sandal-strap, their arms and legs were sheathed in scales of gold. And so, ready for peaceful show or mortal combat,—his heroes and ambassadors,—they bided the monarch's careful review.

"Health to you, my brothers! and to you, my children!" he said with satisfaction. "What of the morning? How looks the sun?"

"Like the beginning of a great day, O king, which we pray may end happily for you," replied Cuitlahua.

"It is the work of Huitzil'; doubt not! I have called you, O my children, to see how well my fame will be maintained. I wish to show Malinche a power and beauty such as he has never seen, unless he come from the Sun itself. Earth has but one valley of Anahuac, one city of Tenochtitlan: so he shall acknowledge. Have you directed his march as I ordered?"

And Cacama replied, "Through the towns and gardens, he is to follow the shore of the lake to the great causeway. By this time he is on the road."

Then Montezuma's face flushed; and, lifting his head as it were to look at objects afar off, he said aloud, yet like one talking to himself,—

"He is a lover of gold, and has been heard speak of cities and temples and armies; of his people numberless as the sands. Oh, if he be a man, with human weaknesses,—if he has hope, or folly of thought, to make him less than a god,—ere the night fall he shall give me reverence. Sign of my power shall he find at every step: cities built upon the waves; temples solid and high as the hills; the lake covered with canoes and gardens; people at his feet, like stalks in the meadow; my warriors; and Tenochtitlan, city of empire! And then, if he greet me with hope or thought of conquest,—then"— He shuddered.

"And then what?" said Cuitlahua, upon whom not a word had been lost.

The thinker, startled, looked at him coldly, saying,—

"I will take counsel of the gods."

And for a while he returned to his *choclatl*. When **next he** looked up and spoke, his face was bright and smiling.

"With **a** train, my children, **you** are to go in advance of me, **and** meet Malinche at Xoloc. Embrace him, speak to him honourably, return with him, **and** I will be at the first bridge outside the city. Cuitlahua and Cacama, be near when he steps forward to salute me. I will lean upon your shoulders. Get you gone now. Remember Anahuac!"

Shortly afterward a train of nobles, magnificently arrayed, issued from the palace, and marched down the great street leading to the Iztapalapan causeway. The housetops, the porticoes, even the roofs and towers of temples, and the pavements and cross streets, were already occupied by spectators. At the head of the procession strode the four heralds. Silently they marched, in silence the populace received them. The spectacle reminded **very** old men of the day the great Axaya' was borne in mournful pomp to Chapultepec. Once only there was a cheer, or, rather, a war-cry from the warriors looking down from **the** terraces of **a** temple. So the cortège passed from the city; so, through a continuous lane of men, they moved along the causeway; so they reached the gates of Xoloc, at which the two dykes, **one** from Iztapalapan, the other from Cojohuaca, intersected each other. There they halted, waiting for Cortes.

And while the train was on the road, out of one **of** the gates **of** the royal garden passed a palanquin, borne by four slaves in the king's livery. The occupants were the princesses Tula and Nenetzin, with Yeteve in attendance. In any of the towns of old Spain there would have been much remark upon the style of carriage, but no denial of their beauty, or that they were Spanish born. The elder sister was thoughtful and anxious; the younger kept constant look-out; the priestess, at their feet, wove the flowers with which they were profusely supplied into *ramilletes*, and threw them to the passers-by. The slaves, when in the great street, turned to the north.

"Blessed Lady!" cried Yeteve. "Was the like ever seen?"

"What is it?" asked Nenetzin.

"Such a crowd of people!"

Nenetzin looked out again, saying, "I wish I could see a noble **or** a warrior."

"That may not be," said Tula. "The nobles are gone to receive Malinche, the warriors are shut up in the temples."

"Why so?

"They may be needed."

"Ah! was it thought there is much danger? But look, see!" And Nenetzin drew back alarmed, yet laughing.

There was a crash outside, and a loud shout, and the palanquin stopped. Tula drew the curtain quickly, not knowing but that the peril requiring the soldiery was at hand. A vendor of little stone images,—*teotls*, or household gods,—unable to get out of the way, had been run upon by the slaves, and the pavement sprinkled with the broken heads and legs of the luckless *lares*. Aside, surveying the wreck, stood the pedlar, clad as usual with his class. In his girdle he carried a mallet, significant of his trade. He was uncommonly tall, and of a complexion darker than the lowest slaves. While the commiserate princess observed him, he raised his eyes; a moment he stood uncertain what to do; then he stepped to the palanquin, and from the folds of his tunic drew an image elaborately carved upon the face of an agate.

"The good princess," he said, bending so low as to hide his face, "did not laugh at the misfortune of her poor slave. She has a friendly heart, and is loved by every artisan in Tenochtitlan. This carving is of a sacred god, who will watch over and bless her, as I now do. If she will take it, I shall be glad."

"It is very valuable, and maybe you are not rich," she replied.

"Rich! When it is told that the princess Tula was pleased with a *teotl* of my carving, I shall have patrons without end. And if it were not so, the recollection will make me rich enough. Will she please me so much?"

She took from her finger a ring set with a jewel that, in any city of Europe, would have bought fifty such cameos, and handed it to him.

"Certainly; but take this from me. I warrant you are a gentle artist."

The pedlar took the gift, and kissed the pavement, and, after the palanquin was gone, picked up such of his wares as were uninjured, and went his way well pleased.

At the gate of the temple of Huitzil' the three alighted, and made their way to the *azoteas*. The lofty place was occupied by pabas and citizens, yet a sunshade of gaudy feather-work was pitched for them close by the eastern verge, overlooking the palace of Axaya', and commanding the street up which the array was to come. In the area below, encompassed by the *Coatapantli*, or Wall of Serpents, ten thousand warriors were closely ranked, ready to march at beat of the great drum hanging in the tower. Thus, comfortably situated, the daughters of the king awaited the strangers.

When Montezuma started to meet his guests, the morning was far advanced. A vast audience, in front of his palace, waited to catch a view of his person. Of his policy the mass knew but the little gleaned from a thousand rumours,—enough to fill them with forebodings of evil. Was he going out as king **or** slave? At last he came, looking their ideal of a child of the Sun, and ready for the scrutiny. Standing in the portal, he received their homage ; **not one** but kissed the ground before him.

He stepped **out, and the sun, as** if acknowledging his **presence,** seemed to pour **a double** glory about him. In the time **of** despair and overthrow **that** came, alas ! too soon, those who **saw him,** in that moment **of** pride, spread his arms in general **benediction,** remembered his princeliness, and spoke **of** him **ever after in the** language of poetry. The *tilmatli,* looped at **the** throat, **and** falling gracefully from his shoulders, was beaded **with** jewels and precious stones ; the long, dark-green plumes in his *panache* drooped with pearls ; his sash was in keeping with the mantle ; **the** thongs of his sandals were edged with gold, and the soles were entirely of gold. Upon his breast, relieved against the rich embroidery of his tunic, symbols of the military orders of the realm literally blazed with gems.

About the royal palanquin, in front of the portal, **bareheaded** and barefooted, stood **its** complement of bearers, lords **of the first** rank, proud of the service. Between the carriage **and the** doorway a carpet of white cloth was stretched : common **dust might** not soil his feet. As he stepped out, he was saluted by a **roar of** attabals and conch-shells. The music warmed his blood ; **the** homage was agreeable to him,—was to his soul what incense is **to** the gods. He gazed proudly around, and **it was** easy to see how much he was in love with his own royalty.

Taking his place in the palanquin, the cortège moved slowly **down** the street. In advance walked stately caciques, with wands, clearing the way. The carriers of the canopy, which was separate from the carriage, followed next ; and behind them, reverently, and with downcast faces, marched an escort of armed lords indescribably splendid.

The street traversed was the same Malinche was to traverse. Often and again did **the** subtle monarch look to paves and housetops, and to the canals and temples. Well he knew the cunning guest would sweep them all, searching for evidences of his power ; that nothing would escape examination ; that the myriads of spectators, the extent of the city, its position in the lake, and thousands of things not to be written, would find places in the calculation inevitable if the visit were with other than peaceful intent.

At a palace near the edge of the city the escort halted to abide the coming.

Soon, from the lake, a sound of music was heard, more plaintive than that of the conchs.

"They are coming, they are coming! The *teules* are coming!" shouted the people; and every heart, even the king's, beat quicker. Up the street the cry passed, like a hurly gust of wind.

CHAPTER VIII.

THE ENTRY.

It is hardly worth while to eulogize the Christians who took part in Cortes' crusade. History has assumed their commemoration. I may say, however, they were men who had acquired fitness for the task by service in almost every clime. Some had tilted with the Moor under the walls of Granada; some had fought the Islamite on the blue Danube; some had performed the first Atlantic voyage with Columbus; all of them had hunted the Carib in the glades of Hispaniola. It is not enough to describe them as fortune-hunters, credulous, imaginative, tireless; neither is it enough to write them soldiers, bold, skilful, confident, cruel to enemies, gentle to each other. They were characters of the age in which they lived, unseen before, unseen since; knights-errant, who believed in hippogriff and dragon, but sought them only in lands of gold; missionaries, who complacently broke the body of the converted that Christ might the sooner receive his soul; palmers of pike and shield, who, in care of the Virgin, followed the morning round the world, assured that Heaven stooped lowest over the most profitable plantations.

The wonders of the way from the coast to Iztapalapan had so beguiled the little host that they took but partial account of its dangers. When, this morning, they stepped upon the causeway, and began the march out into the lake, a sense of insecurity fell upon them, like the shadow of a cloud; back to the land they looked, as to a friend from whom they might be parting for ever; and as they proceeded, and the water spread around them, wider, deeper, and up-bearing denser multitudes of people, the enterprise suddenly grew in proportions, and challenged their self-sufficiency. Yet, as I have heard them confess, they did not wake to a perfect comprehension of their situation, and its dangers and difficulties, until they passed the gates of Xoloc: then Tenoch-

titlan **shone** upon them,—a city of enchantment! And then each
one felt that to advance was like marching in the face of death,
at the same time each one saw that there was no hope except in
advance. Every hand grasped closer the weapon with which it
was armed, while the ranks were intuitively closed. What most
impressed them, they said, was the silence of the people; a word,
a shout, a curse, or a battle-cry would have been a relief from the
fears and fancies that beset them; as it was, though in the midst
of myriad life, they heard only their own tramp, or the clang
and rattle of their own arms. As if aware of the influence, and
fearful of its effect upon his weaker followers, Cortes spoke to the
musicians, and trumpet and clarion burst into a strain **which,**
with beat of **drum** and clash of cymbal, was heard in **the city.**

"*Ola,* **Sandoval,** Alvarado! Here, at my right **and left!**"
cried Cortes.

They spurred forward at the call.

"Out of the way, dog!" shouted Sandoval, thrusting **a** naked
tamane over the edge of the dyke with the butt of his lance.

"By my conscience, señores," Cortes said, "I think true
Christian in a land of unbelievers never beheld city like this!
If **it be** wrong to the royal good knight, Richard of England, or
that valorous captain, the Flemish Duke Godfrey, may the saints
pardon me; but I daresay the walled towns they took—and, for
that matter, I care not if you number Antioch and the Holy City
of the Sepulchre among them—were not to be put in comparison
with this infidel stronghold."

And as they ride, listening to his comments, let me bring **them**
particularly to view.

They were in full armour, except that Alvarado's squire carried
his helmet for him. In preparation for the entry, their skilful
furbishers had well renewed the original lustre of helm, gorget,
breastplate, glaive, greave, and shield. The plumes in their
crests, like the scarfs across their breasts, had been carefully
preserved for such ceremonies. At the saddle-bows hung heavy
hammers, better known as battle-axes. Rested upon the iron
shoe, and balanced in the right hand, each carried a lance, to
which, as the occasion was peaceful, a silken pennon was
attached. The horses, opportunely rested in Iztapalapan, and
glistening **in** mail, trod the causeway as if conscious of the terror
they inspired.

Cortes, between his favourite captains, rode with lifted visor,
smiling and confident. His complexion was bloodless and ashy,
a singularity the more noticeable on account of his thin black
beard. The lower lip was seamed with a scar. He was of fine
stature, broad-shouldered and thin, but strong, active, and
enduring. His skill in all manner of martial exercises was

extraordinary. He conversed in Latin, composed poetry, wrote unexceptionable prose, and, except when in passion, spoke gravely and with well-turned periods.[1] In argument he was both dogmatic and convincing, and especially artful in addressing soldiers, of whom, by constitution, mind, will, and courage, he was a natural leader. Now, gay and assured, he managed his steed with as little concern and talked carelessly as a knight returning victorious from some joyous passage of arms.

Gonzalo de Sandoval, not twenty-three years of age, was better-looking, having a larger frame and fuller face. His beard was auburn, and curled agreeably to the prevalent fashion. Next to his knightly honour, he loved his beautiful chestnut horse, Motilla.[2]

Handsomest man of the party, however, was Don Pedro de Alvarado. Generous as a brother to a Christian, he hated a heathen with the fervour of a crusader. And now, in scorn of Aztecan treachery, he was riding unhelmed, his locks, long and yellow, flowing freely over his shoulders. His face was fair as a gentlewoman's, and neither sun nor weather could alter it. Except in battle, his countenance expressed the friendliest disposition. He cultivated his beard assiduously, training it to fall in ringlets upon his breast,—and there was reason for the weakness, if such it was; yellow as gold, with the help of his fair face and clear blue eyes, it gave him a peculiar expression of sunniness, from which the Aztecs called him *Tonatiah*, child of the Sun.[3]

And over what a following of cavaliers the leader looked when, turning in his saddle, he now and then glanced down the column,—Christobal de Oli, Juan Velasquez de Leon, Francisco de Montejo, Luis Marin, Andreas de Tapia, Alonzo de Avila, Francisco de Lugo, the Manjarezes, Andreas and Gregorio, Diego de Ordas, Francisco de Morla, Christobal de Olea, Gonzalo de Dominguez, Rodriques Magarino, Alonzo Hernandez Carrero,—most of them gentlemen of the class who knew the songs of Rodrigo, and the stories of Amadis and the Paladins!

And much shame would there be to me if I omitted mention of two others,—Bernal Diaz del Castillo, who, after the conquest, became its faithful historian, and Father Bartolomé de Olmedo,[4] sweet singer, good man, and devoted servant of God, the first to whisper the names of Christ and the Holy Mother in the ear of New Spain. In the column behind the cavaliers, with his assistant, Juan de las Varillas, he rode bareheaded, and clad simply in a black serge gown. The tinkle of the little silver bell, which the soldiers, in token of love, had tied to the neck of

---

[1] Bernal Diaz, *Hist. of the Conq. of Mexico.*
[2] *Ib.*   *Ib.*   [4] *Ib.*

his mule, sounded, amid the harsher notes of war, like a gentle reminder of shepherds and grazing flocks in peaceful pastures near Old World homes.

After the holy men, in care of a chosen guard of honour, the flag of Spain was carried ; and then came the artillery, drawn by slaves ; next, in close order, followed the crossbowmen and arquebusiers, the latter with their matches lighted. Rearward still, in savage pomp and pride, strode the two thousand Tlascalans, first of their race to bear shield and fly banner along the causeway into Tenochtitlan. And so the Christians, in order of battle, but scarcely four hundred strong, marched into a capital of full three hundred thousand inhabitants, swollen by the innumerable multitudes of the valley.

As they drew nigh the city, the cavaliers became silent and thoughtful. With astonishment, which none of them sought to conceal, they gazed at the white walls and crowded houses, and, with sharpened visions, traced against the sky the outlines of temples and temple-towers, more numerous than those of papal Rome. Well they knew that the story of what they saw so magnificently before them would be received with incredulity in all the courts of Christendom. Indeed, some of the humbler soldiers marched convinced that all they beheld was a magical delusion. Not so Cortes.

"Ride on, gentlemen, ride on !" he said. "There is a question I would ask of a good man behind us. I will rejoin you shortly."

From the artillerists he singled a soldier.

"Martin Lopez ! Martin Lopez !"

The man came to him.

"Martin, look out on this lake. Beareth it resemblance to the blue bays on the southern shore of old Spain ? As thou art a crafty sailor, comrade mine, look carefully."

Lopez raised his motion, and, leaning on his pike, glanced over the expanse.

"Señor, the water is fair enough, and, for that, looks like bayous I have seen without coming so far ; but I doubt if a two-decker could float on it long enough for Father Olmedo to say mass for our souls in peril."

"Peril ! Plague take thee, man ! Before the hour of vespers, by the Blessed Lady, whose image thou wearest, this lake, yon city, its master, and all thou seest here, not excepting the common spawn of idolatry at our feet, shall be the property of our sovereign lord. But, Martin Lopez, thou hast hauled sail and tacked ship in less room than this. What sayest thou to sailing a brigantine here ?"

The sailor's spirit rose ; he looked over the lake again.

"It might be done ! It might be done !"

"Then, by my conscience, it shall be! Confess thyself an admiral to-night."

And Cortes rode to the front. Conquest might not be, he saw, without vessels; and, true to his promise, it came to pass that Lopez sailed, not one, but a fleet of brigantines on the gentle waters.

When the Christians were come to the first bridge outside the walls, their attention was suddenly drawn from the city. Down the street came Montezuma and his retinue. Curious as they were to see the arch-infidel, the soldiers kept their ranks; but Cortes, taking with him the cavaliers, advanced to meet the monarch. When the palanquin stopped, the Spaniards dismounted. About the same time an Indian woman, of comely features, came forward.

"Stay thou here, Marina," said Cortes. "I will embrace the heathen, then call thee to speak to him."

"*Jésu!*" cried Alvarado. "There is gold enough on his litter to furnish a cathedral."

"Take thou the gold, señor; I choose the jewels on his mantle," said De Ordas.

"By my patron saint of excellent memory!" said Sandoval, lisping his words, "I think, for noble cavaliers, ye are easily content. Take the jewels and the gold; but give me that train of stalwart dogs, and a plantation worthy of my degree here by Tezcuco."

So the captains talked.

Meantime, the cotton cloth was stretched along the dyke. Then on land and sea a hush prevailed.

Montezuma came forward, supported by the lords Cuitlahua and Cacama. Cortes met him half-way. When face to face, they paused, and looked at each other. Alas for the Aztec then! In the mailed stranger he beheld a visitant from the Sun,—a god! The Spaniard saw, wrapped in the rich vestments, only a man,— a king, yet a heathen! He opened his arms; Montezuma stirred not. Cuitlahua uttered a cry to Huitzil', and caught one of the extended arms. Long did Cortes keep in mind the cacique's look at that moment; long did he remember the dark-brown face, swollen with indignation and horror. Alvarado laid his hand on his sword.

"Peace, Don Pedro!" said Cortes. "The knave knows nothing of respectable customs. Instead of taking to thy sword, bless the Virgin that a Christian knight hath been saved the sin of embracing an unbeliever. Call Marina."

The woman came, and stood by the Spaniard, and in a sweet voice interpreted the speeches. The monarch expressed delight at seeing his visitors, and welcomed them to Tenochtitlan; his manner and courteous words won even Alvarado. Cortes answered, acknowledging surprise at the beauty and extent of the city; and, in token of his gratification at being at last before a king so rich and powerful, begged him to accept a present. Into the royal hand he then placed a string of precious stones, variously coloured, and strongly perfumed with musk. Thereupon the ceremony ended. Two of the princes were left to conduct the strangers to their quarters. Resuming his palanquin, Montezuma himself led the procession as far as his own palace.

And Cortes swung himself into the saddle. "Let the trumpets sound. Forward!"

Again the music,—again the advance; then the pageant passed from the causeway and lake into the expectant city.

Theretofore, the Christians had been silent from discipline, now they were silent from wonder. Even Cortes held his peace. They had seen the irregular towns of Tlascala, and the pretentious beauty of Cholula, and Iztapalapan, in whose streets the lake contended with the land for mastery, yet were they unprepared for Tenochtitlan. Here, it was plain, wealth and power and time and labour, under the presidency of genius, had wrought their perfect works, everywhere visible: under foot, a sounding bridge, or a broad paved way, dustless, and unworn by wheel or hoof; on the right and left, airy windows, figured portals, jutting balconies, embattled cornices, porticoes with columns of sculptured marble, and here a palace, there a temple; overhead pyramidal heights crowned with towers and smoking braziers, or lower roofs, from which, as from hanging gardens, floated waftures sweet as the perfumed airs of the Indian isles; and everywhere, looking up from the canals, down from the porticoes, houses, and pyramids, and out of the doors and windows, crowding the pavement, clinging to the walls,—everywhere the PEOPLE! After ages of decay I know it has been otherwise; but I also know that conquerors have generally found the builders of a great state able and willing to defend it.

"St. James absolve me, señor! but I like not the coldness of these dogs," said Monjarez to Avila.

"Nor I," was the reply. "Seest thou the women on yon balcony? I would give my helmet full of ducats, if they would but once cry, '*Viva España!*'"

"Nay, that would I if they would but wave a scarf."

The progress of the pageant was necessarily slow; but at last the spectators on the temple of Huitzil' heard its music; at last the daughters of the king beheld it in the street below them.

"Gods of my fathers!" thought Tula, awed and trembling; "what manner of beings are these?"

And the cross-bowmen and arquebusiers, their weapons and

N

glittering iron caps, the guns, and slaves that dragged them, even the flag of Spain,—objects of mighty interest to others,— drew from Nenetzin but a passing glance. Very beautiful to her, however, were the cavaliers, insomuch that she cared only for their gay pennons, their shields, their plumes nodding bravely above their helms, their armour of strange metal, on which the sun seemed to play with a fiery love, and their steeds, creatures tamed for the service of gods. Suddenly her eyes fixed, her heart stopped : pointing to where the good Captain Alvarado rode, scanning, with upturned face, the great pile, "O Tula, Tula !" she cried. "See ! there goes the blue-eyed warrior of my dream !"

But it happened that Tula was at the moment too much occupied to listen or look. The handsome vendor of images, standing near the royal party, had attracted the attention of Yeteve, the priestess.

"The noble Tula is unhappy. She is thinking of"—

A glance checked the name.

Then Yeteve whispered, "Look at the image-maker."

The prompting was not to be resisted. She looked, and recognised Guatamozin. Not that only ; through his low disguise, in his attitude, his eyes bright with angry fire, she discerned his spirit, its pride and heroism. Not for her was it to dispute the justice of his banishment. Love scorned the argument. There he stood, the man for the time ; strong-armed, stronger-hearted, prince by birth, king by nature, watching afar off a scene in which valour and genius entitled him to prominence. Then there were tears for him, and a love higher, if not purer, than ever.

Suddenly he leaned over the verge, and shouted, "Al-a-lala ! Al-a-lala !" and with such energy that he was heard in the street below. Tula looked down, and saw the cause of the excitement,—the Tlascalans were marching by ! Again his cry, the same with which he had so often led his countrymen to battle. No one took it up. The companies inside the sacred wall turned their faces, and stared at him in dull wonder. And he covered his eyes with his hands, while every thought was a fierce invective. Little he then knew how soon, and how splendidly, they were to purchase his forgiveness !

When the Tlascalans were gone, he dropped his hands, and found the—mallet ! So it was the artisan, the image-maker, not the 'tzin, who had failed to wake the army to war ! He turned quickly, and took his way through the crowd, and disappeared ; and none but Tula and Yeteve ever knew that, from the *teocallis*, Guatamozin had witnessed the entry of the *teules*.

And so poor Nenetzin had been left to follow the warrior of her dream ; the shock and the pleasure were hers alone.

The palace of Axaya' faced the temple of Huitzil' on the west. In one of the halls Montezuma received Cortes and the cavaliers ; and all their lives they recollected his gentleness, courtesy, and unaffected royalty in that ceremony. Putting a golden collar around the neck of his chief guest, he said, " This palace belongs to you, Malinche, and to your brethren. Rest after your fatigues ; you have much need to do **so.** In a little while I **will** come again."

And when he was gone, straightway the guest **so** honoured proceeded to change the palace into a fort. Along **the** massive walls that encircled it he stationed sentinels ; at every gate planted cannon ; and, like the enemy he was, he began, and from that time enforced, a discipline sterner than before.

The rest of the day the citizens, from the top of the temple, kept incessant watch upon the palace. When the shades of evening were collecting over the city, and the thousands, grouped along the streets, were whispering of the incidents they had seen, **a** thunderous report broke the solemn stillness ; and they looked at each other, and trembled, and called the evening guns of Cortes " Voices of the Gods."

BOOK FIVE

CHAPTER I.

PUBLIC OPINION.

GUATAMOZIN, accompanied by Hualpa, left the city a little after nightfall. Impressed, doubtless, by the great event of the day, the two journeyed in silence, until so far out that the fires of the capital faded into a rosy tint low on the horizon.

Then the 'tzin said, "I am tired, body and spirit; yet must I go back to Tenochtitlan."

"To-night?" Hualpa asked.

"To-night; and I need help."

"What I can, O 'tzin, that will I."

"You are weary also."

"I could follow a wounded deer till dawn, if you so wished."

"It is well."

After a while the 'tzin again spoke.

"To-day I have unlearned all the lessons of my youth. The faith I thought part of my life is not; I have seen the great king conquered without a blow!"

There was a sigh such as only shame can wring from a strong man.

"At the Chalcan's, where the many discontented meet to-night, there will be," he resumed, "much talk of war without the king. Such conferences are criminal; and yet there shall be war."

He spoke with emphasis.

"In my exile without a cause," he next said, "I have learned to distinguish between the king and country. I have even reflected upon conditions when the choosing between them may become a duty. Far be they hence! but when they come, Anahuac shall have her son. To accomplish their purpose, the lords in the city rely upon their united power, which is nothing; with the signet in his hand, Maxtla alone could disperse their

forces. There is that, however, by which what they seek can be
wrought rightfully,—something under the throne, not above it,
where they are looking, and only the gods are,—a power known
to every ruler as his servant when wisely cared for, and his
master when disregarded ; public opinion we call it, meaning the
judgment and will of the many. In this garb of artisan, I have
been with the people all day, and for a purpose higher than sight
of what I abhorred. I talked with them. I know them. In
the march from Xoloc there was not a shout. In the awful
silence, what of welcome was there? Honour to the people !
Before they are conquered the lake will wear a red not of the
sun ! Imagine them of one mind, and zealous for war : how
long until the army catches the sentiment ? Imagine the streets
and temples resounding with a constant cry, 'Death to the
strangers !' how long until the king yields to the clamour ? O
comrade, that would be the lawful triumph of public opinion ;
and so, I say, war shall be."

After that the 'tzin remained sunk in thought until the canoe
touched the landing at his garden. Leaving the boatmen there,
he proceeded, with Hualpa, to the palace. In his study, he said,
"You have seen the head of the stranger whom I slew at
Nauhtlan. I have another trophy. Come with me."

Providing himself with a lamp, he led the way to what seemed
a kind of workshop. Upon the walls, mixed with strange
banners, hung all kinds of Aztec armour ; a bench stood by one
of the windows, covered with tools ; on the floor lay bows,
arrows, and lances, of such fashion as to betray the experi-
mentalist. The corners were decorated, if the term may be used,
with effigies of warriors preserved by the process peculiar to the
people. In the centre of the room, a superior attraction to Hualpa,
stood a horse, which had been subjected to the same process, but
was so lifelike now that he could hardly think it dead. The
posture chosen for the animal was that of partial repose, its head
erect, its ears thrown sharply forward, its nostrils distended, the
forefeet firmly planted ; so it had, in life, often stood watching
the approach or disappearance of its comrades. The housings
were upon it precisely as when taken from the field.

"I promised there should be war," the 'tzin said, when he
supposed Hualpa's wonder spent, "and that the people should
bring it about. Now I say, that the opinion I rely upon would
ripen to-morrow, were there not a thick cloud about it. The
faith that Malinche and his followers are *teules* has spread from
the palace throughout the valley. Unless it be dispelled, Anahuac
must remain the prey of the spoiler. Mualox, the keeper of the
old Cû of Quetzal', taught me long ago, that in the common mind
mystery can only be assailed by mystery ; and that, O comrade,
is what I now propose. This nameless thing here belonged to the

stranger **whom I** slew at Nauhtlan. Come closer, and lay **your**
hand upon it ; mount it, and you may know how its master felt
the day he rode it to death. There is his lance, there his shield,
here his helm and whole array ; take them, and learn what little
is required to make a god of a man."

For a moment he busied himself getting the property of the
unfortunate Christian together ; then he stopped before the
Tihuancan, saying, "Let others choose their parts, O comrade.
All a warrior may do, that **will** I. If the Empire must die, it
shall be like a fighting man,—a hero's song for future minstrels.
Help me now. We will take the trophy to the city, and set it
up in the *tianguez* along with the shield, arms, and armour.
The rotting head in the summer-house **we** will fix near **by on**
the lance. To-morrow, when the traders **open** their stalls, **and**
the thousands so shamelessly sold come **back** to **their** barter-
ing and business, a mystery shall **meet them** which no man can
look upon and afterwards believe **Malinche** a god. I see the
scene,—the rush of the people, their surprise, their pointing
fingers. I hear the eager questions, ' What are they ?' 'Whence
came they ?' I hear the ready answer, 'Death to the strangers !'
Then, O comrade, will begin the Opinion, by force of which,
the gods willing, we shall yet hear the drum of Huitzil'. Lay
hold now, and let us to the canoe with the trophies."

"If it be heavy as it seems, good 'tzin," said Hualpa, stooping
to the wooden slab which served **as** the base of the effigy, "I
fear we shall be overtasked."

"It is not heavy ; two children could carry it. A **word** more
before we proceed. In what I propose there is a peril aside from
the patrols in **the** *tianguez.* Malinche will hear of "—

Hualpa **laughed.** "Was ever a victim sacrificed before he **was**
caught ?"

"Hear further," said the 'tzin gravely. "I took the king to the
summer-house, and showed him the head, which he will recognise.
Your heart as well as mine may pay the forfeit. Consider."

"Lay hold, O 'tzin ! Did you not but now call me comrade ?
Lay hold !"

Thereupon they carried the once good steed out to the landing. Then the 'tzin went to the kiosk for the Spaniard's
head, while Hualpa returned to the palace for the arms and
equipments. The head, wrapped in a cloth, was dropped in the
bow of the boat, and the horse and trappings carried on board.
Trusting in the gods, the *voyageurs* pushed off, **and were** landed,
without interruption, near the great *tianguez.*

CHAPTER II.

A MESSAGE FROM THE GODS.

"It is done!" said the 'tzin in a whisper. "It is done! One more service, O comrade, if"—

"Do not spare me, good 'tzin. I am happiest when serving you."

"Then stay in the city to-night, and be here early after the discovery. Take part with the crowd, and, if opportunity offer, direct it. I must return to my exile. Report when all is over. The gods keep you! Farewell."

Hualpa, familiar with the square, went to the portico of the Chalcan ; and as the lamps were out, and the curtains of the door drawn for the night, with the privilege of an *habitué* he stretched himself upon one of the lounges, and, lulled by the fountain, fell asleep.

A shout awoke him. He looked out to see the day breaking in gloom. The old sky of blue, in which the summer had so long and lovingly nestled, was turned to lead ; the smoke seemed to have fallen from the temples, and, burdening the atmosphere, was driving along slowly and heavily, like something belonging to the vanishing night. Another cry, louder than the first ; then the door, or rather the screen, behind him was opened, and the Chalcan himself came forth.

"Ah, son of my friend!— Hark! Some maudlin fellow hallooes. The fool would like to end his sleep, hard enough out there, in the temple. But you,—where have you been ?"

"Here, good Xoli, on this lounge."

"The night? Ah! the *pulque* was too much for you. For your father's sake, boy, I give you advice : to be perfectly happy in Tenochtitlan, it is necessary to remember, first, how the judges punish drunkenness ; next, that there is no pure liquor in the city except in the king's jars, and— There, the shout again ! two of them ! a third !"

And the broker also looked out of the portico.

"Holy gods, what a smoke! There go some sober citizens, neighbours of mine,—and running. Something of interest ! Come, Hualpa, let us go also. The times are wonderful. You know there are gods in Tenochtitlan besides those we worship. Come !"

"I am hungry."

"I will feed you to bursting when we get back. Come on."

As they left the portico, people were hastening to the centre of the square, where the outcry was now continuous and growing.

"Room for the Chalcan!" said a citizen already on the ground. "Let him see what is here fallen from the clouds."

Great was the astonishment of the broker when his eyes first rested on the stately figure of the horse, and the terrible head on the lance above it. Hualpa affected the same feeling, but, having a part to play, shouted, as in alarm,—

"It is one of the fighting beasts of Malinche! **Beware, O** citizens! Your lives may be in danger."

The crowd, easily persuaded, fell back.

"Let us get arms!" shouted **one.**

"Arms! Get arms!" then rose in full chorus.

Hualpa ventured nearer, and cried out, "The beast is dead!"

"Keep off, boy!" said Xoli, himself at **a** respectable distance. "Trust it not ; such things do not die."

Never speech more opportune for the Tihuancan.

"Be it of the earth or Sun, I tell you, friends, it is dead!" he replied more loudly. "Who knows but that the holy Huitzil' has set it up here to be seen of all of us, that we may know Malinche **is** not a god. Is there one among you who has a javelin?"

A weapon was passed **to him** over the heads of the fast increasing crowd.

"Stand aside! I will see."

Without more ado, the adventurer thrust deep **in** the horse's flank. Those directly about held their breath from fear ; and when the brute stirred not, they looked at each other, not knowing what to say. That it was dead, was past doubt.

"Who will gainsay me now?" continued Hualpa. **"It is** dead, and so is he to whom yon head belonged. Gods **fall not** so low."

It was one of those moments when simple minds are easily converted to any belief.

"Gods they are not," said a voice in the throng ; "but whence came they?"

"And who put them here?" asked another.

Hualpa answered swiftly,—

"Well said! The gods speak not directly to those whom they would admonish or favour. And if this be the handiwork of Huitzil',—and what more likely?—should we not inquire if it have a meaning? It may be **a** message. Is there a reader of pictures among you, friends?"

"Here is one!"

"Let him come! Make way for him!"

A citizen, from his dress a merchant, was pushed forward.

"What experience have you?"

"I studied in the *calmecac!"* [1]

The man raised his eyes to the head on the lance, and they became transfixed with horror.

"Look, then, to what we have here, and, saying it is a message from the holy Huitzil', read it for us. Speak out, that all may hear."

The citizen was incapable of speech, and the people cried out, "He is a shame to the heroic god! Off with him, off with him!"

But Hualpa interfered. "No. He still believes Malinche a god. Let him alone! I can use him." Then he spoke to the merchant. "Hear me, my friend, and I will read. If I err, stop me."

"Read, read!" went up on all sides.

Hualpa turned to the group as if studying it. Around him fell the silence of keen expectancy. •

"Thus writes Huitzil', greatest of gods, to the children of Anahuac, greatest of peoples!"—so Hualpa began. "'The strangers in Tenochtitlan are my enemies, and yours, O people. They come to overthrow my altars, and make you a nation of slaves. You have sacrificed and prayed to me, and now I say to you, Arise! Take arms before it is too late. Malinche and his followers are but men. Strike them, and they will die. To convince you that they are not gods, lo! here is one of them dead. So, I say, slay them, and everything that owns them master, even the beasts they ride!'—Ho, friend, is not that correct?"

"So I would have read," said the merchant.

"Praised be Huitzil'!" cried Hualpa devoutly.

"Live the good god of our fathers! Death to the strangers!" answered the people.

And amid the stir and hum of many voices, the comrade of the 'tzin, listening, heard his words repeated, and passed from man to man; so that he knew his mission done, and that by noon the story of the effigy would be common throughout the city, and in flight over the valley, with his exposition of its meaning accepted and beyond counteraction.

After a while the Chalcan caught his arm, saying, "The smell is dreadful to a cultivated nose sharpened by an empty stomach. Snuff for one, breakfast for the other. Let us go."

Hualpa followed him.

"Who is he? who is he?" asked the bystanders eagerly.

"Him! Not know him! It is the brave lad who slew the tiger and saved the king's life."

And the answer was to the exposition like an illuminated seal to a royal writ.

Morning advanced, curtained with clouds; and, as the account of the spectacle flew, the multitude in the *tianguez* increased, until there was not room left for business. All who caught the news hurried to see the sight, and for themselves read the miraculous message of Huitzil'. The clamour of tongues the while was like the clamour of waves, and not singularly; for thus was fought the first great battle,—the battle of the mysteries,—and with this result: if a believer in **the** divinity of Cortes looked once at the rotting head on the lance, he went away of the 'tzin's opinion, impatient for war.

About noon a **party of Spaniards,** footmen, armed, and out inspecting the **city,** entered **the** square. The multitude daunted them not the least. Talking, sometimes laughing, they sauntered along, **peering into the** open booths and stalls, and watching **with** practised **eyes for** gold.

"Holy mass!" exclaimed one of them, **stopping.** "The heathen are **at** sacrifice."

"Sacrifice, saidst thou? This is their market-place."

"That as thou wilt. I tell thee they have been at worship. **My** eyes are not dim as my mother's, who was past fifty the day **we** sailed from Cuba,—may the saints preserve her! If they were, yet could I swear that yonder hangs the head of a victim."

Over the restless crowd they looked at the ghastly object, eager yet uncertain.

"Now I bethink me, the poor wretch who hath suffered the death may have been one of the half-assoilzied sons of Tlascala. If we are in a stronghold of **enemies,** as I have concluded from the wicked, Carib looks of **these savages, Heaven** and St. James defend us! We are a score **with weapons; in the** Mother's **name, let us to** the bloody sign!"

The unarmed mass into which, without further consideration, they plunged, was probably awed by the effrontery of the **move-ment,** for the leader had not once occasion to shorten his advancing step. Halted before the spectacle, they looked first at the horse, then **at** the head. Remembrance was faithful: in one, they recognised the remains of **a** comrade; in the other, his property.

"Arguella, Arguella! Good captain! Santa Maria!" burst from them.

As they gazed, tears of pity and rage filled their eyes, and coursed down their bronzed cheeks.

"Peace!" said the sterner fellow, at whose suggestion they had come. "Are ye soldiers, or whimpering women? Do as I bid! Save your tears for Father Bartolomé to mix with masses for the poor fellow's soul. Look to the infidels! I will take down the head."

He lowered the lance, and took off the loathsome object.

"We will carry it to the Señor Hernan. It shall have burial, and masses, and a cross. Hands to the horse **now!** Arguella loved it well; many a day I have **seen** him **comb** its mane kindly **as** if it had been the locks of **his sweetheart.** Nay, it is too unwieldy. Let it stand, but take the armour. Hug the good sword close. Heaven willing, it shall redden in the carcases of some of these hounds of hell. Are we ready? To quarters, then! As we go, mark the unbelievers, and cleave the first that lifts a hand or bars the way."

They reached the old palace in safety. Needless to depict the grief and rage of the Christians at sight of the countenance of the unfortunate Arguella.

CHAPTER III.

HOW ILLS OF STATE BECOME ILLS OF SOCIETY.

By this time, Io' the prince had acquired somewhat of the importance of a man. Thanks to Hualpa and his own industry, he could hurl a javelin, strike stoutly with a *maquahuitl*, and boast of skill with the bow. As well he might, he smiled at thought of the maternal care, and from his sisters demanded a treatment due to one of his accomplishments and dignity.

The day after the incidents narrated in the preceding chapter, he entered Tula's apartment, and requested her to dismiss her attendants.

"Sit down, my brother," she said when they were alone. "You look vexed. What has happened?"

Going to a table close by, he commenced despoiling a vase of flowers. She repeated the question.

"I am glad," he answered, "to find one whom the coming of the strangers has not changed."

"What now?"

"I have been again and again to see Nenetzin, but she refuses me. Is she sick?"

"Not that I know."

"Then why is she so provoking?"

"My brother, you know not what it is for a girl to find her lover. Nenetzin has found hers."

"It is to talk about him I want to see her."

"You know him! How? when?"

"Do I not see him every day? Is he not my comrade?"

"Your comrade!"

"The lord Hualpa. He came to you once with a message from the 'tzin."

To a woman, the most interesting stories are those that have to do with the gentle passion. Seeing his mistake, she encouraged it.

"Yes, I remember him. He is both brave and handsome."

Io' left the vase, and came to her side. His curiosity was piqued.

"How came you to know he was her **lover?** **He** would hardly confess it to me."

"Yet he did tell you?" she answered evasively.

"Yes. One day, tired of practising with our slings, we lay down in the shade of a ceiba-tree. We talked about what I should do when I became a man. I should be a warrior, and command armies, and conquer Tlascala; he should be a warrior also, and in my command. That should not be, I told him, **as** he would always be the most skilful. He laughed, but not **as** merrily as I have heard him. Then he said, 'There are many things you will have learned by that time; such as what rank is, and especially what it is to be of the king's blood.' I asked him why he spoke so. He said he would tell me some day, but not then. And I thought of the time we went to meet you at the *chinampa*, and of how he gave you a vase from the 'tzin, and one to Nenetzin from himself. Then I thought I understood him, but insisted on his telling. He put me off; at last he said he was **a** foolish fellow, and, in his lonely haunts in Tihuanco, had acquired a habit of dreaming, which was not broken as he would like. He had first seen Nenetzin at the Quetzal' combat, **and** thought her handsomer than any one he had ever met. The day on the lake he ventured to speak to her; she smiled, and **took** his gift; and since that he had not been strong enough to **quit** thinking about her. It was great folly, he said. 'Why so?' I **asked** him. He hid his face in the grass, and answered, '**I am the son** of a merchant; she is of the king's blood, and would mock me.' 'But,' said I, 'you are now noble, and owner of a palace.' He raised his head, and looked at me; had she been there, she would **not** have mocked him. 'Ah,' he said, 'if I could only get her to cease thinking of me as the trader's son!' 'Now you are foolish,' I told him. 'Did you not win your rank by fighting? Why not fight for'—Nenetzin, I was about to say, but he sprang up and ran off, and it was long before I could get him to speak of her again. The other day, however, he consented to let me try and find out what she thought of him. To-morrow I rejoin him; and if he asks me about her, what can I say?"

"So you wished to help your poor comrade? Tell me what you intended saying to her."

"I intended to tell her how I was passing **the** time, and **then** to praise him for his courage and skill, his desire to be great, **his** gentleness— Oh, there are a thousand things to **say!**"

Tula smiled sorrowfully. "Did you imagine **she** would learn to love him from that?"

"Why not?" asked Io' innocently.

"I cannot explain now; time will teach you. My brother, long will an Aztec woo before he wins our wayward sister!"

"Well," he said, taking her hand, "what I wanted to say to her will come better from you. Ah, if you but knew him as I and the 'tzin do!"

"Does the 'tzin so love him?"

"Was he not a chosen messenger to you?"

She shook her head doubtfully. "I fear she is beyond our little arts. Fine speeches alone will not do. Though we painted him fair as Quetzal', and set the picture before her every hour of the day, still it would not be enough. Does he come often to the city?"

"Never, except for the 'tzin."

"We must get them together. Let me see,—ah yes; the *chinampa!* We have not been there for a long time, and that will be an excuse for going to-morrow. You can bring the lord Hualpa, and I will take a minstrel, and have him sing, and tell stories of love and lovers."

She stopped, and sighed, thinking, doubtless, how the 'tzin's presence would add to the pleasure of the meeting. At that moment the curtain of the door was flung aside, and Nenetzin herself came in, looking vexed and pouting.

"Yesterday was too much for my sister," said Tula pleasantly. "I hope she is well again."

"I slept poorly," was the reply.

"If you are sick, we will send to the temples"—

"No; I hate the herb-dealers."

"What ails you, Nenetzin?" asked Io', irritated.

"Who would not be ailing, afflicted as I have been? One graceless fellow after another calling to see me, until I am out of patience!"

Io' coloured, and turned away.

"But what if they had news," said Tula,—"something from the strangers?"

Nenetzin's face brightened. "What of them? Have they waited on our father?"

"Have they, Io'?" Tula asked.

He made no answer; he was angry.

"Well, well! what folly! You, Io', I shall have to send back to the 'tzin; and, Nenetzin—fie! the young lords would be afraid to see you now."

"The monkeys!"

Io', without a word, left the room.

"You are too hard, Nenetzin. Our brother wants to be treated like a man. Many of the young lords are his friends. When you came in, he was telling me of the fine fellow who saved our father's life."

Nenetzin appeared uninterested.

"From Io's account, he must be equal to the 'tzin. Have you forgotten him?"

"I have his vase somewhere."

"Somewhere? I hope you have **not** lost it. I received one at the same time; there mine is,—that one filled with flowers."

Nenetzin did not look.

"When he made you the gift, I think he meant more than a compliment. He is a lover to be proud of; and, sister, a smile might win him."

"I do not care for lovers."

"Not care to be loved?"

Nenetzin **turned** to **her** with tearful eyes. **"Just now you said** Io' wanted **to be** treated as a man; for the same **reason**, O Tula, I want to be treated **as** a woman. I do want to be **loved, but not** as children are."

Tula put her arm around her lovingly. "Never mind. I will **learn** better afterwhile. I treat you as a child from habit, and **because of the** warm, sweet love of our childhood. Oh that the **love would** last always!"

They were silent then, each intent upon her separate thought, **both** unconscious that the path theretofore so peacefully travelled together was now divergent, and that the fates were leading them apart for ever. Of all the evil angels of humanity, that one is the most cruel whose mission it is **to** sunder the loves of the household.

"Nenetzin, you have been crying,—over what? Lean on me, confide in me!"

"You will make light of what I say."

"When was I a jester? You have had ills before, childish **ills**; **if** I did not mock them, am I likely to laugh at your woman's troubles?"

"But this **is** something you cannot help."

"The gods can."

"A god is the trouble. I saw him, **and love** him better than any our father worships."

Bold confirmation that of **the elder** sister's fears. "You saw him?" she asked musingly.

"And know him by **name**. *Tonatiah, Tonatiah:* is it not pretty?"

"Are you not afraid?"

"Of what? Him? Yes, but he is so handsome! You saw **him** also. Did you not notice his white forehead, and the brightness of his blue eyes, the sunshine of his face? As against him, ah, Tula, what are the lords you would have me love?"

"He is our father's enemy."

"His guest; he came by invitation."

"All the gods of our race threaten him."

"Yet I love him, and would quit everything to follow him."

"Gods ask not the love we give each other."

"You mean he would despise me. Never! I am the daughter of a king."

"You are mad, Nenetzin."

"Then love is madness, and I am very mad. Oh, I was so happy yesterday! Once I thought he saw me. It was when he was passing the *coatapantli*. The base artisan was shouting, and he heard him, or seemed to, for he raised his glance to the *azoteas*. My heart stood still; the air brightened around me; if I had been set down in the Sun itself, I could not have been happier."

"Have you mentioned this to the queen Acatlan?"

"Why should I? I will choose my own love. No one, not even my mother, would object to the king Cacama: why should she when my choice is nobler, handsomer, mightier than he?"

"What do you know of the strangers?"

"Nothing. He is one of them: that is enough."

"I meant of their customs: marriage, for instance."

"The thought is new."

"Tell me, Nenetzin: would you go with him, except as his wife?"

She turned away her glowing eyes, confused. "I know not what I would do. If I went with him except as his wife, our father would curse me, and my mother would die. I shudder; yet I remember how his look from a distance made me tremble with strange delight."

"It was magic, like Mualox's."

"I do not know. I was about to say, if such was his power over me at a distance, what may it be near by? Could I refuse to follow him, if he should ask me face to face, as we now are?"

"Avoid him, then."

"Stay here, as in prison! Never look out of doors for fear of seeing him whom I confess I so love! And then, the music, marching, banquets: shall I lose them, and for such a cause?"

"Nenetzin, the strangers will not abide here in peace. War there will be. The gods have so declared, and in every temple preparation is now going on."

"Who told you so?" the girl asked tremulously.

"This morning I was in the garden, culling flowers. I met Mualox. He seemed sad. I saluted him, and gave him the sweetest of my collection, and said something about them as a cure for ills of the mind. 'Thank you, daughter,' he said; 'the ills I mourn are your father's. If you can get him to forego his thoughts of war against Malinche, do so at any price. If flowers influence him, come yourself, and bring your maidens, and gather them all for him. Leave not a bud in the garden.' 'Is he so bent on war?' I asked. 'That is he. In the temples every hand

is making ready.' 'But my father counsels otherwise.' **The old**
man shook his head. 'I know every purpose of his soul.'"

"And is that all?" asked Nenetzin.

"No. Have you not heard what took place in the *tianguez* this
morning?"

And Tula told of the appearance of the horse and the stranger's
head; how nobody knew who placed them there; how they were
thought to have come from Huitzil', and with what design; and
how the wish for war was spread, until the beggars in the street
were clamouring. "War there will be, O my sister, right around
us. Our father will lead the companies against Malinche. The
'tzin, Cuitlahua, Io', and all we love best of our countrymen **will**
take part. O Nenetzin, of the children of the Sun, will you alone
side with the strangers? *Tonatiah* may slay our great father."

"And yet I would go with him," the girl said slowly, and **with**
sobs.

"Then you are not an Aztec," cried Tula, pushing her away.

Nenetzin stepped back speechless, and, throwing her scarf over
her head, turned to go.

The elder sister sprang up, conscience-struck, and caught
her. "Pardon, Nenetzin. I did not know what I was saying.
Stay"—

"Not now. I cannot help loving the stranger."

"The love shall not divide **us; we are** sisters!" And Tula
clung to her passionately.

"Too late, too late!" sobbed Nenetzin.

And she passed out the door; the curtain dropped behind her;
and Tula went to the couch, and wept as if her heart **were**
breaking.

Not yet have all the modes in which ills of state become ills **of**
society been written.

CHAPTER IV.

ENNUYÉ IN THE OLD PALACE.

"Father, holy father!—and by my sword, as belted knight,
Olmedo, I call thee so in love and honour,—I have heard thee
talk in learned phrase about the saints, and quote the sayings **of**
monks, mere makers of books, which I will swear are for the
most part dust, or, at least, not half so well preserved as the bones
of their scribblers,—I say I have thus heard thee talk and quote
for hours at **a** time, until I have come to think thy store of know-

ledge is but jargon of that kind. Shake thy head! Jargon, I say a second time."

"It is knowledge that leadeth to righteousness. *Bien quisto!* Thou wouldst do well to study it," replied the padre curtly.

A mocking smile curled the red-haired lip of the cavalier. "Knowledge truly! I recollect hearing the Señor Hernan once speak of thee. He said thou wert to him a magazine, full of learning precious as breadstuffs."

"Right, my son! Breadstuffs for the souls of sinners irreverent as "—

"Out with it!"

"As thou."

"*Picaro!* Only last night thou didst absolve me, and, by the Palmerins, I have just told my beads!"

"I think I have heard of the Palmerins," said the priest gravely; "indeed, I am certain of it; but I never heard of them as things to swear by before. Hast thou a license as coiner of oaths?"

"*Cierto,* father, thou dost remind me of my first purpose; which was to test thy knowledge of matters, both ancient and serious, outside of what thou callest the sermons of the schoolmen. And I will not take thee at disadvantage. Oh no! If I would play fairly with the vilest heathen, and slay him with none but an honest trick of the sword, surely I cannot less with thee."

"Slay me!"

"That will I,—in a bout at dialectics. I will be fair, I say. I will begin by taking thee in a field which every knight hath traversed, if, perchance, he hath advanced so far in clerkliness as to read,—a field divided between heralds, troubadours, and poets, and not forbidden to monks; with which thou shouldst be well acquainted, seeing that, of late days at least, thou hast been more prone to knightly than saintly association!"

"Santa Maria!" said Olmedo, crossing himself. "It is our nature to be prone to things sinful."

"I smell the cloister in thy words. Have at thee! Stay thy steps."

The two had been pacing the roof of the palace during the foregoing passage. Both stopped now, and Alvarado said, "Firstly,—nay, I will none of that; numbering the heads of a discourse is a priestly trick. To begin, by my conscience!—ho, father, that oath offends thee not, for it is the Señor Hernan's, and by him thou art thyself always ready to swear."

"If thou wouldst not get lost in a confusion of ideas, to thy purpose quickly."

"Thank thee. Who was Amadis de Gaul?"

"Hero of the oldest Spanish poem."

"Right!" said the knight, stroking his beard. "And who was Oriana?"

"Heroine of the same story; more particularly, **daughter of** Lisuarte, king of England."

"Thou didst reprove me for swearing **by** the Palmerins; **who** were they?"

"Famous knights, who founded chivalry by going about slaying dragons, working charities, and overthrowing armies of heathen, for the Mother's sake."

"Excellently answered, by my troth! I will have to lead thee into deeper water. Pass we the stories of Ruy Diaz, and Del Carpio, and Pelayo. I will even grant that thou hast heard of Hernan Gonzales; **but** canst thou tell in how many ballads his prowess hath been sung?"

Olmedo was silent.

"Already!" cried Alvarado, exultant. "Already! By **the** cross on my sword, I have heard of thirty. But to proceed. Omitting Roland, and Roncesvalles, and the brethren of the Round Table, canst thou tell me of the Seven Lords of Lares?"

"No. But there is a Lord of whom I can tell thee, and of **whom** it will be far more profitable for thee to inquire."

"I knew a minstrel—a rare fellow—who had a wondrous voice and memory, and who sang fifteen songs all about the Lords of Lares; and he told me there were as many more. Oh for the time of the true chivalry, when our Spanish people were song-lovers, and honour was **of** higher esteem than gold! In one respect, Olmedo, I am more Moslem **than** Christian."

The padre crossed himself.

"Mahomet—so saith history—taught his warriors that Paradise lieth **in** the shape of crossing scimitars,—as unlike thy **doctrine** as a stone is unlike a plum. *Picaro!* It pleaseth **me**; it hardeneth the heart and grip; it is more inspiring than clarions and drums."

Olmedo looked into the blue eyes of the knight, now unusually bright, and said, "Thou didst jest at my knowledge; now I ask thee, son, is it not better to have a mind full of saintly lore than **one** which nothing holds but swords and lances and high-bred steeds? What dost thou know but war?"

"The taste of good wine," said Alvarado seriously; "and, by Sta. Agnes, holy father, I would I had my canteen full! the smoke from these dens is turning me into a Dutch sausage. Look to the towers of yon temple,—the great one just before **us**. How the clouds ascending from them poison the morning air! When my sword is at the throats of the fire-keepers, Heaven help me to slay them!"

Alvarado then took the tassels of the cord around the good man's waist, and pulled him forward. "Come briskly, father! This roof is all the field left us for exercise; and much do I fear that **we** will dream many times of green meadows before we see

them again." Half dragging him, the knight lengthened his
strides. "Step longer, father! Thou dost mince the pace, like
a woman."

"Hands off, irreverent!" cried the padre, holding back.
"My feet are not iron-shod, like thine."

"What! Didst thou not climb the mountains on the way
hither barefooted? And dost now growl at these tiles? Last
night Sandoval shod his mare, the gay Motilla, with silver, which
he swore was cheaper, if not better, than iron. When next we
take a morning trot, like this, *cierto*, I will borrow two of the
precious shoes for thee."

Olmedo's gown, of coarse black woollen serge, was not a
garment a Greek, preparing for a race, would have chosen ; the
long skirts hampered his legs ; he stumbled, and would have
fallen, but for his tormentor.

"Stay thee, father! Hast been drinking? Not here shouldst
thou kneel unless in prayer ; and for that, bethink thee, housetops are for none but Jews." And the rough knight laughed
heartily. "Nay, talking will tire thee," he continued. "Take
breath first. If my shield were at hand, I would fan thee. Or
wouldst thou prefer to sit? or, better still, to lie down? Do so,
if thou wouldst truly oblige me ; for, by my conscience! as Cortes
sweareth, I have not done testing thy knowledge of worthy
things outside the convent libraries. I will take thee into a new
field, and ask of the Moorish lays ; for, as thou shouldst know, if
thou dost not, they have had their minstrels and heroes as fanciful
and valiant as infidels ever were ; in truth, but little inferior to
the best of old Castile."

Olmedo attempted to speak.

"Open not thy mouth, father, except to breathe. I will talk
until thy tire is over. I was on the Moors. A fine race they
were, bating always their religion. Of their songs, thou hast
probably heard that mournful roundelay, the Loves of Gazul and
Abindarraez ; probably listened to Tales of the Arabian Nights,
or to verses celebrating the tournaments in the Bivarrambla.
Certainly, thou hast heard recitals of the recontres, scimitar in
hand, between the Zegris and Abencerrages. By Sta. Agnes!
they have had warriors fit for the noblest songs. At least, father,
thou knowest"— He stopped abruptly, while a lad mounted the
roof and approached them, cap in hand.

"Excellent señor, so it please thee, my master hath somewhat
to say to thee in his chamber below. And"—crossing himself to
Olmedo—"if the holy father will remember me in his next
prayer, I will tell him that Bernal Diaz is looking for him."

"Doth thy master want me also?"

"That is Diaz's message."

"What can be in the wind now?" asked Alvarado musingly.

"Hadst thou asked me that question "—

"Couldst thou have answered? Take the chance! **What** doth thy master intend?"

"Look, Don Pedro, and thou, good father," replied the page,— "**look** to the **top** of yon pile so ridiculously called a temple **of** "—

"Speak it, as thou lovest me," cried Alvarado.

"Wilt thou pronounce it after me?"

"That will I ; though, *cierto*, I will not promise my horse if I fail."

"*Huitzilpotchli*," said the boy slowly.

"The saints defend us !" exclaimed the knight, crossing **him-self**. "Where didst thou get so foul a name?"

"Of **the** Doña Marina. Well, the Señor Hernan, my master, designeth visiting those towers, and seeing what horrors they hold."

Olmedo's countenance became unusually grave. "Holy Mother, keep his temper in check, that nothing rash be done !"

Alvarado received the news differently. "Thou art a good boy, Orteguilla," he said. "I owe thee a ducat. Remind me of the debt when next thou seest me with gold. *Espiritu Santo !* Now will I take the rust out of my knees, and the dull out of my head, and the spite from my stomach ! Now will I give my sword, that hath hungered so long, to surfeit on the heart-eaters ! *Bien quisto !* What jargon didst thou use a moment ago when speaking of the temple?"

"*Huitzilpotchli*," said the boy, laughing.

"Murrain take the idol, if only for his name's sake ! **Come ;** we shall have a good time."

The knight turned to descend. Orteguilla caught him by **the** mantle. "A word, Don Pedro."

"*Picaro !* A thousand of them, quickly !"

"Thou didst promise me a ducat "—

"Truly, and thou shalt have it. Only wait till the division cometh, and thy master saith to me, 'Take thy share.'"

"Thou hearest, father ?"

"**How !** Dost doubt **me ?**"

The boy stepped back. "No ; Alvarado's promise is good against the world. But dost thou not think the Señor Hernan will attack the temple?"

"*Cierto*, with horse, foot, guns, Tlascalans, and all."

"He goeth merely on a visit, and by invitation of Montezuma, the king."

Olmedo's face relaxed, and he rubbed his hands ; but the captain said dismally, "By invitation ! *Picaro !* Instead of the ducat, that for thy news !" And he struck open-handedly at the page, but with such good-will that the latter gave him wide margin the rest of the day.

CHAPTER V.

ALVARADO FINDS THE LIGHT OF THE WORLD.

THERE was a bluster of trumpets and drums, and out of the main gate of the palace in which he was lodged, under the eyes of a concourse of spectators too vast to be nearly estimated, Cortes marched with the greater part of his Christians. The column was spirited, even brilliant. Good steeds had improved with rest; while good fare, not to speak of the luxury of royal baths, had reconstituted both footmen and riders. At the head, as guides, walked four commissioners of the king,—stately men, gorgeous in *escaupils* and plumed helms.

The Spaniards were full of glee, vented broad exaggerations, and manifested the abandon I have seen in sailors ashore the first time after a long voyage.

"Be done, good horse!" said Sandoval to Motilla, whose blood warmed under the outcry of trumpet and clarion. "Be done!"

Montejo laughed. "Chide her not! She feels the silver on her heels as a fine lady the ribbons on her head."

"No," said Alvarado, laying his lance half in rest; "Motilla is a Christian, and the scent of the pagan is in her nostrils."

"Up with thy lance, *Señor Capitan!* The guides, if they were to look back, would leave us without so much as good day."

"*Cierto*, thou'rt right! But how pleasant it would be to impale two of them at once!"

"Such thy speculation? I cannot believe thee. I have been thy comrade too long," said Leon gravely.

Alvarado turned curtly, as if to say, "Explain thyself."

"The gold in their ears and on their wrists, señor,—there were thine eyes. And thou didst look as if summing up,—ear-rings, four; bracelets, six; sundries, three; total, thirteen ounces pure. Confess thee, confess thee!"

The laugh was loud and long.

I have already given the reader an idea of the *tianguez*, or market, whither Cortes, by request, was first conducted. It is sufficient to say now, that the exhibition of the jewellers attracted most attention; in front of their booths many of the footmen actually broke ranks, determined to satisfy themselves if all they there saw was indeed of the royal metal. Years after, they vaunted the sight as something surpassing all the cities of Europe could display.

Cortes occupied himself questioning the guides; for which purpose Marina was brought forward. Nothing of importance escaped him.

At one of the corners, while the interpreter was in the midst of a reply, Cortes' horse suddenly stopped, startled by an obstacle in the way. Scarcely a lance-length off, pictures of terror, stood four slaves, richly liveried, and bearing a palanquin crowned by a green *panache.*

"By Our Lady, I will see what is here contained!"

So saying, Alvarado spurred impetuously forward. The guides threw themselves in his way; he nearly rode one of them down; and, laughing at the fright of the slaves, he drew aside the curtain of the carriage, and peered in.

"*Jesu!*" he cried, dropping the cloth, and reining his horse back.

"Hast thou the fiend there, or only a woman?" asked Cortes.

"A paragon, an houri, your excellency! What a rude fellow I have been! She is frightened. Come hither, Marina. Say to the girl"—

"Not now, not now!" said Cortes abruptly. "If she is pretty, thou wilt see her again."

Alvarado frowned.

"What! angry?" continued the general. "Out on thee, captain! How can an untaught infidel, though paragon and houri, understand knightly phrases? What the merit of an apology in her eyes? Pass on!"

"Perhaps thou'rt right. Stand aside! Out of the way there!" And, as if to make amends, he cleared a passage for the slaves and their burden.

"To the devil all of ye!" he replied to the laughter of his comrades. "Ye did not see her, nor know ye if she is old or young, harridan or angel."

From the market, the column marched back to the great temple, with which, as it rose broad and high like a terraced hill between the palace they occupied and the sun at rising, they were somewhat familiar. Yet, when fairly in view of the pile, Cortes called Olmedo to his side.

"I thank thee, Father Bartolomé. That thou art near, I feel better. A good surcoat and shield, as thou knowest, give a soldier confidence in battle; and so, as I come nigh yon abomination, full of bloody mysteries, called worship, and carven stones, called gods,—may they be accursed from the earth!—I am pleased to make use of thee and thy holiness. Doubtless the air of the place is thick with sorceries and evil charms; if so, thy crucifix hath more of safeguard than my sword. Ride nearer, father, and hearken, that thou mayest answer what more I have to say. Would not this pile look the better of a cross upon every tower?"

"Thy zeal, my son, I commend, and thy question strictly hath but one answer," Olmedo replied. "The impulse, moreover, is to do at once what thou hast suggested. Roll away a stone, and in its bed plant a rose, and the blooming will be never so sweet; and so, never looketh the cross so beautiful as when it taketh the place of an idol. And for the conversion of heathen, the Holy Mother careth not if the worship be under Christian dome or in pagan chamber."

"Sayest thou so?" said Cortes, checking his horse. "By my conscience, I will order a cross!"

"Be not so fast, I pray you. What armed hand now putteth up, armed hand must keep; and that is war. May not the good end be reached without such resort? In my judgment we should first consult the heathen king. How knowest thou that he is not already inclined to Christian ways! Let us ask him."

Cortes relaxed the rein, and rode on convinced.

Through the gate of the *coatapantli*, amid much din and clangour, the entire column entered the yard of the temple. On a pavement, glassy-smooth, and spotless as a good housewife's floor, the horsemen dismounted and the footmen stood at rest. Then Cortes, with his captains and Marina, approached the steps, where he was received by some pabas, who offered to carry him to the *azoteas*, — a courtesy he declined with many protestations of thanks.

At the top, under a green canopy, and surrounded by courtiers and attendants, Montezuma stood, in the robes of a priest, and with only his sceptre to indicate his royalty.

"You have my welcome, Malinche. The ascent is wearisome. Where are the pabas whom I sent to assist you?"

The monarch's simple dignity affected his visitors, Cortes as much as the others.

"I accept thy welcome, good king," he replied, after the interpretation. "Assure thyself that it is given to a friend. The priests proffered their service as you directed; they said your custom was to be carried up the steps, which I grant accords with a sovereign, but not with a warrior, who should be superior to fatigue."

To favour a view of the city, which was after a while suggested, the king conducted Cortes to the southern side of the *azoteas*, where were also presented a great part of the lake, bordered with white towns, and the valley stretching away to the purple sierras. The train followed them with mats and stools, and erected the canopy to intercept the sun; and, thus at ease, the host explained, and the guest listened. Often, during the descriptions, the monarch's eyes rested wistfully on his auditor's face; what he sought, we can imagine; but well I ween there was more revelation in a cloudy sky than in that bloodless countenance. The demeanour of the Spaniard was courtierly; he failed not to follow every gesture of the royal hand ; and if the meaning of what he heard was lost because of the strange language, the voice was not. In the low, sad intonations, unmarked by positive emphasis, he divined more than the speaker read in his face,—a soul goodly in all but its irresolution. If now and then the grave attention relaxed, or the eye wandered from the point indicated, it was because the city and lake, and the valley to the mountains, were in the visitor's mind more a military problem than a picture of power or beauty.

The interview was at length interrupted. Two great towers crowned the broad *azoteas* of the temple, one dedicated to Tezca', the other to Huitzil'. Out of the door of the latter issued a procession of pabas, preceded by boys swinging censers, the smoke of which was sickening sweet. Tlalac, the *teotuctli*, came last, walking slowly, bareheaded, barefooted, his gown trailing behind him, its sleeves and front, like his hands and face, red with the blood of recent sacrifice. While the gloomy train gathered about the astonished Christians, the heathen pontiff, as if unconscious of their presence, addressed himself to the king. His words were afterwards translated by Marina.

"To your application, O king, there is no answer. What you do will be of your own inspiration. The victims are removed ; the servants of the god, save whom you see, are in their cells. If such be thy will, the chamber is ready for the strangers."

Montezuma sat a moment hesitant, his colour coming and going ; then, feeling the gaze of his guest upon him, he arose, and said kindly, but with dignity, "It is well. I thank you." Turning to Cortes, he continued, "If you will go with me, Malinche, I will show you our god, and the place in which we celebrate his worship. I will explain our religion, and you may explain yours. Only give me respect for respect."

Bowing low, Cortes replied, "I will go with thee, and thou shalt suffer no wrong from the confidence. The hand or tongue that doeth grievance to anything pertaining to thy god or his worship shall repeat it never." The last sentence was spoken with a raised voice, and a glance to the captains around ; then, observing the frowns with which some of them received the notice, he added, almost without a pause, to Olmedo, "What saith the Church of Christ ?"

"That thou hast spoken well, for this time," answered the priest, kissing the crucifix chained to his girdle. "Go on. I will go with thee."

Then they followed the king into the sanctuary, leaving the *teotuctli* and his train on the *azoteas.*

I turn gladly from that horrible chamber. With quite as much satisfaction, I turn from the conversation of the king and Cortes. Not even the sweet voice of Marina could make the

Aztec theogony clear, or the Catholic commentary of the Spaniard interesting.

Alvarado approached the turret door with loathing. Staggered by the stench that smote him from within, he stopped a moment. Orteguilla, the page, pulled his mantle, and said, "I have news for thee. Wilt thou hear?"

"*Picaro!* To-morrow, if the Mother doth spare me so long, I will give thee a lash for every breath of this sin-laden air thou makest me draw with open mouth. As thou lovest life, speak, and have done!"

"What if I bring thee a message of love?"

"If thou couldst bring me such a message from a comely Christian maiden, I would kiss thee, lad."

Orteguilla held out an exquisite *ramillete.* "Seest thou this? If thou carest, and wilt follow me, I will show thee an infidel to swear by for ever."

"Give me the flowers, and lead me to the infidel. If thou speakest truly, thy fortune is made; if thou liest, I will fling thee from the temple."

He turned from the door, and was conducted to the shade of the turret of Tezca'.

"I was loitering after the tall priest, the one with the bloody face and hands,—what a monster he is!" said the page, crossing himself,—"when a slave came in my way, offering some flowers, and making signs. I spoke to him. 'What do you want?' 'Here is a message from the princess Nenetzin.' 'Who is she?' 'Daughter of the great king.' 'Well, what did she say?' 'She bade me'—and, *Señor Capitan,* these are almost his words—'she bade me give these flowers to one of the *teules,* that he might give them to *Tonatiah*—him with the red beard.' I took the present, and asked, 'What does the princess say to the *Tonatiah?*' 'Let him read the flowers,' the fellow answered. I remembered then that it is a custom of this people to send messages in that form. I asked him where his mistress was; he told me, and I went to see her."

"What of her? Is she handsome?"

"Here she is; judge thou."

"Holy Mother! 'Tis the girl I so frightened on the street. She is the pearl of the valley, the light of the world!" exclaimed Alvarado. "Stay thou, sir page. Interpret for me. I will speak to her."

"Simply, then. Thou knowest I am not so good an Aztec as Marina."

Nenetzin was sitting in the shade of the turret. Apart several paces stood her carriage-bearers. Her garments of finest cotton, white as snow, were held close to her waist by a green sash. Her ornaments—necklace, bracelets, and anklets—were of gold, enriched by *chalchuites*. Softest sandals protected her feet; and the long scarf, **heavy** with embroidery, and half covering her **face**, fell from her head to the mat of scarlet feathers upon which **she** was sitting.

When the **tall** Spaniard, in full armour, **except** the helmet, stopped **thus** suddenly before her, the large eyes dilated, the blood left her cheeks, and she shrank almost **to** the roof. Was it not as if the dream, **so** strange in the coming, had vitalized its subject and sent it **to her, a** fate the more irresistible because of its peculiarities,—the **blue** eyes, the forehead womanly white, the hair long and **waving**, the beard dyed, apparently, in **the** extremest brightness **of the** sun,—all so unheard of among **the** brown and olive children of Anahuac? And **what** if **the fate** had come demandingly? Refuse! Can the chrysalis, **joyous in** the beauty **of** wings just perfected, refuse the sun?

The cavalier could not mistake the **look** with which **she** regarded him. In pity for her fear, **in** admiration of her beauty, in the native gallantry of his soul, **he** knelt, and took her hand **and** kissed it; then, giving it back, and looking into her face **with** an expression as unmistakeable as her own, he said,—

"My beautiful princess must not be afraid. I would die sooner than harm her."

While the page interpreted, as best he could, the captain smiled so winsomely that she sat up, and listened with a smile in return. She was won, and—shall we say lost? The future comes rapidly now to answer for itself.

"Here is the message," **Alvarado** continued, "which **I could** not read; but if it meant to **tell** me of love, what **better can I** than **give it** back to tell the same story for me?"

He kissed the flowers, and laid them before her. Picking **them up,** she said, with a laugh, "*Tonatiah* is a poet,—a god and a poet."

He heard the interpretation, and **spoke again,** without relaxing his ardent gaze.

"*Jesu Christo!* That one so beautiful should be an infidel! She shall not be,—by the Holy Sepulchre, she shall not! Here, lad, take off the chain which is about my neck. It hath an iron crucifix, the very same my mother—rested be her soul!—gave me, with her blessing and prayer, what time I last bade her farewell."

Orteguilla took off **the** chain and crucifix, and put them in **the** cavalier's hand.

"Will my beautiful princess deign **to** receive these gifts from me, her slave for ever? And in my presence will she put them on? And for my sake, will she always wear them? They have God's blessing, which cannot be better bestowed."

Instead of laying the presents down **to be** taken or not, this time he held them out **to her** directly; and she took them, and, childlike, hung them **around** her neck. In the act, the scarf fell, and left bare her **head** and face. He saw the glowing countenance, and was **about to speak** further, when Orteguilla stopped him.

"Moderate thyself, I pray thee, **Don Pedro.** Look at the **hounds**; they are closing us in. The **way** to the turret is already cut off. Have a care, I pray!"

The tone of alarm had instant effect.

"How! Cut off, sayest thou, lad?" And Alvarado sprang up, **his hand** upon his **sword.** He swept the circle with a falcon's glance; **then,** turning **once** more to the girl, he said, resuming the tenderness of voice **and manner,** "By what name **may** I know my love hereafter?"

"Nenetzin,—the princess Nenetzin."

"Then farewell, Nenetzin. Ill betide the man or fortune that **keepeth** thee from me hereafter! May I forfeit life, and the Holy **Mother's** love, if I see thee not again! Farewell."

He kissed his mailed hand to her, and, facing the array of **scowling pabas, strode to** them, and through their circle, with a **laugh of knightly scorn.**

At the door of the turret of Huitzil' he said to the page, "The love **of** yon girl, heathen no longer, but Christian, by the cross she weareth,—her love, and the brightness of her presence, for the foulness and sin of this devil's den,—what **an** exchange! *Valgame Dios!* Thou shalt have the ducat. She **is the** glory of the world!"

CHAPTER VI.

THE IRON CROSS.

"**My lord** Maxtla, go see if there be none coming this way now."

And while the chief touched the ground with his palm, the **king** added, as to himself, and impatiently, "Surely it is time."

"**Of whom** speak you?" asked Cuitlahua, standing by. Only **the brother** would have so presumed.

The **monarch looked into the** branches **of the** cypress-tree above him; he **seemed holding the** words in **ear,** while he followed **a** thought.

They were in the grove **of** Chapultepec **at the** time. About them were the famous trees, apparently **old** as the hill itself, with trunks so massive **that** they had likeness to things of cun-**ning** labour, products **of** some divine art. The **sun** touched them here and there with slanting yellow rays, by contrast deepening the shadows that purpled the air. From the gnarled limbs the grey moss drooped, like listless drapery. Nesting birds sang from the topmost boughs, and parrots, flitting to and fro, lit the gloaming with transient gleams of scarlet and gold : yet the effect of the place was mysterious ; the hush of the solitude softened reflection into dreaming ; the silence was a solemn presence in which speech sank to a whisper, and laughter would have been profanation. In such primeval temples men walk with Time, as in paradise Adam walked with God.

"I am waiting for the lord Hualpa," the king at last replied, turning his sad eyes to his brother's face.

"Hualpa!" said Cuitlahua, marvelling, as well he might, to find the great king waiting for the merchant's son, so lately a simple hunter.

"Yes. He serves me in an affair of importance. His appointment was for noon ; he tarries, I fear, in the city. Next time I will choose an older messenger."

The manner of the explanation was that of one who has in mind something of which he desires to speak, yet doubts the wisdom of speaking. So the cacique seemed to understand, for he relapsed into silence, while the monarch again looked upwards. Was the object he studied in the sky or in his heart?

Maxtla returned ; saluting, he said, "The lake is thronged with canoes, O king, but none come this way."

The sadness of the royal face deepened.

"Montezuma, my brother," said Cuitlahua.

"Well."

"Give me a moment's audience."

"Certainly. The laggard comes not ; the rest of the day is yours." And to Maxtla he said, "In the palace are the queens, and the princesses Tula and Nenetzin. Inform them that I am coming."

When the chief was gone, the monarch turned to Cuitlahua, smiling. "Yes, the rest of the day is yours, and the night also ; for I must wait for the merchant's son ; and our mother, were she here, would say it was good of you to share my waiting."

The pleasantry and the tender allusion were hardly observed by the cacique. "I wished to call your attention to Iztlil', the Tezcucan," he said gravely.

"Iztlil'? what of him now?"

"Trouble. What else can come of him? Last night, at the house of Xoli, the Chalcan, he drank too much *pulque*, quarrelled with the good man's guests, and abused everybody loyal,—abused you, my brother. I sent a servant to watch him. You must know—if not, you should—that all Tenochtitlan believes the Tezcucan to be in alliance with Malinche and his robbers."

"Robbers!" said Montezuma, starting.

The cacique went on. "That he has corresponded with the Tlascalans is well understood. Only last night he spoke of a confederacy of tribes and cities to overturn the empire."

"Goes he so far?" exclaimed the king, now very attentive.

"He is a traitor!" replied Cuitlahua emphatically. "So I sent a servant to follow him. From the Chalcan's, he was seen go to the gates of the palace of Axaya'. Malinche received him. He is there now."

The two were silent a while, the cacique observing the king, the king gazing upon the ground.

"Well," said the latter at length, "is that all?"

"Is it not enough?"

"You are right. He must be arrested. Keep close watch on the gates of the palace, and, upon his coming out, seize him, and put him safely away in the temple."

"But if he comes not out?"

"To-morrow, at noon, if he be yet within, go to Malinche and demand him. Here is your authority."

At that, the monarch took from a finger of his left hand a ring of gold, set with an oval green malachite, on which his likeness was exquisitely cut.

"But," said the other, while the royal hand was outstretched, "if Malinche refuses your demand?"

"Then—then"— And the speaker paused so long that his indecision was apparent.

"Behind the refusal,—see you what lies there?" asked Cuitlahua bluntly.

The king reflected.

"Is it not war?" the cacique persisted.

The hand fell down, and closed upon the signet.

"The demand is just, and will not be refused. Take the ring, my brother; we will at least test Malinche's disposition. Say to him that the lord Iztlil' is a traitor; that he is conspiring against me; and that I require his person for punishment. So say to him; but go not yet. The messenger I await may bring me something to make your mission unnecessary."

The cacique smiled grimly. "If the Tezcucan is guilty, so is Malinche," he said. "Is it well to tell him what you know?"

"Yes. He will then be careful; at least, he will not be deceived."

"Be it so," said Cuitlahua, taking the ring. "I will bring you his answer; then"—

"Well?"

"Bear with me, O king. The subject I now wish to speak of is a tender one, though I know not why. To win the good-will of the **Tezcucan,** was not Guatamozin, our nephew, banished **the** city?"

"Well?"

"Now that the Tezcucan is lost, why should not the 'tzin return? He is a happy man, O my brother, who discovers an enemy ; happier is he who, at the same time, discovers a friend."

Montezuma studied the cacique's face, then, with his eyes upon the ground, walked on. Cuitlahua went with him. Past the great trees, under the grey moss, up the hill to the summit, and along the summit to the verge of the rocky bluff, they went. At the king's side, when he stopped, was a porphyritic rock bearing, in bas-relief, his own image and that of his father. Below him, westwardly, spread the placid lake ; above it, the setting sun ; in its midst, a fair child on a fair mother's breast, Tenochtitlan.

"See ! a canoe goes swiftly round yon *chinampa ;* now it out-strips its neighbours, and turns this way. How the slaves bend to the paddles ! My laggards at last !"

The king, while speaking, rubbed his hands gleefully. For **the time,** Cuitlahua and his question were forgotten.

"The **lord** Hualpa has company," observed the brother quietly.

"Yes. Io'."

Another spell of silence, during which both watched the canoe.

"Come, let us to the palace. Lingering here is useless." And with another look to the city and lake, and a last one at the speeding vessel, yet too far off to be identified, the king finally turned away. And Guatamozin was still an exile.

Tecalco and Acatlan, the queens, and Tula, **and** their atten-dants, sitting on the *azoteas* of the ancient house, taking the air of the declining day, arose to salute the monarch and his brother. The latter took the hand of each, saying, "The gods of our fathers be good **to** you." Tula's forehead he touched with his lips. His countenance, like his figure and nature, Indian in type, softened somewhat under her glance. He knew her sorrow, and in sympathy thought of the 'tzin, and of the petition in his behalf as yet unanswered.

" All are not here, one is absent,—Nenetzin. Where is she? I may not sleep well without hearing her laugh once more."

Acatlan said, "You are very good, my lord, to remember my child. She chose to remain below."

"She is not sick, I hope?"

"Not sick, yet not well."

"Ah ! the trouble is of the mind, perhaps. How **old is she** now?"

"Old enough to be in love, if that is your meaning."

Cuitlahua smiled. "That is not **a** sickness, but a happiness ; so, at least, the minstrels say."

"What ails Nenetzin?" asked the king.

Acatlan cast down her eyes and hesitated.

"Speak! What ails her?"

"I hardly know. She hardly knows herself," the queen answered. "If I am to believe what she tells me, the lord Cuitlahua is right; she is in love."

"With Tula, I suppose," said the king, laughing.

"Would it were! She says her lover is called *Tonatiah.* Much I fear, however, that what she thinks love is really a delusion, wrought by magic. She is not herself. When did Malinche go to the temple?"

"Four days ago," the king replied.

"Well, the *teule* met her there, and spoke to her, and gave her a present. Since that, like a child, she has done little else than play with the trinket."

Montezuma became interested. He seated himself, and asked, "You said the spell proceeds from the present: why do you think so?"

"The giver said the gift was a symbol of his religion, and whoever wore it became of his faith, and belonged to his god."

"Mictlan!" muttered Cuitlahua.

"Strange! What is the thing?" the king persisted.

"Something of unknown metal, white, like silver, about a hand in length, and attached to a chain."

"Of unknown metal,—a symbol of religion! Where is the marvel now?"

"Around the child's neck, where I believe it has been since she came from the temple. Once she allowed me to see if I could tell what the metal was, but only for a moment, and then her eyes never quit me. She sits hours by herself, with the bauble clasped in both hands, and sighs, and mopes, and has no interest in what used to please her most."

The king mused a while. The power of the strangers was very great; what if the gift was the secret of the power?

"Go, Acatlan," he said, "and call Nenetzin. See that she brings the charm with her."

Then he arose, and began moodily to walk. Cuitlahua talked with Tecalco and Tula. The hour was very pleasant. The sun, lingering above the horizon, poured a flood of brilliance upon the hill and palace, and over the flowers, trailing vines, and dwarfed palm and banana trees, with which the *azoteas* was provided.

Upon the return of the queen with Nenetzin, the king resumed his seat. The girl knelt before him, her face very pale, her eyes full of tears. So lately a child, scarce a woman, yet so weighted with womanly griefs, the father could not view her except with compassion; so he raised her, and, holding her hand, said, "What is this I hear, Nenetzin? Yesterday I was thinking of sending you to school. Nowadays lovers are very exacting; they require of their sweethearts knowledge as well as beauty; but you outrun my plans, you have a lover already. Is it so?"

Nenetzin looked down, blushing.

"And no common lover either," continued the king. "Not a 'tzin, or a cacique, or a governor; not a lord or a prince,—a god! Brave child!"

Still Nenetzin was silent.

"You cannot call your lover by name, nor speak to him in his language; nor can he speak to you in yours. Talking by signs must be tedious for the uses of love, which I understand to be but another name for impatience; yet you are far advanced; you have seen your beloved, talked with him, and received—what?"

Nenetzin clasped the iron cross upon her breast firmly,—not as a good Catholic, seeking its protection, for she would have laid the same hands on Alvarado rather than Christ,—and for the first time she looked in the questioner's face straight and fearlessly. A moment he regarded her; in the moment his smile faded away; and for her it came never again—never.

"Give me what you have there," he said sternly, extending his hand.

"It is but a simple present," she said, holding back.

"No, it has to do with religion, and that not of our fathers."

"It is mine," she persisted, and the queen mother turned pale at sight of her firmness.

"The child is bewitched," interposed Cuitlahua.

"And for that I should have the symbol. Obey me, or"—

Awed by the look, now dark with anger, Nenetzin took the chain from her neck, and put the cross in his hand: "There! I pray you, return them to me."

Now, the cross as a religious symbol was not new to the monarch,—in Cozumel it was an object of worship; in Tabasco it had been reverenced for ages as emblematic of the God of Rain; in Palenque, the Palmyra of the New World, it is sculptured on the fadeless walls, and a child held up to adore it (in the same picture) proves its holy character: it was not new to the heathen king; but the cross of Christ was; and singularly enough, he received the latter for the first time with no thought of saving virtues, but as a problem in metallurgy.

"To-morrow I will send the trinkets to the jewellers," he said, after close examination. "They shall try them in the fire. Strange, indeed, if, in all my dominions, they do not find whereof they are made."

He was about to pass the symbol to Maxtla, when a messenger came up, and announced the lord Hualpa and the prince Io'. Instantly, the cross and Nenetzin, and her tears and troubles, vanished out of his mind.

CHAPTER VII.

THE CHRISTIANS IN THE TOILS.

"LET the *azoteas* be cleared of all but my family. You, my brother, will remain."

So saying, the king arose, and began walking again. As he did so the cross slipped from his fingers, and fell, ringing sharply upon the roof. Nenetzin sprang forward and picked the symbol up.

"Now, call the messengers."

When the chief was gone, the monarch stepped to Cuitlahua, and, laying a hand upon his arm, said, "At last, O brother, at last! The time so long prayed for is come. The enemy is in the snare, and he is mine. So the god of our fathers has promised. The messengers bring me his permission to make war."

"At last! Praised be Huitzil'!" exclaimed Cuitlahua, with upraised hands and eyes.

"Praised be Huitzil'!" cried Tula, with equal fervour.

"Malinche began his march to Tenochtitlan against my order, which, for a purpose, I afterwards changed to invitation. Since that my people, my army, the lords, the pabas, the Empire, have upbraided me for weakness. I only bided my time, and the assent of Huitzil'. And the result? The palace of Axaya' shall be the tomb of the insolent strangers."

As he spoke, the monarch's bosom swelled with the old warrior spirit.

"You would have had me go meet Malinche, and in the open field array my people to be trodden down by his beasts of war. Now, ours is the advantage. We will shut him in with walls of men as well as of houses. Over them he may ride, but the first bridge will be the end of his journey; it will be raised. Mictlan take our legions, if they cannot conquer him at last!"

He laughed scornfully.

"In the temples are seventy thousand fighting men, gathered unknown to all but Tlalac. They are tired of their prison, and cry for freedom and battle. Two other measures taken, and the war begins,—only two. Malinche has no stores; he is dependent upon me for to-morrow's bread. What if I say, not a grain of corn, not a mouthful of meat shall pass his palace gate? As to the other step,—what if I bid you raise the bridges? What then? His beasts must starve; so must his people, unless they can fly. Let him use his engines of fire; the material he serves them with cannot last always, so that want will silence them also. The measures depend on my word, which, **by** the blessing of Huitzil', I will speak, and "—

"When ?" asked Cuitlahua earnestly.

"To-morrow "—

"The day, O my kingly brother !—the day **will** be memorable in Anáhuac for ever !"

The monarch's eyes flashed with evil fire. "It shall be so. Part of the invaders will **not** content me ; none shall escape,—not one ! In the world shall **not** one be left !"

All present listened eagerly. Nenetzin alone gave no sign of feeling, though she heard every word.

The couriers **now** appeared. Over their uniforms was the inevitable *nequen.* Instead of helms, they wore broad bands, ornamented with **plumes and** brilliants. At their backs hung their shields. The prince, proud and happy, kissed his mother's hand, and nodded to his sisters. Hualpa went to the king, and knelt in salute.

"I have been waiting since noon," **said** Montezuma coldly.

"We pray your pardon, O king, good master. The fault **was** not ours. Since yesterday at noon we have not ate, or drank, or slept ; neither have we been out of the great temple, except to embark and come here, which was with all possible speed."

"It is well. Arise ! What **says the god ?**"

Every ear was strained to hear.

"We followed your orders in all things, O king. **In** the temple we found the *teotuctli,* and the pabas of the city, with many from Tezcuco and Cholula."

"Saw you Mualox, of the old Cû of Quetzal' ?"

"Mualox was not there."

The king waved his hand.

"We presented ourselves to the *teotuctli,* and gave him your message ; **in** proof of our authority, we showed him the signet, which **we now** return."

The **seal was** taken in silence.

"In presence, then, of all the pabas, the sacrifices were begun. I counted the victims,—nine hundred in all. The afternoon and night, and to-day, to the time of our departure, the service lasted. The sound of prayer from the holy men was unintermitted and loud. I looked once to the palace of Axaya', and saw the *azotcas* crowded with the strangers and their Tlascalans."

The king and the lord Cuitlahua exchanged glances **of** satisfaction.

"At last the labours of the *teotuctli* were rewarded. **I saw** him tear a heart from a victim's breast, and study the signs ; then, with a loud cry, he ran and flung the heart into the fire before the altar of Huitzil' ; and all there joined in the cry, which was of rejoicing, and washed their hands in the blood. The holy man then came to me, and said, 'Say to Montezuma, the wise king, that Huitzil', the Supreme God, has answered, and bids him begin the war. Say to him, also, to be of cheer; for the land shall be delivered from the strangers, and the strangers shall be delivered to him, in trust for the god.' Then he stood in the door of the sanctuary, and made proclamation of the divine will. And that was all, O king."

"To Huitzil' be the praise!" exclaimed the king piously.

"And to Montezuma the glory!" said Cuitlahua.

And the queens and Tula kissed the monarch's hand, and at his feet Io' knelt, and laid his shield, saying,—

"A favour, O king, a favour!"

"Well."

"Let not my years be counted, but give me a warrior's part in the sacred war."

And Cuitlahua went to the suppliant, and laid a hand upon his head, and said, his massive features glowing with honest pride, "It was well spoken, O my brother, well spoken. The blood and spirit of our race will survive us. I, the oldest, rejoice, and, with the youngest, pray: give us each to do a warrior's part."

Brighter grew the monarch's eyes.

"Your will be done," he said to Io'. "Arise!" Then looking toward the sun, he added, with majestic fervour, "The inspiration is from you, O holy gods! Strengthen it, I pray, and help him in the way he would go." A moment after, he turned to Cuitlahua. "My brother, have your wish also. I give you the command. You have my signet already. To-morrow the drum of Huitzil' will be beaten. At the sound, let the bridges next the palace of Axaya' on all the causeways be taken up. Close the market to-night. Supplies for one day more Malinche may have, and that is all. Around the *teocallis*, in hearing of a shell, are ten thousand warriors; take them, and, after the beating of the drum, see that the strangers come not out of the palace, and that nothing goes through its gates for them. But until the signal, let there be friendship and perfect peace. And"—he looked around slowly and solemnly—"what I have here spoken is between ourselves and the gods."

And Cuitlahua knelt and kissed his hand, in token of loyalty.

While the scene was passing, as the only one present not of the royal family, Hualpa stood by, with downcast eyes; and as he listened to the brave words of the king, involving so much of weal or woe to the realm, he wondered at the fortune which had brought him such rich confidence, not as the slow result of years of service, but, as it were, in a day. Suddenly the monarch turned to him.

"Thanks are not enough, lord Hualpa, for the report you bring. As a messenger between me and the mighty Huitzil', you shall have reason to rejoice with us. Lands and rank you have, and a palace; now,"—a smile broke through his seriousness,—"now I will give you a wife. Here she is." And to the amazement of all, he pointed to Nenetzin. "A wild bird, by the Sun! What say you, lord Hualpa? Is she not beautiful? Yet," he became grave in an instant, "I warn you that she is self-willed, and spoiled, and now suffers from a distemper which she fancies to be love. I warn you, lest one of the enemy, of whom we were but now talking, lure her from you, as he seems to have lured her from us and our gods. To save her, and place her in good keeping, as well as to bestow a proper reward, I will give her to you for wife."

Tecalco looked at Acatlan, who governed her feelings well; possibly she was satisfied, for the waywardness of the girl had of late caused her anxiety, while, if not a prince, like Cacama, Hualpa was young, brave, handsome, ennobled, and, as the proposal itself proved, on the high road to princely honours. Tula openly rejoiced; so did Io'. The lord Cuitlahua was indifferent; his new command, and the prospects of the morrow, so absorbed him that a betrothal or a wedding was a trifle. As for Hualpa, it was as if the flowery land of the Aztec heaven had opened around him. He was speechless; but in the step half taken, his flushed face, his quick breathing, Nenetzin read all he could have said, and more; and so he waited a sign from her,—a sign, though but a glance or a motion of the lip or hand. And she gave him a smile,—not like that the bold Spaniard received on the temple, nor warm, as if prompted by the loving soul,—a smile, witnessed by all present, and by all accepted as her expression of assent.

"I will give her to you for wife," the monarch repeated, slowly and distinctly. "This is the betrothal; the wedding shall be when the war is over, when not a white-faced stranger is left in all my domain."

While yet he spoke, Nenetzin ran to her mother, and hid her face in her bosom.

"Listen further, lord Hualpa," said the king. "In the great business of to-morrow I give you a part. At daylight return to the temple, and remain there in the turret where hangs the drum of Huitzil'. Io' will come to you about noon, with my command; then, if such be its effect, with your own hand give the signal for which the lord Cuitlahua will be waiting. Strike so as to be heard by the city, and by the cities on the shores of the lake. Afterwards, with Io', go to the lord Cuitlahua. Here is the signet again. The *teotuctli* may want proof of your authority."

Hualpa, kneeling **to receive the** seal, kissed the monarch's hand.

"And now," the latter said, addressing himself to Cuitlahua, "the interview is ended. You have much **to do.** Go. The gods keep you."

Hualpa, at last released, went and paid homage to his betrothed, and was made still more happy by her words, and the congratulations of the queens.

Tula alone lingered at the king's side, her large eyes fixed appealingly on his face.

"What now, Tula?" he asked tenderly.

And she answered, "You have need, O king and good father, of faithful, loving **warriors.** I know of one. He should be here, but **is** not. Of to-morrow, its braveries and sacrifices, the minstrels will sing for ages **to come;** and the burden of their songs will be how nobly the people **fought,** and died, and conquered for **you.** Shall the opportunity be **for** all but him? Do not so wrong yourself, be not so cruel **to—to** me," she said, clasping her hands.

His look of tenderness vanished, and he walked away, and from the parapet of the *azoteas* gazed long and fixedly, apparently observing the day dying in the west, or the royal gardens that stretched out of sight from **the base of the** castled hill.

She waited expectantly, **but** no answer came,—none **ever** came.

And when, directly, she joined the group about Nenetzin and Hualpa, and leaned confidingly upon Io', **she** little thought that his was the shadow darkening her love; that the dreamy monarch, looking forward **to the** succession, saw in the far future a struggle for the **crown** between the prince and the 'tzin; that for the former, **hope there** was not, except **in** what might now be done; and **that yet** there was not hope, **if** the opportunities of war **were as open to** the **one** as **to** the other. So the exile continued.

CHAPTER VIII.

ADMITTING that the intent with which **the** Spaniards came to Tenochtitlan took from them the sanctity accorded by Christians to guests, and at the same time justified any measure in prevention,—a subject belonging **to the casuist** rather than the teller of a story,—their situation has now **become so** perilous, **and** possibly so interesting to my sympathetic reader, that he may be anxious to enter the old palace, and see what they are doing.

The dull report of the evening gun had long since spent itself over the lake, and along the gardened shores. So, too, mass had been said in the chapel, newly improvised, and very limited for such high ceremony ; yet, as Father Bartolomé observed, roomy enough for prayer and penitence. Nor had the usual precautions against surprise been omitted ; on the contrary, extra devices in that way had been resorted to ; the guards had been doubled ; the horses stood caparisoned ; by the guns at the gates low fires were burning, to light, in an instant, the matches of the gunners ; and at intervals, under cover of the walls, lay or lounged detachments of both Christians and Tlascalans, apparently told off for battle. A yell without or a shot within, and the palace would bristle with defenders. A careful captain was Cortes.

In his room, once the audience-chamber of the kings, paced the stout *conquistador*. He was alone, and, as usual, in armour, except of the head and hands. On a table were his helm, iron gloves, and battle-axe, fair to view, as was the chamber, in the cheerful, ruddy light of a brazen lamp. As he walked, he used his sword for staff ; and its clang, joined to the sharp concussion of the sollerets smiting the tessellated floor at each step, gave notice in the adjoining chamber, and out in the *patio*, that the general—or, as he was more familiarly called, the Señor Hernan— was awake and uncommonly restless. After a while the curtains of the doorway parted, and Father Bartolomé entered without challenge. The good man was clad in a cassock of black serge, much frayed, and girt to the waist by a leathern belt, to which hung an ivory cross and a string of amber beads. At sight of him Cortes halted, and, leaning on his sword, said, " Bring thy bones here, father ; or, if such womanly habit suit thee better, rest them on the settle yonder. Anyhow, thou'rt welcome. I assure thee of the fact in advance of thy report."

" Thank thee, señor," he replied. " The cross, as thou mayst have heard, is proverbially heavy ; but its weight is to the spirit, not the body, like the iron with which thou keepest thyself so constantly clothed. I will come and stand by thee, especially as my words must be few, and to our own ears."

He went near, and continued in a low voice, and rapidly, " A deputation, appointed to confer with thee, is now coming. I sounded the men. I told them our condition ; how we are enclosed in the city, dependent upon an inconstant king for bread, without hope of succour, without a road of retreat. Following thy direction, I drew the picture darkly. Very soon they began asking, ' What thinkest thou ought to be done ?' As agreed between us, I suggested the seizure of Montezuma. They adopted the idea instantly ; and, that no consideration like personal affection for the king may influence thee to reject the proposal, the deputation cometh, with Diaz del Castillo at the head."

A gleam of humour twinkled in Cortes' eyes.

"Art sure they do not suspect me as the author of the scheme?"

"They will urge it earnestly as their own, and support it with arguments which"—the father paused a moment—"I am sure thou wilt find irresistible."

Cortes raised himself from the sword, and indulged a laugh while he crossed the room and returned.

"I thank thee, father," he said, resuming his habitual gravity. "So men are managed; nothing more simple, if we do but know how. The project hath been in my mind since we left Tlascala; but, as thou knowest, I feared it might be made of account against me with our imperial master. Now it cometh back as business of urgency to the army, to which men think I cannot say nay. Let them come; I am ready."

He began walking again, thumping the floor with his sword, while Olmedo took possession of a bench by the table. Presently there was heard at the door the sound of many feet, which you may be sure were not those of slippered damsels; for, at the bidding of Cortes, twelve soldiers came in, followed by several officers, and after them yet other soldiers. The general went to the table and seated himself. They ranged themselves about him, standing.

And for a time the chamber went back to its primitive use; but what were the audiences of Axaya' compared with this? Here was no painted cotton, or feather-work gaudy with the spoils of humming-birds and parrots: in their stead, the gleam and lustre blent with the brown of iron. One such Christian warrior was worth a hundred heathen chiefs. So thought Cortes, as he glanced at the faces before him, bearded, mustachioed, and shaded down to the eyes by well-worn morions.

"Good evening, gentlemen and soldiers," he said kindly, but without a bow. "This hath the appearance of business."

Diaz advanced a step, and replied,—

"Señor, we are a deputation from the army, appointed to beg attention to a matter which to us looketh serious; enough so, at least, to justify this appearance. We have been, and are, thy faithful soldiers, in whom thou mayest trust to the death, as our conduct all the way from the coast doth certify. Nor do we come to complain; on that score be at rest. But we are men of experience; a long campaign hath given us eyes to see and ability to consider a situation; while we submit willingly to all thy orders, trusting in thy superior sense, we yet think thou wilt not take it badly, nor judge us wanting in discipline and respect, if we venture the opinion that, despite the courtesies and fair seeming of the unbelieving king, Montezuma, we are, in fact, cooped up in this strong city as in a cage."

"I see the business already," said Cortes; "and, by my conscience! ye are welcome to help me consider it. Speak out, Bernal Diaz."

"Thank thee, señor. The question in our minds is, What shall be done next? We know that but few things bearing anywise upon our expedition escape thy eyes, and that of what is observed by thee nothing is forgotten; therefore, what I wish, first, is to refer some points to thy memory. When we left Cuba, we put ourselves in the keeping of the Holy Virgin, without any certain purpose. We believed there was in this direction somewhere a land peopled and full of gold for the finding. Of that we were assured when we set out from the coast to come here. And now that we are come, safe from so many dangers, and hardships, and battles, we think it no shame to admit that we were not prepared for what we find, so far doth the fact exceed all our imaginings; neither can we be charged justly with weakness or fear, if we all desire to know whether the expedition is at an end, and whether the time hath arrived to collect our gains, and divide them, and set our faces homeward. There are in the army some who think that time come; but I, and my associates here, are not of that opinion. We believe, with Father Olmedo, that God and the Holy Mother brought us to this land, and that we are their instruments; and that, in reward for our toils, and for setting up the cross in all these abominable temples, and bringing about the conversion of these heathen hordes, the country, and all that is in it, are ours."

"They are ours!" cried Cortes, dashing his sword against the floor until the chamber rang. "They are ours, all ours; subject only to the will of our master, the Emperor."

The latter words he said slowly, meaning that they should be remembered.

"We are glad, señor, to hear thy approval so heartily given," Diaz resumed. "If we are not mistaken in the opinion, and, following it up, decide to reduce the country to possession and the true belief,—something, I confess, not difficult to determine, since we have no ships in which to sail away,—then we think a plan of action should be adopted immediately. If the reduction can be best effected from the city, let us abide here, by all means; if not, the sooner we are beyond the dykes and bridges, and out of the valley, the better. Whether we shall remain, señor, is for thee to say. The army hath simply chosen us to make a suggestion, which we hope thou wilt accept as its sense; and that is, to seize the person of Montezuma, and bring him to these quarters, after which there will be no difficulty in providing for our wants and safety, and controlling, as may be best, the people, the city, the provinces, and all things else yet undiscovered."

"*Jesu Christo!*" exclaimed Cortes, like one surprised. "Whence got ye this idea? Much I fear the devil is abroad again." And he began to walk the floor, using long strides, and muttering to himself; retaking his seat, he said,—

"The proposition hath a bold look, soldiers and comrades, and for our lives' sake requireth careful thought. That we can govern the Empire through Montezuma, I have always held, and with that idea I marched you here, as the cavaliers now present can testify; but the taking and holding him prisoner,—by my conscience! ye out-travel me, and I must have time to think about the business. But, gentlemen,"—turning to the Captains Leon, Ordas, Sandoval, and Alvarado, who, as part of the delegation, had stationed themselves behind him,—"ye have reflected upon the business, and are of made-up minds. Upon two points I would have your judgments: first, can we justify the seizure to his Majesty the Emperor? secondly, how is the arrest to be accomplished? Speak thou, Sandoval."

"As thou knowest, Señor Hernan, what I say must be said bluntly, and with little regard for qualifications," Sandoval replied, lisping. "To me the seizure is a necessity, and as such justifiable to our royal master, himself so good a soldier. I have come to regard the heathen king as faithless, and therefore unworthy, except as an instrument in our hands. I cannot forget how we were cautioned against him in all the lower towns, and how, from all quarters, we were assured he meant to follow the pretended instructions of his god, allow us to enter the capital quietly, then fall upon us without notice and at disadvantage. And now that we are enclosed, he hath only to cut off our supplies of bread and water, and break down the bridges. So, señor, I avouch that, in my opinion, there is but one question for consideration, Shall we move against him, or wait until he is ready to move against us? I would rather surprise my enemy than be surprised by him."

"And what sayest thou, Leon?"

"The good Captain Sandoval hath spoken for me, señor. I would add, that some of us have to-day noticed that the king's steward, besides being insolent, hath failed to supply our tables as formerly. And from Aguilar, the interpreter, who hath his news from the Tlascalans, I learn that the Mexicans certainly have some evil plot in progress."

"And yet further, captain, say for me," cried Alvarado impetuously, "that the prince now with us—his name— The fiend take his name!"

"Thou wouldest say, the prince of Tezcuco; never mind his name," Cortes said gravely.

"Ay, never mind his name," Olmedo repeated, with a scarce perceptible gleam of humour. "At the baptism to-morrow I will give him something more Christian."

"As ye will, as ye will!" Alvarado rejoined impatiently. "I was about to say, that the Tezcucan averreth most roundly that the yells we heard this afternoon from the temple over the way signified a grand utterance from the god of war, and, of opinion that we will now be soon attacked, he refuseth to go into the city again."

"And thou, Ordas?"

"Señor," that captain replied, "I am in favour of the seizure. If, as all believe, Montezuma is bent to make war upon us, the best way to meet the danger is to arrest him in time. The question, simply stated, is, His liberty, or our lives? Moreover, I want an end to the uncertainty that so vexeth us night and day,—worse, by far, than any battle the heathen can offer."

Cortes played with the knot of his sword, and reflected.

"Such, then, is the judgment of the army," he finally said. "And such, gentlemen, is mine also. But is that enough? What we do as matter of policy may be approved of man, even our imperial master, of whom I am always regardful; but, as matter of conscience, the approval of Heaven must be looked for. Stand out, Father Bartolomé! Upon thy brow is the finger of St. Peter, at thy girdle the cross of Christ. What saith the Church?"

The good man arose, and held out the cross, saying,—

"My children, upon the Church, by Christ himself, this solemn 'hest hath been placed, good for all places, to be parted from never: 'Go ye into all the world, and preach the gospel to every creature.' The way hither hath been through strange seas and deadly climates. Hear me, that ye may know yourselves. Ye are the swords of the Church. In Cempoalla she preached; so in Tlascala; so in Cholula; and in all she cast out false gods, and converted whole tribes. Only in this city has the gospel not been proclaimed. And why? Because of a king who to-day, almost in our view, sacrificed men to his idols. Swords of the Church, which go before to make smooth her path, Christ and the Holy Mother must be taught in yon temple of sin. So saith the Church!"

There was much crossing of forehead and breast, and "Amen," and the sweet name "Ave Maria" sounded through the chamber, not in the murmur of a cathedral response, but outspokenly as became the swords of Christ. The sensation was hardly done when some one at the door called loudly for Alvarado.

"Who is he that so calleth? the captain asked angrily. "Let him choose another time."

The name was repeated more loudly.

"Tell the mouther to seek me to-morrow."

A third time the captain was called.

"May the devil fly away with the fellow! I will not go."

"Bid the man enter," said Cortes. "The disturbance is strange."

A soldier appeared, whom Alvarado, still angry, addressed. "How now? Dost thou take me for a kitchen-girl, apprenticed to answer thee at all times? What hast thou? Be brief. This goodly company waiteth."

"I crave thy pardon, captain. I crave pardon of the company," the soldier answered, saluting Cortes. "I am on duty at the main gate. A little while ago, a woman"—

"*Picaro!*" cried Alvarado contemptuously. "Only a woman!"

"Peace, captain! Let the man proceed," said Cortes, whose habit it was to hear his common soldiers gravely.

"As I was about saying, señor, a woman came running to the gate. She was challenged. I could not understand her, and she was much scared, for behind her on the street was a party that seemed to have been in pursuit. She cried, and pressed for admittance. My order is strict,—Admit no one after the evening gun. While I was trying to make her understand me, some arrows were shot by the party outside, and one passed through her arm. She then flung herself on the pavement, and gave me this cross, and said 'Tonatiah, Tonatiah!' As that is what the people call thee, Señor Alvarado, I judged she wanted it given to thee for some purpose. The shooting at her made me think that possibly the business might be of importance. If I am mistaken, I again pray pardon. Here is the cross. Shall I admit the woman?"

Alvarado took the cross, and looked at it once.

"By the saints! my mother's gift to me, and mine to the princess Nenetzin!" Of the soldier he asked, in a suppressed voice, "Is the woman old or young?"

"A girl, little more than a child."

"'Tis she! Mother of Christ, 'tis Nenetzin!"

And through the company, without apology, he rushed. The soldier saluted, and followed him.

"To the gate, Sandoval! See the rest of this affair, and report," said Cortes quietly. "We will stay the business until you return."

———

CHAPTER IX.

TRULY WONDERFUL—A FORTUNATE MAN HATH A MEMORY.

Two canoes, tied to the strand, attested that the royal party, and Io' and Hualpa, were yet at Chapultepec, which was no doubt as pleasant at night, seen of all the stars, as in the day, kissed by the softest of tropical suns.

That the lord Hualpa should linger there was most natural. Raised, almost as one is transported in dreams, from hunting to warriorship; from that again to riches and nobility; so lately contented, though at peril of life, to look from afar at the house in which the princess Nenetzin slept; now her betrothed, and so pronounced by the great king himself,—what wonder that he loitered at the palace? Yet it was not late,—in fact, on the horizon still shone the tint, the last and faintest of the day,— when he and Io' came out, and, arm in arm, took their way down the hill to the landing. What betides the lover? Is the mistress coy? Or runs he away at call of some grim duty?

Out of the high gate, down the terraced descent, past the avenue of ghostly cypresses, until their sandals struck the white shells of the landing, they silently went.

"Is it not well with you, my brother?" asked the prince, stopping where the boats, in keeping of their crews, were lying.

"Thank you for that word," Hualpa replied. "It is better even than comrade. Well with me? I look my fortune in the face, and am dumb. If I should belie expectation, if I should fall from such a height! O Mother of the World, save me from that! I would rather die!'

"But you will not fail," said Io' sympathetically.

"The gods keep the future; they only know. The thought came to me as I sat at the feet of Tula and Nenetzin,—came to me like a taste of bitter in a cup of sweets. Close after followed another even stronger,—how could I be so happy, and our comrade over the lake so miserable? We know how he has hoped and worked and lived for what the morrow is to bring: shall he not be notified even of its nearness? You have heard the sound of the war-drum: what is it like?"

"Like the roll of thunder."

"Well, when the thunder crosses the lake, and strikes his ear, saying, 'Up, the war is here!' he will come to the door, and down to the water's edge; there he must stop; and as he looks wistfully to the city, and strains his ear to catch the notes of the combat, will he not ask for us, and accuse us of forgetfulness? Rather than that, O my brother, let my fortune all go back to its giver."

"I understand you **now**," said the prince softly.

"Yes," Hualpa continued, "I am to be at the temple by the break of day ; but the night is mine, and I will go to the 'tzin my first friend, of Anahuac the soul, as Nenetzin is the flower."

"And I will go with you."

"No, you cannot. You have not permission. So farewell."

"Until to-morrow," said Io'.

"In the temple," answered Hualpa.

CHAPTER X.

HOW THE IRON CROSS CAME BACK.

Io' stayed at the landing awhile, nursing the thought left him by his comrade. And he **was** still there, the plash of the rowers of the receding canoe in **his ear**, when the great gate of the palace gave exit to another person, this time a girl. **The** guards on duty paid her no **attention**. She was clad simply and poorly, and carried a basket. **Around the** hill were scores of gardeners' daughters like her.

From the avenue **she turned** into a path which, through one **of** the fields below, led **her to** an inlet of the lake, where the market-people **were accustomed** to moor their canoes. The stars gave light, but **too feebly to reclaim** anything from the darkness. Groping amongst **the vessels**, she at length entered one, and, seating herself, **pushed clear** of the **land**, and **out in the** lake toward **the glow in the** sky beneath **which reposed the** city.

Like the night, **the** lake was calm ; **therefore, no fear for the** adventuress. The boat, under her hand, had **not the speed of the** king's when driven by his twelve practised **rowers ; yet she was** its mistress, and it obeyed her kindly. **But why the journey?** Why **alone** on the water at such a time?

Half an hour of steady work. The **city** was, of **course, much** nearer. **At the same** time, the labour began to tell ; **the reach of** her paddle **was not so** great as at the beginning, nor was **the dip** so deep ; **her** breathing **was** less free, and sometimes she **stopped** to draw a dripping hand across her forehead. **Surely** this **is not** a gardener's daughter.

Voyageurs now **became** frequent. Most of **them** passed by with the salutation usual **on** the lake,—"The blessings of the gods upon you !" Once she was in danger. A canoe full of singers, and the singers full of *pulque*, came down at speed upon her **vessel**. Happily, the blow was given obliquely ; the crash suspended the song ; the wassailers sprang to their feet ; seeing only a girl, and no harm done, they drew off, laughing. "Out with your lamp next time !" shouted one of them. A law of the lake required some such signal at night.

In the flurry of the collision, a *tamane*, leaning over the bow of the strange canoe, swung a light almost in the girl's face. With a cry, she shrank away ; as she did so, from her bosom fell a shining cross. To the dull slave the symbol told no tale ; but, good reader, we know that there is but one maiden in all Anahuac who wears such a jewel, and we know for whom she wears that one. By the light of that cross we also know the weary passenger is not a gardener's daughter, but Nenetzin the princess.

And the wonder grows. What does the 'tzin Nene—so they called her in the days they swung her to sleep in the swinging cradle—out so far alone on the lake? And where goes she in such guise, this night of all others, and now when the kiss of her betrothed is scarcely cold on her lips ! Where are the slaves? Where the signs of royalty? As prayed by the gentle *voyageurs*, the blessings of the gods may be upon her, but much I doubt if she has her mother's, almost as holy.

Slowly now she wins her way. The paddle grows heavier in her unaccustomed hands. On her brow gathers a dew which is neither of the night nor the lake. She is not within the radius of the temple lights, yet stops to rest, and bathe her palms in the cooling waves. Later, when the wall of the city, close by, stretches away on either side, far reaching, a margin of darkness under the illuminated sky, the canoe seems at last to conquer ; it floats at will idly as a log ; and in that time the princess sits motionless as the boat, lapsed in reverie. Her purpose, if she has one, may have chilled in the solitude or weakened under the labour. Alas, if the purpose be good ! If evil, help her, O sweet Mary, Mother !

The sound of paddles behind her broke the spell. With a hurried glance over her shoulder, she bent again to the task, and there was no more hesitation. She gained the wall, and passed in, taking the first canal. By the houses, and through the press of canoes, and under the bridges, to the heart of the city, she went. On the steps bordering a basin close to the street which had been Cortes' line of march the day of the entry, she landed, and, ascending to the thoroughfare, set out briskly, basket in hand, her face to the south. With never a look to the right or left, never a response to the idlers on the pavement, she hurried down the street. The watchers on the towers sung the hour ; she scarcely heard them. At last she reached the great temple. A glance at the *coatapantli*, one at the shadowy sanctuaries, to be sure of the locality ; then her eyes fell upon the palace of Axaya', and she stopped. The street to this point had been

thronged with people ; here there were none ; the strangers were
by themselves. The main gate of the ancient house stood half
open, and she saw the wheels of gun-carriages, and now and then
a Christian soldier pacing his round, slowly and grimly ; of the
little host, he alone gave signs of life. Over the walls she heard
the stamp of horses' feet, and once a neigh, shrill and loud. The
awe of the Indian in presence of the white man seized her, and
she looked and listened, half frightened, half worshipful, with
but one clear sense, and that was of the nearness of the Tonatiah.

A sound of approaching feet disturbed her, and she ran across
to the gate ; at once the purpose which had held her silent on the
azoteas, which prompted her ready acquiescence in the betrothal
to Hualpa, which had sustained her in the passage of the lake,
was revealed. She was seeking her lover to save him.

She would have passed through the gateway but for a number
of lances dropped with their points almost against her breast.
What with fear of those behind and of those before her, she
almost died. On the pavement, outside the entrance, she was
lying when Alvarado came to the rescue. The guard made way
for him quickly ; for in his manner was the warning which
nothing takes from words, not even threats ; verily, it had been
as well to attempt to hinder a leaping panther. He threw the
lances up, and knelt by her, saying tenderly, " Nenetzin, Nenetzin,
poor child ! It is I,—come to save you ! "

She half arose, and, smiling through her tears, clasped her
hands, and cried, " Tonatiah ! Tonatiah ! "

There are times when a look, a gesture, a tone of the voice, do
all a herald's part. What need of speech to tell the Spaniard
why the truant was there ? The poor disguise, the basket, told
of flight ; her presence at that hour said, " I have come to thee ; "
the cross returned, the tears, the joy at sight of him, certified her
love ; and so, when she put her arm around his neck, and the
arrow, not yet taken away, rattled against his corslet, to his heart
there shot a pain so sharp and quick it seemed as if the very soul
of him was going out.

He raised her gently, and carried her through the entrance.
The rough men looking on saw upon his cheek what, if the
cheek had been a woman's, they would have sworn was a tear.

" Ho, Marina ! " he cried to the wondering interpreter. " I
bring thee a bird dropped too soon from the nest. The hunter
hath chased the poor thing, and here is a bolt in its wing. Give
place in thy cot, while I go for a doctor, and room with thee,
that malice hurt not a good name."

And at the sight the Indian woman was touched ; she ran to
the cot, smoothed the pillow of feathers, and said, " Here, rest her
here, and run quickly. I will care for her."

He laid her down tenderly, but she clung to his hand, and said to Marina, " He must not go. Let him first hear **what I have to say."**

" But you are hurt."

" It is nothing, nothing. He must stay."

So earnestly did she speak, that the captain changed his mind. " Very well. What is spoken in pain should be spoken quickly. I will stay."

Nenetzin caught the assent, and went on rapidly. " Let him know that to-morrow at noon the drum in the great temple will be beaten, and the bridges taken up, and then there will be war."

" By the saints ! she bringeth doughty news," said Alvarado in his voice of soldier. " Ask her where she got it ; ask her, as you love us, Marina."

" From my father,—from the king himself."

" And this is child of Montezuma !" cried Marina.

" The princess Nenetzin," said the cavalier. " But stay not so. Ask her when and where she heard the news."

" To-day, at Chapultepec."

" What of the particulars ? How is the war to be made ? What are the preparations ?"

" The lord Cuitlahua is to take up the bridges. Maize and meat will be furnished to-morrow only. About the great temple now there are ten thousand warriors for an attack, and elsewhere in the city there are seventy thousand more."

" Enough," said Alvarado, kissing **the** little **hand. "Look** now to the hurt, Marina. Bring the light **; mayhap we can take** the bolt away ourselves."

Marina knelt, and examined the wounded arm, and **shortly** held up the arrow.

" Good !" the cavalier said. " Thou art a doctor, indeed, Marina. In the schools at home they give students big-lettered parchments. I will do better by thee ; I will cover the arm that did this surgery with bracelets of gold. Run now, and bring cloth and water. The blood thou seest trickling here is from her heart, which loveth me too dearly to suffer such waste. Haste thee ! haste thee !"

They bathed the wound, and applied the bandages, though all too roughly to suit the cavalier, who, thereupon, turned to go, saying, " Sit thou there, Marina, and leave her not, except to do her will. Tell her I will return, and to be at rest, for she is safe as in her father's house. If any do but look at her wrongfully, they shall account to me. So, by my mother's cross, I swear !"

And he hurried back to the audience-chamber, **where** the council was yet in session. While he related what had been told by Nenetzin, a deep silence pervaded the assemblage, and the brave men, from looking at each other, turned, with singular unanimity, to Cortes; who, thus appealed to, threw off his affectation, and, standing up, spoke so as to be heard by all,—

"Comrades, soldiers, gentlemen, let there be no words more. The step you have urged upon me, in the name of the army, I hesitated to take. I grant you, I hesitated; but not from love of the soft-tongued, lying, pagan king. Bethink ye. We left Cuba hastily, as ye all remember, because of a design to arrest us there as malefactors and traitors. Now, when our enemies in that island hear from our expedition, and have told them all its results,—the wealth we have won, and the country, cities, peoples, and empire discovered,—envy and jealousy will pursue us, and false tongues go back to Spain, and fill the ears of our royal master with reports intended to rob us of our glory and despoil us of our hire. How could I know but the seizure in question might be magnified into impolicy and cruelty, and furnish cause for disgrace, imprisonment, and forfeiture. For that I hesitated. This news, however, endeth doubt and debate. The over-cunning king hath put himself outside of mercy or compassion; we are compelled to undo him. So far, well. Let me remind ye now, that the news of which I speak hath in it a warning which it were sinful not to heed. Yesterday the great infidel was at our mercy; not more difficult his capture then than a visit to his palace; but now, in all the histories of bold performances, nothing bolder,—nothing of the Cid's, nothing of King Arthur's. In the heart of his capital we are to make prisoner him the head of millions, the political ruler and religious chief, not merely secure in the love and fear of his subjects, but in the height of his careful preparation for war, in the centre of his camp, within call, nay, under the eyes, of his legions, numbering thousands where we number tens. Take ye each, my brave brethren, the full measure of the design, and then tell me, in simple words, how it may be best done. And among ye, let him speak who can truly say, I dare do what my tongue delivereth. I wait your answer."

And in the chamber there again fell a hush so deep that those present might well have been taken for ghosts. The idea as first seen by them was commonplace; under his description, it became heroic; and struggling, as he suggested, to measure it each for himself, all were dumb.

"Good gentlemen," said Cortes, smiling, "why so laggard now? Speak, Diaz del Castillo. Offer what thou canst."

The good soldier, and afterward good chronicler, of the conquest and its trials, this one among the rest, replied, "I confess, señor, the enterprise is difficult beyond my first thought. I confess, also, to more reflection about its necessity than its achievement. To answer truthfully, at this time I see but one

way **to the** end ; and **that** is, to invite the monarch **here** under
some sufficient pretence, and then lay hands on him."

"Are **ye** all of the same minds, gentlemen?"

There was a murmur of assent, whereupon **Cortes arose from**
leaning upon his sword, and said sharply,—

"To hear ye, gentlemen, **one** would think the summer all
before us in which to interchange courtesies with the royal
barbarian. What is the fact? At noon to-morrow our hours of
grace expire. A beat of drum, and then assault, and after that,"—
he paused, looking grimly round the circle,—"and after that,
sacrifices to the gods, I suppose."

There was a general movement and outcry. **Some griped**
their arms, others crossed themselves. Cortes **saw and pressed**
his advantage.

"I shall not take your advice, Bernal Diaz,—not I, by my
conscience! Heaven helping me, I expect to see old Spain
again ; and more, I expect to take these comrades back with me,
rich in glory and gold." Then, to the officers behind him, he
said, **in** his ordinary tone of command, "Ordas, do thou bid the
carpenters prepare quarters in this palace for Montezuma and his
court ; and let them begin their work to-night, for he will be our
guest before noon to-morrow. And thou, Leon, thou, Lugo,
thou, Avila, and thou, Sandoval, **get ye** ready to go with me to
the "—

"And I?" asked Alvarado.

"Thou shalt go also."

"And the army, señor?" Diaz suggested.

"The army shall remain in quarters."

Never man's manner more calm, never man more absolutely
assured. The listeners warmed with admiration. As unconscious
of the effect he was working, he went on,—

"I have shown the difficulties of the enterprise ; now I say
further, the crisis of the expedition is upon us : if I succeed, all
is **won ; if** I fail, all is lost. In such strait, what should we do
between **this** and then? Let us not trust in our cunning and
strength : we are Christians ; as such, put we our faith in Christ
and the Holy Mother. Olmedo, father, go thou to the chapel,
and get ready the altar. The night to confession and prayer ;
and let the morning find **us on** our knees shrieved and blessed.
We are done, comrades. **Let** the chamber be cleared. To the
chapel all."

And they did the bidding cheerfully. All night **the** good
father was engaged in holy work, confessing, shrieving, praying.
So the morning found them.

CHAPTER XI.

THE CHRISTIAN TAKES CARE OF HIS OWN.

HUALPA returned to the city about the time the stars which, in
that clime and season, herald the morning take their places in
the sky. He had lightened his heart, and received the sympathy
of a lover in return; he had told the great things done and promised by the king, and sorrowed that his friend could take no
part in the events which, he imagined, were to make the day
heroic for ever; and now, his enthusiasm of youth sobered by
the plaints to which he had listened while traversing the dusky
walks of the beautiful garden, he climbed the stairs of the
teocallis. Before the day was fairly dawned, he was at his
post, waiting, dreaming of Nenetzin, and hearkening to the
spirit-songs of ambition, always so charming to unpractised
souls.

And the lord Cuitlahua perfected his measures. On all the
dykes, and at the entrance of all the canals, guards were stationed.
The bridges nearest the palace occupied by the strangers were
held by chosen detachments. Except those thus detailed, the
entire military in the city were pent in the temples. And to
all, including the lord steward, the proper orders were confided.
All awaited the signal.

And the king, early in the night, ignorant of the flight of
Nenetzin, had come from Chapultepec to his palace in the capital.
He retired as he was wont, and slept the sleep as restful to a
mind long distracted by irresolution as to a body exhausted by
labour; such slumber as comes to him who, in time of doubt,
involving all nearest interests, at last discovers what his duty is,
and, fully determined, simply awaits the hour of performance,
trustful of the action taken, and of the good-will of the god or
gods of his faith.

On the side of the Christians, the preparation, more simple,
was also complete. From mass the little host went to breakfast, then to arms. The companies formed; even the Tlascalans
behaved as if impressed with a sense that their fate had been
challenged.

To the captains, again convoked in the audience-chamber,
Cortes detailed his plan of operation. His salutation of each
was grave and calm. Though very watchful, they heard him
without question; and when they went out, they might have
said, The hour of trial is come, and now will be seen which
holds the conquering destiny,—the God of the Christian or that
of the Aztec.

From the council, Alvarado went first to Marina ; finding that Nenetzin slept, he joined his companions in the great court, where, gay and careless, he carolled a song, and twirled his sword, and, in thought of smiling fortune and a princely Indian love, walked complacently to and fro. And so wait, ready for action, the Christian lover and the heathen,—one in the palace, the other in the temple,—both in fancy lord of the same sweet mistress.

At the stated hour, as had been the custom, the three lords came, in splendid costume, and with stately ceremonial, bringing the king's compliments, and asking Cortes' will for the day. And they returned with compliments equally courteous and deceptive, taking with them Orteguilla, the page, instructed to inform the monarch that directly, if such were the royal pleasure, Malinche would be happy to visit him in his palace.

A little later there went out parties of soldiers, apparently to view the city ; yet the point was noticeable that, besides being fully armed, each was in charge of a chosen subordinate. Later, the army was drawn up, massed in the garden ; the matches of the gunners were lighted ; the horsemen stood at their bridles ; the Tlascalans were stationed to defend the outer walls. De Oli, Morla, Marin, and Monjarez passed through the lines in careful inspection.

"Heardest thou when the drum was to be sounded ?" asked De Oli, looking to the sun.

"At noon," answered Marin.

"Three hours yet, as I judge. Short time, by Our Lady !"

The party was impatient. To their relief, Cortes at last came out, with his five chosen cavaliers, Sandoval, Alvarado, Leon, Avila, and Lugo. As he proceeded to the gate, all eyes turned to him, all hearts became confident,—so much of power over the weak is there in the look of one master spirit.

At the gate he waited for the Doña Marina.

"Are ye ready, gentlemen ?"

"All ready," they replied.

"With thee, De Oli, I leave the command. At sight or sound of attack or combat, come quickly. Charge straight to the palace, lances in the lead. Bring our horses. Farewell. Christ and the Mother for us !" And with that, Cortes stepped into the street.

For a time the party proceeded silently.

"Is not this what the pagans call the beautiful street ?" Sandoval asked.

"Why the question ?"

"I have gone through graveyards not more deserted."

"Thou'rt right," said Lugo. "By Our Lady ! when last we

went this way, I remember the pavements, doors, porticoes, and roofs were crowded. Now, not a woman or a child."

"In faith, señor, we are a show suddenly become stale."

"Be it so," replied Leon sneeringly. "We will give the public a new trick."

"*Mirad, señores!*" said **Cortes.** "Last night, all through **this** district, particularly along the street, there went patrols, removing the inhabitants, and making ready for what the drum is advertised to let loose upon us. **Don** Pedro, thy princess hath told the truth." And, looking back to the towers of the *teocallis*, he added, after a fit of laughter, "The fools, the swine! They have undone themselves; or, rather," — his face became grave on the instant, — "the Holy Mother hath undone them for us. Give thanks, gentlemen, our emprise is already won! Yonder the infidel general hath his army in waiting for the word of the king. Keep we that **unspoken or** undelivered, — only that, — and the way of **our** return, prisoner in hand, will be as clear of **armed men as the** going is."

The customary guard **of** nobles kept the portal of the palace; the antechamber, however, was crowded to its full capacity with unarmed courtiers, through whom the Christians passed with grave assurance. To acquaintances Cortes bowed courteously. Close by the door of the audience-chamber he found Orteguilla conversing with Maxtla, who, at sight of him, knelt, and, touching the floor with his palm, offered to conduct the party to the royal **presence;** such were his orders. Cortes stopped an instant.

"Hath the king company?" he asked Orteguilla.

"None of account, — a boy and three or four old **men.**"

"He is ours. Let us on, gentlemen!"

And forthwith they passed under the curtains held aside for them by Maxtla.

On **a dais** covered with a carpet of *plumaje* the monarch sat. **Three venerable** men stood behind him. At his feet, a little to the right, **was the** prince Io', in uniform. A flood of light poured through a window on the northern side of the chamber, and fell full on the group, bringing out with intense clearness the rich habiliments of the monarch and every feature of his face. The Christians numbered the attendance, and, trained to measure dangers and **discover** advantages by a glance, smiled at the confidence **of** the treacherous heathen. Upon the stillness, broken only by their ringing tread, **sped** the voice of Cortes.

"Alvarado, Lugo, **all of ye, watch well** whom we **have here.** On your lives, see that the boy escape not."

Montezuma kept his seat.

"The gods keep you this pleasant morning," he **said.** "I am glad to see you."

They bowed to him, and Cortes replied,—

"We thank thee, good king. May the **Holy** Virgin, of our Christian faith, have thee in care. Thus **pray** we, than whom thou hast no truer servants."

"If you prefer to sit, I will have seats brought."

"We thank thee again. In the presence of our master it is the custom to stand, and he would hold us discourteous if we did otherwise before a sovereign friend **as dear to** him as thou art, great king."

The monarch waved his hand.

"Your master is no doubt a rare and excellent **sovereign,**" he said, then changed the subject. "The lords, whom I **sent to** you this morning, reported that all goes well with you in the palace. I hope so. If anything is wanted, **you** have only to speak. My provinces are at your service."

"**The** lords reported truly."

"I am very glad. Thinking **of** you, Malinche, and studying to make your contentment perfect, I have wondered if you have any amusements **or** games with which to pass the time."

As there were not in **all the** New World, however **it** might be in the Old, more desperate gamblers than the cavaliers, they looked at each other when the translation was concluded, and smiled at the simplicity of the speaker. Nevertheless, Cortes replied, with becoming gravity,—

"We have **our** pastimes, good king, as all must **have** ; for without them nature hath ordered that the body shall grow old and the mind incapable. Our pastimes, however, relate almost entirely to war."

"That is labour, Malinche."

"So is hunting," said Cortes, smiling.

"My practice is not," answered the monarch, taking the remark **as** an allusion to his own love of **the** sport, and laughing. "The lords drive the game to me, and my pleasure is in exercising the skill required to take it. Some day you must go with me to my preserves **over** the lake, and I will show you my modes. But I did not mean **that** kind of amusement. I will explain **my** meaning. Io'," he **said** to the prince, who had arisen, "bid Maxtla bring hither the silver balls. I will teach Malinche to play *totoloque.*"

"Have a care, gentlemen!" **said Cortes,** divining the speech from the action of the speaker. "**The lad must stay.** And thou, Marina, tell him so."

The comely, gentle-hearted Indian woman hastened tremulously to say, "Most mighty king, Malinche bids me tell thee that

he has heard of the beautiful game, and will be glad to learn it,
but not now. He wishes the prince to remain."

One step Io' had in the meantime taken,—but one ; in front
of him Leon stepped, hand on sword, and menace on his brow.
The blood fled the monarch's face.

"Go not," he at length said to the boy ; and to Cortes, "I do
not understand you, Malinche.'

The time of demand was come. Cortes moved nearer the dais,
and replied, his eyes fixed coldly and steadily on those of the
victim,—

"I have business with thee, king ; and, until it is concluded,
thou, the prince, and thy counsellors must stay. Outcry, or
attempt at escape, will be at peril of life."

The monarch sat upright, pale and rigid ; the ancients dropped
upon their knees. Io' alone was brave ; he stepped upon the
platform, as if to defend the royal person. Then, in the same
cold, inflexible manner, Cortes proceeded,—

"I have been thy guest, false king, long enough to learn thee
well. The power which, on all occasions, thou has been so careful
to impress upon me hath but made thy hypocrisy the more
astonishing. Listen, while I expose thee to thyself. We started
hither at thy invitation. In Cholula, nevertheless, we were set
upon by the army. No thanks to thee that we are alive to-day.
And, in the same connection, when thou wert upbraided for
inviting us, the lords and princes were told that such was the
instruction of one of thy bloody gods, who had promised here in
the capital to deliver us prisoners for sacrifice."

Montezuma offered to speak.

"Deny it not, deny it not !" said Cortes, with the slightest
show of passion. "In god or man, such perfidy cannot be
excused. But that is not all. Say nothing about the command
sent the troops near Tuzpan to attack my people ; nor about
the demand upon townships under protection of my royal
master for women and children to feed to thy hungry idols ;
now"—

Here the king broke in upon the interpreter,—

"I do not understand what Malinche says about my troops
attacking his people at Tuzpan."

"Thy governor killed one of my captains."

"Not by my order."

"Then make good the denial, by sending for the officer who
did the murder, that he may be punished according to the
wickedness of his crime."

The king took a signet from his wrist, and said to one of his
counsellors, "Let this be shown to the governor of that province.
I require him to come here immediately, with all who were
concerned with him at the time spoken of by Malinche."

The smile with which the monarch then turned to the Spaniard **was** lost upon him, for he continued, pitilessly as before,—

"The punishment of the governor is not enough. I **accuse** thee further. Thou treacherous king! Go with me **to the** temple, and now—this instant—I will **show** thee thy brother, with an army at call, waiting thy signal to attack us in the palace where so lately we received thy royal welcome."

The listener started from his seat. Upon his bewildered faculties flashed the remembrance of how carefully and with what solemn injunction he had locked his plans of war in the breasts of the members of his family, gathered about him on the *azoteas* at Chapultepec. His faith in them forbade suspicion. Whence then the exposure? And to the dealer in mysteries Mystery answered, "The gods!" If his former faith in the divinity of the stranger came not back, now, at least, he knew him sustained by powers with which contention were folly. He sank down again; his head dropped upon his struggling breast; —**HE** WAS CONQUERED!

And **the** stern Spaniard, as **if** moved by the sight, said **in a** softened voice,—

"I know not of thy religion; but there is a law of ours—a mercy of the dear Christ who hath us in his almighty keeping— by which every sin may be atoned by sacrifices, not of innocent victims, but of the sinner's self. In the world I come from, so much is the law esteemed, that kings greater than thou have laid down their crowns, the better to avail themselves of its salvation. Thou art an unbeliever, and I may do wrong,—if so, I **pray** pardon of the Holy Ghost that heareth me,—I may do wrong, I say, but, infidel as thou art, if thou wilt obey the precept, thou shalt have the benefit of the privilege. I do not want war which would end in thy destruction and the ruin of thy city and people; therefore I make thee a proposal. Hear me!"

The unhappy king raised his head, and listened eagerly.

"Arise, and go with us to our quarters, and take up thy abode there. King shalt thou continue. Thy court can go with thee, and thou canst govern from one palace as well as another. To make an end of speech,"—and Cortes raised his hand tightly clenched,—"to make an end of speech, finally and plainly, choose now: go with us or die! I have not brought these officers without a purpose."

All eyes centred on the pale face of the monarch, and **the** stillness of the waiting was painful and breathless. At last, from the depths of his tortured soul, up rose a sparkle of resentment.

"Who ever heard of a great prince, like myself, voluntarily leaving his own palace to become a prisoner in the hands of a stranger?"

"Prisoner! Not so. Hear me again. Court, household, and power, with full freedom for its exercise, and the treatment due a crowned prince,—all these shalt thou have. So, in my master's name, I pledge thee."

"No, Malinche, press me not so hardly. Were I to consent to such a degradation, my people would not. Take one of my sons rather. This one,"—and he laid his hand on Io's shoulder,—"whom I love best, and have thought to make my successor. Take him as hostage; but spare me this infamy."

The debate continued; an hour passed.

"Gentlemen, why waste words on this wretched barbarian?" exclaimed Leon at last, half drawing his sword, while his face darkened with dreadful purpose. "We cannot recede now. In Christ's name, let us seize him, or plunge our swords in his body!"

The captains advanced, baring their swords; Cortes retired a step, as if to make way for them. Brief time remained for decision. Trembling and confused, the monarch turned to Marina, and asked, "What did the *teule* say?"

As became a gentle woman, fearful lest death be done before her, she replied,—

"O king, I pray you make no further objection. If you yield, they will treat you kindly; if you refuse, they will kill you. Go with them, I pray you."

Upon the advance of the captains, Io' stepped in front of the king; as they hesitated, either waiting Cortes' order or the answer to Marina's prayer, he knelt, and clasped his father's knees, and cried tearfully,—

"Do not go, O king! Rather than endure such shame, let us die!"

Stupefied, almost distraught, the monarch seemed not to hear the heroic entreaty. His gaze was on the face of Cortes, now as impenetrable and iron-like as the armour on his breast. "The gods have abandoned me!" he cried despairingly. "I am lost! Malinche, I will go with you!" His head drooped, and his hands fell nerveless on the chair.

The boy arose, and turned to the conquerors, every feature convulsed with hate.

"Thanks, good king, thanks!" said Cortes, smiling. "Thou hast saved my soul a sin. I will be thy friend till death!"

Thereupon he stepped forward and kissed the royal hand, which fell from his lips as if palsied—I will not say profaned —by the touch. And, one after another, Leon, Lugo, Avila, Alvarado, and Sandoval approached, and knelt on the dais, and in like manner saluted the fallen prince.

"Are you done, Malinche?" the victim asked, when somewhat revived.

"What I wish now, above all things," was the reply, spoken with rare pretence of feeling, "is to be assured, good king, that we are forgiven the pain we have caused thee, since, though of our doing, it was not of our will as much as of the ambition of some of thy own lords and chiefs. What I desire next is, that thy goodness may not be without immediate results. I and my officers, thy son and these counsellors, are witnesses that thou didst consent to my proposal out of great love of peace and thy people. To secure the object,—noble beyond praise,—the lords here in the palace, and those of influence throughout the provinces, must be convinced that thou dost go with me of thine own free will ; not as prisoner, but as trusted guest returning the favour of guest. How to do that best is in thy knowledge more than mine. Only, what thy judgment approveth, set about quickly. We wait thy orders."

"Io', uncles," said Montezuma, his eyes dim with tears, "as you love me, be silent as to what has here taken place. I charge you that you tell it to no man, while I live. Bid Maxtla come."

Summoning all his strength to meet the shrewd eyes of the chief, the monarch sat up with a show of cheerfulness.

"Bring my palanquin," he said, after Maxtla's salutation ; "and direct some of the elder lords to be ready to accompany me without arms or ceremony. As advised by Huitzil', and these good uncles, I have resolved to go, and for a time abide with Malinche in the old palace. Send an officer, with the workmen, to prepare quarters for my use and that of the court. Publish my intention. Go quickly."

Afterwhile from the palace issued a procession which no man, uninformed, might look upon and say was not a funeral : in the palanquin, the dead ; on its right and left, the guard of honour ; behind, the friends, a long train, speechless and sorrowing. The movement was quiet and solemn ; three squares and as many bridges were passed, when, from down the street, a man came running with all speed. He gained the rear of the cortège, and spoke a few hurried words there ; a murmur arose, and spread, and grew into a furious outcry,—a moment more, and the cortège was dissolved in tumult. At the last corner on the way, the cavaliers had been joined by some of the armed parties, who, for the purpose, had preceded them into the city in the early morning ; these closed firmly around, a welcome support.

"*Mirad !*" cried Cortes loudly. "The varlets are without arms. Let no one strike until I say so."

The demonstration increased. Closer drew the mob, some adjuring the monarch, some threatening the Christians. That an understanding of the situation was abroad was no longer doubtful ; still **Cortes** held his men in check, for he knew, if blood were shed now, **the common-sense** of the people would refuse the story he so relied upon,—that the king's coming was voluntary.

"**Can** our guest," he **asked** of Sandoval, "be sleeping the while?"

"Treachery, señor."

"By God's love, captain, **if** it so turn out, **drive** thy sword first of all things through him !"

While yet he spoke, **the** curtains of the carriage **were** drawn aside ; the carriers **halted** instantly ; and, of the concourse, all the natives **fell upon their** knees, and became still, so that the **voice of the monarch** was distinctly heard.

"**The noise** disturbs me," he said in ordinary tone. "Let the street be cleared."

The lords whom he addressed kept **their faces to** the ground.

"What is the cause of the clamour ?"

No one answered. **A frown was gathering upon his** face, when an **Aztec sprang up, and drew near him.** He **was** dressed as a citizen of the lower class. At the side of the carriage he stopped, and touched the pavement with his palm.

"**Guatamozin !**" said the king, more **in astonishment than anger.**

"**Even so. O** king,—father,—to **bear a soldier's part to-day,** I have dared your judgment." **Lifting** his eyes to the monarch's, he endured his gaze steadily, but at the same time with such an expression of sympathy that reproof was impossible. "I am prepared for any sentence ; but first, let me know—let these lords and all the people **know, is this going in** truth **of** your own free will ?"

Montezuma regarded him fixedly, but not in wrath.

"I conjure you, uncle, father, king,—I **conjure** you, by our royal blood, by **our** country, by all the gods,—are **these** strangers **guests** or guards? Speak,—I **pray you,** speak but one word."

The poor stricken monarch **heard,** and was penetrated by the tone of **anguish ;** yet he replied,—

"**My brother's** son insults me by his question. I am **still the king,—free** to go and come, **to reward** and punish."

He would have spoken further, and kindly, but for **the inter-ruption** of Cortes, who cried impatiently,—

"**Ho, there !** Why this delay? Forward !"

And thereupon **Avila stepped rudely** and insolently between the king and the 'tzin. The **latter's** broad **breast** swelled, and his eyes blazed ; he seemed like a tiger **about to leap.**

"Beware !" said **the** king, **and the warning was in** time. "Beware ! Not here, not now !"

The 'tzin turned to him with a quick, anxious look of inquiry ; **a revulsion of** feeling ensued ; he **arose,** and said with bowed head, " I understand. O king, if we help **not** ourselves, we are lost. 'Not here, not now.' I catch the permission." Pointing to Avila, he added, "This man's life **is in** my hands, but I pass it by ; thine, O uncle, **is** the most precious. We will punish **these** insolents, but *not here ;* **we** will give you rescue, but *not **now**.* Be of cheer."

He stepped aside, **and** the melancholy cortège passed on, leaving **the** lords and people **and** the Empire, as represented by them, in **the** dust. Before the *teocallis,* under the eyes of Cuitlahua, within hailing distance of the ten thousand warriors, the doughty cavaliers bore their prize unchallenged.

And through the gates **of** the **old** palace, through the files **of** Spaniards in order of **battle** waiting, they also carried what they thought was the Empire, won without a blow, to be parcelled at pleasure,—its lands, its treasures, its cities, and its people.

BOOK SIX.

CHAPTER I.

THE LORD HUALPA FLEES HIS FORTUNE.

THE 'tzin Guatamo sat at breakfast alone in his palace near Iztapalapan. The fare was simple,—a pheasant, bread of maize,
oranges and bananas, and water from the spring; and the repast
would have been soon despatched but for the announcement, by a
slave in waiting, of the lord Hualpa. At mention of the name,
the 'tzin's countenance assumed a glad expression.

"The lord Hualpa! The gods be praised! Bid him come."

Directly the visitor appeared at the door, and paused there, his
eyes fixed upon the floor, his body bent, like one half risen from
a salutation. The 'tzin went to him, and, taking his hand, said,—

"Welcome, comrade! Come and account for yourself. I know
not yet how to punish you; but, for the present, sit there and eat.
If you come from Tenochtitlan this morning, you must bring with
you the appetite which is one of the blessings of the lake. Sit,
and I will order your breakfast."

"No, good 'tzin, not for me, I pray you. I am from the lake,
but do not bring any blessing."

The 'tzin resumed his seat, looking searchingly and curiously at
his guest, and pained by his manner and appearance. His face
was careworn; his frame bent and emaciated; his look constantly
downward; the voice feeble and of uncertain tone,—in short, his
aspect was that of one come up from a battle in which shame and
grief had striven with youth of body and soul, and, fierce as the
struggle had been, the end was not yet. He was the counterpart
of his former self.

"You have been sick," said the 'tzin afterwhile.

"Very sick, in spirit," replied Hualpa, without raising his eyes.

The 'tzin went on. "After your desertion, I caused inquiry to
be made for you everywhere,—at the Chalcan's, and at your
palace. No one could give me any tidings. I sent a messenger

239

to Tihuanco, and your father was no better informed. Your truancy has been grievous to your friends, no less than to yourself. I have a right to call you to account."

"So you have; only let us to the garden. The air outside is sweet, and there is a relief in freedom from walls."

From habit, I suppose, they proceeded to the arena set apart for military exercise. No one was there. The 'tzin seated himself on a bench, making room for Hualpa, who still declined the courtesy, saying,—

"I will give an account of myself to you, brave 'tzin, not only because I should, but because I stand in need of your counsel. Look for nothing strange; mine is a simple story of shame and failure. You know its origin already. You remember the last night I spent with you here. I do, at least. That day the king made me happier than I shall ever be again. When I met you at the landing, the kiss of my betrothed was sweet upon my lips, and I had but one sorrow in the world,—that you were an exile, and could not take part, as you so wished and deserved, in the battle which my hand was to precipitate next noon. I left you, and by dawn was at my post in the temple. The hours were long. At last the time came. All was ready. The ten thousand warriors chosen for the assault were in their quarters. The lord Cuitlahua was in the tower of Huitzil', with the *teotuctli* and his pabas, at prayer. We awaited only the king's word. Finally, Io' appeared. I saw him coming. I raised the stick, my blood was warm, another instant and the signal would have been given"— Hualpa's voice trembled, and he stopped.

"Go on," said the 'tzin. "What restrained you?"

"I remembered the words of the king,—'Io' will come to you at noon with my commands,'—those were the words. I waited. 'Strike!' said Io'. 'The command,—quick!' I cried. 'As you love life, strike!' he shouted. Something unusual had taken place; I hesitated. 'Does the king so command?' I asked. 'Time never was as precious! Give me the stick!' he replied. But the duty was mine. 'With your own hand give the signal,'— such was the order. I resisted, and he gave over the effort, and, throwing himself at my feet, prayed me to strike. I refused the prayer also. Suddenly he sprang up, and ran out to the verge of the temple overlooking the street. Lest he should cast himself off, I followed. He turned to me, as I approached, and cried with upraised hands, 'Too late, too late! We are undone. Look where they carry him off!' 'Whom?' I asked. 'The king—my father—a prisoner!' Below, past the *coatapantli*, the royal palanquin was being borne, guarded by the strangers. The blood stood still in my heart. I turned to the prince; he was gone. A sense of calamity seized me. I ran to the tower, and called the lord Cuitlahua, who was in time to see the procession. I shall never forget the awful look he gave me, or his words." Hualpa again paused.

"What were they?" asked the 'tzin.

"'My lord Hualpa,' he said, 'had you given the signal when Io' came to you first, I could have interposed my companies and saved him. It is now too late; he is lost. May the gods forgive you! A ruined country cannot.'"

"Said he so?" exclaimed the 'tzin indignantly. "By all the gods, he was wrong!"

At these words, Hualpa for the first time dared look into the 'tzin's face, surprised, glad, yet doubtful.

"How?" he asked. "Did you say I was right?"

"Yes."

Tears glistened in the Tihuancan's eyes, and he seized and kissed his friend's hand with transport.

"I begin to understand you," the 'tzin said still more kindly. "You thought it your fault that the king was a prisoner; you fled for shame."

"Yes,—for shame."

"My poor friend!"

"But consider," said Hualpa,—"consider how rapidly I had risen, and to what height. Admitting my self-accusations, when before did man fall so far and so low? What wonder that I fled?"

"Well, you have my judgment. Seat yourself, and hear me further."

Hualpa took the seat this time; after which the 'tzin continued. "The seizure was made in the palace. The king yielded to threats of death. He could not resist. While the strangers were bearing him past the *teocallis*, and you were looking at them, their weapons were at his throat. Had you yielded to Io's prayer, and given the signal, and had Cuitlahua obeyed, and with his bands attempted a rescue, your benefactor would have been slain. Do not think me dealing in conjectures. I went to him in the street, and prayed to be allowed to save him; he forbade me. Therefore, hold not yourself in scorn; be happy; you saved his life a second time."

Again Hualpa gave way to his gratitude.

"Nor is that all," the 'tzin continued. "In my opinion, the last rescue was nobler than the first. As to the lord Cuitlahua, be at rest. He was not himself when he chid you so cruelly; he now thinks as I do; he exonerates you; his messengers have frequently come, asking if you had returned. So, no more of shame. Give me now what else you did."

The sudden recall to the past appeared to throw Hualpa back; his head sank upon his breast again, and for a time he was silent. At length he replied, "As I see now, good 'tzin, I have been very foolish. Before I go on, assure me that you will listen with charity."

"With charity and love."

"I have hardly the composure to tell what more I did; yet the story will come to you in some form. Judge me mercifully, and let the subject be never again recalled."

"You have spoken."

"Very well. I have told you the words of the lord Cuitlahua; they burnt me, like fire. Thinking myself for ever disgraced, I descended from the *azoteas* to the street, and there saw the people's confusion, and heard their cries and curses. I could not endure myself. I fled the city, like a guilty wretch. Instinctively I hurried to Tihuanco. There I avoided every habitation, even my father's. News of evil travels fast. The old merchant, I knew, must needs hear of the king's seizure and what I regarded as my crime. So I cared not to meet his eyes. I passed the days in the jungles hunting, but the charm of the old occupation was gone; somehow my arrows flew amiss, and my limbs refused a long pursuit. How I subsisted, I scarcely know. At last, however, my ideas began to take form, and I was able to interrogate myself. Through the king's bounty, I was a lord, and owner of a palace; by his favour, I further reflected, Nenetzin was bound to me in solemn betrothal. What would she think of me? What right had I, so responsible for his great misfortune, to retain his gifts? I could release her from the odious engagement. At his feet I could lay down the title and property; and then, if you refused me as a soldier or slave, I could hide myself somewhere; for the grief-struck and unhappy, like me, earth has its caverns and ocean its islands. And so once more I hurried to Tenochtitlan. Yesterday I crossed the lake. From the Chalcan I heard the story which alone was needed to make my humiliation complete,—how Nenetzin, false to me, betrayed the great purpose of her father, betook herself to the stranger's house, adopted his religion, and became his wife or—spare me the word, good 'tzin. After that, I lost no time, but went to the palace, made way through the pale-faced guards at the gate and doors, each of whom seemed placed there to attest the good king's condition and my infamy. Suitors and lords of all degrees crowded the audience-chamber when I entered, and upon every face was the same look of sorrow and dejection which I had noticed upon the faces of the people whom I passed in the street. All who turned eyes upon me appeared to become accusers, and say, 'Traitor, behold thy victim!' Imagine the pressure upon my spirit. I made haste to get away,—unseemly haste. What my salutation was I hardly know. I only remember that, in some form of speech, I publicly resigned all his honourable gifts. I remember, also, that when I took what I thought was my last look at him,—friend, patron, king, father,—may the gods, who have forbidden the relation, forgive the allusion!—I

could not see him for tears. My heart is in my throat **now; then**
it nearly choked me. And so ends my account. And once more,
true friend, I come to you, Hualpa, the Tihuancan, without title,
palace, or privilege ; without distinction, except as the hero and
victim of a marvellous fortune."

The 'tzin was too deeply touched, too full **of** sympathy, to reply
immediately. He arose, and paced the arena awhile. Resuming
his seat again, he asked simply, "And what said the king ?"

" To what ?"

" Your resignation."

" He refused **to take back his** gifts. They could not revert, he
said, except for **crime.**"

" And he **was right.** You should have known him better. A
king **cannot** revoke a gift in any form."

After a spell of silence, the 'tzin spoke again.

" One matter remains. You are not guilty, as you supposed ;
your friends have not lost their faith in you. Such being the case,
it were strange if your feelings are as when you came here ; and
as purposes too often follow feelings, I ask about the future.
What do you intend ?—what wish ?"

" I see you understand me well, good 'tzin. **My folly has** been
so great that I feel myself unworthy **to** be my **own master.** I
ought not to claim a purpose, much less **a** wish. I came to your
door seeking to be taken back **into service ; that was all the**
purpose I had. I rely upon **your exceeding kindness.**"

Hualpa moved as if to kneel ; but the **'tzin caught** him, **and**
said, "Keep your seat." And rising, he **continued** severely,
"**Lord Hualpa,**—for such you still are,—all men, even the best,
are criminals ; but, as for the most part their crimes **are** against
themselves, we take no notice of them. In that sense you are
guilty, and in such degree that you deserve forfeiture of all the
king refused to take back. But pass we that,—pass the folly, the
misconduct. I will not take you into service ; you have your
old place of friend and comrade, more fitting your rank."

Hualpa's face brightened, and he answered,—

" Command me, O 'tzin ! With you I **can** be brave warrior,
good citizen, true friend ; without you, I am nothing. Whatever
the world thinks **of me,** this I know,—I can reinstate myself in
its good opinion **before** I can in my own. Show me the **way**
back to self-respect ; restore me that, and I will be your **slave,**
soldier, comrade,—what you will."

" It is well," said Guatamozin, smiling at his earnestness,—" it
is well. I can show you the way. Listen. The war, about
which we have so often talked, thanks to the gods ! is finally at
hand. The public opinion has done its work. The whole nation
would throw itself upon the strangers to-morrow, but for the king,
who has become their shield ; and he must be rescued ; other-

wise, we must educate the people to see in him an enemy to be removed. We cannot spare the time for that, and consequently have tried rescue in many ways, so far in vain. To-morrow we try again. The plot is arranged, and cannot fail, except by the king's own default. Reserving explanation, I congratulate you. You are in time; the good fortune clings to you. To-morrow I will set your feet in the way you seek."

Hualpa gazed at him doubtingly. "To-morrow!" he said. "Will you trust me so soon, and in a matter so high?"

"Yes."

"Will my part take me from you?"

"No."

"Then I thank you for the opportunity. On the *teocallis*, that dreadful morning, I lost my assurance; whether it will ever return is doubtful; but with you, at your side, I dare walk in any way."

"I understand you," the 'tzin replied. "Go now, and get ready. Unless the king fail us, we will have combat requiring all our strength. To the bath first, then to breakfast, then to find more seemly garments, then to rest. I give you to midnight. Go."

CHAPTER II.

WHOM THE GODS DESTROY THEY FIRST MAKE MAD.

THE morning after Hualpa's return, Xoli, the Chalcan, as was his wont, passed through his many rooms, making what may be called a domestic reconnaissance.

"What!" he cried, perplexed. "How is this? The house is empty! Where are all the lords?"

The slaves to whom he spoke shook their heads.

"Have there been none for breakfast?"

Again they shook their heads.

"Nor for *pulque?*"

"Not one this morning," they replied.

"Not even for a draught of *pulque!* Wonderful!" cried the broker, bewildered and amazed. Then he hurried to his steward, soliloquizing as he went, "Not one for breakfast; not even a draught of *pulque!* Holy gods! to what is the generation coming?"

The perplexity of the good man was not without cause. The day the king removed to the palace of Axaya', the royal hospitality went with him, and had thenceforth been administered there; but, though no less princely and profuse than before, under the new *régime* it was overshadowed by the presence of the strangers, and for that reason became distasteful to the titled personages accustomed to its enjoyment. Consequently, owners of palaces in the city betook themselves to their own boards ; others, especially non-residents, quartered with the Chalcan ; as a further result, his house assumed the style of a *meson*, with accommodations equal to those of the palace ; such, at least, was the disloyal whisper, and I am sorry to say Xoli did not repudiate the impeachment as became a lover of the king. And such eating, drinking, playing, such conspiring and plotting, such political discussion, such transactions in brokerage went on daily and nightly under his roof as were never before known. Now all this was broken off. The silence was not more frightful than unprofitable.

" Steward, steward ! " said Xoli to that functionary, distinguished by the surpassing whiteness of his apron, " what has befallen ? Where are the patrons this morning ? "

" Good master, the most your slave knows is, that last night a paba from the great temple passed through the chambers, after which, very shortly, every guest departed."

" A paba, a paba ! " and Xoli was more than ever perplexed. " Heard you what he said ? "

" Not a word."

" About what time did he come ? "

" After midnight."

" And that is all you know ? "

The steward bowed, and Xoli passed distractedly to the front door, only to find the portico as deserted as the chambers. Sight of the people beginning to collect in the square, however, brought him some relief, and he hailed the first passing acquaintance.

" A pleasant morning to you, neighbour."

" The same to you."

" Have you any news ? "

" None, except I hear of a crowd of pabas in the city, come, as rumour says, from Tezcuco, Cholula, Iztapalapan, and other lake towns."

" When did they come ? "

" In the night."

" Oho ! There's something afoot," and Xoli wiped the perspiration from his forehead.

" So there is," the neighbour replied. " The king goes to the temple to worship to-day."

A light broke in upon the Chalcan. " True, true ; I had forgotten."

" Such is the talk," the citizen continued. " Will you be there? Everybody is going."

"Certainly," answered **Xoli** drily. "**If I** do not go, every-body will not be there. Look for me. The gods keep you!"

And with that he re-entered his house, satisfied, but not altogether quieted; wandering restlessly from chamber to chamber, he asked himself continually, "Why so many pabas? And why do they come in the night? And what can have taken the lords away so silently, and at such a time,—without **breakfast**, with-**out even a** draught of *pulque?*"

Invariably these interrogatories were followed by appeals to the great ebony jar of snuff; after sneezing, he would **answer** himself, "Pabas for worship, lords and soldiers for fighting; but pabas and soldiers together! Something is afoot. I will stay at home, and patronize myself. And yet—and yet—they might have told me something about it!"

. . . . . .

About ten o'clock—to count **the time as** Christians do—the **king** issued from the old palace, going **in** state to the *teocallis,* **attended** by a procession of courtiers, warriors, and pabas. He **was** borne in an open palanquin, shaded by the detached canopy, the whole presenting a spectacle of imperial splendour.

The movement was **slow** and stately, through masses **of** people **on the** pavements, under the gaze of other thousands on the **housetops**; but neither the banners, **nor the** music, nor the pomp, **nor the** king himself, though fully exposed to view, **amused** or deceived the people; for at the right and left **of** the carriage walked Lugo, Alvarado, Avila, and Leon; **next,** Olmedo, dis-tinguishable from the native clergy **by his** shaven crown, and the cross he carried aloft **on** the shaft of **a** lance; after him, conclud-ing the **procession, one** hundred and fifty Spaniards, ready for battle. **Priesthood, — king, —** the strangers! Clearer, closer, **more inevitable, in the eyes of** the people, arose the curse of Quetzal'.

When the monarch alighted at **the foot** of the first stairway of the temple, **the** multitude far **and** near knelt, and so remained **until the** pabas, delegated for the purpose, took him in their arms **to carry** him to the *azoteas.* Four times in the passage of the **terraces the cortège** came in **view** from the side toward the palace, climbing, **as it were, to the Sun**;—dimmer the holy symbols, fainter the **solemn music; and** each time the people knelt. **The** unfortunate going to worship was still the great king!

A detachment **of** Christians, under De Morla, preceded the procession as an advance-guard. Greatly were they surprised at what they found on **the** *azoteas.* Behind Tlalac, at the head **of** the last stairway, were **a score or** more **of** naked boys, swinging **smoking** censers; yet farther toward **the** tower or sanctuary of **Huitzil'** was an assemblage of dancing priestesses, veiled, rather **than dressed,** in gauzy robes and scarfs. From the steps to the

door of the sanctuary a passage-way had been left ; elsewhere the
sacred area was occupied by pabas, drawn up in ranks close and
scrupulously ordered. Like their pontiff, each of them **wore a**
gown of black ; but while his head was bare, theirs were covered
by hoods. Thus arranged,—silent, motionless, more like phantoms
than men,—they both shocked and disquieted the Spaniards.
Indeed, so sensible were the latter of the danger of their position,
alone and unsupported in the face of an array so dismal and solid,
that many of them fell to counting their beads and muttering *Aves.*

A savage dissonance greeted the king when he was set down on
the *azoteas*, and simultaneously the pabas burst into a hymn, and
from the urn **over the** tower a denser column of smoke arose, slow
mounting, but **ere** long visible throughout the valley. Half
bending, he received the blessing of Tlalac ; then the censer-
bearers swept around him ; then, too, jangling silver bells and
beating calabashes, the priestesses began to dance ; in the midst
of the salutation, the arch-priest, moving backward, conducted
him slowly toward the entrance of the sanctuary. At his side
strode the four cavaliers. The escort of Christians remained
outside ; yet the pabas knew the meaning of their presence, and
their hymn deepened into a wail ; the great king had gone before
his god—a prisoner !

The interior of the sanctuary was **in** ordinary condition : the
floor and the walls black with the blood of victims ; the air foul
and sickening, despite the smoking censers and perfuming pans.
The previous visit had prepared the cavaliers for these horrors ;
nevertheless, a cry broke from them upon their entrance. In a
chafing-dish before the altar, four human hearts were slowly
burning to coals !

" *Jesu Christo !* " exclaimed Alvarado. " Did not **the** pagans
promise there should be no sacrifice ? Shrieve me never, if I
toss **not** the contents of yon dish into the god's face ! "

" **Stay !** " **cried** Olmedo, seizing his arm. " Stir not ! The
business **is mine.** As thou lovest God,—the **true** God,—get thee
to thy place ! "

The father spoke firmly, **and the captain,** grinding his teeth
with rage, submitted.

The pedestal **of** the idol was **of** stone, square in form, and
placed in the centre of the sanctuary. Several broad steps, front-
ing the doorway,—door there was not,—assisted devotees up to **a**
platform, upon which stood a table curiously carved, and resting,
as it were, under the eyes of the god. The chamber, bare of
furniture, was crowded with pabas, kneeling and hooded and
ranked, like their brethren outside. The cavaliers took post by
the entrance, with Olmedo between them and the altar. Two
priests, standing on the lower step, seemed waiting to assist in the
ceremonial, although, at the time, apparently absorbed in prayer.

Tlalac led the monarch by the hand up the steps.

"O king," he said, "the ears of the god are open. He will hear you. And as to these companions in devotion,"—he pointed to the assistants as he spoke,—"avoid them not: they are here to pray for you; if need be, to die for you. If they speak, be not surprised, but heed them well; what they say will concern you, and all you best love."

Thereupon the arch-infidel let go the royal hand, and descended the steps, moving backward; upon the floor he continued his movement. Suddenly he stopped, turned, and was face to face with Olmedo; all the passions of his savage nature blazed in his countenance. In reply, the Christian priest calmly held up the cross, and smiled, and was content.

Meantime the monarch kissed the altar, and, folding his hands upon his breast, was beginning to be abstracted in prayer, when he heard himself addressed.

"Look not this way, O king, nor stir; but listen."

The words, audible throughout the chamber, proceeded from the nearest devotee,—a tall man, well muffled in gown and hood. The monarch controlled himself, and listened, while the speaker continued in a slow, monotonous manner, designed to leave the cavaliers, whom he knew to be observing him, in doubt whether he was praying or intoning some part of the service of the occasion,—

"It is in the streets and in the palaces, and has gone forth into the provinces, that Montezuma is the willing guest of the strangers, and that, from great love of them and their society, he will not come away, although his Empire is dissolving, and the religion of his fathers menaced by a new one; but know, O king, that the chief and caciques refuse to credit the evil spoken of you, and, believing you a prisoner, are resolved to restore you to freedom. Know further, O king, that this is the time chosen for the rescue. The way back to the throne is clear; you have only to go hence. What says the king? The nation awaits his answer."

"The throne is inseparable from me,—is where I am, under my feet always," answered the monarch coldly.

"And there may it remain for ever!" said the devotee with fervour. "I only meant to pray you to come from amongst the strangers, and set it once more where it belongs,—amongst the loving hearts that gave it to you. Misunderstand me not, O king. Short time have we for words. The enemy is present. I offer you rescue and liberty."

"To offer me liberty is to deny that I am free. Who is he that proposes to give me what is mine alone to give? I am with Huitzil'. Who comes thus between me and the god?"

From the pabas in the chamber there was a loud murmur; but as the king and devotee retained their composure, and, like praying men, looked steadily at the face of Huitzil', the cavaliers remained unsuspicious observers of what was to them merely a sinful ceremony.

"I am the humblest, though not the least loving, of all **your** subjects," the devotee answered.

"The name?" said the king. **"You ask me to go hence:** whither and with whom?"

"Know me without speaking **my name, O king.** I am your brother's son."

Montezuma was visibly affected. Afterwhile he said,—

"Speak further. Consider what you have said true,—that **I** am a prisoner, that the strangers present are my guards,—what are the means of rescue? Speak, that I may judge of them. Conspiracy is abroad, and I do not choose to be blindly led from what is called my prison to a tomb."

To the reasonable demand the 'tzin calmly replied, "That you **were** coming to worship to-day, and the conditions upon which **you** had permission to come, I learned from the *teotuctli*. I saw **the** opportunity, and proposed to attempt your rescue. In Tlalac **the** gods have a faithful servant, and you, O king, a true lover. When you were received upon the *azoteas*, you did not fail to notice the pabas. Never before in any one temple have there been **so** many assembled. They are the instruments of the rescue."

"The instruments!" exclaimed the **king,** unable **to repress his** scorn.

The 'tzin interposed hastily. "Beware! Though **what we say** is not understood by the strangers, their faculties are **sharp, and** very little may awaken their suspicion and alarm; and **if our** offer be rejected, better for you, O king, that they go hence ignorant of their danger and our design. Yes, if your conjecture were true, if we **did** indeed propose to face the *teules* with barehanded pabas, **your scorn** would be justified; but know that the concourse on the *azoteas* is, **in** fact, of chiefs and caciques, whose gowns do **but conceal their** preparation for battle."

A pang contracted the monarch's face, and his hands closed harder upon his breast; possibly he shuddered **at** the necessity so thrust upon him, of deciding between Malinche whom he feared, and the people whom he so loved.

"Yes," continued the 'tzin, "here are the chosen of the realm, —the noblest and the best,—each with his life in his hand, **an** offering to you. What need of further words? You have not forgotten the habits of war; you divine the object of the concourse of priests; you understand they **are** formed **in** ranks, that, upon a signal, they may throw themselves **as** one man **upon** the strangers. Here in the sanctuary **are** fifty more with *maquahuitls;* behind them a door has been constructed to pass you quickly to the *azoteas;* they will help me keep the door, and

stay pursuit, while you descend to the street. And now, O king,
said I not rightly? What have you to do more than go hence?
Dread not for us. In the presence of Huitzil', and in defence of
his altar, we will fight. If we fall in such glorious combat, he
will waft our souls straightway to the Sun."

"My son," the king answered after a pause, "if I were a
prisoner, I would say you and the lords have done well; but,
being free and pursuing my own policy, I reject the rescue.
Go your ways in peace; leave me to my prayers. In a few days
the strangers will depart; then, if not sooner, I will come back
as you wish, and bring the old time with me, and make all the
land happy."

The monarch ceased. He imagined the question answered and
passed; but a murmur, almost a groan, recalled him from the
effort to abstract himself. And then the *teotuctli*, exercising his
privilege, went to him, and, laying a hand upon his arm, and
pointing up to the god, said,—

"Hearken, O king! The strangers have already asked you to
allow them to set up an altar here in the house of Huitzil', that
they may worship their god after their manner. The request
was sacrilege; listening to it, a sin; to grant it would make you
accursed for ever. Save yourself and the god, by going hence as
the lords have besought. Be wise in time."

"I have decided," said the poor king in a trembling voice,—
"I have decided."

Tlalac looked to the 'tzin despairingly. The appeal to the
monarch's veneration for the god of his fathers had failed; what
else remained? And the 'tzin for the first time looked to the
king, saying sorrowfully,—

"Anahuac is the common mother, as Huitzil' is the father.
The foot of the stranger is heavy on her breast, and she cries
aloud, 'Where is Montezuma? Where is the Lord of the Earth?
Where is the Child of the Sun?'"

And silence hung heavy in the sanctuary, and the waiting was
painful. Again the 'tzin's voice,—

"A bride sits in the house waiting. Love puts its songs in her
mouth, and kindles her smiles with the dazzle of stars. But the
bridegroom lingers, and the evening and the morning bring him
not. Ah, what is she, though ever so beautiful and sweet-singing,
when he comes not, and may never come? O king, you are the
lingering lord, and Anahuac the waiting bride; as you love her,
come."

The fated king covered his face with his hands, as if, by
shutting out the light, to find relief from pangs too acute for
endurance. Minutes passed,—minutes of torture to him, and of
breathless expectancy to all present, except the cavaliers, who,
unconscious of peril, watched the scene with indifference, or

rather the scornful curiosity natural to men professing a purer and diviner faith. At last his hand dropped, and he said with dignity,—

"Let this end now,—so I command. My explanation must be accepted. I cannot understand why, if you love me as you say, you should receive my word **with so** little **credit ;** and if you can devote yourselves so entirely to me, why **can you** not believe me capable of equal devotion to myself? Hear me once more. I do not love the strangers. I hope yet to see them sacrificed to Huitzil'. They promise in **a** few days to leave the country, and I stay with them **to** hasten their departure, and, in the meantime, shield you, the **nation,** the temples, and the gods, from their power, which is **past** finding out. Therefore, let no **blow be** struck **at them, here** or elsewhere, without my order. **I am** yet the king. **Let** me have peace. Peace **be** with **you ! I have** spoken."

The 'tzin looked once to heaven, as if uttering a last appeal, **or** calling it to witness a vow, then he fell upon his knees ; he, too, had despaired. And, as if the feeling were contagious, the *teotuctli* knelt, and in the sanctuary there was stillness consistent with worship, save when some overburdened breast relieved itself by a sigh, a murmur, or a groan.

And history tells how Montezuma remained **a** little while **at** the altar, and **went** peacefully back to his residence with **the** strangers.

CHAPTER III.

THE PUBLIC OPINION MAKES WAY.

IN the *tianguez*, one market-day, there was an immense crowd, yet trade was dull ; indeed, comparatively nothing in that way was being done, although the display of commodities was rich and tempting.

"Holy gods ! what is to become of us ?" cried a Cholulan merchant.

"You ! You are rich. Dullness of the market cannot hurt you. But I,—I am going to ruin."

The second speaker was a slave-dealer. Only the **day before,** he had, at great cost, driven into the city a large **train of his** "stock" from the wilderness beyond the Great River.

"Tell me, my friend," said a third party, addressing the slave-dealer, though in hearing of the whole company, "heard you ever of a slave owning a slave ?'

"Not I."

"Heard you ever of a man going into the market to buy a slave, when he was looking to become one himself?"

"Never."

"You have it then,—the reason nobody has been to your exhibition."

The bystanders appeared to assent to the proposition, which all understood but the dealer in men, who begged an explanation.

"Yes, yes. You have just come home. I had forgotten. A bad time to be abroad. But listen, friend." The speaker quietly took his pipe from his mouth, and knocked the ashes out of the bowl. "We belong to Malinche; you know who he is."

"I am not so certain," the dealer replied gravely. "The most I can say is, I have heard of him."

"Oh, he is a god"—

"With all a man's wants and appetites," interposed one.

"Yes, I was about to say that. For instance, day before yesterday he sent down the king's order for three thousand *escaupiles*. What need"—

"They were for his Tlascalans."

"Oh, possibly. For whom were the cargoes of cotton cloth delivered yesterday?"

"His women," answered the other quickly.

"And the two thousand sandals?"

"For his soldiers."

"And the gold of which the market was cleaned last week? and the gold now being hunted in Tustepec and Chinantla? and the tribute being levied so harshly in all the provinces,— for whom are they?"

"For Malinche himself."

"Yes, the god Malinche. Slave of a slave! My friend," said the chief speaker to the slave-dealer, "there is no such relation known to the law, and for that reason we cannot buy of you. Better go back with all you have, and let the wilderness have its own again."

"But the goods of which you spoke; certainly they were paid for," said the dealer, turning pale.

"No. There is nothing left of the royal revenue. Even the treasure which the last king amassed, and walled up in the old palace, has been given to Malinche. The Empire is like a man, in one respect, at least,—when beggared, it cannot pay."

"And the king?"

"He is Malinche's too."

"Yes," added the bystander; "for nowadays we never see his signet, except in the hands of one of the strangers."

The dealer in men drew a long breath, something as near a sigh as could come from one of his habits, and said, "I remember

Mualox and his prophecy ; and, hearing these things, **I know not** what to think."

"We have yet one hope," said the chief **spokesman, as if** desirous of concluding the conversation.

"**And** that ?"

"**Is the** 'tzin Guatamo."

.   .   .   .

"What luck, Pepito ?"

"Bad, very bad."

The questioner was the wife of the man questioned, who had just returned from the market. Throwing aside his empty baskets, **he sat down** in the shade of a bridge spanning one of the canals, **and, locking** his hands across his bare knees, looked gloomily **in the water.** His **canoe,** with others, **was close at** hand.

The wife, without seeming to notice his dejection, busied herself setting out their dinner, which was humble as them-**selves,** being of boiled maize, tuna figs, and *tecuitlatl,* or cheese of the lake. When the man began to eat, he began to talk,—a peculiarity **in** which he was not altogether singular.

"Bad luck, very bad," he repeated. "I took my baskets to the old stand. The flowers were fresh **and** sweet, gathered, you know, only last night. The market was full **of** people, many **of** whom I knew to be rich enough to buy **at two** prices ; they came, and looked, and said, 'They are very **nice,** Pepito, very nice,' but did not offer to buy. By and by the sun went up, and stood overhead, and still no purchaser, not even an offer. It was very discouraging, I tell you ; and it would have been much more so if I had not pretty soon noticed that the market-people around me, fruiterers and florists, were doing **no** better than I. Then I walked about to see my friends ; and in the porticoes and booths, as elsewhere in the square, no trade ; plenty of people, but no trade. The jewellers had covered their fronts with flowers,—I never saw richer,—you should have been there !—and crowds stood about breathing the sweet perfume ; but as to purchasing, they did nothing of the sort. In fact, may the *millou*[1] of our little house fly away to-night if, in the whole day, I saw **an** instance of trade, or so much as a cocoa-bean pass from one hand to another !"

"It has been **so many** days now, only not quite so bad, Pepito," the wife said, struggling to talk cheerfully. "What did they say was the cause ? Did any one speak of that ?"

"Oh yes, everybody. Nothing else was talked. 'What is the **use** of working ? Why buy or sell ? We have no longer a king **or** country. We are all slaves now. We belong to Malinche. Afterwhile, because we are poor, he will take **us** off to some of

[1] Household god of the **lowest grade.**

his farms, like that one he has down in Oajaca, and set us to
working, and keep the fruits, while he gives us the pains. No,
we do not want anything; the less we have, the lighter
will be our going down.' That is the way the talk went
all day."

For the first time the woman threw off her pretence of cheerfulness, and was still, absorbed in listening and thinking.

"Belong to Malinche! We? And our little ones at home?
Not while the gods live!" she said confidently.

"Why not? You forget. Malinche is himself a god."

A doubt shook the strong faith of the wife; and soon, gloomy
and hopeless as Pepite, she sat down by him, and partook of the
humble fare.

.   .   .   .

"The nation is dying. Let us elect another king," said an old
cacique to a crowd of nobles, of whom he was the centre, in the
pulque chamber of the Chalcan. Bold words, which half a year
before would have been punished on the spot; now they were
heard in silence, if not with approbation. "A king has no right
to survive his glory," the veteran continued; "and how may one
describe his shame and guilt, when, from fear of death, he suffers
an enemy to use him, and turn his power against his people!"

He stopped, and for a time the hush was threatening; then
there was clapping of hands, and voices cried out,—"Good,
good!"

"May the gods forgive me, and witness that the speech was
from love of country, not hatred of Montezuma," said the cacique
deferentially.

"Whom would you have in his place? Name him!" shouted
an auditor.

"Montezuma,—if he will come back to us."

"He will not; he has already refused. Another,—give us
another!"

"Be it so!" said the veteran with decision. "My life is forfeit
for what I have said. The cell that holds the king Cacama and
the good lord Cuitlahua yawns for me also. I will speak."
Quaffing a bowl of *pulque*, he added, "Of all Anahuac, O my
brothers, who, with the fewest years, is wisest of head and
bravest of heart, and therefore fittest to be king in time like
this?"

The question was of the kind that addresses itself peculiarly to
individual preferences,—the kind which has afflicted the world
with its saddest and greatest wars; yet, strange to say, the company, as with one voice, and instantly, answered,—

"The 'tzin, the 'tzin! Guatamo, the 'tzin!"

.   .   .   .

In the evening time three pabas clomb the stairs by which the top of the turret of Huitzil' on the *teocallis* was reached from the *azoteas*. Arrived at the top, they found there the night-watcher, who recognised the *teotuctli*, and knelt to him.

"Arise, and get you down now," the arch-priest **said**; "**we** would be alone awhile."

On a pedestal of stone, or rather of many stones, rested the brazier, or urn, that held the sacred fire. In it crackled the consuming faggots, while **over** it, with unsteady brilliancy, leaped the flames which, **for so** many leagues away, were as a beacon in the valley. The three stopped in the shadow of the urn, and might have studied the city, or those subjects greater and more fascinating,—mysteries now, to-night, for ever,—Space, and its children, the Stars; but it was not to indulge a common passion or uncertain speculations that Tlalac had brought from their temples **and** altars his companions, the high priests of Cholula and Tezcuco. And there for a long time they remained, **the** grave and holy servants of the gods of the New World, talking earnestly, on what subject and with what conclusion we **may** gather.

"He is of us no longer," said Tlalac impressively. "He has abandoned his people; to a stranger he has surrendered himself, his throne and power; he spends his days learning, from **a new** priesthood, a new creed, and the things that pertain **to a god of** whom everything is unknown to us, except that he **is the enemy** of our gods. I bore his desertion patiently, **as we always bear** with those we love. By permission, as you heard, **he came one** day **to** worship Huitzil'; the permission was on condition that there should be no sacrifices. Worship without sacrifice, my brethren! Can such thing be? When he came, he was offered rescue; the preparations were detailed to him; he knew they could not fail; the nobles begged him to accept the offer; I warned him against refusal: yet, of choice, he went back to Malinche. Then patience almost forsook me. Next, as you also know, came the unpardonable sin. In the chamber below—the chamber sanctified by the presence of the mighty Huitzil'—I will give you to see, if you wish, a profanation the like of which came never to the most wicked dream of the most wicked Aztec,—an altar to the new and unknown God. And to-morrow, if you have the curiosity, I will give you to see the further sight,— a service mixed of singing and prayer, by priests of the strange God, at the same time, and side by side with the worship of our gods,—all with the assent—nay, by order—of Montezuma. Witness these crimes once, and your patience will go quickly, whereas **mine** went slowly; but it is gone, and in its stead **lives** only the purpose to do what the gods command."

"Let **us** obey the gods!" said the reverend high priest of Cholula.

"Let us obey the gods!" echoed his holy brother of Tezcuco.

"Hear me, then," said **Tlalac** with increased fervour. "I will give their command. 'Raise up a **new king**, and save yourselves, by **saving our** worship in the land!' so the **gods say.** And I am ready."

"But the law," said the Tezcucan.

"By the law," answered Tlalac, "there **can be kings** only in the order of **election.**"

"And so?"

"Montezuma—*must*—DIE!"

Tlalac said these terrible words slowly, but firmly.

"And who will be the instrument?" they asked.

"Let us trust the gods," he answered. "For love of them men go down to death every day; and of the many lovers, doubt not some one will be found to do their bidding."

And so it was agreed.

. . . .

And so, slowly but surely, the public opinion made its way, permeating all classes, — labourers, merchants, warriors, and priests.

CHAPTER IV.

THE 'TZIN'S FAREWELL TO QUETZAL'.

If I were writing **history, it** would delight me to linger over the details of Cortes' management after the arrest of Montezuma; for in them were **blent,** fairly as ever before seen, the grand diversities of war, politics, and governmental administration. Anticipating interference from the headquarters in Cuba, he exercised all his industry and craft **to recommend himself** directly to his **Majesty,** the Emperor Charles. The interference **at** last came in the form of a grand expedition **under** Panfilo de Narvaez; but in the interval—a period of little **more than five** months—he had practically **reduced** the new discovery to **possession, as attested** by numerous **acts** of sovereignty,—such, for **instance, as the coast** of the gulf **surveyed; colonies** established; **plantations opened** and worked **with profit;** tribute levied; high officials arrested, disseized, and **executed;** the collection and division of a treasure greater than ever before seen **by Christians in the** New World; communication with the **capital secured** by armed brigantines on the lakes; the **cross set up and** maintained in the *teocallis;* and last, and, **by custom** of the civilised world, most **absolute.** Montezuma brought to acknowledge vassalage and swear allegiance to the Emperor; and withal, so perfect was the administration of affairs, that a Spaniard, though alone, was as safe in the defiles between Vera Cruz and Tenochtitlan as he would have been in the *caminos reales* of old Spain, as free in the great *tianguez* as on the quay of Cadiz.

Narvaez's expedition landed in May, six months after Cortes entered Tenochtitlan; and to that time I now beg to advance my reader.

Cortes himself is down in Cempoalla; having defeated Narvaez, he is lingering to gather the fruits of his extraordinary victory. In the capital, Alvarado is commanding, supported by the Tlascalans, and about one hundred and fifty Christians. Under his administration affairs have gone rapidly from bad to worse; and in selecting him for a trust so delicate and important, Cortes has made his first serious mistake.

At an early hour in the evening Mualox came out of the sanctuary of his Cû, bearing an armful of the flowers which had been used in the decoration of the altar. The good man's hair and beard were whiter than when last I noticed him; he was also feebler, and more stooped; so the time is not far distant when Quetzal' will lose his last and most faithful servant. As he was about to ascend the stairway of the tower, his name was called, and, stopping, he was overtaken by two men.

"Guatamozin!" he exclaimed in surprise.

"Be not alarmed, father, but put down your burden, and rest awhile. My friend here, the lord Hualpa, has brought me news which calls me away. Rest, therefore, and give me time for thanks and explanation."

"What folly is this?" asked Mualox hastily, and without noticing Hualpa's salutation. "Go back to the cell. The hunters are abroad and vigilant as ever. I will cast these faded offerings into the fire, and come to you."

The 'tzin was in the guise of a paba. To quiet the good man's alarm, he drew closer the hood that covered his head, remarking, "The hunters will not come. Give Hualpa the offerings; he will carry them for you."

Hualpa took them, and left; then Mualox said, "I am ready to hear. Speak."

"Good father," the 'tzin began, "not long since, in the sanctuary there, you told me—I well remember the words—that the existence of my country depended upon my action; by which I understood you to prefigure for me an honourable, if not fortunate, destiny. I believe you had faith in what you said; for on many occasions since you have exerted yourself in my behalf. That I am not now a prisoner in the old palace with Cacama and the lord Cuitlahua is due to you; indeed, if it be

true, as I was told, that the king gave me to Malinche to be
dealt with as he chose, I owe you my life. These are the greatest
debts a man can be bound for ; I acknowledge them, and, if the
destiny should be fortunate as we hope, will pay them richly :
but now all I can give you is my thanks, and what I know you
will better regard,—my solemn promise to protect this sacred
property of the holy Quetzal'. Take the thanks and the promise,
and let me have your blessing. I wish now to go."

"Whither?" asked Mualox.

"To the people. They have called me ; the lord Hualpa
brings me their message."

"No, you will not go," said the paba reproachfully. "Your
resolution is only an impulse ; impatience is not a purpose ; and
—and here are peace, and safety, and a holy presence."

"But honour, father"—

"That will come by waiting."

"Alas!" said the 'tzin bitterly, "I have waited too long
already. I have most dismal news. When Malinche marched
to Cempoalla, he left in command here the red-haired chief
whom we call Tonatiah. This, you know, is the day of the
incensing of Huitzil'"—

"I know, my son,—an awful day ! The day of cruel sacrifice,
itself a defiance of Quetzal'."

"What!" said Guatamozin in angry surprise. "Are you not
an Aztec?"

"Yes, an Aztec, and a lover of his god, the true god, whose
return he knows to be near, and'—to gather energy of expression,
he paused, then raised his hands as if flinging the words to a
listener overhead—"and whom he would welcome, thought he
land be swimming in the blood of unbelievers."

The violence and incoherency astonished the 'tzin, and as he
looked at the paba fixedly, he was sensible for the first time of a
fear that the good man's mind was affected. And he considered
his age and habits, his days and years spent in a great cavernous
house, without amusement, without companionship, without
varied occupation ; for the thinker, it must be remembered,
knew nothing of Tecetl or the world she made so delightful.
Moreover, was not mania the effect of long brooding over wrongs,
actual or imaginary ? Or, to put the thought in another form,
how natural that the solitary watcher of decay, where of all
places decay is most affecting, midst antique and templed
splendour, should make the cause of Quetzal' his, until at last,
as the one idea of his being, it mastered him so absolutely that a
division of his love was no longer possible. If the misgiving had
come alone, the pain that wrung the 'tzin would have resolved
itself in pity for the victim, so old, so faithful, so passionate ; but
a dreadful consequence at once presented itself. By a strange

fatality, the mystic had been taken into the royal councils, where, from force of faith, he had gained faith. Now,—and this was the dread,—what if he had cast the glamour of his mind **over** the king's, and superinduced a policy which had for object and end the peaceable transfer of the nation to the strangers?

This thought thrilled the 'tzin indefinably, and in a moment his pity changed to deep distrust. To master himself, he walked away; coming back, he said quietly, "The day you pray for has come; rejoice, if you can."

"I do not understand you," said Mualox.

"I will explain. This **is** the day of the incensing of Huitzil', which, you know, has been celebrated for ages as a festival religious **and** national. This morning, as customary, lords and priests, personages the noblest and most venerated, assembled in the courtyard of the temples. To bring the great wrong out in clearer view, I ought to say, father, that permission to celebrate had been asked of Tonatiah, and given,—to such a depth have we **fallen**! And, as if to plunge us into a yet lower deep, he forbade **the** king's attendance, and said to the *teotuctli*, 'There shall be no sacrifice.'"

"No victims, no blood!" cried Mualox, clasping his **hands**. "Blessed be Quetzal'!"

The 'tzin bore the interruption, though with an **effort**.

"In the midst of the service," he continued, "when the yard was most crowded, and the revelry gayest, and the good company most happy and unsuspecting, dancing, singing, feasting, suddenly Tonatiah and his people rushed upon them, and began to kill, and stayed not their hands until, of all the revellers, not one was left alive; leaders in battle, ministers at the altar, old and young, —all were slain!! [1] Oh, such a piteous sight! The court is a pool of blood. Who will restore the flower this day torn from the nation? **O** holy gods, what have we done **to** merit such calamity?"

Mualox listened, his hands still clasped.

"Not one left alive! Not one, did you say?"

"Not one."

The paba arose **from** his stooping, and upon the 'tzin flashed the old magnetic flame.

"What have you done, **ask you?** Sinned against the true and only god."

"I?" said the 'tzin, for the moment shrinking.

"The nation,—the nation, blind to its crimes, no less blind **to** the beginning of its punishment! What you call calamity, I call vengeance. Starting in the house of Huitzil',—the god for **whom** my god was forsaken,—it will next go to the **city**; and if

[1] Sahagun, *Hist. de Nueva Esp.* Gomara, *Cronica.* Prescott, *Conq. of Mexico.*

the lords so perish, how may the people escape? Let them tremble! He is come, he is come! I knew him afar, I know him here. I heard his step in the valley, I see his hand in the court. Rejoice, O 'tzin! He has drunk the blood of the sacrificers. To-morrow his house must be made ready to receive him. Go not away! Stay and help me! I am old. Of the treasure below I might make use to buy help; but such preparation, like an offering at the altar, is most acceptable when induced by love. Love for love. So said Quetzal' in the beginning; so he says now."

"Let me be sure I understand you, father. What do you offer me?" asked the 'tzin quietly.

"Escape from the wrath," replied Mualox.

"And what is required of me?"

"To stay here, and, with me, serve his altar."

"Is the king also to be saved?"

"Surely; he is already a servant of the god's."

Under his gown the 'tzin's heart beat quicker, for the question and answer were close upon the fear newly come to him, as I have said; yet, to leave the point unguarded in the paba's mind, he asked,—

"And the people: if I become what you ask, will they be saved?"

"No. They have forgotten Quetzal' utterly."

"When the king became your fellow-servant, father, made he no terms for his dependants, for the nation, for his family?"

"None."

Guatamozin dropped the hood upon his shoulders, and looked at Mualox sternly and steadily; and between them ensued one of those struggles of spirit against spirit in which glances are as glittering swords, and the will holds the place of skill.

"Father," he said at length, "I have been accustomed to love and obey you. I thought you good and wise, and conversant with things divine, and that one so faithful to his god must be as faithful to his country; for, to me, love of one is love of the other. But now I know you better. You tell me that Quetzal' has come, and for vengeance; and that, in the fire of his wrath, the nation will be destroyed; yet you exult, and endeavour to speed the day by prayer. And now, too, I understand the destiny you had in store for me. By hiding in this gown, and becoming a priest at your altar, I was to escape the universal death. What the king did, I was to do. Hear me now: I cut myself loose from you. With my own eyes I look into the future. I spurn the destiny, and for myself will carve out a better one by saving or perishing with my race. No more waiting on others! no more weakness! I will go hence and strike"—

"Whom?" asked Mualox impulsively. "The king and the god?"

"He is not my god," said the 'tzin, interrupting him in turn. "The enemy of my race is my enemy, whether he be king or god. As for Montezuma,"—at the name his voice and manner changed, —"I will go humbly, and, from the dust into which he flung them, pick up his royal duties. Alas! no other can. Cuitlahua is a prisoner; so is Cacama; and in the courtyard yonder, cold in death, lie the lords who might with them contest the crown and its tribulations. I alone am left. And as to Quetzal',—I accept the doom of my country,—into the heart of his divinity I cast my spear! So, farewell, father. As a faithful servant, you cannot bless whom your god has cursed. With you, however, be all the peace and safety that abide here. Farewell!"

"Go not, go not!" cried Mualox, as the 'tzin, calling to Hualpa, turned his back upon him. "We have been as father and son. I am old. See how sorrow shakes these hands, stretched toward you in love."

Seeing the appeal was vain, the paba stepped forward and caught the 'tzin's arm, and said, "I pray you stay,—stay. The destiny follows Quetzal', and is **close** at hand, and brings in its arms the throne."

Neither the tempter nor the temptation moved the 'tzin; he called Hualpa again. Then the holy man let go his arm, and said sadly, "Go thy way,—one scoffer more! Or, if you stay, hear of what the god will accuse you, so that when your calamity comes, as come it will, you may not accuse him."

"I will hear."

"Know, then, O 'tzin, that Quetzal', the day he landed **from** Tlapallan, took you in his care; a little later, he caused **you to** be sent into exile"—

"Your god did that!" exclaimed the 'tzin. "And why?"

"Out of the city there was safety," replied Mualox sententiously; **in** a moment he continued, "Such, I say, was the beginning. Attend to what has followed. After Montezuma went to dwell with the strangers, the king of Tezcuco revolted, and drew after him the lords of Iztapalapan, Tlacopan, and others; to-day they are prisoners, while you are free. Next, aided by Tlalac, you planned the rescue of the king by force in the *teocallis;* for that offence the officers hunted you, and have not given over their quest; but the cells of Quetzal' are deep and dark; I called you in, and yet you are safe. To-day Quetzal' appeared amongst the celebrants, and to-night there is mourning throughout the valley, and the city groans under the bloody sorrow; still you are safe. A few days ago, in the old palace of Axaya', the king assembled his lords, and there he and they became the avowed subjects of a new king, Malinche's master; since that the people, in their ignorance, have rung the heavens with their curses. You alone escaped **that** bond; so that, if

Montezuma were to join his fathers, asleep in Chapultepec, whom would soldier, priest, and citizen call to the throne? Of the nobles living, how many are free to be king! And of all the empire, how many are there of whom I might say, 'He forgot not Quetzal'?' One only. And now, O son, ask you of what you will be accused, if you abandon this house and its god? or what will be forfeit, if now you turn your back upon them? Is there a measure for the iniquity of ingratitude? If you go hence for any purpose of war, remember Quetzal' neither forgets nor forgives; better that you had never been born."

By this time Hualpa had joined the party. Resting his hand upon the young man's shoulder, the 'tzin fixed on Mualox a look severe and steady as his own, and replied, "Father, a man knows not himself; still less knows he other men; if so, how should I know a being so great as you claim your god to be? Heretofore I have been contented to see Quetzal' as you have painted him,—a fair-faced, gentle, loving deity, to whom human sacrifice was especially abhorrent; but what shall I say of him whom you have now given me to study? If he neither forgets nor forgives, wherein is he better than the gods of Mictlan? Hating, as you have said, the sacrifice of one man, he now proposes, you say, not as a process of ages, but at once, by a blow or a breath, to slay a nation numbering millions. When was Huitzil' so awfully worshipped? He will spare the king, you further say, because he has become his servant; and I can find grace by a like submission. Father,"—and as he spoke the 'tzin's manner became inexpressibly noble,—"father, who of choice would live to be the last of his race? The destiny brings me a crown: tell me, when your god has glutted himself, where shall I find subjects? Comes he in person or by representative? Am I to be his crowned slave or Malinche's? Once for all, let Quetzal' enlarge his doom; it is sweeter than what you call his love. I will go fight; and, if the gods of my fathers—in this hour become dearer and holier than ever—so decree, will die with my people. Again, father, farewell!"

Again the withered hands arose tremulously, and a look of exceeding anguish came to the paba's help.

"If not for love of me, or of self, or of Quetzal', then for love of woman, stay."

Guatamozin turned quickly. "What of her?"

"O 'tzin, the destiny you put aside is hers no less than yours."

The 'tzin raised higher his princely head, and answered, smiling joyously,—

"Then, father, by whatever charm, or incantation, or virtue of prayer you possess, hasten the destiny,—hasten it, I conjure you. A tomb would be a palace with her, a palace would be a tomb without her."

And with the smile still upon his face, and the resolution yet in his heart, he again, and for the last time, turned his back upon Mualox.

CHAPTER V.

THE CELLS OF QUETZAL' AGAIN.

"A victim! A victim!"

"Hi, hi!"

"Catch him!"

"Stone him!"

"Kill him!"

So cried a mob, at the time in furious motion up the beautiful street. Numbering hundreds already, it increased momentarily, and howled as only such a monster can. Scarce eighty yards in front ran its game,—Orteguilla, the page.

The boy was in desperate strait. His bonnet, secured by a braid, danced behind him; his short cloak, of purple velvet, a little faded, fluttered as if struggling to burst the throat-loop; his hands were clenched; his face pale with fear and labour. He ran with all his might, often looking back; and as his course was up the street, the old palace of Axaya' must have been the goal he sought,—a long, long way off for one unused to such exertion and so fiercely pressed. At every backward glance, he cried, in agony of terror, "Help me, O Mother of Christ! By God's love, help me!" The enemy was gaining upon him.

The lad, as I think I have before remarked, had been detailed by Cortes to attend Montezuma, with whom, as he was handsome and witty, and had soon acquired the Aztecan tongue and uncommon skill at *totoloque,* he had become an accepted favourite; so that, while useful to the monarch as a servant, he was no less useful to the Christian as a detective. In the course of his service he had been frequently entrusted with his royal master's signet, the very highest mark of confidence. Every day he executed errands in the *tianguez,* and sometimes in even remoter quarters of the city. As a consequence he had come to be quite well known, and to this day nothing harmful or menacing had befallen him, although, as was not hard to discern, the people would have been better satisfied had Maxtla been charged with such duties.

On this occasion,—the day after the interview between the 'tzin and Mualox,—while executing some trifling commission in the market, he became conscious of a **change in** the demeanour of those whom he met; of courtesies, there were none; he was not once saluted; even the jewellers with **whom he** dealt viewed him **coldly, and** asked not a word about **the king; yet,** unaware of **danger, he** went to the portico of the Chalcan, **and sat** awhile, **enjoying the shade** and the fountain, and **listening to the** noisy **commerce without.**

Presently he heard a din of conchs and attabals, **the martial music of the Aztecs.** Somewhat startled, and half hidden by the curtains, **he looked** out, **and** beheld, coming from the direction of the king's palace, a procession bearing ensigns and banners of all shapes, designs, and colours.

At the first sound **of the** music, **the** people, of whom, as usual, **there were great** numbers in the *tianguez*, quitted their occupa**tions, and ran to meet** the spectacle, which, without halting, **came swiftly down to the** Chalcan's; **so** that there passed within **a few feet of the adventurous page a procession** rarely beautiful,— a procession **of warriors marching in deep files, each one** helmeted, and with **a shield at his back, and a banner in his** hand,—an army with banners.

At **the** head, apart from the **others, strode a chief whom all eyes** followed. Even Orteguilla **was** impressed with his appearance. He wore **a tunic** of very brilliant feather-work, the skirt of which fell **almost to** his knees; from the skirt **to** the ankles his lower limbs **were bare;** around the ankles, **over** the thongs of the sandals, were **rings of furbished silver;** on his left arm he carried a shield of **shining metal, probably brass,** its rim fringed with locks of **flowing hair, and in the centre the device of an owl,** snow-white, **and wrought of the plumage of the bird;** over his **temples, fixed firmly in the golden head-band, there were wings of a parrot, green as emerald,** and half **spread. He exceeded his followers in stature,** which appeared **the greater by reason of the long Chinantlan spear** in his right hand, **used as a staff. To the whole was added an** air severely grand **; for,** as he **marched, he looked neither to the** right **nor** left,—apparently too absorbed to notice **the people, many** of whom even knelt upon his approach. From **the cries that saluted the** chief, together with the descriptions **he had often heard of** him, Orteguilla recognised Guatamozin.

The procession well-nigh **passed, and the young** Spaniard was studying the devices **on** the ensigns **when a hand** was laid upon his shoulder; turning quickly to the **intruder, he** saw the prince **Io',** whom he was in the habit **of meeting daily in** the audience-**chamber** of the king. The prince **met his smile and pleasantry with a sombre** face, and said coldly,—

"You have been kind to the king, my father; he loves you; on your hand I see his signet; therefore I will serve you. Arise, and begone; stay not a moment. You were never nearer death than now."

Orteguilla, scarce comprehending, would have questioned him, but the prince spoke on.

"The chiefs who inhabit here are in the procession. Had they found you, Huitzil' would have had a victim before sunset. Stay not; begone!"

While speaking, Io' moved to the curtained doorway from which he had just come. "Beware of the people in the square; trust not to the signet. My father is still the king; but the lords and pabas have given his power to another,—him whom you saw pass just now before the banners. In all Anahuac Guatamozin's word is the law, and that word is—War." And with that he passed into the house.

The page was a soldier, not so much in strength as experience, and brave from habit; now, however, his heart stood still, and a deadly coldness came over him; his life was in peril. What was to be done?

The procession passed by, with the multitude in a fever of enthusiasm; then the lad ventured to leave the portico, and start for his quarters, to gain which he had first to traverse the side of the square he was on; that done, he would be in the beautiful street, going directly to the desired place. He strove to carry his ordinary air of confidence; but the quick step, pale face, and furtive glance would have been tell-tales to the shopkeepers and slaves whom he passed, if they had been the least observant. As it was, he had almost reached the street, and was felicitating himself, when he heard a yell behind him. He looked back, and beheld a party of warriors coming at full speed. Their cries and gestures left no room to doubt that he was their object. He started at once for life.

The noise drew everybody to the doors, and forthwith everybody joined the chase. After passing several bridges, the leading pursuers were about seventy yards behind him, followed by a stream of supporters extending to the *tianguez* and beyond. So we have the scene with which the chapter opens.

The page's situation was indeed desperate. He had not yet reached the king's palace, on the other side of which, as he knew, lay a stretch of street frightful to think of in such a strait. The mob was coming rapidly. To add to his horror, in front appeared a body of men armed and marching toward him; at the sight, they halted; then they formed a line of interception. His steps flagged; fainter, but more agonizing, arose his prayer to Christ and the Mother. Into the recesses on either hand, and into the doors and windows, and up to the roofs, and down into the canals, he cast despairing glances; but chance there was not; capture was certain, and then the—SACRIFICE!

That moment he reached a temple of the ancient construction,—properly speaking, a Cû,—low, broad, massive, in architecture not unlike the Egyptian, and with steps along the whole front. He took no thought of its appearance, nor of what it might contain; he saw no place of refuge within; his terror had become a blind, unreasoning madness. To escape the sacrifice was his sole impulse; and I am not sure but that he would have regarded death in any form other than at the hands of the pabas as an escape. So he turned, and darted up the steps; before his foremost pursuer was at the bottom, he was at the top.

With a glance he swept the *azoteas*. Through the wide, doorless entrance of a turret, he saw an altar of stainless white marble, decorated profusely with flowers; imagining there might be pabas present, and possibly devotees, he ran around the holy place, and came to a flight of steps, down which he passed to a courtyard bounded on every side by a colonnade. A narrow doorway at his right hand, full of darkness, offered him a hiding-place.

In calmer mood, I doubt if the young Spaniard could have been induced alone to try the interior of the Cû. He would at least have studied the building with reference to the cardinal points of direction; now, however, driven by the terrible fear, without thought or question, without precaution of any kind, taking no more note of distance than course, into the doorway, into the unknown, headlong he plunged. The darkness swallowed him instantly; yet he did not abate his speed, for behind him he heard—at least he fancied so—the swift feet of pursuers. Either the dear Mother of his prayers, or some ministering angel, had him in keeping during the blind flight; but at last he struck obliquely against a wall; in the effort to recover himself, he reeled against another; then he measured his length upon the floor, and remained exhausted and fainting.

CHAPTER VI.

LOST IN THE OLD CÛ.

THE page at last awoke from his stupor. With difficulty he recalled his wandering senses. He sat up, and was confronted everywhere by a darkness like that in sealed tombs. Could he be blind? He rubbed his eyes, and strained their vision; he saw nothing. Baffled in the appeal to that sense, he resorted to another ; he felt of his head, arms, limbs, and was reassured ; he not only lived, but, save a few bruises, was sound of body. Then he extended the examination : he felt of the floor, and, stretching his arms right and left, discovered a wall, which, like the floor, was of masonry. The cold stone, responding to the touch, sent its chill along his sluggish veins ; the close air made breathing hard ; the **silence** absolutely lifeless,—and in that respect so unlike what we **call** silence in the outer world, which, after all, is but **the time** chosen by small things, the entities of the dust and grass **and** winds, for their hymnal service, heard full-toned **in** heaven, **if not** by us,—the dead, stagnant, unresonant silence, **such** as haunts the depths of old **mines, and** lingers in the **sunken** crypts of abandoned castles, **awed and** overwhelmed his soul.

Where was he ? How came he there ? With head drooping, and hands and arms resting limp upon the floor, weak in body **and** spirit, he sat a long time motionless, struggling to recall the past, which came slowly, enabling him to see the race again with all its incidents : the enemy in rear, the enemy in front ; the temple stairs, with their offer of escape ; the *azoteas*, the court, the dash into the doorway under the colonnade,—all came back slowly, I say, bringing a dread that **he** was lost, and that, in a frantic effort to avoid death in one form, he had run open-eyed to embrace it in another even more horrible.

The dread gave him strength. He arose to his feet, and **stood** awhile, straining his memory to recall **the** direction of the **door** which had admitted him to the passage. Could he find **that** door, he would wait a fitting time to slip from the temple ; **for** which he would trust the Mother, and watch. But now, what was done must needs be done quickly ; for, though but an ill-timed fancy, he thought he felt a sensation of hunger, indicating that **he had been a** long time lying there ; how long, of course, he **knew** not.

Memory served him illy, or rather not at all ; so that nothing would do now but to feel his way **out**. Oh for a light, if only a spark from **a** gunner's match, or **the** moony gleam of a Cuban glow-worm !

As every faculty **was** now **alert,** he was conscious of the importance of the start ; **if that were** in the wrong direction, every inch would be from **the** door, and, possibly, toward his grave. First, then, was he in a hall or a chamber ? He hoped the former, for then there would be but two directions from which to choose ; and if he took the wrong one, **no** matter ; he had only **to keep** on until the fact was made clear by **the** trial, and then **retrace** his steps. "Thanks, O Holy Mother ! In the darkness **thou art** with thy children **no** less than in the day !"

And with the pious words, he crossed himself, forehead and breast, and set about the work.

To find if he were in a passage,—that was the first point. He laid his hand upon the wall again, and started in the course most likely, as he believed, to take him to the daylight, never before so beautiful to his mind.

The first step suggested a danger. There might be traps in the floor. He had heard the question often at the camp-fire, What is done with the bodies of the victims offered up in the heathen worship? Some said they were eaten; others, that there were vast receptacles for them in the ungodly temples,— miles and miles of catacombs, filled with myriads of bones of priests and victims. If he should step off into a pit devoted to such a use! His hair bristled at the thought. Carefully, slowly, therefore, his hands pressed against the rough wall, his steps short, one foot advanced to feel the way for the other, so he went, and such was the necessity.

Scarcely three steps on he found another dilemma. The wall suddenly fell away under his hand; he had come to the angle of a corner. He stopped to consider. Should he follow the wall in its new course? It occurred to him that the angle was made by a crossing of passages, that he was then in the square of their intersection; so the chances of finding the right outlet were three to one against him. He was more than ever confused. Hope went into low ebb. Would he ever get out? Had he been missed in the old palace? If hostilities had broken out, as intimated by the prince Io', would his friends be permitted to look for him in the city? The king was his friend, but, alas! his power had been given to another. No, there was no help for him; he must stay there as in his tomb, and die of hunger and thirst,—die slowly, hour by hour, minute by minute. Already the fever of famine was in his blood,—next to the fact is the fancy. If his organism had begun to consume itself, how long could he last? Never were moments so precious to him. Each one carried off a fraction of the strength upon which his escape depended; each one must, therefore, be employed. No more loitering; action, action! In the darkness he looked to heaven, and prayed tearfully to the Mother.

The better to understand his situation, and what he did, it may be well enough to say here, that the steps by which he descended into the courtyard faced the west; and as, from the court, he took shelter in a door to his right, the passage must have run due north. When, upon recovery from the fainting spell, he started to regain the door, he was still in the passage, but unhappily followed its continuation northward; every step, in that course, consequently, was so much into instead of out of the labyrinth. And now, to make the situation worse, he weakly clung to the wall, and at the corner turned to **the right**; after which his painful, toilsome progress was to the east, **where the** chances were sure to be complicated.

If the reader has ever tried **to pass through a strange hall** totally darkened, he can imagine **the** young Spaniard in **motion.** Each respiration, each movement, was doubly loud; the slide and shuffle of the feet, changing position, filled the rockbound space with echoes, which, by a cooler head than his, might have made tell the width and height **of** the passage, and something of its depth. There **were times** when the sounds seemed startlingly like the noise of **another** person close by; then he would stop, lay hand **on his dagger,** the only weapon he had, and listen nervously, **undetermined** what to do.

In **the course** of the tedious movement, **he** came **to** narrow **apertures at** intervals in the wall, which he surmised to be doors **of** apartments. Before some of them he paused, thinking they might be occupied; but nothing came from them, or was heard within, but the hollow reverberations usual to empty chambers. The crackle of cement under **foot and** the crevices **in** the wall filled with **dust** assured him **that a long** time had passed since **a** saving hand had been there; yet **the** evidences that the old pile had once been populous made **its** present desertion all the more impressive. Afterwhile he began to wish for the appearance of somebody, though an enemy. **Yet farther** on, when the awful silence and darkness fully kindled **his** imagination, and gave him for companionship the spirits of the pagans who had once—how far back, who could say?—made **the** cells animate with their prayers and orgies, the yearning for the company **of** anything living and susceptible of association became **almost** insupportable.

Several times, as he advanced, he came to cross passages. Of **the** distance made, he could form no idea. Once he descended a flight of **steps,** and at **the** bottom judged himself a storey below the level **of the court** and street; reflecting, however, that he could not have clomb **them on** the way in without some knowledge of them, he **again** paused for consideration. The end of the passage **was not** reached: he could not say the door he sought **was not there**; he simply believed not; still he resolved to go back to the starting-point and begin anew.

He set out bravely, and proceeded with less caution **than in** coming. Suddenly he stopped. He had neglected to count **the** doors and intersecting passages along the way; consequently **he** could not identify the starting-point when **he** reached it. Merciful God! *he was now indeed* LOST!

For **a** time he struggled against the conviction; but when the condition was actually realized, a paroxysm seized him. He raised his hands wildly, and shouted, "*Ola! Ola!*" The cry smote the walls near by until they rang again, and, flying down the passage, died lingeringly in the many chambers, leaving him so shaken by the discordance that he cowered nearly to the floor, as if, instead of human help, he had conjured a demon, and looked for its instant appearance. Summoning all his resolution, he again shouted the challenge, but with the same result; no reply except the mocking echoes—no help! He was in a tomb, buried alive! And at that moment, resulting doubtless from the fever of mind and body, he was conscious of the first decided sensation of thirst, accompanied by the thought of running water, cool, sweet, and limpid; as if to add to his torture, he saw then, not only that he was immured alive, but how and of what he was to die. Then also he saw why his enemies gave up the pursuit of the passage-door. Lost in the depths of the Cû, out of reach of help, groping here and there through the darkness, in hours condensing years of suffering, dead, finally, of hunger and thirst,—was he not as much a victim as if formally butchered by the *teotuctli?* And if, in the eyes of the heathen god, suffering made the sacrifice appreciable, when was there one more perfect?

"No, no!" he cried; "I am a Christian, in care of the Christian's God. I am too young, too strong. I can walk—if need be, run; and there are hours and days before me. I will find the door. Courage, courage! And thou, dear, blessed Mother! if ever thou dost permit a shrine in the chapel of this heathen house, all that which the Señor Hernan may apportion to me thou shalt have. Hear my vow, O sweet Mother, and help me!"

How many heroisms, attributed to duty, or courage, or some high passion, are in fact due to the utter hopelessness, the blindness past seeing, the fainting of the soul called despair! In that last motive what mighty energy! How it now nerved Orteguilla! Down the passage he went, and with alacrity. Not that he had a plan, or with the mind's eye even saw the way,—not at all. He went because in motion there was soothing to his very despair; in motion he could make himself believe there was still a hope; in motion he could expect each moment to hail the welcome door and the glory of the light.

CHAPTER VII.

HOW THE HOLY MOTHER HELPS HER CHILDREN.

I DOUBT not my reader is gentle, good, and tender-hearted, easily moved by tales of suffering, and nothing delighting in them; and that, with such benignant qualities of heart and such commendable virtues of taste, he will excuse me if I turn from following the young Spaniard, who has now come to be temporarily a hero of my story, and leave to the imagination the details of the long round of misery he endured in his wanderings through the interior of the old Cû.

Pathologists will admit they are never at fault **or loss** in the diagnosis of cases of hunger and thirst. Whether considered as disease or accident, their marks are unmistakeable, and their symptoms before dissolution, like their effects afterwards, invariable. Both may be simply described as consumption of the body by **its** own organs; precisely as if, to preserve life, one devoured his **own** flesh and drank his own blood. Not without reason, therefore, the suicide, what time he thinks of his crime, always, when possible, chooses some mode easier and more expeditious. The gradations to the end **are,** an intense desire for food and drink; a fever, accompanied by exquisite **pain;** then delirium; finally, death. It is in the second and **third stages** that the peculiarities show most strangely; then the mind cheats the body with visions of Tantalus. If the sufferer be thirst-stricken, he is permitted to see fountains and sparkling streams, and water **in** draughts and rivers; if he be starving, the same mocking fancy spreads Apician feasts before his eyes, and stimulates the intolerable misery by the sight and scent of all things delicious and appetizing. I have had personal experience of the anguish and delusions of **which I** speak. I know what they are. I pray the dear Mother, who **has** us all in holy **care,** to keep them far from my gentle friends!

A day and night in the temple,—another **day** and night,—morning of the third day, and we discover the page sitting upon the last of a flight of steps. No water, no food, in all that time. He slept once; how long, he did not know. A stone floor does not conduce to rest, even where there is sleep. All that time, too, the wearisome search for the door; groping **along** the wall, feeling the way ell by ell; always at fault and lost utterly. His condition can be understood **almost without** the aid of description. He sits on the step **in a kind of** stupor; his cries for help have become a dull, unmeaning moan; before him pass the fantasies of food and water; and could the light—the

precious, beautiful light, **so long sought, so** earnestly prayed and
struggled for—fall upon him, **we should have a** sad picture of the
gay youth who, in the market, sported **his** velvet **cloak** and
feathered bonnet, and half disdainfully flashed the royal signet in
the faces of the wondering merchants,—**the** picture of a despairing
creature whom much misery **was** rapidly bringing down **to** death.

And of his thoughts, or, rather, the vagaries that had **taken** the
place of thoughts,—ah, **how** well they can **be divined !** Awhile
given to the far-off native land, and the loved **ones** there,—**land
and loved ones never again** to be seen ; then to **the New** World,
full of all things strange ; but mostly to his **situation, lost** so
hopelessly, **suffering so** dreadfully. There were yet **ideas of**
escape, **reawakenings of the energy of** despair, but less **frequent**
every hour ; indeed, **he was becoming** submissive to the fate. **He**
prayed **also ;** but **his** prayers had more relation to the life **to**
come than to this one. To die **without** Christian rite, to leave
his bones in such unhallowed place **!** **Oh for one** shrieving word
from Father Bartolomé **!**

In the midst of his wretchedness, **and of the** sighs and sobs and
tears which were its actual expression, **suddenly** the ceiling overhead, and all the **rugged sides of the** passage above the line of the
upper step of the stairway at the foot **of which he was** sitting,
were illumined by **a faint, red glow of light. He started to** his
feet. Could it be **? Was it not a delusion ? Were not his** eyes
deceiving him **? In the darkness he had seen** banquets **and** the
chambers thereof, **and had heard the** gurgle of pouring **wine** and
water. Was not this **a** similar trick of the imagination **? or had**
the Blessed **Mother** at last heard his supplications ?

He looked steadily **;** the glow deepened. Oh, wondrous **charm of**
life **!** To be, **after dying so** nearly, brought back **with such**
strength, so **quickly, and by** such a trifle **!**

While he **looked, his doubts gave way to certainty. Light**
there was,—essential, revealing, **beautiful light. He clasped his**
hands, and the tears of despair became **tears of joy ;** all the hopes
of his being, which in the dreary hours **just passed had gone out**
as stars go **behind a** spreading cloud, **rose up whirring like a flock**
of startled **birds,** and, filling all his heart, **once more** endued him
with strength of mind and body. He passed **his hands across his**
eyes : **still the** light remained. Surer than a fantasy, **good as a**
miracle, **there it** was, growing brighter, and approaching, **and that,**
too, by the very passage in which he was standing **; whether**
borne by man or spirit, friend or foe, **it would** speedily reach **the**
head of the steps, and then—

Out of the very certainty of aid at hand, **a reaction of feeling
came.** A singular caution seized him. What if those bearing
the light were enemies **?** Through the glow dimly lighting the
part of the passage below the stairway, he looked eagerly for a

place for concealment. Actually, though starving, the prospect of
relief filled him with all the instincts of life renewed. A door
caught his eye. He ran to the cell and hid, but in position to
see whomsoever might pass. He had no purpose ; he would wait
and see,—that was all.

The light approached slowly,—in his suspense, how slowly !
Gradually the glow in the passage became a fair illumination.
There were no sounds of feet, no forerunning echoes ; the coming
was noiseless as that of spirits. Out of the door, nevertheless, he
thrust his head, in time to see the figure of a man on the upper
step, bareheaded, barefooted, half wrapped in a cotton cloak, and
carrying a broad wooden tray or waiter, covered with what seemed
table-ware ; the whole brought boldly into view by the glare of a
lamp fastened, like a miner's, to his forehead.

The man was alone ; with that observation, Orteguilla drew
back, and waited, his hand upon his dagger. He trembled with
excitement. Here was an instrument of escape ; what should he
do ? If he exposed himself suddenly, might not the stranger
drop his burden, and run, and in the race extinguish the lamp ?
If he attacked, might he not have to kill ? Yet the chance must
not be lost. Life depended upon it, and it was therefore precious
as life.

The man descended the steps carefully, and drew near the cell
door. Orteguilla held his breath. The stepping of bare feet
became distinct. A gleam of light, almost blinding, flashed
through the doorway, and, narrow at first but rapidly widening,
began to wheel across the floor. At length the cell filled with
brightness ; the stranger was passing the door, not a yard away.

The young Spaniard beheld an old man, half naked, and bearing
a tray. That he was a servant was clear ; that there was no
danger to be apprehended from him was equally clear : he was
too old. These were the observations of a glance. From the
unshorn, unshaven head and face, the eyes of the lad dropped to
the tray ; at the same instant the smell of meat, fresh from the
coals, saluted him, mixed with the aroma of chocolate, still smoking, and sweeter to the starving fugitive than incense to a devotee.
Another note : the servant was carrying a meal to somebody, his
master or mistress. Still another note : the temple was inhabited,
and the inhabitants were near by. The impulse to rush out and
snatch the tray, and eat and drink, was almost irresistible. The
urgency there is in a parched throat and in a stomach three days
empty cannot be imagined. Yet he restrained himself.

The lamp, the food, the human being—the three things most
desirable—had come, and were going, and the page still undetermined what to do. Instinct and hunger and thirst, and a dread
of the darkness and of the death so lately imminent, moved him

to follow, and he obeyed. He had cunning enough left to take off his boots. That done, he stepped into the passage, and, moving a few paces behind, put himself in the guidance of the servant, sustained by a hope that daylight and liberty were but a short way off.

For a hundred steps or more the man went his way, when he came to a great flat rock or flag cumbering the passage; there he stopped, and set down the tray; and, taking the lamp from the fastening on his head, he knelt by the side of a trap or doorway in the floor. Orteguilla stopped at the same time, drawing, as a precaution, close to the left wall. Immediately he heard the tinkling of a bell, which he took to be a signal to some one in a chamber below. His eyes fixed hungrily upon the savoury viands. He saw the slave fasten a rope to the tray, and begin to lower it through the trap; he heard the noise of the contact with the floor beneath: still he was unresolved. The man arose, lamp in hand, and without more ado, as if a familiar task were finished, started in return. And now the two must come within reach of each other; now the page must discover himself or be discovered. Should he remain? Was not retreat merely going back into the terrible labyrinth? He debated; and, while he debated, chance came along and took control. The servant, relieved of his load, walked swiftly, trying, while in motion, to replace the lamp over his forehead; failing in that, he stopped; and, as fortune ordered, stopped within two steps of the fugitive. A moment,—and the old man's eyes, dull as they were, became transfixed; then the lamp fell from his hand and rolled upon the floor, and with a scream he darted forward in a flight which the object of his fear could not hope to outstrip. The lamp went out, and darkness dropped from the ceiling and leaped from the walls, reclaiming everything.

Orteguilla stood overwhelmed by the misfortune. All the former horrors returned to plague him. He upbraided himself for irresolution. Why allow the man to escape? Why not seize, or, at least, speak to him? The chance had been sent, he could now see, by the Holy Mother; would she send another? If not, and he died there, who would be to blame but himself? He wrung his hands, and gave way to bitter tears.

Eventually the unintermitting craving of hunger aroused him by a lively suggestion. The smell of the meat and chocolate haunted him. What had become of them? Then he remembered the ringing of the bell, and their disappearance through the trap. There they were; and more,—somebody was there enjoying them! Why not have his share? Ay, though he fought for it! Should an infidel feed while a Christian starved? The thought lent him new strength. Such could not be God's will. Then, as often happens, indignation begat a certain shrewdness to discern **points,** and put them together. The temple was not vacant, as he **at first** feared. Indeed, its tenants were thereabouts. Neither **was he** alone; on the floor below he had **neighbours.** "Ave Maria!" he cried, and crossed himself.

His neighbours, he thought,—advancing to another conclusion, —his neighbours, whoever they were, had communication with the world; otherwise, they would perish, as he was perishing. Moreover, the old servant was the medium of the communication, and would certainly come again. Courage, courage!

A sense of comfort, derived from the bare idea of neighbourship with something human, for the time at least, lulled him into forgetfulness of misery.

Upon his hands and knees, he went to the **great stone and to** the edge of the trap.

"*Salvado! Soy salvado!* I am saved!" **And** with tears of joy he rapturously repeated the sweet salutation **of the** angels to the Virgin. *The space below was lighted!*

The light, as he discovered upon a second look, came through curtains stretched across a passage similar to the one he was in, and was faint, but enough to disclose **two** objects, the sight of which touched him with a fierce delight, — the tray on the floor, its contents untouched, and **a rope** ladder by which to descend.

He lost no time now. Placing his dagger between his teeth, he swung off, though with some trouble, and landed safely. At his feet, then, lay a repast to satisfy the daintiest appetite,—fish, white bread, chocolate, in silver cups and beaten into honeyed **foam,** and fruits from vine and tree. He clasped his hands and **looked to** Heaven, and, as became a pious Spaniard, restrained the maladies that afflicted him while he said the old Paternoster,— dear, hallowed utterance taught him in childhood by the mother who but for this godsend would have lost him for ever. Then he stooped to help himself, and while his hand was upon the bread the curtain parted, and he saw, amidst a flood of light pouring in over her head and shoulders, a girl, very young and very beautiful.

CHAPTER VIII.

THE PABA'S ANGEL.

IF I were writing a tale less true, or were at all accomplished in the charming art of the story-teller, which has come to be regarded as but little inferior to that of the poet, possibly I could have disguised the incidents of the preceding chapters so as to have checked anticipation. But many pages back the reader no doubt discovered that the Cû in which the page took shelter was that of Quetzal'; and now, while to believe I could, by any arrangement or conceit consistent with truth, agreeably surprise a friend, I must admit that he is a dull witling who failed, at the parting of the curtain as above given, to recognise the child of the paba,— Tecetl, to whom, beyond peradventure, the memory of all who follow me to this point has often returned, in tender sympathy for the victim of an insanity so strange or—as the critic must decide—a philosophy so cruel.

Now, however, she glides again into the current of my story, one of those wingless waifs which we have all at one time or another seen, and which, if not from heaven, as their purity and beauty suggest, are at least ready to be wafted there.

I stop to say that, during the months past, as before, her life had gone sweetly, pleasantly, without ruffle or labour or care or sickness, or division, even, into hours and days and nights,—a flowing onward, like time,—an existence so serenely perfect as not to be a subject of consciousness. Her occupation was a round of gentle ministrations to the paba. Her experience was still limited to the chamber, its contents and expositions. If the philosophy of the venerable mystic—that ignorance of humanity is happiness—was correct, then was she happy as mortal can be, for as yet she had not seen a human being other than himself. Her pleasure was still to chatter and chirrup with the friendly birds; or to gather flowers and fashion them into wreaths and garlands to be offered at the altar of the god to whom she herself had been so relentlessly devoted; or to lie at rest upon the couch, and listen to the tinkling voices of the fountain, or join in their melody. And as I do not know why, in speaking of her life, I should be silent as to that part which is lost in slumber, particularly when the allusion will help me illustrate her match-less innocency of nature, I will say further that sleep came to her as to children, irregularly and in the midst of play, and waking was followed by no interval of heaviness, or brooding over a daily task, or bracing the soul for a duty. In fact, she was still a child; though, not to be thought dealing with anything seraphic,

I will add that in the months past she had in height become quite womanly, while the tone of her voice had gained an equality, and her figure a fulness, indicative of quick maturity.

Nor had the "World" undergone any change. The universal exposition on the walls and ceiling remained the same surpassing marvel of art. At stated periods, workmen had come, and, through the shaft constructed for the purpose, like those in deep mines, lifted to the *azoteas* such plants and shrubs as showed signs of suffering for the indispensable sun ; but as, on such occasions, others were let down, and rolled to the vacant places, there was never an abatement of the garden freshness that prevailed in the chamber. The noise of the work disturbed the birds, but never Tecetl, whose spirit during the time was under the mesmeric Will of the paba.

There was a particular, however, in which the god who was supposed to have the house in keeping had not been so gracious. A few days before the page appeared at the door,—exactness requires me to say the day of the paba's last interview with Guatamozin, — Mualox came down from the sanctuary in an unusual state of mind and body. He was silent and exhausted ; his knees tottered, as, with never a smile or pleasant word or kiss in reply to the salutation he received, he went to the couch to lie down. He seemed like one asleep ; yet he did not sleep, but lay with his eyes fixed vacantly on the ceiling, his hand idly stroking his beard.

In vain Tecetl plied all her little arts : she sang to him, caressed him, brought her vases and choicest flowers and sweetest singing-birds, and asked a thousand questions about the fair, good Quetzal',—a topic theretofore of never - failing interest to the holy man.

She had never known sickness,—so kindly had the god dealt by her. Her acquaintance with infirmity of any kind was limited to the fatigue of play, and the weariness of tending flowers and birds. Her saddest experience had been to see the latter sicken and die. All her further knowledge of death was when it came and touched a plant, withering leaf and bud. To die was the end of such things ; but they—the paba and herself—were not as such ; they were above death : Quetzal' was immortal, and, happy souls ! they were to serve him for ever and ever. Possessed of such faith, she was not alarmed by the good man's condition ; on the contrary, taking his silence as a wish to be let alone, she turned and sought her amusements.

And as to his ailment. If there be such a thing as a broken heart, his was broken. He had lived, as noticed before, for a single purpose, hope of which had kept him alive, survivor of a mighty brotherhood. That hope the 'tzin in the last interview took away with him; and an old man without a hope is already dead.

Measuring time in the chamber by its upper-world divisions, noon and night came, and still the paba lay in the dismal coma. Twice the slave had appeared at the door with the customary meals. Tecetl heard and answered his signals. Meantime—last and heaviest of misfortunes—the fire of the temple went out. When the sacred flame was first kindled is not known; relighted at the end of the last great cycle of fifty-two years, however, it had burned ever since, served by the paba. Year after year his steps, ascending and descending, had grown feebler; now they utterly failed. "Where is the fire on the old Cû?" asked the night-watchers of each other. "Dead," was the answer. "Then is Mualox dead."

And still another day like the other; and at its close the faded hands of the sufferer dropped upon his breast. Many times did Tecetl come to the couch, and speak to him, and call him father, and offer him food and drink, and go away unnoticed. "He is with Quetzal'," she would say to herself and the birds. "How the dear god loves him!"

Yet another, the fourth day; still the sleep, now become a likeness of death. And Tecetl,—she missed his voice, and the love-look of his great eyes, and his fondnesses of touch and smile; she missed his presence also. True, he was there, but not with her; he was with Quetzal'. Strange that they should forget her so long! She hovered around the couch, a little jealous of the god, and disquieted, though she knew not by what. She was very, very lonesome.

And in that time what suspense would one familiar with perils have suffered in her situation! If the paba dies, what will become of her? We know somewhat of the difficulties of the passages in the Cû. Can she find the way out alone? The slave will doubtless continue to bring food to the door, so that she may not starve; and at the fountain she will get drink. Suppose, therefore, the supplies come for years, and she live so long; how will the solitude affect her? We know its results upon prisoners accustomed to society; but that is not her case: she never knew society, its sweets or sorrows. With her the human life of the great outside world is not a thing of conjecture, or of dreams, hopes, and fears, as the future life with a Christian; she does not even know there is such a state of being. Changes will take place in the chamber; the birds and plants, all of life there besides herself, will die; the body of the good man, through sickening stages of decay, will return to the dust, leaving a ghastly skeleton on the couch. Consequently, hers will come to be a solitude without relief, without amusement or occupation or society, and with but few memories, and nothing to rest a hope upon. **Can a mind** support itself, any more than a body? In other words, if Mualox dies, how long until she becomes what **it** were charity to kill? Ah, never mortal more dependent or more terribly threatened! Yet she saw neither the cloud nor its shadow, but followed her pastimes as usual, and sang her little songs, and slept when tired,—a simple-hearted child.

I am not an abstractionist; and the reader, whom I charitably take to be what I am in that respect, has reason to be thankful; for the thought of this girl, so strangely educated,—if the word may be so applied,—this pretty plaything of a fortune so eccentric, opens the gates of many a misty field of metaphysics. But I pass them by, and, following the lead of my story, proceed to say that, in the evening of the fourth day of the paba's sickness, the bell, as usual, announced the last meal at the door of the chamber. Tecetl went to the couch, and, putting her arms around the sleeper's neck, tried to wake him; but he lay still, his eyes closed, his lips apart,—in appearance, he was dying.

"**Father, father, why do you stay** away so long?" she said. "Come **back,—speak to me,—say** one word,—call **me once more!**"

The dull ear heard not; the hand used to caressing was still.

Tenderly she smoothed the **white beard** upon his breast.

"Is Quetzal' angry with **me? I love** him. Tell him how lonely I am, and that the birds are not enough to keep **me** happy when you stay so long; tell him how dear you **are** to **me.** Ask him to let you come back now."

Yet no answer.

"O Quetzal', fair, beautiful god! hear me," she continued. "Your finger is on his lips, or he would speak. Your veil is over his eyes, **or** he would see me. I **am** his child, and love him so much; and he is hungry, and here are bread and meat. Let him come for a little while, and I will love you more than ever."

And so she prayed and promised, but in **vain.** Quetzal' was obdurate. With tears fast flowing, she arose and stood by the couch, and gazed upon the face now sadly changed by the long abstinence. And as she looked, there came upon her own face a new expression, that which the very young always have when at the side of the dying,—half dread, half curiosity,—wonder **at** the manifestation, awe of the power that invokes it,—the look we can imagine on the countenance of a simple soul in the presence of Death interpreting himself.

At last she turned away, and went to the door. Twice she hesitated, **and** looked back. Wherefore? Was she pondering

the mystery of the deep sleep, or expecting the sleeper to awake,
or listening to the whisper of a premonition fainter in her ears
than the voice of the faintest breeze? She went on, nevertheless;
she reached the door, and drew the curtain; and there, in the
full light, was Orteguilla.

That we may judge the impression, let us recall what kind of
youth the page was. I never saw him myself, but those who
knew him well have told me he was a handsome fellow: tall,
graceful, and in manner and feature essentially Spanish. He
wore at the time the bonnet and jaunty feather and the purple
mantle of which I have spoken, and under that a close black
jerkin, with hose to correspond; half-boots, usual to the period,
and a crimson sash about the waist, its fringed ends hanging
down the left side, completed his attire. Altogether, a goodly
young man; not as gay, probably, as some then loitering
amongst the *alamedas* of Seville; for rough service long continued
had tarnished his finery and abused his complexion, to say
nothing of the imprints of present suffering; yet he was enough
so to excite admiration in eyes older than Tecetl's and more
familiar with the race.

The two gazed at each other, wonderstruck.

"Holy Mother!" exclaimed Orteguilla, the bread in his hand.
"Into what world have I been brought? Is this a spirit thou
hast sent me?"

In his eyes, she was an angel; in hers, he was more. She
went to him, and knelt, and said, "Quetzal', dear Quetzal',—
beautiful god! You are come to bring my father back to me.
He is asleep by the fountain."

In her eyes the page was a god.

The *paba's* descriptions of Quetzal' had given her the ideal of a
youth like Orteguilla. Of late, moreover, he had been constantly
expected from Tlapallan, his isle of the blest; indeed, he had
come,—so the father said. And the house was his. Whither
would he go, if not there? So, from tradition oft repeated, from
descriptions coloured by passionate love, she knew the god; and
as to the man,—between the image and his maker there is a likeness; so saith a book holier than the *teoamoxtli*.

The page, as we have seen, was witty and shrewd, and
acquainted well with the world; his first impression went
quickly; her voice assured him that he was not come to any
spirit land. The pangs of hunger, for the moment forgotten,
returned, and I am sorry to say that he at once yielded to
their urgency, and began to eat as heroes in romances never
do. When the edge of his appetite was dulled, and he could
think of something else, an impulse of courtesy moved him, and
he said,—

"I crave thy pardon, fair mistress. I have been so much an animal as to forget that this food is thine, and required to subsist thee, and, perhaps, some other inhabiting here. I admit, moreover, that ordinarily the invitation should proceed from the owner of the feast; but claim thy own, and partake with me; else it may befall that in my great hunger thy share will be wanting. Fall to, I pray thee."

Still kneeling, she stared at him, and, folding her hands upon her breast, replied, "Quetzal' knows that I am his servant. Let him speak so that I may understand."

"*Por cierto!*—it is true! What knoweth she of my mother tongue?"

And thereupon, in the Aztecan, he asked her to help herself.

"No," said she. "The house and all belong to you. I am glad you have come."

"Mine! Whom do you take me for?"

"The good god of my father, to whom I say all my prayers,— Quetzal'!"

"Quetzal', Quetzal'!" he repeated, looking steadily in her face; then, as if assured that he understood her, he took one of the goblets of chocolate, and tried to drink, but failed; the liquid had been beaten into foam.

"In the world I come from, good girl," he said, replacing the cup, "people find need of water, which, just now, would be sweeter to my tongue than all the honey in the valley. Canst thou give me a drink?"

She arose, and answered eagerly, "Yes, at the fountain. Let us go. By this time my father is awake."

"So, so!" he said to himself. "Her father, indeed! I have eaten his supper or dinner, according to the time of day outside, and he may not be as civil as his daughter. I will first know something about him." And he asked, "Your father is old, is he not?"

"His beard and hair are very white. They have always been so."

Again he looked at her doubtingly. "Always, said you?"

"Always."

"Is he a priest?"

She smiled, and asked, "Does not Quetzal' know his own servant?"

"Has he company?"

"The birds may be with him."

He quit eating, and, much puzzled by the answer, reflected.

"Birds, birds! Am I so near daylight and freedom? Grant it, O Blessed Mother!" And he crossed himself devoutly.

Then Tecetl said **earnestly,** "**Now** that you have eaten, good Quetzal', come and let us go **to** my father."

Orteguilla made up his **mind speedily:** he could not do worse than go back the way he came ; **and** the light here was so beautiful, and the darkness there so **terrible ;** and here was company. Just then, also, as a further inducement, he heard the **whistle of** a bird, and fancied he distinguished the smell of flowers.

"A garden," he said in his soul,—"a garden, **and** birds, and liberty !" The welcome thought thrilled him inexpressibly. "Yes, **I will go ;**" and, aloud, "I am ready."

Thereupon she **took his** hand, and put the curtains aside, and led him into **the paba's W**orld, never but once before seen by a stranger.

This time forethought **had not** gone in advance to prepare for **the** visitor. The master's eye was dim, **and** his careful hand still, **in the** sleep by the fountain. The **neglect** that darkened the fire on the turret was gloaming the lamps in the chamber ; one by **one they** had gone out, as all would have gone but **for** Tecetl, to **whom the** darkness and the **shadows** were hated enemies. Never**theless, the** light, falling **suddenly upon** eyes so long filled with **blackness** as his had been, **was blinding** bright, insomuch that **he clapped his** hand over his **face.** Yet she led him on eagerly, saying,—

"Here, here, good Quetzal'. Here by **the fountain he lies.**"

All her concern was for the paba.

And through the many pillars of stone, and along a walk bounded by shrubs and all manner of dwarfed tropical trees, half blinded by the light, but with the scent of flowers and living vegetation in his nostrils, and the carol of birds in his ears, and full of wonder unspeakable, he was taken, without pause, to the fountain. At sight of the sparkling jet his fever of thirst raged **more** intensely than **ever.**

"**Here** he is. **Speak to him,—call him back to me !** As you **love him,** call **him back, O** Quetzal' !"

He scarcely heard her.

"**Water, water !** Blessed Mother, I see it again ! A cup,— quick,—a cup !"

He **seized one on the table,** and drank, and drank again, crying **between each breath,** "To the Mother the praise !" Not until **he was fully satisfied did** he give ear to the girl's entreaty.

Looking to **the couch, whither** she had gone, **he** saw the figure of the paba **stretched out** like a corpse. He approached, and, searching the face, and laying his hand upon the breast over **the** heart, asked in a low voice, "How **long** has your father been asleep ?"

"A long time," she replied.

"*Jesu Christo!* He is dead, and she does **not know it!**" he thought, amazed at her simplicity.

Again he regarded her closely, and for the first time was struck by her beauty of face and form, by the brightness of her eyes, by the hair, wavy on the head and curling over the shoulders, by the simple, childish dress and sweet voice; above all, by the innocence and ineffable purity of her look and manner, all then discernible in the full glare **of the** lamps. And with what feeling he made discovery of her loveliness may be judged passably well by the softened tone in which he said, "Poor girl! your father will never, **never** wake."

Her eyes opened wide.

"Never, never **wake! Why?**"

"He **is** dead."

She looked at him wistfully, and he, **seeing** that she did not understand, added, "He **is** in heaven; **or, as he himself would** have said, in the Sun."

"Yes, but you will let him come back."

He took note of the trustful, beseeching look with which she accompanied the words, and shook his head, and, returning to the fountain, took a seat upon a bench, reflecting.

"What kind of girl is this? Not know death when he showeth so plainly! Where hath she been living? And I am possessed of St. Peter's **keys.** I open heaven's gate to let the heathen out! By the bones **of the saints! let** him get there first! The devil hath him!"

He picked up a withered flower lying by the bowl **of the** fountain, and went back to Tecetl.

"You remember how beautiful this was when taken **from the** vine?"

"Yes."

"What ails it **now?**"

"It is dead."

"Well, did you ever **know one of these, after** dying, to come back to life?"

"No."

"No more can thy father regain his life. He, too, is dead. From what you see, he will go to dust; therefore, leave him now, and let **us** sit by the fountain, and talk of escape; **for** surely you know the way out of this."

From the flower she looked to the dead, and, comprehending the illustration, sat by the body and cried. And so it happened that knowledge of death was her first lesson in life.

And he respected her grief, and went and took **a** bench by the basin, and thought.

"Quetzal', Quetzal',—who is he? A god, no doubt; yes, the one of whom the king so liveth in dread. I have heard his name. And I am Quetzal'! And this is his house—that is, my house! A scurvy trick, by St. James! Lost in my own house,—a god lost in his own temple!"

And as he could then well afford, being full-fed, he laughed at the absurd idea; and, in such mood, fell into a reverie, and grew drowsy, and finally composed himself on the bench, and sank to sleep.

CHAPTER IX.

LIFE IN THE PABA'S WORLD.

WHEN the page awoke, after a long, refreshing sleep, he saw the fountain first, and Tecetl next. She was sitting a little way off, upon a mat stretched on the floor. A number of birds were about her, whistling and coquetting with each other. One or two of very beautiful plumage balanced themselves on the edge of the basin, and bathed their wings in the crystal water. Through half-shut eyes he studied her. She was quiet,—thinking of what? Of what do children think in their waking dreams? Yet he might have known, from her pensive look and frequent sighs, that the fountain was singing to deaf ears, and the birds playing their tricks before sightless eyes. She was most probably thinking of what he had so lately taught her, and nursed the great mystery as something past finding out; many a wiser head has done the same thing.

Now, Orteguilla was very sensible of her loveliness; he was no less sensible, also, that she was a mystery out of the common way of life; and had he been in a place of safety, in the palace of Axaya', he would have stayed a long time, pretending sleep, in order to study her unobserved. But his situation presently rose to mind; the yellow glow of the lamps suggested the day outside; the birds, liberty; the fountain and shrubbery, the world he had lost; and the girl, life,—his life, and all its innumerable strong attachments. And so, in his mind, he ran over his adventures in the house. He surveyed all of the chamber that was visible from the bench. The light, the fountain, the vegetation, the decorated walls,—everything in view dependent upon the care of man. Where so much was to be done constantly, **was** there not something to be done **at** once,—something to save life? There were the lamps: how were they supplied? They might go out. And, *Jesu Christo!* the corpse of the paba! He sat up, as if touched by a spear: there it was, in all the repulsiveness of death.

The movement attracted the girl's attention; she arose, and waited for him to speak.

"Good morning,—if morning it **be**," he said.

She made no reply.

"Come here," he continued. "**I** have some questions to ask."

She drew **a few steps** nearer. A bird with breast of purple and wings of **snow flew** around her for a while, then settled upon her hand, **and was** drawn close to her bosom. He remembered, from Father Bartolomé's reading, how the love **of** God once before **took a** bird's form; and forthwith his piety and superstition hedged her about with sanctity. What with **the** white wings upon her breast, and the whiter **innocency within,** she **was safe as** if bound by walls of **brass.**

"Have **no** fear, I pray you," he said, misinterpreting her respectful sentiment. "You and I are two people in a difficult strait, and, if I mistake not, much dependent upon each other. A God, of whom you never heard, but whom I will tell you all about, took your father away, and **sent** me in his stead. The road thither, I confess, has been **toilsome** and dreadful. Ah me, I shudder at the thought!"

He emphasized his feelings **by a true Spanish shrug of the** shoulders.

"This is a strange place," he next said. "**How** long **have you been** here?"

"I cannot say."

"**Can you** remember coming, and who brought you?"

"No."

"You must have been a baby." He looked **at her** with pity. "Have you never been elsewhere?"

"No, never."

"Ah, by the Mother that keeps me! Always here! And the sky, and sun, and stars, and all God's glory of nature, seen in the valleys, mountains, and rivers, and seas,—have they been denied you, poor girl?"

"I have seen them **all**," she answered.

"Where?"

"On the ceiling and walls."

He looked up at the former, and noticed its **excellence** of representation.

"Very good,—beautiful!" he said, in **the way** of criticism. "Who did **the** work?"

" Quetzal'."

" And who is Quetzal' ? "

" Who should know better than the god **himself ?** "

" Me ? "

" Yes."

Again he shrugged his shoulders.

" My name, then, is Quetzal'. Now, what **is yours ?** "

" Tecetl."

" **Well, then, Tecetl, let me** undeceive you. In the first place, I **am not Quetzal', or any god.** I am a man, as your father there **was.** My name **is Orteguilla ;** and for the time I am page to the great king Montezuma. And before long, if I live, and get **out** of this place, as I **most devoutly pray,** I will be a soldier. In the next place you are a **girl, and soon** will be a woman. You have been cheated of life. By God's help, I will take you out of this. Do you understand me ? "

" No ; unless men and gods are the same."

" **Heaven** forbid ! " He crossed himself fervently. " **Do** you **not know** what men are ? "

" **All** my knowledge of things **is from the pictures on the** walls, and what else you see **here.**"

" *Jesu Christo !* " he cried in open **astonishment.** " And did the good man never tell you of **the world** outside,—of its creation, and its millions upon millions **of** people ? "

" No."

" Of the world in which you may find the originals of all that is painted **on the walls, more** beautiful than colours can make them ? "

He received **the** same reply, but, still incredulous, went on.

" Who takes care of these plants ? "

" My father."

" **A servant** brings your food **to the door—may he do** so again ! **Have you not seen** him ? "

" No."

" Where does the oil that feeds the lamps come from ? "

" From Quetzal'."

Just then a lamp went out. He arose hastily, and saw that the contents of the cup were entirely consumed. " Tecetl, **is there plenty** of oil ? Where do you keep it ? Tell me."

" In a jar, **there by** the door. While you **were asleep I** refilled the cups, **and now the jar** is empty."

He turned pale. Who **better** than he **knew the** value of the liquid that saved them **from the** darkness so horribly peopled by hunger and thirst ? If exhausted, where **could they get more ?** Without further question, he went through the chamber, and collected **the** lamps, and put **them** all **out** except one. Then he brought the jar from the door, and poured the oil **back**, losing not a drop.

Tecetl remonstrated, and cried when she saw the darkness invade the chamber, blotting out the walls, and driving the birds to their perches, or to the fountain yet faintly illuminated. But he was firm.

"Fie, fie!" he said. "You should laugh, not cry. Did I not **tell** you about the world above this, so great, and so full of people like ourselves? And **did** I not promise to take you there? I **am** come in your father's stead. Everything must contribute to our escape. We must think of nothing else. Do you understand? This chamber is but one of many, in a house big as a mountain, and full of passages in which, if we get lost, we might wander days and days, and then not get out, unless we had a light to show us the way. So we must **save** the oil. When this supply gives out, as it soon will if we are not careful, the darkness that so frightens you will come and swallow us, **and we** shall die, as did your father there."

The last suggestion sufficed; **she** dried **her** tears, and drew **closer** to him, as if to say, "I **confide** in you; save me."

Nature teaches fear of death; **so** that separation from the breathless thing upon the **couch was** not like parting from Mualox. Whether she **touched his** hand or looked in his **face** now, "Go hence, go hence!" was what **she** seemed to **hear.** The stony repulsion that substituted his **living love reconciled** her to the idea **of** leaving **home, for** such **the chamber** had been to her.

Here **I** may as **well** confess the page began to do a great **deal of** talking,—a consequence, probably, of having a good listener; **or** he may have thought it a duty to teach all that was necessary to prepare his disciple for life in the new world. In the midst of a lecture, the tinkle of a bell brought him to a hasty pause.

"Now, O Blessed Mother, now I am happy! Thou hast not **forsaken** me! I shall see the sun again, and brave old Spain. **Live** my heart!" he cried, as **the** last tinkle trembled and died **in** the silence.

Seeing that she regarded him with surprise, he said, in her tongue, "I was thanking the Mother, Tecetl. She will save **us** both. Go now, and bring the breakfast,—I say breakfast, **not** knowing better,—and while we eat I will tell you why I am **so** glad. When you have heard me, you will be glad as I am."

She went at once, and, coming back, found him bathing his **face** and head in the water of the basin,—a healthful **act,** but not **one to** strengthen the idea of his godship. She placed **the** tray upon **the** table, and helped him to napkin and comb; then they took places opposite each other, with the lamp between them;

whereupon she had **other proof of his kind** of being ; for it is difficult to think of **a** deity **at table**, eating. The Greeks felt the incongruity, and dined their gods on nectar and ambrosia, leaving us to imagine them partaken in **some other** than the ordinary, vulgar way. Verily, Tecetl **was becoming** accustomed **to** the stranger !

And while they ate, he explained his plans, and **talked** of the **upper** world, and described its wonders **and** people, until, her **curiosity** aroused, she plied him with questions ; and, as point **after point was** given, **we** may suppose nature asserted itself, and **taught her, by what** power there is in handsome **youth, with** its **bright** eyes, **smooth face, and** tongue more winsome than **wise,** that **life in** the **said world** was a desirable exchange for **the** monotonous drifting to **which she** had been so long subjected. We may also suppose that she **was not** slow to observe the differ- ence between Mualox and the page ; which **was** that between age and youth, or, more philosophically, that between a creature to be **revered and** a creature to be admired.

* * * * * * * *

CHAPTER X.

THE ANGEL BECOMES A BEADSWOMAN.

THE point-line at the **foot of** the last chapter I **called** in as an easy bridge by which to cross an interval of two days,—a trick never to be resorted to except when there is nothing of interest to record, as was the case here.

Orteguilla occupied the interval **very** industriously, if not pleasantly. He had in hand two tasks,—one to instruct Tecetl **about** the world **to** which he had vowed **to** lead her ; the other **to fix upon a** plan of **escape. The first he found** easy, the latter **difficult ; yet** he had **decided, and** his preparations for the attempt, **sufficient,** he thought, **though** simple, lay upon the floor by the **fountain.** A lamp shed a **dim** light over the scene.

"So, so, Tecetl ; are we ready now ?" he asked.

"You are the master," she replied.

"Very good, I will be assured."

He went through a thorough **inspection.**

"Here are the paint and brush ; **here the oil** and lamp ; here **the** bread and meat, and **the calabash of** water. So far, good, **very good.** And here **is the mat,—very** comfortable, Tecetl, if you have to make your bed upon a stone in the floor. **Now**, are **we** ready ?"

"Yes, if you say so."

"Good again ! The Mother is with us. Courage ! You shall see the sun and sky, or I am not **a** Spaniard. Listen, now, and I will explain."

They took seats upon **the** bench, this time together ; for the strangeness was well-nigh gone, and they had come to have an interest in a common purpose.

"You must know, then, that I have two reliances : first, the man who brings the tray **to** the door ; next, the Blessed Mother.

"I will begin with the first," he said after a pause. "The man is a slave, and, therefore, easy to impose upon. If he is like his class, **from** habit, he asks no questions of his superiors. Your father—I speak from what you have told me—was thoughtful and dreamy, and spoke but little to anybody, and seldom, if ever, **to** his servants. You are not well **versed** in human nature ; one **day, no** doubt, you will be ; then you will be able to decide **whether** I am right in believing that the traits of master and slave, which I have mentioned, are likely to help us. I carried your father's body over to the corner yonder,—you were asleep **at** the time,—and laid it upon the floor, as **we** Christians serve our dead. I made two crosses, and **put** one upon his lips, the other on his breast ; he will sleep **all the** better for them. As you would have done, had you been present, I also covered him with flowers. One other thing I did."

He took a lamp, and was gone a moment.

"Here are your father's gown and hood," he said, coming back. "I doubt whether they would sell readily in the market. He will never need them again. I took them to help save your life,—a purpose for which he would certainly have given them, had **he** been alive. I will put them on."

He laid his bonnet on the bench ; then took off his boots, and put on the gown,—a garment of coarse black *manta*, loose in body and sleeves, and hanging nearly to the feet. Tying the cord about his waist, and drawing the hood over his head, he walked away a few steps, saying,—

"Look at me, Tecetl. Your father was very old. Did **he** stoop much—as much **as** this ?"

He struck the good man's habitual posture, and, in a moment after, his slow, careful gait. At the sight she could not repress her tears.

"What, crying again !" he said. "I shall be ashamed of you soon. If we fail, then you may cry, and—I do **not** know but that **I** will join you. People who weep much cannot hear as they ought, and I want you to hear every **word**. To go on,

U

then : in this guise I mean to wait for the old slave. When he
lets the tray down, I will be there to climb the ladder. He
will see the hood and gown, and think me his old master. He
will not speak, nor will I. He will let me get to his side, and
then"—

After reflection, he continued,—

"Ah, Tecetl! you know not what troubles women sometimes
are. Here am I now. How easy for me, in this guise, to follow
the slave out of the temple! The most I would have to do would
be to hold my tongue. But you,—I cannot go and leave you ;
the Señor Hernan would not forgive me, and I could not forgive
myself. Nevertheless, you are a trouble. For instance, when
the slave sees you with me, will he not be afraid, and run ? or,
to prevent that, shall I not have to make him a prisoner ? That
involves a struggle. I may have to fight him, to wound him.
I may get hurt myself, and then—alas! what would become
of us ?"

Again he stopped, but at length proceeded,—

"So much for that. Now for my other reliance,—the Blessed
Lady. If the slave escapes me, you see, Tecetl, I must trust to
what the infidels call Fortune,—a wicked spirit, sometimes good,
sometimes bad. I mean we shall then have to hunt the way out
ourselves ; and having already tried that, I know what will
happen. Hence these preparations. With the paint I will
mark the corners we pass, that I may know them again ; the
lamp will enable me to see the marks and keep the direction ;
if we get hungry, here are bread and meat, saved, as you know,
from our meals ; if we get thirsty, the calabash will be at hand.
That is what I call trusting to ourselves ; yet the Blessed Mother
enabled me to anticipate all these wants and provide for them,
as we have done ; therefore I call her my reliance. Now you
have my plans. I said you were my trouble ; you cannot work,
or think, or fight ; yet there is something you can do. Tecetl,
you can be my pretty beadswoman. I see you do not know what
that is. I will explain. Take these beads."

While speaking, he took a string of them from his neck.

"Take these beads, and begin now to say, 'O Blessed Mother,
beautiful Mother, save us for Christ's sake !' Repeat ! Good !"
he said, his eyes sparkling. "I think the prayer never sounded
as sweetly before ; nor was there ever cavalier with such a beadswoman. Again."

And again she said the prayer.

"Now," he said, "take the string in your own hand,—thus ;
drop one bead,—thus ; and keep on praying, and for every
prayer drop one bead. Only think, Tecetl, how I shall be comforted, as I go along the gloomy passages, to know that right

behind me comes one, so lately a heathen, but now a Christian, at every step calling on the Mother. Who knows but we shall be out and in the beautiful day before the beads are twice counted? If so, then shall we know that she cared for us; and when we reach the palace we will go to the chapel with good Father Bartolomé, and say the prayer together once for every bead on the string. So I vow, and do you the same."

"So I vow," she said with a pretty submission.

Then, by ropes fixed for the purpose, he raised the calabash and mat and bundle of provisions, and swung them lightly over his shoulders. Under his arm he took an earthen vase filled with oil.

"Let us to the door now. The slave should be there. Before we start, look around: you are leaving this place for ever."

The thought went to her heart.

"Oh, my birds! What will become of them?"

"Leave them to God," he replied laconically.

There were tears and sobs, in the midst of which he started off, lamp in hand. She gave a look to the fountain, within the circle of whose voice nearly all her years had been passed. In her absence it would play and sing, would go on as of old; but in her absence who would be there to see and hear? In the silence and darkness it would live, but nevermore for her.

And she looked to the corner of the chamber where Orteguilla had carried the body of the paba. Her tears attested her undiminished affection for him. The recollection of his love outlived the influence of his will. His world was being abandoned, having first become a tomb, capacious and magnificent, — his tomb. But Quetzal' had not come. Broken are thy dreams, O Mualox, wasted by thy wealth of devotion! Yet, at this parting, thou hast tears, —first and last gift of love, the sweetest of human principles and the strongest, —stronger than the will; for if the latter cannot make God of a man, the former can take him to God.

And while she looked, came again the bird of the breast of purple and wings of snow, which she placed in her bosom; then she followed the page, saying trustfully, "O Blessed Mother, beautiful Mother, save us for Christ's sake!"

Outside the curtain door he deposited his load, and carefully explained to Tecetl the use of the ladder. Then he placed a stool for her.

"Sit now; you can do nothing more. Everything depends on the slave: if he behaves well, we shall have no need of these preparations, and they may be left here. But whether he behave well or ill, remember this, Tecetl, —cease not to pray; forget not the beads."

And so saying, he tossed a stout cord up through the trap;
then, leaving the lamp below, he clomb to the floor above. His
anxiety may be imagined. Fortunately the waiting was not
long. Through the gallery distantly he saw a light, which—
praise to the Mother!—came his way. He descended the ladder.

"He comes, and is alone. Be of cheer, Tecetl; be of cheer,
and pray. Oh, if the Mother but stay with us now!"

Faster fell the beads.

When the sound of footsteps overhead announced the arrival
of the slave, Orteguilla put his dagger between his teeth, drew
the hood over his head, and began to ascend. He dared not look
up; he trusted in the prayers of the little beadswoman, and
clomb on.

His head reached the level of the floor, and with the trap
gaping wide around, he knew himself under the man's eyes.
Another moment, and his hand was upon the floor; slowly he
raised himself clear of the rope; he stood up, then turned to the
slave, and saw him to be old and feeble, and almost naked; the
lamp was on his forehead, the tray at his feet; his face was
downcast, his posture humble. The Spaniard's blood leaped
exultantly; nevertheless, carefully and deliberately, as became
his assumed character, he moved to one side of the passage, to
clear the way to the trap. The servant accepted the movement,
and without a word took the lamp from his head, crossed the
great stone, fixed the ropes, and stooped to lower the tray.

Orteguilla had anticipated everything, even this action, which
gave him his supreme advantage; so he picked up the cord lying
near, and stepped to the old man's side. When the tray was
landed below, the latter raised himself upon his knees; in an
instant the cord was around his body; before he understood the
assault, escape was impossible.

Orteguilla, his head yet covered by the hood, said calmly, "Be
quiet, and you are safe."

The man looked up and replied, "I am the paba's servant
now, even as I was when a youth. I have done no wrong, and
am not afraid."

"I want you to live. Only move not."

Then the page called, "Tecetl! Tecetl!"

"Here," she answered.

"Try, now, to come up. Be careful lest you fall. If you need
help, tell me."

"What shall I do with the bread and meat, and"—

"Leave them. The Mother has been with us. Come up."

The climbing was really a sailor's feat, and difficult for her;
finally, she raised her head through the trap. At the sight, the
slave shrank back, as if to run. Orteguilla spoke to him.

" Be not afraid of the child. I have raised her to **help** me take care of the temple. We are going to the chapel now."

The man turned to him curiously; possibly he **detected a** strange accent under the hood. When, on her part, Tecetl saw him, she stopped, full of wonder as of fear. Old and ugly as he **was,** he yet confirmed **the** page's story, and brought the new **world** directly to her. So a child stops **and** regards the first person met at the door of **a** strange house,—attracted, curious, afraid.

" Come on," said Orteguilla.

She raised her hand overhead, and held up the bird **with the** white wings.

" Take it," **she** said.

Used as he was to wonderful things in connection with his old master, the servant held back. A girl and a bird from the cells,— a mystery, indeed !

" Take it," said Orteguilla.

He did so ; whereupon the page assisted her to the floor.

" **We** are almost there,—almost," he said cheerfully. " Have you kept count of the prayers ? Let me see the beads."

She held out the rosary.

" Ten beads more,—ten **prayers yet. The** Mother is with us. Courage ! "

Then of the slave **he** asked,—

" How is the day without ? "

" There is not a cloud in the sky."

" Is it morning or evening ? "

" About midday."

" Is the city quiet ? "

" I cannot say."

" Very well. Give the girl her bird, and lead to the courtyard."

And they started, the slave ahead, held in check by the cord in the Spaniard's hand. The light was faint and unsteady. Once they ascended a flight of steps, and twice changed direction. When the page saw the many cells on either side, and the number of intersecting passages, all equal in height and width, and bounded by the same walls of rough red stone, he understood how he became lost ; and with a shuddering recollection **of** his wanderings through the great house, he could not sufficient**ly** thank the Providence that was now befriending him.

They clomb yet another stairway, and again changed direction ; after that, a little farther walk, and Orteguilla caught sight **of** a doorway penetrated by a pure white light, which he recognised as day. Words cannot express his emotion ; his spirit could hardly be controlled ; he would have shouted, sung, danced,— anything **to** relieve himself of this oppression of happiness. But he thought, if he were out of the temple, he would not yet be out of danger; that he had to make way, by the great street from which he had been driven, to the quarters of his friends before he could promise himself rest and safety; the disguise was the secret of his present good fortune, and must help him further. So he restrained himself, saying to Tecetl,—

"For the time, cease your prayers, little one. The world I promised to bring you to is close by. I see the daylight."

There was indeed a door into the *patio*, or court-yard, of the temple. Under the lintel the page lingered a moment,—the court was clear. Then he gave the cord into the servant's hand, with the usual parting salutation, and stepped once more into the air, fresh with the moisture of the lake and the fragrance of the valley. He looked to the sky, blue as ever, and through its serenity up sped his grateful Ave Maria. In the exulting sense of rescue he forgot all else, and was well across the court to the steps leading to the *azoteas*, when he thought of Tecetl. He looked back, and did not see her; he ran to the door; she was there. The bird had fallen to the floor, and was fluttering blindly about; her hands were pressed hard over her face.

"What ails you?" he asked petulantly. "This is not a time to halt and cry. Come on."

"I cannot"—

"Cannot! Give me your hand."

He led her through the door, under the colonnade, out into the court.

"Look up, Tecetl, look up! See the sky, drink the air. You are free!"

She uncovered her eyes; they filled as with fiery arrows. She screamed, staggered as if struck, and cried, "Where are you? I am lost, I am blind!"

"*O Madre de Dios!*" said Orteguilla, comprehending the calamity, and all its inconveniences to her and himself, "help me, most miserable of wretches,—help me to a little wisdom!"

To save her from falling, he had put his arm around her; and as they stood thus,—she the picture of suffering, and he overwhelmed by perplexity,—help from any quarter would have been welcome; had the slave been near, he might have abandoned her; but aid there was not. So he led her tenderly to the steps, and seated her.

"How stupid," he said in Spanish,—"how stupid not to think of this! If, the moment I was born, they had carried me out to take a look at the sun, shining as he is here, I would have been blinder than any beggar on the Prado, blinder than the Bernardo of whom I have heard Don Pedro tell. My nurse was a sensible woman."

Debating what to do, he looked at Tecetl; and for the first time since she had come out of the door, he noticed her dress,— simply a cotton chemise, a skirt of the same reaching below the knees, a blue sash around the waist,—very simple, but very clean. He noticed, also, the exceeding delicacy of her person, the transparency of her complexion, the profusion of her hair, which was brown in the sun. Finally, he observed the rosary.

"She is not clad according to the laws which govern high-born ladies over the water; yet she is beautiful, and, by the Mother! she is a Christian. Enough. By God's love, I, who taught her to pray, will save her, though I die. Help me, all the saints!"

He adjusted the hood once more, and, stooping, said in his kindliest tone, "Pshaw, Tecetl, you are not blind! The light of the sun is so much stronger than that of your lamps that your eyes could not bear it. Cheer up, cheer up! And now put your arm around my neck. I will carry you to the top of these steps. We cannot stay here."

She stretched out her arms.

"Hark!" he cried. "What is that?"

He stood up and listened. The air above the temple seemed full of confused sounds; now resembling the distant roar of the sea, now the hum of insects, now the yells of men.

"*Jesu!* I know that sound. There,—there!"

He listened again. Through the soaring, muffled din came another report, as of thunder below the horizon.

"It is the artillery! By the mother that bore me, the guns of Mesa!"

The words of Io', spoken in Xoli's portico, came back to him.

"Battle! As I live, they are fighting on the street!"

And he, too, sat down, listening, thinking. How was he to get to his countrymen?

The sounds overhead continued, at intervals intensified by the bellowing guns. Battle has a fascination which draws men as birds are said to be drawn by serpents. They listen; then wish to see; lingering upon the edge, they catch its spirit, and finally thrill with fierce delight to find themselves within the heat and fury of its deadly circle. The page knew the feeling then. To see the fight was an overmastering desire.

"Tecetl, poor child, you are better now?"

"I dare not open my eyes."

"Well, I will see for you. Put your arms around my neck."

And with that he carried her up the steps. All the time, he gave ear to the battle.

"Listen, Tecetl; hear that noise! A battle is going on out in the street, and seems to be coming this way. I will lead you into the chapel here,—a holy place, so your father would have said. In the shade, perhaps, you can find relief."

"How pleasant the air is!" she said as they entered.

"Yes, and there is Quetzal',"—he pointed to the idol,—"and here the step before the altar upon which, I venture, your father spent half his life in worship. Sit and rest until I return."

"Do not leave me," she said.

"A little while only. I must see the fight. Some good may come of it,—who knows? Be patient; I will not leave you."

He went to the door. The sounds were much louder and nearer. All the air above the city apparently was filled with them. Amongst the medley he distinguished the yells of men and peals of horns. Shots were frequent, and now and then came the heavy, pounding report of cannon. He had been at Tabasco, at Tzimpantzinco, and in the three pitched battles in Tlascala, and was familiar with what he heard.

"How they fight!" he said to himself. "Don Pedro is a good sword and brave gentleman, but—ah! if the Señor Hernan were there, I should feel better: he is a good sword, brave gentleman, and wise general also. Heaven fights for him. Ill betide Narvaez! Why could he not have put off his coming until the city was reduced? *Jesu!* The sounds come this way now. Victory! The guns have quit, the infidels fly, on their heels ride the cavaliers. Victory!"

And so, intent upon the conflict, insensibly he approached the front of the temple, before described as one great stairway. On the topmost step he paused. A man looking at him from the street below would have said, "It is only a paba;" and considering, further, that he was a paba serving the forsaken shrine, he would have passed by without a second look.

What he looked down upon was a broad street, crowded with men,—not citizens, but warriors, and warriors in such splendour of costume that he was fairly dazzled. Their movement suggested a retreat, whereat pride dashed his eyes with the spray of tears; he dared not shout.

More and more eagerly he listened to the coming tumult. At last, finding the attraction irresistible, he descended the steps.

The enemy were not in rout. They moved rapidly, but in ranks extending the width of the street, and perfectly ordered. The right of their column swept by the Spaniard almost within arm's reach. He heard the breathing of the men, saw their arms,—their shields of quilted cotton, embossed with brass; their armour, likewise of quilted cotton, but fire-red with the blood of the cochineal; he saw their musicians, drummers, and conch-blowers, the latter making a roar ragged and harsh, and so loud that a groan or death-shriek could not be heard; he saw, too, their chiefs, with helms richly plumed or grotesquely adorned with heads of wild animals, with *escaupiles* of plumage, gorgeous as hues of sunset, with lances and *maquahuitls*, and shields of bison-hide or burnished silver, mottoed and deviced like those of Christians; amongst them, also, he saw pabas, bareheaded, without arms, frocked like himself, singing wild hymns, or chanting wilder epics, or shouting names of heroic gods, or blessing the brave and cursing the craven,—the Sun for the one, Mictlan for the other. The seeing all these things, it must be remembered, was very different from their enumeration; but a glance was required.

The actual struggle, as he knew, was at the rear of the passing column. In fancy he could see horsemen plunging through the ranks, plying sword, lance, and battle-axe. And nearer they came. He could tell by the signs, as well as the sounds; by the files beginning to crowd each other; by the chiefs, labouring to keep their men from falling into confused masses. At length the bolt of a cross-bow, striking a man, fell almost at his feet. Only the hand of a Spaniard could have launched the missile.

"They come,—they are almost here!" he thought, and then, "*O Madre de Dios!* If they drive the infidels past this temple, I am saved. And they will. Don Pedro's blood is up, and in pursuit he thinks of nothing but to slay, slay. They will come; they are coming! There—*Jesu Christo!* That was a Christian shout!"

The cross-bow bolts now came in numbers. The warriors protected themselves by holding their shields over the shoulder behind; yet some dropped, and were trampled under foot. Orteguilla was himself in danger, but his suspense was so great that he thought only of escape; each bolt was a welcome messenger, with tidings from friends.

The column, meantime, seemed to become more disordered; finally, its formation disappeared utterly; chiefs and warriors were inextricably mixed together; the conch-blowers blew hideously, but could not altogether drown the yells of the fighting men.

Directly the page saw a rush, a parting in the crowd as of waters before a ship; scores of dark faces, each a picture of dismay, turned suddenly to look back; he also looked, and over the heads and upraised shields, half obscured by a shower of stones and arrows, he saw a figure which might well have been taken for the fiend of slaughter,—a horse and rider, in whose action there were a correspondence and unity that made them for the time one fighting animal. A frontleted head, tossed up for a forward plunge, was what he saw of the horse; a steel-clad form, swinging a battle-axe with the regularity of a machine, now to the right, now to the left of the horse's neck, was all he saw of the rider. He fell upon his knees, muttering what he dared not shout, "Don Pedro, brave gentleman! I am saved! I am saved!" Instantly he sprang to his feet. "O my God! Tecetl,—I had almost forgotten her!"

He climbed the steps again fast as the gown would permit.

"My poor girl, come; the Mother offers us rescue. Can you not see a little?"

She smiled faintly, and replied, "I cannot say. I have tried to look at Quetzal' here. He was said to be very beautiful; my father always so described him; but this thing is ugly. I fear I cannot see."

"It is a devil's image, Tecetl, a devil's image,—Satan himself!" said the page vehemently. "Let him not lose us a moment; for each one is of more worth to us than the gold on his shield there. If you cannot see, give me your hand. Come!"

He led her to the steps. The infidels below seemed to have held their ground awhile, fighting desperately. Eight or ten horsemen were driving them, though slowly; if one was struck down, another took his place. The street was dusty as with the sweeping of a whirlwind. Under the yellow cloud lay the dead and wounded. The air was alive with missiles, of which some flew above the temple, others dashed against the steps. It looked like madness to go down into such a vortex; but there was no other chance. What moment Don Pedro might tire of killing, no one could tell; whenever he did, the recall would be sounded.

"What do I hear? What dreadful sounds!" said Tecetl, shrinking from the tumult.

"Battle," he answered; "and what that is I have not time to tell; we must go down and see."

He waited until the fighting was well past the front of the old Cû, leaving a space behind the cavaliers clear of all save those who might never fight again; then he threw back the hood, loosed the cord from his waist, and flung the disguise from him.

"Now, my pretty beadswoman, now is the time! Begin the prayer again: 'O Mother, beautiful Mother, save us for Christ's sake!' Keep the count with one hand; put the other about my neck. Life or death,—now we go!"

He carried her down the steps. Over a number of wounded wretches who had dragged themselves, half dead, out of the blood **and** trample, he crossed the pavement. **A** horseman caught **sight** of him, and rode to his side, and lifted the battle-axe.

"Hold, señor! I am Orteguilla. *Viva España!*"

The axe dropped harmless; up went the visor.

"In time, boy,—in time! An instant more, **and** thy soul had been in Paradise," **cried Alvarado,** laughing heartily. "What hast thou there? **Something from** the temple? But stay not to answer. To **the rear, fast as** thy legs **can** carry thee! Faster! Put the baggage **down.** We are tired of the slaughter; but for thy sake **we** will **push** the dogs a little farther. Begone! Or stay! **Arrows are thicker** here than curses in hell, and **thou** hast **no armour. Take my** shield, which I have not used **to-day.** Now **be** off!"

Orteguilla set the girl upon her feet, took the shield, and proceeded to buckle it upon his arm, while Alvarado rode into the fight again. A moment more, and he would have protected **her** with the good steel wall. Before he could complete the preparation, he heard a cry, quick, shrill, and sharp, that seemed **to** pierce his ear like a knife,—the cry by which one in battle announces himself death-struck,—the cry once heard, never forgotten. He raised the shield,—too late! she reeled and fell, dragging him half down.

"What ails **thee** now?" he **cried in Spanish,** forgetting himself. "What ails thee? **Hast thou looked at** the sun again?"

He lifted her head upon his knee.

"Mother of Christ, she is slain!" he cried in horror.

An arrow descending had gone through her neck to **the heart.** The blood gushed from her mouth. He took her in **his** arms and carried her to the steps of the temple. As he laid her down, she tried **to** speak, **but** failed; then she opened her eyes wide: the light poured into them **as** into the windows of an empty house; **the** soul was gone,—she was dead!

In so **short a** space habitant of three worlds,—when was there the like?

From the peace **of** the old chamber to the din of battle, from the din of **battle** to the calm of paradise,—brief time, short way!

From the sinless **life to the** sinful she had come; from the sinful life sinless she **had** gone; and in the going, **what fulness** of the mercy of God!

I cannot say the Spaniard loved her; most likely **his** feeling was the simple affection we all have for things gentle and helpless,—a bird, a lamb, a child; now, however, **he** knelt over her with tears; and as he did so, he saw **the rosary,** and that all the beads but one were wet **with her** blood. He took the string from the slender neck, and **laid** her head upon the stone, and thought the unstained bead **was** for a prayer uncounted, — a prayer begun on earth and finished in heaven.

CHAPTER XI.

THE PUBLIC OPINION PROCLAIMS ITSELF—BATTLE.

"How now! thou here yet? In God's name, what madness hast thou? Up, idiot! up, and fly, or in mercy I will slay thee here!"

As he spoke, Alvarado touched Orteguilla with the handle of his axe. The latter sprang up, alarmed.

"*Mira, señor!* She is just dead. I could not leave her dying. I had **a vow.**"

The cavalier looked at **the dead** girl; **his heart softened.**

"I give thee honour, lad, I give thee honour. Hadst thou left her living, shame would have been to thee for ever. But waste **not** time in maudlin. Hell's **spawn is loose.**" With raised visor, he **stood in** his stirrups. "See, far as eye **can reach,** the street is full! And hark to their yells! Here, mount behind **me; we** must go at speed."

The infidels, faced about, were coming back. **The** page gave them one glance, then caught the hand reached out to him, and, placing his foot on the captain's, swung himself behind. At a word, up the street, over the bridges, by the palaces and temples, the horsemen galloped. The detachment at the head of which they had sallied from the palace—gunners, arquebusiers, and cross-bowmen—had been started in return some time before. Upon overtaking them, Alvarado rode to a broad-shouldered fellow, whose grizzly beard overflowed the chin-piece of his morion.

"Ho, Mesa! the hounds **we** followed **so** merrily were only feigning; **they** have turned upon us. Do thou take the rear with **thy guns.** We will to the front, and cut a path to the gate. Follow **closely.**"

"Doubt **not, captain. I** know **the trick. I caught it** in Italy."

"*Cierto!* What **thou knowest not** about a gun is not worth the knowing," Alvarado **said; then** to the page, "Dismount, lad, **and** take place with these. **What** we have ahead may require **free man** and free horse. *Picaro!* If anybody is killed, thou **hast** permission to use his arms. What say **ye,** *compañeros mios?*"

he cried, facing the detachment,—"what say ye? Here I bring one whom we thought roasted and eaten by the cannibals in the temples. Either he hath escaped by miracle, **or** they are not judges of bones good to mess upon. He is without arms; will ye take care of him? I leave him my shield; will **ye** take care **of** that also?"

And Najerra, the hunchback, **replied, "The shield we will** take, señor; but"—

"But what!"

"Señor, may a Christian lawfully take what the infidels have refused?

And they looked **at** Orteguilla, and laughed roundly,—the bold, confident adventurers. In the midst of the jollity, however, down the street came a sound deeper than that of the guns,—a sound of abysmal depth, like thunder, but without its continuity, —a divided, throbbing sound, such **as** has been heard in the throat of a volcano. Alvarado threw up his visor.

"What now?" asked Serrano, first to speak.

"One, two, three,—I have it!" the captain replied. "Count ye the strokes,—one, two, three. By the bones of the saints, the drum in the great temple! Forward, comrades! Our friends are in peril! If they are lost, so are **we.** Forward, in Christ's name!"

Afterwards they became **familiar with** the sound; but **now,** heard the first time in battle, every man of them was **affected.** They moved off rapidly, and there was no jesting,—none **of the** grim wit with which old soldiers sometimes cover the **nervousness** preceding the primary plunge into a doubtful fight.

"Close the files. Be ready!" shouted Serrano.

And ready they were,—matches lighted, steel-cords full **drawn.** Every drum-beat welded them a firmer unit.

The roar of the combat in progress around the palace had been all the time audible to the returning party; now they beheld the *teocallis* covered with infidels, and the street blockaded with them, while a cloud of smoke, slowly rising and slowly fading, bespoke the toils and braveries of the defence enacting under its dun shade. Suddenly, Alvarado stood in his stirrups,—

"*Ola!* what have we here?"

A body of Aztecs, in excellent order, armed with spears **of** unusual length, and with a front that swept the street from **wall** to wall, was marching swiftly to meet him.

"There is wood enough in those spears to build **a ship,"** said a horseman.

A few steps on another spoke,—

"If I may be allowed, señor, I suggest that Mesa be called up to play upon them awhile."

But Alvarado's spirit rose.

"No; there is an enemy fast coming behind us; turn thy ear in that direction, and thou mayest hear them already. We cannot wait. Battle-axe and horse first; if they fail, then the guns. Look to girth and buckle!"

Rode they then without halt or speech until the space between them and the coming line was not more than forty yards.

"Are ye ready?" asked Alvarado, closing his visor.

"Ready, señor."

"Axes, then! Follow me. Forward! *Christo y Santiago!*"

At the last word, the riders loosed reins, and, standing in their stirrups, bent forward over the saddle-bow, as well to guard the horse as to discover points of attack; each poised his shield to protect his breast and left side,—the axe and right arm would take care of the right side; each took up the cry, *Christo y Santiago;* then, like pillars of iron on steeds of iron, they charged. From the infidels one answering yell, and down they sank, each upon his knee; and thereupon the spears, planted on the ground, presented a front so bristling that leader less reckless than Alvarado would have stopped in mid-career. Forward, foremost in the charge, he drove, right upon the brazen points, a score or more of which rattled against his mail or that of his steed, and glanced harmlessly, or were dashed aside by the axe whirled from right to left with wonderful strength and skill. Something similar happened to each of his followers. A moment of confusion,—man and beast in furious action, clang of blows, splintering of wood, and battle-cries,—then two results: the Christians were repulsed, and that before the second infidel rank had been reached; and while they were in amongst the long spears, fencing and striking, clear above the medley of the *mêlée* they heard a shout, *Al-a-lala! Al-a-lala!* Alvarado looked that way,—looked through the yellow shafts and brazen points. Brief time had he; yet he beheld and recognised the opposing leader. Behind the kneeling ranks he stood, without trappings, without a shield even; a *maquahuitl*, edged with flint, sharp as glass, hard as steel, was his only weapon; behind him appeared an irregular mass of probably half a thousand men, unarmed and almost naked. Even as the good captain looked, the horde sprang forward, and by pressing between the files of spearmen, or leaping panther-like over their shoulders, gained the front. There they rushed upon the horsemen, entangled amidst the spears,—to capture, not slay them; for, by the Aztec code of honour, the measure of a warrior's greatness was the number of prisoners he brought out of battle, a present to the gods, not the number of foemen he slew. The rush was like that of wolves upon a herd of deer. First to encounter a Christian was the

chief. The exchange of blows was incredibly quick. **The** horse
reared, plunged blindly, then rolled upon the ground ; **the** flinty
maquahuitl, surer than the axe, had broken its leg. A cry,
sharpened by mortal terror,—a Spanish cry for help, in the
Mother's name. Christians and infidels looked that way, **and**
from the latter burst a jubilant yell,—

"The 'tzin ! The 'tzin !"

The successful leader **stooped** and wrenched the shield from
the fallen man ; **then he** swung the *maquahuitl* twice, and
brought it down **on the** mailed head of the horse : the weapon
broke in pieces ; **the steed** lay still for ever.

Now Alvarado **was** not the man to let the cry of a comrade **go**
unheeded.

"Turn, gentlemen ! One of us is down ; **hear ye** not the name
of Christ and the Mother ? To the rescue ! **Charge !** *Christo y
Santiago !"*

Forward the brave men spurred ; **the** spears closed around
them **as** before, while the unarmed foe, encouraged by the 'tzin's
achievement, redoubled their efforts to drag them from their
saddles. In disregard of blows, given fast as skilled hands could
rise and fall, some flung themselves upon the legs and necks of
the horses, where they seemed to cling after the axe had spattered
their brains or the hoofs crushed their bones ; some caught the
bridle-reins and hung **to them** full weight ; **others** struggled
with the riders directly, hauling at **them,** leaping behind them,
catching sword-arm and shield ; and **so did** the peril finally grow
that the Christians were forced to give up the rescue, the better
to take care of themselves.

"God's curses upon the dogs !" shouted Alvarado, **in fury** at
sight of the Spaniard dragged away. "Back, some **of** ye, who
can, **to** Serrano ! Bid him advance. Quick, or we too are lost !"

No **need ; Serrano** was coming. To the very spears he
advanced, **and** opened with cross-bow and arquebus ; yet the
infidels remained firm. Then the dullest of the Christians
discerned the 'tzin's strategy, and knew well, if **the** line in front
of them were not broken before the companies coming up the
street closed upon their rear, they **were** indeed lost. So, at the
word, Mesa came, his guns charged to the muzzles. To avoid his
own people, he sent one piece to the right of the centre of combat,
and the other to the left, and trained both to obtain the deepest
lines of cross-fire. The effect was indescribable ; yet the lanes
cloven through the kneeling ranks were instantly refilled.

The 'tzin became anxious.

"Look, Hualpa !" he said. "The companies **should be** up by
this time. Can you see them ?"

"The smoke is too great ; I cannot see."

Some of his people attacking the horsemen began to retreat behind the spearmen. He caught up the axe of the Spaniard, and ran where the smoke was most blinding. In a moment he was at the front;—clear, inspiring, joyous even, rose his cry. He rushed upon a bowman, caught him in his arms, and bore him off with all his armour on. A hundred ready hands seized the unfortunate. Again the cry,—

"The 'tzin! The 'tzin!"

"Another victim for the gods!" he answered. "Hold fast, O my countrymen! Behind the strangers come the companies. Do what I say, and Anahuac shall live."

At his word, they arose; at his word again, they advanced with levelled spears. Faster the missiles smote them. The horsemen raged; each Spaniard felt unless that line were broken his doom was come. Alvarado fought, never thinking of defence. The bowmen and arquebusiers recoiled. Twice Mesa drew back his guns. Finally, Don Pedro outdid himself, and broke the fence of spears; his troop followed him; right and left they plunged, killing at every step. At places, the onset of the infidels slackened, halted; then the ranks began to break into small groups; at last they dropped their arms, and fairly fled, bearing the 'tzin away in the mighty press for life. At their backs rode the vengeful horsemen, and behind the horsemen, over the dead and shrieking wretches, moved Serrano and Mesa.

And to the very gates of the palace the fight continued. A ship in its passage displaces a body of water; behind, however, follows an equal reflux: so with the Christians, except that the masses who closed in upon their rear outnumbered those they put to rout in front. Their rapid movement had the appearance of flight; on the other hand, that of the infidels had the appearance of pursuit. The sortie was not again repeated.

Seven days the assault went on: a week of fighting, intermitted only at night, under cover of which the Aztecs carried off their dead and wounded,—the former to the lake, the latter to the hospitals. Among the Christians some there were who had seen grand wars; some had even served under the Great Captain; but, as they freely averred, never had they seen such courage, devotion, and endurance, such indifference to wounds and death, as here. At times the struggle was hand to hand; then, standing upon their point of honour, the infidels perished by scores in vain attempts to take alive whom they might easily have slain; and this it was,—this fatal point of honour,—more than superiority in any respect, that made great battles so bloodless to the Spaniards. Still, nearly all of the latter were wounded, a few disabled, and seven killed outright. Upon the Tlascalans the losses chiefly fell ; hundreds of them were killed ; hundreds more lay wounded in the chambers of the palace.

The evening of the seventh day, the 'tzin, standing on the western verge of the `teocallis`, from which he had constantly directed the assault, saw coming the results which could alone console him for the awful sacrifice of his countrymen. The yells of the Tlascalans were not as defiant as formerly ; the men of iron, the Christians, were seen to sink wearily down at their posts, and sleep, despite the tumult of the battle ; the guns were more slowly and carefully served ; and whereas, before Cortes' departure there had been three meals a day, now there were but two : the supply of provisions was failing. The ancient house, where constructed of wood, showed signs of demolition ; fuel was becoming scant. Where the garrison obtained its supply of water was a marvel. He had not then heard of what Father Bartolomé afterwards celebrated as a miracle of Christ,—the accidental finding of a spring in the middle of the garden.

Then the assault was discontinued, and a blockade established. Another week, during which nothing entered the gates of the palace to sustain man or beast. Then there was but one meal a day, and the sentinels on the walls began to show the effect.

One day the main gate opened, and a woman and a man came out. The 'tzin descended from his perch to meet them. At the foot of the steps they knelt to him,—the princess Tula and the prince Io'.

"See, O 'tzin," said the princess,—"see the king's signet. We bring you a message from him. He has not wherewith to supply his table. Yesterday he was hungry. He bids you reopen the market, and send of the tributes of the provinces without stint,— all that is his kingly right."

"And if I fail?" asked Guatamozin.

"He said not what, for no one has ever failed his order."

And the 'tzin looked at Io'.

"What shall I do, O son of the king?"

In all the fighting, Io' had stayed in the palace with his father. Through the long days he had heard the voices of the battle calling to him. Many times he walked to the merlons of the *azoteas*, and saw the 'tzin on the temple, or listened to his familar cry in the street. And where,—so ran his thought the while,—where is Hualpa? Happy fellow! What glory he must have won,—true warrior-glory to flourish in song for ever! A heroic jealousy would creep upon him, and he would go back miserable to his chamber.

"One day more, O 'tzin, and all there is in the palace—king and stranger alike—is yours," Io' made answer. "More I need not say."

"Then you go not back?"

"No," said Tula.

"No," said Io'. "I came out to fight. Anahuac is our mother. Let us save her, O 'tzin!"

And the 'tzin looked to the sun; his eyes withstood its piercing splendours awhile, then he said calmly,—

"Go with the princess Tula where she chooses, Io'; then come back. The gods shall have one day more, though it be my last. Farewell."

They arose and went away. He returned to the *azoteas*.

Next day there was not one meal in the palace. Starvation had come. And now the final battle, or surrender! Morning passed; noon came; later, the sun began to go down the sky. In the streets stood the thousands,—on all the housetops, on the temple, they stood,—waiting and looking, now at the leaguered house, now at the 'tzin seated at the verge of the *teocallis*, also waiting.

Suddenly a procession appeared on the central turret of the palace, and in its midst Montezuma.

"The king! the king!" burst from every throat; then upon the multitude fell a silence, which could not have been deeper if the earth had opened and swallowed the city.

The four heralds waved their silver wands; the white carpet was spread, and the canopy brought and set close by the eastern battlement of the turret; then the king came and stood in the shade before the people. At sight of him and his familiar royalty the old love came back to them, and they fell upon their knees. He spoke, asserting his privileges; he bade them home, and the army to its quarters. He promised that in a short time the strangers, whose guest he was, would leave the country; they were already preparing to depart, he said. How wicked the revolt would then be! How guilty the chiefs who had taken arms against his order! He spoke as one not doubtful of his position, but as king and priest, and was successful. Stunned, confused, uncertain as to duty, nigh broken-hearted, the fighting people and disciplined companies arose, and, like a conquered mob, turned to go away.

Down from his perch rushed the 'tzin. He put himself in the midst of the retiring warriors. He appealed to them in vain. The chiefs gathered around him, and knelt, and kissed his hands, and bathed his feet with their tears; they acknowledged his heroism,—they would die with him; but while the king lived, under the gods, he was master, and to disobey him was sacrilege.

Then the 'tzin saw, as if it were a god's decree, that Anahuac and Montezuma could not both live. ONE OR THE OTHER MUST

DIE! And, never so wise as in his patience, he submitted, and told them,—

"I will send food to the palace, and cease the war now, **and** until **we** have the voice of Huitzil' to determine what we **shall** do. **Go,** collect the companies, and put them in their quarters. This **night** we will to Tlalac; together, from his sacred lips, **we** will **hear** our fate and our country's. Go now. At midnight come **to** the *teocallis.*"

At midnight the sanctuary of Huitzil' was crowded; so was all the *azoteas.* Till the breaking of dawn the sacrifices continued. At last the *teotuetli*, with a loud cry, ran and laid a heart in the fire before the idol; then turning to the spectators, he said in **a** loud voice,—

"Let the war go on! So saith the mighty Huitzil'! **Woe to** him who refuses to hear!"

And the heart that attested **the will was the heart of** a Spaniard.

BOOK SEVENTH.

CHAPTER I.

THE HEART CAN BE **WISER THAN** THE HEAD.

I WILL now ask the reader to make a note of the passage of a fortnight. By so doing he will find himself close upon the 24th of June,—another memorable **day** in the drama of the conquest.

'Tzin Guatamo, as is already known, had many times proven himself a warrior after the manner of his country, and, in consequence, had long been the idol **of** the army; now he gave token of a ruling faculty which brought the whole people **to** his feet; so that in Tenochtitlan, for the first time in her history, were **seen a** sceptre unknown to the law and **a** royalty not the king's.

He ruled in the valley everywhere, except in the palace of Axaya'; and around that **he** built works, and set guards, and **so** contrived that nothing passed in or out without his permission. His policy was to wait patiently, and in the meantime organize the nation for war; and the nation obeyed him, seeing that in obedience there was life; such, moreover, was the will of Huitzil'.

As may **be** thought, the Christians thus pent up fared illy; in fact, they would have suffered before the fortnight was gone but for the king, who stinted himself and his household in order to divide with his keepers the supplies sent in for his use.

In the estimation of the people of the empire, it was great glory to have shut **so** many *teules* in a palace, and held them there; but the success did not deceive the 'tzin: in his view, that achievement was not the victory, but only the beginning of the war; every hour he had news of Malinche, the real antagonist, who had the mind, the will, and the hand of a warrior, and was coming with another army, more numerous, if not braver, than the first **one**. In pure, strong love there is an element akin to

the power of prophecy,—something that **gives the** spirit eyes to
see what is to happen. **Such an** inspiration quickened the 'tzin,
and told him Anahuac was not saved, though **she** should be : if
not, the conquerors should **take** an empty **prize** ; he would **leave**
them nothing,—so he swore,—neither gods, **gold**, slaves, city, nor
people. He set about the great idea by inviting the New World
—I **speak** as a Spaniard—to take part in **the struggle. And** he
was answered. To the beloved city, turned into a **rendezvous for**
the **purpose,** flocked the fighting vassals of the great caciques, **the**
men of the cities and their dependencies, the *calpulli,* **or** tribes
of the loyal provinces, and, mixed with them, wild-eyed **bands**
from **the Unknown, the wildern**esses,—in all, a multitude **such**
as had never been seen in the valley. At the altars he had **but**
one prayer, "Time, time, O gods **of my fathers!** Give me time!"
He knew the difference between a **man** and **a** soldier, and that,
likewise, between a multitude and **an** army. As he used the
word, time meant organization and discipline. He not only
prayed, he worked ; and into his work, as into his prayers, he
poured all his soul.

The organization **was simple :** first, **a company of** three **or** four
hundred men ; next, **an** army of thirty **or** forty companies,—a
system **which** allowed the preservation **of** the identity of tribes
and cities. **The** companies of Cholula, for example, were separate
from those **of** Tezcuco ; while the Acolmanes marched and fought
side by side with the Coatopees, but under their own chiefs and
flags. The system also gave him a number of armies, and he
divided them,—one to raise supplies, another to bring the supplies
to the depôts, a **third** to prepare material of war ; the fourth was
the active or fighting division ; and each was subject to take the
place of the other. To the labour of so many hands, systematized
and industriously exerted, though for a fortnight, almost **every-**
thing is possible. One strong will, absolutely operative **over**
thousands, is nearer omnipotency than anything else human.

The climate of the valley, milder and more equable than that
of Naples, permits the bivouac in all seasons. The sierra west
of the capital, and bending around it like a half-drawn bow, is
marked on its interior or city side by verdant and watered vales,
—these were **seized** ; and the bordering cliffs, which theretofore
had shaded **the** toiling husbandman, or been themselves the scenes
of the hun**ter's** daring, **now** hid the hosts of New World's **men,**
in the bivouac, **biding the** day of battle.

War, good reader, **never** touches anything **and** leaves it as it
was. And the daughter of the **lake,** fair Tenochtitlan, was no
exception to the law. The young master, having reduced the
question of strategy to the formula, **a** street **or** a plain, chose the
street, and thereby dedicated the city to all **of** ruin or horror the
destroyer could bring. Not long, therefore, until its presence

could **have** been detected by the idlest glance : **the streets were** given up to the warriors ; the palaces were deserted by **families ;** houses conveniently situated for the use were turned into **forts ;** the shrubbery garnishing roofs that dominated the main **streets** concealed heaps of stones made **ready** for the hand ; the bridges were taken up, or put in **condition** to be **raised** ; the canoes **on** the lakes were multiplied, **and** converted **to the** public service ; the great markets were suspended ; **even** the sacred temples were changed into **vast** arsenals. When **the** 'tzin, going hither and thither, **never idle, observed the** change, **he** would sigh, but say to himself, " **'Tis well.** If we win, we can restore ; if we lose,— if we lose,—**then, to** the strangers, waste, to the waters, welcome !"

And **up and down,** from city to bivouac and back again, passed the minstrels, singing of war, and the pabas, proclaiming the oracles and divine promises ; and the services in the temples were unintermitted,—those in the *teocallis* were especially grand ; the smoke from its turrets overhung the city, and at night the fire of Huitzil', a new star reddening in the sky, was seen from the remotest hamlet in the valley. The 'tzin had faith in moral effects, and he studied them, and was successful. The army soon came to have, like himself, but one prayer,—" Set us before the strangers ; let us fight !"

And the time they prayed for was come.

.   .   .   .

The night of the 23rd of **June** was pleasant as night can be in that region of pleasant nights. The sky was clear and starry. The breeze abroad brought coolness to outliers **on** the house-tops, without threshing the lake to the **disturbance** of its *voyageurs.*

Up in the north-eastern part of the little sea lay a *chinampa* at anchor. Over its landing, at the very edge of the water, burned a flambeau of resinous pine. Two canoes, richly decorated, swung at the mooring. The path from the landing to the pavilion was carpeted and lighted by lamps pendent in the adjoining shrub-**bery.** In the canoes the slaves lay at rest, talking idly, and in low voices crooning Indian songs. Close by the landing, on **a** bench, over which swayed the leaves of an immense banana-tree, rested a couple of warriors, silent, and nodding, as it were, to the nodding leaves. From the rising to the setting of the day's **sun,** many a weary league, from the city to the vales of the sierra **in** which bivouacked the hope of Anahuac, had they travelled,— Hualpa and Io'. One familiar with the streets **in** these **later** days, **at** sight of them would have said, " Beware ! the 'tzin **is** here-away." The three were almost as one,—so had **their** friendship grown. The pavilion, a circular canopy, **spread** like a Bedouin's tent, was brightly lighted ; and there, in **fact,** was the 'tzin, with Tula and Yeteve, the priestess.

Once before, I believe, I described this pavilion ; and now I know the imagination of the reader will give the floating garden richer colours than lie within compass of my pen ; will surround it with light, and with air delicious with the freshness of the lake and the exhalations of the flowers ; will hover about the guardian palm and willow trees, the latter with boughs lithe and swinging and leaves long and fine as a woman's locks ; will linger about the retreat, I say, and, in thought of its fitness for meeting of lovers, admit the poetry and respect the passion of the noble Aztec.

Within, the furniture was as formerly ; there were yet the carven stools, the table with its bowl-like top, now a mass of flowers, a couch draped with brilliant plumage, the floor covered with matting of woven grasses, the hammock, and the bird-cage, —all as when we first saw them. Nenetzin was absent, and, alas! might never come again.

And if we enter now, we shall find the 'tzin standing a little apart from Tula, who is in the hammock, with Yeteve by her side. On a stool at his feet is a waiter of ebony, with spoons of tortoise-shell, and some *xicaras*, or cups, used for chocolate.

Their faces are grave and earnest.

"And Malinche?" asked Tula, as if pursuing a question.

"The gods have given me time ; I am ready for him," he replied.

"When will he come?"

"Yesterday, about noon, he set out from Tezcuco, by way of the shore of the lake ; to-night he lodges in Iztapalapan ; to-morrow, marching by the old causeway, he will re-enter the city."

"Poor, poor country!" she said after a long silence.

The words touched him, and he replied in a low voice, "You have a good heart, O Tula,—a good heart and true. Your words were what I repeat every hour in the day. You were seeing what I see all the time"—

"The battle!" she said, shuddering.

"Yes. I wish it could be avoided ; its conditions are such that against the advantage of arms I can only oppose the advantage of numbers ; so that the dearest of all things will be the cheapest. I must take no account of lives. I have seen the streets run with blood already, and now— Enough! we must do what the gods decree. Yet the slaughter shall not be, as heretofore, on one side alone."

She looked at him inquiringly.

"You know the custom of our people to take prisoners rather than kill in battle. As against the Tlascalans and tribes, that was well enough ; but new conditions require new laws, and my order now is, Save nothing but the arms and armour of the strangers. Life for life as against Malinche! **And I could** conquer him, but "—

He stopped, and their glances met,—his full **of fire, hers** sad and thoughtful.

"Ah, Tula! your woman's **soul** prompts **you** already of whom I would speak,—the king."

"Spare me," she said, covering **her face** with her hands. **"I** am his child; I love him yet."

"So I know," he replied; "and I would not have you do else. The love is proof of fitness to be loved. Nature cannot be silenced. He is not as near to me as to you; yet I feel the impulse that moves you, though in a less degree. In memory, he is a part of my youth. For that matter, who does not love him? He has charmed the strangers; **even** the guards at his chamber-door have been known to weep at sight of his sorrow. And the heroes who so lately died before his prison-gates, did **not** they love him? And those who will die to-morrow and the next day, what else may be said of them? In arms here, see the children of the valley. What seek they? In their eyes, he is Anahuac. And yet"—

He paused again; her hands had fallen,—her cheeks glistened with tears.

"If I may not speak plainly now, I may not ever. Strengthen yourself to hear me, and hear me pitifully. To begin, you know that I have been using the king's power without his permission,— that, I say, you know and have forgiven, because the usurpation was not of choice but necessity, and to save the empire; but you will hear now, for the first time probably, that I could have been king in fact."

Her gaze became intent, and she listened breathlessly.

"Three times," he continued,—"three times have the caciques, for themselves and the army, offered me the crown. The last time, they were accompanied by the electors,[1] and deputations from all the great cities."

"And you refused," she said confidently.

"Yes. I will not deny the offer was tempting,—that for the truth. I thought of it often; and at such times came revenge, and told me I had been wronged, and ambition, whispering of glory, and, with ready subtlety, making acceptance appear a duty. But, Tula, you prevailed; your love was dearer to me than the crown. For your sake I refused the overture. You never said so,—there was no need of the saying,—yet I know **you** could never be queen while your father lived."

Not often has a woman heard such a story **of** love, or been given such proofs of devotion; her face mantled, and she dropped her gaze, saying,—

[1] The monarchy was elective. Prescott, *Conq. of Mexico*, Vol. I., p. 24.

"Better to be so loved than to be queen. If not here, O 'tzin, look for reward in the Sun. Surely the gods take note of such things!"

"Your approval is my full reward," he replied. "But hear me further. What I have said was easy to say; that which I go to now is hard, and requires all my will; for the utterance may forfeit not merely the blessing just given me, but your love,— more precious, as I have shown, than the crown. You were in the palace the day the king appeared and bade the people home. The strangers were in my hand at the time. Oh, a glad time,— so long had we toiled, so many had died! Then he came, and snatched away our triumph. I have not forgotten, I never can forget the disappointment. In all the labour of the preparation since, I have seen the scene, sometimes as a threat, sometimes as a warning, always a recurring dream whose dreaming leaves me less resolved in the course I am running. Continually I find myself saying to myself, 'The work is all in vain; what has been will be again; while he lives, you cannot win.' O Tula, such influence was bad enough of itself. Hear now how the gods came in to direct me. Last night I was at the altar of Huitzil', praying, when the *teotuctli* appeared, and said, ''Tzin Guatamo, pray you for your country?' 'For country and king,' I answered. He laid his hand upon my shoulder. 'If you seek the will of the god with intent to do what he imposes, hear then: The king is the shield of the strangers; they are safe while he lives; and if he lives, Anahuac dies. Let him who leads choose between them. So the god says. Consider!' He was gone before I could answer. Since that I have been like one moving in a cloud, seeing nothing clearly, and the duty least of all. When I should be strongest, I am weakest. My spirit faints under the load. If the king lives, the empire dies; if it is to die, why the battle and its sacrifices? This night have I in which to choose; to-morrow, Malinche and action! Help me, O Tula, help me to do right! Love of country, of king, and of me,—you have them all. Speak."

And she answered him,—

"I may not doubt that you love me; you have told me so many times, but never as to-night. I thank you, O 'tzin! Your duties are heavy. I do not wonder that you bend under them. I might say they are yours by gift of the gods, and not to be divided with another, not even with me; but I will give you love for love, and, as I hope to share your fortunes, I will share your trials. I am a woman, without judgment by which to answer you; from my heart I will answer."

"From your heart be it, O Tula."

"Has the king heard the things of which you have spoken?"

"I cannot say."

"Does he know you were offered the crown?"

"No; the offer was treason."

"Ah, poor king, proud father! **The love** of the people, that of which you were proudest, is lost. **What** wretchedness awaits you!"

She bowed her head, and there was a silence broken only by her sobs. The grief spent itself; then she said earnestly,—

"I know him. He, too, **is a** lover of Anahuac. More than once he has exposed himself to death for her. Such loves age not, nor do they die, except with the hearts they animate. There was a time—but now— No matter, I will try. 'Let him **who** leads choose:' **was not** that the decree, good 'tzin?"

"Yes," **he replied.**

"Must **the choice** be made to-night?"

"I may delay until to-morrow."

"To-morrow; what time?"

"Malinche will pass the causeway in the cool of the morning; by noon he will have joined his people in the old palace: the decision must then be made."

"Can you set me down at the gate before he passes in?"

The 'tzin started. "Of the old palace?" he asked.

"I wish to see the king."

"For what?"

"To tell him the things **you have told me** to-night."

"All?"

"Yes."

His face clouded with dissatisfaction.

"Yes," she continued calmly; "that, as becomes a king, **he** may choose which shall live,—himself or Anahuac."

So she answered the 'tzin's appeal, and the answer was from her heart; **and,** seeing of what heroism she dreamed, his dark eyes glowed **with** admiration. Yet his reply **was** full of hopelessness.

"I give you honour, **Tula,—I** give you honour for the thought; but forgive me if I think you beguiled by your love. There was a time when he was capable of what you have imagined. Alas! he is changed; he will never choose,—never!"

She looked at him reproachfully, and said, with a sad smile, "Such changes are not always of years. Who is he that to-night, only to-night, driven by a faltering of the will, which in the king my father is called weakness, brought himself prayerfully to a woman's feet, and begged her to divide with him a burden imposed upon his conscience by a decree of the gods? Who is he, indeed? Study yourself, O 'tzin, and commiserate him, and bethink you, if he choose not, it will be yours to choose for him. His duty will then become yours, to be done without remorse and"—

She hesitated, and held out her hand, as if to say, "And I can love you still."

He caught the meaning of the action, and went to her, and kissed her forehead tenderly, and said,—

"I see now that the heart can be wiser than the head. Have your way. I will set you down at the gate, and of war there shall be neither sign nor sound until you return."

"Until I return! Maybe I cannot. Malinche may hold me prisoner."

From love to war,—the step was short.

"True," he said. "The armies will await my signal of attack, and they must not wait upon uncertainties."

He arose and paced the floor, and when he paused he said firmly,—

"I will set you down at the gate in the early morning, that you may see your father before Malinche sees him. And when you speak to him, ask not if I may make the war—on that I am resolved; but tell him what no other can,—that I look forward to the time when Malinche, like the Tonatiah, will bring him from his chamber, and show him to the people, to distract them again. And when you have told him that, speak of what the gods have laid upon me, and then say that I say, 'Comes he so, whether of choice or by force, the dread duty shall be done. The gods helping me, I will strike for Anahuac.' And if he ask what I would have him do, answer, 'A king's duty to his people,—die that they may live!'"

Tula heard him to the end, and buried her face in her hands, and there was a long silence.

"Poor king! poor father!" she said at last. "For me to ask him to die! A heavy, heavy burden, O 'tzin!"

"The gods help you!" he replied.

"If Malinche hold me prisoner, how will the answer avail you?"

"Have you not there two scarfs,—the one green, the other white?"

"Yes."

"Take them with you, and from the roof, if your father resolve not, show the green one. Alas, then, for me! If in its stead you wave the white one, I shall know that he comes, if so he does, by force, and that"—his voice trembled—"*it is his will Anahuac should live.*"

She listened wistfully, and replied, "I understand: Anahuac saved means Montezuma lost. But doubt him not, doubt him not; he will remember his glory's day, and die as he has lived."

An hour later, and the canoe of the 'tzin passed into one of the canals of the city. The parting on the *chinampa* may be imagined. Love will have its way even in war.

CHAPTER II.

THE CONQUEROR ON THE CAUSEWAY AGAIN.

As predicted by the 'tzin, the Spaniards set out early next morning—the morning of the 24th of June—by the causeway from Iztapalapan, already notable in this story.

At their head rode the Señor Hernan, silent, thoughtful, and not well pleased ; pondering, doubtless, the misconduct of the *adelantado* in the old palace to which he was marching, and the rueful condition it might impose upon the expedition.

The cavaliers next in the order of march, which was that of battle, rode and talked as men are wont when drawing nigh the end of a long and toilsome task. This the leader at length interrupted,—

"Señores, come near. Yonder ye may see the gate of Xoloc," he continued when they were up. "If the heathen captains think to obstruct our entry, they would do well, now that our ships lie sunken in the lake, to give us battle there. Ride we forward to explore what preparations, if any, they have made."

So they rode, at quickened pace, arms rattling, spurs jingling, and found the gate deserted.

"*Viva compañeros !*" cried Cortes, riding through the shadow of the battlements. "Give the scabbards their swords again. There will be no battle ; the way to the palace is open. And, waiting till the column was at their heels, he turned to the trumpeters, and shouted cheerily, "*Ola*, ye lazy knaves ! Since the march began, ye have not been heard from. Out now, and blow !—blow as if ye were each a Roland, with Roland's horn. Blow merrily a triumphal march, that our brethren in the leaguer ahead may know deliverance at hand."

The feeling of the chief spread rapidly : first, to the cavaliers ; then to the ranks, where soon there were shouting and singing ; and, simultaneous with the trumpetry, over the still waters sped the minstrelsy of the Tlascalans. Ere long they had the answer of the garrison ; every gun in the palace thundered welcome.

Cortes settled in his saddle smiling : he was easy in mind ; the junction with Alvarado was assured ; the city and the king were his, and he could now hold them ; nevertheless, back of his smile there was much thought. True, his enemies in Spain would halloo spitefully over the doughty deed he had just done down in Cempoalla. No matter. The Court and the Council had pockets, and he could fill them with gold,—gold by the caravel, if necessary ; and for the pacification of his most Catholic master, the Emperor, had he not the New World ? And over the schedule of guerdons sure to follow such a gift to such a master he lingered compla-

cently, as well he might.   Patronage, **and titles,** and high employ-
ments, and lordly estates danced before **his eyes, as** danced the
un's glozing upon the crinkling **water.**

One thought, however,—only one,—brought him trouble.
The soldiers of Narvaez were new men, **ill-**disciplined, footsore,
grumbling, discontented, disappointed.   **He** remembered the
roseate pictures by which they had been won from their leader
before the battle was joined.   "The Empire was already in
possession ; there would be no fighting ; the march would be **a**
promenade through grand landscapes, and by towns and cities,
whose inhabitants would meet them in processions, loaded **with**
fruits and flowers, tributes of love and fear,"—so he had **told**
them through his spokesmen, Olmedo the priest and Duero **the**
secretary.   Nor failed he now to recall the chief inducements **in**
the argument,—the charms of the heathen capital, and the easy
life there waiting—a life whose sole vexation would be appor-
tionment of the lands conquered and the gold gathered.   And
the wonderful city,—here it was, placid as ever ; and neither the
valley, **nor** the lake, nor the summering climate, nor the abundance of which he had spoken, failed his description ; nothing was
wanting but *the people*, THE PEOPLE !   Where were they ?   He
looked at the prize ahead ; gyres of smoke, slowly rising and
purpling **as** they rose, **were** all the proofs of life within its walls.
He swept the little sea with angry eyes ; **in** the distance **a canoe,**
stationary, and with a solitary occupant, and he a spy !   **And**
this was the grand reception promised the retainers of Narvaez !
He struck his mailed thigh with his mailed hand fiercely, and,
turning in his saddle, looked back.   The column was moving
forward compactly, the new men distinguishable by the freshness
of their apparel and equipments.   "*Bien !*" he said with a grim
smile and cunning solace,—"*Bien !* they will fight for life, if not
for majesty and **me.**"

Close by the wall Father Bartolomé overtook him, and, after
giving rein to his mule and readjusting his hood, said gravely,
"If the tinkle of my servant's bell disturb not thy musing,
señor,—I have been through the files, and bring thee wot of the
new men."

"Welcome, **father,**" said Cortes, laughing.   "I am not an evil
spirit to fly **the** exorcisement of thy bell, not I ; and so **I bid**
thee welcome.   **But** as for whereof thou comest to tell, no more,
I pray.   I know of what the varlets speak.   And as I am a
Christian, I blame them not.   We promised them much, and—
this is all : fair sky, fair land, strange city,—and all without
people !   Rueful enough, I grant ; but, **as** matter more serious,
what say the veterans ?   Came they within **thy** soundings ?"

"Thou mayest trust them, señor.   Their tongues go with their
swords.   They return to the day of our first entry here, and with

excusable enlargement tell what they saw then in contrast with
the present."

"And whom blame they for the failure now?"

"The Captain Alvarado."

Cortes' brows dropped, and he became thoughtful again, and in
such temper rode into the city.

Within the walls, everywhere the visitors looked, were signs of
life, but nowhere a living thing; neither on the street, nor in
the houses, nor on the housetops,—not even a bird in the sky.
A stillness possessed the place, peculiar in that it seemed to
assert a presence, and palpably lurk in the shade, lie on the
doorsteps, issue from the windows, and pervade the air; giving
notice, so that not a man, new or veteran, but was conscious that
in some way he was menaced with danger. There is nothing
so appalling as the unaccountable absence of life in places
habitually populous; nothing so desolate as a deserted city.

"*Por Dios!*" said Olmedo, toying with the beads at his side;
"I had rather the former reception than the present. Pleasanter
the sullen multitude than the silence without the multitude."

Cortes made him no answer, but rode on abstractedly, until
stopped by his advance-guard.

"At rest!" he said angrily. "Had ye the signal? I heard it
not.

"Nor did we, señor," replied the officer in charge. "But,
craving thy pardon, approach, and see what the infidels have
done here."

Cortes drew near, and found himself on the brink of the first
canal. He swore a great oath; the bridge was dismantled. On
the hither side, however, lay the timbers, frame, and floor. The
tamanes detailed from the guns replaced them.

"Bartolomé, good father," said Cortes confidentially, when the
march was resumed, "thou hast a commendable habit of holding
what thou hearest, and therefore I shame not to confess that I,
too, prefer the first reception. The absence of the heathen and
the condition of yon bridge are parts of one plan, and signs certain
of battle now ready to be delivered."

"If it be God's will, amen!" replied the priest calmly. "We
are stronger than when we went out."

"So is the enemy, for he hath organized his people. The
hordes that stared at us so stupidly when we first came—be the
curse of the saints upon them!—are now fighting men."

Olmedo searched his face, and said coldly, "To doubt is to
dread the result."

"Nay, by my conscience! I neither doubt nor dread. Yet I
hold it not unseemly to confess that I had rather meet the brunt
on the firm land, with room for what the occasion offers. I like
not yon canal, with its broken bridge, too wide for horse, too deep

for weighted man; it putteth us to disadvantage, and hath a
hateful reminder of the brigantines, which, as thou mayest
remember, we left at anchor, mistresses of the lake; in our
absence they have been lost,—a most measureless folly, father!
But let it pass, let it pass! The Mother—blessed be her name!—
hath not forsaken us. Montezuma is ours, and"—

"He is victory," said Olmedo zealously.

"He is the New World!" answered Cortes.

And so it chanced that the poor king was centre of thought for
both the 'tzin and his enemy,—the dread of one and the hope of
the other.

CHAPTER III.

LA VIRUELA.

A LONG interval behind the rear-guard—indeed, the very last of
the army, and quite two hours behind—came four Indian slaves,
bringing a man stretched upon a litter.

And the litter was open, and the sun beat cruelly on the man's
face; but plaint he made not, nor motion, except that his head
rolled now right, now left, responsive to the cadenced steps of his
bearers.

Was he sick or wounded?

Nathless, into the city they carried him.

And in front of the new palace of the king they stopped, less
wearied than overcome by curiosity. And, as they stared at the
great house, imagining vaguely the splendour within, a groan
startled them. They looked at their charge; he was dead! Then
they looked at each other, and fled.

And in less than twice seven days they too died, and died
horribly; and, in dying, recognised their disease as that of the
stranger they had abandoned before the palace,—the small-pox,
or, in the language which hath a matchless trick of melting everything, even the most ghastly, into music, la viruela of the Spaniard.

The sick man on the litter was a negro,—first of his race on the
continent!

And, most singular, in dying he gave his masters another servant stronger than himself, and deadlier to the infidels than
swords of steel,—a servant that found way everywhere in the
crowded city, and rested not. And everywhere its breath, like its
touch, was mortal; insomuch that a score and ten died of it where
one fell in battle.

Of the myriads who thus perished, one was a KING.

CHAPTER IV.

MONTEZUMA A PROPHET—HIS **PROPHECY.**

SCARCE five weeks before, **Cortes** sallied from the palace with seventy soldiers, ragged, yet curiously bedight with gold and silver ; now he returned full-handed, at his back thirteen hundred infantry, a hundred horse, additional guns and Tlascalans. Surely he could hold what **he had** gained.

The garrison **stood in** the courtyard to receive him. Trumpet replied to trumpet, **and** the reverberation of drums shook the ancient house. When all were assigned to quarters, the ranks were broken, and the veterans—those who had remained, and those who had followed their chief—rushed clamorously into each **other's** arms. Comradeship, with its strange **love,** born of **toil and** danger **and** nursed by red-handed battle, asserted itself. **The men** of Narvaez looked on indifferently, **or** climbed the **palace,** and from the roof surveyed the vicinage, especially the **great** temple, apparently as forsaken as the city.

And **in** the courtyard Cortes met Alvarado, saluting him coldly. The latter excused his conduct as best he could ; but the palliations were unsatisfactory. The general turned from him with bitter denunciations ; and, as he did so, a procession approached : four nobles, carrying silver **wands** ; then a **train in** doubled files ; then Montezuma, in the royal regalia, splendid **from** head **to** foot. The shade of the canopy borne above him wrapped his person in purpled softness, but did not hide that other shadow discernible in the slow, uncertain step, the bent form, the wistful eyes,—the shadow of the coming fate. Such of his family as shared his captivity brought up the cortège.

At the sight, Cortes waited : his blood was hot, and his head filled with the fumes of victory ; from a great height, as it were, he looked upon the retinue and its sorrowful master ; and his eyes wandered fitfully from the Christians, worn by watching and hunger, to the sumptuousness of the infidels ; so that, when the monarch drew nigh him, the temper of his heart was as the temper of his corselet.

"I salute you, O Malinche, **and** welcome your return," **said** Montezuma according **to the** interpretation of Marina.

The Spaniard heard **him** without a sign of recognition.

"The good Lady of **your** trust has had you in **care** ; she has given you the victory. I congratulate you, Malinche."

Still the Spaniard was obstinate.

The king hesitated, dropped his eyes under **the** cold stare, and was frozen into silence. Then Cortes turned **upon** his heel, and, without a word, sought his chamber.

Y

The insult was plain, and the witnesses, Christian and infidel, were shocked ; and, while they stood surprised, Tula rushed up and threw her arms around the victim's neck and laid her head upon his breast. The retinue closed around them, as if to hide the shame ; and thus the unhappy monarch went back to his quarters,—back to his captivity, to his remorse, and the keener pangs of pride savagely lacerated.

For a time he was like one dazed ; but, half waking, he wrung his hands, and said feebly, "It cannot be, it cannot be ! Maxtla, take the counsellors and go to Malinche, and say that I wish to see him. Tell him the business is urgent, and will not wait. Bring me his answer, omitting nothing."

The young chief and the four nobles departed, and the king relapsed into his dazement, muttering, "It cannot be, it cannot be !"

The commissioners delivered the message. Olid, Leon, and others who were present, begged Cortes to be considerate.

"No," he replied ; "the dog of a king would have betrayed us to Narvaez ; before his eyes we are allowed to hunger. Why are the markets closed ? I have nothing to do with him."

And to the commissioners he said, "Tell your master to open the markets, or we will for him. Begone !"

And they went back and reported, omitting nothing, not even the insulting epithet. The king heard them silently ; as they proceeded, he gathered strength ; when they ceased, he was calm and resolved.

"Return to Malinche," he said, "and tell him what I wished to say : that my people are ready to attack him, and that the only means I know to divert them from their purpose is to release the lord Cuitlahua, my brother, and send him to them to enforce my orders. There is now no other of authority upon whom I can depend to keep the peace and open the markets ; he is the last hope. Go."

The messengers departed ; and when they were gone the monarch said, "Leave the chamber now, all but Tula."

At the last outgoing footstep she went near and knelt before him ; knowing, with the divination which is only of woman, that she was now to have reply to the 'tzin's message, delivered by her in the early morning. Her tearful look he answered with a smile, saying tenderly, "I do not know whether I gave you welcome. If I did not, I will amend the fault. Come near."

She arose, and, putting an arm over his shoulder, knelt closer by his side ; he kissed her forehead, and pressed her close to his breast. Nothing could exceed the gentleness of the caress, unless it was the accompanying look. She replied with tears and such breaking sobs as are only permitted to passion and childhood.

"Now, if never before," he continued, "you are my best beloved, because your faith in me fell not away with that of all the world besides; especially, O good heart!—especially because you have to-day shown **me** an escape from my intolerable misery and misfortunes,—for which may the gods who have abandoned **me** bless you!"

He stroked the dark locks under his hand lovingly.

"Tears? Let there be none for me. I am happy. I have been unresolved, drifting with uncertain currents, doubtful, yet hopeful, seeing nothing and imagining everything; waiting, sometimes on men, sometimes on the gods,—and that so long,—ah, so long! But now the weakness is past. Rejoice with me, O Tula! In this hour I have recovered dominion over myself; with every faculty restored, the very king whom erst you knew, I will make answer to the 'tzin. Listen well. I give you my last decree, after which I shall regard myself as lost to the world. If I live, I shall never rule again. Somewhere in the temples I shall find **a** cell like that from which they took me **to** be king. The sweetness of the solitude I remember yet. There I will wait for death; and **my** waiting shall be so seemly that his **coming** shall be as the coming of a restful sleep. Hear, **then,** and these words give the 'tzin: Not as king to subject, **nor as** priest to penitent, but as father to son, I send him my blessing. Of pardon I say nothing. All he has done for Anahuac, and all he hopes to do for her, I approve. Say to him, also, that in the last hour Malinche will come for me to go with him to the people, and that I will go. Then, I say, let the 'tzin remember what the gods have laid upon him, and with his own hand do the duty, that it may be certainly done. A man's last prayer belongs to the gods, his last look to those who love him. In dying, there is no horror like lingering long amidst enemies."

His voice trembled, and he paused. She raised her eyes **to his** face, which was placid, but rapt, as if his spirit had been caught by **a** sudden vision.

"To the world," he **said** in **a little** while, "I have bid farewell. I **see** its vanities go from me one by one; last in the train, **and most** glittering, most loved, Power,—and in its hands is my **heart.** A shadow creeps upon me, darkening all without, but brightening all within; and in the brightness, lo, my People and their Future!"

He stopped again, **then** resumed,—

"The long, long cycles—two—four—eight—pass away, and **I** see the tribes newly risen, like the trodden grass, and in their midst **a** Priesthood and a Cross. An age of battles more, and lo! the Cross but not the priests; in their stead Freedom and God!"

And with the last word, as if to indicate **the** Christian God, **the** report of **a** gun without broke the spell **of** the seer. The two started, and looked at each other, listening for what might follow ; but there was nothing more, and he went on quietly talking to her.

"I know the children of the Aztec, crushed now, will live, and more,—after ages of wrong suffered by them, they will rise up, and take their place—a place of splendour—amongst the deathless nations of the earth. What I saw was revelation. Cherish the words, O Tula ! repeat them often ; make them an utterance of the people, a sacred tradition ; let them go down with the generations,—one of which will at last rightly interpret the meaning of the words FREEDOM and GOD, now dark to my understanding ; and then, not till then, will be the new birth and new career. And so shall my name become of the land a part, suggested by all things,—by the sun mildly tempering its winds ; by the rivers singing in its valleys ; by the stars seen from its mountain-tops ; by its cities and their palaces and halls : and so shall its red races, of whatever blood, learn to call me father, and in their glory, as well as misery, pray for and bless me."

In the progress of this speech his voice grew stronger, and insensibly his manner ennobled ; at the conclusion his appearance was majestic. Tula regarded him with awe, and accepted his utterances, not as the song habitual to the Aztec warrior at the approach of death, nor as the rhapsody of pride soothing itself ; she accepted them as prophecy and as a holy trust,—a promise to be passed down through time, to a generation of her race, the first to understand fully the simple words—FREEDOM and GOD. And they were silent a long time.

At length there was a warning at the door ; the little bells filled the room with music strangely inharmonious. The king looked that way, frowning. The intruder entered without *nequen*. As he drew near the monarch's seat, his steps became slower, and his head drooped upon his breast.

"Cuitlahua ! my brother !" said Montezuma, surprised.

"Brother and king !" answered the cacique, as he knelt and placed both palms upon the floor.

"You bring me a message. Arise and speak."

"No," said Cuitlahua, rising. "I have come to receive your signet and orders. I am free. The guard is at the door to pass me through the gate. Malinche would have me go and send the people home, and open the markets ; he said such were your orders. But from him I take nothing, except liberty. But you, O king, what will you,—peace or war ?"

Tula looked anxiously at the monarch ; would the old vacillation return ? He replied firmly and gravely,—

"I have given my last order as king. Tula will go with you from the palace, and deliver it to you."

He arose while speaking, and gave the cacique a ring ; then

for a moment he regarded the two with suffused eyes, and said, "I divide my love between you and my people. For their sake, I say, go hence quickly, lest Malinche change his mind. You, O my brother, and you, my child, take my blessing and that of the gods! Farewell!"

He embraced them both. To Tula he clung long and passionately. More than his ambassadress to the 'tzin, she bore his prophecy to the generations of the future. His last kiss was dewy with her tears. With their faces to him, they moved to the door; as they passed out, each gave a last look, and caught his image then,—the image of a man breaking because he happened to be in God's way.

CHAPTER V.

HOW TO YIELD A CROWN.

As the guard passed the old lord and the princess out of the gate opposite the *teocallis*, the latter looked up to the *azoteas* of the sacred pile, and saw the 'tzin standing near the verge. Taking off the white scarf that covered her head, and fell from her shoulders after passing once around her neck, she gave him the signal. He waved his hand in reply, and disappeared.

The lord Cuitlahua, just released from imprisonment and ignorant of the situation, scarcely knowing whither to turn, yet impatient to set his revenge in motion, accepted the suggestion of Tula, and accompanied her to the temple. The ascent was laborious, especially to him; at the top, however, they were received by Io' and Hualpa, and with every show of respect conducted to the 'tzin. He saluted them gravely, yet affectionately. Cuitlahua told him the circumstances of his release from imprisonment.

"So," said the 'tzin, "Malinche expects you to open the market and forbid the war; but the king,—what of him?"

"To Tula he gave his will; hear her."

And she repeated the message of her father. At the end, the calm of the 'tzin's temper was much disturbed. At his instance she again and again recited the prophecy. The words "Freedom and God" were as dark to him as to the king, and he wondered at them. But that was not all. Clearly, Montezuma approved the war; that he intended its continuance was equally certain: unhappily, there was no designation of a commander. And in thought of the omission, the young chief hesitated; never did

ambition appeal to him more strongly; but he brushed the
allurement away, and said to Cuitlahua,—

"The king has been pleased to be silent as to which of us
should govern in his absence; but we are both of one mind; the
right is yours naturally, and your coming at this time, good
uncle, looks as if the gods sent you. Take the government,
therefore, and give me your orders. Malinche is stronger than
ever." He turned thoughtfully to the palace below, over which
the flag of Spain and that of Cortes were now displayed. "He
will require of us days of toil and fighting, and many assaults.
In conquering him there will be great glory, which I pray you
will let me divide with you."

The lord Cuitlahua heard the patriotic speech with glistening
eyes. Undoubtedly he appreciated the self-denial that made it
beautiful; for he said, with emotion, "I accept the government,
and, as its cares demand, will take my brother's place in the
palace. Do you take what else would be my place under him in
the field. And may the gods help us each to do his duty!"

He held out his hand, which the 'tzin kissed in token of fealty,
and so yielded the crown; and as if the great act were already
out of mind, he said,—

"Come now, good uncle,—and you also, Tula,—come both of
you, and I will show what use I made of the kingly power."

He led them closer to the verge of the azoteas, so close that
they saw below them the whole western side of the city, and
beyond that the lake and its shore, clear to the sierra bounding
the valley in that direction.

"There," said he in the same strain of simplicity,—"there, in
the shadow of the hills, I gathered the people of the valley, and
the flower of all the tribes that pay us tribute. They make an
army the like of which was never seen. The chiefs are chosen;
you may depend upon them, uncle. The whole great host will
die for you."

"Say, rather, for us," said the lord Cuitlahua.

"No, you are now Anahuac;" and, as deeming the point
settled, the 'tzin turned to Tula. "O good heart," he said, "you
have been a witness to all the preparation. At your signal, given
there by the palace gate, I kindled the piles which yet burn, as
you see, at the four corners of the temple. Through them I spoke
to the chiefs and armies waiting on the lake-shore. Look now,
and see their answers."

They looked, and from the shore and from each pretentious
summit of the sierra saw columns of smoke rising and melting
into the sky.

"In that way the chiefs tell me, 'We are ready,' or 'We are
coming.' And we cannot doubt them; for see! a dark line on the
white face of the causeway to Cojohuacan, its head nearly touching

the gates **at** Xoloc ; and another from Tlacopan ; **and** from the
north a third ; and yonder on the lake, in the shadow of Chapultepec, a yet deeper shadow."

" I see them," said Cuitlahua.

"And I," said Tula. "What are they ?"

For the first time the 'tzin acknowledged a passing sentiment ;
he raised his head and swept the air with a haughty gesture.

"What are they ? Wait a little, and you shall see the lines on
the causeways grow into ordered companies, and the shadows
under Chapultepec become a multitude of canoes ; wait a little
longer, and you shall see the companies fill all the great streets,
and the canoes girdle the city round about ; wait a little longer,
and you **may** see **the** battle."

And **silence fell** upon the three,—the silence, however, in
which **hearts beat** like drums. From point to point they turned
their eager eyes,—from the causeways to the lake, from the lake
to the palace.

Slowly the converging lines crawled toward the city ; slowly
the dark mass under the royal hill, sweeping out on the lake,
broke into divisions ; slowly **the** banners came into view, of
every colour and form, and then **the** shields and uniforms, until
at last each host **on** its **separate way** looked like an endless
unrolling ribbon.

When the column approaching by the causeway from Tlacopan
touched the city with its advance, it halted, waiting for the
others, which, having farther to march, **were** yet some distance
out. Then the three on the *teocallis* separated : the princess
retired to her *chinampa ;* the lord Cuitlahua, with some nobles
of the 'tzin's train, betook himself to the new palace, there **to**
choose a household ; the 'tzin, for purposes of observation, remained **on** the *azoteas.*

And all the time the threatened palace was a picture of peace :
the flags hung idly down ; only the sentinels were in motion,
and they gossiped with each other, or lingered lazily at places
where **a** wall or a battlement flung them **a** friendly shade.

CHAPTER VI.

IN THE LEAGUER.

By and by a Spaniard came out through the main gateway of the
palace ; after brief leave-taking with the guard there, he walked
rapidly down the street. The 'tzin, observing that the man was
equipped for a journey, surmised him to be a courier, and smiled

at the confidence of the master who sent him forth alone at such a time.

The courier went his way, and the great movement proceeded.

After a while Hualpa and Io' came down from the turret where, under the urn of fire, they too had been watching, and the former said,—

"Your orders, O 'tzin, are executed. The armies all stand halted at the gates of the city, and at the outlet of each canal I saw a division of canoes lying in wait."

The 'tzin looked up at the sun, then past meridian, and replied, "It is well. When the chiefs see but one smoke from this temple they will enter the city. Go, therefore, and put out all the fires except that of Huitzil'."

And soon but one smoke was to be seen.

A little afterwards there was a loud cry from the street, and, looking down, the 'tzin saw the Spanish courier, without morion or lance, staggering as he ran, and shouting. Instantly the great gate was flung open, and the man taken in; and instantly a trumpet rang out, and then another and another. Guatamozin sprang up. The alarm-note thrilled him no less than the Christians.

The palace, before so slumberous, became alive. The Tlascalans poured from the sheds that at places lined the interior of the parapet, and from the main building forth rushed the Spaniards, —bowmen, slingers, and arquebusiers; and the gunners took post by their guns, while the cavalry clothed their horses and stood by the bridles. There was no tumult, no confusion; and when the 'tzin saw them in their places—placid, confident, ready—his heart beat hard: he would win,—on that he was resolved,—but ah, at what mighty cost!

Soon, half drowned by the voices of the captains mustering the enemy below, he heard another sound rising from every quarter of the city, but deeper and more sustained where the great columns marched. He listened intently. Though far and faint, he recognised the *susurrante*,—literally the commingled war-cries of almost all the known fighting tribes of the New World. The chiefs were faithful; they were coming,—by the canals, and up and down the great streets, they were coming; and he listened, measuring their speed by the growing distinctness of the clamour. As they became nearer, he became confident, then eager. Suddenly everything,—objects far and near, the old palace and the hated flags, the lake, and the purple distance, and the unflecked sky,—all melted into mist, for he looked at them through tears. So the Last of the 'Tzins welcomed his tawny legions.

While he indulged the heroic weakness, Io' and Hualpa re-

joined him. About the same time Cortes and some of his cavaliers
appeared on the *azoteas* of the central and higher part of the
palace. They were in armour, but with raised visors, and seemed
to be conjecturing one with another, and listening to the portentous sounds that now filled the welkin. And as the 'tzin, in
keen enjoyment, watched the wonder that plainly possessed the
enemy, there was a flutter of gay garments upon the palace, and
two women joined the party.

"Nenetzin!" said Io' in a low voice.

"Nenetzin!" echoed Hualpa.

And sharper grew his gaze, while down stooped the sun to
illumine the face of the faithless, as, smiling the old smile, she
rested lovingly upon Alvarado's arm. He turned away and
covered his head. But soon a hand was laid upon his shoulder,
and he heard a voice,—the voice of the 'tzin,—

"Lord Hualpa, as once before you were charged, I charge you
now. With your own hand make the signal. Io' will bring
you the word. Go now." Then the voice sank to a whisper:
"Patience, comrade. The days for many to come will be days of
opportunity. Already the wrong-doer is in the toils; yet a little
longer. Patience!"

The noise of the infidels had now come to be a vast uproar,
astonishing to the bravest of the listeners. Even Cortes shared
the common feeling. That war was intended he knew; but he
had not sufficiently credited the Aztec genius. The whole valley
appeared to be in arms. His face became a shade more ashy as
he thought, either this was of the king, or the people were capable
of grand action without the king; and he griped his sword-hand
hard in emphasis of the oath he swore, to set the monarch and
his people face to face; that would he, by his conscience!—by
the blood of the saints!

And as he swore, here and there upon the adjacent houses
armed men showed themselves; and directly the heads of columns
came up, and, turning right and left at the corners, began to
occupy all the streets around the royal enclosure.

If one would fancy what the cavaliers then saw, let him first
recall the place. It was in the heart of the city. Eastward
arose the *teocallis*,—a terraced hill in fact, and every terrace a
vantage-point. On all other sides of the palace were edifices
each higher than its highest part, and each fronted with a wall
resembling a parapet, except that its outer face was in general
richly ornamented with fretwork and mouldings and arches and
grotesque corbels and cantilevers. Every roof was occupied by
infidels; over the sculptured walls they looked down into the
fortress, if I may so call it, of the strangers.

As the columns marched and countermarched in the streets
thus beautifully bounded, they were a spectacle of extraordinary

animation. Over them played the semi-transparent shimmer or
thrill of air, so to speak, peculiar to armies in rapid movement,—
curious effect of changing colours and multitudinous motion. The
Christians studied them with an interest inappreciable to such as
have never known the sensations of a soldier watching the foe
taking post for combat.

Of arms there were in the array every variety known to the
Aztecan service,—the long-bow ; the javelin ; slings of the ancient
fashion, fitted for casting stones a pound or more in weight ; the
maquahuitl, limited to the officers ; and here and there long
lances with heads of bronze or sharpened flint. The arms, it
must be confessed, added little to the general appearance of the
mass,—a deficiency amply compensated by the equipments. The
quivers of the bowmen and the pouches of the slingers, and the
broad straps that held them, to the person were brilliantly
decorated. Equally striking were the costumes of the several
branches of the service : the fillet, holding back the long, straight
hair, and full of feathers, mostly of the eagle and turkey, though
not unfrequently of the ostrich,—costly prizes come, in the way
of trade, from the far *llanos* of the south ; the *escaupil*, of
brightest crimson ; the shield, faced with brazen plates and
edged with flying tufts of buffalo hair, and sometimes with
longer and brighter locks, the gift of a mistress or a trophy of
war. These articles, though half barbaric, lost nothing by contrast with the naked dark-brown necks and limbs of the warriors,
lithe and stately men, from whom the officers were distinguished
by helmets of hideous device and mantles indescribably splendid.
Over all shone the ensigns, *indicia* of the tribes : here a shining
sphere ; there a star, or a crescent, or a radial sun ; but most
usually a floating cloth covered with blazonry.

With each company marched a number of priests, bareheaded
and frocked, and a corps of musicians, of whom some blew
unearthly discords from conchs, while others clashed cymbals
and beat atabals fashioned like the copper tam-tams of the Hindoos.

Even the marching of the companies was peculiar. Instead of
the slow, laborious step of the European, they came on at a pace
which, between sunrise and sunset, habitually carried them from
the bivouac twenty leagues away.

And as they marched, the ensigns tossed to and fro ; the priests
sang monotonous canticles ; the cymbalists danced and leaped
joyously at the head of their companies ; and the warriors in the
ranks flung their shields aloft and yelled their war-cries, as if
drunk with happiness.

As the inundation of war swept around the palace, a cavalier
raised his eyes to the temple.

"*Valgame Dios !*" he cried in genuine alarm. "The levies of
the valley are not enough. Lo, the legions of the air !"

On the *azoteas*, where but the moment before only the 'tzin and Io' were to be seen, there were hundreds of caparisoned warriors; and as the Christians looked at them, they all knelt, leaving but one man standing; simultaneously the companies on the street stopped, and, with those on the housetops, hushed their yells, and turned up to him their faces countless and glistening.

"Who is he?" the cavaliers asked each other.

Cortes, cooler than the rest, turned **to** Marina : **"Ask** the princess Nenetzin if she knows him."

And Nenetzin **answered,—**

"The 'tzin **Guatamo."**

As **the two** chiefs surveyed each other in full recognition, down **from the** sky, as it were, broke an intonation so deep, that **the** Christians were startled, and the women fled **from** the roof.

"*Ola!*" **cried** Alvarado with **a** laugh. **"I have heard** that thunder **before.** Down with your visors, **gentlemen, as ye** care for the faces your mothers love !"

Three times Hualpa struck the great drum in the sanctuary of Huitzil'; and as the last intonation rolled down over the city, the clamour of the infidels broke out anew, and into the enclosure of the palace they poured a cloud of missiles so thick, that place of safety there was not anywhere outside the building.

To this time the garrison had kept silence ; now, standing each at his post, they answered. In the days of the former siege, besides preparing banquettes for the repulsion of escalades, they had pierced the outer walls, generally but little higher than a man's head, with loop-holes and embrasures, out of which the guns, great and small, were suddenly pointed and discharged. No need of **aim** ; outside, not farther than the leap of the flames, stood the assailants. The effect, especially of the artillery, was dreadful ; and the prodigious noise, and the dense, choking smoke, stupefied **and** blinded the masses, so unused to such enginery. And from the wall they shrank staggering, and thousands turned to fly ; but in pressed the chiefs and the priests, and louder rose the clangour of conchs and cymbals : the very density of the multitude helped stay **the** panic.

And down from the temple came the 'tzin, not merely to **give** the effect of his presence, but to direct the assault. In **the** sanctuary he had arrayed himself : his *escaupil* and *tilmatli*, of richest feather-work, fairly blazed ; his helm and shield sparkled ; and behind, scarcely less splendid, walked Io' and Hualpa. He crossed the street, shouting his war-cry. At sight **of** him men struggling to get away turned to fight again.

Next the wall of the palace the shrinking of the infidels had left a clear margin ; and there, the better to be seen by his people, the 'tzin betook himself. In front of the embrasures he cleared the lines of fire, so that the guns were often ineffectual; he directed attention to the loopholes, so that the appearance of an arbalist or arquebus drew a hundred arrows to the spot. Taught by his example, the warriors found that under the walls there was a place of safety; then he set them to climbing: for that purpose some stuck their javelins in the cracks of the masonry; some formed groups over which others raised themselves; altogether the crest of the wall was threatened in a thousand places, insomuch that the Tlascalans occupied themselves exclusively in its defence; and as often as one raised to strike a climber down, he made himself a target for the quick bowmen on the opposite houses.

And so, wherever the 'tzin went he inspired his countrymen; the wounded, and the many dead and dying, and the blood maddened instead of daunting them. They rained missiles into the enclosure; upon the wall they fought hand to hand with the defenders; in their inconsiderate fury, many leaped down inside, and perished instantly,—but all in vain.

Then the 'tzin had great timbers brought up, thinking to batter in the parapet. Again and again they were hurled against the face of the masonry, but without effect.

Yet another resort. He had balls of cotton steeped in oil shot blazing into the palace-yard. Against the building, and on its tiled roof, they fell harmless. It happened, however, that the sheds in which the Tlascalans quartered consisted almost entirely of reeds, with roofs of rushes and palm-leaves; they burst into flames. Water could not be spared by the garrison, for the drought was great; in the extremity, the Tlascalans and many Christians were drawn from the defences, and set to casting earth upon the new enemy. Hundreds of the former were killed or disabled. The flames spread to the wooden outworks of the wall. The smoke almost blotted out the day. After a while a part of the wall fell down, and the infidels rushed in; a steady fire of arquebuses swept them away, and choked the chasm with the slain; still others braved the peril; company after company dashed into the fatal snare uselessly, as waves roll forward and spend themselves in the gorge of a sea-wall.

The conflict lasted without abatement through long hours. The sun went down. In the twilight the great host withdrew,— all that could. The smoke from the conflagration and guns melted into the shades of night; and the stars, mild-eyed as ever, came out one by one to see the wrecks, heaped and ghastly, lying in the bloody street and palace-yard.

All night the defenders lay upon their arms, or, told off in working parties, laboured to restore the breach.

All night the infidels collected their dead and wounded,

thousands in number. They did not offer to attack,—custom forbade that; yet over the walls they sent their vengeful warnings.

All night the listening sentinels on the parapet noted the darkness filled with the sounds of preparation from every quarter of the city. And they crossed themselves, and muttered the names of saints and good **angels,** and thought shudderingly of the morrow.

CHAPTER VII.

IN THE **LEAGUER YET.**

GUATAMOZIN took little rest that night. The very uncertainty of the combat multiplied his cares. It was not to be supposed that his enemy would keep to the palace, content day after day with receiving assaults; that was neither his character nor his policy. To-morrow he would certainly open the gates, and try conclusions in the streets. The first duty, therefore, was to provide for such a contingency. So the 'tzin went along all the streets leading to the old palace, followed by strong working-parties; and where the highest houses fronted each other he stopped, and thereat the details fell to making barricades and carrying stones and logs to the roofs. As a final measure of importance, he cut passages through the walls of the houses and gardens, that companies might be passed quickly and secretly from one thoroughfare to another.

Everywhere he found great cause for mourning; but the stories of the day were necessarily lost in the demands of the morrow.

He visited his caciques, and waited on the lord Cuitlahua to take his orders; then he passed to the temples, whence, as he well knew, the multitudes in great part derived their inspiration. The duties of the soldier, politician, and devotee discharged, he betook himself to the *chinampa*, and to Tula told the heroisms of the combat and his plans and hopes; there he renewed his own inspirations.

Toward morning he returned to the great temple. Hualpa and Io', having followed him throughout his round, spread their mantles on the roof and slept: he could not; between the work of yesterday and that to come, his mind played pendulously, and with such forceful activity as forbade slumber. From the quarters of the strangers, moreover, he heard constantly the ringing of hammers, the neighing and trampling of steeds, and voices of direction. It was a long night to him; but at last over the crown of the White Woman the dawn flung its first light into the valley; and then he saw the palace, its walls manned, the gunners by their pieces, and in the great court lines of footmen, and at the main gate horsemen standing by their bridles.

"Thanks, O gods!" he cried. "Walls will not separate my people from their enemies to-day!"

With the sunrise the assault began,—a repetition of that of the day before.

Then the guns opened; and while the infidels reeled under the fire, out of the gates rode Cortes and his chivalry, a hundred men-at-arms. Into the mass they dashed. Space sufficient having been won, they wheeled southward down the beautiful street, followed by detachments of bowmen and arquebusiers and Tlascalans. With them also went Mesa and his guns.

When fairly in the street, environed with walls, the 'tzin's tactics and preparation appeared. Upon the approach of the cavalry the companies took to the houses; only those fell who stopped to fight or had not time to make the exit. All the time, however, the horsemen were exposed to the missiles tossed upon them from the roofs. Soon as they passed, out rushed the infidels in hordes, to fall upon the flanks and rear of the supporting detachments. Never was Mesa so hard pressed; never were helm and corselet so nearly useless; never gave up the ghost so many of the veteran Tlascalans.

At length the easy way of the cavalry was brought to a stop; before them was the first barricade,—a work of earth and stones too high to be leaped, and defended by Chinantlan spears, of all native weapons the most dreaded. Nevertheless, Cortes drew rein only at its foot. On the instant his shield and mail warded off a score of bronzed points, whirled his axe, crash went the spears,—that was all.

Meantime, the eager horsemen in the rear, not knowing of the obstacle in front, pressed on,—the narrow space became packed; then from the roofs on the right hand and the left descended a tempest of stones and lances, blent with beams of wood, against which no guard was strong enough. Six men and horses fell there. A cry of dismay arose from the pack, and much calling was there on patron saints, much writhing and swaying of men and plunging of steeds, and vain looking upward through bars of steel. Cortes quitted smashing spears over the barricade.

"Out! out! Back, in Christ's name!" he cried.

The jam was finally relieved.

Again his voice,—

"To Mesa, some of ye; bring the guns! Speed!"

Then he, too, rode slowly back; and, sharper than the shame of retreat, sharper than the arrows or the taunts of the foe, sharper than **all** of them together, was the sight of the six riders in their armour left to quick despoilment,—they and their good steeds.

It was not easy for Mesa to come; but he did, opening within a hundred feet of the barricade. Again and again he fired; **the** smoke wreathed blinding white about him.

"What sayest thou now?" asked Cortes impatiently.

"That thou mayest **go,** and thou wilt. The saints go with thee!"

The barricade was **a ruin.**

At the first bridge again there was a fierce struggle; **when** taken, the floor was heaped with dead and wounded infidels.

And so for hours. Only at the last gate, that opening on **the** causeway to Iztapalapan, did Cortes stay the sally. There, riding to the rear, now become the front, he started in return. Needless **to** tell how well the Christians fought, **or** how devotedly the pagans resisted and perished. Enough **that** the going back was more difficult than the coming. Four **more** of the Spaniards perished on the way.

At a late hour that night Sandoval entered Cortes' room, and gave him a parchment. The chief went to the lamp and read; then, snatching his sword from the table, he walked to and fro, as was his wont when much disturbed; only his strides were longer, and the gride of the weapon on the tiled floor more relentless than common.

He stopped abruptly.

"Dead, ten of them! And their horses, captain?"

"Three were saved," replied Sandoval.

"By my conscience, I like it not! And thou?"

"I like it less," said the captain naïvely.

"What say the men?"

"They demand to **be led from** the city **while yet** they have strength to go."

Cortes frowned **and** continued his walk. When next he stopped, he said, **in the** tone of a man whose mind was made up,—

"Good-night, captain. See that the sentinels sleep not; and, captain, as thou goest, send hither Martin Lopez, and mind him to bring one or two of his master carpenters. Good-night."

The mind of the leader, never so quick as in time of trouble, had in the few minutes reviewed the sortie. True, he had broken through the barricades, taken bridge **after** bridge, and driven the enemy often as they opposed him; he had gone triumphantly to the very gates of the city, and returned, and joined Olmedo in unctuous celebration of the achievement; yet the good was not as clear and immediate **as at** first appeared.

He recalled the tactics of his enemy: **how,** on his approach, they had vanished from the street and assailed him from the roofs; how, when he had passed, they poured into the street again, and flung themselves hand to hand upon the infantry and artillery. And the result,—ten riders and seven horses were dead; of the Tlascalans in the column nearly all had perished; every Christian foot-soldier had one or more wounds. At Cempoalla he himself had been hurt in the left hand; now he was sore with contusions. He set his teeth hard at thought of the moral effect of the day's work; how it would raise the spirit of the infidels, and depress that of his own people. Already the latter were clamouring to be led from the city,—so the blunt Captain Sandoval had said.

The enemy's advantage was in the possession of the houses. The roofs dominated the streets. Were there no means by which he could dominate the roofs? He bent his whole soul to the problem. Somewhere he had read or heard of the device known in ancient warfare as *mantelets*,—literally, a kind of portable roof, under which besiegers approached and sapped or battered a wall. The recollection was welcome; the occasion called for an extraordinary resort. He laid the sword gently upon the table, gently as he would a sleeping child, and sent for Lopez.

That worthy came, and with him two carpenters, each as rough as himself. And it was a picture, if not a comedy, to watch the four bending over the table to follow Cortes, while, with his dagger-point, he drew lines illustrative of the strange machine. They separated with a perfect understanding. The chief slept soundly, his confidence stronger than ever.

Another day,—the third. From morn till noon and night the clamour of assault and the exertion of defence, the roar of guns from within, the rain of missiles from without,—Death every-where.

All the day Cortes held to the palace. On the other side, the 'tzin kept close watch from the *teocallis*. That morning early he had seen workmen bring from the palace some stout timbers, and in the great courtyard proceed to frame them. He plied the party with stones and arrows; again and again, best of all the good bowmen of the valley, he himself sent the shafts at the man who seemed the director of the work; as often did they splinter upon his helm or corselet, or drop harmless from the close links of tempered steel defending his limbs. The work went steadily on, and by noon had taken the form of towers, two in number, and high as ordinary houses. By sunset both were under roof.

When the night came the garrison were not rested; and as to the infidels, the lake received some hundreds more of them, which was only room made for other hundreds as brave and devoted.

Over the palace walls the besiegers sent words ominous and disquieting, and not to be confounded with the half-sung formulas of the watchers keeping time on the temples by the movement of the stars.

"Malinche, Malinche, we are a thousand to your one. Our gods hunger for vengeance. You cannot escape them."

So the Spaniards heard in their intervals of unrest.

"Oh, false sons of Anahuac, the festival is making ready ; your hearts are Huitzil's ; the cages are open to receive you."

The Tlascalans heard, and trembled.

The fourth day. Still Cortes kept within the palace, and still the assault ; nor with all the slaughter could there be perceived any decrease either in the number of the infidels or the spirit of their attack.

Meantime the workmen in the courtyard clung to the construction of the towers. Lopez was skilful, Cortes impatient. At last they were finished.

That night the 'tzin visited Tula. At parting, she followed him to the landing. Yeteve went with her. "The blessing of the gods be upon you!" she said ; and the benediction, so trustful and sweetly spoken, was itself a blessing. Even the slaves, under their poised oars, looked at her and forgot themselves, as well they might. The light of the great torch, kindled by the keeper of the *chinampa*, revealed her perfectly. The head slightly bent and the hands crossed over the breast helped the prayerful speech. Her eyes were not upon the slaves, yet their effect was ; and they were such eyes as give to night the beauty of stars, while taking nothing from it, neither depth nor darkness.

The canoe put off.

"Farewell," said Io'. His warrior-life was yet in its youth.

"Farewell," said Hualpa. And she heard him, and knew him thinking of his lost love.

In the 'tzin's absence the garrison of the temple had been heavily reinforced. The *azoteas*, when he returned, was covered with warriors, asleep on their mantles, and pillowed on their shields. He bade his companions catch what slumber they could, and went into the grimy but full-lighted presence-chamber, and seated himself on the step of the altar. In a little while Hualpa came in, and stopped before him as if for speech.

"You have somewhat to say," said the 'tzin kindly. "Speak."

"A word, good 'tzin, a single word. Io' lies upon his mantle ; he is weary, and sleeps well. I am weary, but cannot sleep. I suffer"—

"What?" asked the 'tzin.

"Discontent."

"Discontent!"

"O 'tzin, to follow you and win your praise has been my greatest happiness ; but as yet I have done nothing by myself. I pray you, give me liberty to go where I please, if only for a day."

"Where would you go?"

"Where so many have **tried and failed**,—over the wall, into the palace."

There was a long silence, during which **the** supplicant looked on the floor, and the master at him.

"**I** think I understand you," the latter at **length** said. "To-**morrow I** will give you answer. Go now."

Hualpa touched the floor with his palm, and left **the** chamber. The 'tzin remained thoughtful, motionless. An hour passed.

"Over the wall, into the palace!" he said musingly. "**Not** for country, **not for** glory,—**for** Nenetzin. Alas, poor lad! From his life she has taken the **life. Over the** wall into the—Sun. To-morrow comes swiftly; **good or ill, the** gifts it brings are from the gods. Patience!"

And upon the step he spread his mantle, and slept, muttering, "Over the wall, into the palace, and she has **not** called him! Poor lad!"

CHAPTER VIII.

THE BATTLE OF THE MANTAS.

The report of a **gun awoke** the 'tzin **in** the morning. The great uproar of the assault, now become familiar to him, filled the chamber. He knelt on the step and prayed, **for** there was a cloud upon his spirit, and over the idol's stony face there seemed **to be** a cloud. He put **on** his helm and mantle; **at** the door Hualpa offered him his arms.

"No," he said; "bring me those we took from the stranger."

Hualpa marked the gravity of his manner, and with a rising **heart** and a smile, the first seen on his lips for many a day, he brought **a** Spanish shield and battle-axe, and gave them to him.

Then **the** din below, bursting out in greater volume, drew the 'tzin to **the** verge of the temple. The warriors made way for him reverently. He looked down into the square, and through a **veil** of smoke semilucent saw Cortes and his cavaliers charge the ranks massed in front **of the** palace gate. The gate stood open, and a crowd of the Tlascalans **were** pouring out of **the** portal, hauling **one** of the towers whose **construction** had been **the** mystery of the **days last** passed. They **bent low to the work,** and cheered each other with their war-cries; **yet the** *manta*—so called by Cortes— moved slowly, as if loath to **leave. In the same** manner the other tower **was** drawn out of the court; **then, side** by side, both were started **down** the street, which **they filled so** nearly that room was hardly left for the detachments that guarded the Tlascalans on the flanks.

The fighting ceased, and silently the enemies stared at the spectacle,—such power is there in curiosity.

At sight of the structures, rolling, rocking, rumbling, and creaking dismally in every wheel, Cortes' eyes sparkled firelike through his visor. The 'tzin, on the other hand, was disturbed and anxious, although outwardly calm; for the objects of the common wonder were enclosed on every side, and he knew as little what they contained as of their use and operation.

Slowly they rolled on, until past the intersection of the streets; there they stopped. Right and left of them were beautiful houses covered with warriors for the moment converted into spectators. A hush of expectancy everywhere prevailed. The 'tzin shaded his eyes with his hand and leant eagerly forward. Suddenly, from the sides of the machine next the walls, masked doors dropped out, and guns, charged to the muzzle, glared over the housetops—then swept them with fire.

A horrible scream flew along the street and up to the *azoteas* of the temple; at the same time, by ladders extended to the coping of the walls, the Christians leaped on the roofs, like boarders on a ship's deck, and mastered them at once; whereupon they returned, and were about taking in the ladders, when Cortes galloped back, and, riding from one to the other, shouted,—

"Ordas! Avila! *Mirad!* Where are the torches I gave ye? Out again! Leave not a stone to shelter the dogs! Leave nothing but ashes! *Pronto, pronto!*"

The captains answered promptly. With *flambeaux* of resinous pine and cotton, they fired all the wood-work of the interior of the buildings. Smoke burst from the doors and windows; then the detachments retreated, and were rolled on without the loss of a man.

Behind the *mantas* there was a strong rearguard of infantry and artillery; with which, and the guards on the flanks, and the cavaliers forcing way at the front, it seemed impossible to avert, or even interrupt, an attack at once so novel and successful.

The smoke from the burning houses, momentarily thickening and widening, was seen afar, and by the heathen hailed with cries of alarm. Not so Cortes; riding everywhere, in the van, to the rear, often stopping by the *mantas*, which he regarded with natural affection, as an artist does his last work, he tasted the joy of successful genius. The smoke rising, as it were, to heaven, carried up his vows not to stop until the city, with all its idolatries, was a heap of ashes and lime,—a holocaust to the Mother such as had never been seen. The cheeriness of his constant cry, "*Christo, Christo y Santiago!*" communicated to his people, and they marched laughing and fighting.

Opposition had now almost ceased; at the approach of the *mantas*, the housetops were given up without resistance. A general panic appeared to have seized the pagans; they even vacated the street, so that the cavaliers had little else to do than ride leisurely, turning now and then to see the fires behind them and the tall machines come lumbering on.

As remarked, when the *mantas* stopped at the intersection of the streets, the 'tzin watched them eagerly, for he knew the time had come to make their use manifest; he saw a door drop, and the jet of flame and smoke leap from a gun; he heard the cry of agony from the housetops and the deeper cry from all the people. To the chiefs around him he said, with steady voice, and as became a leader,—

"Courage, friends! We have them now. Malinche is mad to put his people in such traps. Lord Hualpa, go round the place of combat and see that the first bridge is impassable; for there, unless the towers have wings and can fly, they must stop. And to you, Io',"—he spoke to the lad tenderly,—"I give a command and sacred trust. Stay here, and take care of the gods."

Io' kissed his hand, and said fervently, "May the gods care for me as I will for them!"

To other chiefs, calling them by name, he gave directions for the renewal of the assault on the palace, now weakened by the sortie, and for the concentration of fresh companies in the rear of the enemy, to contest their return.

"And now, my good lord," he said to a cacique, grey-headed, but of magnificent frame, "you have a company of Tezcucans, formerly the guards of king Cacama's palace. Bring them, and follow me. Come."

A number of houses covering quite half a square were by this time on fire. Those of wood burned furiously; the morning, however, was almost breathless, so that the cinders did little harm. On the left side of the street stood a building of red stone, its front profusely carved, and further ornamented with a marble portico,—a palace, in fact, massively built, and somewhat higher than the *mantas*. Its entrances were barricaded, and on the roof, where an enemy might be looked for, there was not a spear, helm, or sign of life, except some fan-palms and long banana-branches. Before the stately front the *mantas* were at length hauled. Immediately the door on that side was dropped and the ladder fixed, and Avila, who had the command, started with his followers to take possession and apply the torch. Suddenly the coping of the palace-front flamed with feathered helms and points of bronze.

Avila was probably as skilful and intrepid as any of Cortes' captains; but now he was surprised: directly before him stood

Guatamozin, whom every Spaniard had come to know and respect as the most redoubted of all the warriors of Anahuac; and he shone on the captain a truly martial figure, confronting him with Spanish arms, a shield with a face of iron and a battle-axe of steel. Avila hesitated; and as he did so, the end of the ladder was lifted from the wall, poised a moment in the air, then flung off.

The 'tzin had not time to observe the effect of the fall, for a score of men came quickly up, bringing a beam of wood as long and large as the spar of a brigantine; a trailing rope at its further end strengthened the likeness. Resting the beam on the coping of the wall, at a word they plunged it forward against the *manta*, which rocked under the blow. A yell of fear issued from within. The Tlascalans strove to haul the machine away, but the Tezcucans from their height tossed logs and stones upon them, crushing many to death, and putting the rest in such fear that their efforts were vain. Meantime, the beam was again shot forward over the coping, and with such effect that the roof of the *manta* sprang from its fastenings, and nearly toppled off.

The handiwork so rudely treated was not as stout as the ships Martin Lopez sailed on the lake. It was simply a square tower, two stories high, erected on wheels. The frame was enclosed with slabs, pinned on vertically and pierced with loopholes. On the sides there were apertures defended by doors. The roof, sloping hip-fashion, had an outer covering of undressed skins as protection against fire. The lower floor was for the Tlascalans, should they be driven from the drag-ropes; in the second story there was a gun, some arquebusiers, and a body of pikemen to storm the housetops; so that altogether the contrivance could hardly stand hauling over the street, much less a battery like that it was then receiving. At the third blow it became an untenable wreck.

"Avila!" cried Cortes. "Where art thou?"

The good captain, with four of his bravest men, lay insensible, if not dead, under the ladder.

"Mercy, O Mother of God, mercy!" groaned Cortes; next moment he was himself again.

"What do ye here, men? Out and away before these timbers tumble and crush ye!"

One man stayed.

"The gun, señor, the gun!" he protested.

Spurring close to the door, Cortes said, "As thou art a Christian, get thee down, comrade, and quickly! I can better spare the gun than so good a gunner."

Then the beam came again, and with a great crash tore away the side of the *manta*. The gun rolled backward, and burst through the opposite wall of the room. The veteran disappeared.

By this time all eyes were turned to the scene. The bowmen and arquebusiers in the column exerted themselves to cover their unfortunate comrades. Upon the neighbouring houses a few infidels, on the watch, yelled joyously, "The 'tzin! the 'tzin!" From them the shout, spread through the cowering army, became, indeed, a battle-cry significant of success.

To me, good reader, the miracles of the world, if any there be, are not the things men do in masses, but the sublimer things done by one man over the many; they testify most loudly of God, since without Him they could not have been. I am too good a Christian to say this of a heathen; nevertheless, without the 'tzin his country had perished that morning. Back to the roofs came the defenders, into the street poured the companies again; no leisure now for the cavaliers. With the other *manta* Ordas moved on gallantly, but the work was hard; at some houses he failed, others he dared not attack. From front to rear the contest became a battle. In the low places of the street and pavement the blood flowed warm, then cooled in blackening pools. The smoke of the consuming houses, distinguishable from that of the temples, collected into a cloud and hung wide-spread over the combat. The yells of Christians and infidels, fusing into a vast monotone, roared like the sea. Twice Mesa went to the front,—the cavaliers had need of him,—twice he returned to the rear.

The wrath of the Aztecs seemed especially directed against the Tlascalans tugging at the ropes of the *manta;* as a consequence, their quilted armour was torn to rags, and so many of them were wounded, so many killed, that at every stoppage the wheels were more difficult to start; and, to make the movement still more slow and uncertain, the carcases of the dead had to be rolled or carried out of the way; and the dead, sooth to say, were not always Aztecs.

Luis Marin halted to breathe.

"*Ola, compañero!* What dost thou there?"

"By all the saints!" answered Alvarado, on foot, tightening his saddle-girth. "Was ever the like? It hath been strike, strike,—kill, kill,—for an hour. I am dead in the right arm from finger to shoulder. And now here is a buckle that refuseth its work. *Caramba!* My glove is slippery with blood!"

And so, step by step,—each one bought with a life,—the Christians won their way to the first bridge: the floor was gone! Cortes reined his horse, bloody from hoof to frontlet, by the edge of the chasm. Since daybreak fighting, and but a square gained! The water, never so placid, was the utmost limit of his going. He looked at the *manta*, now, like that of Avila, a mocking failure. He looked again, and a blasphemy beyond the absolution of Olmedo, I fear, broke the clenching of his jaws,—not for the machines, or the hopes they had raised, but the days their construction lost him. As he looked, through a rift in the cloud still rising along the battle's track he saw the great temple; gay banners and gorgeous regalia, all the splendour **of** barbaric war, filled that view and inspired him. To the cavaliers, close around and in waiting, he turned. The arrows smote his mail and theirs, **yet** he raised his visor: the face was calm, **even** smiling, for the **will** is **a** quality apart from mind and passion.

"We will go back, **gentlemen**," he said. "The city is on fire,— enough for one day. **And hark** ye, gentlemen. We have had enough of common **blood. Let** us go now and see of what the heathen gods are made."

His hearers **were in the** mood; they raised their shields and shouted,—

"To the **temple!** To the temple! For the love **of** Christ, **to** the temple!"

The cry sped down the column; and as the men caught its meaning they faced about of their own will. Wounds, weariness, and disappointments were forgotten; the rudest soldier became **a** zealot on the instant. "*Al templo! Adelante, adelante!*" rose **like a** new chorus, piercing the battle's monotone.

Cortes stood in his stirrups, and lo! the enemy, ranked close, like corn in the full ear, yet outreaching his vision,—plumed, bannered, brilliant, and terrible.

"Close and steady, swords of the Church! What ye see is but grass for the cutting. Yonder is the **temple** we seek! Follow me. *Adelante! Christo y Santiago!*"

So saying, he spurred in deep amongst the infidels.

CHAPTER IX.

OVER THE WALL—INTO THE PALACE.

THE duty Hualpa had been charged with by the 'tzin was not difficult of performance; for the bridges of the capital, even those along the beautiful street, were much simpler structures than they appeared. When he had seen the balustrades and flooring and the great timbers that spanned the canal—the first one south of the old palace—torn from their places and hauled off by the canoemen whom he had collected for the purpose, he returned to the temple to rejoin his master.

The assault upon the palace, when he reached that point, was more furious than at any previous time. The companies in the street were fighting with marvellous courage, while the missiles from the *azoteas* and westward terraces of the temple and all the houses around literally darkened the air. Amidst the clamour Hualpa caught at intervals the cry, "The 'tzin, the 'tzin!" He listened, and all the loyal thousands seemed shouting, "The 'tzin, the 'tzin! *Al-a-lala!*"

"Has anything befallen the 'tzin?" he asked of an acquaintance.

"Yes, thanks to Huitzil'! He has broken one of Malinche's towers to pieces, and killed everybody in it."

Hualpa's love quickened suddenly. "Blessed be all the gods!" he cried, and, passing on, ascended to the *azoteas*. It may have been the battle, full of invocations, as battles always are; or it may have been that Io', in full enjoyment of his command and so earnest in its performance, stimulated his ambition; or it may have been the influence of his peculiar sorrow, the haunting memories of his love, and she, its star, separated from him by so little,—something made him restless and feverish. He talked with the caciques and priests; he clomb the turret, and watched the smoke go softly up and hide itself in the deeper blue of the sky; with Io', he stood on the temple's verge, and witnessed the fight, at times using bow and sling; but nothing brought him relief. The opportunity he had so long desired was here calling him, and passing away. Oh for an hour of liberty to enact himself!

Unable to endure the excitement, he started in search of the 'tzin, knowing that wherever he was there was action, if not opportunity. At that moment he saw a cacique in the street plant a ladder against the wall of the palace not far from the main gate. The Tlascalans defending at that point tried to throw it off, but a shower of stones from the terrace of the temple deluged them, and they disappeared. Up went the cacique, up went his followers; they gained the crest; then the conflict passed from Hualpa's view.

"Io'," he said, "when the 'tzin comes back, tell him I have gone to make a way for him through yon wall."

"Have a care, comrade, have a care!"

Hualpa put an arm around him, and replied, smiling, "There is one over the wall now: if he fears not, shall I? And then"—he whispered low—"Nenetzin will despise me if I come not soon."

A dawning fell upon Io', and from that time he knew the power of love.

"The gods go with you! Farewell."

Hualpa set about his purpose deliberately. Near the door of the presence-chamber there was a pile of trophies, shields, arms, and armour of men and horses; he made some selections from the heap, and carried them into the chamber. When he came out, under his *panache* there was a steel cap, and under his mantle a cuirass; and to some dead Spaniard he was further beholden for a shield and battle-axe,—the latter so-called, notwithstanding it had a head like a hammer and a handle of steel pointed at the end and more than a yard in length.

Thus prepared, he went down into the street and forced his way to the ladder planted near the gate; thence to the crest of the wall. A hundred arrows splintered against his shield as he looked down upon the combat yet maintained by the brave cacique at the foot of the banquette.

The wall, as I think I have elsewhere said, was built of blocks of wrought stone, laid in cement only a little less hard than the stone, and consequently impervious to any battery against its base; at the same time, taken piece by piece from the top, its demolition was easy. Hualpa paused not; between the blocks he drove the pointed handle of his axe: a moment, and down fell the capping-stone; another followed, and another. Alike indifferent to the arrows of the garrison and the acclamations of the witnesses outside, looking neither here nor there, bending every faculty to the task, he did in a few minutes what seemed impossible: through a breach wide enough for the passage of a double sedan, foemen within and without the wall saw each other.

And there was hastening thither of detachments. Up the ladder and over the wall leaped the devoted infidels, nothing deterred by waiting swords and lances; striking or dying, they shouted, "The 'tzin, the 'tzin! *Al-a-lala!*" Live or die, they strove to cover the stedfast workman in the breach.

De Olid, at the time in charge of the palace, drew nigh, attracted by the increasing uproar.

"Ye fools! Out on ye! See ye not that the dog is hiding behind a Christian shield! Run, fly, bring a brace of arque-busiers! Bring the reserve guns! Upon them, gentlemen! Swords and axes! The Mother for us all! *Christo, Christo!*"

And on foot, and in full armour, he pushed into the press; for, true to his training, he saw that the labourer behind the shining shield was more worthy instant notice than the hordes clamber-ing over the wall.

Still the breach widened and deepened, and every rock that tumbled from its place contributed to the roadway forming on both sides of the wall to facilitate the attack. But now the guns were coming, and the arquebusiers made haste to plant their pieces, against which the good shield might not defend. Suddenly Hualpa stood up, his surcoat whitened with the dust of the mortar; without a word he descended to the street: the work was done,—*a way for the 'tzin was ready!* Scarcely had he touched the pavement before the guns opened; scarcely had the guns opened before the gorge was crowded with infidels rushing in. The palace, wanting the column absent with Cortes, was in danger. To the one point every Christian was withdrawn; even the sick and wounded staggered from the hospital to repel the attack. With all his gallantry, De Olid was beaten slowly back to the house. Cursed he the infidels, prayed he the return of Cortes,—still he went back. In the midst of his perplexity a messenger came to tell him the enemy was breaking through the wall of the western front.

Hualpa had not only made another breach,—De Olid found him inside the enclosure, with a support already too strong for the Tlascalans.

The fight the good captain was called to witness was that of native against native; and, had the peril been less demanding, he would have enjoyed its novelties. An astonishing rattle of shields and spears, mixed with the clash of *maquahuitls*, and a deafening outcry from the contending tribes saluted him. Over the fighting lines the air was thick with stones and flying javelins and tossing banners. Quarter was not once asked. The grim combatants engaged each other to conquer or die. Hither and thither danced the priests, heedless of the danger, now cursing the laggards, now blessing the brave. And at times so shrilly blew the conchs that where they were nothing might be heard but the shriller medley of war-cry answering war-cry.

I doubt if the captain took other note of the fight than its menace to the palace; and if he prayed the return of Cortes a little more fervently than before, it was not from fear or confusion of mind; for straightway he appealed to that arm which had been the last and saving resort of the Christians in many a former strait. Soon every disengaged gun was in position before the western door of the palace, loaded full of stones not larger than birds' eggs, and trained, through the crowd, upon the breach, —and afterwards there were those who charged that the captain did not wait for all his Tlascalans to get out of the way. The guns opened with united voices; palace and paved earth trembled; and the smoke, returning upon the pieces, enveloped everything, insomuch that the door of the house was not to be seen, nor was friend distinguishable from enemy.

If my reader has been in battle, he knows the effect of that fire too well to require description of me; he can hear the cries of the wounded and see the ghastly wrecks on the pavement; he can see, too, the recoil of the Aztecs, and the rush of the Tlascalans, savagely eager to follow up their advantage. I leave the scene to his fancy, and choose rather to go with a warrior who, availing himself of the shrouding of the smoke, pushed through the throng behind the guns, and passed into the palace. His steps were hurried, and he looked neither to the right nor left ; **those whom** he brushed out of the way had but time to see him pass, **or to** catch an instant's view of a figure of motley appurtenances,— **a** Christian shield and battle-axe, a close cap of steel, and the gleam of a corselet under the colourless tatters of a surcoat **of** feather-work,—a figure impossible to identify as friend **or foe.** The reader, however, will recognise Hualpa coming out of **the** depths of the battle, but going—whither ?

Once before, as may **be** remembered, he had been in the ancient house,—the time when, in **a** fit of shame and remorse, he had come to lay **his** lordship **and** castle at the king's feet. Then he had entered **by** the eastern portal, and passed to the royal presence under guidance ; this time his entry was from the west, and he was alone, and unacquainted with the vast interior, its halls, passages, courts, and chambers. In his first visit, moreover, peace had been the rule, and he could not go amiss for friends ; now the palace was a leaguered citadel, and he could hardly go amiss for enemies.

Whatever his purpose, he held boldly on. **It is** possible he **counted** on the necessities of the battle requiring, as in fact they **did, the** presence of every serviceable man of the garrison. The **few he** met passed him in haste, and without question. He avoided the courts and occupied rooms. In the heart of the building he was sensible that the walls and very air vibrated to the roar without ; and as **the** guns in the eastern front answered those in the western, he was advised momentarily of the direction in which he was proceeding, and that his friends still maintained the combat.

Directly three men passed clad in *nequen;* they were talking earnestly, and scarcely noticed him. After them came another, very old, and distinguished by a green *maxtlatl* over his white tunic,—one of the king's counsellors.

"Stay, uncle," said Hualpa,—"stay ; **I** have a question to ask you."

The **old man** seemed **startled.**

"Who are you ?" he inquired.

Hualpa did not appear to hear him, but asked, "Is not the princess Nenetzin with the king, her father ?"

"Follow this hall **to its** end," replied the ancient coldly. "She is there, but **not with** the king, her father. Who is **he,**" he continued after **a pause,**—"who is he that asks for the **false** princess ?"

With a groan Hualpa passed on.

The hall ended in a small *patio,* which at sight declared itself a retreat for love. The walls were finished with a confusion of arabesque moulding, brilliantly and variously coloured ; the tracery around the open doors and windows was a marvel of the art ; there were flowers on the floor, and in curious stands, urns, and swinging baskets ; there were also delicate vines and tropical trees dwarfed for the place, amongst which one full-grown banana lifted its long branches of velvet green, and seemed to temper the light with dewy coolness ; in the centre there was a dead fountain. Indeed, the *patio* could have been but for the one purpose. Here, walled in from the cares of empire, where only the day was bold enough to come unbidden, the wise Axaya' and his less fortunate successors, Tecociatzin and Avizotl, forgot their state, and drank their cups of love, and were as other men.

All the beauty of the place, however, was lost on Hualpa. He saw only Nenetzin. She was sitting at the time in a low sedilium, her white garments faintly tinted by the scarlet stripes of a canopy extended high overhead, to protect her from the too ardent sun.

At the sound of his sandals she started ; and as he approached her, she arose in alarm. In sooth, his toilet was not that most affected for the wooing of women ; he brought with him the odour of battle ; and as he knelt but a little way from her, she saw there was blood upon his hands and upon the axe and shield he laid beside him.

"Who are you ?" she asked.

He took off the steel cap and shapeless *panache*, and looked up in her face.

"The lord Hualpa !" she exclaimed. Then a thought flashed upon her mind, and with terror in every feature, she cried, "Ah, you have taken the palace ! And the Tonatiah ?"—she clasped her hands despairingly,—"dead ? a captive ? Where is he ? I will save him. Take me to him."

At these words, the uncertain expression with which he had looked up to her upon baring his head changed to utter hopelessness. The hurried sentences tore his heart like talons. For this he had come to her through so much peril ! For this he was then braving death at her feet ! His head sank upon his breast, and he said,—

"The palace is not ours. The Tonatiah yet lives, and is free."

With a sigh of relief, she resumed her seat, asking,—

"How came you here ?"

He answered without raising his eyes, "The keepers of the palace are strong ; they can stay the thousands, but they could not keep me out."

The face of the listener softened ; she saw his love, and all his heroism, but said coldly,—

"I have heard that wise men do such things only of necessity."

"I do not pretend to wisdom," he replied. "Had I been wise, I would not have loved you. Since our parting at Chapultepec, where I was so happy, I have thought you might be a prisoner here, and in my dreams I have heard you call me. **And a** little while ago, on the temple, I said to Io', 'Nenetzin **will** despise me if I come not soon.' Tell me, O Nenetzin, that you **are a** prisoner, and I will take you away. Tell **me** that the **stories** told of you on the streets are **not** true, and "—

"What stories?" she asked.

"Alas that it should **be mine to tell** them!—and to you, Nenetzin, my beautiful!"

With a strong effort, he put down the feeling, and went on,—

"There be those who say that the good king, your father, is in this prison by your betrayal; they say, too, that you are the keeper of a shrine unknown to the gods of Anahuac; and yet more shamelessly, they say you abide here with the Tonatiah, unmindful of honour, father, or gods known or unknown. Tell me, O Nenetzin, tell me, I pray **you,** that these are the tales of liars. If you cannot be mine, **at least** let me go hence with **cause** to think you in purity like the **snow** on the mountain-top. My heart is at your feet,—oh, crush me not utterly!"

Thereupon she arose, with flushed face and flashing eyes, never so proud, never so womanly.

"Lord Hualpa, were you more **or** less to me than you **are,** I would make outcry, and have you sent to death. You **can-** not understand me; yet I will answer—because of the **love** which brought you here, I will answer."

She went into **a** chamber, and returning, held up the **iron** cross,—more precious to her, I fear, as the gift of Alvarado **than** as the symbol of Christ.

"Look, lord Hualpa! This speaks to me of a religion better than that practised in the temples, and of a God mightier than all those known in Anahuac,—a God whom it is useless to resist, who may not be resisted,—the only God. There, in my chamber, is an altar to Him, upon which rests only this cross and such flowers as I can gather here in the morning; that is the shrine of which you have heard upon the street. I worship at no other. As to the king, I did come and tell the strangers of the attack he ordered. Lord Hualpa, to me, as is the destiny of every woman, the hour came **to** choose between love and father. I could not else. What harm **has** come **of** my choice? Is not the king safe?"

At that moment, the noise which had all the time **been** heard in the *patio*, as of a battle up in the air, swelled **trebly** loud. The tendrils of the vines shook; the floor trembled.

"Hark!" she said with an expression of dread. "Is he not **safer** than that other for whom I forsook him? Yet I thought **to** save them both; and saved they shall **be!**" she added with a confident smile. "The God I worship **can** save them, and He will."

Then she became silent; and as he could tell by her face that
she was struggling with a painful thought, he waited, listening
intently. At length she spoke, this time with downcast eyes,—

"It would be very pleasant, O Hualpa, to have you go away
thinking me pure as snow on the mountain-top. And if—if I
am not, then in this cross"—and she kissed the symbol tearfully—"there is safety for me. I know there is a love that can
purify all things."

The sensibilities are not alike in all persons; but it is not
true, as some philosophers think, that infidels, merely because
they are such, are incapable of either great joy or great grief.
The mother of El Chico reviled him because he took his last
look at Granada through tears; not less poignant was the sorrow
of Hualpa, looking at his love, by her own confession lost to him
for ever: his head drooped, and he settled down and fell forward
upon his face, crushed by the breath of a woman,—he whom a
hundred shields had not sufficed to stay!

For a time nothing was heard in the *patio* but the battle.
Nenetzin stirred not; she was in the mood superinduced by pity
and remorse, when the mind merges itself in the heart, and is
lost in excess of feeling.

At length the spell was broken. A woman rushed in, clapping
her hands joyfully, and crying,—

"Be glad, be glad, O Nenetzin! Malinche has come back, and
we are saved!"

And more the Doña Marina would have said, but her eyes fell
upon the fallen man, and she stopped.

Nenetzin told his story,—the story women never tire of
hearing.

"If he stays here, he dies," said Marina, weeping.

"He shall not die. I will save him too," said Nenetzin; and
she went to him, and took his hands, bloody as they were, and
by gentle words woke him from his stupor. Mechanically he
took his cap, shield, and mace, and followed her,—he knew not
whither.

And she paused not until he was safely delivered to Maxtla, in
the quarters occupied by the king.

CHAPTER X.

THE WAY THROUGH THE WALL.

"AL TEMPLO, *al templo!* to the temple!" shouted Cortes as he charged the close ranks of the enemy. "*Al templo!*" answered the cavaliers, plunging forward in chivalric rivalry.

And from the column behind them rolled the hoarse echo, with the words of command superadded,—

"*Al templo! Adelante, adelante!*—forward!"

Not a Spaniard there but felt the inspiration of the cry,—felt himself a soldier of Christ, marching to a battle of the gods, the true against the false; yet the way was hard, harder than ever; so much so, indeed, that the noon came before Cortes at last spurred into the space in front of the old palace.

The first object to claim attention there was the temple against which the bigotry of the Christians had been so suddenly and shrewdly directed,—shrewdly, because in the glory of its conquest the failure of the *mantas* was certain to be forgotten. In such intervals of the fight as he could snatch, the leader measured the pile with a view to the attack. Standing in his stirrups, he traced out the path to its summit, beginning at the gate of the *coatapantli*, then up the broad stairs and around the four terraces to the *azoteas*,—a distance of nearly a mile, the whole crowded with warriors, whose splendid regalia published them lords and men of note, in arms to die, if need be, for glory and the gods. As he looked, Sandoval rode to him.

"Turn thine eyes hither, señor,—to the palace, the palace!"

Cortes dropped back into his saddle, and glanced that way.

"By the Mother of Christ, they have broken through the wall!"

He checked his horse.

"Escobar," he said calmly, through his half-raised visor, "take thou one hundred men, the last in the column, and attack the temple. Hearest thou? Kill all thou findest! Nay, I recollect it is a people with two heads, of which I have but one. Bring me the other, if thou canst find him,—I mean the butcher they call the high priest. And more, Señor Alonzo: when thou hast taken the idolatrous mountain, burn the towers, and fear not to tumble the bloody gods into the square. Thy battle will be glorious. On thy side God, the Son, and Mother! Thou canst not fail."

"And thou, Olea," he added to another, "get thee down the street, and hasten Mesa and his supports. Tell them the infidels are at the door of the palace, and that the Captain Christobal hath scarce room to lift his axe. And further,—as speed is

everything now,—bid **Ordas** out with the gun, and fire the
manta, which hath done **its work. Spare not** thy horse!"

With the last word, **Cortes** shut his visor, and, gripping his
axe, spurred to the front, shouting,—

"To the palace, gentlemen! for love **of Christ and** good comrades. Rescue, rescue!"

Down **the column** sped the word,—then **forward** resistlessly,
through **the** embattled gate, into the enclosure; and **none** too
soon, for, **as Cortes** had said, though at the time **witless of** the
truth, **the Aztecs were** threatening the very doors of **the** palace.

Escobar, elated with the task assigned him, arranged **his**
men and made ready for the assault. The infidels beheld his
preparation with astonishment. **All eyes,** theretofore bent upon
the conflict in the palace yard, **now fixed upon** the little band so
boldly proposing to scale the sacred **heights. A cry** came up the
street: "The 'tzin, the 'tzin!" then the 'tzin himself **came; and**
as he passed through the gate of the *coatapantli,* the thousands
recognised him, and breathed freely. "The 'tzin has come! The
gods are safe!" so they cheered each other.

The good captain led his men to the gate of the *coatapantli.*
With difficulty he gained entrance. As if to madden the infidels,
already fired by a zeal as great as his own, the dismal thunder
of the great drum of Huitzil' rolled down from the temple, over-
whelming all other sounds. **Slowly he penetrated** the enclosure;
closely his command **followed him—yet not all of** them; before
he reached the **stairway he was fighting for, the** hundred were
but ninety.

Twenty minutes,—thirty: at last Escobar set his foot on the
first step of the ascent. There he stopped; a shield of iron
clashed against his; his helmet rang with a deadly blow. When
he saw light again, he was outside the sacred wall, borne away by
his retreating **countrymen, of whom not one re-entered the palace**
unwounded.

Cortes, meantime, with sword and axe, cleared the palace **of**
assailants; and, **as if the day's work** were done, he prepared **to**
dismount. Don Christobal, holding his stirrup, said,—

"*Cierto, señor,* thou art welcome. I do indeed kiss thy hand.
I thank thee."

"Not so, **captain, not** so. By my conscience, **we** are the
debtors! **I will hear** nothing else. It is true we came not a
moment too soon,"—he glanced at the breach in the wall, and
shook his head gravely,—"but—I speak what **may** not be gainsaid
—thou hast saved the palace."

More he would have said in the same strain, but that a sentinel
on the roof cried out,—

"*Ola, señores!*"

"**What wouldst thou?**" asked Cortes quickly.

"I am an old soldier, Señor Hernan"—

"To the purpose, varlet, to the purpose!"

"— whom much experience hath taught not to express himself hastily; therefore, if thy orders were well done, señor, whither would our comrades over the way be going?"

"To the top of the temple," said Cortes gravely, while all around him laughed.

"Then I may say safely, señor, that they will go round the world before they arrive there. They come this way fast as men can who have to"—

A long, exulting cry from the infidels cut the speech short; and the party, turning to the temple, saw it alive with waving sashes and tossing shields.

"To horse, gentlemen!" said Cortes quietly, but with flashing eyes. "Satan hath ruled yon pile long enough. I will now tilt with him. Let the trumpets be sounded! Muster the army! God's service hath become our necessity. Haste ye!"

Out of the gate, opened to receive Escobar and his bruised followers, marched three hundred chosen Christians, with as many thousand Tlascalans. In their midst went Olmedo, under his gown a suit of armour, in his hand a lance, and on that a brazen crucifix. Other ensign there was not. Cortes and his cavalry led the column, which was of all the arms except artillery; that remained with De Olid, to take care of the palace.

And never was precaution more timely; for hardly had the gate closed upon the outgoers before the good captain sent his garrison to the walls, once more menaced by the infidels.

The preparations of Escobar, as we have seen, had been under Io's view; so the prince, divining the object, drew after him a strong support, and hastened to keep the advantage of the stairways. On one of the eastern terraces he met the 'tzin ascending. There was hurried salutation between them.

"Look you for Hualpa?" asked Io', observing the 'tzin search the company inquiringly.

"Yes. He should be here."

The boy's face and voice fell.

"I would he were, good 'tzin. He left me on the *azoteas*. With the look of one who had devoted himself, he embraced me. His last words were, 'Tell the 'tzin I have gone to make for him a way into the palace.'" And thereupon Io' told the story through, simply and sorrowfully; at the end the listener kissed him, and said,—

"I will find the way he made for me."

There was a silence, very brief, however, for a burst of yells from below warned them of the fight begun. Then the 'tzin, recalled to himself, gave orders.

"Care of the gods is mine now. Leave me these friends, and

go, and, with the people at command, bring stones and timbers, all you find, and heap them ready for use on the terraces at the head of each stairway. Go quickly, so may you earn the double blessing of Huitzil' and Tezca' !"

In a little time the 'tzin stood upon the last step of the lowest stairway ; nor did he lift hand until Escobar, half spent with exertion, confronted him shield to shield. The result has been told.

And then were shown the qualities which, as a fighting man, raised the 'tzin above rivalry amongst his people. The axe in his hand was but another form of the *maquahuitl ;* and that his shield was of the Christian style mattered not,—he was its perfect master. With a joyous cry, he rushed upon the arms outstretched to save the fallen captain ; played his shield like a shifting mirror ; rose and fell the axe, now in feint, now in foil, but always in circles swifter than eye could follow : striking a victim but once, he amazed and dazzled the Spaniards, as in the Moorish wars El Zagel, the Moor, amazed and dazzled their fathers. Nor did he want support. His followers, inspired by his example, struggled to keep pace with him. On the flanks poured the masses of his countrymen, in blind fury, content if with their naked hands they could clutch the weapons that slew them. Such valour was not to be resisted by the lessening band of Christians, who yielded, at first inch by inch, then step by step ; at length, in disorder, almost in rout, they were driven from the sacred enclosure.

The victory was decided ; the temple was safe and the insult punished ! The air shook with the deep music of the drum ; in the streets the companies yelled as if drunk ; the temple was beautiful with waving sashes and tossing shields and banners ; and on the *azoteas* of the great pile, in presence of the people, the priests appeared and danced their dance of triumph,—a horrible saturnalia. The fight had been a trial of power between the gods Christian and Aztec, and lo, Huitzil' was master !

The 'tzin felt the sweetness of the victory, and his breast filled with heroic impulses. Standing in the gate of the *coatapantli,* he saw the breach Hualpa had made in the wall enclosing the palace, noticed that the ascent to the base of the gorge was easy, and the gorge itself now wide enough to admit of the passage of several men side by side. The temptation was strong, the possibilities alluring, and he fixed his purpose.

"It is the way he made for me, and I will tread it. Help me, O God of my fathers !"

So he resolved, so he prayed.

And forthwith messengers ran to the chiefs on the four sides of the palace with orders for them to pass the wall. From the dead Spaniards the armour was stripped and arms taken ; and the robbers, fourteen caciques, men notable for skill and courage, stood up under cuirass and helm or morion, and with pike and battle-axe of Christian manufacture, covered, nevertheless, with pagan trappings.

Still standing in the gateway, the 'tzin **saw the** companies in the street begin the assault. Swelled their war-cries as never before, for the inspiration of the victory was upon them also; rattled the tambours, brayed the conchs, danced the priests, and from the temple and housetops poured the missiles in a darkening cloud. Within his view **a** hundred ladders were planted, and crowded with **eager** climbers. At the gorge of the breach men struggled with **each other** to make the passage first. He called a messenger.

"Take this ring to the prince Io'," he said. "Tell him the house of the gods is once more in his care." Then to his chosen caciques he turned, saying, "Follow me, O countrymen!"

With that, he walked swiftly to the breach; calm, collected, watchful, silent, he walked. His companions shouted his war-cry. From mouth to mouth it passed, thrilling and inspiring,—

"Up, up, Tlateloco! Up, **up, over** the wall! The 'tzin is with us!"

Meantime the besieged were **not** idle; over the crest of **the** parapet the Tlascalans fought successfully; through the **ports** and embrasures the Christians kept up their **fire** of guns **great** and small. Nevertheless, to the breach the 'tzin went **without** stopping.

"Clear the way!" he cried.

The guns within made answer; a shower of blood drenched him from head to foot. Except of the dead, the way was clear! A rush through the slippery gorge,—a shout,—and he was inside the enclosure, backed by his caciques. And as he went in, Cortes passed out, marching to storm the temple.

No doubt or hesitation on the 'tzin's part now; no looking about, uncertain what to do, while bowmen and gunners made a mark of him. He spoke to his supporters, and with them faced **to** the right, and cleared the banquette of Tlascalans. Over the wall, thus cleared, and through the breach leaped his people; and as they came, the iron shields covered them, and they multiplied rapidly.

About eight hundred Spaniards, chiefly Narvaez' men, defended the palace. They fought, but not with the spirit of the veterans, and were pushed slowly backward. As they retired, **wider** grew the space of undefended wall,—like waves over **a** ship's side, in poured the companies; the Aztecs fell by scores, **yet** they increased by hundreds.

Again the sick and wounded staggered from their quarters; again De Olid brought his reserves into action; again the volleys shook the palace, and wrapped it in curtains of smoke, whiter and softer than bridal veils : still the infidels continued to master the walls and the space within. By and by the gates fell into their hands ; and then, indeed, all seemed lost to the Christians.

The stout heart of the good Captain Christobal was well tempered for the trial. To the windows and lesser entrances of the buildings he sent guards, stationing them inside ; then, in front of the four great doors, he drew his men back, and fought on, so that the palace was literally girt with a belt of battle.

An hour like that I write of seems a long time to a combatant ; on this occasion, however, one there was, not a combatant, to whom, possibly, the time seemed much longer. In his darkened chamber sat the king, neither speaking nor spoken to, though surrounded by his court. He must have heard the cries of his people ; knowing them so near, in fancy at least he must have seen their heroism and slaughter. Had he no thought in sympathy with them ? no prayer for their success ? no hope for himself even ? Who may answer ?—so many there are dead in the midst of life.

At length the 'tzin became weary of the mode of attack, which, after all, was but a series of hand-to-hand combats along length-ened lines that might last till night, or, indeed, as long as there were men to fill the places of the fallen. To the companies crowding the conquered space before the eastern front of the palace he passed an order : a simultaneous forward movement from the rear took place ; the intervals between the ranks were closed up ; a moment of fusion,—a pressure ; then a welding together of the whole mass followed. After that, words may not convey the scene. The unfortunates who happened to be engaged were first pushed, then driven, and finally shot forward, like dead weights. Useless all skill, useless strength ; the opposite lines met ; blood flew as from a hundred fountains ; men, impaled on opposing weapons, died, nailed together face to face. As the only chance for life, very many fell down and were smothered.

The defenders broke in an instant. Back, back they went,— back to the guns, which for a time served as breakwaters to the wave ; then past the guns, almost to the wall, forced there by the awful impetus of the rush.

The truly great leaders of men are those who, invoking storms, stand out and brave them when they come. Such was Guata-mozin. The surge I have so faintly described caught him foremost in the fighting line of his people, and flung him upon his antagonists. With his shield he broke the force of the collision ; the cuirass saved him from their points ; close wedged amongst them, they could not strike him. Tossed like so much drift, backward they went, forward he. Numbers of them fell and disappeared. When at last the impetus of the movement was nigh spent, he found himself close by the principal **door** of the palace. But one man stood before him,—a warrior with *maquahuitl* lifted **to** strike. The 'tzin raised his shield and caught the blow ; **then,** upon his knee, he looked up and saw the face and heard **the** exulting yell of—-Iztlil', the Tezcucan ! Whirled the weapon again. The noble Aztec summoned all his spirit ; death glared upon him through the burning eyes of his hated rival ; up, clear to vision, rose all dearest things,—gods, country, glory, love. Suddenly the raised **arm** fell—down dropped the *maquahuitl ;* and upon the shield **down** dropped Iztlil' himself, carrying the **'tzin** with him.

The Tezcucan seemed dead.

A friendly hand helped the 'tzin to his feet. He was conscious, **as he arose,** of a strange calm in the air ; the clamour and furious **stir of** the combat were dying away ; he stood in the midst of enemies, but they were still, and did not even look at him. A shield not his own covered his breast ; **he** turned, and lo ! the **face** of Hualpa !

"Whence came you ?" asked the 'tzin.

"From the palace."

"Thanks "—

"Not now, not now," said Hualpa in a low voice. "The gods who permitted me to save you, **O** 'tzin, have not been able to save themselves. Look ! to the temple ! "

His eyes followed Hualpa's directing finger, and the same astonishment that held his enemies motionless around him, the same horror that, in the full tide of successful battle, had so instantly stayed his countrymen, seized him also. He stood transfixed,—a man turned to stone !

The towers of the temple were in flames ; and, yet more awful, the **image** of Huitzil', rolled to the verge of the *azoteas,* was tottering to **its** fall ! A thousand hands were held up instinctively, —a groan,—a long cry,—and down the stairway and terraces, grinding and crashing, thundered the idol. Tezca' followed after, and the sacrificial stone. Then the religion of the Aztecs was ended for **ever** !

As if to **assure the** great fact, when next the spectators raised their eyes **to the** *azoteas,* lo ! Olmedo and his crucifix ! The faithful servant of Christ had performed his mission : he **had** burst the last gate and gained the last mountain in the way ; and now, with bared head and face radiant with sublime emotion, he raised the symbol of salvation high up in view of all the tribes, and, **in** the name of his Master, and for his Master's Church, for ever, by that simple ceremony, took **possession** of the New World.

And, marvellous to relate further, the tribes, awed if not con-

quered, bowed their heads in peace. Even the companies in the
palace yard marched out over their dead, and gave up the victory
so nearly won. Guatamozin and Hualpa followed them, but with
their faces to the foe. Needless the defiance : as they went, not a
word was spoken, not a hand lifted. For the time, all was peace.

CHAPTER XI.

BATTLE IN THE AIR.

As Cortes, at the head of his column, drew near the gate of the
coatapantli, he saw the enclosure and the terraces on that side of
the temple occupied by warriors, and the edge of the *azoteas* above
lined with *pabas*, chanting in dismal harmony with the deep
music of the great drum. Ensigns and symbols of unknown
meaning and rich regalia pranked the dull grey faces of the pile
with holiday splendours. Little note, however, gave he to the
beautiful effect.

"God helping us," he said to his cavaliers, and with such
gravity that they knew him unusually impressed with the task
before them,—"God helping us, gentlemen, we will do a deed
now that hath no likeness in the wars of men. Commend we
ourselves each, and all who follow us, to the holy Christ, who
cometh yonder on the staff of Father Olmedo."

So saying, he reversed his sword and carried the crossed handle
softly and reverently to the bars of his helmet, and all who heard
him did likewise.

In front of the gate, under a shower of arrows, he stopped to
adjust the armlets of his shield, for his hand was yet sore ; then,
settling in his saddle again, he spurred his horse through the
entrance into the enclosure.

Right into the mass waiting to receive him he broke, and whom
his sword left untouched the trained steed bore down. After him
charged the choicest spirits of the conquest, animated with generous rivalry and the sublime idea that this time the fight was for
God and His Church. And so, with every thrust of sword and
every plunge of horse, out rang their cries.

"On, on, for love of Christ ! Death to the infidels ! Down
with the false gods !"

On the side of the infidels there was no yielding, for the ground
was holy ground to them. When their frail weapons were
broken, they flung themselves empty-handed upon the nearest

rider, or under the horses, and, dying even, tried to hold fast
locked the hoofs that beat them to death. In their aid, the pavement became heaped with bodies, and so slippery **with** blood that
a number of the horses fell down ; and in such cases, **if** the rescue
came not quickly, they and their riders were lost. Indeed, **so**
much did this peril increase that Cortes, when his footmen were
fairly in the yard, dismounted the horsemen the better to **wage**
the fight.

At length resistance ceased ; the enclosure was won. The
marble floor bore awful evidences of the prowess of one party and
the desperation of the other.

The Christians took up their wounded and carried them
tenderly to the shade, for the sun blazed down from the cloudless
sky.

Around Cortes gathered the captains, resting themselves.

"The Tlascalans must hold the yard," he said, well pleased, and
with raised visor. "That charge I commit to thee, Lugo."

Lugo bared his face, and said sullenly,—

"Thou knowest, señor, that I am accustomed to obey thee
questionless ; but this liketh me not. I"—

"By the love of Christ"—

"Even so, señor," said Lugo, interrupting him in turn. "I feel
bidden by love of Christ to go up and help cast down the accursed
idols."

The face of the crafty leader changed quickly.

"*Ola*, father!" he said. "Here is one malcontent, **because I**
would have him stay and take care of us while we climb the **stair-**
ways. What sayest thou?"

Olmedo answered solemnly, "What ye have in mind now,
señores—the disgrace of the false gods who abide in this temple
of abominations—is what hath led us here. And now that the
end is at hand, the least circumstance is to be noted ; for the wise
hear God **as** often in the small voice as in the thunder. Doubt
not, doubt **not** ; the prompting of the good captain is from Him.
Be this lower duty to the unassoilzied Tlascalans ; go we as the
love of Christ calleth. Verily, he who doeth this work well,
though his sins be many as the sands of the sea, yet shall he
become as purity itself, and be blessed for ever. Take thy
measures quickly, señor, and let us be gone."

"Amen, amen!" said the cavaliers ; and Cortes, crossing himself, hastened in person to make dispositions for the further
emprise.

The Tlascalans he set to hold the *coatapantli* from attack
without. To the arquebusiers and cross-bowmen he gave orders
to cover him with their fire while he climbed the stairways and
was driving the enemy around the terraces. When the *azoteas*
was gained, they were to ascend and take part in the crowning

struggle for the sanctuaries. The cavalry, already dismounted, were to go with him in the assault. To the latter, upon rejoining them, he said,—

"In my judgment, gentlemen, the fighting we go to now is of the kind wherein the sword is better than axe or lance ; therefore put away all else."

He took place at the head, with Alvarado and Sandoval next him in the column.

"And thou, father?" he asked.

Olmedo raised his crucifix, and, looking up, said,—

"*Hagase tu voluntad en la tierra asi como en el cielo.*" [1] Then to Cortes, "I will follow these my children."

"Forward, then ! Christ with us, and all the saints !" cried Cortes. "*Adelante ! Christo y Santiago !*"

In a moment they were swiftly climbing the lower stairway of the temple.

Meantime Io', from the *azoteas*, kept watch on the combats below. Two figures charmed his gaze,—that of Cortes and that of the 'tzin,—both, in their separate ways, moving forward slowly but certainly. Before he thought of descending, the Christians were in the precinct of the *coatapantli*, and after them streamed the long line of Tlascalans.

As we have seen, the prince had been in battles, and more than once felt the joyous frenzy nowhere else to be found ; but now a dread fell upon him. Did Malinche's dream of conquest reach the gods? Again and again he turned to the sanctuaries, but the divine wrath came not forth,—only the sonorous throbs of the drum. Once he went into the presence-chamber, which was full of kneeling *pabas*. The *teotuctli* stood before the altar praying. Io' joined in the invocation ; but miracle there was not, neither was there help : for when he came out, all the yard around the temple was Malinche's.

Then Io' comprehended that this attack, unlike Escobar's, was of method ; for the ways of succour, which were also those of retreat, were all closed. The supreme trial had come early in his career. His spirit arose ; he saw himself the stay of the religion of his fathers ; the gods leaned upon him. On the roof and terraces were some two thousand warriors, the fighting children of the valley : Tezcucans, with countless glorious memories to sustain their native pride ; Cholulans, eager to avenge the sack of their city and the massacre of their countrymen ; Aztecs, full of the superiority of race and the inspiration of ages of empire. They would fight to the last man. He could trust them, as the 'tzin had trusted him. The struggle, moreover, besides being of special interest on account of its religious character, would be in mid-air, with the strangers and all the tribes and companies as

---

[1] Thy will be done on earth as it is in heaven.

witnesses. So, with his caciques, he went down to the landing at
the top of the lower stairway.

A yell saluted Cortes when, at the head of the cavaliers, he
appeared on the steps, and, sword in hand and shield overhead,
commenced the perilous ascent. At the same time javelins and
spears began to rain upon the party from the first terrace. Up
they hurried. Half the height was gained and not a man hurt,—
not a foot delayed! Then, slowly at first, but with longer leaps
and increasing force, a block of stone was started down the stairs.
Fortunately, the steps were broad, having been built for the
accommodation of processions. Down sped a warning cry; down
as swiftly plunged the danger. Olmedo saw three figures of men
in iron follow it headlong to the bottom; fast they fell, but not
too fast for his words of absolution; before the victims touched
the pavement, their sins were forgiven, and their souls at rest in
Paradise.

The stones and timbers placed on the landing by the 'tzin's
order were now laid hold of, and rolled and dragged to the steps
and hurled down. Thus ten Christians more were slain. Even
Cortes, deeming escape impossible, turned his battle-cry into a
prayer, and not in vain! From below the arquebusiers and
cross-bowmen suddenly opened fire, which they kept so close
that on the landing the dead and wounded speedily outnumbered the living.

"The saints are with us! Forward, swords of the Church!"
cried Cortes.

Before the infidels recovered from their panic, he passed the
last step and stood upon the terrace. And there, first in front of
him, first to meet him, was Io', whom pride and zeal would not
permit to retire.

The meeting—combat it can hardly be called—was very brief.
The blades of Io's *maquahuitl* broke at the first blow. Cortes
replied with a thrust of the sword,—quick but true, riving both
the shield and the arm. A cacique dragged the hapless boy out
of reach of the second thrust, and took his place before the
conqueror.

The terrace so hardly gained was smoothly paved, and wide
enough for ten men to securely walk abreast; on the outer side
there was no railing or guard of any kind, nothing but a descent
of such height as to make a fall certainly fatal. Four times the
smooth, foot-worn pavement extended around the temple, broken
in its course by six grand stairways, the last of which landed on
the *azoteas*, one hundred and fifty feet above the level of the
street. Such was the highway of the gods, up which the
adventurous Christians essayed to march, fighting.

"To my side, Sandoval! And ye, Alvarado, Morla, Lugo,
Ordas, Duero,—to my side!" said Cortes, defending himself the

while. "Make with me a line of shields across the way. Let me
hear your voices. **No battle-cry** here but Christ and St. James!
When ye are ready, **shout, that I** may hear **ye!**"

One by one the brave gentlemen took their places; then rose
the cry, "*Christo y Santiago! Christo y Santiago!*"

And then the voice of Cortes,—

"Forward, my friends! Push the dogs! **No** quarter! *Christo
y Santiago!*"

Behind **the** line of shields moved the other **cavaliers,** eager to
help when help should be needed.

And then were shown **the** excellences of the sword in a master's
hand. The best shields **of the** infidels could not bar its point; **it**
overcame resistance **so** quietly **that** men fell wounded, or slain
outright, before they thought themselves **in** danger; it won the
terrace, and **so** rapidly that the Christians were themselves
astonished.

"*Ola, compañeros!*" said Cortes, who **in the fiercest** *mêlée* was
still **the** watchful captain. "*Ola!* Yonder riseth the second
stairway. That the heathen may **not use the** vantage against us,
keep we close to this pack. On their **heels!** Closer!"

So they mounted the steps of the second stairway fighting; and
the crowd which they kept between **them** and the enemy on the
landing was a better cover even than **the** fire of the bowmen and
arquebusiers. And so **the** terraces were **all** taken. Of the eight
other Christians who fell under the **stones** and **logs rolled** upon
them from the heights above, two lived **long enough** to be shrived
by the faithful Olmedo.

The *azoteas* of the temple **has been already described** as a broad,
paved area, unobstructed **except by the sacrificial** stones and the
sanctuaries **of Huitzil' and Tezca'. A more** dreadful place for
battle **cannot be** imagined. **The** coming and going of worshippers, singly **or** in processions, **and** of barefooted pabas, **to**
whom the dizzy height was all the world, had worn its surface
smooth as furbished iron. If, as the combat rolled slowly around
the terraces, rising higher, and nearer the chiefs and warriors on
the summit,—**if,** in faintness of heart **or** hope, they looked for a
way of escape, **the** sky and the remote horizon were all they saw:
escape **was** impossible.

With **many** others disabled **by** wounds, Io' ascended **to** the
azoteas in **advance** of the fight; not in despair, but as the faithful
might, never doubting that, when the human effort failed, Huitzil'
the Omnipotent would defend himself. He passed through the
ranks, and with brave words encouraged the common resolve to
conquer or die. Stopping upon the western verge, he looked
down upon the palace, and lo! there was a rest in the assault,
except where the 'tzin fought, with his back to the temple; and
the thousands **were** standing still, their faces upturned,—each

where the strange truce found him,—to behold the hunted gods in some majestic form at last assert their divinity. **So Io'** knew, by the whisperings of his own faith.

Again he turned prayerfully to the sanctuaries. **At that** instant Cortes mounted the last step of the last stairway,—after him **the** line of shields, and all the cavaliers,—after them again, Olmedo with his crucifix ! Then was wrought an effect, simple enough of itself, but so timely that the good man—forgetful that the image of Christ dead on the cross is nothing without the story of His perfect love and sorrowful death—found believers when he afterwards proclaimed it a miracle. He held the sacred effigy up **to** be seen by all the infidels : they gazed at it as at a god unfriendly to their gods, and waited in awe for the beginning of **a** struggle between the divine rivals ; and while they waited, Cortes and his cavaliers perfected their formation upon the *azoteas*, and the bowmen and arquebusiers began to climb **the second** stairway of the ascent. The moment of advantage was **lost to the** Aztecs, and they paid the penalty.

Io' waited with the rest : from crucifix to sanctuary, and **sanctuary** to crucifix, he turned ; yet the gods nursed their power. **At** last he awoke ; too late ! there was no escape. Help of man was not possible, and the gods seemed to have abandoned him.

"Tezcuco ! Cholula ! Tenochtitlan ! **Up, up,** Tlateloco, up !"

Over the *azoteas* his words rang piercing clear, and through **the** ranks towards the Christians he rushed. The binding of the spell was broken. Shook the banners, pealed war-cry, conch, and atabal,—and the battle was joined.

"Hold fast until our brethren come ! then shall our swords drink their fill ! *Christo y Santiago !*"

Never was the voice of Cortes more confident.

Need, nevertheless, had the cavaliers for all their strength and skill, even the nicest cunning of fence and thrust. Every joint of their harness was searched by javelin and spear, and the clang of *maquahuitls* against the faces of their shields was as the noise of a thousand *armeros* at work. The line swayed and bent before the surge, now yielding, now recovering, at times ready to **break,** and then—death awaited them all on the terraces below. **For** life they plied their swords,—no, not for life alone ; behind **them** to and fro strode Olmedo.

"Strike, and spare not !" he cried. "Lo ! **the** gates of hell yonder, but they shall not prevail. Strike **for** Holy Church, whose swords ye are ! For Holy Cross, **and room** to worship above the Baals of heathendom ! For glory here, and eternal life hereafter !"

So he cried **as** he strode ; and the crucifix on his lance and the saintly words on his lips were better than trumpets, better than a hundred Cids in reserve.

The great drum, which had been for a while silent, at this juncture burst out again ; and, still more to inflame the infidels, forth from the sanctuaries the pabas poured, and dispersed themselves, leaping, dancing, singing, through the ranks. Doubtless they answered the Christian priest, promise for promise, and with even greater effect ; the calm and self-possessed among their people became zealots and the zealots became frantic madmen.

At last the bowmen and arquebusiers appeared upon the scene. When Cortes saw them,—their line formed, matches lighted, bows drawn,—he drew out of the combat to give them directions.

"*Viva compañeros!*" he said with a vivacity peculiar to himself ; "I bid ye welcome. The temple and its keepers are ours. We with swords will now go forward. Keep ye the stairway, and take care of our flanks. Ply your bolts,—ply them fast,—and spare not a cur in the kennel !"

They made no answer, spake not a word. Stolidly, grimly, they gazed at him under their morions ; they knew their duty, and he knew them. Once more he turned to the fight.

"To the sanctuaries !" he shouted to the cavaliers. "We have come for the false gods : let us at them. Charge, gentlemen. Christ with us ! Forward all !"

Back came their response, "Forward ! *Christo y Santiago !*"

They advanced their shields suddenly ; the play of their swords redoubled ; the weapons in front of them splintered like reeds ; war-cries half uttered turned to screams ; under foot blood ran like water, and feathered panoply and fallen men, dying and dead, blotted out the pavement. Surprised, bewildered, baffled, the bravest of the infidels perished ; the rest gave way or were pushed helplessly back ; and the dismay thus excited rose to panic when the bowmen and arquebusiers joined in the combat. A horrible confusion ensued. Hundreds threw away their arms and ran wildly around the *azoteas ;* some flung themselves from the height ; some climbed the sanctuaries ; some took to piteous imploration of the doomed idols ; others, in blind fury, rushed empty-handed upon the dripping swords.

Steadily, as a good craft divides the current and its eddies, Cortes made way to the sanctuaries, impatient to possess the idols, that, at one blow, he might crush the faith they represented ; after which he made no doubt of the submission of the nations in arms. A rare faculty that which in the heat of battle can weave webs of policy, and in the mind's eye trace out lines of wise conduct.

When at last the end was nigh, such of the pabas as survived withdrew themselves from the delirious mob and assembled around the sacrificial stones. Some of them were wounded ; on many the black gowns hung in shreds; all of them had one purpose more, usually the last to linger in an enthusiast's heart. There, where they had witnessed so many sacrifices, and, in eager observance of auguries, overlooked or savagely enjoyed the agony of the victims, they came themselves to die,—there the sword found them; and from their brave, patient death we may learn that Satan hath had his martyrs as well as Christ.

About the same time another body collected in the space before the presence-chamber of Huitzil'. They were the surviving caciques, with Io' in their midst. Having borne him out of the fray, they now took up a last position to defend him and the gods.

Upon them also the battle had laid a heavy hand: most of them were hurt and bleeding; of their beautiful regalia only fragments remained; some were without arms of any kind, some bore headless javelins or spears, a few had *maquahuitls*. Not a word was spoken: they too had come to die, and the pride of their race forbade repining.

They saw the last of the pabas fall; then the rapacious swords, to complete the work, came to them. In the front strode Cortes. His armour shone brightly, and his shield, though spotted with blood, was as a mirror from which the sun's rays shot like darts into the eyes of the infidels attracted by its brightness.

Suddenly three warriors, unarmed, rushed upon him; his sword passed through one of them; the others caught him in their arms. So quick, so bold and desperate was the action that, before he could resist or his captains help him, he was lifted from his feet and borne away.

"Help, gentlemen! Rescue!" he cried.

Forward sprang Sandoval, forward Alvarado, forward the whole line. The caciques interposed themselves. Played the swords then never so fast and deadly,—still the wall of men endured.

Cortes with all his armour was a cumbrous burden; yet the warriors bore him swiftly toward the verge of the *azoteas*. No doubt of their purpose: fair and stately were the halls awaiting them in the Sun if they but took the leap with him! He struggled for life, and called on the saints, and vowed vows. At the last moment, one of them stumbled and fell; thereupon he broke away, regained his feet, and slew them both.

In the door of the sanctuary of Huitzil', meantime, Io' stood, biding the sure result of the unequal struggle. Again and again he had striven to get to the enemy; but the devoted caciques closed their circle against him as compactly as against them. Nearer shone the resistless blades,—nearer the inevitable death. The rumble and roar of the drum poured from the chamber in mighty throbs; at times he caught glimpses of the *azoteas* strewn with bloody wreck. A sense of the greatness of the calamity seized him, followed by the sudden calm which, in brave men dying, is more an accusation of fate than courage, resignation, or despair; upon his faculties came a mist; he shouted the old war-cry of the 'tzin, and scarcely heard himself. The loves and hopes that had made his young life beautiful seemed to rise up and fly away, not in the air-line of birds, but with the slow, eccentric flight of star-winged butterflies. Then the light faded and the sky darkened; he reeled and staggered, but, while falling, felt himself drawn into the presence-chamber, and looking up saw the face of the *teotuctli*, and heard the words, " I loved your father, and he loved the god, who may yet save us. Come, come !" The loving hands took off his warlike trappings, and, covering him with the frock of a paba, set him on the step of the altar at the feet of the god; then the darkness became perfect, and he knew no more.

Directly there was a great shout within the chamber, blent with the clang of armour and iron-shod feet; the *teotuctli* turned, and confronted Olmedo, with Cortes and the cavaliers.

The Christian priest dropped his lance to the floor, threw back his cowl, raised his visor, and, pointing to the crucifix, gazed proudly into the face of the infidel pontiff, who answered with a look high and scornful, as became the first and last servant of a god so lately the ruler of the universe. And while they faced each other, the beating of the drum ceased and the clamour stilled, until nothing was heard but the breathing of the conquerors, tired with slaughter.

Then Cortes said,—

" Glory to Christ, whose victory this is ! Thou, father, art His priest, let thy will be done. Speak !"

Olmedo turned to that quarter of the chamber where, by permission of Montezuma, a Christian shrine and cross had been erected: shrine and cross were gone ! Answered he then,—

" The despoiler hath done his work. Vengeance is mine, saith the Lord. Take this man," pointing to the *teotuctli*, "and bind him, and lead him hence."

Alvarado stepped forward, and took off the massive silver chain which he habitually wore twice encircling his neck and falling down low over his breast-plate; with it he bound the wrists of the prisoner, who once, and once only, cast an appealing glance up to the stony face of the idol. As they started to lead him off, his eyes fell upon Io'; by a sign and look of pity he directed their attention to the boy.

" He is not dead," said Sandoval after examination.

" Take him hence also," Olmedo ordered. " At leisure to-morrow we can learn what importance he hath.

Hardly were the captives out when the chamber became a

scene of wild iconoclasm. The smoking censers were overthrown ; the sculpturings on the walls were defaced ; the altar **was** rifled of the rich accumulation of gifts ; faggots snatched from **the** undying **fires in** front of the sanctuaries were applied to the carved and gilded wood-work ; and amid the smoke, and with shouting and laughter and the noisy abandon of schoolboys at play, the zealots despoiled the gigantic image of its ornaments and treasure, —of the bow and golden arrows in its hands, the feathers of humming-birds on its left foot, the necklace of gold and silver hearts, the serpent enfolding its waist in coils glistening with pearls and precious stones. A hundred hands then pushed the monster from its sitting-place, and rolled it out of the door, and finally off the *azoteas*. Tezca' shared the same fate. The greedy flames mounted to the towers, and soon not a trace of the ages **of** horrible worship remained, except the smoking walls of the ruined sanctuaries.

Down from the heights marched the victors ; into the palace they marched ; and not a hand was raised against them on the way,—the streets were almost deserted.

" *Bien !* " said Cortes, as he dismounted once more in front of **his** quarters. " *Muy bien !* We have their king and chief priests ; we have burned their churches, disgraced their gods, and slain their nobles by the thousand. The war is over, gentlemen ; let us to our couches. Welcome **rest** ! welcome peace ! "

And the weary army, accepting his words as verity, went to rest, though the sun flamed in the brassy sky. But rest there was not. Ere dreams could follow slumber, the trumpets sounded, and the battle was on again, fiercer than ever.

The sun set, and the night came ; then the companies thought to rest ; but Cortes, made tireless by rage, went out after them, and burned a vast district of houses.

And the flames so filled the sky with brilliance that the sun seemed to have stood still just below the horizon.

During the lurid twilight, Olmedo laid away, in shallow graves dug for them in the palace garden, more than fifty Christians, of whom six-and-forty perished on the temple and its terraces.

CHAPTER XII.

IN THE INTERVAL OF THE BATTLE—LOVE.

THE *chinampa*, at its anchorage, swung lightly, like an Indian cradle pendulous in the air. Over it stooped the night, its wings of darkness brilliant with the plumage of stars. The fire in the city kindled by Cortes still fitfully reddened the horizon in that direction,—a direful answer to those who, remembering the sweetness of peace in the beautiful valley, prayed for its return with the morning.

Yeteve, in the hammock, had lulled herself into the sleep of dreams; while in the canoe Hualpa and the oarsmen slept the sleep of the warrior and labourer,—the sleep too deep for dreams. Only **Tula** and the 'tzin kept vigils.

Just outside the canopy, in sight of the meridian stars, and where the night winds came sighing through the thicket of flowers, a *petate* had been spread for them; and now she listened, while he, lying at length, his head in her lap, talked of the sorrowful time that had befallen.

He told her of the *mantas* and their destruction; of how Hualpa had made way to the presence of Nenetzin, and how she had saved his life; and as the narrative went on, the listener's head drooped low over the speaker's face, and there were sighs and tears which might have been apportioned between the lost sister and the unhappy lover. He told of the attack upon the palace and of the fall of Iztlil', and how, when the victory was won, Malinche flung the gods from the temple, and so terrified the companies that they fled.

"Then, O Tula, my hopes fell down. A people without gods, broken in spirit, and with duty divided between two kings, are but grass to be trodden. And Io',—so young, so brave, so faithful"—

He paused, and there was a long silence, devoted to the prince's memory. Then he resumed,—

"In looking out over the lake, you may have noticed that the city has been girdled with men in canoes,—an army, indeed, unaffected by the awful spectacle of the overthrow of the gods. I brought them up, and in their places sent the companies that had failed me. So, as the sun went down, I was able to pour fresh thousands upon Malinche. How I rejoiced to see them pass the wall with Hualpa and grapple with the strangers! All my hopes came back again. That the enemy fought feebly was not a fancy. Watching, wounds, battle, and care have wrought upon them. They are wasting away. A little longer—two days—a day even,—patience, sweetheart, patience!"

There was silence again,—the golden silence of lovers, under the stars, hand in hand, dreaming.

The 'tzin broke the spell to say, in **lower tones and with longer** intervals,—

"Men must worship, O Tula, and there **can** be no worship without faith. So I had next to renew the sacred fire and restore the gods. The first **was** easy: I had only to start a flame from the embers of the sanctuaries; the fire that burned them was borrowed from that kept immemorially on the old altars. The next duty was harder. The images were not of themselves more estimable than other stones; neither were the jewels that adorned them more precious than others of the same kind: their sanctity was from faith **alone.** The art of arts is to evoke the faith of men : **make** me, **O** sweetheart, make me master of that art, and, as the **least of** possibilities, I will make gods of things least godly. In the places where they had fallen, at the foot of the temple, I **set the** images up, and gave each **an** altar, with censers, holy fire, **and all the** furniture of worship. **By** and by they shall be raised **again to** the *azoteas ;* and when **we** renew the empire, we will **build for** them sanctuaries richer **even** than those of Cholula. If **the** faith of our people demand more, then"—

He hesitated.

"Then, what?" she asked.

He shuddered, and said, lower than ever, "I will **unseal the** caverns of Quetzal', and—more I cannot answer now."

The influence of Mualox was upon him yet.

"And if that fail?" she persisted.

Not until the stars at the time overhead had passed and **been** succeeded by others as lustrous did he answer,—

"And if that fail? Then we will build a temple,—one without images,—a temple to the One Supreme God. So, O Tula, shall the prophecy of the king your father be fulfilled in our day."

And with that up sprang a breeze **of** summery warmth, lingering awhile to wanton with the tresses of the willow, and swing the flowery island half round the circle of its anchorage; and from the soothing hand on his forehead, or the reposeful motion of the *chinampa*, the languor of **sleep** stole upon his senses; yet recollection of the battle and **its** cares was hard to be put away.

"I should have told you," he said in a vanishing voice, **"that** when the companies abandoned us, I went first to **see our** uncle, the lord Cuitlahua. The guards at the door refused me admittance; the king was sick, they said."

A tremor shook the hand on his forehead, **and** larger grew the great eyes bending over him.

2 B

"Did they say of what he was sick?" she asked.

"Of the plague."

"And what is that?"

"Death," he answered, and next moment fell asleep.

Over her heart, to hush the loudness of its beating, she clasped her hands; for out of the chamber of the almost forgotten, actual as in life, stalked Mualox the paba saying, as once on the temple he said, "You shall be queen in your father's palace." She saw his beard of fleecy white and his eyes of mystery, and asked herself again and again, "Was he indeed a prophet?"

And the loving child and faithful subject strove hard to hide from the alluring promise, for in its way she descried two living kings, her father and her uncle; but it sought her continually, and found her, and at last held her as a dream holds a sleeper—held her until the stars heralded the dawn, and the 'tzin awoke to go back to the city, back to the battle,—from love to battle.

CHAPTER XIII.

THE BEGINNING OF THE END.

"LEAVE the city, now so nearly won! Surely, father, surely thou dost jest with me!"

So Cortes said as he sat in his chamber, resting his arm on the table, the while Olmedo poured cold water on his wounded hand.

The father answered without lifting his face,—

"Go, I say, that we may come back assured of holding what we have won."

"Sayest thou so,—thou! By my conscience, here are honour, glory, empire! Abandon them, and the treasure, a part of which, as thou knowest, I have already accounted to his Majesty? No, no; not yet, father! I cannot—though thou mayest—forget what Velasquez and my enemies, the velveted minions of the court, would say."

"Then it is as I feared," said Olmedo, suspending his work, and tossing his hood farther back on his shoulders,—"it is as I feared. The good judgment which hath led us so far so well, and given riches to those who care for riches, and planted the Cross over so many heathen temples, is at last at fault."

The father's manner was solemn and reproachful. Cortes turned to him inquiringly,

"Señor, thou knowest I may be trusted. Heed me. I speak for Christ's sake," continued Olmedo. "Leave the city we must. There is not corn for two days more; the army is worn down with wounds and watching; scarcely canst thou thyself hold an axe; the men of Narvaez are mutineers; the garden is full of graves, and it hath been said of me that, for want of time, I have shorn the burial service of essential Catholic rites. And the enemy, señor, the legions that broke through the wall last evening, were new tribes for the first time in battle. Of what effect on them were yesterday's defeats? The gods tumbled from the temple have their altars and worship already. Thou mayest see them from the central turret."

The good man was interrupted. Sandoval appeared at the door.

"Come," said Cortes impatiently.

The captain advanced to the table, and saluting, said in his calm, straightforward way,—

"The store for the horses is out; we fed them to-night from the rations of the men. I gave Motilla half of mine, and yet she is hungry."

At these words the hand Olmedo was nursing closed, despite its wound, as upon a sword-hilt, vice-like, and up the master arose, brow and cheek grey as if powdered with ashes, and began to walk the floor furiously; at last he stopped abruptly.

"Sandoval, go bid the captains come. I would have their opinions as to what we should do. Omit none of them. Those who say nothing may be witnesses hereafter."

The order was given quietly, with a smile even. A moment the captain studied his leader's face, and I would not say he did not understand the meaning of the simple words; for of him Cortes afterwards said, "He is fit to command great armies."

Cortes sat down, and held out the hand for Olmedo's ministrations; but the father touched him caressingly, and said, when Sandoval was gone,—

"I commend thee, son, with all my soul. Men are never so much on trial as when they stand face to face with necessity; the weak fight it, and fall; the wise accept it as a servant. So do thou now."

Cortes' countenance became chill and sullen. "I cannot see the necessity"—

"Good!" exclaimed Olmedo. "Whatsoever thou dost, hold fast to that. The captains will tell thee otherwise, but"—

"What?" asked Cortes with a sneer. "The treasure is vast, —a million *pesos* or more. Dost thou believe they will go and leave it?"

But Olmedo was intent upon his own thought.

"*Mira!*" he said. "**If the** captains **say** there is a necessity, do thou put in thy **denial**; stand **on thy** opinion boldly; and when thou givest up at last, yield **thee to** that other necessity, the demand of the army. And so"—

"And so," Cortes said with a smile, **which was** also a sneer,— "and so **thou** wouldst make a servant **of one** necessity by invoking another."

"**Yes**; another which may be admitted without **danger** or dishonour. Thou hast the idea, my son."

"So be it, so be it,—*aguardamonos!*"

Thereupon Cortes retired within himself, and the father began again to nurse the wounded hand.

And by and by the chamber was filled with captains, soldiers, and caciques, whose persons, darkly visible in the murky light, testified to the severity of the situation: rusted armour, ragged apparel, faded trappings, bandaged limbs, countenances heavy with anxiety or knit hard by suffering,—such were the evidences.

In good time Cortes arose.

"*Ola*, my friends," he said bluntly. "**I have heard** that there are among ye many who think the time **come to give** the city and all we have taken back to the infidels. I have sent for ye that I may know **the** truth. **As** the matter concerneth interests of our royal **master** aside from **his** dominion,—property, for example,—the Secretary Duero will make note of all that passeth. Let him come forward and take place here."

The secretary seated himself by the table with manuscript and pen.

"Now, gentlemen, begin."

So saying, **the** chief dropped back **into his seat,** and held the sore hand to Olmedo for further care,—never speech more bluff, **never face more** calm. For a time nothing was heard but the **silvery tinkle** of the falling water. **At** length one was found sturdy enough **to** speak; others followed him; and at last, when **the opinion** was taken, not a voice **said stay**; on the contrary, the **clamour to** go was, by some, indecently **loud.**

Cortes then stood up.

"**The opinion is all one way. Hast thou so written, Señor** Duero?"

The secretary **bowed.**

"Then write again,—write that I, Hernan Cortes, to this retreat said, No; write that, if I yield my judgment, it is not **to** any necessity **of** which we have heard as coming from the enemy, but to the demand of my people. Hast thou so written?"

The **secretary** nodded.

" Write again, that upon this demand I ordered Alonzo Avila and Gonzalo Mexia to take account of all the treasure belonging to our master, the most Christian king ; with **leave to** the soldiers, when the total hath been perfected and the retreat made ready, to help themselves from the balance, as each one may wish. Those gentlemen will see that their task be concluded by noon to-morrow. Hast written, Duero ?"

" Word for word," answered the secretary.

" Very well. And now,"—Cortes raised his head and spoke loudly,—"and now, rest and sleep who can. This business is bad. Get ye gone !"

And when they were alone, he said to Olmedo,—

" I have done ill"—

" Nay," said the father, smiling, "thou hast done well."

"*Bastante*,—we shall see. Never had knaves such need of all **their** strength as when this retreat is begun ; yet of what account **will** they be when loaded down with the gold they cannot consent **to** leave behind ?"

" Why then the permission ?" **asked the** father.

Cortes smiled blandly.

" If I cannot make them friends, by my conscience ! I can **at** least seal their mouths in the day of my calamity."

Then bowing his head, he added,—

" Thy benediction, father."

The blessing was given.

" Amen !" said Cortes.

And the priest departed ; but the steps of the iron-hearted soldier were heard long after,—not quick and determined as usual, **but** slow and measured, and with many and long pauses between. So ambition walks when marshalling its resources ; so walks a heroic soul at war with itself and fortune ! He flung himself upon his couch at last, saying,—

" In my quiver there are two bolts **left. The** saints help me ! I will speed them first."

CHAPTER XIV.

THE KING BEFORE HIS PEOPLE AGAIN.

GUATAMOZIN'S call at the royal palace to see the king Cuitlahua had not been without result. When told that the monarch was too sick **of** the plague **to** be seen, he called for the officer who had charge of the accounts of tribute received for the royal support.

"Show me," said the 'tzin, "how much corn was delivered to Montezuma for Malinche."

A package of folded *aguave* leaves was brought and laid at the accountant's feet. In a moment he took out a leaf well covered with picture-writing and gave it to the 'tzin, who, after study, said to a cacique in waiting, "Bring me one of the couriers," and to another, "Bring me wherewith to write."

When the latter was brought, he sat down, and, dipping a brush into a vessel of liquid colour, drew upon a clear, yellow-tinted leaf a picture of a mother duck leading her brood from the shore into the water; by way of signature, he appended in one corner the figure of an owl in flight. On five other sheets he repeated the writing; then the missives were given each to a separate courier with verbal directions for their delivery.

When he left the palace, the 'tzin laid his hand upon Hualpa's shoulder, and said joyfully,—

"Better than I thought, O comrade. Malinche has corn for one day only!"

The blood quickened in Hualpa's heart, as he asked, "Then the end is near?"

"To-morrow, or the next day," said the 'tzin.

"But Montezuma is generous"—

"Can he give what he has not? To-night there will be delivered for his use and that of his household, whom I have had numbered for the purpose, provisions for one day, not more."

"Then it is so! Praised be the gods! and you, O my master, wiser than other men!" cried Hualpa with upraised face, and a gladness which was of youth again, and love so blind that he saw Nenetzin,—not the stars,—and so deaf that he heard not the other words of the 'tzin,—

"The couriers bear my orders to bring up all the armies. And they will be here in the morning."

.   .   .   .

. In the depth of the night, while Cortes lay restlessly dreaming, his sentinels on the palace were attracted by music apparently from every quarter; at first so mellowed by distance as to seem like the night singing to itself; afterwhile swollen into the familiar dissonant minstrelsy of conch and atabal, mixed with chanting of many voices.

"O ho!" shouted the outliers on the neighbouring houses, —"O ho, accursed strangers! Think no more of conquest,—not even of escape; think only of death by sacrifice! If you are

indeed *teules,* the night, though deepened by the smoke of our
burning houses, cannot hinder you from seeing the children of
Anahuac coming in answer to the call of Huitzil'. If you are
men, open wide your ears that you **may** hear their paddles on the
lake and their tramp on the causeway. O victims! one day
more, then—the sacrifice!"

Even the Christians, leaning **on** their lances and listening, felt
the heaviness of heart which is all of fear the brave can know,
and crossed themselves and repeated such paternosters as they
could recollect.

And so it was. The reserve armies which had been reposing
in the vales behind Chapultepec all marched to the city; and
the noise of their shouting, drumming, and trumpeting, when
they arrived and began to occupy its thoroughfares and strong
places, was like the roar of the sea.

To the garrison, under arms meantime, and suffering from the
influence of all they heard, the dawn was **a** long time coming;
but at last the sun came, and poured its full light over the
leaguered palace and courtly precincts.

But the foemen stood idly looking at each other; for in the
night Cortes, on his side, had made preparations for peace. Two
caciques went from him to the king Cuitlahua, proposing **a**
parley; and the king replied that he would come in the morning
and hear what he had to say. **So** there was truce as well as
sunshine.

"Tell me truly, Don Pedro,—as thou art a gentleman, tell **me,**
—didst thou ever see a sight like this?"

Whereupon Alvarado, who, with others, was leaning against
the parapet which formed part of the battlements of the eastern
gate of the palace, looked again, and critically, over that portion
of the square visible from his position, and replied, "I will
answer truly and lovingly, as if thou wert my little princess
yonder in the *patio.* Sight like this I never saw, and," he
added, with a quizzical smile, **"never care to see** again."

Orteguilla persisted,—

"Nay, didst thou ever see anything that surpassed it?"

Once more Alvarado surveyed the scene,—of men a myriad, in
the streets rank upon rank; so on the houses and temple,—
everywhere the glinting of arms and the brown faces of warriors
glistening above their glistening shields; everywhere *escaupiles*
of flaming red, and banners; everywhere the ineffable beauty
and splendour of royal war. The good captain withdrew his
enamoured gaze slowly.

"No, never!" he said.

Even he, the prince of gibes and strange oaths, forgot his tricks
in presence of the pageant.

While the foemen looked at each other so idly, up the beautiful street came heralds announcing Cuitlahua. Soon his palanquin, attended by a great retinue of nobles, was brought and set down in front of the eastern gate of the palace. Upon its appearance the people knelt and touched the ground with their palms. Then there was a blare of Christian trumpets, and Cortes, with Olmedo and Marina, came upon the turret.

The heralds waved their silver wands; the hush became absolute; then the curtains of the palanquin were rolled away, and the king turned his head languidly and looked up to Cortes, who raised his visor and looked down on him, and in the style of a conqueror demanded peace and quick return to obedience.

"If thou dost not," he said, "I will make thy city a ruin."

The shrill voice of Marina, interpreting, flew wide over the space, so peopled, yet so still; at the last word there was a mighty stir, but the heralds waved their wands, and the hush came back.

On Cuitlahua's face the pallor of sickness gave place to a flush of anger; he sat up, and signed to Guatamozin, and upon his shoulder laid his hand trustingly, saying,—

"My son, lend me your voice; answer."

The 'tzin, unmindful that the breath he drew upon his cheek was the breath of the plague, put his arm around the king, and said, so as to be heard to the temple's top,—

"The king Cuitlahua answers for himself and his people. Give ear, O Malinche! You have desolated our temples and broken the images of our gods; the smoke of our city offends the sky: your swords are terrible,—many have fallen before them, and many more will fall; yet we are content to exchange in death a thousand of ours for one of yours. Behold how many of us are left; then count your losses, and know that you cannot escape. Two suns shall not pass until, amidst our plenty, we shall laugh to see you sick from hunger. For further answer, O Malinche, as becomes the king of his people, Cuitlahua gives you the war-cry of his fathers."

The 'tzin withdrew his arm, and, snatching the green *panache* from the palanquin, whirled it overhead, crying, "Up, up, Tlateloco! Up, Tlateloco!"

At sight of the long feathers streaming over the group like a banner, the multitude sprang to foot, and with horrible clamour and a tempest of missiles drove the Christians from the turret.

And of the two bolts in Cortes' quiver, such was the speeding of the FIRST ONE!

.   .   .   .

An hour passed,—an hour of battle without and dispute within the palace.

To Cortes in his chamber then came Orteguilla, reporting.

"I gave the king the message, señor; and he bade me tell **thee** thy purpose is too late. He will not come."

The passion-vein[1] on Cortes' neck and forehead rose and **stood** out like a purple cord.

"The heathen dog!" he cried. "Will not! He is a slave, and shall come. By the holy blood of Christ, he shall come, or die!"

Then Olmedo spoke,—

"If thou wilt hear, señor, Montezuma affects me and the good Captain Oli tenderly; suffer us to go to him and see what **we** can do."

"So be it, so be it! If thou canst bring him, in God's name, **go!** If he refuse, then—I have sworn! Hearken to the hell's **roar** without! Let me have report quickly. I will wait thee **here.** Begone!"

Olmedo started. Cortes caught his sleeve and looked at him fixedly.

"*Mira!*" he **said** in a whisper. "As thou lovest me do this work well. If he fail—if he fail"—

"Well?" said Olmedo in the same tone.

"Then—then get thee to prayers! Go."

The audience chamber whither Oli and the priest betook themselves, with Orteguilla to interpret, was crowded with courtiers, who made way for them to the dais upon which Montezuma sat. They kissed his hand, and, declining the invitation to be seated, began their mission.

"Good king," said the father, "we bring thee a message from Malinche; and as its object is to stay the bloody battle which is so grievous to us all, and the slaughter which must otherwise go on, **we** pray thy pardon if we make haste to speak."

The monarch's face chilled, and, drawing **his** mantle close, he said coldly,—

"I am listening."

Olmedo proceeded,—

"The Señor Hernan commiserates the hard lot which compels thee to listen here to the struggle which hath lasted so many days, and always with the same result,—the wasting of thy people. The contest hath become a rebellion against thee as well as against his sovereign and thine. Finally there will be no one left to govern,—nothing, indeed, but an empty valley and a naked lake. In pity for the multitude, he is disposed **to** help save them

[1] Bernal Diaz, *Hist. de la Conq.*

from their false leaders. He hath sent us, therefore, to **ask** thee to join him in one **more effort to that** end."

"Said he how I could help **him?**" **asked the** king.

"Come and speak to the people, and disperse them, as once before thou didst. And to strengthen thy **words,** and as his part of the trial, he saith thou mayest pledge him **to leave** the city as **soon as the** way is open. Only let there be **no delay.** He is in **waiting to** go with thee, good king."

The **monarch** listened intently.

"**Too late—too late!**" he cried. "The ears of my people are turned **from me. I am king in** name and form only; the power is another's. **I am lost,—so is** Malinche. I will not go. Tell him so."

There was a stir in the chamber, and a groan from the bystanders; but the messengers remained looking at **the** poor king, as at one who had rashly taken a fatal vow.

"Why **do** you stay?" he continued with a glowing face. "What more **have I to** do with Malinche? **See** the state **to** which my serving him has already reduced me."

"**Remember** thy people!" said Olmedo solemnly.

Flashed the monarch's eyes as he answered,—

"**My brave people!** I hear them now. They are in arms to **save themselves; and** they will not believe me or the promises of Malinche. I have spoken."

Then Oli moved a step towards the dais, and, kissing the royal hand, said with suffused eyes,—

"Thou knowest **I love** thee, O king; and I say, *if thou carest for thyself,* go."

Something **there was in the** words, in the utterance, probably, **that** drew the **monarch's** attention: leaning forward, he studied the cavalier curiously; over his face the while came the look **of a** man suddenly called by his fate. His lips parted, his eyes fixed; **and** but that battle has voices which only the dead may **refuse to hear, his** spirit would have drifted off into unseemly **reverie. Recalling** himself with an effort, he arose, and said, half smiling,—

"**A** man, much **less** a king, is unfit **to** live when **his friends** think **to move him** from his resolve by appeals to his fears." And, rising and drawing himself to his full stature, he added, so **as to** be heard throughout the chamber, "Very soon, if not now, you will understand me when **I** say I do not care for myself. I desire to die. Go, my friends, and tell Malinche that **I** will do as **he asks, and** straightway."

Oli and Olmedo kissed **his** hands and withdrew; whereupon he **calmly** gave his orders.

Very soon the 'tzin, who was directing **the battle from a** point

near the gate of the *coatapantli*, saw a warrior appear on the
turret so lately occupied by Cortes, and wave a royal *panache*.
He raised his shield overhead at once, and held it there until on
his side the combat ceased. The Christians, glad of a breathing
spell, quit almost as soon. All eyes then turned to the turret ;
even the combatants who had been fighting hand to hand across
the crest of the parapet ventured to look that way, when, according to the usage of the infidel court, the heralds came, and to the
four quarters of the earth waved their silver wands.

Too well the 'tzin divined the meaning of the ceremony. "Peace,"
he seemed to hear, and then, "Lover of Anahuac, servant of the
gods,—choose now between king and country. Now or never!"
The ecstasy of battle fled from him ; his will became infirm as a
child's. In the space between him and **the** turret the smoke **of**
the guns curled and writhed sensuously, each moment growing
fainter and weaker, as did the great purpose to which he thought
he had steeled himself. When he brought the shield down, his
face was that of a man whom long sickness had laid close to the
gates of death. Then came the image of Tula, and then the royal
permission **to** do what the gods enjoined,—nay, more than permission, a charge which left the deed to his hand, that there
might be no lingering amongst the strangers. "O sweetheart,"
he said to himself, "if this duty leave me stainless, whom may I
thank but you?"

Then he spoke to Hualpa, though with a choking voice,—

"The king is coming. I must go and meet him. Get **my**
bow, and stand by me with an arrow in place for instant use."

Hualpa moved away slowly, watching the 'tzin ; then he returned, and asked, in a manner as full of meaning as the words
themselves,—

"Is there not great need that the arrow should be very true?"

The master's eyes met his as he answered, "Yes ; be careful."

Yet the hunter stayed.

"O 'tzin," he said, "his **blood is not in** my **veins.** He is only
my benefactor. Your days are not numbered, like mine, and as
yet you are blameless ; for the sake of the peace that makes life
sweet, I pray you let my hand do this service."

And the 'tzin took his hand, and replied fervently,—

"There is nothing so precious as the sight that is quick to see
the sorrows of others, unless it be the heart that hurries to help
them. After this, I may never doubt your love ; but the duty is
mine,—made so by the gods,—and he has asked it of me. Lo,
the heralds appear!"

"He has asked it of you! that is enough;" **and Hualpa stayed**
no longer.

Upon **the** turret the carpet was spread and the canopy set up, and forth came a throng of cavaliers and infidel lords, the latter splendidly bedight ; then appeared Montezuma and Cortes.

As the king moved forward, a cry, blent of all feelings—love, fear, admiration, hate, reverence—burst from the great audience ; after which only Guatamozin and Hualpa, in front of the gate, were left standing.

And such splendour flashed from the monarch's person, from his sandals of gold, tunic of feathers, *tilmatli* of white, and *copilli*[1] inestimably jewelled ; from his face and mien issued such majesty that, after the stormy salutation, the multitude became of the place a part, motionless as the stones, the dead not more silent.

With his hands crossed upon his breast he stood awhile, seeing and being seen, and all things waited for him to speak ; even the air seemed waiting, it was so very hushed. He looked to the sky, flecked with unhallowed smoke ; to the sun, whose heaven, just behind the curtain of brightness, was nearer to him than ever before ; to the temple, place of many a royal ceremony, his own coronation the grandest of all ; to the city, beautiful in its despoilment ; to the people, for whom, though they knew it not, he had come to die. At last his gaze settled upon Guatamozin, and as their eyes met, he smiled ; then shaking the *tilmatli* from his shoulder, he raised his head and said, in a voice from which all weakness was gone, his manner never so kingly,—

" I know, O my people, that you took up arms to set me free, and that was right ; but how often since then have I told you that I am not a prisoner ; that the strangers are my guests ; that I am free to leave them when I please, and that I live with them because I love them ? "

As in a calm a wind sometimes blows down and breaks the placid surface of a lake into countless ripples, driving them hither and thither in sparkling confusion, these words fell upon the listening mass ; a yell of anger rose, and from the temple descended bitter reproaches.

Yet the 'tzin was steady ; and when the outcry ended, the king went on,—

" I am told your excuse now is, that you want to drive my friends from the city. My children, here stands Malinche himself. He hears me say for him that, if you will open the way, he and all with him will leave of their own will."

Again the people broke out in revilements, but the monarch waved his hand angrily, and said,—

" As I am yet your king, I bid you lay down your arms "—

Then the 'tzin took the ready bow from Hualpa ; full to the ear he drew the arrow. Steady the arm, strong the hand,—an

[1] The crown.

THE FAIR GOD. 381

instant, and the deed was done! In the purple shadow of the canopy, amidst his pomp of royalty, Montezuma fell down, covered, when too late, by a score of Christian shields. Around him at the same time fell a shower of stones from the temple.

Then, with a shout of terror, the companies arose as at a **word** and fled, and, panic-blind, tossed the 'tzin here and there, and finally left him alone in the square with Hualpa.

"All is lost!" said the latter disconsolately.

"Lost!" said the 'tzin. "On the temple yonder lies Malinche's last hope. No need now to assail the palace. When the king comes out, hunger will go in and fight for us."

"But the people,—where are they?"

The 'tzin raised his hand and pointed to the palace.

"So the strangers have asked. See!"

Hualpa turned, and saw the gate open and the cavaliers begin to ride forth.

"Go they this way, or yon," continued the 'tzin, "they will **find** the same answer. Five armies hold the city; a sixth keeps the lake."

Down the beautiful street the Christians rode unchallenged until they came to the first canal. While restoring the bridge there, they heard the clamour of an army, and lo! out of the gardens, houses, and temples, far as the vision reached, the infidels poured and blocked the way.

Then the cavaliers rode back, and took the way to Tlacopan. There, too, the first canal was bridgeless; and as they stood looking across the chasm, they heard the same clamour and beheld the same martial apparition.

Once more they rode, this time up the street toward the northern dyke, and with the same result.

"*Ola*, father!" said Cortes, returned to the palace; "we may not stay here after to-morrow."

"Amen!" cried Olmedo.

"Look thou to the sick and **wounded ; such** as can march or move, get them ready."

"And the others?" asked the good man.

"Do for them what thou dost for the dying. Shrieve them!"

So saying, the Christian leader sank on his seat, and gave himself to sombre thought.

He had sped his *second and*—LAST BOLT!

The rest of the day was spent in preparation for retreat.

CHAPTER XV.

THE DEATH OF MONTEZUMA.

Again Martin Lopez had long conference with Cortes; after which, with his assistant carpenters, he went to work, and until evening time the echoes of the courtyard danced to the sounds of saw and hammer.

And while they worked, to Cortes came Avila and Mexia.

"What thou didst entrust to us, señor, we have done. Here is a full account of all the treasure, our royal master's included."

Cortes read the statement, then called his chamberlain, Christobal de Guzman.

"Go thou, Don Christobal, and bring what is here reported into one chamber, where it may be seen of all. And send hither the royal secretaries, and Pedro Hernandez, my own clerk."

The secretaries came.

"Now, Señores Avila and Mexia, follow my chamberlain, and in his presence and that of these gentlemen take from the treasure the portion belonging to his Majesty the Emperor. Of our wounded horses, then choose ye eight, and of the Tlascalans, eighty, and load them with the royal dividend, and what more they can carry; and have them always ready to go. And as leaving anything of value where the infidels may be profited is sinful, I direct,—and of this let all bear witness, Hernandez for me, and the secretaries for his Majesty,—I direct, I say, that ye set the remainder apart accessible to the soldiers, with leave to each one of them to take therefrom as much as he may wish. Make note, further, that what is possible to save all this treasure hath been done. Write it, good gentlemen, write it; for if any one thinketh differently, let him say what more I can do. I am waiting to hear. Speak!"

No one spoke.

And while the division of the large plunder went on, and afterwards the men scrambled for the remainder, Montezuma was dying.

In the night a messenger sought Cortes.

"Señor," he said, "the king hath something to ask of you. He will not die comforted without seeing you."

"Die, sayest thou?" and Cortes arose hastily. "I had word that his hurts were not deadly."

"If he die, señor, it will be by his own hand. The stones

wrought him but bruises ; and if he would let the bandages alone the arrow-cut would shortly stop bleeding."

"Yes, yes," said Cortes. "Thou wouldst tell **me that** this barbarian, merely from being long a king, hath a spirit of **such** exceeding fineness that, though the arrow had not cut him deeper than thy dull rowel marketh thy horse's flank, yet would he die. Where is he now?"

"In the audience chamber."

"*Bastante!* I will see him. Tell him so."

Cortes stood fast, **thinking.**

"This man hath **been** useful **to** me ; may not some profit be eked out of him dead? So many saw him get his wounds, and so many will see him die of them, that the manner of his taking off may not be denied. What if I send his body out and indict his murderers? If I could take from them the popular faith even, then—— By my conscience, I will try the trick!"

And taking his sword and plumed hat and tossing a cloak over his shoulder, he sought the audience chamber.

There was no guard at the **door.** The little bells, as he threw aside the curtains, greeted him accusingly. Within all was shadow, except where a flickering lamplight played over and around the dais ; nevertheless he saw the floor covered with people, some prostrate, others on their knees or crouching face down ; and the grim speculator thought, as he passed slowly **on,** "Verily, this king must also have been **a** good man **and a** generous."

The couch of the dying monarch was on the dais in the accustomed place of the throne. At one side stood the ancients ; at the other his queens knelt, weeping. Nenetzin hid her face in his hand, and sobbed as if her heart were breaking ; she had been forgiven. Now and then Maxtla bent over him to cleanse his face of the flowing blood. A group of cavaliers were off a little way, silent witnesses ; and as Cortes drew near, Olmedo, who had been in prayer, extended toward the sufferer the ivory cross worn usually at his girdle.

"O king," said the good man imploringly, "thou hast yet a moment of life, which, I pray thee, waste not. Take this holy symbol upon thy breast, cross thy hands upon it, and say after me : I believe in one God, the Father Almighty, in our Lord Jesus Christ, the only begotten Son of God, and in the Holy Ghost, the Lord and Giver of Life. Then pray thou : O God the Father of Heaven, O God the Son, Redeemer of **the** World, O God the Holy Ghost, O Holy Trinity, One God, **have** mercy upon my soul! Do these things, say these **words, O** king, and thou shalt live after thy bones have gone to **dust.** Thou shalt live for **ever,** eternally happy."

Courtiers and cavaliers, the queens, Nenetzin, even Cortes, watched the monarch's waning face; never yet were people indifferent to the issue — the old, old issue — of true god against false. Marina finished the interpretation; then he raised his hand tremulously and put the holy sign away, saying,—

"I have but a moment to live, and will not desert the faith of my fathers now."

A great sigh of relief broke from the infidels; the Christians shuddered and crossed themselves; then Cortes stepped to Olmedo's side.

"I received your message, and am here," said he sternly. He had seen the cross rejected.

The king turned his pale face and fixed his glazing eyes upon the conqueror; and such power was there in the look that the latter added, with softening manner, "What I can do for thee I will do. I have always been thy true friend."

"O Malinche, I hear you, and your words make dying easy," answered Montezuma, smiling faintly.

With an effort he sought Cortes' hand, and, looking at Acatlan and Tecalco, continued,—

"Let me entrust these women and their children to you and your lord. Of all that which was mine, but now is yours,— lands, people, empire,—enough to save them from want and shame were small indeed. Promise me; in the hearing of all these, promise, Malinche."

Taint of anger was there no longer on the soul of the great Spaniard.

"Rest thee, good king!" he said with feeling. "Thy queens and their children shall be my wards. In the hearing of all these, I so swear."

The listener smiled again; his eyes closed, his hand fell down; and so still was he that they began to think him dead. Suddenly he stirred, and said faintly, but distinctly,—

"Nearer, uncles, nearer."

The old men bent over him, listening.

"A message to Guatamozin,—to whom I give my last thought as king. Say to him that this lingering in death is no fault of his; the aim was true, but the arrow splintered upon leaving the bow. And, lest the world hold him to account for my blood, hear me say, all of you, that I bade him do what he did. And in sign that I love him, take my sceptre and give it to him"—

The voice fell away, yet the lips moved; lower the ancients stooped,—

"Tula and the Empire go with the sceptre," he murmured, and they were his last words,—his will.

A wail from the women proclaimed **him** dead.

The unassoilzied great may not see heaven; they pass **from** life into history, where, as in a silent sky, they shine for ever and ever. **So** the light of the Indian king comes to us, a glow rather than a brilliance; for of all fates his was the saddest. Better not to be than to become the ornament of another's triumph. Alas for him whose death is an immortal sorrow!

Out of the palace-gate in the early morning passed the lords of the court in procession, carrying the remains of the monarch. The bier was heavy with royal insignia; nothing of funeral circumstance was omitted; honour to the dead was policy. At the same time the body was delivered, Cortes indicted the murderers; the ancients through whom he spoke were also the bearers of the dead king's last will. Back to the bold Spaniard, therefore, came the reply,—

"Cowards, who at the last **moment beg for peace! you are not two suns away** from **your own graves! Think only of them!**"

And while Cortes was listening to the answer, the streets about the palace filled with companies, and crumbling parapet and solid wall shook under the shock of a new assault.

Then Cortes' spirit arose.

"Mount, gentlemen!" he cried. "The hounds come scrambling for the scourge; shame on us if we do not meet them! And hearken! The prisoners report a plague in the city, of which the new king is dying, and hundreds are sick. It is the small-pox."

"*Viva la viruela!*" shouted Alvarado.

The shout spread through the palace.

"Where God's curse is," continued Cortes, "Christians need not stay. To-night we will go. To clear the way **and** make this day memorable let us ride. Are ye ready?"

They answered joyously.

Again the gates were opened, and, with **a** goodly following **of** infantry, into the street they rode. Nothing withstood them; they passed the canals by repairing the bridges or filling up the chasms; they rode the whole length of the street until the causeway clear to Tlacopan was visible. St. James fought at their head; even the Holy Mother stooped from her high **place** and threw handfuls of dust in the enemy's eyes.

In the heat of the struggle suddenly the companies **fell** back and made open space around the Christians; then came word that commissioners from king Cuitlahua waited in the palace to treat **of peace.**

"The heathen is an animal!" said Cortes, unable to repress his exultation. "To cure him of temper and win his love, there is nothing like the scourge. Let us ride back, gentlemen."

In the courtyard stood four caciques, stately men in peaceful garb. They touched the pavement with their palms.

"We are come to say, O Malinche, that the lord Cuitlahua, our king, yields to your demand for peace. He prays you to give your terms to the pabas whom you captured on the temple, that they may bring them to him forthwith."

The holy men were brought from their cells, one leaning upon the other. The instructions were given; then the two, with the stately commissioners, were set without the gate, and Cortes and his army went to rest, never so contented.

They waited and waited; but the envoys came not. When the sun went down, they knew themselves deceived; and then there were sworn many full, round, Christian oaths—none so full, so round, and so Christian as Cortes'.

A canoe, meantime, bore Io' to Tula. In the quiet and perfumed shade of the *chinampa* he rested, and soothed the fever of his wound.

Meanwhile also a courier from the *teotuctli* passed from temple to temple; short the message, but portentous,—

"Blessed be Huitzil', and all the gods of our fathers! And, as he at last saved his people, blessed be the memory of Montezuma! Purify the altars, and make ready for the sacrifice, for to-morrow there will be victims!"

CHAPTER XVI.

ADIEU TO THE PALACE.

At sunset a cold wind blew from the north, followed by a cloud which soon filled the valley with mist; soon the mist turned to rain; then the rain turned to night, and the night to deepest darkness.

The Christians, thinking only of escape from the city, saw the change of weather with sinking hearts. With one voice they had chosen the night as most favourable for the movement, but they had in mind then a semi-darkness warmed by south winds and brilliant with stars; not a time like this so unexpectedly come upon them,—tempest added to gloom, icy wind splashing the earth with icy water.

Under the walls the sentinels cowered shivering and listening, and, as is the habit of wanderers surrounded by discomforts and miseries, musing of their homes so far away and of the path thither; on the land so beset, on the sea so viewless. Recalled to present duty, they saw nothing but the fires of the nearest temple faintly iridescent, and heard only the moans of the blast and the pattering of the rain, always so in harmony with the spirit when it is oppressed by loneliness and danger.

Meantime the final preparation for retreat went on with the completeness of discipline.

About the close of the second watch of the night, Cortes, with his personal attendants,—page, equerry, and secretaries,—left his chamber and proceeded to the eastern gate, where he could best receive reports, and assure himself, as the divisions filed past him, that the column was formed as he had ordered. The super-structure of the gate offered him shelter; but he stood out, bridle in hand, his back to the storm. There he waited, grimly silent, absorbed in reflections gloomy as the night itself.

Everything incident to the preparation which required light had been done before the day expired; outside the house, therefore, there was not a spark to betray the movement to the enemy; in fact, nothing to betray it except the beat of horses' hoofs and the rumble of gun-carriages, and they were nigh drowned by the tempest. If the saints would but help him clear of the streets of the city, would help him to the causeway even, without bringing the infidels upon him, sword and lance would win the rest: so the leader prayed and trusted the while he waited.

"My son, is it thou?" asked a man close at his side.

He turned quickly, and replied, "Father Bartolomé! Welcome! What dost thou bring?"

"Report of the sick and wounded."

"I remember, I remember! Of all this bad business, by my conscience! no part so troubled me as to say what should be done with them. At the last moment thou wert good enough to take the task upon thyself. Speak! what did thy judgment dictate? What did thy conscience permit?"

The good man arranged his hood, the better to shield his face from the rain, and answered,—

"Of the Christians, all who are able will take their places in the line; the very sick will be borne by Tlascalans; the litters are ready for them."

"Very well," said Cortes.

"The Tlascalans"—

"*Cierto*, there the trouble began!" and Cortes laid his hand heavily on the priest's shoulder. "Three hundred and more of them too weak to rise from the straw, which yet hath not kept their bones from bruising the stony floor! Good heart, what didst thou with them?"

"They are dead."

"Mother of God! Didst thou kill them?" Cortes gripped the shoulder until Olmedo groaned,—"didst thou kill them?"

The father shook himself loose, saying, "There is no blood on my hands. The Holy Mother came to my help; and this was the way. Remembrance of the love of Christ forbade the leaving one Christian behind; but the heathen born had no such appeal; they must be left,—necessity said so. I could not kill them. By priestly office, I could prepare them for death; and so I went from man to man with holy formula and sacramental wafer. The caciques were with me the while, and when I had concluded they spoke some words to the sufferers: then I saw what never Christian saw before. Hardly wilt thou believe me, but, señor, I beheld the poor wretches, with smiles, bare their breasts, and the chiefs begin and thrust their javelins into the hearts of all there lying."

An exclamation of horror burst from Cortes.

"'Twas murder, murder! What didst thou?"

Olmedo replied quickly, "Trust me, my son, I rushed in and stayed the work until the victims themselves prayed the chiefs to go on. Not even then did I give over my efforts,—not until they made me understand the purpose of the butchery."

"And that? Haste thee, father. What thou tellest will stagger Christendom!"

Again Cortes caught the priest's shoulder.

"Nay," said the latter, shrinking back, "thy hand is hard enough without its glove of steel."

"Pardon, father; but"—

"In good time, my son, in good time! What, but for thy impatience, I would have said ere this is, that the object was to save the honour of the tribe, and, by killing the unfortunates, rescue them from the gods of their enemy. Accordingly, the bands who are first to enter the palace to-night or to-morrow will find treasure,—much treasure, as thou knowest,—but not one victim."

The father spoke solemnly, for in the circumstance there was a strain of pious exaltation that found an echo in his own devoted nature; greatly was he shocked to hear Cortes laugh.

"*Valgame Dios!*" he cried, crossing himself; "the man blasphemes!"

"Blasphemes, saidst thou?" and Cortes checked himself. "May the saints forget me for ever if I laughed at the tragedy thou wert telling! I laughed at thy simplicity, father."

" Is this a time for jesting?" asked Olmedo.

"Good father," said Cortes gravely, "the bands **that take** the palace to-night or to-morrow will find no treasure,—not enough to buy a Christmas ribbon for a country girl. Look now. I went to the treasure-room a little while before coming here, and there I found the varlets of Narvaez loading themselves with bars of silver and gold; they had sacks and pouches belted to their waists and shoulders, and were filling them to bursting. Possibly some gold-dust spilled on the floor may remain for those who succeed **us**; but nothing more. Pray thou, good priest, good friend, pray thou that the treasure be not found in the road we travel to-night."

A body of men crossing the courtyard attracted Cortes; then four horsemen approached, and stopped before him.

" Is **it** thou, Sandoval?" he asked.

" Yes, señor."

" And Ordas, Lugo, and Tapia?"

" Here," they replied.

" And thy following, Sandoval?"

" The cavaliers of Narvaez whom thou gavest me, one hundred chosen soldiers, and the Tlascalans to the number thou didst order."

"*Bien!* Lead out of the gate, and halt after **making what** thou deemest room for the other divisions. Christ **and St. James** go with thee!"

" Amen!" responded Olmedo.

And so the vanguard passed him,—a **long** succession **of** shadowy files that he heard rather than **saw.** Hardly **were** they gone when another body approached, **led by an** officer on foot.

" Who **art** thou?" asked Cortes.

" Magarino," the man replied.

" Whom have you?"

" One hundred and fifty Christians, and **four** hundred Tlascalans."

" And **the** bridge?"

" We have it here."

" As thou lovest life and honour, captain, heed **well thine** orders. Move on, and join thyself to Sandoval."

The bridge spoken of was a portable platform of hewn plank bolted **to** a frame of stout timbers, designed to pass the column over the three canals intersecting the causeway to Tlacopan, which in the sally of the afternoon had been found to be bridgeless. If the canals were deep as had been reported, well might Magarino be charged with particular care!

In the order of march next came the centre **or** main body,

Cortes' immediate command. The baggage was in their charge, also the greater part of the **artillery**, making of itself a long train, and one of vast interest ; for, though in the midst of a confession of failure, the leader did not abate his **intention** of conquest,— such was a peculiarity of his genius.

"Mexia, Avila, good gentlemen," he said, halting the royal treasurers, "let me assure myself of what beyond peradventure ye are assured."

And he counted the horses and men bearing away the golden dividend of the Emperor, knowing if what they had in keeping were safely lodged in **the royal** depositories, there was nothing which might not be condoned,—not usurpation, defeat even. Most literally, they bore his fortune.

A moment after there came upon **him a** procession of motley **composition** : disabled Christians ; servants, mostly females, carrying **the** trifles they most affected,—here **a** bundle of wearing apparel, **there a** cage **with** a bird ; prisoners, amongst others the **prince Cacama**, heart-broken by his misfortunes ; women of importance and **rank**, comfortably housed in curtained palanquins. **So** went Marina, her slaves side by side with **those** of Nenetzin, in whose mind the fears, sorrows, and **emotions of** the thousands setting out in the march had no place, for Alvarado had wrapped her in his cloak, and lifted her into the carriage, and left a kiss on her lips, with a promise of oversight and protection.

As if to make good **the** promise, almost on the heels of her slaves rode the deft cavalier, blithe of spirit because of the happy chance which made the place of the lover that of duty also. Behind him, well apportioned of Christians and Tlascalans, and **much the** largest of the divisions, moved the rearguard, of which **he and Leon were chiefs.** His bay mare, Bradamante, however, **seemed** not to **share his** gaiety, but tossed her head, and champed the bit, and frequently shied as **if** scared.

"Have done, **my** pretty girl !" he said to her. "Frightened, art thou ? 'Tis **only** the wind, ugly **enough**, I trow, but nothing worse. **Or art thou** jealous ? *Verguenza !* To-morrow she shall find thee **in the** green pasture, and kiss thee as I will her."

"*Ola*, captain !" said Cortes, approaching him. "To **whom** speakest thou ?"

"To my mistress, **Bradamante**, señor," he **replied**, checking the rein impatiently. "Sometimes she hath **airs** prettier, as thou knowest, than the prettinesses of **a** woman ; but now — So ho, girl !—now she—Have done, I say !—**now** she hath a **devil**. And where she got it I know not, unless from the knave **Botello**."[1]

---

[1] A reputed soothsayer.

"What of **him**? Where is he?" asked Cortes with sudden interest.

"Back with Leon, talking, as is his wont, about certain subtleties, nameless by good Christians, but which he nevertheless calleth prophecies."

"What saith the man now?"

"Out of the mass of his follies, I remember three: that thou, señor, from extreme misfortune shalt at last attain great honour; that to-night hundreds of **us** will be lost,—which last I can forgive in him, if only his third prediction come **true.**"

"And that?"

"Nay, señor, except as serving to **show** that the rogue hath **in** him a savour of uncommon fairness, **it** is the least important **of** all; he saith he himself will be amongst the lost."

Then Cortes laughed, saying, "Wilt thou never be done with thy quips? Lead on. I will wait here **a** little longer."

Alvarado vanished, being **in** haste to recover his place behind Nenetzin. Before Cortes, then, with the echoless tread of panthers **in** the glade, hurried the long array of Tlascalans; after them the cross-bowmen and arquebusiers, their implements clashing against their heavy armour; yet he stood silent, pondering the words of Botello. Not until, with wheels grinding and shaking the pavement, the guns reached him did he wake from his thinking.

"Ho, Mesa, well met!" he said to the veteran, whom he distinguished amid a troop of slaves dragging the first piece. "This is not a night like those in Italy where thou didst learn the cunning of thy craft; yet there might be worse for us."

"*Mira*, señor!" and Mesa went to him, and said in a low voice, "What thou saidst was cheerily spoken, that I might borrow encouragement; and I thank thee, for I have much need of all the comfort thou hast to give. A poor return have I, señor. If the infidels attack us, rely not upon the **guns,** not even mine: if the wind did not whisk the priming away, **the** rain would drown it,—and then,"—his voice sank to a whisper,—"*our matches will not burn!*"

At that moment a gust dashed Cortes with water, and for the first time he was chilled,—chilled until his teeth chattered; for simultaneously a presentiment of calamity touched him with what, in a man less brave, would have been fear. He saw how, without the guns, Botello's **second** prediction was possible! Nevertheless he replied,—

"The saints can help their own in the dark **as** well as in the light. Do thy best. To-morrow thou shalt **be** captain."

Then Cortes mounted his horse, and took his shield, and to his wrist chained his battle-axe: still he waited. A company of horsemen brushed past him, followed by **a** solitary rider.

"Leon!" said Cortes.

The cavalier stopped, and replied,—

"What wouldest thou, señor?"

"Are the guards withdrawn?"

"All of them."

"And the sentinels?"

"I have been to every post; not a man is left."

Cortes spoke to his attendants, and they, too, rode off; when they were gone, he said to Leon,—

"Now we may go."

And, with that, together they passed out into the street. Cortes turned and looked towards the palace, now deserted; but the night seemed to have snatched the pile away, and in its place left a blackened void. Fugitive as he was, riding he knew not to what end, he settled in his saddle again with a sigh—not for the old house itself, nor for the comfort of its roof, nor for the refuge in time of danger; not for the Christian dead reposing in its gardens, their valour wasted and their graves abandoned, nor for that other victim there sacrificed in his cause, whose weaknesses might not be separated from a thousand services and a royalty superbly Eastern: these were things to wake the emotions of youths and maidens, young in the world, and of poets, dreamy and simple-minded. He sighed for the power he had there enjoyed,—the weeks and months when his word was law for an empire of shadowy vastness, and he was master, in fact, of a king of kings,— immeasurable power now lost, apparently for ever.

CHAPTER XVII.

THE PURSUIT BEGINS.

In the afternoon the king Cuitlahua, whose sickness had greatly increased, caused himself to be taken to Chapultepec, where he judged he would be safer from the enemy and better situated for treatment by his doctors and nurses. Before leaving, however, he appointed a deputation of ancients, and sent them, with his signet and a message, to Guatamozin.

The 'tzin, about the same time, changed his quarters from the *teocallis*, now but a bare pavement high in air, to the old Cû of Quetzal'. That the strangers must shortly attempt to leave the city he **knew** ; so, giving up the assault on the palace, he took measures to destroy them, if possible, while in retreat. The road they would move by was the only point in the connection about which he was undecided. Anyhow, they must seek the land by one of the causeways. Those by Tlacopan and Tepejaca were the shortest ; therefore he believed one or the other of them would **be** selected. Upon that theory, he accommodated all his preparations to an attack from the lake, while the foe were outstretched on the narrow dyke. As sufficient obstructions in their front, he relied upon the bridgeless canals ; their rear he would himself assail with a force chosen from the matchless children of the capital, whose native valour was terribly inflamed by the ruin and suffering they had seen and endured. The old Cû was well located **for** his part of the operation ; and there, in the sanctuary, surrounded by a throng of armed caciques and lords, the deputies of the king Cuitlahua found him.

If the shade of Mualox lingered about the altar of the peaceful god, no doubt it thrilled to see the profanation of the holy place ; if it sought refuge in the cells below, alas ! they were filled by an army in concealment ; and if it went farther, down to what the paba, in his poetic madness, had lovingly called his World, alas again ! the birds were dead, the shrubs withered, the angel gone ; only the fountain lived, of Darkness a sweet voice singing in the ear of Silence.

So the 'tzin being found, this was the message delivered **to** him from the king Cuitlahua :—

"May the gods love you as I do ! I am sick with the sickness **of** the strangers. Come not near me, lest you be taken also. I go to Chapultepec to get ready for death. If I die, the Empire **is** yours. Meantime, I give you all power."

Guatamozin took the signet, and was once more master, if not king, in the city of his fathers. The deputies kissed his hand ; the chiefs saluted him ; and when the tidings reached the companies below, the cells rang **as** never before, **not even** with the hymns of their first tenants.

While yet the incense of the ovation sweetened the air about him, he looked up at the image of the god,—web of spider on its golden sceptre, dust on its painted shield, dust bending its plumes of fire ; he looked up into the face, yet fair and benignant, and back to him rushed the speech of Mualox, clear as if freshly spoken : "Anahuac, the beautiful,—her existence, and the glory and power that make it a thing of worth, are linked to your action. O 'tzin, your fate and hers, and that of the many nations, is one and the same !" and the beating of his pulse quickened thrice ; for now he could see that the words were prophetic of his country saved by him.

Then up the broad steps of the Cû, into the sanctuary and through the crowd, rushed Hualpa ; **the rain** streamed from his quilted armour ; and upon the floor in front of the 'tzin, with **a** noise like the fall of a heavy hammer, **he** dropped the butt of a lance to which was affixed a Christian sword-blade.

"At last, at last, O 'tzin !" he said ; "the **strangers are in the** street, marching toward Tlacopan."

The company hushed their very breathing.

"All of them ?" asked the 'tzin.

"All but the dead."

Then on the 'tzin's **lip a smile,** in his eyes a flash **as of** flame.

"Hear **you, friends ?"** he said. "**The time** of vengeance has **come. You know your places and duty.** Go, each one. May the **gods go with you !"**

In a moment he and Hualpa were **alone.** The latter bent his head, and, crossing his hands upon his breast, said,—

"When the burden of my griefs has been greatest, and I cried out continually, O 'tzin, you have held me back, promising that my time would come. I doubt not your **better** judgment, but—but I **have** no more patience. My enemy is abroad, and she whom I cannot forget goes with him. Is not the time come ?"

Guatamozin laid his hand on Hualpa's.

"Be glad, O comrade ! The time has come ; and, as you have prepared for it like a warrior, go now and get the revenge so long delayed. I give **you more** than permission,—I give you my prayers. Where are the people who are to go with you ?"

"In the canoes, waiting."

They were silent awhile. Then **the 'tzin** took **the lance and** looked **at the long,** straight blade admiringly ; **under its blue** gleam lay the **secret** of its composition, by which the few were able to mock the many, and ravage the capital and country.

"**Dread nothing ;** it will conquer," he said, handing the weapon back.

Hualpa kissed his hand and replied, "**I** thought to make return for your preferments, O 'tzin, by serving you well when you were king ; but the service need not be put off so long. I thank the gods for this night's opportunity. If I come not with the rising of the sun to-morrow, Nenetzin can tell you my story. Farewell !"

With his face to his benefactor, he moved away.

"Have a care for yourself !" said the 'tzin, regarding him earnestly. "And remember there must be no sign of attack until **the** strangers have advanced to the first causeway. I will look for you to-morrow. Farewell !"

While yet the 'tzin's thoughts went out compassionately after his unhappy friend, up from **their** irksome hiding in the cells

came the companies he **was** to lead,—a long army in white tunics
of quilted cotton. At their head, the uniform covering a Christian cuirass, and with Christian helm and battle-axe, he marched;
and so, through the darkness and the storm, the pursuit began.

CHAPTER XVIII.

LA NOCHE TRISTE.

THE movement **of** the fugitive army **was** necessarily slow.
Stretched out in **the** street, it formed a column of irregular front
and great depth. A considerable portion was of non-combatants,
such as the sick and wounded, the servants, women, and prisoners;
to whom might be added the Indians carrying the baggage and
ammunition, and laboriously dragging the guns. The darkness,
and the rain beaten into the faces of the sufferers by the wind,
made the keeping order impossible; at each step the intervals
between individuals and between the divisions grew wider and
wider. After crossing two or three of the bridges, a general **con-**
fusion began to prevail; the officers, in dread of the enemy, **failed**
to call out, and the soldiers, bending low to protect their faces,
and hugging their arms or their treasure, marched in dogged
silence, indifferent to all but themselves. Soon what was **at** first
a fair column in close order became an irregular procession; here
a crowd of all the arms mixed, there a thin line of stragglers.

It is a simple thing, I know, yet nothing has **so** much to do
with what we habitually call our spirits **as the** condition in
which we are at the time. Under an open **sky**, with the breath
of a glowing morning in our nostrils, **we** sing, laugh, and **are**
brave; but let the cloud hide the blue expanse and cover **our**
walk with shadow, and we shrink within ourselves; **or worse,**
let the walk be in the night, through a strange place, with rain
and cold added, and straightway the fine thing we call courage
merges itself into a sense of duty, or sinks into humbler concern
for comfort and safety. So, not a man in all the column—not
a cavalier, not a slave—but felt himself oppressed by the circumstances of the situation; those who only that afternoon had
charged like lions along that very street now yielded to the in-
definable effect, and were weak of heart even to timidity. The
imagination took hold of most of them, especially of the humbler

class, and, lining the way with terrors all its own, reduced them
to the state when panic rushes in to complete what fear begins.
They started at the soughing of the wind; drew to strike each
other; cursed the rattle of their arms, the hoof-beats of the
horses, the rumble of the carriage-wheels; on the houses, vaguely
defined against the sky, they saw sentinels ready to give the
alarm, and down the intersecting streets heard the infidel
legions rushing upon them; very frequently they stumbled over
corpses yet cumbering the way after the day's fight, and then
they whispered the names of saints and crossed themselves:
the dead, always suggestive of death, were never so much so to
them.

And so, for many squares, across canals, past palaces and
temples, they marched, and nothing to indicate an enemy; the
city seemed deserted.

"Hist, señor!" said Duero, speaking with bated breath.
"Hast thou not heard of the army of unbelievers that, in the
night, while resting in their camp, were by a breath put to
final sleep? Verily, the same good angel of the Lord hath been
here also."

"Nay, *compadre mio*," replied Cortes, bending in his saddle.
"I cannot so persuade myself. If the infidels meant to let us
go, the going would not be so peaceful. From some housetop
we should have had their barbarous farewell,—a stone, a lance,
an arrow, at least a curse. By many signs,—for that matter, by
the rain which, driven through the visor bars, is finding its way
down the doublet under my breastplate,—by many signs, I
know we are in the midst of a storm. Good Mother forfend,
lest, bad as it is, it presage something worse!"

At that moment a watcher on the *azoteas* of a temple near by
chanted the hour of midnight.

"Didst hear?" asked Cortes. "They are not asleep! Olmedo!
father! Where art thou?"

"What wouldst thou, my son?"

"That thou shouldst not get lost in this Tophet; more especially, that thou shouldst keep to thy prayers."

And about that time Sandoval, at the head of his advanced
guard, rode from the street out on the open causeway. Farther
on, but at no great distance, he came to the first canal. While
there, waiting for the bridge to be brought forward, he heard
from the lake to his right the peal, long and loud, of a conch-
shell. His heart, in battle stedfast as a rock, throbbed faster;
and with raised shield and close-griped sword he listened, as
did all with him, while other shells took up and carried the
blast back to the city, and far out over the lake.

In the long array none failed to interpret the sound aright;

all recognised a signal of attack, and halted, the **slave** by his prolong, the knight on his horse, each one as the moment found him. They said not a word, but listened; and **as** they heard the peal multiply countlessly in every direction,—now close by, now far off,—surprise, the first emotion, turned to dismay. Flight,—darkness,—storm,—and **now** the infidels! "May God have mercy on us!" murmured the brave, making ready to fight. "May God **have** mercy on **us!**" echoed the timid, ready to fly.

The play of the wind upon the lake seemed somewhat neutralized by the density of the rain; still the waves splashed lustily against the grass-grown sides of the causeway; and while Sandoval was wondering if there were many who, in frail canoes, would venture upon the waste at such a time, another sound, heard, **as** it were, under that of the conchs, yet too strong to be confounded with wind or surging water, challenged his attention; then he was assured.

"Now, gentlemen," he said, "get ye ready; they are coming. Pass the word, and ride one to Magarino,—speed to him—speed him here! His bridge laid now were worth a hundred lives!"

As the yells of the infidels—or, rather, their yell, for the many voices rolled over the water in one great volume—grew clearer their design became manifest.

Cortes touched Olmedo,—

"Dost thou remember the brigantines?"

"What of them?"

"Only, father, that what will happen to-night would not **if** they were afloat. Now shall we pay the penalty of their loss. *Ay de mi!*" Then he said aloud to the cavaliers, Morla, Olid, Avila, and others. "By my conscience! a dark day for us was that in which the lake went back **to** the heathen,—brewer, it, of this darker night! An end of loitering! Bid the trumpeters blow the advance! **One ride** forward, to hasten Magarino; another to the rear, that the division may be closed up. No space for the dogs to land from their canoes. Hearken!"

The report of **a** gun, apparently back **in** the city, reached them.

"They are attacking the rearguard! Mesa spoke then. **On** the right hear them, and on the left! Mother of God! if our people stand not firm now, better prayers for our souls than fighting for our lives!"

A stone then struck Avila, startling the group with its clang upon his armour.

"A slinger!" cried Cortes. **"On the** right here,—can **ye see** him?"

They looked that way, but saw nothing. Then the sense of helplessness in exposure smote them, and, knightly as they were, they also felt the common fear.

"Make way! Room, room!" shouted Magarino, rushing to the front, through the advance-guard. His Tlascalans were many and stout; to swim the canal, with ropes to draw the bridge after them, to plant it across the chasm, were things achieved in a moment.

"Well done, Magarino! Forward, gentlemen,—forward all!" So saying, Sandoval spurred across; after him, in reckless haste, his whole division rushed. The platform, quivering throughout, was stauncher than the stone revetments upon which its ends were planted; calcined by fire, they crumbled like chalk. The crowd then crossing, sensible that the floor was giving way under them, yelled with terror, and in their frantic struggle to escape toppled some of them into the canal. None paused to look after the unfortunates; for the shouting of the infidels, which had been coming nearer and nearer, now rose close at hand, muffling the thunder of the horses plunging on the sinking bridge. Moreover, stones and arrows began to fall in that quarter with effect, quickening the hurry to get away.

Cortes reached the bridge at the same time the infidels reached the causeway. He called to Magarino; but before the good captain could answer, the waves to the right hand became luminous with the plashing of countless paddles, and a fleet of canoes burst out of the darkness. Up rose the crews, ghost-like in their white armour, and showered the Christians with missiles. A cry of terror,—a rush,—and the cavaliers were pushed on the bridge, which they jammed deeper in the rocks. Some horses, wild with fright, leaped into the lake, and, iron-clad, like their riders, were seen no more.

On the farther side Cortes wheeled about, and shouted to his friends. Olmedo answered, so did Morla; then they were swept onward.

Alone, and in peril of being forced down the side of the dyke, Cortes held his horse to the place. The occasional boom of guns, a struggling fire of small arms, and the unintermitted cries of the infidels, in tone exultant and merciless, assured him that the attack was the same everywhere down the column. One look he gave the scene near by,—on the bridge, a mass of men struggling, cursing, praying; wretches falling, their shrieks shrill with despair; the lake whitening with assailants! He shuddered, and called on the saints; then the instinct of the soldier prevailed.

"*Ola*, comrades!" he cried. "It is nothing. Stand, if ye

love life. Stand and fight, **as ye so well know how!** Holy
Cross! *Christo y Santiago!*"

He spurred into the thick of **the** throng. In vain,—the
current was too strong; the good **steed** seconded him with hoof
and frontlet; now he prayed, now cursed; **at** last he yielded,
seeing that on the other side of **the** bridge was Fear, on his side
Panic.

When the signal **I have** described, **borne from** the lake to
the city, began to **resound** from temple **to temple,** the rearguard were yet many squares from the causeway, and had, for
the most part, become merely **a** procession of drenched and
cowering stragglers. The sound alarmed them; and divining
its meaning, they assembled in accidental groups, and so hurried
forward.

Nenetzin and Marina, yet in company, were also startled by
the noisy shells. The latter stayed not to question or argue;
at her word, sharply spoken, her slaves followed fast after the
central division, and rested not until they had gained a place
well in advance of the non-combatants, whose slow and toil-
some progress she had shrewdly dreaded. Not so Nenetzin: the
alarm proceeded from her countrymen; feared she, therefore,
for her lover; and when, vigilant as he was gallant, he rode
to her, and kissed her hand, and spoke to her in lover's phrase,
she laughed, though not understanding **a** word, and bade **her**
slaves stay with him.

Last man in the column was Leon, brave gentleman, good
captain. With his horsemen, he closed upon the artillery.

"Friend," he said to Mesa, "the devil is in the night. **As**
thou art familiar with wars as Father Olmedo with mass, **how**
readest thou the noise we hear?"

The veteran, walking at the moment between two of his guns,
replied,—

"Interpret we each for himself, señor. **I am** ready to fight.
See!"

And drawing his cloak aside, **he** showed the ruddy spark of a
lighted match.

"As thou seest, **I am** ready; yet"—and **he** lowered his
voice—"I shame **not** to confess that I wish **we** were well out
of this."

"Good soldier art thou!" **said Leon.** "I will stay with thee.
A la Madre todos!"

The exclamation had scarcely passed his lips when **to their**
left and front the darkness became peopled with men in **white,**
rushing upon them, and shouting, "Up, up, Tlatelolco! *O O
luilones, luilones!*"[1]

---

[1] Bernal Diaz, *Hist. de la Conq.*

"Turn thy guns quickly, **Mesa, or we are** lost!" cried Leon ; and **to** his comrades, "Swords **and axes**! Upon them, gentlemen! *Santiago, Santiago!*"

The veteran as promptly resolved himself **into** action. **A word** to his men,—then he caught a wheel with **one** hand and swung the carriage round, and applied the match. **The gun** failed fire, but up sprang a hissing flame, and in its lurid **light out** came all the **scene** about : the infidels pouring into the street, the Tlascalans and many Spaniards in flight, Leon charging almost alone, and right amongst the guns a fighting man—by his armour, half pagan, half Christian ; all this Mesa saw, and more,—that the slaves had abandoned the ropes, and that of the gunners the few who stood their ground were struggling for life hand **to** hand ; still **more**, that **the** gun he was standing by looked point-blank into the densest ranks of the foe. Never **word** spoke he ; repriming the piece, he applied the match again. **The** report shook the earth, and was heard and recognised by **Cortes** out on **the causeway** ; but it was the veteran's last shot. To **his** side sprang **the 'tzin** : in his ear a war-cry, on his morion a blow, and under **the** gun he died. **When** Duty **loses** a good servant, Honour **gains a** hero.

The fight—or, rather, the struggle of the few against the many—went on. The 'tzin led his people boldly, and they failed him not. **Leon** drew together all he could of Christians **and** Tlascalans ; **then**, as game to be taken at leisure, his **enemy** left him. **Soon** the fugitives following Alvarado heard a strange cry **coming** swiftly after them, " *O, O luilones! O luilones!* "

And through **the** rain and the night, doubly **dark in** the canals, Hualpa **sped** to the open lake, followed by nine canoes, fashioned for **speed**, each driven by six oarsmen, and carrying **four warriors** ; so there were with him nine-and-thirty chosen **men, with linked** mail under their white tunics and swords of **steel on their** long lances,—arms and armour of the Christians.

Off the causeway, beyond the first canal, he waited, until the **great flotillas**, answering his signal, **closed** in on the right hand **and left** ; **then** he started for the **canal**, chafing at **the** delay of **his** vessels.

"Faster, **faster**, my men !" he said aloud ; then **to** himself, "Now will I wrest her from the robber, and after that she will give me her love **again**. Oh happy, happy hour !"

He sought the canal, thinking, doubtless, that the Christians would find it impassable, and that in their front, as the place of safety, they would most certainly place Nenetzin. There, into the press **he** drove.

"Not here ! Back, my men !" he shouted.

The chasm was bridged.

And marvelling at the skill of the strangers, which overcame difficulties **as** by magic, and trembling lest they should escape and his love be lost to him after all, he turned his canoe, if possible **to** be the **first** at the next canal. Others of his people were going in **the same** direction, but he outstripped them.

"Faster, faster!" he cried; and the paddles threshed the water,—wings of the lake-birds not more light and free. Into the causeway he bent, so close as to hear the tramp of horses; sometimes shading his **eyes** against the rain, and looking up, he saw the fugitives, **black** against the clouds,—strangers and Tlascalans,—plumes of men, but never scarf of woman.

Very soon the people on the causeway heard his call to the boatmen and the plash of the paddles, and they quickened their pace.

"*Adelante! adelante!*" cried Sandoval, **and** forward dashed the cavaliers.

"Oh, **my men, land us at the** canal before the strangers come up, and **in** my palace **at ease you shall** eat and drink all your lives! Faster, faster!"

So Hualpa urged his rowers, and in their sinewy hands the oaken blades bent like bows.

Behind dropped the footmen,—even the Tlascalans; and, weak from hunger and wounds, behind dropped some of the horses. Shook the causeway, foamed the water. A hundred yards,— and the coursers of the lake were swift as the coursers of the land; half a mile,—and the appeal of the infidel and the cheering cry of the Christian went down the wind on the same gale. At last, as Hualpa leaped from his boat, Sandoval checked his horse,—both **at** the canal.

Up the dyke the infidels clambered to the attack. And there was clang of swords and axes and rearing and plunging of steeds; then the voice of the good captain,—

"God's curse upon them! They have our shields!"

A horse, pierced to the heart, leaped blindly down the bank, and from the **water** rose the rider's imploration: "Help, help, comrades! **For** the **love** of Christ, **help**! I am drowning!"

Again Sandoval,—

"*Cuidado,*—beware! They have our swords on their lances!" Then, observing his horsemen giving ground, "Stand fast! Unless we hold the canal for Magarino, all is lost! Upon them! *Santiago, Santiago!*"

A rally and a charge! The sword-blades did their work well; horses, wounded to death or dead, began to cumber the causeway, and the groans and prayers of their masters caught under them were horrible to hear. Once, with laughter and taunting jests, the infidels retreated down the slope ; and once some of them, close pressed, leaped into the canal. The lake received them kindly ; with all their harness on they swam ashore. Never was Sandoval so distressed.

Meantime, the footmen began to come up ; and as they were intolerably galled by the enemy, who sometimes landed and engaged them hand to hand, they clamoured for those in front to move on. "Magarino ! The bridge, the bridge ! Forward !" With such cries, they pressed upon the horsemen and reduced the space left them for action.

At length Sandoval shouted,—

"*Ola,* all who can swim ! Follow me !"

And, riding down the bank, he spurred into the water. Many were bold enough to follow ; and though some were drowned, the greater part made the passage safely. Then the cowering, shivering mass left behind without a leader became an easy prey ; and steadily, pitilessly, silently, Hualpa and his people fought,— silently, for all the time he was listening for a woman's voice, the voice of his beloved.

And now, fast riding, Cortes came to the second canal, with some cavaliers whom he rallied on the way ; behind him, as if in pursuit, so madly did they run, followed all of the central division who succeeded in passing the bridge. The sick and wounded, the prisoners, even king Cacama and the women, abandoned by their escort, were slain and captured,—all save Marina, rescued by some Tlascalans, and a Spanish Amazon, who defended herself with sword and shield.

At points along the line of flight the infidels intercepted the fugitives. Many terrible combats ensued. When the Christians kept in groups, as did most of the veterans, they generally beat off the assailants. The loss fell chiefly upon the Tlascalans, the cross-bowmen, and arquebusiers, whose arms the rain had ruined, and the recruits of Narvaez, who, weighted down by their treasure and overcome by fear, ran blindly along, and fell almost without resistance.

One great effort Cortes made at the canal to restore order before the mob could come up.

"God help us !" he cried at last to the gentlemen with him. "Here are bowmen and gunners without arms, and horsemen without room to charge. Nothing now but to save ourselves ! And that we may not do, if we wait. Let us follow Sandoval. Hearken to the howling ! How fast they come ! And by my conscience, with them they bring the lake alive with fiends ! Olmedo, thou with me ! Come, Morla, Avila, Olid ! Come, all who care for life !"

And through the *mêlée* they pushed, through the murderous lancers, down the bank,—Cortes first, and good knights on the right and left of the father. There was plunging and floundering of horses, and yells of infidels, and the sound of deadly blows, and from the swimmers shrieks **for** help, now to comrades, now to saints, now to Christ.

"Ho, Sandoval, right glad am I to find thee!" said Cortes on the farther side of the canal. "Why waitest thou?"

"For the coming of the bridge, señor."

"*Bastante!* Take what thou hast, and gallop to the next canal. I will **do thy** part here."

And, dripping **from** the plunge in the lake, chilled by the calamity more than by the chill wind, and careless of the stones and arrows that hurtled about him, he faced the fight, and waited, saying simply, "O good Mother, hasten Magarino!"

Never prayer more hearty, never prayer more needed! For the central division had passed, and Alvarado had come and gone, **and** down the causeway to the city no voice of Christian was to be heard; at hand, only the infidels with their melancholy cry, of unknown import, "*O, O luilones! O, O luilones!*" Then Magarino summoned his Tlascalans and Christians to raise the bridge. How many of them had died the death of the faithful, how many had basely fled, he knew not; the darkness covered the glory as well as the shame. To work he went. And what sickness of the spirit, what agony ineffable seized him! The platform was too fast fixed in the rocks to be moved! Awhile he fought, awhile toiled, awhile prayed; all without avail. In his ears lingered the parting words of Cortes, and he stayed though his hope was gone. Every moment added to the dead and wounded around him, yet he stayed. He was the dependence of the army: how could he leave the bridge? His men deserted him; at last he was almost alone; before him was a warrior whose shield when struck gave back the ring of iron, and whose blows came with the weight of iron; while around closer and closer circled the white uniforms of the infidels; then he cried,—

"God's curse upon the bridge! What mortals can, my men, we have done to save **it**; enough now, if we save ourselves!"

And, drawn by the great law, supreme in times of such peril, they came together, and retired across the bridge.

Then rose the cry, "*Todo es perdido!* All is lost! The bridge cannot be raised!" And along the causeway from mouth to mouth the warning flew, of such dolorous effect as not merely to unman all who heard it, but to take from them the instincts to which life so painfully entrusts itself when there is no judgment left. Those defending themselves quitted fighting, and turned to fly; except the gold, which they clutched all the closer, many flung away everything that impeded them, even the arquebuses, so precious in Cortes' eyes; guns dragged safely so far were rolled into the lake or left on the road; the horses caught the contagion, and, becoming unmanageable, ran madly upon the footmen.

When the cry, outflying the fugitives with whom it began, reached the thousands at the second canal, it had somewhere borrowed a phrase yet more demoralizing. "The bridge **cannot** be raised! All is lost! *Save yourselves, save yourselves!*" Such was its form there. And about that time, as ill-fortune ordered, the infidels had gathered around the fatal place until, by their yells and missiles, there seemed to be myriads of them. Along the causeway their canoes lay wedged in, like a great raft; and bolder grown, they flung themselves bodily on the unfortunates, and strove to carry them off alive. Enough if they dragged them down the slope,—innumerable hands were ready at the water's edge to take them speedily beyond rescue. Momentarily, also, the yell of the fighting men of Tenochtitlan, surging from the city under the 'tzin, drew nearer and nearer, driving the rear upon the front, already on the verge of the canal with barely room for defence against Hualpa and his people. All that held the sufferers passive, all that gave them endurance, **the** virtue rarer and greater than patience, was the hope of the coming of Magarino; and the announcement, at last, that the bridge could not be raised was as the voice of doom over their heads. Instantly they saw death behind them, and life nowhere but forward,—so always with panic. An impulse moved them,— they rushed on, they pushed each with the might of despair. "Save yourselves, save yourselves!" they screamed; **at** the same time no one thought of any but himself.

To make the scene clear to the reader, he should remember that **the** causeway was but eight yards across its superior slope; while the canal, about as wide, and crossing at right angles, was on both sides walled with dressed masonry to the height, probably, of twelve **feet,** with water at least deep enough to drown a horse. Ordinarily the peril of the passage would have been scorned by a stout swimmer; but, alas! such were not all who must make the attempt now.

The first victims of the movement I have described were those in the front fighting Hualpa. No time for preparation: with shields on their arms, if footmen, on their horses, if riders,—a struggle on the verge, a cry for pity, a despairing shriek, and into the yawning chasm they were plunged; nor had the water time to close above their heads before as many others were dashed in upon them.

Cortes, on the farther side, could only hear what took place in the canal, for the darkness hid it from view ; yet he knew that at his feet was a struggle for life impossible to be imagined except as something that might happen in the heart of the vortex left by a ship foundering at sea. The screams, groans, prayers, and execrations of men ; the neighing, snorting, and plunging of horses ; the bubbling, hissing, and plashing of water ; the writhing and fighting,—a wretch a moment risen, in a moment gone, his death-cry half uttered ; the rolling of the mass, or rather its impulsion onward, which, horrible to think, might be the fast filling up of the passage ; now and then a piteous appeal for help under the wall, reached at last (and by what mighty exertion !) only to mock the hopes of the swimmers,—all this Cortes heard, and more. No need of light to make the scene visible ; no need to see the dying and the drowning, or the last look of eyes fixed upon him as they went down, a look as likely to be a curse as a prayer ! If never before or never again, his courage failed him then ; and turning his horse he fled the place, shouting as he went,—

"*Todo es perdido !* all is lost ! Save yourselves, **save yourselves !**"

And in his absence the horror continued,—continued until the canal from side to side was filled with the bodies of men and horses, blent with arms and ensigns, baggage, and guns and gun-carriages, and munitions in boxes and carts—the rich plunder of the Empire, royal fifth as well as humbler dividend—and all the paraphernalia of armies, infidel and Christian ; filled, until most of those who escaped clambered over the warm and writhing heap of what had so lately been friends and comrades. And the gods of the heathen were not forgotten by their children ; for sufferers there were who, snatching at hands offered in help, were dragged into canoes and never heard of more. Tears and prayers and the saving grace of the Holy Mother and Son for them ! Better death in the canal, however dreadful, than death in the temples,—for the soul's rest, better !

Slowly along the causeway, meantime, Alvarado toiled with the rearguard. Very early he had given up Leon and Mesa, and all with them, as lost. And, to say truth, little time had he to think of them ; for now, indeed, he found the duties of lover and soldier difficult as they had been pleasant. Gay of spirit, boastful, but not less generous and brave, skilful and reckless, he was of the kind to attract and dazzle the adventurers with whom he had cast his lot ; and now they were ready to do his bidding, **and** equally ready to share his fate, life or death. Of them he constituted a bodyguard for Nenetzin. Rough riders were they, yet around her they formed, more careful of her than themselves ; against **them** rattled and rang the **stones** and arrows ; against them dashed the infidels landed from their canoes; sometimes a cry announced a hurt, sometimes a fall announced a death; but never hand of foe or flying missile reached the curtained carriage in which rode the little princess.

Nor can it be said that Alvarado, so careful as lover, failed his duty as captain. Sometimes at the rear, facing the 'tzin; sometimes, with a laugh or a kiss of the hand, by the palanquin; and always his cry, blasphemous yet cheerful, "*Viva á Christo! Viva Santa Cruz! Santiago, Santiago!*" So from mistress and men he kept off the evil bird Fear. The stout mare Bradamante gave him most concern; she obeyed willingly,—indeed, seemed better when in action,—yet was restless and uneasy, and tossed her head, and —unpardonable as a habit in the horse of a soldier—cried for company.

"So-a, girl!" he would say, as never doubting that she understood him. "What seest thou that I do not? or is it what thou hearest? Fear! If one did but say to me that thou wert cowardly, better for him that he spoke ill of my mother! But here they come again! Upon them now! Upon them, sweetheart! *Viva á Christo! Viva la Santa Cruz!*"

And so, fighting, he crossed the bridge; and still all went well with him. Out of the way he chased the foe; on the flanks they were beaten off; only at the rear were they troublesome, for there the 'tzin led the pursuit.

Finally, the rearguard closed upon the central division, which, having reached the second canal, stood, in what condition we have seen, waiting for Magarino. Then Alvarado hurried to the palanquin; and while there, now checking Bradamante, whose uneasiness seemed to increase as they advanced, now cheering Nenetzin, he heard the fatal cry proclaiming the loss of the bridge. On his lips the jest faded, in his heart the blood stood still. A hundred voices took up the cry, and there was hurry and alarm around him, and he felt the first pressure of the impulsive movement forward. The warning was not lost.

"*Ola*, my friends!" he said, at once aroused. "Hell's door of brass hath been opened, and the devils are loose! Keep we together"—

As he spoke the pressure strengthened, and the crowd yelled, "*Todo es perdido!* Save yourselves!"

Up went his visor, out rang his voice in fierce appeal,—

"Together let us bide, gentlemen. We are Spaniards, and in our saddles, with swords and shields. The foe are the dogs who have bayed us so to their cost for days and weeks. On the right and left, as ye are! Remember, the woman we have here is a Christian; she hath broken the bread and drunken the wine; her God is our God; and if we abandon her, may He abandon us!"

Not a rider left his place. The division went to pieces, and rushed forward, sweeping all before it except the palanquin; as a boat in a current, that floated on,—fierce the current, yet placid the motion of the boat. And, nestled warm within, Nenetzin heard the tumult as something terrible afar off.

And all the time Hualpa kept the fight by the canal. Hours passed. The dead covered the slopes of the causeway; on the top they lay in heaps; the canal choked with them: still the stream of enemies poured on, roaring and fighting. Over the horrible bridge he saw some Tlascalans carry two women,—neither of them Nenetzin. Another woman came up and crossed, but she had sword and shield, and used them, shrilly shouting the **war**-cries of the strangers. Out towards the land the battle followed **the** fugitives,—beyond the third canal even,—and everywhere victory! Surely, the Aztecan gods had vindicated themselves; and for the 'tzin there was glory immeasurable. But where was Nenetzin? where the hated Tonatiah? Why came they not? In the intervals of the slaughter he began to be shaken by visions **of** the laughing lips and dimpled cheeks of the loved face out in **the** rain crushed by a hoof or a wheel. At other times, when the awful chorus of the struggle swelled loudest, he fancied he heard her voice in agony of fear and pain. Almost he regretted not having sought her, instead of waiting as he had.

Near morning, from **the** causeway toward the city he heard two cries,—" *Al-a-lala!* " one, " *Viva á Christo!* " the other. Friend most loved, foe most hated, woman most adored! How good the gods **were** to send them! His spirit rose, all its strength returned.

Of his warriors, six were with the slain; the others he called together, and said,—

"The 'tzin comes, and the Tonatiah. Now, O my friends, I claim your service. But forget not, I charge you, forget not her of whom I spoke. Harm her not. Be ready to follow me."

He waited until the guardians of the palanquin were close by, —until he heard their horses' tread; then he shouted, "Now, O my countrymen! Be the 'tzin's cry our cry! Follow me. *Al-a-lala, al-a-lala!*"

The rough riders faced the attack, thinking it a repetition of others they had lightly turned aside on the way; but when their weapons glanced from iron-faced shields, and they recognised the thrust of steel, when their horses shrank from the contact or staggered with mortal hurts, and some of them fell down dying, then they gave way to a torrent of exclamations so seasoned with holy names that they could be as well taken for prayers as curses. Surprised, dismayed, retreating, with scarce room for defence and none for attack, still they struggled to maintain themselves.

Sharp the clangour of axes on shields, merciless the thrust of the blades,—cry answered cry. Death to the horse, if he but reared ; to the rider death, if his horse but stumbled. Nevertheless, step by step the patient Indian lover approached the palanquin. Then that which had been as a living wall around the girl was broken. One of her slaves fell down, struck by a stone. Her scream, though shrill with sudden fear, was faint amid the discordances of storm and fight ; yet two of the combatants heard it and rushed to the rescue. And now Hualpa's hand **was on** the fallen carriage—happy moment ! "*Viva á Christo ! Santiago, Santiago !*" thundered Alvarado. The exultant infidel looked up : right over him, hiding the leaden sky,—a dark impending danger,—reared Bradamante. He thrust quickly, and the blade on the lance was true ; with a cry, in its excess of agony almost human, the mare reared, fell back, and died. As she fell, one foot, heavy with its silver shoe, struck **him to the** ground ; and would that were all !

"*Ola*, comrades !" cried Alvarado, upon his feet again, to some horsemen dismounted like himself. "Look ! the girl is dying ! Help me ! as ye hope for life, stay and help me !"

They laid hold of the mare and rolled her away. **The morning** light rested upon the place feebly, as if afraid of its own revelations. On the causeway, in the lake, in the canal, were many horrors to melt a heart of stone ; one fixed Alvarado's gaze.

"Dead ! she is dead !" he said, falling upon his knees and covering his eyes with his hands. "O Mother of Christ ! What have I done that this should befall **me ?**"

Under the palanquin,—its roof **of aromatic cedar**, thin as tortoiseshell, and its frame of bamboo, light as the cane of the maize, all a heap of fragments now,—under the wreck lay Nenetzin. About her head the blue curtains of the carriage were wrapped in accidental folds, making the pallor of the face more pallid ; **the** lips so given to laughter were dark with **flowing blood** ; and the eyes had looked their love the last time ;—**one** little hand rested palm upward upon the head **of a dead warrior,** and in it shone the iron cross of Christ. Bradamante had crushed her to death ! And this, the crowning horror of the melancholy night, was what the good mare saw on the way that her master did not,—so the master ever after believed.

The pain of grief was new to the good captain ; while yet it so overcame him, a man laid a hand roughly on his shoulder, and said,—

"Look thou, señor ! She is in Paradise ; while of those who, at thy call, stayed to help thee save her but seven are left. If not thyself, up and help us !"

The justice of the rude appeal aroused him, and he retook his

sword and shield and joined in the fight,—eight against the
many. About them closed the lancers ; facing whom one by one
the brave men died, until only Alvarado remained. Over the
clashing of arms then rang the 'tzin's voice,—

"It is the Tonatiah! Take him, O my children, but harm him
not ; his life belongs to the gods !"

Fortunately for Alvarado a swell of Christian war-cries and
the beat of galloping horses came, about the same time, from the
farther side of the canal to distract the attention of his foemen.
Immediately Cortes appeared, with Sandoval, Morla, Avila, and
others,—brave gentlemen come back from the land, which they
had safely gained, to save whom they might of the rearguard.
At the dread passage all of them drew rein except Morla ; down
the slope of the dyke he rode, and, spurring into the lake, through
the canoes and floating *debris*, he headed to save his friend. Useless the gallantry ! The assault upon Alvarado had ceased,—
with what purpose he knew. Never should they take him alive !
Hualpa's lance, **of** great length, was lying at his feet. Suddenly,
casting away his sword and shield, he snatched up his enemy's
weapon, broke the ring that girdled him, ran to the edge of
the canal, and vaulted in air. Loud the cry of the Christians,
louder that of the infidels ! An instant he seemed to halt in
his flight ; an instant more, and his famous feat was performed,
—the chasm was cleared, and he stood amongst his people saved.

Alas for Morla ! An infidel sprang down the dyke, and, by
running and leaping from canoe to canoe, overtook him while in
the lake.

"Sword and shield, Señor Francisco ! Sword and shield !
Look ! The foe is upon thee !"

So he was warned ; but quick the action. First, a blow with a
Christian axe : down sank the horse ; then a blow upon the helmet,
and the wave that swallowed the steed received the rider also.

"*Al-a-lala !*" shouted the victor.

"The 'tzin, the 'tzin !" answered his people ; and forward they
sprang, over the canoes, over the bridge of the dead,—forward to
get at their hated enemies again.

"Welcome art thou !" said Cortes to Alvarado. "Welcome as
from the grave, whither Morla—God rest his soul !—hath gone.
Where is Leon ?"

"With Morla," answered the captain.

"And Mesa ?"

"Nay, Señor Hernan, if thou stayest here for any of the rearguard, know that I am the last of them."

"*Bastante !* Hear ye, gentlemen ?" said Cortes. "Our duty
is done. Let **us** to the land again. Here is my foot, here my
hand : mount, captain, and quickly !"

Alvarado took the seat offered behind Cortes, and the party set out in retreat again. Closely, across the third canal, along the causeway to the village of Popotla, the 'tzin kept the pursuit. From the village, and from Tlacopan the city, he drove the bleeding and bewildered fugitives. At last they took possession of a temple, from which, as from a fortress, they successfully defended themselves. Then the 'tzin gave over, and returned to the capital.

And his return was as the saviour of his country,—the victorious companies behind him, the great flotillas on his right and left, and the clouds overhead rent by the sounding of conchs and tambours and the singing and shouting of the proud and happy people.

Fast throbbed his heart, for now he knew, if the crown were not indeed his, its prestige and power were; and amidst fast-coming schemes for the restoration of the empire, he thought of the noble Tula, and then,—he halted suddenly.

"Where is the lord Hualpa?" he asked.

"At the second canal," answered a cacique.

"And he is"—

"Dead!"

The proud head drooped, and the hero forgot his greatness and his dreams; he was the loving friend again, and as such, sorrowing and silent, repassed the second canal and stood upon the causeway beyond. And the people, with quick understanding of what he sought, made way for him. Over the wrecks of the battle,—sword and shield, helm and breastplate, men and horses, —he walked to where the lover and his beloved lay.

At sight of her face, more childlike and beautiful than ever, memory brought to him the sad look, the low voice, and the last words of Hualpa, "If I come not with the rising sun to-morrow, Nenetzin can tell you my story,"—such were the words. The iron cross was yet in her hand, and the hand yet rested on the head of a warrior lying near. The 'tzin stooped and turned the dead man over, and lo! the lord Hualpa. From one to the other the princely mourner looked; a mist, not of the lake or the cloud, rose and hid them from his view; he turned away,— *she had told him all the story.*

In a canoe, side by side, the two victims were borne to the city, never to be separated. At Chapultepec they were laid in the same tomb; so that one day the dust of the hunter, with that of kings, may feed the grass and colour the flowers of the royal hill.

He had found his fortune!

Here the chronicles of the learned Don Fernando abruptly terminate. For the satisfaction of the reader, a professional story-teller would no doubt have devoted several pages to the careers of some of the characters whom he leaves surviving the catastrophe. The translator is not disposed to think his author less courteous than literators generally; on the contrary, the books abound with evidences of the tender regard he had for those who might chance to occupy themselves with his pages; consequently, there **must** have been a reason for the apparent neglect in question.

If the worthy gentleman were alive, and the objection made to him in person, he would most likely have replied, "Gentle critic, what you take for neglect was but a compliment to your intelligence. The characters with which I dealt were for the most part furnished me by history. The few of my own creation were exclusively heathen, and of them, except the lord Maxtla and Xoli, the Chalcan, disposition is made in one part or another of the story. The two survivors named, it is to be supposed, **were** submerged in the ruin that fell upon the country after the **conquest was** finally completed. The other personages being real, **for** perfect satisfaction as to them, permit me, with the profoundest respect, to refer you to your histories again."

The translator has nothing to add to the explanation except brief mention that the king Cuitlahua's reign lasted but two months in all. The small-pox, which desolated the city and valley, and contributed, more than any other cause, to the ultimate overthrow of the Empire, sent him to the tombs **of** Chapultepec. Guatamozin then took the vacant throne, and **as** king exemplified still further the qualities which had made him already the idol of his people and the hero of his race. Some time also, but whether before or after his coronation we are not told, he married the noble Tula,—an event which will leave the readers of the excellent Don Fernando in doubt **whether** Mualox, the paba, was not more prophet than monomaniac.

THE END.

MORRISON AND GIBB, EDINBURGH,
PRINTERS TO HER MAJESTY'S STATIONERY OFFICE.

DICTIONARIES.

In large crown 8vo, price 3s. 6d., cloth gilt; or half-bound, 5s.
Ditto, half-bound, with Patent Index, 6s.; or half-calf, 7s. 6d.

NUTTALL'S STANDARD DICTIONARY OF THE ENGLISH LANGUAGE. New Edition, thoroughly Revised and Extended throughout by the Rev. JAMES WOOD. Containing all the Newest Words, 100,000 References, with full Pronunciation, Etymology, Definition, Technical Terms, Illustrations, &c.

Large demy 18mo, 288 pp., price 1s., cloth gilt, Illustrated.

WALKER'S PEARL DICTIONARY. Edited throughout from **the** most recent approved Authorities, by P. A. NUTTALL, LL.D.

In crown 8vo, price 1s., cloth gilt, Illustrated.

JOHNSON'S SHILLING DICTIONARY MODERNIZED. Edited from the most approved Authorities.

In crown 48mo, price 1s., cloth limp, 640 pp.; roan 2s.

WARNE'S BIJOU DICTIONARY. Pearl type, with Portrait of Dr. JOHNSON. Edited from the Authorities of JOHNSON, WALKER, WEBSTER, RICHARDSON, WORCESTER, SHERIDAN, &c.

In demy 18mo, cloth boards, price 6d., 290 pp.,
WARNE'S POPULAR EDITION OF

WALKER'S PRONOUNCING DICTIONARY, with WEBSTER'S Definitions and WORCESTER'S Improvements.

In 24mo, price 1s., cloth; or 1s. 6d., French morocco, gilt edges.

WORCESTER'S POCKET DICTIONARY. Illustrated.

In imperial 4to, price 31s. 6d., cloth; or half russia, cloth sides, 42s.

WORCESTER'S DICTIONARY OF THE ENGLISH LANGUAGE. With New Supplement to 1881.

In square 16mo, cloth boards, 2s. 6d. each.

FRENCH. NUGENT'S PRONOUNCING. By BROWN and MARTIN.
GERMAN. WILLIAMS' PRONOUNCING.

BIJOU TREASURIES.

In 48mo, price 1s. 6d., cloth gilt; or roan, pocket-book style, 2s. 6d.

THE BIJOU CALCULATOR AND MERCANTILE TREASURY. Containing Ready Reckoner, Interest Tables, Trade and Commercial Tables, and all Forms, &c., used in Business, 640 pp.

In 48mo, price 1s. 6d., cloth gilt; or roan, pocket-book style, 2s. 6d.

THE BIJOU GAZETTEER OF THE WORLD. New and Revised Edition. Briefly describing, as regards Position, Area, and Population, every Country and State; their Sub-divisions, Provinces, Counties, Principal Towns, Villages, Mountains, Rivers, Lakes, Capes, &c. 30,000 References. By W. R. ROSSER and W. J. GORDON.

In 48mo, price 1s. 6d., cloth gilt; or roan, pocket-book style, 2s. 6d.

BIJOU BIOGRAPHY OF THE WORLD: A Reference Book of the Names, Dates, and Vocations of the Distinguished Men and Women of Every Age and Nation. By WILLIAM JOHN GORDON.

FREDERICK WARNE & CO.'S

COMPLETE LIST OF

THE CHANDOS CLASSICS.

A SERIES OF STANDARD WORKS IN POETRY BIOGRAPHY,
HISTORY, THE DRAMA, &c.

In large crown 8vo, stiff wrapper.
STYLE A.—Ditto, cloth gilt (handsome design).
STYLE B.—(Library Style), very neat, plain blue cloth, with label,
uncut edges.

---

1 Shakespeare's Works.
2 Longfellow's Poetical Works.
3 Byron's   Ditto
4 Scott's   Ditto
5 Arabian Nights, The.
6 Eliza Cook's Poetical Works.
7 Legendary Ballads.
8 Burns' Poetical Works.
9 Johnson's Lives of the Poets.
10 Dante, The Vision of. By CARY.
11 Moore's Poetical Works.
12 Dr. Syntax's Three **Tours.**
13 Butler's Hudibras.
14 **Cowper's** Poetical Works.
15 Milton's   Ditto
16 Wordsworth's Ditto
17 Hawthorne's Twice-Told Tales.
18 England, HALLAM & DE LOLME.
19 The Saracens. GIBBON and
    OCKLEY.
20 Lockhart's Spanish Ballads and
    Southey's Romance of the **Cid.**
21 Robinson Crusoe.
22 Swiss Family Robinson.
23 Mrs. Heman's Poetical Works.
24 Grimm's **Fairy** Tales.

25 Andersen's (Hans) Fairy Tales.
26 Scott's Dramatists & Novelists.
27 Scott's Essays.
28 Shelley's Poetical Works.
29 Campbell's   Ditto
30 Keats'   Ditto
31 Coleridge's Ditto
32 Pope's Iliad. FLAXMAN's Illus.
33 Pope's Odyssey. Ditto.
34 Hood's Poems.
35 Representative Actors.
36 Romance of History—England.
37   **Ditto**   **France.**
38   **Ditto**   Italy.
39   Ditto   Spain.
40   Ditto   India.
41 **German Literature.**
42 Don Quixote, Life and Adventures
    of.
43 Eastern Tales.
44 The Book of Authors.
45 Pope.
47 Goldsmith's Poems, &c.
48 The Koran. Complete.
49 Oxenford's French Songs.
50 Gil Blas, The Adventures of.

THE CHANDOS CLASSICS—*Continued.*

NOTICE.—These Volumes (†) are not supplied in stiff wrapper, 1s. 6d.

FREDERICK WARNE & CO., Publishers,

HANDY INFORMATION BOOKS.

In crown 8vo, cloth gilt, price 2s. 6d. each.

BY A MEMBER OF THE ARISTOCRACY.

THE MANNERS AND RULES OF GOOD SOCIETY. Fourteenth and thoroughly Revised Edition. (New Tpye.)

SOCIETY SMALL TALK; or, What to Say, and When to Say it. Eighth Edition.

THE MANAGEMENT OF SERVANTS: A Practical Guide to the Routine of Domestic Service. Third Edition.

PARTY GIVING ON EVERY SCALE; or, The Cost of Entertainments. Second Edition.

THE LETTER WRITER OF MODERN SOCIETY. Second Edition.

FOOD AND FEEDING. By Sir Henry Thompson, F.R.C.S. Fifth Revised Edition.

MENUS MADE EASY; or, How to Order Dinner, and give the Dishes their French names. By Nancy Lake. Third Edition.

THE HOME, as it Should be: Its Duties and Amenities. By L. Valentine. Second Edition.

OUR SONS: How to Start Them in Life. By Arthur King. Second Edition.

HOW WE ARE GOVERNED; or, The Crown, the Senate, and the Bench. By Fonblanque. Fifteenth Edition, thoroughly revised by Smalman Smith.

HINTS ON BUSINESS: Financial and Legal. By R. Denny Urlin, F.S.S. A very useful book about Investments, Income, and other matters.

HEALTH, BEAUTY, AND THE TOILET: Letters to Ladies from a Lady Doctor. By Anna Kingsford, M.D., Paris. Second Edition.

In crown 8vo, price 2s. 6d., cloth gilt.

THE ELECTRIC LIGHT IN OUR HOMES. By Robert Hammond (The Hammond Electric Light and Power Supply Company, Limited). With Original Illustrations and Photographs.

HANDY MANUALS.

In crown 8vo, price 2s. 6d., cloth gilt; or picture boards, 2s.

THE DOMESTIC EDUCATOR (formerly entitled The Young Woman's Book): A Gathering of Useful Information in Household Matters, Taste, Duties, Study, &c. With Practical Illustrations.

In large crown 8vo, price 2s. 6d., cloth gilt; or picture boards, 2s.

BEST OF EVERYTHING. By the Author of "Enquire Within." Containing 1,800 Useful Articles on how to obtain "The Best of Everything," with a Special Calendar for the Cook and Gardener for each Month.

Bedford Street, Strand.